NINTH CITY
BURNING

NINTH CITY
BURNING

J. PATRICK BLACK

ACE
NEW YORK

ACE
Published by Berkley
An imprint of Penguin Random House LLC
375 Hudson Street, New York, New York 10014

Copyright © 2016 by J. Patrick Duffy

ACE is a registered trademark and the A colophon is a trademark of
Penguin Random House LLC.

Library of Congress Cataloging-in-Publication Data

Names: Black, J. Patrick, author.
Title: Ninth City burning / J. Patrick Black.
Description: First edition. | New York : Ace Books, 2016.
Identifiers: LCCN 2016009793 | ISBN 9781101991442 (hardback)
Subjects: LCSH: Human-alien encounters—Fiction. | BISAC: FICTION / Science Fiction /
Adventure. | FICTION / Science Fiction / Military. | GSAFD: Science fiction.
Classification: LCC PS3602.L2846 N56 2016 | DDC
813/.6—dc23
LC record available at https://lccn.loc.gov/2016009793

International edition ISBN: 9780399585722

First Edition: September 2016

Printed in the United States of America
1   3   5   7   9   10   8   6   4   2

Cover illustration by Matthew Griffin
Cover design by Adam Auerbach
Book design by Kristin del Rosario

For you.
Yes, you, the one reading these words right now.
This book was made for you.
Here it is.

ACKNOWLEDGMENTS

The list of people to whom this book owes its existence could easily fill a volume twice its size. A few, however, do stand out:

My friends and family, particularly my mother and sister, for their understanding and tolerance, and for offering me all the encouragement I was willing to accept.

Kirby Kim, whose influence in this book's publication goes incalculably beyond an agent's wonted duties; his wise advice and keen critical eye brought out something immeasurably finer than I could have produced alone. I prefer not to think of where I would be without his inexhaustible enthusiasm, patience, diplomacy, and talent.

Brenna English-Loeb, for her insights and suggestions, which helped shape this story from its earliest stages.

Jon Cassir, whose guidance and savvy made me feel at home in foreign realms of media.

Jessica Wade, editor and literary wizard; her understanding of books is so deep as to border at times on the telepathic, and it was through her considerable skill that this one was able to become what it truly wanted to be. She shepherded me through many a tough decision and toward many a winning idea, and kindly allowed me to believe I'd had the latter all on my own.

Isabel Farhi and Julie Mianecki, kind voices even when I was delinquent with my assignments.

Tim Durbin, who took the time to be succinct.

Adam Auerbach, for his wonderful cover design, and Matthew Griffin, for his magnificent art.

Sara Schwager, who provided the right (correct) words where they were mislaid or lacking, and a few others of very welcome encouragement.

Alexis Nixon, who helped me to be heard in a noisy world.

Ritsuko Okumura, for leading me to distant lands.

And all the people at Ace, Berkley, and Penguin Random House who, though I never saw them at work, were essential in bringing this book into being.

NINTH CITY
BURNING

PART ONE

MULTIPLICATION OF IMPOSSIBILITIES

ONE

JAX

We're only a few minutes into our quiz when the sirens start, and the first thing I feel is relief, even though I know that's totally wrong, totally not how I should feel. I can still remember the panic, the terror that used to come over me when I heard the atmospheric-incursion siren, the signal that our city is under attack. And I know that's how all the kids around me must be feeling this very second. But it's different for me now. Once the first shock of the wailing siren passes, it's true I'm afraid, too, but it isn't the same kind of fear I used to feel. It's more like fear of letting everyone down, and even that's not so bad yet, though I know it's going to get worse. But for a moment, just a moment, there was that relief because I'm totally not prepared for this quiz, which I know is crazy because what kind of person is like, *Oh great, I won't have to take a quiz because everybody is going to die.*

I'm not a bad student, really. Even in biology, which is the subject of this quiz, which is about photosynthesis, which is how plants turn sunlight into energy. The trouble is, whenever I sit down to study, I end up picking up the Academy Handbook. It isn't a long book, but each time I finish I just flip back to the beginning, like maybe if I read it one more time, I'll find the answer I need. Like maybe I just missed it the other hundred million times. But even though the Handbook has all the rules for life at the Academy, it doesn't tell me the one thing I really need to know. Oh, and there's nothing about photosynthesis, either.

"Pencils down, Cadets." That's Danyee, our rhetor. Everyone in Sixth Class Section E has her for biology, physics, and irrational mechanics. She had been pacing the rows of desks, looking over our shoulders one by one, but at the sound of the siren, she walked to the front of the room. "In line by the door, please," she says, her voice calm, almost cheerful, like this is just another lesson.

All around, there is the sound of chairs creaking from beneath desks. Near the back of the room, a girl gives a little squeal of panic: Her pencil is still scribbling away. She smacks it down like someone swatting a fly, then glances up to see if anyone's noticed. We all have, including Rhetor Danyee, who takes the girl by the hand and leads her to the line of cadets forming by the door. Using an artificed pencil during any kind of test is totally against the rules, as anyone who'd even picked up the Academy Handbook would know. On a normal day, this girl would be in for some big-time trouble, but not today. Rhetor Danyee, who is usually pretty tough, gives the girl's hand a reassuring squeeze before ushering her into line. If they're still alive tomorrow, they can talk about punishment then.

I'm cadet 6-E-12, meaning Sixth Class Section E Seat Twelve, so I take my place twelfth from the door. As I walk down the line, I can feel the other cadets watching me—not staring because you're supposed to be face forward when you're in formation, but from the corners of their eyes. My uniform is the same gray as any other cadet's, and on my collar I have the same six black pips as everyone in Sixth Class, but there isn't a person in this city who would mistake me for a normal kid. The symbol I wear at my neck, a golden circle with a second circle inside, is just a reminder. During school hours, everyone is expected to pretend like I'm just another student at the Academy, but that's all they can really do: pretend.

Over the past few months, I've gotten used to everyone's looking at me differently, gotten used to setting off whispers everywhere I go. It isn't like people are mean to me. If anything, they're extra, extra nice. Actual officers will stop and salute me, or congratulate me, or ask to shake my hand. I've made a lot of friends since starting at the School of Rhetoric, and my friends from before are still my friends. The kids in Section E seem proud to have me, usually. But not today. Today, things are different. Today, everyone's nervous. They know that in a little while, their lives could depend on me.

Of all the eleven- and twelve-year-olds who came back from Sequester, I'm the only one who turned out to be fontani, and as the youngest fontanus in the city, it's my job to stand for all of us during an attack. The last line of defense. In ten minutes, all of Ninth City could be gone, and I will have to fight, to protect whoever is left. And that's the look the other cadets are giving me now: They're wondering if they can trust me with their lives, this kid with his long nose and curly dirt-brown hair, who's somehow skinny and a little pudgy at the same time, who's in the bottom half of his class in chin-ups and push-ups, and don't even ask about the five-kilometer run. Who's never been really, really good at anything. They're seeing the same Jax they've known for twelve years, only now I'm somehow supposed to protect them from complete destruction. Even Rhetor Danyee seems tense. I don't blame them: I wish they didn't have to depend on me, either.

When all the cadets of Section E are in line, Danyee opens the door, and we file out of the classroom, forming two columns of ten, everyone moving smoothly in time. Each of us has been doing atmospheric-incursion drills practically since we learned to walk. As a section, our best time is classroom to shelter in three minutes and forty-two seconds. It's all so familiar, I almost forget this is the real thing. But only almost.

The hall of East Wing is filled with sections just like ours, kids walking calmly two by two with a rhetor at the front. The rhetors stand out by their black legionary's uniforms and because they're older, most around twenty years old, like Danyee. Some of the rhetors for the upper classes are even older than that, but not for the Dodos, which is the general Academy term for sixth-classers. The rumor is that rhetors aren't allowed to teach the younger kids anymore once they've been on their first tour.

No one speaks or looks anywhere but straight ahead; the only sound is the rhythmic clacking of our Academy dress shoes and the wail of the attack siren. The siren is an artifice, designed so that it's nearly impossible to ignore, a sound that seems to come right out of the air, like water gathering on the side of a glass. I wonder sometimes whether it could be an actual wail—like someone really screaming. That's how artifices are: No matter how precisely they're designed, you can never really be sure what they'll do.

We follow the flow of cadets down the wide stone stairway of East Wing as far as the ground floor, but where everyone else continues on to the lower levels, Danyee leads us to the main foyer. She brings us to a halt in front of the tall stone arch, like the threshold of a huge door but blocked with a massive slab of white stone, its translucent surface faintly glowing with the light outside. "Section E adjutant," she says, turning to face us. "Report."

Elessa leaves her place in the column to stand up front. "Cadet Adjutant

Elessa reporting, ma'am," she says. "Sixth Class Section E all present and in good condition." On our first day at the School of Rhetoric, when Danyee told us to elect a section adjutant, everyone was sure it would be Bomar. On the School's entrance evaluations, Bomar scored higher than anyone in our section in leadership. "Ninety-seventh percentile," he would say about ten times a day, just in case anyone forgot. Bomar decided his high score meant anything he wanted to do was automatically good leadership; at lunch, he liked to order people to give him their dessert rations "for the good of the section." Elessa was the first one to say what we all already knew: that school would be miserable with Bomar as adjutant. After that, the choice was obvious. Elessa is smart and organized, and she can do an insane number of chin-ups. When the vote came in, she won 19–1. Elessa always seems to know what to do—she would have made a good fontana, I bet. Instead, Ninth City got me.

"Section E is yours," Danyee tells Elessa. "Take your cadets to East Wing Shelter and report to your Centurio Aspirant."

"Yes, ma'am." Elessa turns on her heel to face us. "Cadets, with me," she says, and sets off. The other cadets of Section E follow, until only I am left.

Danyee gives me a small nod and an even smaller smile, then approaches the arch with its huge wall of stone. As she does, a dark shape appears in the white surface: the outline of a man, like the shadow of someone standing on the other side. It holds up one arm, waving at us to stop, and a voice comes out of the wall. "An atmospheric-incursion alert is in effect," it says, deep and booming and sort of echoing in the same way as the siren still wailing through the air. "The Academy of Ninth City is closed until further notice. All personnel are to report to their designated shelters. This is not a drill."

The voice pauses a moment, then begins its message again, but stops when Danyee places her palm against the white stone. "Rhetor Danyee of the Academy," she says, "escorting Fontanus Jaxten to the Forum."

The voice stops, then, after a moment, it says, "Pass."

All at once, the wall of white vanishes like clearing mist, and we're looking out onto a courtyard of stone paths and wide lawns, empty and bright beneath a cloudy sky. The door reappears behind us as soon as we're outside; I don't hear it happen, but when I look back, it's there.

Danyee has taken a small metal disk from her pocket. It's a storage device, I know, made to hold artifices, and given to her for the sole purpose of bringing me to the Forum during an attack. I could get there just as fast by myself, but the Academy can be very strict—and sometimes kind of unreasonable—when it comes to what cadets are and aren't allowed to do on their own. I actually kind of like it better this way.

"Ready, Cadet?" Danyee asks.

I think she might actually be nervous, but I can't tell for sure. "Ready, ma'am," I say.

Danyee passes two fingers over the surface of the disk, and suddenly everything is a blur, the ground rushing beneath us like wind, walkways and stairways and hallways whirling around us with the speed of a cyclone.

When the world settles back again, Danyee and I are standing in front of another stone archway, easily twice as tall as the last one, opening onto a wide stone plaza. I feel Danyee's hand settle onto my shoulder. We pass beneath the arch, and she steps back and salutes. "This is as far as I go, sir," she says. This whole procedure is in my Handbook, part of a special appendix added just for me. It always feels weird when adults address me as "sir," but now that we're off Academy grounds, I outrank Danyee by quite a bit.

"Yes, ma'am," I say, returning her salute. "I'll take it from here."

But instead of leaving, Danyee kneels and hugs me hard. "Good luck, sir," she whispers. "We're all rooting for you."

The hug takes me completely by surprise. Nowhere in the Handbook—not even in the special appendix—does it mention hugging, let alone hugging a superior officer. As far as I know, hugging is completely nonregulation. I mumble something that sounds like, "Thanks," and Danyee lets me go, smiling sadly. She salutes once more, then she's gone in a gust of wind.

TWO

JAX

t's only then that I hear the quiet. The siren is silenced here, and the Forum, usually so crowded you can hardly breathe, is completely empty. The stone plaza seems to go on forever, the huge buildings bordering each side like distant mountains on the horizon.

I take a long breath, close my eyes, and for a moment the gray light of the Forum is gone, and I'm standing in a field of green grass under a clear blue sky. The sun is warm on my face, the air fresh. Distantly, I can hear people cheering—they might even be chanting my name. If I have to fight, this is where I'll do it.

Feeling a bit more confident, I open my eyes and make for the monstrous fountain in the center of the plaza. The first assignment any cadet gets at the School of Rhetoric is writing an essay about this fountain and how it represents the history and ideals of our city. The fountain has five levels, all swirling with people carrying swords and rifles and flags, some of them supposed to be real historical people, some whole groups of people, some abstract things like Honor and Duty and Courage, who stand out because they're usually not wearing clothes. The essay has become sort of a joke at the Academy because the rhetors basically just tell you what to write. The fountain's official name is the Font of the Principate, but most people just call it Old Fife.

Molded into one edge of the fountain is a gigantic chair, known as Macduff among Academy cadets, who spend a lot of time trying to fit as many people as possible onto it at once. The most I've ever seen was twenty-five, kids all stacked on each other's shoulders into this teetering tower. But the real name is the Seat of the Champion. "Champion" is an old title, from before the Legion started, but it still has symbolic meaning, which I guess is what the fountain is all about. And, at least for now, the Champion of Ninth City is me.

I'm able to stay on the Seat of the Champion for about ten seconds before I start to completely freak out. At first, it's not so bad. The stone is cold and a little damp from one of the sprinkling showers that have been passing over the city, but I don't mind. I lean back, looking up at the sky, then I hear Bomar saying, "I can't believe that kid Jax ended up being the one. Out of everybody. He can barely finish a five-K, and we're supposed to trust him to defend the city? It's like a sick joke."

It was our first day at Rhetoric. I'd been just outside the door to the classroom when I heard people talking inside. What Bomar said didn't surprise me—he hadn't really been keeping his opinion a secret. The surprise was what happened next.

"Shut up, Bomar. You're just jealous." That was Elessa. She isn't an overly nice person, but she's fair, and I was glad we'd elected her section adjutant. But then she said, "And anyway, it won't really be Jax. Fontani have another personality or something that does the fighting."

"It's gotta be some tough personality *or something* to make up for Jax," Bomar said. "Otherwise, we might as well just kill ourselves now, save Romeo the trouble."

Elessa didn't disagree. Other voices joined in, and I realized most of the section was in there. No one wanted me fighting for them.

I think of Danyee hugging me and saying, "We're all rooting for you." I bet she wishes she had someone else instead, though. I know I do.

The Academy Handbook talks a lot about courage. It says it's OK to be afraid, that fear is just part of bravery. It says you'll know what to do when the time comes, you just have to trust your training. But it doesn't tell you what to do while you're waiting, alone under an open sky, sure everyone you've ever met is going to die because you're not strong enough to save them.

When the people at Sequester told me I might be fontani, I was sure there'd been a mistake somewhere. Fontani are supposed to be the best of the best, and I'm about as close to average as you can get. But they were right. I thought I'd feel different after I shaded that first time, like maybe I'd just *know* what to do, but I didn't, and I still don't. At night sometimes when I can't sleep, I'll get up and look at myself in the mirror, to see if there's any proof I've really changed, but it's always the same me.

All of a sudden, it's like I can't breathe, like the air has turned to rock. My heart feels like it's rolling full speed down a hill, bumping all the way, and I get the serious feeling that I'm about to throw up.

I close my eyes, take a deep breath, and try to summon up that big green sunny field the way Charles, my special-sessions instructor, taught me. I see the grass spreading out all around, but this time there's no sun anywhere. The sky is deep gray, almost black, and it's raining balls of slush like icy spit. The grass begins to wilt and turn brown, and suddenly there are bare patches everywhere, and I'm sinking into the cold mud, first to my ankles, then my knees . . .

I snap my eyes open and scramble off the fountain, determined not to leave a pile of throwup beneath the Seat of the Champion. Once I'm up and sure I'm back in Ninth City, I feel a bit better but still not good. I hobble around the edge of the Forum, totally out of breath, passing the buildings that make up the four sides of the plaza one by one: the Academy, the Basilica of the Legion, the Praetorium, the Hall of the Principate.

I'm on my third lap and still feeling like I'm three Ks into the worst five-K of all time when I hear something strange echoing down one of the tall passageways that run through the Hall of the Principate—pretty much the most unlikely sound in the world: laughter. Not even thinking about why, I follow the sound through the passage to the opposite side of the building, out onto a wide terrace. Ninth City spreads out below, Old Town, with its spiraling streets, the serious-looking stone towers of the newer districts, the battle spires rising like claws, and the hulking City Guns—huge cannons the size of buildings, some over two hundred meters tall. Charles calls them "literal skyscrapers."

At first I think the laughter must have been some trick of the wind, then I see them: legionaries, three of them, two men and a woman. For a couple of seconds, I just stare, trying to figure out what they're doing here. They should be at their posts, getting ready to fight. And then I see the insignia on their collars, the peaked symbol marking them as Officers Aspirant from the School of Philosophy. They're younger than I thought, maybe around Rhetor Danyee's age, which I guess makes sense because she's an OA, too. But that still doesn't explain why they're *here*.

"You're supposed to be at the shelters." I just blurt it out. All three turn to look at me, clearly taken by surprise.

The first to recover himself is one of the boys, the tallest of the three, lanky, with dark skin and a lean, handsome face. He has dark hair, longer than male cadets usually choose to wear it. "Well, look who it is," he says, showing off an easy smile. "Fontanus Jaxten. Seat of the Champion a little soggy for you?"

"You were supposed to go to the shelters," I repeat, sounding idiotic. It's only after I've opened my mouth that I think how close he was to the truth.

The other boy is tall, too, and kind of bronze-colored all over, with muscles that seem to bulge straight through his uniform. "Jaxten, really?" he asks, adjusting a pair of silver-rimmed glasses like he's trying to bring me into focus. "Fantastic. Get over here, champ. Have a drink with us."

I notice the little silver cup each is holding, and the pair of glass bottles, both mostly full of a pale amber liquid, on the stone by their feet. "Is that Fizz?" Fizz is a drink cadets make using aquavee and flavor packets. The Handbook says it's sometimes called Gurgle or Foamy, and lists it as a Category Four Restricted Substance.

"Now, let's remember our manners," says the first boy. "I think we ought to introduce ourselves to young Jaxten before we go offering him any Category Four Restricted Substances."

"I know who you are," I say, because I do. "You're Vinneas. And you"— I turn to the other boy—"you're Imway." Imway looks surprised and impressed, but Vinneas only grins as if I've just given the correct answer to a math problem. "You're in the Handbook," I explain, "in the section for Executive OAs."

Vinneas is Procurator of the Academy, which is like the rhetor of all rhetors, basically in charge of every cadet here. Imway is the top-ranked OA in the Equites Aspirant, the most elite fighting unit at the Academy. Every cadet in Ninth City knows these two.

"Sounds like we're famous, Way," Vinneas says, still grinning. "The Handbook! It doesn't get much better than that."

The girl, meanwhile, is watching me with something between impatience and sarcasm. She's a lot smaller than the other two, with bright blue eyes, wavy black hair pinned up at odd angles, and a way-more-than-regulation number of earrings. "Um," I say, squirming a bit under her gaze, "I don't know who you are."

Imway and Vinneas start laughing, like this is the funniest thing they've ever heard.

"Now that you mention it," Imway says between laughs, "I don't recognize her, either—Vinneas, who is this girl?"

"I don't know—I thought you invited her!"

The girl watches them with obvious annoyance. "Nice to meet you," she says to me. "I'm Kizabel, but my friends call me Kiz." She glances at the boys, now leaning on one another like they're about to fall over laughing. "None of them are here right now."

"Aw, Kiz, we didn't mean it," Vinneas says, wrapping an arm playfully around her. "I'll have you know, Jaxten, that our girl here has a vast number of remarkable talents." Imway snorts at this; Kizabel tries to kick him, but Vinneas holds her back.

"For example," he says pointedly, "she is undoubtedly the most sought-after artifex at the Academy, arguably in the entire city. I'll bet you've used some of her artifices without even knowing it. A lot of philosophers around here would kill to work with her."

"If only she didn't keep failing her general exams," Imway concludes, still smirking. Something metallic bounces off his arm, and I see Kizabel has thrown her cup at him. She's trying to pull herself loose from Vinneas, snarling like she's going to rip Imway's head off.

"Did you finish that already?" Imway says, picking up the cup and examining it. "I'm not giving this back, you know. You're too much of an angry drunk."

"I'm not drunk, you stupid oaf," Kiz growls. She jabs Vinneas in the ribs, making him loosen his grip, then ducks past him and charges straight at Imway. It doesn't seem like a very good plan. He's twice her size at least, and he holds her off with one arm, not flinching even when she starts punching and kicking him and calling him things that would have gotten her a whole lot of disciplinary work hours if any of her supervising officers were here.

"Pay attention, Jaxten," Vinneas says, rubbing his side but grinning, too. "This is how grown-ups settle their differences."

"Shut up, Vinn," Kizabel yells. "You're next!"

Vinneas raises his hands in surrender. "Forget I said anything." While Kizabel goes on punching Imway, Vinneas leans toward me and kind of half whispers, "Kizabel's sense of honor demands a token show of force. Nothing to worry about so long as nobody breaks into their repertoire of artifices."

Just then there's a kind of buzzing-popping sound, and Imway's glasses go flying into the air. He stumbles back, blinking and looking between Kizabel and his glasses, which have landed at the other end of the balcony. "Oh, so it's going to be like that, is it?" he says.

Kizabel is taking off her earrings and putting them in her pocket. "Yup."

"Now's about when we might want to take cover," Vinneas says.

"You have to get to the shelters!" I shout. I'd actually almost forgotten where I was until Vinneas mentioned taking cover. We're in the middle of an attack. "If the city is hit—"

"We're not worried," Imway says casually. I'd looked away from him and Kizabel for maybe half a second when I thought about the shelters, and now he's somehow gotten her in a headlock. Her face is bright red from trying to squeeze out, but Imway is acting like there's nothing strange going on. "We've got you to protect us, right, champ? Nothing's getting past Fontanus Jaxten. You're gonna—"

"Will you *shut up*?" Kizabel breaks in. Even though she's been yelling at Imway pretty much since I got here, this is the first time she's sounded really, actually mad. Imway lets go of her immediately, and she stands up, using her fingers to comb back her hair, which is pretty messed up from the headlock. "Come on. Look at the kid."

That sick, airless feeling is back, and I feel hot, sort of quivery, like my legs are going to melt. It shouldn't be me out here. The Seat of the Champion is made for people like Imway and Vinneas, and Kizabel, too, people who are smart and brave and amazing. Not some random kid.

"Hey, Jaxten," Kizabel says, coming over to me. "It's OK."

I'm afraid I'll start crying, which in front of these three would be even worse than throwing up.

"We're all scared," Kizabel is saying. "That's why we're up here."

"Definitely," Imway agrees.

"I don't get it," I say, shaking my head. Is it that, with me as Champion, they're so sure they're going to die that they might as well not bother with the shelters—save Romeo the trouble, like Bomar said?

"If the city is hit, it won't matter whether we're in the shelters or not," Vinneas says.

"What do you mean?" I look up at him, confused, but all he does is calmly finish his drink.

"Vinn." There's a warning in Kizabel's voice.

"He's been told he has to protect the city, Kiz. He should at least know what he's defending." He looks at me. "What do you think, Jax? Can I call you Jax?"

I'm not sure how to answer, but I say, "OK."

"Excellent," he says, setting down his cup. "So here's the thing, Jax. Those shelters were built a long time ago, before we knew quite what kind of firepower Romeo had at his disposal. As it turns out, nothing we can build would be strong enough to survive what he's throwing at us. Down there, up here, we're all cooked either way. Except for you, of course," he adds with a grin. "You're about the most indestructible thing this side of a black hole."

"But if that's true, why—"

"Why stick you in the Forum, when you could be off with the rest of the defense force?" he says. "To keep the city running, mostly, and the City Guns firing. After you, those guns are our best chance of coming out of this with all our atoms still attached. And I suppose it doesn't hurt to let people imagine they're safe. The prospect of imminent certain death can have a soggying effect on morale."

For some reason, hearing this makes me feel better. I don't know why. I mean, it's awful if all those people think they're safe when they're not. But if they do die, at least it won't be because I did something wrong. "But how do you know?" I ask. "About the shelters, I mean."

"One of the drawbacks to being good with numbers," Vinneas says.

"One of the drawbacks to having friends who are good with numbers," Imway adds, giving Kiz a light shove that still almost knocks her over.

"We're not the only ones, of course," Kizabel says, after shoving Imway back, then kicking him in the shins. "All the city officials know, more or less."

"And now you." Vinneas leans over the railing. "The three of us figure no one needs us at the shelters, and anyway, we all work in different parts of the city, so it's pretty unlikely we'd end up in the same place during an attack. We decided we'd rather be together."

"And since there's no one around," Imway says, refilling his and Vinneas's cups, "we thought we'd make a little party of it."

"The view from here definitely beats the shelters, too," Kizabel adds. "Those places creep me out."

"What my friend here means to say is that in confined spaces, people are more likely to notice you're drunk," Imway clarifies.

"I am not *drunk*!" Kizabel snarls, punching him with each word.

"Beats the Seat of the Champion, too," I say, because it's true.

"I can't believe they make you just sit there by yourself and wait." Kizabel sounds really disgusted at the idea.

"It's tradition. It's in the Handbook."

"Oh, right, the *Handbook*. The sum of all the world's truth and knowledge."

"Sure is." Imway laughs, raising his cup so he and Vinneas can toast.

Kizabel ignores them. "Let's make this the new tradition. Anytime that siren goes off, you meet us here. We'll even bring something for you that isn't a Category Four Restricted Substance."

"I always said Kiz comes up without our best ideas," Vinneas says. "What about it, Jax?"

"OK," I say. "It's a deal." And it's strange, but for the first time since the attack began, I feel like I really could fight.

Eventually, Kizabel convinces Imway to return her cup. They offer me a drink, too, but I don't take it—I've never had aquavee before, and I'm not sure what it'll do to me. If I do have to meet Romeo today, I want to make him pay. For a while we're all quiet, looking out over Ninth City, weirdly peaceful in the gray light. It's always pretty impressive, especially when you're way up in the Forum, with the tall stone buildings spreading out below, but I'd never really thought of it as beautiful until now. The air is warm but clear, washed clean from the rain, with little wisps of mist floating past, and with the whole city silent like this, I can almost imagine I'm high in the mountains somewhere, far away from everything.

And then the City Guns begin to move. The ground shakes as all around they turn and point their massive barrels into the sky.

Vinneas has taken a small watch from his pocket. He glances at the numbers, then up at the clouds. "Here we go," he says.

"Something else we've figured out, Jax," Imway says. "If Romeo doesn't get us within twenty minutes of the incursion, he won't get us at all."

All across Ninth City, the guns begin to fire, each one burning with a blinding flash, slashing upward with pillars of light that leave wide holes in the clouds where they cut through, enough to see blue sky and shafts of sunlight.

Suddenly, Kizabel winds up and throws her cup into the air over the city. "Come and get us, Romeo, you asshole!" she screams. "What are you waiting for? We're right here!"

"Imway was right," Vinneas says to me. "She's a complete lightweight."

But Imway is shouting, too. "Yeah, let's go! What's wrong, Romeo—you scared?"

And before I know it, I'm shouting with them. "You just try it! I'll break your stupid face!" I decide if we make it out of this, I'll need to think of something better to yell next time.

"Show us what you've got!"

"Our boy Jax is gonna tear you a new one!"

We keep yelling, and the ground rumbles with each shot of the City Guns, faster and faster, like a gigantic drum, until they're coming so fast and so loud, we can't hear our own shouts.

Beside me, Vinneas is still watching the time.

THREE

NAOMI

We reach the crossing just as the clouds that have been trailing our caravan now for a day and a night finally overtake us, scattering the cold air with flakes as small and bright as stars. Whoops and shouts go up all along the line of wagons to greet the first snow of winter. I have heard it is otherwise among the mighty townships and the northern tribes, but for us Walkers, winter has always been the happiest season.

Mama sits beside me in the front of our wagon, quietly smoking her pipe while I keep Chester, our cart horse, to his duties. Baby Adam hides in back, his bravado of the past days having lasted only to the first sight of the high pass, whereupon he near about wet his britches. I have told him to get out and walk awhile so he can see just how wide and strong the ridge is, but he prefers to cover his head with blankets. Leon, our rat terrier, is whimpering to console him. I will admit the path feels much worse than it looks, rocking us this way and that and setting the pots and pans hanging in our wagon to clattering, and I am glad we are fifth in line through the ravine and not first.

"Come up and keep us company, cowboy," Mama calls. "We're just about over the ridge." This enticement is enough to lure my brother into the open, perhaps because Mama has not called him Baby Adam, a title he likes not at all but which has stuck to him well past his baby years. Baby is seven now and too fond of coddling. He still has the fine blond hair he was born wearing, firm evidence in my opinion that he remains in most respects an infant, and I plan on referring to him as such until he shows me wrong. He comes out carrying the fiddle he inherited from Papa, proof his courage is not fully restored. Torturing that poor instrument and the ears of anyone within hearing is a balm for Baby's soul, it seems, because he plays only when he's anxious or afraid. Soon, Leon is beside him, singing along, and between the two of them and the pots still banging with each bump of the wagon, they set up a racket wanting only a chorus of devils to complete a full demonic symphony.

It is to this unmelodious anthem that the scouts return. They appear at the edge of the ravine, horses and riders breathing clouds into the freezing air, the rock walls sparkling with crystalline frost, and a moment later, we hear the bugle sounding through the mountains, signaling that they have encountered no danger, that the way ahead is clear. Once again, the caravan sets up a cheer. Even Chester senses the excitement, and it is all I can do to keep him from charging ahead. The snow is still sparse, but I know there is ice lurking beneath the thin white lace laid over the ground.

The scouts are waiting for us as we round the pass. The ridge widens and levels, and with a tumble into the ravine not so likely, Baby and Leon leave off their caterwauling, the last of their wails fading as my sister, Rae, trots up on Envy, her piebald mare.

"I hope you've got another song in you, Baby," Rae says, smiling at him with her warm, suede-brown eyes. "I told the scouts you would play us into New Absalom."

Baby mutely shakes his head and holds out his arms, asking to be picked up and forgetting all about the fiddle, which nearly bounces from the wagon at the next bump.

"Damn it, Baby!" I shout, grabbing for the fiddle. "You break this thing, and I'll have your guts for garters!" I have watched my sister unman our coda's meanest rowdies with the same words and less, but my little brother appears hardly to have heard.

Rae meanwhile has lifted Baby onto the saddle in front of her and placed her hat on his head. Only with Rae does Adam truly earn his title, nor will she quit spoiling him no matter how much I get after her for it.

"Mm sorry," says Baby Adam, plainly not sorry.

"How about you, Sunshine?" Rae asks. Rae is about the only one who still uses this name for me. I nearly reply that my name is Naomi or hers is Puddinghead, but unlike Baby Adam, I have the sense not to get upset when someone calls me something I don't like.

"How about me what?" I ask, sharper than I intend. The pair of us have been bickering the better part of a month, and I was prepared for some chiding or rebuke. But my sister is not the sort to come at you sideways. If she means to start a fight, she will lay in right away, and just now she seems as merry as you please.

Rae shakes the snow from her matted braids, hair the brown-gold of burned sugar. Her tanned face is flushed from the cold, her scarf stiff with frozen breath. She is nineteen and beautiful, even by the standards of the townships, where girls are rumored to bathe almost daily and can generally be counted upon to have all their teeth. "How about you play for us? I promised the scouts we'd have a tune. You're too kind a girl to make your big sister a liar."

Rae is highly peculiar when it comes to my fiddling. She could easily play for herself, and yet hardly a day goes by in which she does not try to cajole a song out of me, usually on some pretext, as lately I have wearied of acting her personal minstrel. I would offer some mean remark if I thought meanness would discourage her, but it is not possible to hurt Rae's feelings as far as I have seen, and anyway, it turns out today I do feel like playing, even like the fiddle wants me to play; I could almost swear I hear it humming to me on its own. So I tell Rae sure and hand Mama Chester's reins and set the old fiddle to my arm.

The tune I have in mind is slow and somewhat mournful but also happy, what Papa called a waltz. It is an old song well-known among our coda, and only a few notes have passed before people begin to sing, first in the wagons closest to us—Jasper Hollis and his family just ahead, and the Silva girls with their husbands and Alicia Silva's new baby boy—and then others up and down the line, until all fifteen wagons are mooning and crooning along with my fiddle, and it is thus that we come finally to New Absalom and our winter rest.

For the past three seasons, my coda has traveled all up and down the continent trading and foraging and tending our small herds, and never have we remained in one place more than a few nights running. To stop longer would be to hazard attack from the tribes that claim those lands as their territory, most of whom are hostile to anyone not their own and consider caravans like ours fat and tempting plunder. Even on the move, we are often called upon to defend ourselves, but we are as a rule better armed than most tribesmen and unwilling to surrender our wagons without demanding payment up front in blood, and once our assailants realize this, we are generally deemed not worth the trouble. But in the wintertime, most everything north of the bridgelands is covered in snows so savage that attempting a trek of any distance is to invite death into your own boots, and even the fiercest warriors will not venture far from their lodges. So when the cold comes, we Walkers take the provisions we have spent the year gathering to some snowbound roost and wait out the cold months in safety.

New Absalom is the finest of our winter refuges, though at first sight it looks like little more than an overgrown ruin. The sprawling shrubbery and tall grass is a careful deception, however, planted deliberately to make it seem as if New Absalom's last inhabitants left long ago and with no intention of returning. Once the brush and dirt are cleared away, we will have a town of grand stone homes seemingly untouched by time.

This place is what my people call a shroomtown, owing to the way everything from buildings to roads to walls to stairways seems to have sprouted like so many mushrooms from the ground. We have encountered other such localities in our wanderings, but never one so intact or so secluded. Nor have we ever succeeded in puzzling out the means by which such structures were raised. Once, Randy Tinker Bose tried digging under the wall of a shroomhouse and discovered it was fused to the living rock beneath. His conclusion was that the builders of New Absalom were somehow able to command Nature herself to grow houses the way she might grow mountains or trees, though presumably a bit more quickly. Everyone agreed this was a damn-fool notion, but to date it remains our only explanation. What we do know is that shroomhouses are sturdy and comfortable, more so even than the houses they have in the townships, which are impressive to look at but still made with nails and planks and other common materials, much the same as our own wagons.

By tomorrow night, we will be fully settled in New Absalom, and there will be a feast and a bonfire to celebrate the start of winter, but tonight we are quiet and somber, settling together in the huge rock fortress we call Everett's Palace, a fanciful name that stuck as fanciful names often do. Despite its generous proportions, the Palace holds heat well, and a few small fires warm it nicely. I roll up in my blankets, planning to make a show of sleeping, though I expect the real article will be hard to come by.

Tomorrow will be my first ride with the scouts, who are charged with venturing ahead of the caravan to survey the path and flush out danger. Rae put up a fuss when I announced my intention to ride, though she had no right to whatever. Any member of our coda is permitted to become a scout at the onset of her thirteenth winter, and stay as long as the others will have her. But Rae considered her own judgment sufficient to keep me with the wagons and would not hear otherwise. My sister's temper is never to be trifled with, but this was one of the few times I have seen her in so black a rage. She would have had me forever nannying Baby and laundering everyone's underthings had Reaper Thom not finally succeeded in talking her down. I have been thin with her ever since. Who she thinks she is to make exceptions to our coda's laws I cannot say. Rae herself was fully two months younger than I am now when she first joined the scouts, and she is counted among their best. I intend to be every bit as good and have spent many a sleepless night pondering just how I will achieve this lofty aim.

It thus comes as a surprise when I awake and realize half the night has already passed. The upstairs chamber where we have bedded down with some of the Hollises is dark save for a few rambling embers, and I lie there listening to the breathing of sleepers dreaming quiet dreams. And then I hear something else, a kind of metallic winding, and notice Rae's bed has not been slept in.

I find her seated by a window in the hall, looking out into the clear night. I'm sure she hasn't seen me, but then she says, "Hey there, Sunshine. What's the matter? Not sleepy?"

The windows of shroomhouses seem thin and flimsy but are harder than any glass I have ever encountered. Outside, the clouds have cleared, allowing moonlight to fall bright into the hall. "Is the storm over?"

"Not quite. It's just resting a bit."

"Are there moon babies out?" I regret speaking as soon as the words leave my mouth. Moon babies are colorful blooms of light found in the vicinity of the Moon on some clear nights, often in the company of angel's stitches and sparrow fires and other similar displays. They make a grand spectacle, and the number of times I have witnessed them could be counted on one hand. It is said they are more commonly seen from New Absalom, but likely that is just another of the superstitions surrounding this place, and I fear by asking I have shown myself the silly girl I am trying so hard to prove I am not.

"Just the plain old Moon," Rae says.

"Then what are you doing?"

She turns her face to me, smiling. "Thinking about winter. There's a book of stories I've been meaning to finish. And I think I'll carve a set of chess for Baby." She sighs happily. "You go on back to bed. Big day tomorrow. I'll be along in a minute."

Rae is in a fine mood, our quarrels of the past days seemingly forgotten. I am not so quick to relinquish a grudge, but like all my sister's passions, her happiness is catching, and as I crawl beneath my covers, I feel a smile climbing my face.

Not until I am teetering on the edge of sleep do I recall the sound of winding metal that drew me from my bed and picture Rae beside the window, and see the pistol in her hand, and hear the ratcheting as she worked the action over and over and over and over.

□————□

FOUR

NAOMI

When next I open my eyes, morning has arrived, and I am surrounded by empty bedrolls and cool ashes and bodies bustling as they ready for the day. Breakfast is well under way in the great hall, everyone seated at long tables loudly devouring hotcakes. Most will spend their day clearing the town, heavy labor and cold but work all are eager to begin. I spot a place next to Baby Adam and have annexed one of his hotcakes before he registers my arrival.

"You give that back!" he shouts, grabbing.

I pretend confusion, my mouth full. "Give what back, Baby?"

"I'm not a *baby*!" I have chewed enough of his meal now that he no longer wants it returned, and so Baby tries to bite me instead. "And you're a big old priss, Miss Priss!" We all have names for one another in my family, and this is Baby's for me.

"Careful there, little man. You don't have so many sisters you can afford to just go eating them willy-nilly." Rae has arrived with a tall stack of hot-cakes, all dripping goat butter and burned-sugar syrup. She makes remuneration to Baby for his lost cake and plops the rest in front of me. I tuck in with gusto, both because I'm famished and because I am anxious to get going, but when I'm done, Rae makes me drink a big glass of goat milk before I am allowed to leave, insisting I'll need the energy. I am so full of nerves that I neglect even to remind her that I can feed myself, thank you very much. I finish in one great gulp and run to put on my boots and wool-ens and leathers and run back to the hall.

Mama is waiting with packs for me and Rae, each with a lunch of hard-boiled eggs and a sandwich made with thick-cut bacon and no little grease, one bottle of milk and one of whiskey, plus blankets in case we are caught outside tonight. She gives Rae her pack and Rae bows to receive a kiss on the forehead. "Come back to me, sweet girl," Mama says.

"I will, Mama," Rae replies softly.

Mama removes my hat to kiss me on the crown of my head. She and I are colored alike, freckly with eyes and hair shaded like coffee, though if Mama's brew would keep you up all night, mine is milkier and not so potent. "Come back to me, sweet girl," she says.

"I will, Mama."

This is no idle promise or needless benediction. It is the duty of the scouts to spare our coda peril by facing that peril first. If there is violence waiting beyond the safety of our camp, the scouts will bear the worst of it. We were fortunate this year not to lose a single soul, though at the summer gathering, Timothy Sullivan did convince some poor, misguided girl to marry him and left our coda for hers. But if we ever imagine partings are always so cheerful, we have the tablets to tell us otherwise.

The tablets are tall wooden slabs, all carved with the names of friends and family lost to the wilderness, taken by sickness or cold or by our enemies. Among the names are three Rae carved herself: Everett Ochre, which is Papa's name, and those of our brother and sister, Jesse and Delilah Ochre, all three taken in a raid by Leafcoat warriors eight years ago. The tablets are hinged like cabinets and have shelves holding candles and pictures and toys and other tokens of remembrance. No one leaves the safety of our camp without first touching them for luck. Much of our coda's history is held in those tablets, and as I follow Rae from the great hall, my hand running across the wooden grain, I feel the warmth of memory beneath my palm.

The other scouts are at the gun racks set just inside the arch of Everett's Palace, jostling and joking as they shoulder their rifles. I hang back, not wanting to get in the way, suddenly remorseful for stealing Baby's breakfast. I feel much the baby myself now, unsure how to find my way in. Rae shoves and laughs with the rest, but when she turns away, I see she has my gun beneath her arm.

"Cleaned it this morning," she says, presenting me with the rifle. "And this is for you." In her other hand is a pistol, a revolving sixer, new and dimly gleaming, with a textured wooden handle.

"Where did you get it?" I ask, awed. I had expected to be stuck with one of the old rusty things used for practice.

"At that township a few days back." Rae is plainly pleased with herself, and for good reason. Townspeople are notoriously stingy when it comes to their weapons, and coaxing the tiniest peashooter from them is a lengthy and expensive production.

"But how did you pay for it?"

She flashes me a jaunty smile. "My secret. Go ahead—put it on." The pistol has its own leather holster, which Rae helps affix to my belt. The gun hangs heavily, frightening and reassuring both. "Good girl," Rae says, when I'm set. "Now go saddle up Jumbo."

Rae must have known how I would feel about riding Jumbo, which is likely why she gave me my present first. I often imagine myself out with the scouts, and always I am atop some swift and spirited steed—Sherlock or Cloud or Roadster, or Rae's own Envy. Jumbo is a plump, dappled gray, a sturdy and reliable mount but rarely moved to quick action. Rae claims he is among the wisest animals she has ever known, but he strikes me as indolent and something of a smart aleck.

In my twelve years of life, I have learned only one thing for certain about horses, which is this: All else being equal, they would rather not have you on their back. Unless you are Rae, that is; horses seem to consider carrying my sister a privilege. It takes little time for Jumbo and me to reach cross-purposes: I want him to take his bridle, whereas he would rather put his nose under my hat and munch my hair. Much to my humiliation, Rae comes to help me. From her, Jumbo accepts the bridle as though it were a candied apple.

"You do as I say unless Thom tells you otherwise," she instructs as we go to join the other scouts. "Twelve isn't too old for a spanking, and that's the best you'll get if Mama hears you've been goofing."

"I won't goof," I mutter, angry Rae thought such a warning necessary. Winter outings are a kind of audition for new scouts, and if I prove a liability, I won't be invited to stay on when we set out again in the spring. I know better than to mar my chances by making some ignorant or frivolous display.

The other nine scouts are waiting on their mounts, all slung up with packs and rifles. They call out to Rae and offer me exaggerated compliments on my new gun. But all joviality flees the moment Reaper Thom appears.

Reaper Thom Mancebo is our coda's boss scout, a bachelor of some fifty years, with a hard, lined face and a beard of wild black wires. However many of our people raiders have taken over the years, it is merely a fraction of the enemies Thom himself has mowed down. It is said he ships so many souls to hell, the Devil ought to put him on commission. He is dire and imposing and dangerous, with the bearing of a starved lion. I can think of no two people less alike than Reaper Thom and Rae, yet the two of them are close as kin.

Reaper Thom is not one for grandiose speeches. He tells us only that we will be riding as far as the Great Ridge and not to get cocky just because most of the terrain was scouted yesterday. Several tribes claim these mountains as their territory, and a single outrider is enough to bring an entire war party down on New Absalom. Leafcoats, Downeasters, What-Whats, and Niagaras have all been spotted in past years, and with winter now upon us, no tribesman will pass up the opportunity to pillage our stores.

"I want you all keen. Any antics are to be saved for tonight," Thom growls. "Sally Fisher has prepared three barrels of her special brew and promised a mug waiting for each of you. If I get the idea anyone is celebrating before that tap goes in, said person will be returning to New Absalom on foot and without boots. Understood?"

The scouts convey their understanding with a shout, and we are off into the woods and slopes of the mountain. Overnight, the world has become a whirl of crisp, glittering white, ankle-deep powder that will make quarry easy to track but also leave clear sign to anyone tracking us. But today our task is seeking, not hiding, so on balance the snow is more help than hindrance.

We all dearly hope the trails will show nothing of any humans save ourselves because if there are strangers in these woods, we will have little choice but to uproot rather than risk a raid in the deep of winter. The mood is tense as we sift between the snowy trees, tenser still as we pass the limit of yesterday's scouting into land none in our coda has seen these past five years. But by lunchtime it seems our only neighbors are deer and rabbits, and spirits begin to rise. Even Reaper Thom looks in danger of breaking into a grin as we approach the Great Ridge.

The Great Ridge is the far boundary of scouting from New Absalom, a wall of rock that sweeps up from the mountainside, then plummets into a valley below, the drop so steep and sheer that only the hardiest raiders could hope to climb it and afterward would be in little shape to cause us trouble. I know this place from stories: The Ridge is a favorite subject of the scouts, though not as much as the land beyond, which they name the Valley of Endless Summer. It is said that winter never touches this country, that the meadows are always flowering, the trees always heavy with fruit. I have never put much stock in such tales, thinking they were only the scouts funning us littler kids, and so I am astonished indeed to find the Ridge just as they described: the high plateau of mountain, and below, the fields and woodlands as lush and verdant as if summer had just reached its peak. Snow is falling again, but over the valley it vanishes, as if encountering a border beyond which winter cannot pass.

"It's something, isn't it, Sunshine?" Rae says as we look down over the Valley of Endless Summer.

"It's just like you said."

"Don't sound so surprised!" She laughs. "Not everything I say is some tale, you know! I do have a little useful advice for you now and then."

I am about to ask her to name another instance of this useful advice, but just then we hear someone calling for Thom, and I can tell from the sound, the news is not good. Rae and I have left our horses to climb the Ridge, and we slide back down the icy slope to join the others.

Simon Grumble has made an unsettling discovery. Off beyond a stand of trees there is a breach in the Ridge wide enough for several men to pass and fissures in the rock below that seem to create a path down into the valley. This in itself would be nothing but enticement to a dangerous adventure, one to be argued over and likely abandoned in favor of Sally Fisher's brew, were it not for the signs of violence all around the breach. The rock walls are scorched black in places, or stained brown with blood, and beneath the snow we find broken arrows and spent shell casings, rags of bloodied cloth, what appear to be shards of bone, and human teeth.

Discussion ensues. The carnage here is not fresh, but it is new enough that whoever left it could yet be nearby. The only way out of the mountains goes through New Absalom, meaning either the shedders of this blood departed just before we arrived, or they are still roaming these ridges, or else they descended into the valley. The consensus among the scouts is that we cannot stay the winter with such danger lurking. We will have to leave New Absalom behind—that is clear enough. In the morning, we will load our wagons again and set out for another of our hidden refuges, only now we will be moving in winter, harried by snow and frost and cold. It is a drastic shift in our fortunes and hard news to take.

I am mulling through these and similarly dismal thoughts when I hear

Rae speak up. "I will go and look," she says, glancing first at me, then at the other scouts. "It could be whoever fought here died afterward, and the bodies were taken by wolves or other scavengers. I will go down into the valley and see if they have left any trace. I won't need to travel far—only a few miles. If I find nothing, and you find nothing more along the Ridge, then maybe we stay the night here on watch, and in the morning get a few good workers from New Absalom to help seal up this hole." She nods toward the breach. "So what if someone did go down there? No reason we have to let them back up."

Rae has hardly finished speaking before every one of the scouts has volunteered to accompany her. No one wants to leave New Absalom behind if by some extra effort we can make it secure. Only Reaper Thom is reluctant, but eventually he agrees to Rae's plan, sending Lester Silva and Apricot Bose, our two fastest runners, down with her. Half-Moon Hollis takes a party of three to follow the Ridge as far as the cliffs at the edge of the mountain, while the rest of us remain behind to make camp.

There is no more jollity among the scouts, only a grim, businesslike manner as we set to our tasks. I am charged with assembling makings for a fire, to be lit once the Ridge and valley are cleared, and this I do methodically, gathering and splitting wood and constructing a cone of tinder to incubate the flames. I have just finished stacking my kindling when Half-Moon comes crashing through the woods and about flattens the whole pile. Before I can voice even a single curse, he makes an urgent motion with his hand: the signal for enemies nearby.

The other scouts gather around as Half-Moon confers with Thom in low tones, describing a party of Niagaras spotted about two miles down the Ridge. Five at least, but with campfires enough to spell some twenty more.

I do not wait for him to go into further detail but make straight for our signaling bugle. If Niagaras attack this ridge, Rae and the others will be trapped down in the valley. They must be warned, and without delay. But before I can bring the horn to my lips, Reaper Thom seizes my arm. "It won't do her any good, girl," he says. "The Niagaras will answer that call long before your sister does. All we can do is hope they don't come this way and beat them back if hoping proves insufficient."

Reaper studies my face until he is sure I understand, then takes the bugle from me. Around us, the scouts are readying for a fight, checking their weapons, scouring the camp to build covered firing posts. But as soon as I am sure Thom is occupied, I turn and run, making for the breach. I do understand him about the bugle, but I take issue with his opinion that all I can do for Rae is wait and possibly fire a shot or two into a crowd of Niagaras.

No one gives chase, nor does anyone try to call me back. As I descend, it seems a head or two pokes over the cliff to see where I have gone, but I am moving too quickly to say for sure, more concerned with what is below than above, more with what is ahead than behind.

□────────□

FIVE

NAOMI

Wide cracks spread down the Ridge from the breach all the way to the ground, allowing easy footing through the wall of smooth stone. The land at the bottom is just as snowy as at the top, which surprises me until I consider the width of this valley. Summer must be gathered around toward its middle. In the snow, I have no trouble discerning the tracks Rae and the rest have left behind, and I set off at a run, pistol bouncing at my side.

I cross white fields and sparse woodlands of barren trees, a river crusted in ice and marshes of slushy ponds and snowcapped reeds. Now and then I catch a breath of unseasonably warm air, but that is my only whiff of fair weather. I have begun to think the Valley of Endless Summer is some strange fraud or illusion when I come upon a sight that stops me dead.

There, across an expanse of bare ground shrouded in snow and ringed with skeletal trees, is a bold green meadow of tall grass and bobbing flowers. The greenness begins abruptly, shooting up over the snow, as though pressing at that border of winter I imagined from the Ridge above. Only it seems this border has begun to fail: Snow drifts lightly over the meadow, collecting on thick grass blades and the bright faces of flowers. I do not like this place, I realize; it makes me uneasy. But Rae's tracks lead directly into the meadow, and I can see where the scouts passed through, parting strands of tall grass and shaking snow loose to leave a path through the white dusting, and so I force myself on.

Not long after that, the screaming begins.

Without warning, an unearthly wail descends out of the sky like a swooping banshee. I have never heard anything so awful. The vague fear I felt crossing the border of winter flares into panic, and suddenly I am running headlong, thinking only of finding a place to hide. I stagger to a stop beneath a wide and leafy tree, glad for protection from the echoing sky. The screaming has not ceased, but it is dimmer here, more distant. As I lean there, panting and shivering with fear, I realize Rae's trail is nowhere in sight. Moreover, my sense of direction has become so muddled that I can no longer be sure which way I came. I am well and truly lost.

There is a clearing beyond my tree, and I venture forth carefully, hoping for some familiar landmark but finding none. Even the sun has hidden behind a bank of clouds. I have crept some distance from cover when, at the corner of my eye, I catch a scattering of dark birds taking flight, and when I turn to see what has startled them, I find a man watching me from the edge of the woods.

He is small but densely built, clad in furs, with a bow over one shoulder and a spear in his hand. His hair is yellow, as is his braided beard, though the face above seems blue in color. Niagaras, I recall, are said to paint their bodies blue and white before going into battle. Slowly, deliberately, the man begins striding toward me across the clearing, eyes set on me all the while as he wades through the grass.

I run, mustering what remains of my energy and breath to make for the nearby trees, never considering that this might be exactly what the yellow-bearded man wants of me until a second man has leapt forth to scoop me up. This new man is large and strong enough to hold me with little effort, and I am like a rabbit snatched in a sight hound's jaws, legs kicking uselessly at the air. I can do nothing but scream, and presently this recourse is denied me as well when a thick, hairy paw is folded across my mouth.

"Now then, girl, there'll be none of that," my captor says, his voice deep and too chipper for a man possessing such a violent grip. He has the musky smell of a wet dog and jagged designs decorating the backs of his hands, crude things quite at odds with the gentlemanly cadence of his speech.

I attempt another scream, but my efforts prove doubly useless: Not only does this man's meaty palm reduce my shout to a bumblebee's hum, but I am answered by the hearty laughter of more Niagaras, strolling from the woods to join the man with the yellow beard. I count no fewer than ten, at least two with old rifles slung over their shoulders, before the man restraining me heaves me around so that I am looking straight into his unpleasant face. His long hair and a beard are the dull brown of wood bark, his blue eyes set deep in pink cheeks etched with intricate blue markings—a color I see now comes not from paint but tattooing.

"I would be more obliging if I were you, young miss," my captor says, holding me at arm's length, as I have made certain efforts to bite and kick him. "Be advised that my associates have already erected a secure perimeter. As you are alone and without recourse in this situation, we have elected to take you into protective custody. We will overlook your attempts to flee heretofore as mere misdemeanor, but any further resistance will be seen as a willful and intentional act of aggression, and your cooperation will thereafter be subject to coercive efforts, which may result in severe and grievous harm to you. Do you understand?"

Truthfully, I did not follow much of what this man has said, but his demeanor, and the set of his teeth, file-sharpened to points, tell me more clearly than any flowery words that I am in dire circumstances.

"You are lucky I and my associates happened to surveil you out in the woods. There are things in this valley far worse than us. Let us cease and desist this disorderly conduct, now, and after that we can—"

I do not get to hear what this brute has planned, for at that moment, a rifle's crack echoes across the clearing, loud and abrupt over the sky's waning scream. The blue-eyed man releases his grip, and I fall breathless to the cold grass. When I raise my head, I see one of the Niagara men, a long-armed scarecrow with a shaved head, sway and fall to the side, his face a mask of gory red. Around him, his fellows crouch as though ducking hailstones, weapons raised to attack. I watch one Niagara shoulder his rifle, a rusty piece but functional enough to fire with a puff of smoke and another loud crack.

To my startled brain, it seems I must be the target, and I hold my breath for the impact of the bullet, only to find that my enemies have other, more dangerous concerns. My blue-eyed captor has not dropped me out of surprise or fear, but to pull a set of cruel-looking hatchets from his waistband. He swings them up, pivoting in the direction of the first gunshot, but midway through his turn he utters an oath, and a second later, his furs and face and the air around him are red with spraying blood.

Above him stands Rae, blade drawn, red speckles across her cheeks. The blue-eyed man goes to one knee, then falls, and she has put her knife in him twice more—a stuttering puncture, quick as a woodpecker's rattle—before he hits the earth, throat and side bubbling blood.

I make to jump up and rush for Rae's familiar embrace, but even as I get one shaking leg beneath me, Rae has taken the collar of my coat and thrown me hard onto the snowy turf. When I cry out in alarm, her only answer is to order me in cold, deadly tones to stay down and keep quiet.

Surprise silences me then as much as anything else. Rae has never spoken to me like this, even in the worst of our fights. I am accustomed to the scalding flashes of her temper, but what I see in her now is different, something icy and sharp. She sets one hand on my breastbone to hold me in place and presses a knee painfully into my hip to further discourage any struggling. From my back, I have a good view of her face, her jaw set, the blue-eyed man's blood trailing to her chin, and the idea comes to me that this is a person I have never met in my life. Rae pays me no notice whatever, instead discarding her knife and reaching for the pistol at her belt. Over my staring eyes, she levels the gun and begins to fire slowly and methodically at something I cannot see.

It is about then that I begin to perceive the noise and chaos around me: the wild cries and the whizzing of arrows and the clatter of guns. I count three shots from Rae's pistol, then she rises, stepping over me and striding ahead into the clearing. Finally free to move, I get to my knees and push myself up, turning just in time to see my sister, still firing, advancing on the crowd of Niagaras, though only two of them now remain standing. Rae shoots again, and this number is reduced to one. The last to fall is the yellow-bearded man who chased me here, his empty bow sliding from his hand as he clutches a hole Rae has opened in his chest.

For a while there is only the sky's scream, fading like an echo, and I have time to survey how the scenery around me has changed. The clearing is now scattered with arrows and axes and the bodies of men who only minutes before had been leering and grinning at me, the grass flattened and upset by gunfire and running feet. My sister is the lone figure still upright, her long coat sluiced with blood, pistol hanging at her side, standing motionless in the center of the clearing with specks of snow drifting around her, like she has spotted some quarry and is daring it to move first.

"Rae?" I call, my voice hoarse from screaming and her hand against my throat.

Rae turns sharply, and for a moment it is as if she does not know who I am. Then her face shifts with recognition, like I am someone she met long ago but has only just managed to locate in her memory. Without another word she is upon me, and I must tell her several times that I am all right before she even seems to hear me and several more times before she will quit asking if I am hurt and inspecting me to confirm I am free of injury.

A whistle goes up from the woods behind us, and I see Lester and Apricot there among the trees, rifles in hand. I realize with a bolt that they must have been the ones firing at these Niagaras, that while I lay pinned to the grass, a skirmish was taking place all around me, that Rae had used her body to shield me from the exchange of arrows and bullets.

At this thought of the Niagaras, I am reminded of the errand that brought me here in the first place. I rush to tell Rae about the enemies Half-Moon discovered on the Ridge, but she stops me.

"We know, Sunshine," she says, her voice warm now, the last of that dark, chilly aspect I saw in her melting away. "Caught wind of these boys and their crew not far from here. Only they aren't Niagaras. They're Nworkies."

"Nworkies?" I hazard a glance at the man Rae has just cut down. "What would Nworkies be doing this far north?"

"Beats me, but they're Nworkies all right. Look for yourself."

The blue-eyed man has gone still, the gush of blood at his neck slowed to a trickle. Rae takes his hand and turns it. There, among the dark tattoos underneath, is the mark all Nworkie warriors wear:

I ♥
NY

"Come on, Sunshine. Lester and Apricot are waiting for us."

Our friends have faded into the trees, rifles ready to cover our retreat. I watch as Rae retrieves her hat and wipes her knife on the grass, then I follow her into the forest, willing myself not to look back at the clearing and the remnants of the bloody scene played out there.

We decide to take the long way back to the Ridge, heading farther into the valley and doubling back to avoid the main body of Nworkies, which Lester guesses to be nearly fifty in number. "Soon as we saw them, we knew there would be no staying at New Absalom," he says. "I'm glad Half-Moon had to bring you the bad news first."

We run at a good clip, Rae first, then me, with Lester and Apricot behind, guns drawn. The sound of screaming is by now only a whisper, but the warm breezes, once only an occasional hint of sweet air, have picked up, growing stronger the more we move into the valley. We see nothing more of the Nworkies, and I think we are about to begin circling back around when suddenly Rae shouts, "Stop!"

The tone of her command is such that the rest of us obey immediately. "What is it, Rae?" Apricot asks.

Rae doesn't answer. She has halted midstride, shoulders tensed. When Lester takes a step toward her, she screams, "Don't move!" The fear in her voice catches me more than any command could, but her next words are slow, steady. "It's some trap."

Now that we have stopped, the strangeness of this place becomes apparent. The chill taste of winter is gone, and there is a strange odor, at once like metal and an ocean tide. A warm drizzle has begun to fall, though I recall only a minute ago there was snow in the air.

Rae shifts her feet and slowly begins to turn. Her gun has fallen from her hands, which she holds before her as though she has never seen such things in all her life, and with good reason: Above each of Rae's fingers dances a single white-gold flame, as if she has somehow swapped her digits for candles. I raise my eyes to meet hers, and see the same pale fire licking across her cheeks and forehead, darting in the manner of pink flames over coals. Her voice comes out thin, strained. "You have to go," she says. "You have to go right now."

"Rae," I say, pleading, but she stops me with a scream, a fierce and desperate thing to hear.

"Run!" Rae cries out with all her might even as the flames on her face whirl and spread. In an instant, she is consumed in white-gold fire, fire that burns hotter and brighter until it erupts with a concussion that lifts me from my feet.

I have a glimpse of the woods where my sister once stood, now alight in flames of molten gold, but the sight recedes from me, slowly shrinking until all I can see are dark trees. More woods and meadows pass in the same manner. It is not until I spy tracks below me in the snow that I understand I am being borne along against someone's shoulder and that I am screaming Rae's name. In my ear, I hear Apricot Bose breathing, "She's gone, she's gone, she's gone," in time to her own running feet, then the ground thuds beneath me, and I see the Ridge rising over my head. Could my senses have been so addled as to miss traveling all this way?

"I can't carry you up there," says Apricot breathlessly. "You have to climb, Naomi."

Beside her, Lester is reloading his rifle. He raises it and fires into the trees, summoning up a howl from inside. The Nworkies have given chase, it seems. From the top of the Ridge come answering cracks of gunfire, and a bugle calling. Distantly, my thoughts tell me this can only mean Half-Moon's Niagaras have mounted an attack, and indeed that is the signal sounding: battle already joined.

There is a new sound, too, over the cries and blasts. It is distant at first, but builds in speed and degree until it has become a steady booming, the sort a giant would make running at full tilt. I wait for some monstrous creature to come breaking through the trees, but what I see instead is an even stranger vision: blue lights, thin and sharp as needles, stabbing over the horizon into the sky, each flashing only a moment but so powerfully as to pierce the very clouds.

I know I must rise now, rise and fight, if I am to survive. I make a fist and find the pistol, Rae's present to me, already in my hand.

SIX

TORRO

The last five minutes of your shift are always the worst. I won't say longest because they're each sixty seconds apiece, just like every minute since the beginning of time. They seem longer, sure, but that's not what's so bad about them. What's so bad is that you've been watching the fish rolling around on the conveyor belts for like sixteen hours, getting gutted and beheaded by little blades, then stuffed into cans and drowned in oil and sealed up and cooked to superhigh temperatures and labeled and boxed, and you're just waiting for it all to stop; only when it finally does, you don't feel like it's really over. You *feel* like it's *you* down there on the belts, and the reason everything seems still is because now *you're* the one moving along with all those little fish, waiting for the rotating saw to come and slice your head off. So when the bell rings at the end of the shift, I don't just run off like everybody else. I stay at my station a minute and let my brain work out which way is up and everything. If people ask, I say I'm dizzy, and that's not like a complete lie. But it's also a good excuse to not leave right away.

From my station, I watch everyone filing out, dumping their gloves and goggles and hairnets and aprons in separate containers to be cleaned and sterilized and so forth, all in a rush, like they've got someplace important to be or something, even though the first railbus back to town doesn't leave for fifteen minutes. Most of them are kids about my age, that is, seventeen. Pretty much everybody does a rotation or two at the factories once they get out of school, even if you're like me and you actually made it all the way through. Not like school necessarily gets you anywhere. Or experience, either. There are plenty of people who work the factories their whole lives and never even make foreman, and I bet half of them did as much school as me. I can see a few of them, the lifers, there among the younger kids. Not so many, though. It's just that the older you get, the more likely you'll end up at the Front instead of in good old Settlement 225.

When pretty much everyone is off the factory floor, I head for the door, making sure to go the way that takes me by the cookers, so all the cans I pass are basically ready to go except maybe for the labels. At the last corner, I stumble and knock a whole bunch of cans off the conveyor. I make a big show of being like embarrassed over screwing up the line of production and whatnot, and I'm real careful about picking up every single can and dusting it off and checking it for dents. I put the good cans back on the belt and toss the dented ones into a bin labeled "nonconforming." There are a lot of non-conforming ones.

I've been doing this a couple of times each week since I started over in canning, just denting a few cans here and there so they can't be boxed. I've got a whole bunch of ways to do it. Like I might leave something on the conveyor belt so it gets backed up, and the cans start falling off, or maybe I'll let one of the cardboard storage boxes get a little wet so the bottom falls out when I try to pick it up. Little things like that. I'll bust one or two at my station, too, but only so no one gets suspicious. On my performance reports my error rate is listed as "good," and you only have to be "accept-able" to avoid getting stuck with demerits.

I keep playing up the clumsiness a bit, fumbling with my gloves and apron as I rush to join everyone else filing off the floor. Hardly anyone even looks at me; they're all just this huge, exhausted herd. We lumber out the big doors and over this bridge where you can see half the factory com-plex, just this mammoth stack of boxy buildings and domes and steam spewing everywhere from big tangles of pipes and whatnot.

Somehow, Hexi finds me in the crowd, which is like a feat because I look about the same as everyone else. I mean, I'm a little taller than average, but I have the same short haircut most factory workers choose, my straight black hair cut down to a bristly fuzz, and in my brown floor uniform, I'm not very remarkable. That doesn't keep Hexi from picking me out right away, though.

"Hey, Torro!" Hexi calls in her high little voice. My full name is Troshosho, so you can see why Torro is easier.

Hexi is friendly as anything. Like she could make friends with a rock, and the rock would send her birthday cards. "How do you always find me right away?" I ask her.

"The smell, boyo. What was it today, tuna?"

I was afraid it would be something like that. "Herring."

"I'm only kidding you, don't be so *sen*sitive. Half the people here smell like fish, or didn't you notice? Anyway, at least you can wash the fishiness off with a shower or two. I'm going to be red for a week!" She holds up her hands so I can see the stains she got from canning red beets.

"A shower or *two*? What do you think I do all day?"

"Basically the same thing I do all day. You going to eat? The kiddos are probably waiting for us."

Everyone working at the factories gets two meals here per day plus one credit for the eateries in town. You can use your extra credit here, too, if you happen to be insane. The factory caf is a huge room in the middle of the complex, with rows of tables and servers spooning different colors of slop onto segmented plates. Some of the slop is seasonal, like when we're harvesting potatoes, the starchy slop is slightly better. Fortunately, we're behind our quotas on both red beets and fish, so Hexi and me won't have to eat what we've been canning since like 1600 yesterday.

Today's slop comes in three colors: orange, brown, and green. The orange is like sliced carrots or something, and the brown is mystery meat with mystery gravy. The green could be broccoli or peas, but I'm not going to think too much about it. When Hexi holds out her plate for her serving of slop, I notice her looking at the red splotches on her arms with a lot less like jolliness than before.

"It really doesn't look that bad," I say. "Two more weeks, and we're done anyway. Just twenty more days. Maybe you'll rotate somewhere better." Where I really want to go is the fishing fleet. I guess that's sort of strange given my present feelings on fish. But I just imagine myself out there with nothing but the ocean for a hundred kilometers in every direction, old S-225 nowhere in sight, and I think, that's for me. It's tough work to get, though, fishing. There's a lot to learn, so if you don't get into it early, you probably never will. My chances would have been better if I'd left school a few years ago, which is sort of a dumb way of doing things if you think about it.

"With my luck, I'll probably end up in textiles," Hexi says, sighing.

"At least then I can get dyed a few colors besides red. I really think green is my shade, don't you?"

"You know you never told me how you picked me out back there."

"That? I don't know. I guess you just walk different from everyone else."

"Different how?"

"I don't know, just different. Do you see the kiddos? I'm totally lost."

Hexi has this great brain for remembering people but couldn't find her way out of an empty box. Like she doesn't know where our table is, even though we sit in the same place every single day. It's a good table, so we've got to make a point of claiming it regularly. Spammers, Mersh, and Isslyn are all there already, working away at their piles of slop.

Spammers greets us with his usual "Good morning, chummies!" He likes to be chipper in a sort of sarcastic way. It's his like preferred stance toward life in general.

"What's wrong with Mersh?" Hexi asks as we sit down. Mersh looks like he's on the verge of complete and total collapse.

"Mersh has decided he doesn't need to sleep like the rest of us," says Isslyn. "That's just what we need, some sleep-deprived dickhead running shipments from the fields." Isslyn's actually a sweetie most of the time, but when she thinks you're doing something dumb, she can be a real pain in the ass. She says it's for your own good. "Hel*lo*, Mersh? If you die in some fiery wreck, I'm going to kill you, you hear?"

"I'm not going to crash," Mersh says defensively. "I'm like the best driver in my shift." Mersh is always bragging about how great he is at practically everything, but this might actually be true. Those drivers are terrible. "And it's not my fault if I'm tired. They set the required runs too high. There's no time to sleep." He stabs a little at his slop. "I'm telling you, I'm ready to go and join the Legion."

Nobody says anything to that. We all just kind of look at each other, nervous-like. The Legion is supposed to be this incredible army. They're off fighting the biggest war of all time, and we're expected to be really like pleased about that because the people they're fighting want us all dead. Everyone is always going on about how heroic the Legion is. That's basically required. We're supposed to talk a lot about how grateful we are to be able to work all day and support the war effort. They're always looking for new recruits to go out and fight, but most people aren't too keen on becoming heroes. People from our settlement go all the time, of course, but the thing is, none of them ever come back. Not one. Never. So when Mersh starts talking about joining up, we all get pretty scared. Like, we all *think* about it now and then. If we're sending the Legion all this food and whatnot, they can't have it that bad is what we think. But Mersh is the only one who's ever serious about it. That's what scares us. Mersh is an idiot most of the time, but we've known him forever, and we don't want him to just disappear on us.

"What?" says Mersh, like he knows what we're thinking. "You're telling me the Legion couldn't be better than this?" He looks sort of longingly up at the murals covering the cafeteria walls, which are all huge paintings of these strapping young men and women wearing romantic-looking suits of armor and gazing heroically into the distance, with like sunrises and mountains and waterfalls and whatnot in the background. The same good-looking people appear on posters all around the settlement, sometimes in their armor charging into battle, but sometimes in smart little uniforms building houses or sitting in classrooms or just laughing together. The posters always have slogans like "Fighting for You" and "Be Part of the Adventure" and "Building Your Future."

"Come on, Mersh," Spammers says. "You can't really go in for all that crap." When it comes to the Legion, Spammers is what you'd call a skeptic.

"Yeah," says Isslyn. "Those poor slobs in the Legion are probably looking at paintings of handsome kids working in fields and factories and stuff and thinking how great it is to be *us*."

Everyone else laughs, but Mersh only gets more sullen. "At least they get enough sleep and plenty of food. And after five years with the Legion, you can leave and start a no-quota settlement."

One poster you see everywhere has the slogan "Your Tomorrow Starts Today." There's always a bunch of people walking off into the distance, you can't see where really, and one at the back with a hand out to like invite you along. The person at the back changes from one poster to another. Sometimes it's a tough-looking guy, and sometimes it's this busty girl in a uniform that's probably a few sizes too small. Mersh actually stole one of the posters with the busty girl. He keeps it under his mattress. I bet that's what he's thinking about now, starting a new settlement with that busty girl, who probably isn't even a real person.

"And you believe that *why*?" Spammers is getting angry now.

"Don't you remember the last time the censors came?" Mersh says.

"They had that guy, the one who started Settlement 401. *He'd* been in the Legion."

"And you believe that *why*?" Spammers says again. "Because he had like a scar on his cheek? Haven't you ever wondered why they never bring anyone from Granite Shore?"

Granite Shore is what people here call Settlement 225. It isn't an official name or anything, but it sounds a lot nicer.

"Maybe they just didn't want to come back to this shit hole," Mersh mutters. He's been stabbing and mashing at his slop, but now he stops and smiles this sly smile, like he's got some big secret. "No reason we can't improve things a bit for ourselves, though. Right, kiddos?" He opens his jacket to show us something big and white and craggy. A sugar beet, just sitting there like a bomb.

Hexi instantly starts panicking. "Mersh, what are you *doing*?"

"We always lose a bunch from the truck on the way in." He's just smiling more, like no one would ever believe how smart he is. "This one fell off while I was pulling into the dock. What do you think it's worth?"

"I have no clue what you could mean," I say. I jam a big spoonful of the green slop into my mouth and talk over my food, like I could not care less about his stupid beet. "I guess if anyone catches you stealing, it'll be worth a whole assload of demerits."

"Come on, everyone here steals. What do you think I could trade it for? Think I could get an en-text?"

"This is slander, and we'll have nothing to do with it," Spammers says. "Implying theft is common or acceptable at this factory impugns the integrity of your fellow workers, our foremen, and the factory executives. Keep it up and I'm filing a grievance." Spammers sounds pretty angry, even though everything he's saying is complete crap. I don't know anyone with like a lower opinion of the integrity of his fellow workers, and he's always making fun of people who file grievances. He says you're better off just farting at someone, for all the good grievances do. Mersh is probably thinking the same thing I am because he looks confused and a little mad.

"What you can trade it for is a trip to the Front," I say. "I guess that's fine if you're planning on going anyway."

You can just tell Mersh thought this sugar-beet thing would go over real different, like he'd be this big hero for stealing a stupid beet. He's so disappointed, even Spammers feels sorry for him. "Come on," Spammers says.

"We can drop that turd of yours outside before our next shift, and no one will know the difference. What do you say?" He gets up and pats Mersh on the shoulder. "Only seven hours to go, and the first drink's on me!"

Mersh cheers up a little at that. I'm glad. He's really a good guy, but the things that come out of his mouth sometimes you wouldn't believe. Take this sugar beet, for instance. It's completely worthless unless you've got about a thousand more as well as a working sugar refinery, which Mersh ought to know because Spammers *works* at the stupid refinery. It's the sugar you really want. And what no one saw was that when Spammers got up from the table, he passed me a paper bag with about a kilo of the stuff inside, by the feel of it.

The others all have to go back for their second shift, but Hexi and me have been here since last night, and we're done for a while. "You coming back to the dorms?" Hexi asks as we're leaving the caf.

"No, I've got some things to do in town."

"Oh well, say hi to Camareen for me." The way Hexi says it, it's like she's caught me doing something sneaky. That sort of annoys me. Our friends all know about Camareen and me.

"I'll give her your warmest regards." I'm just glad she doesn't try to come with me. I really do have some things to do, and Hexi can be bad for business.

SEVEN

TORRO

On my way to the railbuses, I stop off at the factory store to get my new uniform. Factory workers are allowed one new uniform every sixty days. If you damage yours before then, you still get a new one, but you get demerits along with it. I always make sure mine rips on like day sixty-two or sixty-three. I know just where to tear it so it's eligible for replacement, but I do it along a seam, so it's easy to fix, too. The box waiting for me at the company store is a little heavier than it should be because there are about twenty slightly dented cans of herring inside.

Mersh wasn't really wrong when he said everybody steals. Really, every-one, from turds like me all the way up to the Prefect. People always put on this huge act of being like appalled and horrified whenever someone gets caught lifting from the factories or warehouses or whatever, but most people aren't really mad about it. In the end, you're only lifting from the Principate.

The Principate is the outfit running that big war and protecting us from our enemies and whatnot. Settlements like old 225 are supposed to send them all the food and supplies and soldiers they need and do it with a smile because without the Prips, we'd all get like marauded and killed. The Prips set quotas to make sure we're working hard and giving up everything we can spare, and we get to keep whatever's left over, Granite Shore does. But the thing is, whenever we beat our quotas, the quotas just go up. So we find ways to get a little for ourselves. Spammers lifts sugar. I dent cans, and my floor foreman, who's supposed to dispose of all the bad cans, he keeps them and gives me part of the haul. We'd all be in a lot of trouble if the wrong people found out, but Spammers and me only deal with the right people, meaning the ones who'd be just as screwed as us if we got caught.

Cranely is one of the right sorts of people. He works as a tailor in the

Town Center, but the basement of his shop is like a warehouse of every-thing from truck parts to canned peaches to shoe soles to dried pasta. Old Cranely is probably the biggest underground dealer in Granite Shore. Spammers and me have been working with him for years.

As soon as Cranely sees me hanging around the entrance to his shop, he starts closing up. It doesn't take long—the place is pretty empty anyway. We go downstairs, and he gets right to sewing up the torn seam in my jacket. He'd charge most people a few service credits for that sort of work, but he does my uniforms for free. It's all part of the deal, I guess. Spammers and me worked everything out with Cranely in advance, back when we first started at the factories, so he pretty much knows what I've brought and what he'll give me. We still haggle a little bit over the weight of the sugar, though, Cranely getting all outraged like I'm trying to lift from him. It's a form of endearment or something. If he were really mad, he'd get very quiet. That's when you want to back off about as fast as you can.

You don't want to mess with Cranely. You just don't. He's sort of an old guy, but there are stories about him that would give you nightmares. Sup-posedly, this one girl once ran off with his half of a trade, and like a day later, she just disappeared. All anyone ever found was a doll that looked just like her, lying in her bed. It had the same haircut and clothes and every-thing, just in miniature. And it turned out it was made from *her* clothes, and *her* hair. Her skin, too, I heard. The stories are all like that. Real grue-some stuff. But Spammers and me are on good terms with Cranely, and we intend to keep it that way.

For the sugar and the fish and my new uniform, which Cranely can alter and sell, I get a whole bunch of condensed milk and canned bread. The guards at the fences make little sandwiches out of that stuff during their night watch. They can't get enough of it. Spammers and me do real good business trading with them. We were sure to tell Cranely all about it, of course, and he doesn't mind missing out on what he'd make selling di-rectly to the guards—he's too old to go running out to the fences at night anyway. We still give him a cut of the profit, though.

Cranely finishes with my jacket pretty quickly. Afterward, you can't even tell it was ripped. You really can't. "You've got that look today, boy," Cranely says. "Got something else for me, haven't you?"

"I think you're going to give me a few more pages, Cranely old man. I can just about guarantee it."

From my pocket I take a pair of glasses. They're not the sort of glasses they give you around here, if you're nearsighted or whatever. Uniform glasses are all thin black plastic, or maybe metal wire if you happen to be pretty important as well as nearsighted. These glasses are basically the same as normal ones, but they look totally different. They're sort of rounder and spotted yellow and brown. The hinges are all rusty, and the lenses are broken, but it doesn't matter to Cranely if the glasses aren't new.

"Where did you get these?" he asks.

"I get to keep a few secrets, right?"

He sort of laughs to himself, saying, "Indeed, indeed," and turning the glasses over in his hands, looking real closely at them. I start to get nervous, like maybe these are just normal glasses. The bivvie girl who traded them to me said she found them deep in hellion territory, but maybe she just got them from some other settlement and like scuffed them up to look like they'd been lying at the bottom of some ruins somewhere. You can't trust those bivvies, not really. I mean, this girl seemed nice enough, but everyone says a bivvie is just a hellion who knows how to use a fork. It took me months to lift all the parts for that gun I traded her, and it would be just like me to end up with some sham artifact glasses. I can be a real sucker some-times.

Finally, Cranely says, "Well, boy, looks like we have something here." He's got his big, toothy smile on, like he always does when I bring him an artifact. I don't know what he does with them, just that he'll pay big for anything not made in the settlements. Cranely puts the glasses away and starts shuffling around his desk. "What was it we agreed? Four pages?"

"Seven." Cranely isn't trying to swindle me. He's just being polite.

"Yes, yes. Seven pages. A fine memory you've got. Keep it sharp, that's my advice." He gets out an envelope and hands it to me. Inside are seven folded pages. That's what I mean about old Cranely. He was always going to give me seven pages. He had them all ready.

I put the envelope into my satchel with about a third of the bread and milk. Spammers will be by later to pick up the rest. Cranely is still chuck-ling to himself as he unlocks the store to let me out. "You come by any-thing else like those glasses, you be sure and bring it here."

"Nine pages, right?" I ask.

Old Cranely just loves that.

After I leave Cranely's, I head for the Square, just a few blocks away.

The whole place is pretty much empty this time of day, since mostly every-one is at work or asleep, but there are a few bureaucrats going in and out of the Office of the Prefect. It's like twice the size of any other building in the Square, and all brick and concrete, with these big tall steps. Real impressive stuff. The bureaucrats kind of look at me as I go up the stairs, like I'm the first factory worker they've ever seen.

The Prefect Building has these two huge staircases right inside the doors, but there are never very many people on the upper floors. Everyone is waiting in line to get into this other big room, where there are even more lines to wait in. That's why you don't see many workers here. We only get one day free every ten, and no one wants to spend it in some dumb line. But for a lot of bureaucrats, that's pretty much their job. Spammers worked awhile at the meat farms, and he said the bureaucrats here look just like pigs at the troughs. That's not so far off, I guess. You can see them all lined up on benches, waiting to talk to someone more important than they are. Talking to someone more important is basically like their food.

I wait in one line to fill out a grievance form, then wait in another line to hand it in. The guy at the window reads it and kind of smiles at me as he gives me my number, 732-00-5. Instead of going to wait on the benches, though, I duck into the hall. It's pretty quiet out there, and I just pace around a bit, listening to my footsteps.

After a while the door opens, and Camareen comes out. "Calling num-ber 732-00-5," she says, then she kisses me.

Camareen and me have been going together for about two years. She's the prettiest girl in the world. I know not everyone would think that. I mean, she's not busty like the girl in Mersh's poster, but I don't care. And anyway, the poster girl isn't real. That's one thing I don't get about Mersh. There are real girls all over the place, and he's obsessed with this girl on a poster. I don't know. Maybe I wouldn't feel that way if I didn't get to see Camareen all the time. She's got these green eyes that look like the ocean on a sunny day, like when you open your eyes underwater and there's sun shining down and you can't stop looking, even though it stings.

"Hi, Camareen."

"And what exactly is *this*?" Camareen holds up my grievance form. She's a junior clerk for the Assistant Sub-Prefect of Production, and I filled out the boxes so the form would go right to her. It's pale green, the form, a very different green from her eyes, sort of like nauseated-looking. At the bottom, where you're supposed to explain your grievance, it says, "Camareen works too much."

"I have some real problems with the way things are run around here," I say.

"I'm taking my ten-minute break now, how's that?"

"It's a start." I wait for her to kiss me again, and while she's doing it, I take the envelope from my satchel. "So I guess I'll have to give you this now."

She kind of goes still, then glares at me. "That better not be what I think it is."

"You probably shouldn't think about it, then."

When she sees what's inside, you can tell she's trying hard to stay mad. "You've got to stop doing this, Torro. There's a war on, in case you didn't notice, and we're all supposed to be doing our part."

"Does that mean you don't want them?"

"Of course I want them, you idiot." She's holding the pages now, and she looks like she's ready to cry. It always seems crazy the way dots and lines on a page can do that to her. She'd never let you know it, but Camareen is really sensitive as anything. "But there are better things you could be doing with your time."

To see her now, though, I don't think there are. The pages I got from Cranely are supposed to be music. To me, the marks look a little like stick people sitting on some mostly empty bleachers, but Camareen can read them as easy as normal words. She plays with our settlement orchestra, even though she sort of hates the music. Prip music is just a lot of booming noise that makes you think of battles and whatnot. It's all about how we're part of this big struggle and how heroic we all are and everything. That sort of music really gets some people. Like during official concerts, you can always see bureaucrats just crying their eyes out. But Camareen hates it. The only reason she plays anything at all is because when she was little, she heard a song that wasn't Prip-approved. It was an old song. Artifact music. So when I found out Cranely had a book of old music, I knew I had to get it from him. He won't trade artifacts for anything except more artifacts, though. That's why I needed the glasses. He's been trading me the book seven pages at a time for a while now.

"So is it any good?" I ask.

Camareen is going through the pages, wiping her eyes with the cuff of her shirt. "Really, really good."

"Sing one for me."

She looks over her shoulder, toward the hallway door. "Not here. Later."

"Just sing a little." I know she will if I keep asking her.

She knows it, too. "All right, just a little."

I don't get to hear the song, though, because just then the muster alarm goes off, so loud I wouldn't have heard her even if she'd screamed.

EIGHT

TORRO

More or less everyone in Granite Shore is part of the settlement militia. You don't go on active duty until you turn fifteen, but as soon as you start school, you're learning to assemble a rifle and stab things with bayonets, all that stuff. People don't mind the training, though. It's not like shipping our quotas to the Prips, because we all know *why* we need the militia. Everybody here's seen a hellion before, or knows someone who has, and we know without the militia, the hellions would be in here just hacking us to pieces in no time.

With that great big war the Legion's supposed to be fighting for us, you sort of wonder sometimes. What they tell us, like in school and telecasts and whatnot, is there's this big empire out there planning to take over the entire world and fill it up with their own people. Anyone else— meaning all of us here at Settlement 225—just gets the old summary execution. Those empire people have some name in their own language, but as far anyone around here's concerned, they're just "the Enemy." Sometimes they're also "wanton aggressors" or "implacable foes" for the purpose of official speeches, but in the posters and murals and whatnot, they're usually just big, creepy, shadowy things with long claws and lots of teeth. The Front, where the Legion is out holding off our implacable foes, is supposed to be real far away, but if the Enemy ever gets through, there'll be no stopping them. That's why we have to support the Legion with everything we've got. But I think now and then everyone around here gets the idea something else must be going on. Like, maybe there isn't a war at all. Maybe it's just something the Prips came up with so we'd work ourselves stupid for them. Maybe if we stopped shipping supplies to the Front, we'd all be just fine because there isn't really any Enemy. No one actually comes out and says it, though, except maybe Spammers when he gets into the aquavee because that's like "criminal sedition" and about the quickest way to land yourself at the Front. But no one ever wonders about the hellions. We all know *they're* real.

Once you hear the muster alarm, you've got fifteen minutes to report to a muster station. That's easy enough for Camareen and me, since the Prefect Building is the muster station for the whole Town Center. We're some of the first outside, so there isn't much of a line at the arsenal lockers beneath the big steps. Most work uniforms are made to double as militia uniforms once you put on your gun vest, but Camareen has to take a jacket for the cold and change into boots. She leaves her shoes in one of the cubbies inside the arsenal, and I leave my satchel. If anyone finds it and sees what's in there, I'll have to just pretend it isn't mine and lose all that milk and bread. It'd be a pain, but better than getting caught.

I've never been around the Square during a muster, and I'm surprised at how many important people there are. I guess it makes sense, since they all work around here, but it's still kind of strange to see all these faces from telecasts and news publications and so forth. There's even Qu, the Prefect, walking around in her muster commander's armband. Right behind her is Ghalo, the Sub-Prefect of Production, Camareen's boss's boss. Both of them are watching us all put on our vests and caps like it's the most exciting thing they've ever seen.

Even though Camareen was still a little mad at me before we heard the muster alarm, I can tell she's forgiven me by the way she squeezes my hand as we wait for everyone to line up. This is only our second muster since we started in the militia for real, and it's scary as anything. Most hellions near Granite Shore have learned to stay away, and even when they try something, the sentries at the outer fences usually take care of them pretty quickly. They don't sound the muster alarm unless they're worried the tower guards won't be able to handle things. Last time they called a muster, a whole bunch of hellions had just charged the fences, trying to break through. They didn't stand a chance, though, those hellions. In the end, only a few militia squads got sent out, and no one I know went with them.

But when the trucks start pulling into the Square, I know we're really going out this time. Camareen's hand tightens around mine, but then Ghalo comes along counting us all off into squads, and I get put in the first load of trucks while Camareen waits for the second. She raises one hand to wave as my squad drives off, and I just watch her getting smaller and smaller. I think about how this could be the last time I ever see her, and there's this punch in my chest, like someone's really punching me. I tell myself they always send out way more militia than they need. Like last time no one got killed at all, except a whole bunch of hellions. It doesn't make me feel any better, though.

I'm so worried about Camareen, I don't even think to be scared or nervous on the ride out. Everyone else in my squad is some clerk or low-level bureaucrat. They sort of look at me but don't say anything. They can tell I'm a factory worker.

Three trucks have already arrived by the time we unload in the open ground beyond the fences. Probably they're from some of the factories or the fields out at the edge of the settlement. The militia captain waiting for us is some bureaucrat by the looks of her—she's got a tie on beneath her vest. I guess she knows what she's doing, though. Her name is Ubstia, and she tells us guard towers five through thirteen have all reported hellions in the woods outside the settlement. They're guessing there could be two hundred hellions or more out there. "Probably an exaggeration," Ubstia says, "but the Prefect wants to take this situation seriously."

Hundreds. I can't stop thinking about it, even when we set off for the woods. Hundreds, boyo. That would be like the biggest attack in years. I'm just glad a few other squads went in ahead of us. There's gunfire off in the woods, and I hope it's us shooting and not them. Hellions are bad enough when they only have bows and arrows and axes and whatnot.

It's sunny out but still cold, and when the wind blows, you can smell smoke. The smell of smoke gets stronger as we go, and pretty soon, it starts to look like we're getting near the fighting. We see one dead hellion only a little way into the trees. He's got on what looks like a suit made out of grass and leaves, and he'd probably be real hard to see out here if he wasn't all covered in blood. A bit farther in we see another dead hellion, then another, until there are dead hellions like everywhere, some looking like they've just gone to sleep, but some looking pretty awful. There's one with about three-fourths of his head gone, and one with her guts fallen out and tangled all over the place. It's not just people, either. There are animals, mostly horses, all in just as bad shape as the hellions.

Eventually, we come up on one of the other squads. I'm thinking they're the ones who must've killed all these hellions, but their captain tells Ubstia the hellions were all dead or dying when they got here. That seems really weird to me. I mean, hellions fight each other all the time. They're supposedly like savages who'll kill just about anyone for no reason whatsoever. I just don't know why they'd do it so close to our settlement when we'd be sure to come out and find them.

The gunfire isn't as loud now, but I can't tell if it's dying out or just farther away. Our two captains decide to move on, to make sure there are no hellions planning to like wait around until night and attack the fences. We all spread out in a line, everyone pretty much in sight of everyone else. The woods are sort of like a dream, just full of things you'd never expect to see in real life. There's this one fat gray horse, sort of pudgy and cute, except he's dead, with all these bullet holes down his back. And this other huge hellion, just gigantic, leaning against a tree, with a little tiny dog attached to his leg. They're both dead. I'm thinking about how weird a sight it is, the big guy and the little dog, when the dog makes a sound. Or I think it does anyway. Sort of a whimper. I'm about to go and look when I hear something else behind me, like a click. When I turn around, there's a gun right in my face.

Some girl has appeared out of nowhere, and she's pointing a pistol at me. I can just see her over the barrel. She has these huge brown eyes, and freckles. *Freckles.* Sometimes I think about how I might die, but I never thought I'd be killed by someone with freckles. She'll do it, though. Shoot me, I mean. I'm sure of it.

Before I can quite think about what to do, Ubstia is there with her rifle, yelling at the girl to put down her gun. Two guys from my squad have started running our way. The girl doesn't even look at them, just keeps her gun pointed right at me. I'm thinking about whether she could really be some crazy bloodthirsty hellion who'd kill me just for fun, when all of a sudden Ubstia drops her gun. This other hellion has come up behind her, and now he's got a knife to her throat and another pistol aimed at me. He's more how I always imagined hellions looking, with like a leathery face and a tangled beard and whatnot. He looks mean as anything.

The man yells something at me, but I don't understand because he's speaking his crazy hellion language. There are hellions all over the place now. Like they've just come out of the trees and bushes and everything. And they all have guns. This one woman has a rifle under each arm, pointed at the two guys who'd been coming to help Ubstia and me.

We're all in real trouble now, us *and* the hellions. Any minute, another squad is going to come through here, and maybe they'll shoot the guy with the knife or the woman with the rifles, maybe they'll kill every hellion here, but those hellions won't go down easy, and this little girl is going to get me first. I don't know how I know it, but I do.

The dead dog whimpers again, but this time I see it's not actually the dog whimpering. There are two eyes looking at me from behind the huge, dead hellion. It all just comes together then, when I see those little brown eyes. I look back at the girl, and she's still got her gun on me. But now I know what to do.

"Hey, little girl," I say. Not in hellion. I'm speaking Aux, the language we use in the settlements. "Can you understand me?"

She doesn't say anything, but her eyes sort of widen.

"So listen, little girl, you've got me, I'll admit it. And you got my kiddos here, too. But see, there's a lot more of us around, and some are gonna come through here pretty soon, and when that happens, they're gonna shoot you. You'll probably shoot me first, but they'll get you eventually, is what I'm saying. So how about this. How about you and your friends all come into the settlement with us. I bet you've come a real long way, and you just wanna rest. You won't have to worry about all these hellions out there. I'll need you to give us those guns, though. We can't let you in if you've got all those guns."

For a while I'm afraid she really doesn't understand me, but then she blinks. It's the first time I've seen her blink. She shouts something in hellion to the others. Old Black Beard with the knife shouts back, and they have a sort of argument, but finally the girl throws down her pistol. "On behalf of my coda, I accept your terms," she says. Her Aux is real good, though she makes some of the words sound a little funny. The others look kind of unsure, but, eventually, they drop their guns, too. The guy with the knife is the last one to do it.

Ubstia calls in the rest of our squad. A few stand with guns ready while the others gather up all the rifles and knives and pistols and so forth on the ground. Things get sort of tense for a second when the girl runs to the big dead man, like Ubstia thinks there's another gun hidden there or something, but I tell her she's just getting the little boy. And sure enough, there's this kid with wispy blond hair hiding behind the dead man. He starts crying hysterically, the boy does, but the girl slaps him hard across the face, like real hard, and he stops.

"You want to tell me how you pulled that off?" Ubstia asks as we're walking back to the trucks. "I've never known a hellion to understand Aux."

"They're not hellions," I say. "They're bivvies." Bivvies do a lot of trading in the settlements, so some of them have learned to speak our language. And as soon as I saw the boy hiding beneath that dead body, I knew these people weren't attacking our settlement. They were running from the hellions. That little girl had been trying to fight them off, using the dead gray horse for cover.

"Right. Well, you probably saved us all from getting killed, so nice work." Ubstia sounds sort of annoyed, though. "I should have figured that out. The old guy probably told me, even."

"You speak bivvie?" I'm pretty impressed. You can always hear bivvies talking in that language of theirs whenever they come to trade. It kind of makes you think they're laughing at you most of the time.

"They teach you a few phrases in captain training, but I couldn't understand a word that guy was saying. I don't even know which language it was."

"You mean like if he was talking bivvie or hellion?" I guess if Ubstia'd known that, we probably wouldn't have had a problem to begin with.

"No, a lot of hellions and bivvies have the same language, but there are a bunch of different ones out there. The tribes around here mostly speak English, but there's some Français and Español, too."

That sort of surprises me. I'd always figured every hellion could talk to every other hellion, and the same for the bivvies, but maybe they have as hard a time understanding *each other* as we do understanding *them*.

"You ever consider being a militia captain?" Ubstia asks. "I could get you into training."

"I just want to go home."

Camareen is there, waiting in the Square when our truck pulls up. She's the only one around—the other squads have all been dismissed, but she waited for me. I guess her squad never even went out. I'm real glad about that, so glad I don't even know what to say. While she kisses me, I write my next grievance in my head. It's about not being kissed enough.

I even forget about my satchel, sitting there in the arsenal locker, until she throws it over my shoulder. She went and got it as soon as they dismissed her squad, and the milk and bread are all still there.

NINE

VINNEAS

Being an eminently important person does have its benefits. You get your own private quarters overlooking the Forum, and you're allowed to skip to the front of just about any line you come across. Cadets are expected to salute you, which combined with line-cutting privileges can result in a few sparkling moments of comedy. There's also a special washroom—two, I've heard, though I haven't quite located the second one. Oh, and the food. The food can be rather spectacular at times.

Curator Ellmore made a special show of laying out all the wonderful perquisites I could expect, now that I'd been named Procurator of the Academy. It took all of thirty-seven seconds. Explanation of my new duties occupied the next four and a half hours. The Curator's point—aptly conveyed by the wry smile she wore while describing some of the more excruciating tasks I could look forward to enjoying—was that the privileges of power should never outweigh the obligations; if they do, there's something wrong. Sure, I'd have access to as many as two glossy and mostly private toilets, but I would also be responsible for every cadet at the Schools of Grammar and Rhetoric, as if they were my own personal Legion. It's hard to enjoy even the most regal toilet when you're facing the migraine-inducing hassles cadets produce on a daily basis. It's the same with all my other lovely perks: They just aren't worth it. Take the food. Occasionally, I am presented with some of the most exquisite delicacies Ninth City has to offer, and never do such remarkable meals in any way make up for the company of those with whom I'm forced to share them.

This evening's cuisine is beef and a kind of shellfish with potatoes and greens, each fresh and individually plated—quite a luxury, given that Academy food is prepared in batches of several hundred servings and without much attention to flavor, presentation, or the distinctions in temperature between, say, soup and ice cream. I picture Kizabel and Imway eating together off their wooden trays, talking with their mouths full and having a wonderful time, then I revise the image, because Imway is on active duty now and would be eating with his escadrille, and Kizabel is likely asleep in her lab, snoring into a bowl of instant curry or noodles. Frankly, I'd rather be either place than here.

One of my duties as Procurator is to act as Curator Ellmore's attaché, which means dining a few times weekly with Command, Ninth City's ruling body, of which the Curator is a part. She's sitting at the head of the room, next to Princept Azemon, the most powerful person in Ninth City, and seems to be thoroughly enjoying herself.

Our venue for tonight's mess is a particularly grand function room at the Hall of the Principate. The ornate flourishes—the fluted columns, the arched ceilings, the densely textured patterns of stone—hearken back to some of the earlier, more exuberant demonstrations of irrational mechanics, before we settled, unimaginatively, on a plain, no-frills style deemed more appropriate for a time of war. No doubt my preference for places like this over Ninth City's more austere outer districts is a symptom of being a soft-bellied academic, as any one of my dinner companions would doubtless be glad to inform me.

I have been seated at a long table of lackeys and petty officers, all of them eagerly talking over the recent battle, playing up their part in our stunning victory. I should be boasting and bragging along with them, I know—part of being Procurator is preparing for command, and in a few years these young men and women will be my colleagues. We'll have to trust one another in combat, each of us staking our lives on the others' talent and ability, and it's a lot easier to take orders from someone you've gotten to know over a steak, I've heard. This is my future, the life I've been preparing for as long as I can remember, the prize for outlasting the cut-throat competition of the Academy's executive track, for being anointed a future leader of the Legion. I'll have a good deal of ambitious posturing in my future to go with my juicy tenderloins and shiny toilets.

But for some reason, I can't bring myself to join the froth of self-congratulation over the ass-kicking we gave Romeo during our most recent encounter. Part of the reason is that I'm not convinced we kicked said ass quite as much as we think. That, and I'm distracted by the man sitting beside me.

He's about twice the age of anyone else at the table, and I haven't seen him at mess before, which means he's probably visiting from another city or else the Front. If that's true, however, he ought to be sitting up with Curator Ellmore, not down here. What really catches my attention, though, is his food. He's forgone tonight's fresh fare in favor of what appears to be pickled fish with sour cream, complemented by circles of brown bread covered—"smeared" is probably the better word—in some gooey white substance the consistency of glue. The effect, especially as he spackles the stuff on, is unsettling to say the least.

So overcome am I with mingled horror and fascination that I don't see Imperator Feeroy coming my way. My first clue that anything might be amiss is the abrupt cessation of all conversation around me. When I look for the source of this unexpected silence, I see the Imperator standing over me, wearing what passes for a smile on his long, thin face. Really, it more resembles the sort of grimace people make in especially cold weather: thin lips, mostly teeth.

"Procurator Vinneas," Imperator Feeroy says, his voice surprisingly basso for such a reedy man. "I'm pleased you were able to attend tonight's mess."

"Thank you, sir. It's an honor to be here."

"I wanted to compliment you on your contribution to yesterday's discussion. You have an insightful mind, and your comments were quite helpful in our deliberations."

"I'm pleased to have been of use."

"Of use indeed." The Imperator's cold-weather grin tightens. "It is encouraging to know we have someone like you in our ranks. You are an impressive young man, and will doubtless make a fine officer once you graduate to active duty. Perhaps sooner than you imagine."

"Thank you, sir."

Imperator Feeroy offers me a stiff nod and departs to take his seat with Curator Ellmore and the rest of Command. The Imperator is one of the Legion's highest officers, second in Ninth City only to the Dux. To have received such praise from him, and publicly, is a major achievement. My tablemates, who have been watching me sidelong with alternating jealousy and awe, return to their chatter, now inflating their part in the other day's action until minor contributions have become essential elements of our victory.

Only the man beside me seems unimpressed. He did not acknowledge Imperator Feeroy's arrival and continued eating throughout the short conversation and ensuing compensatory boasting. Now he wipes his mouth and says to me, low enough that only I hear, "So, what'd you do to *that* guy?"

"What do you mean?" I ask.

He pats speculatively at his belly, a much rounder example than those found on most legionary officers. "The man clearly loathes you. So let's hear it. How'd you piss him off?"

It seems I wasn't the only one who'd noticed something sour in Feeroy's flattery. I know exactly why the Imperator is upset with me. After all, I've only spoken to him once before, and it turned out to be my first big mistake in Ninth City's circles of power.

It happened yesterday, at the Command briefing following the All Clear and subsequent cleanup effort. I would have much preferred a nap, but Curator Ellmore was expected at the Hall of the Principate, and she wanted me with her. I sat in the back, nursing a headache from Imway's extra-potent Fizz and listening to Imperator Feeroy, who had been directing Ninth City's defenses, describe the battle.

Overall, the impression he gave was of a ringing and unmitigated success. The enemy's first incursion was detected at 1437 hours, and by 1551, the last of Romeo's scattered forces had been eradicated. Despite the unusually large enemy contingent, very few of our legionaries were wounded or killed, and Romeo failed to strike a single population center or production facility. The only action my new pal Fontanus Jaxten saw was an ovation from the City Guns and an essentially one-sided wrestling match between Kizabel and Imway.

Most of Command seemed happy to accept the Imperator's account of the battle, but the more I listened, the more I became convinced there was something to this attack other than the glorious rout being paraded out for our admiration. If Feeroy's tallies were correct, Romeo's incursion force had been vastly larger than any we'd seen in recent memory. And yet nothing in Feeroy's report indicated anything more than our standard defensive response. Why hadn't the damage been worse?

I waited for someone to speak up, to ask Feeroy how exactly he'd managed so complete and categorical a victory. No one did. Even after Feeroy opened the room to questions, few people voiced any opinion that wasn't simply a compliment with a question mark at the end. So I raised my hand. "Yes, you there," Feeroy said, pointing. "The young man at the back."

"Vinneas, sir," I answered. "Academy Procurator. I was wondering whether you remarked on any deviation from the enemy's typical behavior during this incursion. Novel or unusual tactics, perhaps, or some indication of a different choice of target."

Feeroy blinked, assuming the baffled and mildly disgusted expression of a man who suspects he has stepped in something unpleasant. "Romeo's tactics have remained static for hundreds of years. This is a war of attrition, *Procurator*," he added, emphasizing my academic title and assuming the air of a teacher weary with a particularly dim-witted student. "The enemy's objective is, and has always been, to cripple our ability to supply our forces at the Front. To that end, he will by necessity target our means of production, either in our cities or outlying settlements. In this instance, he failed in all respects."

Another hand had risen several rows down, and Feeroy turned that way, but I persisted. "Excuse me, sir. You haven't answered my question."

Feeroy now appeared certain there was something nasty on his boot. "My answer is no. There was no change in the enemy's usual pattern of attack, only the strength of his numbers."

"But if that's the case, how do you explain such a tidy victory? If the enemy's tactics haven't changed, and our response hasn't changed, shouldn't a larger enemy force have caused more losses than usual?"

"Our 'tidy victory,' as you call it, can be credited to the fighting spirit of our legionaries." Feeroy was by this point quite unambiguously enraged. "I will say as well that the bravery and sacrifice our soldiers exhibited in this battle deserves better than the abstract musings of an untested academic. Perhaps after you've seen combat, you won't be so quick to criticize good soldiers for a battle they *won*."

I would have liked to tell the Imperator I was criticizing him, not his soldiers, but I'd already used as much of Command's time as I dared, and I still had at least one unanswered question. Fortunately, someone else spoke up and asked just what I wanted to know. "If you please, Imperator," said Princept Azemon, "could you tell us what you mean by the 'sacrifice our soldiers exhibited in this battle'?"

It turned out that there had indeed been something strange about this action. As Imperator Feeroy was forced to explain, the attack had proceeded identically to others in the past only somewhat more slowly. He offered no explanation for Romeo's unusual behavior except to say that the enemy force seemed to "linger." As a result, our legionaries were able to engage far earlier into the attack than was typical and thus completely eradicate the invaders before they could reach any of their targets. The prolonged combat did, however, result in greater than usual cost to our defense capabilities, in terms of the number of units left disabled, even if very few legionaries were actually killed. Feeroy was careful to point out that such damage would in no way disrupt production or supply to the Front, and most of those present agreed that the Legion had nevertheless won a fine victory. Still, Feeroy's achievement had been marred, and it was all my fault.

"Can you tell me what you did wrong back there?" Curator Ellmore asked afterward as we crossed the Forum toward the Academy. I only muttered something more sarcastic than sensible, so she said, "You made Imperator Feeroy appear foolish. You might have learned what you wished to know in some other way, but instead you publicly exposed his ignorance, and that is something I fear he will not forgive." I opened my mouth to tell her I didn't particularly care what Feeroy thought of me, but she said, "There will be times, Vinneas, when making enemies will be unavoidable, but this was not one of those times. Do not set others against you unnecessarily. We have enough enemies as it is."

It looks now like the Curator was right. Feeroy is still angry with me, enough to make a complete stranger curious as to the nature of my offense. "I asked him a question" is the explanation I give the man beside me.

He winces theatrically, sucking air through his teeth like someone observing a particularly bloody scraped knee. "That bad, was it?" he says, as if he's intuited yesterday's entire scene, at the same time grinning to himself and preparing another of his hair-raising treats.

"Do you mind if I ask *you* a question?" I say, not wanting to relive my blunder with Feeroy just now.

"Haven't learned much, have we?"

"What exactly are you eating?"

He pauses, the unappealing morsel almost to his lips, as though only now noticing its presence. "This? It's canned bread, toasted and spread with condensed milk. A favorite in the settlements. Looks wretched, I know, but I can't get enough of it." He pops the milk-sodden bread into his mouth with a prestidigitatory flourish.

"You've been to the settlements?" I say, not caring anymore about the bread. The settlements and their place in the war effort—providing most of the food, raw materials, and soldiers necessary to keep the Legion running—feature only marginally in a standard Academy education, and what little we do learn is superficial at best. I've never met anyone who's actually seen the settlements in person. Tonight's mess is turning out to be rather more interesting than I'd expected.

"Originally from Giant's Run," he says proudly. "That's Settlement 105 to you folks. Spent ten years guarding the fences before I ended up in the Legion. Guard's where I got the taste for crusty milk."

"Crusty milk?"

"That's what we called it, anyway," he says, making himself another. "Each settlement has its own name for the stuff. Milko, goo bread, soggies. In Settlement 361, they cook the milk first to brown it. In Settlement 89, they like to add peanut butter when they can get it. But just about everywhere has some version or other."

I suppose that makes sense. Condensed milk has sugar and fat and protein, a great choice if you already don't get enough to eat. I glance down at my own half-finished meal. "You're with the censors, then," I say to the man. No one else would have seen so much of the settlements.

"Censor Reggidel," he says, extending his hand to shake. "I must say, Procurator Vinneas, it's a pleasure not to be the most hated man in the room for once."

"All part of hospitality in Ninth City," I say. "I suppose it's strange, going back to the settlements as a censor."

"It's a unique perspective, that's for sure." He chuckles. "We always thought we were really putting one over on you boys at the Principate, squirreling away warehouses full of grain and canned meat, then pretending we'd only barely made our quotas. No idea you had that all calculated in."

"Is the corruption really that extensive?"

He chews, talking over his crusty milk. "Oh yeah. Just about everyone's pocketing something somewhere along the line. I don't blame them, though. All part of the process. I used to get my crusty on the black market."

He's right, of course. Barter economies and black markets are practically inevitable given the system we've set up in the settlements. "Have you ever thought of doing things differently?" I ask.

"Sounds like you're going to hit me with some crazy Academy crap," he says with another grin. "Let's hear it."

"What if we were to authorize trade between the settlements? It would allow them to exchange their surplus, which would not only raise the local standard of living but increase overall production."

"It'd never work," Reggidel says dismissively. "For one thing, we don't have the infrastructure for it." He sees me about to object, probably guesses I'm preparing to launch into an explanation of how easy it would be to create a rail system connecting the settlements, and says, "But that isn't the real issue. The real issue is you can't trade goods without transporting people, and you can't transport people without transmitting ideas. And once you start exchanging ideas, administering the settlements gets a lot more complicated. I lived in one of those junk heaps for thirty years, and believe me, if anyone there ever got wind of something like thelemity, it'd be chaos. We don't need that. Not with a war on."

"But that's just what I'm getting at," I say, excited now. "Our whole system is based around the premise that the settlements have to remain ignorant of the true nature of this war. But they're as much a part of it as we are. The more we tell them, the more they'll understand what's at stake and the more motivated they'll be to help."

"That isn't how we've been doing things the last few hundred years, kid, and the old way's worked well enough so far. Haven't you heard? We're winning!" He crunches his last bite of crusty and claps me on the back, pushing back from his seat. "It may take another five centuries, but we'll have Romeo beat sooner or later. Now, if you'll excuse me, I'm going to see about dessert."

That's the standard position on this war of ours, the same whether you're listening to the official political channels or general popular opinion: It'll take some time, but we're winning. We're doing everything right; it's going our way. All we have to do is stay the course, and we'll get there sooner or later.

But if everyone knew what I know, if they'd seen what I've seen, I doubt they'd be so sure.

TEN

VINNEAS

The aftermath of any military action, no matter how small, involves a disproportionate amount of administrative drudgery, like righting a roomful of dominoes, and this incursion was no exception. Add in my experience at Feeroy's briefing to cap off the whole exhausting affair and I was poised on the brink of catatonia. But tired as I was, I couldn't sleep. I'd spent part of the evening reviewing data from the battle, comparing it to other engagements in the past, and what I'd learned did nothing to ease my mind. Back in my quarters, I could only lie awake, the same questions bubbling up again and again. Finally, I realized I would have to work the problem through, and there was only one person who could help me. Maybe one and a half.

There was no guarantee Kizabel would be up so late, but I figured my odds were good enough. She's never had much regard for normal sleep cycles, and lately she's been disappearing into her workshop at extremely odd hours and with very little thought for her regularly scheduled duties and coursework.

Her workshop was sealed when I arrived, a dull metal slab blocking the high threshold, but I'd only been standing outside a moment when a voice said, "Why *hello*, Vinneas. How *are* you? It's been *ages*!" The reflection looking back at me from the metal wall was hazy and indistinct but definitely not mine.

"I'm doing fine, Lady," I said. "Is Kiz in?"

"Of course she's *in*," said the voice, the reflection placing hands on hips in a pose of profound exasperation. "She's *always* in, except when she's off gallivanting with you and that eques boy. And ever since the two of you became so *important*, all she does is loaf around here being a reclusive, antisocial crank, never mind that it's two in the morning and everyone decent is in bed."

"Do you think I could speak to her? It's kind of urgent."

"Why *certainly*, Vinn, I'm just supposed to keep you busy while she straightens up a bit"—the voice paused, the shadow leaning to the side as though listening to something just out of view—"oh, and it seems I wasn't to let you know I'm stalling. Oops! But honestly, Vinneas, it's disgraceful in here. It's just like I'm always telling her—" Another pause. "All right, all right," Lady said with a sigh. "Come in, Vinneas."

With that, the metal door drained away, granting me access to the tall expanse of Kizabel's workshop. It's a cavernous metal bay, like the belly of some monstrous steel beast. The far wall, which opens onto a nearby testing floor, is flat and bare, but just about every other surface is covered in all manner of junk, ranging in size and complexity from huge stone monoliths to tiny and arcane filigrees of wood and metal, all organized according to some principle I've never quite been able to fathom. There is a large area devoted entirely to books, thick tomes and unbound pages in towering stacks and cascading shelves. Another wall is lined with mirrors of every shape and description, and as I passed these, I saw Lady Jane walking beside me where my reflection should have been.

Lady is Kizabel's instara, a thinking artifice used as a sort of spectral assistant. Most instari aren't quite as eccentric as Lady, and Kizabel swears she should have scrapped her long ago, but it's obvious Kiz is fond of her, not to mention that Lady is a marvel of irrational mechanics. I ought to know—I helped design her. Physically, she's an exact replica of Kizabel— or perhaps it's better to say she has all Kizabel's features. Lady doesn't much care for Kizabel's sense of style, however, preferring instead a series of irreverent costumes she changes with her mood. That night she was dressed in a set of old-fashioned pajamas, a sleeping mask pressed to her forehead and her long black hair tied in a ponytail.

Kizabel, meanwhile, stood by one of her cluttered tables, bobbed hair pinned tight to her scalp, work overalls splattered with a glowing blue substance that seemed to fade even as I watched. "This had better be important," she said, and though she sounded angry, her expression was ever so slightly guilty. Only then did I take in the greater-than-usual level of destruction around her workshop. A full row of shelves had been split down the middle, its contents scattered in all directions. Several of Lady's mirrors also exhibited signs of disturbance—chips missing and patterns of spidery fractures. Along the far wall, I noted what appeared to be the imprint of a gigantic foot.

"So," I said, glancing pointedly at the wreckage, "what'cha been up to?"

"Nothing!" Kizabel shouted much too quickly. "I mean, just slaving away for those ungrateful equites. You know. Imway needs someone to patch up his precious FireChaser."

"Yes, I'm still hearing about his encounters with the unincorporated peoples." Imway's first official mission, and his resultant wall-punching frustration, has been the source of much amusement for Kizabel and me. "He can't figure out why they won't just follow orders after he went to all the trouble of capturing them."

Having fun at Imway's expense is perhaps the easiest way to brighten Kizabel's mood, but that night her smile morphed into a sneer halfway through. "Well, you two must have plenty of time to chat about it while you're off being hotshots together," she said. "So what are you doing here? Things getting dull up there in Command?"

"Quite the opposite. I need your help." I waited until the metal door had solidified into place behind me before laying out everything that had happened at yesterday's briefing.

"Are you even allowed to tell me this stuff?" Kizabel asked when I was done. She looked concerned, though more over the problems my story raised than my reckless leaking of privileged information.

"I'm making an executive decision to bring you onto the case."

"I just wish we knew how Romeo was making these incursions in the first place," she mused. The blue stains on her overalls were gone now, and she had unzipped the front and tied the sleeves at her waist, revealing a white T-shirt underneath. "Our countermeasures at the Front should make it impossible for hostiles like that to get anywhere near us. It's like they're appearing out of nowhere."

"That's the thing," I said. "I've been looking into it, and I think I've found a pattern. Nothing that explains how the attacks happen—but maybe *when* they happen."

"Really?" Kizabel had given up being indignant with me by then. She's never been able to listen to an interesting problem without getting excited.

"I was hoping you and Lady could help me work it out."

"Well, *I'm* happy to help," said Lady Jane. She had exchanged her pajamas for recreational gear and commenced alternately jogging in place and stretching her hamstrings, as though in preparation for vigorous exercise. "If Kizabel is going to insist on holding a grudge, you and I can just ignore her."

"Yeah, yeah," Kizabel said, sighing resignedly. "Let's have at it. You want something to drink? It'd be tea. I'm never touching aquavee again."

"She only stopped puking about two hours ago," confided Lady between knee lunges.

We were up all night and well into the following afternoon, testing theories, looking at the data from every angle. Lady is a wonder with heavy calculations (and, incidentally, word games), and she worked the numbers cheerfully while jumping rope and doing ostentatious, one-armed push-ups. By the time we had finished, I was pretty confident about our findings, and what we'd found was grim indeed. Curator Ellmore was the logical outlet for our concerns: She could inform Command of what Kizabel and I had discovered without making us any new enemies. And since I knew she would be at supper tonight, I dragged myself here to enjoy some exquisite food I barely have the stomach to swallow.

When the Curator finally gets up to leave, I abandon my plate of uneaten pie and melted ice cream and hurry after her. "Curator," I say, catching up to her in the hall, "I need to speak with you. In private."

"How fortuitous," she says. "I need to speak with you as well, and I was just on the way to my office."

I don't stop to wonder what business the Curator might have with me. As soon as we're alone, I launch into the discoveries Kizabel and I have made, explaining everything in a rush, feeling somehow that if I don't say it all now, I won't ever get the chance.

Kiz and I have learned two important things about yesterday's attack. The first is that, like all incursions behind our main lines, this one is somehow connected to a major battle at the Front. That was the pattern I had noticed and wanted Kizabel's help parsing out: Whenever the Front sees heavy fighting, we at the rear experience a corresponding attack not long afterward. It wasn't an easy connection to prove, in part because the lag in communication with the Front means we only ever learn about the fighting there *after* the corresponding attack here has already occurred, but the pattern is very real. We've got the data to prove it.

The second thing we learned is that Imperator Feeroy was wrong about Romeo's never changing tactics. Kizabel and I looked at battles going back for years, and when we compared the enemy's behavior to the battle two days ago, it was pretty clear the "lingering" Feeroy described was actually a shift in objective. Romeo never intended on hitting our production facilities—he *wanted* to engage our defenses.

All of which points to one very disturbing conclusion: This isn't the war of attrition we thought we were fighting. Something about it has changed. We'll be able to repair most of the losses incurred during this most recent battle in a matter of months, meaning that if Romeo's goal was really to weaken our defenses, he's almost certainly planning to hit us again, and soon. Whatever success we had in the other day's action, it's too soon to declare victory. This incursion was only the beginning.

"Very compelling," Curator Ellmore says when I've finished. We've been in her office for nearly an hour now, and it's become apparent little if anything I've said has surprised her. "And what actions would you recommend?"

"We should evacuate all cities and settlements we don't have the resources to secure and consolidate our forces until our defenses have been fully restored."

The Curator nods, closing the folder with my report inside. "I advised the very same thing this morning at my meeting with Command. Unfortunately, Princept Azemon decided to follow Imperator Feeroy's recommendation to increase production as a means of bolstering our damaged defenses. The other Principates will do the same."

"But we're spread too thin as it is! We can't possibly expect—"

Curator Ellmore holds up a hand, as though to say there's no use debating what we both already know. "I will make sure the Princept sees your report, but I'm afraid the decision has already been made." The Curator has never looked particularly old to me, though she must be well past eighty. Now, though, I see the lines of worry deepen on her face.

Before I can say anything else, there's a faint chirp in the air just beside the Curator's ear, and she says, apparently to no one, "Yes, thank you. Send him in."

Behind me, the door to Curator Ellmore's office opens, and Censor Reggidel steps in. "Good evening, Curator," he says, taking a seat. "I see you've already brought the boy." He glances at me, reads the befuddlement on my face, and says, "And you haven't told him yet." He shrugs. "I thought he would have guessed."

"Guessed what?" I ask.

"You've been promoted, Vinneas," the Curator says with a resigned smile. "Imperator Feeroy requested you specifically as part of his new initiative. He's put you with the censors. Full senior status. Quite the honor," she adds dryly. "The position carries a rank equivalent to centurio."

I glance at Reggidel, then back to Curator Ellmore. "All of this was decided today?"

Curator Ellmore gives me a long look, and it's all I need to understand what's happened. Imperator Feeroy has classified me as an obstacle, so he's getting rid of me. He brought me onto active duty in the Legion, then promoted me to a post it should have taken years of hard work to achieve—an honor, as the Curator said, but one that will keep me well away from anything happening at Command—all so he could ship me off on the pretense of rewarding merit when what he really wants is to put me at a safe distance, someplace where I won't be able to undermine him.

I get the idea that Reggidel has worked out all of this as well and finds it hilarious. "Welcome to the censors, boy," he says with an avuncular grin. "Looks like we've got a new most hated man in the room."

ELEVEN

NAOMI

There is no time for grieving yet, and until that time comes, I must be strong. In this, Mama has been my example. She was waiting when we clattered into camp, and I watched her face as Reaper Thom told her what had befallen us in our scouting, of the raiders coming fast behind us. And though Mama had only just learned her exquisite daughter Rae was dead, killed in some trap of unknown treachery, she did not cry out or weep as I had done, only nodded, and said, "Then we must saddle the horses." She had heard our bugle call, the signal for enemies approaching, and loaded her guns, but Thom's report made it clear our choice was to leave now or not at all. I knew then that whatever sorrow I carried must be sealed up and stored away. To be a limp and sobbing weight would only put everyone in more danger.

There were some who refused to go, disbelieving Thom's tale of hostile warriors beyond counting, a horde about to descend upon New Absalom, and others who believed but lingered to hitch their wagons, cleaving to the wealth they had spent their lives collecting. They are all gone now, dead or taken, as are many of those who rode out with us, bringing only their weapons and what goods they could carry on their backs. Of more than seventy in our coda who came singing into New Absalom some three days past, barely twenty remain.

We reside now on the outskirts of the last township we visited before coming to New Absalom, a place its inhabitants call Granite Shore. They are wary of us here, making no secret of their opinion that we are thieves by nature and will at the merest opportunity take anything not bolted to the floor. They have put us up in a warehouse, a tall and echoing structure with thin, drafty walls, lately used to store sugar but now holding only a collection of hard pallets for my people to sleep upon. Even these sparse accommodations were offered only grudgingly, after we had surrendered ourselves and were already within the township fences, and it became clear something had to be done with us, as we could not be trusted to wander freely about.

We Ochres, once the smallest clan of our coda by far, now stand about middle in number. The families of Fisher and Silva have been cut down root and branch, and of the Sullivans only Marcus and Jenny remain. Apricot is our last Bose. But Mama's kin, the Hollises, remain strong, as do the Mancebos, and we have enough Simon Gardiners yet that nicknames still serve a purpose. As night comes in, we sit around a fire built of planks salvaged from broken crates, flames wavering in the chilly wind that pushes through our flimsy shelter, and argue through what sparse prospects remain to us.

Our only certainty is that we cannot remain here. We have been told as much by one of the township's magistrates, a man named Ghalo, who appeared this afternoon in a rumbling mechanical coach and demanded to speak with our leader. Reaper Thom was chosen to parley with him, and I was sent as interpreter, for Thom has never learned the language of the townships, and in any case, I had negotiated the cease-fire with these people, which made me something of an ambassador. Thom listened impassively as Ghalo explained how little there was to spare in his township, proclaiming poverty, though he was fat through the face and had strings of meat lodged in his teeth. "We will provide you what we can, but I am afraid we are not a wealthy settlement, and we must ask you to leave soon" was what he said. Through me, Reaper assured the man we would not trouble him long, and in that regard my coda is in full agreement. To subsist on what handouts these people deign to provide fills us with bitter resentment, and we take the little that is offered only because refusing would be to forfeit our lives. Though weary and wounded, we are resolved to set out as soon as we are able. Where we will go is a matter of less certainty.

Simon Grumble Gardiner and his cousins say we should head for the southern territories, where the weather is milder and we stand a chance of surviving in the open, sleeping beneath the sky and subsisting on wild game and forage. A different faction, headed by Gideon and Phoebe Hollis, argues that we ought to go north, making for another winter roost in the hope that others of our people will be settled there and willing to give us succor. The two parties bicker back and forth, and voices speak up in support now of one and now the other, but never saying what we all know to be the truth: that both paths will likely lead to our death. The southern lands are overrun with hostile tribes, and we will be outnumbered and exposed on all sides. In the north, we would stand paltry chance of reaching another haven, and if there is no one waiting when we do, we might as well lie down on the frozen ground and give ourselves up to the cold. Either way, we will have to outrun a winter already prowling close behind, poised to fall upon us with its icicle teeth.

It is not easy to hold back the despair that grows in me as I listen to my coda weigh one manner of death against another. Nor do they remark upon the ravenous tribesmen who chased us from New Absalom, now likely waiting just beyond the township fences, Nworkies and Leafcoats and Niagaras and What-Whats, and still others I could not name by sight, all gathered into a warriors' confederacy unlike any we have ever known. To get even a few miles past the fences would be no small miracle; to survive longer would necessitate still greater wonders. I listen, relying on the trick I have devised for when fear or sadness threatens to overtake me: I put on the face I wear whenever Baby is acting up and I need him to mind me or Mama or his manners. Only now it is not Baby I intend to get in line but my own trembling spirit. Yet I cannot help envisioning the grim road before us, and that is what I am doing when from the warehouse door comes a commotion of shouts and banging.

Simon Rumble Gardiner has discovered a stranger outside our warehouse and pinned the interloper against the metal wall with his big brawler's fists. When I see who Simon has in his grasp, I leave my place by the fire and rush over. "Simon Gardiner!" I shout. "You take your hands off that man, or I'll put a knife your gut!"

"They took our knives," Simon replies. "Took them with our guns."

"I expect I'll make do with a spoon, then."

Simon looks over his shoulder, and I am relieved to see him wearing a grin. "Caught this one prowling outside," he says of his captive. "No telling what manner of mischief he's about."

"Do as she says, Simon," calls Reaper Thom. "That boy means no harm, and I prefer not to give his people cause for quarrel."

With a shrug, Simon releases his grip on the townsman, who staggers back, wearing a look of bemused humor, as if to say being handled so roughly was all in good fun. "Just the girlie I wanted to see," he says to me in the language of the townships. "That's twice you've rescued me now."

It is the man from the woods, the soldier who negotiated the surrender of my coda. He is without his gun and vest, wearing only the formless garb of most township men. "If you wish to continue in my acquaintance, you may call me by my name, which is Naomi Ochre," I inform him.

"Fine with me, Naomi Ochre," he says, smiling. His face is not uncomely, dusky and square of jaw, with white teeth and a bristly cap of dark hair. "My name's Torro, in case you're wondering."

I think to ask what sort of person names a child Torro, but in my experience all township people bear similarly nonsensical names. Instead, I say, "Tell me your business, Torro."

"I brought this for you." He reaches past the warehouse door and presents me with a heavy burlap sack. "You can share it with your people. It's not a huge feast or anything, but it's all edible at least."

The sack is full of canned food. We Walkers occasionally trade for preserves like these, and I recognize portions of meat and fish and vegetables, even bread. I hand the bag back to him. "It is kind of you to offer, but I will not accept your charity."

"Hey, it's not charity," he says, still smiling. "It's kind of like a thank-you, you know? My kiddos were all real happy you didn't just shoot me in the head like you could've. Like, they would have been pretty upset if you had. So when I told them about you, they all wanted to throw something in to bring over here. I think they'll be mad at me if I just bring it back." He shrugs. "If you don't take it, I'll probably just throw it away."

"That would make no sense at all," I say, looking back at the sack. It would be a shame to waste good food, and with my coda going hungry. "Very well. You have my thanks, Torro. Please convey my gratitude to your kiddos as well."

"Yeah, I'll do that," he says, and with one more smile, ducks back into the night.

My coda is at first mistrustful of such unwarranted generosity, nor does the explanation that Torro's gifts are in a sense a blood payment ease their minds. Once I have opened the first can, however, others join me, hunger trumping their caution. What few rations we took from New Absalom amounted to only a mouthful for each of us, and until now, this township has offered only cans of thin broth to warm over our fires. But welcome as this food is, it presses upon us the urgency of our departure all the more, for we know we can expect no more such gifts. If we stay, we must either starve or be reduced to begging and thievery.

In the morning, Thom takes me to speak with one of the armed men who are always posted just in sight of our warehouse. I inform this guard that we intend to leave the township and ask him to summon someone of authority to make the arrangements. Shortly thereafter, five mechanical coaches draw up outside of our warehouse and empty a dozen tall, broad-shouldered men onto the street. All carry guns, though by their bearing it is plain they comprise an honor guard for the woman who emerges from the center coach. Her face and figure are equally stout, and she wears her yellow hair in a tight bun. Ghalo stands behind her, bending to speak into her ear as she surveys those of us who have come outside to witness the spectacle of soldiers and sleek township machines.

I know by now what is expected of me and go to Reaper Thom's side as Ghalo and the woman approach. Ghalo is plainly subservient here, his deference much in contrast to the bluster of his previous visit. "Prefect Qu," he says, "I present Thom, headman of the bivvie caravan, and Naomi, his interpreter." I have noticed that township people have no family names and do not seem to understand their purpose.

Thom replies, and I translate, leaving out most of the scorn his words convey. "Reaper Thom Mancebo wishes to inform you that the time has come for us to leave," I say. "He thanks you for your hospitality and asks that you return our weapons and allow us passage to your borders. If we have anything that would be of value to you, we will gladly trade for ammunition, as our own stores are low."

Qu the Prefect has keen, intelligent eyes, and as I speak, they examine me and Thom in turn. "If you are determined to leave, you are, of course, free to go," she says when I have finished my speech. Her tone is unaccountably solicitous. "But you must be aware of how cold the weather has become, and I'm afraid there may be hellions still camped beyond our fences. You would be far better off remaining at our settlement, at least until winter is over."

Reaper's reaction to hearing our troubles laid out as though we had not yet considered them is ungracious, and I must rephrase carefully. "We have already burdened you too much, and it will be better for us to leave now, before the worst of winter sets in."

"Your concerns are thoughtful, but quite unnecessary," the Prefect says with stalwart cheer. "Here at Settlement 225 we all have a duty to share what we produce. It is not a luxurious life, but we are comfortable enough. You will have shelter and all the food you need."

This offer is so surprising that it takes me some time to form the right words for Thom. His response, though, is plain enough. "What would be required of us?"

"Only that you become citizens of our settlement and share in all the responsibilities of citizenship. Those old enough to work will be asked to work, those of schooling age to attend our schools. You will train with our militia and help defend our settlement from the hellions of the outer wilderness. You will be subject to our laws, and to punishment under those laws if you disturb our peace, the same as every other citizen here, myself included."

Reaper Thom regards the Prefect for a long time, so long that I wonder if he is trying to compose some response in her language, but then he says to me, "Tell her we will consider her offer."

When Prefect Qu has gone, we gather around the ashes of last night's fire, and Thom lays her proposal out. The discussion that follows is fierce. My people are loath to relinquish the sovereignty and freedom of our walking, even for the ease and plenty of township life. Not long ago, I would have named them all fools. As a little girl, my envy for the people of these places, with their fine houses and high walls, was so powerful that I would dream of staying behind after one of our visits, of becoming a town girl myself. But as I grew older, I came to understand that there is something not right about the townships. There is a strange air of fear to these people, and no matter which township you visit, it is always there, this same dread, lurking behind their eyes. It is one reason we never stay long. Nor do we fully credit the Prefect's tale of equality and fairness for all. We can see that some here are high and some low, just as everywhere, and we know we will be among the low. Some in my coda shout that it would be better to die free than live as slaves, but this very argument reminds us what awaits should we refuse the Prefect's offer. It takes the balance of the afternoon, but in the end we are of one mind: We will becomes citizens, yes, but at the first sign of spring, we will put this place to our backs and never return.

I am tasked with communicating our consent to the warehouse guards, and hardly have I spoken the words than a great convoy of mechanical wagons arrives outside our warehouse. Men unload one crate after another filled with all manner of victuals. They tell us there is plenty more to be had, we need only ask. We are given blankets and sturdy cots to keep us off the warehouse floor, and in the morning the man Ghalo returns with a crew of boys and girls who issue each of us a card bearing our name and likeness and date of birth reckoned by some queer calendar, as well as something called our "number of citizenship." We are informed that this is to be our identification and we must carry it at all times. In the coming days, we will be assigned work or a place in school, as befits our age and aptitude, and as space opens up, we will be given housing more fit for human habitation than this warehouse.

The benefits of our bargain with Prefect Qu are so ready and so rich that we are immediately suspicious, but in the face of the relief they bring, it is hard to remain circumspect. It is that night, with my coda sleeping warm and safe around me, that I finally shed the armor of sternness and command I have worn since we left New Absalom, and find my heart has broken so terribly that I think I will never find the pieces.

TWELVE

NAOMI

The tablets bearing the names of our lost and dead were left behind at New Absalom, and it strikes me now that if we are to remain here, this could be the first step toward abandoning our old lives, toward forgetting our very selves. And so that night I take the sides of a discarded crate and begin carving them with every name I can remember, beginning with my sister's, Rachel Ochre. I include all those lost to the marauding warriors in our flight from New Absalom, and because these tablets are mine, I break the old rule that animals are not to be so remembered, and carve in Jumbo, who ran tirelessly for me for two days and fell to Niagara fire only after taking more wounds than a beast twice his size could rightly endure, and Leon the ratter, who died with his teeth in the thigh of a Leafcoat warrior intent on staving in my brother's head. I cannot remember all the names at once, but whenever one comes to me, I find my tablets and etch it on. Others in my coda see what I am doing, and offer up more names I have forgotten. It is slow work, but we have time.

The days pass, and though we expect to be sent to work or school as promised, it is as though the settlement has forgotten us. Our food is delivered daily, and we are given new clothes and a stove that produces blue flames from small metal tanks, but we see neither Qu nor Ghalo again. Torro visits with another delivery of cans, and is pleased to find his gifts are not needed, but the news of my new citizenship puzzles him. He examines my identification with furrowed brow, as though uncertain of its function. "Old Qu must have her reasons," he says. "She never does anything just to be nice. You tell your people to be careful."

Our only other visitors are children who come to hurl stones and hateful words at our warehouse. "Bivvie" is the term we hear most often among the clatter of rocks, the same word Ghalo used for us, if without so much anger and contempt. The children flee at the smallest indication of pursuit but always return before long. It is one day as I sit watching them, listening to their jeers, that the flying monster appears.

I see it first as a shadow sweeping over the ground, silent as a cloud overtaking the sun. The children glance upward and scatter, running as if some terrible misfortune will befall anyone who allows that darkness to touch them. When I follow their gaze, I find a silhouette gliding across the sky with the ease of a swan over still water. It is the largest thing I have ever known to travel under its own power, with the smooth lines of a raindrop and no moving parts I can discern. Far, far above, I think I see something else, a point of blackness like a dark star gazing down, but I cannot say for certain.

Others of my coda have come to look, shielding their eyes and pointing into the bright sky as the thing passes over us. It is plainly no township machine, and the sight of it brings to mind stories passed sometimes between us Walkers of great beasts roaming the continent, enormous lizards or wolves or birds of prey, accounts mostly heard third- or fourth-hand or from men deeply in their cups and dismissed as tall tales by anyone with any sense. But I have seen spears of light rise above the Valley of Endless Summer, and now this creature, so who is to say. I do not think it is quite alive, but there is a strange energy to it I would not expect from something built of plain metal, and I know then that whatever else it might be, this behemoth is a manifestation of the fear I have seen in the people here.

All day we wait for the great floating blot to indicate its intentions, but it merely hangs silent in the sky above us like some strange and alien moon. At night, its surface glows with ribbons of light that remind me of the auroras of the far north, or my few sightings of angel's stitches and sparrow fires. The town around us seems abandoned, and we see not a single citizen until late the following morning, when a convoy of trucks arrives, bringing Ghalo and a number of his men. He begins speaking before we have all had time to gather, as though addressing our warehouse and not the people inside.

"Citizens of Settlement 225," he says, "due to extraordinary and unforeseen events, the Ninth Principate has issued special supplementary quotas, which will include an emergency ancillary draft. Draft numbers will be announced via telecast beginning at 1800 hours tonight. All citizens not yet registered must report to the Office of the Prefect immediately for registration and evaluation by Principate censors."

Ghalo is nearly halfway through his announcement before Thom has been brought out, and I rush to translate, feeling a chill at the words, though there are some, such as "Principate," I do not understand. Around me, I hear others who know the township language interpreting for those who do not. When Thom makes his reply to Ghalo, he does not need me to convey the anger in his words. "Explain your meaning, man."

Ghalo glances at Thom, as if only now apprehending his presence. "These new quotas come as something of a surprise, yes," he says coolly, "but as citizens, I should think you all understand the draft and the reasons behind it."

"We have already agreed to fight for your militia," Thom says. "There is no need to draft us into service."

"Oh yes, you are already part of our *militia*," Ghalo says, slowly, as if speaking to a child. "The Principate censors are here to recruit soldiers for the *Legion*."

Thom offers nothing but a burning glare in reply.

"The Ninth Principate governs this settlement and many others like it," Ghalo continues, now stammering a bit as he goes on, "and it employs a fighting force known as the Legion to ensure our safety. At present, the Legion is engaged in a great war, and soldiers are needed to fight. Our settlement is expected to contribute its share. When the number of volunteers is too few to meet our quota, we are forced to hold a draft."

We have all heard of this war the townships claim to be engaged in. Now and again, we will glimpse a banner bearing images of battle or slogans denouncing a mysterious "Enemy," or catch some reference in overheard talk between townspeople. We consider it impolite to inquire, however, not only because of the effort everyone makes to hide any mention of the war from us—covering their lurid posters of knights and monsters as we ride into town, clamming up whenever we are too obvious in our eavesdropping— but also because in all the years my people have walked the continent, we have never seen evidence of any conflict grander in scale than that perpetrated by warring tribes, nor heard tell of such anyplace outside the townships themselves. Reports of roving giants have far more to them than this supposed "war." We have come to see it as a sort of local tradition, like our own winter festivals, or superstition, as with certain peoples of the lakelands said to believe themselves descended from lions. Either way, to offer up contradiction, especially unsolicited, would be ungracious, and might cost us our welcome and the fruitful trading it brings. But now it seems this township fiction demands some real form of sacrifice.

Angry voices have begun to rise behind me, but Thom silences them with a gesture. "You told us nothing of any conscription," he says.

"Contributing to the war effort is one of the foremost duties of citizenship." Ghalo has assumed the air of a man wronged, as if he has caught Thom cheating in a trade. "As with all responsibilities of citizenship, the draft is clearly outlined in our settlement charter, which can be found at the Office of the Prefect. You or any of your people could have gone to read it at any time. Now," he says, turning his back by way of conclusion and striding toward the trucks, "if you will please ask everyone to form an orderly line, we can have all of you to the Town Center and back in time to watch the telecast tonight."

No orderly line is formed, and we need no settlement charter to tell us we have been sorely deceived. Before Ghalo has taken two steps, my codesmen have erupted in anger at our betrayal. I do not see all of what happens, but I feel the surge at my back as some rush toward Ghalo and his trucks. I hear the shouts, then the thunderous crack as Ghalo's guards fire into the crowd. Thom vanishes from my side, and when I look back, I see him kneeling on the ground, dark blood welling from a wound in his thigh. Despite his injury, there is no mistaking the killing gleam in his eye, and like a striking snake, he rises and jabs his fist into the throat of a guard who has run up behind me.

The guard topples, sputtering, but two more come rushing after. Thom has broken the arm of one and the jaw of the other before a third deals him a blow to the skull with the butt of his rifle, then all three are on him, pinning him to the ground as they bind up his hands. I have watched all of this rooted in place, but now I rush to Thom's aid and am put solidly on my rear by a guard's backhanded slap. That is when the general commotion impresses itself on me, the moans and shrieks of the injured and the indictments of the guards. Several of my codesmen have taken bullet wounds like Thom's, the guards having kept their aim low to avoid a deadly shot, and of these, most are now being led away. Strong hands encircle me, and I see Mama has come to lift me to my feet.

Ghalo, who has moved only a few paces, surveys the violence as though he had expected nothing less. "Your wounded will be treated at the Town Center," he says wearily, "but I am afraid disturbances of this sort carry our harshest penalties." He addresses his next words to me. "I hope you can convince your people to cooperate before this incident gets any worse."

There is little convincing to do. We know this is a battle we cannot win, and those of us able to walk heave ourselves into the trucks. Even Baby Adam must come with us because there will be no one left at the warehouse to watch him. Only those aged fourteen to sixty may be drafted, but for reasons I cannot grasp, anyone nine years or older is required to register. Not even those too old to fruitfully hold a gun are spared, and so Baby Adam rides beside me, his face buried in Mama's skirts.

We have been driving only a short while when the sky is rent by a sound like tearing leather. From my window, I glimpse an aircraft moving low over the nearby buildings, a swift and elegant thing shaped like a diving bird, and while I am certain it is some cousin to the shadowy apparition floating noiselessly above, in its movement and noise it seems more akin to the truck rumbling beneath me.

The metallic falcon vanishes over the horizon of rooftops as our convoy rattles slowly behind. Presently, the blocky forms of factories and silos shrink into the dwellings and shops I recall from my previous visits to the townships. When the trucks finally shudder to a halt, I see we are in the marketplace, where we Walkers do most of our trade. High over the place looms a great showpiece of a building, an edifice of concrete and tall windows, meant, I suppose, to inspire fear and obedience. I take this to be the Office of the Prefect because that is where Ghalo and his men now take us.

Outside, a great mob has gathered, all made up of children—citizens of this settlement registering for the first time, I presume. My coda makes a strange addition, for otherwise the throng contains not a single adult, only a few dull-eyed chaperones standing along the perimeter. As I join the crowd, one man pulls me aside, and I am surprised to see it is Torro. "Hey, Naomi," he says, his head low like a man hoping to avoid recognition, "I need to talk to you."

"What you need is no concern of mine," I growl, pulling free of him. "And I will thank you to keep your hands off me."

"Look, I'd have warned you if I knew, I really would have. I mean, they're only supposed to do the draft once a year, and this year's was like two months ago. They only told us about this one today. People are real mad about it."

"I cannot imagine why anyone would be upset. I have heard forcible recruitment is one of your duties of citizenship."

"Hey, I'm real sorry this happened to you, I really am. Old Qu really pulled a dirty trick on you. I get it. But you've got to listen to me now, or it's going to get a whole lot worse."

"I do not quite see how such a thing is possible."

Torro glances furtively about, first at Ghalo's guards, then at the ponderous building above. "In a few minutes, they're going to take you all into the Prefect Building, and they're going to give you a test."

I regard him skeptically. "What manner of test?"

"That's the thing—they don't tell you. They just ask you a bunch of questions. It's like they know some secret, and they want to see if you know it, too. But what I want to tell you is, if you feel like you can answer any of their questions, don't. Understand?"

"No, Torro, I cannot rightly say that I do."

"It's just, I don't know." He runs his palms over his bristly hair, desperation clouding his face. "It's like, I took the test, too, starting when I was nine and every year until I turned fourteen. And I knew some people who must've told the Prips what they wanted because I never saw them again. So like, you've got to tell your people what I just told you. Don't give the Prips what they want." He raises his eyes to take in my codesmen, all of them watching us with dark expressions. "Is that your brother there? The little guy? You know they're not going to let him come with you, right? He's too young. I can watch him for you if you want."

Ghalo has appeared at the top of the stairs leading into the Office of the Prefect, wielding a loudspeaker to order us inside. "I would sooner trust him to a pack of hungry dogs," I say to Torro.

I turn my back on him and go to join my codesmen. One at a time, we pass through the building's gaping threshold and present our identification to a man seated inside, who ushers us to stand single file in a long, twisting line. I am pondering what might have happened had I simply thrown my identifying card from the back of the truck on the ride here when from behind me someone screams, and I know without looking that it is Baby. He has been refused admittance, just as Torro predicted, and while Mama stands helpless outside, he thrashes wildly at anyone who tries to lay a hand on him. I am able to scold him quiet, but I am terrified of what will happen once Mama and I are locked inside, and he locked out.

"Hello there," someone says behind me. "You must be Naomi." I turn and find myself looking into the face of a slim, green-eyed girl. "My name is Camareen. My friend Torro told me about you." Her voice is soft, with a faint music to it. "Your brother can stay with me if he wants. I'm supervising the line, so he'll be able to see you the whole time." She smiles down at Baby. "Would you like that?"

I am about to tell this Camareen just what she can do with her offer when Baby nods shyly and extends his hand for her to take. Together, they walk to a place outside the ropes bounding the line of children, Baby still tense and frowning but his terror gone. The companionship of a pretty girl has gone a long way toward mending his fears. I, meanwhile, am singled out as a truant and compelled back into line, this time nearer the front. Baby and Camareen have fallen into conversation, and though Ghalo accosts them, intending to learn why Baby is not in line, the girl's smile deflects him as easily as waxed cotton does rain. By small degrees, I move toward the far end of the room, and though I search the line for Mama, I do not see her again before the door there opens, and I am ushered inside.

THIRTEEN

NAOMI

The room beyond seems unaccountably large for its sparse furnishing of a small rug and desk and two men. One, bald on top with bushy chops and sleepless eyes, reclines behind the desk, turning a small card over in his hands. "Come in, then," he says, rasping somewhat. "Naomi, is it? Have a seat, Naomi, this won't take long."

I sit as requested, noting as I do the other figure standing over the weary-eyed man's shoulder. Though tall and regal in bearing, he is younger than I at first imagined, perhaps not much older than Rae. With this thought comes a pang of hurt that hardens quickly into anger, a hardening that must show in my face because the young man has begun to regard me more closely, as though trying to decide where he has seen me before.

"My name is Reggidel," says the older man, offering the card, which I suspect bears my citizen's identity, to his compatriot, who examines it with interest. "This is Vinneas. We both work for the censors of the Ninth Principate. We just want to ask you a few questions, then you can go."

These are my enemies, tricksters and cheats and scoundrels. If Rae were here, she would have them begging for mercy inside of a minute, and I resolve to come as close as I can. I hitch on my armor and glare at them as I would misbehaving children.

Reggidel, meanwhile, has reached behind his desk and produced a wooden case about twice the length of a man's forearm. When he opens it toward me, I see it is filled with several dozen small metals disks. Each is identical to the others, quicksilver lenses small enough to fit in my palm, and yet one, situated unremarkably near the center, is strangely fascinating. I reach for it, unthinking, surprised by the faint tingle of its surface. Its weight as I hold it in my hand seems less physical than sentimental.

"Thank you, Naomi," Reggidel says, closing the case. "You can keep that if you'd like."

It is only then that I recall Torro's warning, not to do what these people want, and realize with a flash of fear that I have done precisely that. I drop the lens like something turned suddenly hot; it lands, spinning, on the table between us and goes on turning far longer than the force of its fall should warrant. "No," I say to Reggidel. "Take it back."

"Hold on to it, in case you change your mind." I have amused Reggidel, if his grin is any indication. "Only one more thing, then we're finished."

He takes out a second case, smaller than the first. The articles inside are far more familiar in appearance than the silver disks: all relics of the type found in long-abandoned places, the ruined cities and settlements scattered up and down the continent. My people collect them for trade in the townships, where they are known to fetch steep prices. This is the largest collection I have yet seen. It is arranged according to no scheme in particular, fine jewelry and delicate machines of ancient design displayed alongside broken cups and scraps of dirty paper.

"Does anything there interest you, Naomi?" Reggidel asks. "You can pick them up if you like. Go ahead."

In truth, one item in particular does seem fascinating: a pair of old horn-rimmed spectacles. The lenses are gone, the frame cracked, but I have an unaccountable desire to try them on. Instead, I force my hands into my lap and keep them there. I will not give myself away a second time. I say to Reggidel, "I have no use for your trash."

He looks into my eyes then, and I hold his gaze until he sits back, still wearing his grin. "Well, Naomi, it looks like we're in luck. How would you like to go on a little trip with us?"

"I will not go anywhere with you," I inform him. "If you have nothing more to say to me, then let me leave."

"That's your choice, I suppose, but hear me out first." He has retrieved the metal disk from its place on the table and begun twirling it between his fingers. "You see, Naomi, I have a feeling you may be a very special girl, and I'm hoping you'll give me the chance to prove I'm right. The trouble is, this place isn't equipped for the sort of test we have in mind."

"And what sort of 'special girl' do you imagine I am?" I ask, putting as much contempt into the question as I am able.

"Unfortunately, I can't tell you that just yet. Our little experiment here isn't nearly as conclusive as we'd like, but that can't be helped. If it turns out you're not what we're looking for, we can have you back here by tomorrow. If you are, we will ask that you accompany us to our city. No more settlement school, no work detail when you turn fifteen. You'll train to be an officer of the Principate."

"I thank you for your offer," I say, all ice, "but I have had enough plush promises from men of your type. If you are finished, I would like to leave."

Reggidel frowns. "Odd. Usually children can't get out of this place fast enough."

"Censor," the boy Vinneas says, "I don't think this young lady was raised in Settlement 225. It would explain why she's never registered, even though she's twelve years old." He hands my identification card back to Reggidel. "You aren't from around here, are you, Naomi?" he asks, and I am surprised to hear him speaking my native tongue. "You're one of the people who call themselves Autumn Walkers."

I nod, dazed. I have never heard my language from one of these townspeople. His accent is strange, but the words are spoken well enough.

"How did you come to be a citizen of Settlement 225?"

"We were tricked," I say. "My coda came here fleeing the winter and hostile tribes. We were offered shelter, but it seems being pressed into service in your Legion is the price of hospitality."

Vinneas appears both angered and embarrassed by my story, a reaction that nearly makes me like him, until I think this, too, may be some ruse.

"It sounds like the Prefect here made Naomi and her people citizens so they would be included in the draft," he says to Reggidel in their township language. "It must have been just after the Principate introduced the new quotas."

Reggidel chuckles with grim amusement. "I'm sorry to hear that," he says. "Looks like those jokers really screwed us on this one."

"Something that might have been avoided if we didn't put such a high premium on ignorance," Vinneas answers, his air that of a man making a point in some ongoing dispute.

Reggidel doesn't reply, merely flips the silver disk once more and pockets it. "The problem, Naomi," he says, "is that we can't take you with us unless you want to go. Oh, I suppose it would be *possible* to bring you along against your will, but it wouldn't be in our interest. Our Legion has plenty of conscripts, but people like you need to be volunteers."

His talk of conscripts and volunteers has reminded me again of my coda, of all those waiting to be drafted, and the others, shot and beaten and bound and carried off to some unknown punishment. I think of Rae and what she would do in my place. "I will make you an offer," I say to Reggidel. "In the room behind me are my mother and brother and other friends dear to me, all brought to be part of your draft. More were taken prisoner on orders of your man Ghalo, who is a liar and a villain. You will ensure that all of these people are released from your draft and every law of this place, and have food and shelter enough to live out the winter in comfort. In the spring, they will be given whatever supplies they require and safe passage from this township. Do that, and I will go wherever you ask."

"Well, Naomi, I'm not sure I can make that kind of promise." Reggidel's mouth has twisted into something half grin, half grimace. "The people here won't be too pleased about our interfering with the way they govern their settlement. We might just try a few others from your—what did you call it? Coda? Maybe one of them will have what we need, along with a little better sense. I've heard the settlement schools aren't exactly pleasant, but at least you'll be able to look forward to working at the factories sixteen hours a day, nine days a week."

I am reminded of the children here, of their slurs and hurled stones, and wonder what sort of life could have bred such meanness. "You have a notion that I am special. Tell me how special."

"If we're right about you, and you really were interested in those glasses there," Vinneas says. "Approximately one in fifteen million." He turns a broad smile on me, and I gather I did not hide my interest quite so well as I imagined. "Give or take a few million."

I regard Reggidel evenly. "If you are willing to make that gamble, sir, you have my blessing."

"You smug little shit," Reggidel says, glaring balefully at Vinneas. "Whose side are you on?"

"As I understand things, we're all on the same side," Vinneas replies, still smiling.

The comment draws a rueful chuckle from Reggidel. "Right you are," he grumbles, as though this is not the first time such words have passed between them. He gives me one more long look, then heaves an exaggerated sigh, throws up his hands in resignation, and closes his case of curios with a slam. "You win, Naomi. It's a deal."

FOURTEEN

TORRO

We all get together in the fourth-floor common room to watch the draft on telecast. Mersh has a room right on fourth, so he gets there early and saves a couch, just lying across it like the big dumb log he is while he's waiting for the rest of us, and then we all squeeze together, Camareen and Hexi and Isslyn in the middle, all locking arms, and me and Mersh squashed on the sides. Spammers shows up last, and he doesn't sit with us, just leans against the wall with his head back, looking real tired. I guess he thinks it's dumb to squeeze onto one couch when there's so much other space. Fourth has the smallest common room in the dorm, and the viewer is kind of crappy, so there aren't that many people here. That's how we wanted it, though. If one of us is going to get called up, we don't want to be packed in with everyone down on first and second.

Right at 1800, the viewer flicks on, and there's Ghalo, sort of blurry and crackly, but definitely Ghalo. Camareen's hand closes around mine, and her fingers are freezing. Her hands can be pretty cold sometimes, but this is different. They're like ice.

Old Ghalo doesn't waste any time. He gets right into drawing the numbers, reading off each one real slow, one digit at a time. The sound in here is pretty good, so we can hear him all right, and I close my eyes and listen, trying real hard not to think about how after tomorrow, I might never see Camareen again.

I'm not a total idiot. It's not like I think Camareen and me will be together forever or anything. We've each got like thirty more years of drafts ahead, and it's pretty definite one of us will get called up eventually. I just want a little more time with her. It doesn't even have to be that long. In a few years, we'll all get moved into double rooms instead of the quads you get just out of school, and Camareen and me want to apply for a place together. And then pretty soon we'll need to start having some babies because every citizen is supposed to have at least two by the time we turn twenty-five. It's sort of like another quota. Most people are pretty unhappy about it, especially the girls, who have to do all the uncomfortable stuff, but Camareen says she doesn't mind as long as it's with me. So if I get called up in ten years, I think I could probably stand it. Or five, maybe. Just not now. Not today. But there isn't anything I can do to stop it. Ghalo just keeps reading off the digits, one after another, all steady and whatnot like a dripping faucet.

Every time Ghalo starts out with a digit that matches one of ours, Camareen squeezes my hand a little. One number actually comes pretty close. The first six digits are the same as Camareen's, and it's like my whole body fills up with cement. My stomach, my lungs, everything. But then digit seven is different, and I don't think I've ever been so relieved in my life. I'm just relieved as anything.

The telecast only lasts about ten minutes, but I'd rather do ten straight shifts at the factory than sit through those ten minutes again, I really would. Finally, Ghalo reads the last number and starts doing his usual speech, telling everyone who got called up to be at the Shipping Station by 0900 tomorrow, but you can hardly hear him because everyone's started like laughing and cheering and whatnot. Camareen hugs me hard and kisses my cheek, and everyone's doing something like that. I even see a few people I don't really like all that much, and we just grin at each other like we're all the best friends in the world.

But then Camareen says my name, and she sounds scared, like really scared. For a second I think maybe I didn't hear one of the numbers, like maybe she got called up after all, but then I see Hexi at the other end of the couch. She's got both hands over her mouth, and tears just rolling down her cheeks like crazy. Isslyn, who's sitting next to her, is rubbing her shoulder and saying, "Hexi? Hexi?" but it's like Hexi doesn't even hear her. Then Hexi starts making this sound, sort of halfway between a hiccup and a scream, and it just gets louder and louder. I start to get pretty scared because Hexi really sounds like she's choking, and she won't say anything or look at us, even though Camareen and Isslyn have both put their arms around her.

Mersh and me, we just stand there like complete morons. I start to think about like what if she runs, just tries to make it past the fences or hides out in a factory basement or something. I imagine Hexi holed up in some storage room, with us bringing her food and everything, even though I know it'd never work. Ghalo's always going on about how no one escapes the draft. The settlement marshals find you no matter what.

Suddenly, from across the room, there's this awful screeching sound, and everyone looks, even Hexi. It's Spammers, dragging a metal chair across the floor. The noise is just terrible, but Spams doesn't seem to care. He plonks the chair right in front of Hexi and sits down. He's got a little satchel with him, and from inside he takes a bottle of yellowy liquid and sets it down with a clink.

"This is some shit, Hex," he says, looking Hexi right in the eyes. He sounds real serious. Spammers is always joking about everything, but he sounds real serious now. "You may be just a number to those lousy Prips, but we love you, got it? We love you, Hex, and we're gonna send you off right." He pulls a stack of little glass cups from his satchel and pours two from the bottle. "I was saving this for something special," he says and offers one glass to Hexi. "You're it."

Hexi just sort of looks at him, like he's a talking dog or something. For a minute, I think she's going to start scream-hiccupping again, but then she grabs the glass and downs it. She wipes her mouth, kind of wincing, and holds out the glass again. "How about one more?"

We all get pretty drunk after that. It turns out Spammers has bottles of aquavee hidden like all over the dorm, and when he realized Hexi'd been called up, he ducked out and grabbed one. The aquavee isn't that great, like it really burns your throat and tastes like crap, but no one complains. Aquavee is real hard to get, and expensive. When we finish the first bottle, Spams gets us a second, and a third. Other kids who'd stayed in the common room after the telecast go and find plastic cups, and pretty soon word gets around that someone up on fourth is giving out aquavee, and people just start stopping by. Some we know, but most are people we've never even talked to. Spammers doesn't care if they're total strangers. He just goes on pouring drinks.

One of the people who shows up later is this guy Gemt. He's one guy I really hate. I can't stand him. He works at the Prefect Building with Camareen, but everybody knows he only got the job because his father is the Sub-Prefect of Production. Ghalo, that is. And yeah, it's not supposed to matter who your parents are. You don't live with them or anything, or even see them that often. We're all one big family in Settlement 225, old Qu likes to say. So when a total moron like Gemt gets a sweet office job and Spammers, who's approximately a million times smarter, ends up in the factories, it's supposed to be some big coincidence that the total moron's father happens to be like the second biggest big shot in the entire settlement. The part that really drives me crazy, though, is that Gemt actually thinks he *earned* his job. He's always talking about how hard he worked in school, just studying all the time when he could have been out having fun, like the rest of us would all be at the Prefect Building, too, if we'd only thought to *try*. It makes me crazy. Every time I see the kid, I want to punch him in the face.

Camareen thinks I'm too hard on Gemt. "You should give him a chance," she'll say sometimes. "Gemt has it rough in his own way. It's not easy being the son of someone everyone hates as much as people hate Ghalo." And maybe she's right, but I don't feel like giving Gemt a chance tonight, that's for sure. So when he starts coming our way, I decide to let Camareen talk to him and go sit with Spammers. He's back in his spot by the wall, sitting cross-legged with like his fifth bottle of aquavee. He starts to pour before I even hold out my glass, and I barely catch the aquavee before it splashes onto the floor.

"We must be guzzling down your whole supply," I say to Spammers.

He raises his glass in a little toast. "There are more important things, right?"

"Yeah." I don't know if Hexi's just forgotten her number got called or what, but she looks like she's having the best night of her life, and it's all thanks to Spammers. He was the only one who got that there was no point trying to convince her everything was going to be fine because it wasn't. "That was real nice what you did, Spams. For Hexi, I mean."

"We've only got one Hexi. Had to make it count." He pours himself another drink, splashing aquavee over the glass. "And hey, I wanted a proper send-off, too."

"What do you mean?" I ask. I don't get an answer, though, because he's busy emptying his glass in one go. "Spams, what are you talking about?"

"I'm going, too," he says, all casual, like it's no big deal. "They got me on demerits."

Demerits are supposed to discourage people from "damaging or diminishing the common good of the settlement," as they say. Anytime you do something wrong or break the rules, like if you steal or start a fight, or you show up to work late or in a messy uniform, you get stuck with a certain number of demerits based on how bad whatever you did was. If you've got too many demerits when the draft comes around, you get called up automatically. They just take your number and put it right at the top of the list.

"They nabbed me building a still. You know, to make aquavee," Spammers says. "It wasn't working yet, but they said it *constituted clear intent toward criminal activity.* Demerits out the ass." He kind of leers at his glass. "Too bad. My stuff would have been way better than this crap."

I think I'd fall over if I wasn't already sitting on the floor. "When?"

"About two weeks ago. I might have been able to work them off, the demerits, I mean, if I'd had all year like I thought. But then the draft came along and, you know."

Yeah, I know. You can erase demerits by doing things that are good for the settlement, things like getting an "excellent" on your performance reviews or volunteering to clean up trash or like writing a patriotic song or whatever. Just being an all-around great citizen of old S-225. Everyone ends up with a few demerits now and then, but we're always sure to get rid of them before the draft. Except this time, no one knew the draft was coming.

"Say the still was part mine," I tell Spams. "Say I was helping you. Maybe that would get you under the limit."

"Awful nice of you, boyo, but they'd never go for it. And even if they did, it wouldn't help. It'd just be both of us off to the Front."

I just sort of lean back against the wall. I can't think of anything to say.

"Listen, kid," Spammers says, "do me a favor and don't tell anyone about me getting called up. It's all right for Hexi, people all crying over her and everything, but I don't think I could take it. All right?"

"All right, Spams. Pour me another drink, will you?"

"Will do, boyo. Will do."

We're there all night, the six of us. No one says it, but I think we've got this idea that as long as we stay together, none of us will have to leave. It's dumb, I know, but anyway, it's how I feel. Even after the aquavee runs out, and everybody else starts wandering off to bed, we stay behind, sometimes not even talking, just sitting together. Later on, Hexi starts like cuddling up to Spams, and I wonder what he's going to do about it. Girls have about zero appeal to old Spammers, something even Hexi knows, but it's also common knowledge she's been after him for years, and tonight's a special occasion, so maybe Spams'll make an exception or whatever. But, eventually, Hex just falls asleep on his shoulder, and Spams announces he's going to go put her to bed. She won't find out he got called up, too, until tomorrow, when they both show up at the Shipping Station. I get this idea that I want to go with them, like to say good-bye, but that's not allowed. So when Spammers picks Hexi up and carries her off, I know it's the last time I'll see either of them. I want to say something else to Spammers, but I promised I wouldn't let anyone know about him getting called up, so we just sort of nod to each other, and that's it.

Isslyn goes next, and Mersh has turned back into a big dumb log, just snoring away on the couch. Camareen's roommates are gone for the night, so we leave for her place, one building over. Outside, it's just getting light, and between the pink sky and the cold air and Camareen warm against me, I actually feel happy. I don't want to feel that way, but I do.

□————————□

FIFTEEN

TORRO

I wake up to this loud banging on the door to Camareen's room, and someone with a very deep voice shouting for us to open up. I'm pretty groggy, my eyes all sticky and my head pounding and everything, and I sort of look around, kind of figuring out where I am and taking stock of things. The clock over the door reads 1021, and for a second I think whoever's doing the banging is telling us to get up and go to work. The whole settlement is supposed to get the day off after the draft, but maybe, since this was a special ancillary draft or whatever, they want us back right away. My last shift would have ended at 0800 anyway, though, so I'd already have missed it, and I'm sort of mulling that over when the door completely busts open, and three guys in uniforms rush into the room.

Before I know it, I've been dragged onto the floor and one guy has his knee on my back and another's tying my wrists with one of those plastic wrist-cuff things they have. Camareen is trying to get to me, but the third guy is standing in her way. When she balls up her fists and starts hitting him, he grabs her arms and kind of locks them around her. That makes me pretty mad. I try to get up, but the guy on my back just twists my arms around, and it hurts so bad, I collapse back down. Then they stand me up anyway, and the guy with the wrist cuffs gets out a card, like an ID card only a little bigger, and holds it next to my face, like comparing me to the picture on the card. Now that I can finally get a look at the three of them, I see they're all wearing the blue uniforms of settlement marshals.

"It's him," says the guy with the card. "Let's go." He and the guy who'd been sitting on my back grab me by the shoulders and haul me out the door while the third guy stays behind to keep Camareen from following. All the way down the hall, I can hear her screaming, "Torro! Torro!"

but every time I try to get away, one of the marshals twists my arm, so I just start kind of insulting them, trying to get them to tell me what the big idea is, dragging me around like this. They just keep on dragging me, though, and eventually we get outside, and they take me to this huge truck and throw me in the back and slam the doors behind me.

It's dark inside, but I can see a few other people, mostly dormitory slobs like me but some older folks, too. They're all real quiet, except one who looks right at me and says, "Torro?"

"Spammers?" It's him all right, but I still ask, because I'm surprised as anything to see him.

"I can't believe *you're* the one they were looking for. We must have been sitting out here half an hour."

"I don't get it," I say, though I'm starting to, and I don't like it one bit.

"Me, either," Spammers says, sort of laughing a little. "I mean, I know why *I'm* here. Figured if old Ghalo wanted me for the draft, I'd make him come and get me. But you, I don't know. They must have made a mistake."

"Yeah, right, a mistake." I know that's what it has to be. There's no reason the marshals should be after me. But then I think about the one guy holding up that picture of me and saying "It's him," and how sure all of them were, and I start to get pretty worried.

It isn't far to the Shipping Station, but it's like the ride takes forever. For one thing, it's real cold in the truck, and the seats are made of metal, and those stupid marshals dragged me off wearing only my shorts and socks, so I'm completely freezing. Also I'm going crazy trying to come up with something to say to make the marshals let me go, and I can't think of a single thing. It doesn't matter much, though. When the truck stops and the doors open, just about everyone in the stupid truck starts yelling how there's been a mistake and they shouldn't be here. The marshals don't even listen. They just start pulling people out, beginning with me because I was the last one in. As the marshals toss Spammers out the back, he shouts, "Thanks for the ride, kiddos!"

The Shipping Station is pretty crowded, but just about everyone is already waiting to board the train, so the long maze of fences leading to the main platform is practically empty. The marshals hurry us through, giving anyone who slows down a hard shove in the back. At the end of the fence maze is a girl with a list of everyone who's supposed to be on the train, and the marshals read off our numbers one at a time. I think of trying to tell the girl I'm here by mistake, but about a hundred people are already doing that, so I keep quiet. What I've decided to do is wait until I find someone in charge, then explain how my number didn't come up and I don't have that many demerits and I didn't volunteer, so, ergo, I should not be joining the stupid Legion. The marshals don't follow us onto the embarking platform, and for a second I think about trying to run, but we're fenced in on all sides. There's nowhere to go but onto the train.

The Shipping Train is about the creepiest thing I've ever seen. It's made to carry everything we make here in S-225, from lumber to sugar to canned herring, so most of it is covered in heavy, metal containers. Only the very back is for carrying people, and what's so creepy is that the only people around are the ones getting shipped off to the Front. As far as anyone can see, there's no one actually driving the train. No marshals, no Prips, no anybody. It's like the train just runs itself. There are all these stories about the Shipping Train, people who say they've seen skeletons working the engines or whatever. I don't believe any of that, but it's still a real creepy train, especially when we're standing around and the doors just open, like it knows we're there, and inside, it's totally empty.

Up above, Ghalo and Qu and a bunch of other important-looking bureaucratic types have gathered on a balcony to see us off. Some real dramatic music is playing, one of the Prip songs with all the drums and trumpets and whatever, and you can tell those bureaucratic types are just loving it, watching us all do our heroic duty and whatnot. It makes me think of Camareen, about how much she would hate this and how worried she must be. I tell myself I'll be fine. I just have to find someone who isn't a complete ass-brained idiot, and'll actually understand I'm not supposed to be here.

I look around for Hexi, but you can't find anyone in this stupid crowd. There are a few people like me and Spammers who're wearing whatever we had on when we went to bed last night, but just about everyone else is in their regular work uniforms. But it's Hexi, so she spots me anyway, as usual.

"Torro!" she shouts, running up to us, "Spammers!" Her eyes are all red and puffy, but she looks more worried than weepy, like she'd been crying before but thought of something more important she had to do. "What are you doing here?"

Spammers gives a little shrug. "Thought we'd stop in to wish you a safe trip, then they wouldn't let us leave."

Hexi just ignores him. "You need something else to wear," she says to me. "I'll see if I can get you a blanket." She does, too. I don't know where she finds it, but a minute later Hexi comes back and throws this thick, heavy blanket onto my shoulders. Hexi's like that. She's so nice, people just want to do things for her. The blanket's stiff and gritty-feeling but a whole lot better than standing there half-naked.

While we wait to file onto the train, Spammers tells Hexi all about getting nabbed building his still and how there was no time to work his demerits off. She's real sympathetic about it, but you can tell she feels a lot better having him here. I don't blame her. The thing about the draft is it makes you feel things you don't want to feel. Like after Spams and Hexi got called up, how I was just glad Camareen and me were still together. Hexi's also pretty mad at Spams for not telling her anything about it until now. "I wanted it to be a surprise," he says with a big, goofy smile.

Hexi agrees it's totally weird that I ended up here, but she's worried, too, because she's never heard of the marshals' taking anyone by mistake. "Maybe they just ask people to keep it quiet," she adds. She says it real quick, like to reassure me. I don't think she believes it, though.

At least there's plenty of room on the train, since this was an emergency ancillary draft and everything, and the Prips didn't want as many recruits as they do for a normal quota. Spammers and Hexi and me get a whole row to ourselves, and we lie across the seats while everyone shuffles past. Suddenly, though, the train gets real quiet. When I look around, people are all staring toward the back of the train. It's obvious why.

Four bivvies have just gotten on. You can tell they're bivvies by their clothes, which have all these bizarre shapes and colors, but it'd be obvious anyway, just from how they stand there, all still and hunched like wild animals. The one in front is about the meanest-looking guy I've ever seen. He's older than the rest, with this long black beard and sunken eyes and tanned face full of scars. The way he looks around the train, it's like he's deciding which of us he'll eat first. The other three are probably a few years older than me, a lady and two guys; I actually recognize one of them, the big guy who sort of manhandled me a bit the first time I visited the bivvie warehouse. He notices me watching him and sort of nods and grins, like we're old pals, and he's remembering all the fun times we've had together. He's limping a bit, I notice, and so is the guy with the beard. All while the bivvies are moving down the aisle, there's no sound except their footsteps. And then they sit down, and all of a sudden the doors snap shut like the train's been waiting for them the whole time.

It's a nasty feeling, hearing the doors close that way, like the train's just chomped down on us. Maybe it'd be better if we'd actually start moving, but we don't. The train just sits there. I see why after a moment. Some Prips are walking along the platform with a bunch of kids. They're all too young for the draft, like maybe ten or eleven, so I guess they must be the ones the Prips picked out with that test of theirs. It makes me think of what it was like going back to school after the first time we met the censors, how people you'd seen a day before were suddenly just gone. What really upsets me, though, is that little girl is with them. Naomi. It makes me pretty sad, seeing her there. She turns and looks through the window, almost right at me, but then I see she's spotted the four bivvies inside the train. She lifts her head as she goes by, just a little, like she's tipping back a hat that isn't there. When I look over to see if any of the bivvies noticed, the old guy is sort of smiling to himself. Two minutes ago, I'd've said he couldn't smile at all, like he was physically incapable, but that's definitely what's happening, or anyway, it's what's happening until he catches me watching. Then it's more like he's imagining how my head'll look hanging on the wall of his house. I decide to just pay attention to my own seat for a while.

The Prips and Naomi and the other kids must be riding in some other part of the train because they don't get on with us. Once they're gone, I'm expecting we'll finally get going, but the train just sits there. People start murmuring and complaining and trying to figure out what's happening, like whether the train is broken or what. I'm about ready to agree with the ones who're saying the Prips just enjoy torturing us when out of nowhere, the doors open again, then shut almost immediately, and the train lurches and starts to move.

People run to the windows as the Shipping Station pulls away, and the factories and warehouses slide by, going faster and faster. But me and Hexi and Spammers, we don't crowd up for one last glimpse of old Settlement 225 because we're staring at the guy who ducked in through the doors just before we set off. It's Mersh.

"There you are," Mersh says, like he's been looking for us all over the place and only just thought to check the train that's leaving the settlement forever.

We all just stare at him, totally surprised, until finally Spammers says, "Mersh, you idiot. You signed up."

It's obvious Spammers is right because Mersh kind of slouches and scowls the way he does whenever Spammers stomps on one of his idiotic ideas. Then he grins a little. "What, you think I'd stay here while you all get to go off with the Legion? Not a chance."

I don't believe it. I really don't. Mersh went and joined the Legion because he was *jealous*. I feel like I should yell at him, call him a stupid moron and everything else I can think of, but the truth is, it's just good to see another friend.

I think Spammers and Hexi feel the same way, like they can't decide whether to strangle old Mersh or hug him. Spams shakes his head and laughs. "Well, kiddo," he says, "it's a good thing you got on the same train as Hex and me. At least now we can keep an eye on you. Fortunately, Torro won't be staying. He's just enjoying the ride."

"The marshals took me by mistake," I tell Mersh.

Mersh furrows his forehead, then grins, like he's caught us playing with him. "Yeah, sure," he says, all sarcastic-like. "Whatever. I know they got you on demerits."

"Mersh, what are you talking about?" Spammers asks.

I was about to say the same thing, but all of a sudden I'm having a hard time talking. I'm having a hard time breathing, too.

"Torro got called up on demerits, same as you." Mersh looks from Spammers to me and back to Spammers, grinning like we're all in on some big joke together. "Come on, don't pretend like he didn't. I mean, I saw the list."

The day after the draft, the Office of the Prefect always posts a list of everyone who got called up for having too many demerits, as like a reminder to follow the rules, because if you're bad for the settlement, here's what happens. They send you to the Front.

"When I heard the marshals got you, I went to the Town Center to look," Mersh is saying, "and there you were. Spams, too, he had a whole pile of demerits, but you, Torro, you had even more, like ten times what it'd take to land you in the Legion. So I decided I'd sign up, too, and just in time. Almost didn't make it." He points a thumb at the door where he jumped in.

I don't think I've ever seen the kid so pleased with himself, but I feel like I'm floating somewhere way up above the train, just going up and up and no matter what I do, I can't get down. This isn't possible. Really, it's not, because I didn't *do* anything. I mean, yeah, I did, I did a lot of things, but I never actually got caught, right?

Suddenly, Spammers says, "Shit, kid." He lets out this long sigh and runs his hands over his head and face. "Shit," he says again. "Torro, kid. You got flipped. Somebody flipped you."

The Prips don't care how we decide who joins the Legion, not as long as we satisfy our quota for soldiers. So if you get drafted but then somehow the quota ends up filled, you don't have to go after all. "Flipping" is what we call it when you purposely get someone called on demerits, so they'll have to take your place at the Front. You never hear about its actually *happening* to anyone, though. It's mostly just a rumor. Even if a spot does get like miraculously filled, it only helps out the last person called in the draft, and it's pretty unlikely whoever's last on the list also happens to know someone they can sell out. But there are supposedly people who'll like collect information so they can go to whoever's been picked last and offer to flip someone for them. You can imagine what someone would pay to get out of going to the Front.

"How'd the list say he got his demerits?" Spammers asks.

Mersh shrugs. "Smuggling. Theft, trafficking stolen and illegal goods, the whole deal. Sounded like you were really into it, kiddo," he says to me.

"Cranely," Spammers hisses through his teeth. "That sneaky old turd."

I go sort of berserk then. I can't help it. I really can't. I start like punching the seat in front of me over and over, just slamming my fist at it as hard as I can. I start yelling, too, I don't know what, I'm going so berserk. Spammers is right. Cranely knew enough to get either of us called up about anytime he wanted. He couldn't flip Spammers, though, because Spammers'd already flipped himself. So that left me. And you can bet old Cranely made some deal with Ghalo to keep from getting in trouble himself, probably gave Ghalo a cut of the price for selling me out. And all because I was dumb enough to do business with Cranely. I thought I could handle him, but it turns out I'm still just a sucker.

Spammers and Hexi are trying to hold me down, but it's hard because I'm going all berserk and whatnot. Eventually, I get tired, though. Going berserk really tires you out. "Easy, kid, just take it easy," Spammers is saying.

But Hexi, she's not actually trying to stop me thrashing around. She's just sort of hugging me tight around the neck. I'm breathing pretty hard, and my nose is running, and I guess I've been sort of crying a bit. I'm about as tired as I've ever felt, so I just sort of curl forward and close my eyes and sit there like that while the train goes on rolling.

SIXTEEN

TORRO

Usually when something goes wrong, I can at least think, like try to work out a way through it, but right now I can't even do that. Inside my head, it's just a mess. All I know is I wrecked everything, just totally wrecked everything. I don't feel like I'm floating anymore. It's more like I'm sliding forward, or that's what I think until I realize it's the train slowing down.

I raise my head and look around, and it's true, the outside isn't whirring by as much, which is weird because I don't think we've been moving all that long. We've still got those tall fences running on both sides of the train, just like at Settlement 225, but beyond that it's all wilderness, trees and fields and hills and everything going on forever. Not a sign of Granite Shore anywhere. I'm thinking maybe I lost track of time, but everyone else looks pretty confused, too.

"What's happening?" I say to Spammers and Hexi and Mersh. My voice is real scratchy from all the yelling I was doing, and it kind of hurts to talk.

"Don't know," Spammers says. "We can't have gone more than fifty kilometers, sixty at the most."

We pass through a big gate beneath another very tall fence, then we're pulling into a station just like the one we left back at Granite Shore, like almost an exact replica, only instead of being surrounded by factories and warehouses and storage yards and so forth, it's in the middle of nowhere.

The train stops, and a few minutes later, the doors open, and the train goes quiet, and all you can hear is the wind and some leaves rustling. If there were really skeletons on this train, now's about the time they'd come out and like chew our heads off or whatever. But that doesn't happen.

What happens instead is the bivvies all get up and walk off the train, just walk right off like it's nothing, like whatever's out there can't be any worse than what's in here. Suddenly, I realize that's about how I feel, too. So I climb over the seat in front of me and follow the bivvies out.

Mersh catches up to me just as I'm leaving the train. "Hey, Torro," he says, "I'm real sorry for what I said. I mean, I thought you knew you'd been called up." He looks sort of sheepish, like it's his fault, what happened to me.

"I'm not mad at you, Mersh," I say. "If you hadn't told me, I'd probably never have found out. Better to hear from one of your boyos, right?"

That makes him pretty happy, or maybe he's just glad I'm not still going berserk. "So listen," he says, "Camareen, she gave me something for you. I would have showed you before but, you know, I wasn't sure what you'd do."

He takes a little envelope out of his jacket and gives it to me. Mersh was right to hold on to it back on the train. I probably would have ripped it to pieces. Inside is a sheet of paper filled with dots and lines. One page of the music I gave to Camareen. At the bottom, in her handwriting, are the words "Come back."

I'm not sure why, but seeing those words makes me feel a whole lot better. I know it's sort of crazy. No one ever comes back from the Front, right? But just then I get the feeling I could be the first one. A second ago, all I wanted was to get off that train, but now I know where I have to go. Home, to Camareen.

Once we're out on the platform, I can see the station really is just a few buildings inside a big, fenced-in circle with wilderness all around. Like, the tracks aren't just passing through to somewhere else. This is the last stop.

Over at the opposite end of the station, a couple of the smaller Prip flying machines are perched on little landing pads like the one behind the Prefect Building back at old S-225. There's a bunch of Prips gathered around, along with Naomi and the other kids from the train. One of the Prips, who's got these real bushy sideburns, is talking to them, gesturing to a bunch of big holes in the ground, more like funnels really, all evenly spaced and ringed in concrete and too deep to see the bottom. As I watch, the guy with the sideburns picks out one of the kids, a boy, and the two walk down into one of the funnels. A minute later, sideburns guy climbs back up, but the kid doesn't.

I'm pretty interested to see what's going to happen next, but some more

Prips, four of them, have shown up on the platform in front of us, and they're telling everyone from the train to form up in rows in an open space down below. They're pretty polite about it, those Prips, not bossy or anything, but they're not like making friendly conversation, either. They just follow us over to where this one lady is standing, and say, "Form up, Recruits!" Except for the bivvies, we've all been training with the settlement militia for years, so we know how to form up pretty good.

I guess this is the start of Legion training. I'm not happy about it, but I *am* just the slightest bit curious. In militia training, the next thing that would happen after forming up was the militia captain would tell us all what worthless turds we were, how we were all like a disgrace to old Settlement 225, and how if we ever went up against real hellions, we'd all probably be skinned alive. So when the lead Prip walks out in front of us, I'm expecting some more of that. She's not all angry and muscly like most of our militia captains were, though. Actually, she looks more like a schoolteacher, sort of thin, with fuzzy grayish hair tied up in a bun. You can tell she's in charge, though, just from the way she stands, so I get ready to be shouted at a bit.

But instead, the lady says, "Welcome, Recruits," and sounds like she means it, to be welcoming, that is. Her voice is sort of soft, but you can still hear it pretty easy. I'm close to the back, and I can hear her just fine.

"My name is Optio Sorril," she says, "and it will be my job to oversee your training and induction into the Legion of Ninth City." She pauses and looks us over a bit. "I am aware that many of you are here against your will," she says, looking right at me, I guess because it's so obvious ending up here wasn't part of my, like, plan for the day. Even Spammers at least had a shirt on when the marshals got him. "What I intend to impress upon you in the coming weeks is that your presence here is not some arbitrary whim. The Legion needs you. All of you. Make no mistake—I will turn you into fighters the likes of which you never imagined, but I will have failed in my duty unless, by the end of your training, every one of you considers yourself a volunteer."

"Sounds like you're ready to graduate, Mersh," Spammers whispers. I don't know how old Sorril hears him, but she does. If we were back in Granite Shore, Spammers'd probably end up doing push-ups or running laps until he fell over, but Sorril just sort of smirks at him and starts pacing back and forth in front of us, like she's waiting for something.

And there is *something* going on, something real strange. It's kind of like when there's a storm coming, only instead of the air swirling around, it feels like the swirling is happening *inside* of you. There's a weird smell, too, sort of briny, but also kind of electric, like you get when one of the machines at the factories shorts out. I'm pretty sure everyone else notices it, too. Only Optio Sorril and the Prips standing with her don't seem very surprised. Optio Sorril has started flexing her hand a bit, like it'd fallen asleep, and the feeling is just coming back.

"In a few moments, you will board the harvester that will take you to Ninth City's Limit Camp," she says. "I suggest you watch as it approaches. Much of what you encounter in the coming days will seem alien to you, but I promise that, like our harvester, in time it will make its own kind of sense."

She points upward, and, of course, we all look. At first I don't see anything, but after a minute I notice something way, way up in the sky. It's the huge Prip flying machine that always shows up just before the draft, only now it's so far away, you can hardly see it. It's getting closer, though, and fast, coming straight down, like a huge boot ready to stomp all of us standing around in the station.

Just then someone starts screaming. I think it must be one of the recruits, but when I look, I see it's Naomi. She's way over by those weird funnels in the ground, and she's just screaming her head off. A couple of Prips are trying to hold on to her, and she's kicking and clawing at them and trying to get away. The way she's screaming, it's like she's trying to tell us something, but I can't hear what.

The bivvies from the train all hear her, too, and right away they push through everyone formed up in front of Optio Sorril and set off running, going straight for Naomi. Optio Sorril calls for them to stop and come back, but she doesn't sound angry or even annoyed. If anything, she's like a little playful. The bivvies don't look back, though, since they're getting ready to grab Naomi and rip every Prip in sight to pieces.

And then something happens I really just can't explain. All of a sudden, Optio Sorril just crashes right into the pack of bivvies. One minute she's standing in front of us, looking like some frail old lady, and the next she's on top of them. She must cover fifty meters in about two seconds. She sends the two bivvies in front flying, though you'd think she'd just bumped into some empty cardboard boxes for how little it slows her down. The other two bivvies, the big guy and the mean guy with the beard, had been going a bit more slowly, still limping on their hurt legs. Now they sort of circle around to come at Optio Sorril from both sides. But she just grabs each one and tosses him on the ground, easy as anything.

I look at Spammers to see if he has any idea what's happening, but he's just watching it all, his mouth a little open. Hexi, too. Mersh has never seen anything so fantastic in his life, you can just tell.

Somehow, the bivvies get back up. I don't know how, after the way old Sorril kicked them around, but they do. They come at Sorril, all four at once, and this time they actually hit her a few times, but it's like she doesn't even feel it. Even when the guy with the beard lands this real nasty punch, she hardly reacts. In a few seconds, the bivvies are all back on the ground, Optio Sorril just standing over them. To look at her, you wouldn't think anything had happened at all.

Little Naomi hasn't stopped screaming all this time. I was pretty distracted while old Sorril was throwing those bivvies all over the place, but now everything's gone quiet, and I can hear Naomi again. She was speaking that bivvie language of hers before, but now she's yelling in Aux, her voice echoing as the Prips try to haul her down into one of those pits. And what's she's screaming is: "Run! You have to run! These men are liars! They have brought you here to kill you!"

SEVENTEEN

NAOMI

I have been a fool to trust these people. There were a hundred signs by which I might have known the truth of them, but I closed my eyes to everything save my desperate hope, and now I fear it will cost me my life. I would have gone to my death wholly ignorant were it not for one final warning, firm proof that these are the men who murdered my sister.

It was perhaps to my advantage that I played such the gawking boob. I had never ridden a train before, and it required an effort to disguise my awe as the landscape outside our windows slithered by. The people of the Principate, as their government is called, were polite and well-mannered, and I convinced myself that my grudge was not with them but with Ghalo and the township of Granite Shore. By the time we arrived at this lonely outpost, I had muffled my misgivings to such an extent that Reggidel's request that I accompany him into some deep, stone-rimmed pit, which he called an "insulation cell," did not seem immediately ludicrous.

Already, I had watched other children who rode with me and our Principate chaperones in the train's front car go dumbly and trustingly down, and so I followed Reggidel, ignoring all the roaring instincts of an animal cut off from her pack. At the bottom was a metal chair, reclined to point toward the sky, and when Reggidel asked me to sit, I obeyed like the gullible child I am. The chair bore clamps to hold my wrists and ankles, and Reggidel might have succeeded in securing me there had the air not begun to crackle and fill with the smell of ocean and rot and brimstone, every sentiment of my soul swirling like a river bottom churned by a passing fish. If I live to be a hundred, I will never forget that sensation, nor the first time I encountered it, in the Valley of Endless Summer.

I rolled clear of the chair and struck out at Reggidel, first toward his face, then in a way men taken unawares will find uniquely painful and disabling. I scrambled upward, but my escape was a short one. Hardly had I mounted the lip of the pit Reggidel had intended to make my grave than I was seized by another Principate man. He did not know I was fighting for my life, and this allowed me to break free, but soon more were upon me, and their strength was unlike anything I have ever felt. It would be no exaggeration to say each had the muscle of twenty men. They held me fast as I watched my loyal codesmen, who though I had bargained for their freedom would not let me go to this strange place alone, laid low by nothing more than some bony grandma. I went on screaming my warning, but all my fight was gone.

I do not know what purpose it serves to bring children all the way to this abandoned place simply to kill us, but I am certain now that we are here for that very reason. And so when the first explosion comes, I am as little surprised as anyone. There is a deep rumble in the earth, and from a nearby pit, where one of my brief acquaintances had been stored, fire erupts as though from the muzzle of some great cannon. A breath later there is a second report, more brittle and sharp in character, and a pit somewhat farther off discharges a blue spray that solidifies briefly into a delicate tree of ice before shattering in a burst of snow.

The conscripts from Granite Shore all witness this terrible display and break into panic. Some lie flat on the ground as though under fire while others cut and run in various directions. To my surprise, the Principate men seem just as alarmed. The two who had seized me with such astonishing strength now drop me in the dirt and beat a hasty retreat. Their comrades back slowly away, as though facing down some raging beast, ordering me in strident tones back into my pit. Reggidel has found his way out and begun waving his arms, shouting for everyone to stand clear. Clear of me, he seems to mean. Somewhere close by, the ground shudders with another detonation.

Above the noise, I hear Reggidel call out, "Stay where you are, Naomi! Just don't move!" If I was ever of a mind to follow instructions from Censor Reggidel, that time has passed. I break toward the train, thinking it my best chance at concealment. My plan is to scale the walls and lose myself in the woods beyond. The Principate men, rather than giving chase, make way as I pass. From the corner of my eye, I see one pull something from his hip and draw a bead on me, but as I turn to look, someone slams into my side, and I abruptly find myself slung over the shoulder of a running body. I am borne across the quaking ground toward one of the falcon-styled flying machines roosting nearby. Only when I have been thrown bodily inside and the door slammed shut do I discover my captor is none other than Vinneas.

"You're heavier than you look, you know that?" He says this in the jaunty way of someone who has suffered a bad scare and wishes to play it off. He inhales deeply, a breath of forced calm, and begins rummaging about the inside of the flying machine. The space is close but comfortable, like a booth intended for meals or intimate conversation. Eventually, Vinneas produces a small can bearing the picture of a redheaded man on the side. "General Ginger," he explains, opening the can with a pneumatic hiss. "It's not bad. Mostly just sugar water with bubbles. Reggidel says it settles his stomach when he flies." He opens a second can and pushes it toward me, then takes a long drink from his. "I don't think it's working very well," he admits, regarding the can askance.

To my shame, I realize I am trembling and near to tears. My nerves are blasted to bits, the memory of my sister's death a gauze clinging to me like a spider's webbing I have walked through and cannot shake off. From outside, another explosion rattles our flying machine.

"You're safe enough, don't worry," Vinneas says, noting my distress. "Everyone will be giving us a little space until they're convinced you're not going to kill me, so we've got a few minutes to chat." He tips his can back, draining it, then takes the one I have left untouched. "So, how about you tell me what all of that was about back there?"

His casual air, however contrived, enrages me. I had begun to think Vinneas an honorable man. He even helped me bargain for the safety of my coda. And yet there he sits, sipping his little can, as if to say he had no part in planning my death.

"I'll admit our insulation cells aren't exactly luxurious," he says conversationally. "*I* certainly wouldn't want to sit down in one of those things. But somehow I don't think the screaming, the kicking Reggidel in the crotch, *et cetera*, was a comment on our decorating."

"You have fooled me for the last time," I say, my voice hoarse and grating in my throat. "I have the measure of you now, you and your people. Kill me if you want, but do not expect me to cooperate."

"Is that so?" He sets down his can, abandoning the pretense of nonchalance.

"I have seen your weaponry at work before, the same as you used on those children, and would have used on me." The story Reggidel told, that this was to be a simple test, now strikes me as nothing but a cruel joke. A test indeed, though I was not the one to be tested. I was merely a target to exercise the Principate's arsenal.

Vinneas makes no effort to conceal his surprise or the keenness of his interest. "When was this?"

"Not long ago." I have the idea that this young man may not know the extent of his people's wickedness, and that finding out will wound him. And so I say, "My sister died in one of your traps."

"Your sister?"

"She was called Rae." I use her name like a charm, invoking it as an emblem of courage. Vinneas would be sorry indeed to find himself trapped with my sister in such close quarters, and if I cannot break him in half the way she would, at least I can put on a look that tells him how pleased I would be to see his insides littering the floor.

Vinneas, for his part, seems dazed, amazed perhaps, like a man who has just discovered that ice and water are, at their base, the same element. In a distant voice, he mutters, "Well, imagine that."

The repeating blasts of the pits outside, once close and fast, have become slow and intermittent, like the last kernels in a pot of corn popped over a fire. I wait for the next to come, but instead hear a hammering at our door. Vinneas draws it open to reveal Censor Reggidel, still somewhat hunched and perturbed to a severe degree.

"That was not very polite, Naomi," he growls. To Vinneas he says, "Looks like you were right about her. Good thing, too. Don't think the Curator would have been very happy with me if I brought her star pupil back in a bucket."

"Naomi and I have been having an exceedingly interesting conversation," Vinneas tells him. His good mood is largely restored, I am sorry to see. He rattles his empty can at Reggidel. "Care to join us? I think there are a few cans of General Ginger left."

"Not now, no," Reggidel responds with exasperation. "We should move on to the final stage as soon as possible." He turns to me. "What do you say, Naomi? Only one more test to go. We'll have to travel a bit, but we'll be moving much more quickly now."

I regard him coldly, feeling the hatred rise anew in my belly. "You are insane if you believe I will ever go anywhere with you again," I say.

"I think we're going to have some trouble securing her cooperation," Vinneas says to Reggidel. "For one thing, she thinks we just tried to kill her." These words come in stark contrast to his mood, which appears near to jubilation. "I don't think our usual demonstration for new recruits is going to do the trick. I've got an idea that might work, but I'll have to borrow the velo. There's something I need from the city."

"This isn't the time, Vinn," Reggidel replies. "The harvester's just about ready to go."

"You'll be glad I went, I promise." Vinneas looks down at me, an absurd grin on his face, as if he intends this promise for me as well. "Naomi, if you're really determined not to go anywhere with us, you should hop out now. I'm about to take off."

Though I suspect I would be better off with Vinneas, I do as he says and climb down from this contraption he calls a velo. It rises smoothly into the air and, after turning a small arc, darts toward the horizon at terrific speed. Strangely, it exhibits none of the whirring effort I remarked in a similar vehicle flying over Granite Shore.

"You weren't entirely wrong, you know," Reggidel says as the velo passes from view. "About someone trying to kill you. I'm pretty sure one of my legionaries might very well have blasted you if Vinneas hadn't shut you up in that velo. Would have been a shame, not to mention extremely embarrassing for me professionally." He glowers disapprovingly at me. "Would it have been so hard to just stay down in that insulation cell like I told you?"

I return his glower. "If you were set on destroying me, I thought I should make you go to some trouble for it."

"Those cells aren't meant to hurt you, Naomi. They're to protect the people around you. Vinneas took a big risk carrying you off like that. He got very lucky."

"I think I have had enough of your tales," I say. My throat has become unaccountably tight, a sharp pain constricting my chest.

"Well, we need something to do while we wait for the harvester to finish loading up. It should only be a few minutes. How about I tell you one more of my tales, and if you're not convinced you want to come with me after that, you can get back on the train and go anywhere you like."

I do not bother with a reply, as I have the notion that I am being mocked. We both know the train has only one destination.

"I'll even hold up my side of the bargain and keep your people out of the draft, whether or not you decide to come along," he says. "I think we've already got the toughest of you for the Legion anyway."

The image returns to me of my codesmen splayed and scattered across the ground like pickup sticks.

"Your people are just fine," Reggidel says, guessing my concern. "They're getting patched up right now. Already good as new, I'd expect. And better than when they showed up here. They aren't the first recruits Ghalo's delivered in less-than-mint condition."

I had not thought to survey this outpost after leaving the velo, but at Reggidel's mention of my codesmen, I look anxiously about for some sign of them, only to discover myself amid a scene so strange that I could easily think myself arrived in another world.

EIGHTEEN

NAOMI

The whalelike monster I had watched descending over us has sunk so low that its ponderous belly now obscures the greater part of the sky. At this near distance, its weightlessness seems all the more unlikely. Long tendrils extend from its side, twisting and groping over the train that brought me from Granite Shore, or so it seems until I look more closely and discern the containers lining the train's spine all thrown open and their contents floating into the sky, apparently of their own volition. Grain spills upward in twirling cords, lithe as a snake rising on its coils. Water, milk, oil, and a dozen other liquids not familiar to me flow like uphill rivers with no other bed than open air, now and then sending up sprays that float as quivering globes before rejoining their respective eddies. Solid goods rise in swarms, orbiting the massive bulb in the sky with an easy synchrony that seems to transform it from gluttonous whale to busy bee-hive, all frantic work and industry. And all of this is accomplished without a single human hand put to work.

Below, the draftees from Granite Shore have mustered once again, and, one at a time, they too begin to float upward, wavering faintly in the manner of rising bubbles until they vanish inside the hive. Against any hope, I search for smaller figures that could be the children who rode with me on the train but find none.

"The harvester should be ready soon," says Censor Reggidel. "Let's sit awhile, shall we?" Despite there being nothing save the ground to serve as a seat, Reggidel looks about as though seeking a set of chairs, apparently deciding upon a stretch of flat rock nearby. From his jacket he produces a thin folding case, which contains a number of the small metal disks he displayed for me back in the township of Granite Shore. Reggidel chooses one disk and begins fussing over it with furrowed brows. He runs a hand across it, then looks about as if expecting some result. When there is none, his confused expression deepens, and he begins muttering to himself, but at last his face clears. "Ah!" he says. "Watch this!"

Again, he runs a hand over the disk, and this time the rocky space beside him abruptly assumes a shivering, liquid quality. He moves his hand once more, and the surface rises as in a splash, solidifying, impossibly, into the shape of two chairs posed opposite one another, each so perfectly formed they could have been sculpted where they stand.

Not so much like mushrooms after all. This is my first thought upon watching the two chairs form. I know then that these people, or others like them, were the ones who raised the shroomtowns. When we wintered in New Absalom and places like it, we were living in their ruins.

"Like that, do you?" Reggidel asks. He has misread my expression, seeing awe when what I feel is more akin to disappointment. "I've got about a hundred of them." He replaces the disk in its case and begins sifting through the others. "Some are pretty showy. I can make a tiny little thunderstorm right over the ground. Comes about up to your knees. How about that?"

"I have no desire to see any more of your tricks."

Reggidel looks up from his case. "They aren't tricks, Naomi," he says. "They're called 'artifices,' and they're meant as a demonstration." He has been working one silver disk in his hand, and with nearly comical mistiming, the area over his head explodes in pink and purple sparks. He ducks, cursing under his breath.

"I hate these stupid things," he mutters. He clicks the case closed, shaking his head, and levels his gaze at me. "You're a smart girl, Naomi. I can tell. You know what's happening here, all around you, it can't be just some illusion. You've seen things that shouldn't be possible, but they're happening anyway. And you have to be curious about how it's done."

I am, of course. I am exceedingly curious, but I will not admit this to Censor Reggidel.

"The truth, Naomi, the real truth, is that we have learned to harness a remarkable power, a power that makes the impossible possible."

Above his head, the contents of the train continue to soar back and forth with an unmistakable sense of purpose. A power, he says, one that renders impossible things real. A power that can create fire or wind or rain from nothing, that can take the massive bulk of this so-called harvester, a thing that should by all rights sit on the earth as heavily as any mountain, and set it in the sky. "You are talking about magic," I say.

"Magic." Censor Reggidel uses the word wistfully, as if it comes from a time fondly remembered, now long past. "Yes, I suppose that's as accurate a description as any. The folks in charge don't much like it, though. Think it encourages too much of a superstitious outlook. The word we use is 'thelemity.'" He regards his case of silver disks, contemplating another demonstration, perhaps. "Thelemity," he repeats. "Think of it as another force of the universe, like gravity. Electricity isn't a bad comparison, actually." He holds up his case of disks. "My little toys here, and that great big harvester floating up above us, none of them would work unless we had a source of thelemity nearby."

"You mean to tell me this outpost of yours is built on some hallowed place, a land inhabited by faeries, where magic is free for the taking." I am all scorn now, having determined to handle Censor Reggidel as I do Baby Adam when he comes round with childish tales of spooks and haints and goblins.

"You aren't too far off," Reggidel says, pleased that I am playing along. "But thelemity doesn't come from any specific place. It comes from people, very special people we call 'fontani.'"

"Fontani," I repeat, making it sound as biting and skeptical as I can. We are speaking his language, the same one used in the townships, but the word sounds familiar. Not unlike our word "fountain."

"Yes, right. There's one up there right now, on that harvester," he says, pointing. He looks purposefully at me. "And if Vinneas and I are right, there's another down here. One more test, and we'll know for sure. But we need your full cooperation, Naomi."

There is no mistaking his meaning. Unbidden, a shiver of excitement slides over me at the prospect of witnessing true magic. I wonder how many other foolish children he has trapped by these same promises. "I have seen what use you make of your power," I say, giving my contempt free rein. "I want no part in it. You would make me a workhorse to be yoked and driven, or else siphon and bottle my spirit and leave me an empty husk."

"No, no, nothing like that," Reggidel says. "This will all make sense once you understand a little more about thelemity. You just need to trust me."

"I will be six feet beneath the earth before I make that mistake again."

Censor Reggidel heaves a heavy sigh. "All right, Naomi. I'll send you back to Settlement 225 if that's what you want."

I cannot say with any surety that this is indeed what I want. My codesmen have volunteered for this Legion when I might have set out with nothing but Papa's old fiddle for company, and I cannot in any conscience abandon them here. But nor can I be a part of Reggidel's schemes. Weariness settles over me, and I finally take one of the shroomchairs. Reggidel watches me silently, seemingly just as tired as I am, and for a time we sit listening to the sound of water and wheat and cans and boxes levitating toward the ship above, until the quiet is broken by a new sound, first a loud roar, then something softer, discernible only as a change in the wind.

"He's back," Censor Reggidel says, rising from his seat and nodding toward an approaching falcon-ship. "Vinneas. He'd better have brought us a miracle."

He has. At first it appears Vinneas has arrived with nothing aside from a grin substantially larger than the one he wore upon his departure. He slings down from his vehicle, the very picture of self-satisfaction, and I feel a sneer form on my face, but then he reaches up to help someone down after him. A tall girl dressed in white. She looks about, disoriented, scanning the terrain around her, then she calls out: "Naomi?" She has not yet seen me, and her voice is thin with panic.

I try to call back to her, but find I cannot. I am unable to move. It is simply one thing too many, and finally I am overcome by everything I have witnessed these past days, the contradictory sights, the multiplication of impossibilities. But then she sees me, and I am caught up in her arms, and she is solid and true and real. "Oh, Sunshine," she says, her voice heavy with tears, "I thought you were gone forever." And though at any other time I would never consent to being lifted up like a child, I do not complain as she holds me and covers my head in kisses, as excessive in her affection as she has always been, returned to me against all promise and reason, my sister, Rae.

PART TWO

COSMIC EMPTINESS IN MY SOUL

NINETEEN

RAE

I opened my eyes to warm rain falling, fine mist dewing the grass and gathering in spheres on the leaves to roll and plunge plopping through the branches. The air was thick but not uncomfortably humid, light clouds drifting eastward, and in the west, the warm hues of sunset. The cold, stark air, the havoc of snowflakes I remembered, had gone without a trace. I could almost imagine I had awakened in some lush paradise, the Elysium Papa was known to discuss in his more whimsical moments, or Valhalla, in which Reaper Thom professed firm and unironical belief.

As my thoughts settled into order, it occurred to me that in an afterlife for the gallant dead, my shirts and britches would likely not be so damp, which was to say soaked through. Moreover, once I took stock of my surroundings, I found them quite familiar in arrangement if not in climate. It seemed far more likely I had remained here for some unknown stretch of time, perhaps one measured in months or years rather than days. A stone maiden sleeping undisturbed as the seasons passed around her. Such fairy-tale notions would come to seem irredeemably silly to me very soon; still later I would decide them entirely appropriate for the place where I had turned up, this juncture between the real and unreal.

The path leading to the spot where I lay shone bright and clear in my mind. I pictured myself standing among the breached mountains over the Valley of Endless Summer, declaring my intention to venture down and confirm the place free of threats, and I cursed myself for every brand of foolish I could name. What I ought to have done was lead the scouts back to New Absalom and see to it our coda was packed up and lit out for Emily's Lake or Black Mills or any other of our winter holdfasts. Coming into this valley was recklessness on a par with the worst of my wild and profligate youth, when I gained a reputation for never turning down a dare. I am on record as running a mile with a live honeybee in my mouth, diving thirty feet to the wreck of some ancient hulk sunk off the southern marshlands, climbing to the top of a ruined monument deep in Nworkie territory, and all other manner of lunacy I thought I had outgrown until I saw the look on Naomi's face as she realized we would likely have to abandon New Absalom. Her disappointment was simply more than I could bear, and I believe it is to blame for my sudden attack of stupidity.

I might even have said I deserved what I got, had I known with any certainty what that was. My last memory was of a strange smell in the air and an internal stirring like the feeling of being secretly watched, then I was swept up by some strange and violent force. The only experience I can name that comes close to matching it was when I was six and nearly drowned. My coda had camped near a beach, and a wave surprised me while I was playing in the surf. I fancied myself a good swimmer, but no matter how hard I fought, my struggles amounted to nothing, and if Papa had not come and dragged me free, I would surely have been carried out to sea. It was the same feeling there in the valley, of being seized by something immeasurably stronger than myself. It took everything I had just to sputter a warning to Naomi and the others before the surge of it overwhelmed me entirely.

My present state was, overall, not nearly so dire as I would have expected, given the events leading up to it. I bore no unaccounted-for cuts or bruises, and what new tears my coat and trousers showed were consistent with a hard fall on rough ground. There was good evidence my clothes had at some point been on fire, but I supposed a little singeing about the hems and collars wasn't bad for a girl who had recently been exploded. My pistol was wedged uncomfortably beneath my back, my rifle basking in the grass a short distance away. Both were loaded and functional. I was short one boot, which turned up after a brief search on hands and knees. My hat, duly charred, had lodged in a tree's lower branches and was easily brought down with the help of a few handy stones.

Once I had established myself as fit to move, I set out for the Ridge. It made no difference whether I had been here an hour or a century—Naomi and the others were making their way back to the breached mountain wall when I saw them last, and if I ever hoped to find them, that was where I had to begin. I forced myself to avoid any conjecture as to what might have befallen them, knowing such thoughts would quickly give way to panic.

The valley's terrain was unchanged as far as I could see. The trees and rivers, hills and marshes, were just as I remembered them, only now they were alive with the song of birds and insects celebrating what was by all appearances a fine summer evening. The rain, already thin, soon ceased completely, and as the air cooled, I quickened my pace. Of the tribal hordes that had previously infested this territory, there was now no sign but a few cold fire pits and abandoned latrines. The sky was making its way past orange to red when over the treetops I saw the mountain ridge rise into view, glowing in the low light.

I do not know what made me look back then. Perhaps there was some sound I did not consciously perceive, or a flutter in the air; perhaps it was that same sense of being watched. Whatever the reason, as I stood measuring the distance left to the mountains, I glanced over my shoulder and beheld something exceedingly strange.

Small, thin clouds were stretching upward from the horizon, twelve of them, all perfectly parallel, all moving in unison, as though some great twelve-fingered hand were scratching its nails across the glowing sky. I am no amateur when it comes to cloud-gazing, but near as I could say, this variety was entirely new, and drawn swifter and straighter than seemed entirely right for Nature's handiwork. I was prepared to count the sight yet another perplexing phenomenon of this bizarre place, an occurance akin to blue thunder or moon babies, but as the needly clouds moved overhead, they suddenly abandoned their forward course and shifted to a widening, circular pattern, like the vortex of a whirlpool. Each coiling cloud now appeared to have something at its tip, a sharp little thorn ripping through the air. They had described several of their widening loops before I understood these were no idle designs but a spiraling dive, one that would bring them down on me in a matter of seconds—a thought that hardly had time to form before three of the smoking pillars peeled away and came crashing down into the forest, directly between me and the Ridge.

The ground shook as though from some heavy impact, the air splitting with the sound of shattered trees. After that, eerie silence. I had thrown myself to the ground, expecting catastrophe, and enjoyed a few moments in the slick mud wondering what on earth had happened before the woods around me burst into pandemonium.

First came the war trumpets. That was the word that formed in my mind, "trumpet," though the sound might as easily have been named a roar, as of a dragon or some other beast of old mythology. The reason I thought of a trumpet was that there seemed to be a message bound up in its sound, like the bugle calls of my coda's scouts. These trumpets spoke of battle joined, of unstoppable victory, of no hope or mercy for the enemy, namely me. The blast rumbled over me, bringing with it fear out of all proportion to anything I could hear or see. I am quite certain I would have dropped my rifle and run from the sound as fast as I could go had I not spotted other figures doing just that, coming toward me through the trees.

Almost before I had time to raise my gun, I was facing down a pack of Leafcoat fighters, bows and hatchets drawn. There were eight of them, enough to take me easily. I might have dispatched one or two, but for a nice set of guns like mine, Leafcoats will trade four or five men and call it a bargain. But these only looked me up and down and hurried on, parting as if I were some inanimate obstacle. The trumpets sounded again, and the fear they summoned up nearly sent me following in the Leafcoats' wake. The woods were thick with fleeing forms now, all flushed from hiding places nearby. That must be what the trumpets are for, I thought: We are being herded.

I chose a route perpendicular to the running crowd, following the direction of the Ridge. My hope was to find some way around whatever was making that terrible sound, but I made little headway before the ground beneath me began to vibrate, a familiar rhythm, though on a scale I had never thought to encounter: footsteps. Something huge was coming my way. I hid myself in a bank of scrubby bushes, curling among the thorns and brambles. I expected at any moment to be ground into the dirt, left a pudding of blood and bones topped with a hat, but the footsteps passed in a flurry of swishing brush and snapping branches, and the trumpets calling terror back and forth soon grew dimmed and distant. I waited until the woods were quiet, then I spooled up the last frayed threads of my courage and ran.

The Ridge, I thought, I had to make the Ridge. The notion had come to me that if the mountains were the boundary of this valley, perhaps the things in this place could not travel beyond it, like a ghoul forbidden to cross running water.

I nearly got there, too. The Ridge was high overhead, glowing in the brilliant sunset, only a small stretch of trees between me and the base of the mountain. And then, so close behind me that the sound tickled the hairs on my neck, one of those awful trumpets sounded. The message had changed. The martial aggression was still there, but now it demanded surrender, proclaimed there would be no escape. I turned, slowly, and faced the thing calling to me.

I did not rightly know what to name it, other than "giant." Its rough shape was that of a man, albeit broader in proportion than average, a blunt head set low on wide shoulders. But it was clearly no man. The scraggy trees growing below the Ridge came hardly to its waist, and though it was only a silhouette against the falling sun, the smooth, hard lines of its frame spoke of some covering much tougher than skin. The only feature I could discern in any detail was its face, though it resembled a human countenance only by its situation at the front of the head. There was no mouth, no eyes, only twisting patterns of glowing red running from crown to chin, the color an exact match to the fiery sunset, an intricate design that curled back on itself like tendrils of smoke. It reminded me, more than anything else, of looking into the grate of a brazier hot with coals. The war trumpet sounded again, and the red glow deepened, like a scowl.

The giant had crept up silently, appearing as if from nowhere. I thought of its brazen trumpeting, the crashing of huge footsteps, and felt certain now all that was merely for show, intended to drive me into some trap, though I could not have guessed the reason. The giants of Papa's stories, with their accustomed hankering for human flesh, were as far from this hard, polished creature as a cart mule was from the mechanical wagons of the townships. But if it wished me to run now, I was happy to oblige.

My first step as I fled was strangely slow, heavier than it should have been; the second was still more ponderous, and on the third, I stumbled. Everything about me had become unaccountably heavy, my limbs taking on the weight of wood, then stone, then metal, until it was a struggle even to remain upright. I went to one knee, fighting to keep my head pointed toward the giant.

I had no doubt it was responsible for the sudden weightiness of the world. I remember thinking this creature had worked some spell or other magic on me, then dismissing the idea as foolish. As it turned out, I was more right than wrong, but just then all I could say for sure was if this kept up, I would break under my own weight. The brim of my hat sagged over my face, my hair hung limp, my cheeks dragged against my jaw. I could hardly lift myself enough to crawl. And so I did what seemed the only thing left. I set my rifle across my leg, its barrel digging into the meat of my thigh, pointed it at the great dark bulk before me, and fired.

Whatever result I expected, it was only a tiny fraction of what actually occurred. My shot landed high of center on the creature and burst into a great globe of flame that lit up the dark woods all around. In the flash of light, I saw the giant was covered in a carapace of interlocking plates, all glossy and in places scriven with symbols I cannot quite discern. The pressure bearing down on me lifted at once, and I succeeded in escaping about ten yards into the forest before an invisible force struck me to the ground. I had the distinct impression of being swatted, like a fly. I rolled, turned, and saw the giant approaching. On its chest, where my rifle blast had hit, a circle of embers glowed like the bowl of a lit pipe.

I stood, fired again. My aim was better this time and the resulting explosion took the giant full in the face, though it seemed the world's newly returned lightness was not fully to my advantage: The rifle's kick was about enough to remove my shoulder. The giant, meanwhile, was neither slowed nor deterred by the new pipe-bowl mark burned into its head.

Again I was felled by some invisible shock, and this time, I ended up some twenty feet distant, with the vague impression of having tumbled from the top of a very high tree. My body rang with pain, the worst of it centered about my leg, which no longer conformed to the usual and expected proportions. Something sharp and jagged had torn through my trousers, and I could guess with reasonable certainty that this was my thighbone.

There was no way I would make the Ridge now. The mere thought of standing brought soupy black pain swimming behind my eyes. My rifle was gone, but I had somehow kept hold of my pistol. I held it low, so that it wouldn't jump from my hand, and fired until it was dry. Even then I didn't let up on the trigger, for whatever good it might have done me. The last picture I beheld with any clarity was of the giant standing over me, sparks dancing like fireflies around its dark shoulders.

TWENTY

RAE

The world went hazy then, and I cannot say for certain whether I became insensible from pain or whether the giant worked another of its tricks on me. Whatever the cause, for a time I lost track of the world, and when I found it again, I was sitting alone in a plain gray room.

The place was small, probably ten feet across, with floor and ceiling and three walls all made of smooth stone, the edges rounded like a bowl set on end. Where the fourth wall would have been, the room opened onto a hallway of the same gray stone, all filled with fuzzy light that came from nowhere in particular, the way sunlight will on days covered in low clouds.

In the hallway, a man dressed smartly in black stood watching me, arms crossed. I say man because of his size—he was tall and muscled like an ox—and his bearing, which was authoritarian and disapproving, as though he suspected me of trampling his prized azaleas—though in truth he could not have been much older than I was. He had short, bronze-colored hair combed back from his forehead, features straight and deeply drawn, high cheekbones and a sloped nose that made me think of a mountain lion, an impression that only deepened as his eyes narrowed at me behind his silver-rimmed spectacles.

"Where am I?" I asked, still quite groggy.

My question had no effect on him that I could see. He only continued to watch me, appraising, over his silver rims. I was preparing to repeat myself when he spoke up in the strangest voice I have ever heard. It was low and rumbling, a bass far deeper than I would have expected, and echoed in a way that seemed wrong for my small room. It reminded me of the voice Papa would use in his stories when he wanted to impersonate a demon or monster. Even stranger, though his words came to me in English, they did not quite match the movement of his lips, as if the sound had changed between there and my ears. What he said was "How did you gain access to the valley?"

I sat there a moment, blinking, then I said, "Who are you? How did I get here?"

That rumbling voice came again. "How did you gain access to the valley?"

"I don't know what you're talking about."

He did not appear to have heard, only went on watching me in that same appraising way. At last, he said, "You will remain here until you answer." He raised a finger, the way you might to hush someone who is about to speak up, and just like that, he vanished.

I spent several moments staring at the place the man in black had occupied before I understood he hadn't truly disappeared but rather that something had appeared between us. There was now a lid to my bowl, a fourth wall where before there had been only empty air. The new barrier was quite solid, as I confirmed by rapping at it with my knuckles, but not stone as I had imagined, or, in any case, unlike any stone I had ever encountered because when I pressed a hand against it, the surface seemed to dissolve. The wall itself was still there, smooth and cold beneath my palm, but it had become clear as glass or flawless ice.

If it wasn't already plain that I was a prisoner, this wall, invisible and immovable, provided the deciding evidence. To make matters worse, my cell, as I now considered it, offered only the sparsest of accommodations. Of particular note was the lack of a bed or anything resembling sanitary facilities. The clothes I had worn into the valley were gone, replaced by a shirt and trousers of some loose, white fabric, comfortable but wholly unsuitable for outdoor wear. A metal ring, about as thick as a finger, hung around my neck, just tight enough that I couldn't take it off. Far more surprising, however, was what I found beneath my clothes.

I had paced half a dozen circles around my little enclosure before it occurred to me that I should not have been able to walk at all. I grasped at my thigh, then undid my trousers for confirmation. My leg was completely healed, straight and strong as ever. Further inspection turned up not a single mark of the battering I had taken in the valley, as if none of it had ever happened. I might have concluded this to be the literal truth—that I had imagined all of it, from the misty summer evening to my battle with the giant—until I discovered that a small cut on my finger, left the night before we arrived at New Absalom by the sharp edge on a can of beans, was also gone. It was as if every little hurt on me had been washed away, down to the chapping at my lips and the rough, cracked ends my boots left on my heels. All that remained was the collection of scars down my right side, what I've come to think of as my unlucky half: thin slices on my ear and neck from a boulder I thought the perfect cover from Dixieman gunfire until it began exploding into sharp little shards; the double-sided puncture through my upper thigh from a Seventy-Sixer's arrow that pinned me to my horse; the knife mark in the shape of a fishhook along my collarbone; and two star-shaped bullet holes above my hip from two equally ill-fated trips through the bridgelands.

I could only assume my captors were responsible for my much-improved condition, which made their oversight in my accommodations all the more perplexing. Surely, people ingenious enough to mend my leg would have thought to provide me with a bed or a toilet.

I was mulling this over when from one of my walls there came a small bubbly noise, like a single drop of water. I stood back, and the wall began to bulge outward, unfurling like an opening flower until it became a narrow, rounded shelf supporting a steaming bowl. The bowl contained a kind of gruel, vaguely orange in color, and in case there was any question as to its intended purpose, a practical if somewhat bulky spoon was provided as well.

The sight of food brought my hunger to life. Reasoning that my captors likely had at their disposal numerous methods of killing me far easier than poisoning, I tucked in without further hesitation. The gruel was better than it looked but needed salt. When I had finished, I set the bowl and spoon back on their shelf, and, at once, all three melted back into the wall.

I turned my attention then to the small bench that constituted my only article of furniture. Thinking of the miraculous arrival of my supper, I began poking and prodding at the wall and was eventually rewarded by the same water-drop tone and the sight of the bench melting away into the surrounding stone. I pressed a finger to the wall again, and the bench reappeared, this time long enough to support a sleeping body. After some experimentation, I discovered I could rearrange my cell into several different configurations, one of which did indeed include a toilet.

I was in the midst of a nap on my bed-sized platform when a deafening noise, somewhere between a bell and a sharp whistle, startled me awake. The man in black had returned. He stood in the hall as before, arms crossed, watching me through narrowed, leonine eyes.

"Look who it is," I said, stretching. "Supper wasn't half-bad, by the way, but if you'd care to improve your recipe, I've got a few ideas."

"How did you gain access to the valley?" he said, the rumbling question exactly the same as the last time I'd heard it.

"You're pretty rude, you know that?" I was annoyed at having my sleep interrupted and about being snuck up on generally. My fourth wall had been opaque when I began my repose, but it seemed when it came to privacy around here, I wasn't the final authority. "And you talk funny."

His response: the same question. "How did you gain access to the valley?"

"Why don't you come on in here and ask? I'll tell you anything you want to know."

I thought I saw something then, a twitch at the edge of his mouth, like he was considering it. And then he said, "How did you gain access to the valley?"

"Fine, fine," I said, disgusted. "Here's how I got into your goddamn valley: I walked. Satisfied? There was a break in the ridge, and I just climbed on down."

His only reaction was to go on looking at me in the same way. As he did not immediately repeat himself, I considered this a small victory, until he happened on a new line of questioning. "Why was there a break in the ridge?" he asked.

"How the hell should I know?" I shouted. I felt like I was dealing with an obstinate child.

"Did you cause the break in the ridge?"

"Of course I didn't! What are you, crazy?"

"I do not believe you."

"Well, I don't give a rat's ass what you believe. I'm telling you the truth."

"I will discover the answer, whether you tell me or not," the voice said, the floor vibrating with the bass of it. "This is your final opportunity to cooperate. Tell me how the ridge was broken."

I crossed my arms, mimicking his pose, and stared at him, pointedly quiet. He nodded, as if understanding my meaning, and came toward me. I had the impression he intended to take me up on the invitation to come into my cell and chat, but then he raised his hand, pressing one finger to the invisible wall. He said something, but the sound had gone out of my cell, and I couldn't hear what, and, anyway, it was plain he wasn't speaking to me because his eyes were focused on the air between us, like a mirror had appeared there, and he was addressing his reflection. As he finished his speech, the space beneath his fingers rippled, and thick tendrils of cloudy red began to spread toward me, twisting and curling like blood poured into water.

I backed away, quite sure I did not want those red clouds to touch me, but my steps took me farther than the distance so few strides should have covered. I found myself on my bench, rolling over to go back to sleep. Then I was up and about, experimenting with my metamorphosing cell, eating a bowl of orangey gruel. In a moment the man in black was standing before me again, only now it was our very first meeting.

Somehow, I was being taken backward through my life, pulled rapidly through one experience after the next. Soon I would be returned to the Valley of Endless Summer, standing before that armored giant, and climbing back up the Ridge, and riding with the scouts, in reverse, to New Absalom. That was what he wanted, the man in black: to see how I had gotten into the valley. But if he saw that, he would see Naomi. He would see the scouts. He could find New Absalom, if he chose, and Mama and Baby Adam and all my family and friends. I did not want to think what he would do then.

I clawed at the visions around me, thrashing the way a person might at a nightmare. Time slowed, grinding with the awful heat of dry gears, and stopped, leaving me in the darkened woods, looking up at the brazier-faced giant.

"It will be unpleasant for you if you resist," said the voice of the man in black, and for a blink I was in my cell again, inky red tentacles swirling all around.

"I reckon it's going to be unpleasant, then," I said.

And then I was back in the forest, only now the flow of time was hot enough to burn, straining to push past as I struggled to hold it back, until all at once the whole world tore away.

And suddenly I am standing in an icy field, snow falling, hearing my sister's terrified voice through the trees . . .

And I am fourteen, slumped on a mound of grass, holding my side as hot blood pulses through my fingers, certain I am going to die . . .

And I am eleven, screaming for help as Leafcoat raiders ride my father down . . .

And I am six, choking on briny water as the tumbling ocean current carries me out, out, out . . .

The sea was all around me, forcing its way into my nostrils just as it had all those years ago, when all at once the water evaporated, and I was in my cell once again. I lay curled on the floor, a little puddle of vomit beside me, which I supposed I'd have to take credit for, there being no one else around who could have supplied it.

From somewhere overhead, that voice rumbled down. "You were warned. I advise you to cooperate from now on. It will be dangerous for you otherwise."

Leaning against the invisible wall, I climbed shakily to my feet, so that I could look into the bespectacled eyes of the man in black. When I had a good view of his face, I spat in it. Spitting is not one of my particular talents—in contests held among the scouts, I regularly place fifth and below—but on this occasion I found a moment of virtuosity: a great gooey gob laced with bile and bits of my supper. Had there been no barrier between us, it would have struck him squarely in the face. As it was, the wad landed with a satisfying splat and oozed obscenely for several inches before something in the wall caused it to bubble and crackle and finally disappear. I decided I had made my position clear enough: I would not allow him one more moment of my past. If he wanted Naomi and Mama and Baby and the rest, he would have to break me first.

I believe he got the message. He allowed me one long look, brimming with contempt, then he was gone.

TWENTY-ONE

RAE

I remained there, glaring at the empty wall, and counted to one thousand in my head to be sure the man in black was really gone before I allowed myself to collapse into bed. I do not know how long I slept, but when I woke, my only company was a new bowl of orange gruel. When that was emptied, there was nothing to do but look at the ceiling and wonder about my coda, and when I did that, my cell would start to shrink; all the air went out of it, and I had the impulse to throw myself at the walls, screaming to be set free. Which, I reasoned, was just what the man in black wanted: for me to know I could just sit here and rot for all he cared. So, instead of thinking, I did push-ups and knee bends until I was too tired to stand, then I ate more gruel and slept. When I couldn't sleep any more, I reprised my exercise routine, adding in jumping jacks.

Sometime later—I wasn't sure how much later, days at the least—I was lying on the floor, working myself up for another round of knee tucks, when a low hum sounded above my head. It was the same variety of sound as the water drip that heralded my food or the shrieking whistle that announced the man in black, and I waited for something to happen, but the hum only came again, and a few seconds after, once more.

Finally, someone said, "Hello? Are you awake in there?" It was a real voice—no menacing rumble but a man's low, rich tones. "You just have to touch the wall there," it said.

I got up and did as the voice asked, partly curious, partly annoyed that its owner believed I hadn't worked out this simple trick.

This new man was taller than the first but slimmer and not so martial in appearance, which made him seem younger, though I suspected the two were around the same age. He had on a suit much like that of his predecessor, black and neatly cut, with a silver-trimmed collar. The low light lent his brown skin a dim luster, his handsome features set in a questioning frown. "Is this a bad time?" he said. "I thought we might have a little chat, but I can come back later if you're busy."

The faint grin he mustered then led me to believe this was meant as humor. I had assumed a look of steely defiance in preparation for the first man in black and decided it would serve just as well for this second visitor. I was determined to give up nothing about myself or my people, but I knew if this fellow wanted to talk, there was nothing I could do to stop him. I went and sat on my bench to wait him out.

Apparently taking my actions as an invitation, he summoned up a chair from the empty floor and sat, as if we were engaged in a pleasant social call. "I hope you'll forgive our accommodations," he said. "We're somewhat over-extended at present, and to be honest, people around here aren't terribly concerned with your comfort, since they believe you're a tribal shaman or warrior priestess intent on conquering our city."

As he was speaking, he produced a small package from his pocket, which he now unwrapped to reveal a sandwich. The ordinariness of it took me by surprise. I had expected some new manner of infernal device. "Would you like to share?" he asked, when he saw me staring. "I doubt I'll finish more than half. It's fluffernutter," he added, plainly considering this nonsense word compelling enticement.

Mama's old lessons in etiquette rose up to betray me, and quite automatically I said, "No, thank you."

"Suit yourself." He took a bite, chewed. "You're not, are you? A shaman or priestess, or planning to overthrow our city? It would help if we could straighten that out right away."

"No, I am not."

"Good, great," he said, smiling as if this were indeed good and great. "For the record, I never thought you were, but you've got quite a few people convinced you're a rather serious threat." He bit again into his sandwich, using his food as a rhetorical pause while he watched for my reaction.

"We've been having some trouble lately, you see," he went on, when he had finished chewing. "The valley where you and I are now is quite isolated from the rest of the world. The mountain range surrounding us on all sides typically discourages any visitors. Some time ago, however, a number of uninvited guests found a way through. Initially, they were considered a mere nuisance, nothing worth worrying over, but it has recently come to our attention that they may have access to a very dangerous sort of power and, well, people around here are concerned."

Again he bit and chewed contemplatively at his sandwich, and this time I took the chance to speak up. "And what does any of that have to do with me?"

"You," he said, after chewing rather longer than seemed necessary, "are in a unique position to tell us how worried we ought to be about this power, since you were observed actually using it."

As I was thinking about that, he took a pocket watch from his coat. "I've got to go," he said, folding up the remainder of his sandwich, "but let's talk again soon. You'll have questions. And you'll probably want a bath. I see you've been exercising."

My white clothes had become stiff and yellowed with sweat, and I assumed he meant impoliteness until he pointed to one of my walls and said, "You just have to touch that part there to get the tub. Run your finger along the side to adjust the water. I'm sure you'll figure it out."

"So," I said as he turned to leave, "you must be Good Cop, then." He regarded me quizzically, brows furrowed. "It's a saying we have," I explained. "Good Cop, Bad Cop. One person comes at you acting the part of marauder and bully, then another turns up friendly as you please, so you'll start trusting and spilling all your darkest secrets."

A slow grin spread across his face. "Vinneas will do," he said. "Bad Cop's name is Imway."

Only after he was gone did I notice my food had arrived; beside my usual bowl was the other half of his sandwich.

The bath worked exactly as promised, and I spent rather more time than necessary soaking, to make up for lost opportunity and also to test my theory that, no matter how long you sat, the water never got cold. Sure enough, my fingers and toes were prunes before I marked the slightest drop in temperature. A new set of clothes and a towel were waiting when I got up, my old wardrobe having likely walked off on its own.

The fluffernutter was better than I expected.

Vinneas returned a day later, as I judged the time required for two more meals, one long nap, and another very extended bath. For this visit he neglected to bring a lunch.

"You know," he said, taking his seat outside my cell, "you never told me your name."

"You didn't ask."

"I'm asking now."

"Rachel," I said. "I go by Rae."

He was silent a moment, as though testing my name for hidden weight and meaning.

"And now that we've been properly introduced," I said, "I'd like to ask you a thing or two."

"Of course," he said. "I can't promise all the answers, but I'm a good enough guesser when the situation calls for it."

"You said I was seen using some kind of power. What did you mean?" I knew I was revealing something merely by asking, but it seemed a fair trade against what there was to learn.

"We call it 'thelemity,'" he said, "the power, that is. 'Force' is probably a better word, like gravity or electromagnetism. It's exceedingly complex—we've been studying thelemity for centuries, and we're still only beginning to understand it. But what you should know is that it's a kind of potential, one certain people can use to affect reality, to use it like an extension of themselves."

"What sort of people?"

"People like you." He shrugged, as if this were a matter of the utmost simplicity. "Our word is 'revenni.' It refers to people who can use thelemity to impose their will upon the world."

"And you think I'm one of these—revenni?" I asked, slowly working over the unfamiliar vocabulary.

"Quite sure, yes. You demonstrated some very impressive talent with thelemity while our defense forces were trying to capture you. I'm sure you noticed your firearms were rather more potent than usual."

I thought back to the woods, to the way my guns seemed to spew comets and stars rather than the bullets I had loaded. "A lot of good it did me."

"You were still pretty thoroughly outgunned," Vinneas said, "though from what I hear, you gave Imway quite a fight."

"Wait," I said, startled. "Are you telling me that thing was *him*?"

"Yes. Imway was in command of the detachment that brought you in. He's an eques. It's a type of warrior," Vinneas added, reading my confusion at yet another strange term. "The closest word in your language is probably 'knight.'"

Knights appeared here and there in Papa's old stories, usually in opposition to all his monsters and dragons. The man in black was not so dissimilar in appearance from the knights I had imagined, though to continue the conceit any further would mean disregarding his character entirely.

"The closest thing in my language is probably 'douche bag,'" I said. Now it was Vinneas's turn to puzzle over my wording. I explained, "It means someone who acts like a jackass because he knows there's no one to stop him from doing as he pleases."

Vinneas's expression made me think I wasn't too far off, but he said, "Imway isn't proud of injuring you. If it makes you feel better, you rather embarrassed him on his first official mission. And you damaged some extremely costly equipment while you were at it."

That did make me feel better, though I wasn't about to admit it. "So that thing was some suit of armor? He was *inside* of it?"

"Exactly. It's called an 'equus.'"

"And your valley," I said, my thoughts gathering speed, "the reason it's summer all the time—you change the weather with your thelemity?"

This question earned me another broad smile. I had become a prized student. "Our power typically doesn't extend far enough into the atmosphere to affect weather patterns, so we can't prevent rain, for example, but we can keep things warm at least."

"Sounds like magic."

"Yes, it does."

"And it only works here, in the valley?"

"Most of the time that's true. We have some control over where our thelemity goes, but generally we keep it here. We built the mountain wall to prevent strangers from stumbling upon it accidentally."

"Why? Anyone gets close, all you have to do is squash them or explode them."

I didn't know how angry I was until the words came out, all harsh and snarling. Vinneas looked rather abashed, which was gratifying. "Of course, I should have started with that," he said, like a man who has made a silly but pardonable mistake. "Not long after you entered the valley, there would have been a strange smell, ozone or phosphorous or something similar, accompanied by a feeling of uneasiness or elation, perhaps both."

"And a second later, I got exploded to kingdom come," I finished for him, my fury returning.

"Exactly. It happens to all revenni the first time you encounter thelemity. How familiar are you with electricity?"

The way he asked made me wonder how much of a savage he thought I was. "I know it well enough."

"Think of yourself as an electric lamp. Before you arrived here, you'd never been plugged in. But then, suddenly, you get a rush of power, and it shorts you out. A power surge. So really, we didn't explode you. You exploded yourself. You were never in any danger, though I expect it ruined your clothes. And it will only happen that one time."

I remained quiet for a while, thinking on what he'd said. "And now I can use that power anytime I want?"

"As long as you have access to thelemity, you'll be able to do some remarkable things unless something happens to interfere with your ability. For example, if you weren't wearing that collar there, you'd have a fairly easy time breaking out of your cell and killing me."

"Break out and kill you?" I said, all false innocence. "I'd never do that."

"I should hope not. I've already written up my report on you for my superiors, and I spent a good three paragraphs describing how you pose no threat whatsoever to our city. It's all part of my recommendation for your release."

"And do you think they'll let me out?"

"Yes," he said, smiling. "I happen to be a remarkably influential person."

By the time he left, I was balanced halfway between thanking him and giving him a good hard slap. He didn't treat me like a criminal, the way the man in black had, but he certainly wasn't about to apologize for my being locked up. I was still glad, though, when he appeared again, another day later as measured in meals and naps.

He dissolved my fourth wall with a touch, like popping a bubble. "Let's go outside," he said.

We ended up in another stone bowl, this one a deal larger than my cell and turned up so that the open end allowed me a view of the tallest buildings I have ever seen, sleek stone shafts like pillars, holding up a sky I hadn't seen in I couldn't say how long.

"About five days," Vinneas explained as he removed the collar from my neck. "You've got to promise not to do anything rash, now, for example, blasting my head off."

"Sure. I bet you could zap me anytime."

"Not at all." He dropped my collar with a clank. "I have about as much control over thelemity as I do over gravity."

"Really? You can't do anything?"

"I'm fairly good with crossword puzzles," he said, "but not with thelemity, no. And before you ask, the word is 'pacifer.' That's the polite way to talk about unexceptional people like me."

That collar had hardly come off before I began to feel different, larger somehow, as though some part of me had diffused into the air. It reminded me of the way steam will rise from your skin after swimming on a cool day, only this cloud seemed to go on and on, and I found that if I tried, I could direct its currents. I flexed one wisp, then another, and, to my astonishment, small swirls of whitish fire began chasing one another across the ground.

"Exciting, isn't it?" Vinneas said. He had a smile on, though I noticed he had stepped deliberately away from the little flames. "I've been told it's like having a thousand sets of tiny hands."

I supposed that was true, though a hand is still something solid, with a wrapping of skin, and this seemed more like smoke. A new appendage entirely, as different from anything I'd ever felt as a set of wings—and yet already it had begun to seem a natural a part of me, as much as any other piece I'd had the past nineteen years.

Vinneas had placed something in the center of our little enclosure: the food bowl from my cell. "Usually, we start people off lifting small weights and folding bits of paper," he said. "But let's see what you can do with this. Go ahead—try to move it."

I eyed the bowl, sizing it up. I couldn't tell how sturdy this new part of me was, and I didn't want to strain or injure it, as I sensed I might if I levered myself improperly.

"Don't worry about breaking it," Vinneas said, meaning the bowl. "It's built to take a lot of punishment. Do your worst."

He had broken my concentration, and I aimed a glare at him that encouraged another few steps back. Returning my attention to the bowl, I gathered my new power around it, and when I judged its strength sufficient for the bowl's weight, I closed it like a fist.

The air surrounding the bowl erupted in a gout of white fire that sent the thing shooting like a bullet into the far wall. I knew I ought to be embarrassed over misjudging my ability so greatly, but I was too preoccupied laughing with the fun of it. The nearest sensation I could name was shooting up a row of glass bottles.

Vinneas had ducked for cover to avoid the bowl's first ricochet, but now he stood, straightening his ruffled uniform. "Well, looks like you won't have any trouble with basic thermal artifices." He went and retrieved the bowl, which was still rolling slowly along one wall. "Let's try that one more time, shall we?"

For such an unexceptional person, Vinneas proved an excellent tutor. By the end of my first lesson in thelemity, I could raise and lower my old gruel bowl at will, as well as produce a gust of wind from nowhere, light the space around my feet with a pair of dancing will-o'-the-wisps, and set small fires with a wave of my hand. Vinneas declared me a natural. "Of course, you'd learn a lot more from someone who could teach from experience," he explained while I gleefully incinerated a number of wood scraps he had brought for this purpose. "We have an entire school here. The Academy. I'm sure they'd be happy to have you."

Burning things lost its appeal at that. For a moment, as I watched the world bend and sparkle under my power, I had forgotten about my family and friends, all the people I loved, lost out in the wilderness. I nearly blurted out everything to Vinneas but caught myself just in time. All I said was "I can't stay."

"I was afraid you would say that, but I had to ask," Vinneas said. "My superiors are satisfied that the people Imway and his squadron took into custody pose no further threat. They will be released into their own territory, but with no memory of this valley or anything that happened here."

"No!" I shouted, unable to hold back my panic. I could survive, I thought, if they set me loose now. I could beat the winter and the roving tribes and find my coda wherever it was. But if they took my memory, I wouldn't even know where to begin. "I have to remember how I got here."

"I'm afraid it isn't up to me." Vinneas did look very sorry, not that it helped any. "We can't risk anyone from outside learning about us, or about thelemity."

"Then I will stay."

He stepped back, like he needed to see all of me to verify my earnestness. "Just like that?"

"Just like that." My plan, formed in that moment, was to attend this school of his only until the opportunity came to slip away.

"Excellent," he said, still plainly dubious of my intentions. "The Academy administrators will want to interview you to verify everything in my report. I'll tell them to contact me if they have any questions."

"Won't you be here?"

"No." He gestured to his collar, where he wore a silver mark shaped something like the letter "C." I recalled seeing others there before, one more like an "A." "I've been promoted."

"Congratulations."

"It isn't much of a promotion," he grumbled, "and it means I'll be away for a good while. I'd been hoping my superiors wouldn't go through with it, but alas. By the time I get back, you'll probably be at the Academy."

Admission turned out to be somewhat stricter than the simple process Vinneas had envisioned. The representatives of this Academy were haughty and pompous and universally under the impression that I was some dangerous savage. They refused to speak to me unless I was collared and locked in my cell, always using that rumbling, otherworldly voice—which I learned was a kind of translator—even after I proved I could speak their language nearly as well as they could. By the time Vinneas returned to visit, I had moved only to a different wing of the same prison.

It was one of the few times I was glad to be locked up because I was in a foul mood when he arrived at my cell, and the grin he had on was so cocky, I would have fancied it a fine target for my fist. But that was until he spoke. What he said flipped my world around more than anything I had seen since coming to this strange place: "So, why didn't you ever tell me you had a sister?"

TWENTY-TWO

JAX

like shooting. I know I'm not supposed to think of it as fun, of course. That's the first thing they tell you when you start weapons training. They show you a lazel, and they say, *This is not a toy.* It's right there in the Academy Handbook, too: "A weapon is a tool of destruction, not amusement." I get it. I do. But shooting is still a little fun. And when you think about it, most things that are really fun *aren't* toys.

The point, I think, is that you shouldn't forget what weapons are for, which is killing. And when you're only shooting a target, it's easy to forget. The one thing you definitely shouldn't do, though, is *look* like you're having fun. Rhetor Croupo, our weapons instructor, is totally the best shot I've ever seen, and when he demonstrated the lazel for us, he looked like he was about to fall asleep, like someone had told him to look at the target but never, ever shoot it. But he still put all ten shots right in the center. A perfect score. Since then, everyone's been doing their best to look as bored as possible.

Today is Section E's first day of live fire. We started weapons training at the same time as all our other lessons at the School of Rhetoric, but for months, all we've been doing is learning about how the weapons work, how to put them together and take them apart, how to handle them, but never actually *using* them. So everyone was pretty excited when we found out we'd be getting to shoot something. We don't even care that our lazels are turned to almost the lowest setting.

The LL-40, also known as the "lazel," is the standard weapon of the Legion. "The legionary's best friend," Croupo calls it. Lazels are issued to everyone in the Legion, though only the milites, the Legion's infantry, really use them in battle. A lazel is basically a tool for focusing and directing thelemity, made so that anyone can use it, even if you're not fontani or revenni. You can load it up with all sorts of different grips and sights and attachments, but basically it's just a dull gray cylinder about forty centimeters long, shaped a little like a tilty letter "L." Inside is something called a "valcov," which gathers up thelemity and turns it into an artifice. What type of artifice depends on the type of valcov, but it's usually something destructive, obviously.

The valcov we're using for practice today creates an artifice called "null." What it does is make things not exist. "Negates the actuality of ordinary matter" was how Croupo put it. Null isn't very exciting to watch—whatever you hit with it just turns sort of blue-white and disappears. There's another artifice called "blast" that makes big, fiery explosions, which is much more interesting, but the thing about explosions is they waste a lot of energy on heat and light and noise. With null, all that energy goes into pure destruction. That's why we mostly use null in battle. If you shoot something with blast, you might blow off a piece or send it flying, but afterward, there'll be a whole lot more left over than if you'd hit it with null instead.

For today's practice, we're shooting at big metal spheres floating low over the ground fifty meters away. Everyone from Sixth Class Section E is lined up along the shooting range, firing away. The lazels have all been hobbled, meaning Rhetor Croupo can control their settings, and the power is turned way down—otherwise even a glancing hit would totally destroy the target. As it is, each shot only takes off a little pea-sized bit. We've each got a hundred shots to put as close as possible to the center of the sphere. Null makes a little crackling noise, like breaking ice or glass, and the range sounds like there are icicles dropping everywhere out of the sky.

Lazels are pretty tricky for beginners because the only way to get them to shoot is to *want* them to shoot. It doesn't work to just think *shoot!* or *fire!* or something like that—it's more like making a fist, or blinking your eyes, or talking. You don't think about it; you just *do* it. If you've never used a lazel before, it can be really hard. I can tell that a lot of the cadets are having trouble because their shots are going off almost randomly, and some kids are swearing to themselves. But I just keep focused on the target, sending off one shot after another.

Rhetor Croupo shouts "Time!" only a few seconds after I've fired my hundredth shot. The hobbles shut down our guns, and we all get up from our firing positions while Croupo calls in the targets. When I see mine, I almost laugh I'm so happy: The middle is full of pea-sized craters. It turns out only seven cadets fired all one hundred shots, and I scored more points than anyone. Croupo leaves Elessa in charge while he goes to reset the range. Most of the section will be doing the same exercise again, but the top five cadets will have moving targets this time.

"That was great, Jax!" says Elessa, looking at my target. She would have had the top score if it weren't for me, but she really does sound happy. Some of the other cadets start congratulating me, too. I don't usually do very well in exercises like this, and they know it's a big deal for me.

"It's because he practices all the time," says Bomar sourly. "That's the only reason Jax is any good. If I had my own lazel, I'd be better than Croupo. I'd have drilled a hole right through my target." Bomar's target looks like an apple after a few bites from a worm, and not a very hungry worm, either. He scored in the bottom five.

Bomar isn't lying about me practicing. I'm officially part of the Legion, so I get a lazel like everyone else. Mine has a lot of weird-looking decorative parts, but it works, and I take it to the range a lot. I wasn't very good at first, but there are always other legionaries there who'll help me out. I wouldn't have said anything about it myself, but now I guess I shouldn't be so proud of scoring higher than kids who've never shot a lazel before—though I bet some of them have. Everyone knows cadets find ways to practice with lazels before they let us have them in class.

"If Jax has a lazel to practice with, why shouldn't he practice?" Elessa says. "Practicing is the only way to get better, and it's not like this is a competition. We're supposed to be learning. He shouldn't have to pretend he's as bad as you just so you'll feel better."

"He shouldn't be practicing at all!" Bomar shouts. His face is all tight and twisted. It's pretty obvious he's actually angry about his low score but would rather yell at me than admit it. "It's not like he's ever going to use a lazel for real! He's just going to be hiding somewhere while we do all the fighting!"

He's kind of right about that. If I ever am in a real battle, I definitely won't be shooting a lazel. I won't have to fight at all if the battle goes the way it's supposed to. I know it's true, and so do all the cadets. Even Elessa agrees, I can tell. She looks over at me, her mouth half-open, like she wants to scold Bomar but doesn't know how.

"We're all on the same side, Bomar," I say. It's something Vinneas told me to remember whenever I felt angry with the other cadets. He says when you're at the Academy, and everyone's being ranked and evaluated and trying to beat each other out for the top spots, it's easy to forget why we're studying and training and taking all these tests in the first place, which is that we've got a war to win. But I bet no one ever got mad at Vinneas for winning at something. He's one of those people who just stand out. And I bet he never had to deal with anyone like Bomar. Or if he did, he knew exactly what to do.

"I don't want you on my side," Bomar says. "If I'm in a fight, I don't want to be anywhere near you. You know why? Because you're *scared*. If things get tough, you'll run off and leave the rest of us to go dark."

Going dark is what legionaries call it when their thelemity fails, and everything it powers—weapons, armor, vehicles, everything—stops working. There are only two ways it can happen: either the source of your thelemity is killed, or it gets too far away for the thelemity to reach you. The very first thing every legionary learns is to protect your source, your fontani, at all costs, because without fontani, you can't fight. But there's nothing you can do about it if your source gets scared and runs away. And if you *are* the source, you've got to stay right up close to the fighting because if you don't, everyone who's depending on you is as good as dead.

"I wouldn't run," I say to Bomar. "I stayed during the last attack, didn't I?" I'm not being totally honest. I wouldn't ever admit it, but while I was out there in the Forum, I did feel like running away. It was only for a second, but I thought about it anyway. I try to sound confident, like there's no question I'd stay and fight, but the thing is, I can't really know for sure.

It's obvious Bomar doesn't believe me. "You'd run," he says, smiling an extremely mean smile. "You know how I know? Because you're a coward. I'll prove it." Still smiling, he runs and grabs his lazel from the firing range, then comes back, pointing it right at me.

"Bomar!" Elessa shouts, using her cadet adjutant's voice. "Lower that weapon!"

Bomar isn't listening. "Look at him!" he says, laughing. "It doesn't even *work*, and he's still scared!"

When he pointed the lazel at me, I flinched and held up my arm to cover my face. I know the lazel won't fire with the hobble on, and even if it did, it couldn't hurt me the way it would the other cadets. But even though I know I'm 100 percent safe, I still don't like having a gun pointed at me.

Bomar's lazel has a trigger attachment, which is a fake trigger meant to help you figure out the feeling that will make a lazel shoot. Eventually, you're supposed to take it off once you don't need it anymore. Now Bomar's jerking the trigger over and over at rapid-fire speed, laughing, and saying, "Look at him! Look at him!"

"Cadet Bomar!" Elessa screams. "Drop your weapon *now*! That's an order!"

Bomar actually does stop, but he's still smiling, like he hasn't heard Elessa at all. "You know, Jax, I've decided you're right," he says, lowering the lazel. "We're on the same side, and there's nothing I can do about it. So I'm going to help you get over being scared." He takes a small silver disk from his pocket and flicks it toward his lazel. There's a little crackling sound, and the hobble breaks to pieces.

Everyone starts yelling then. Most of the cadets run. Even Elessa backs off. Without the hobble, Bomar can shoot the lazel at full power.

I'm the only one who hasn't moved, mostly because I'm so surprised. "How did you do that?" I ask.

"Every idiot knows how to disable one of those things," Bomar scoffs. "But then every idiot knows lazels can't hurt fontani." He points the gun at me again. "Here's your chance, Jax. I'm going to shoot on three. Let's see if you can handle it."

"Bomar," I say, "don't be stupid. You're going to get us both in trouble."

"One!" Bomar yells, starting to laugh again. "Two!"

He pulls the trigger on two. At first nothing happens, but Bomar keeps yanking on the trigger and finally there's an icy crackle as the lazel goes off. The burst of null fizzles out about a meter away from me, before I even think to duck. Bomar hardly notices—he's still trying to shoot me, whooping like it's the most fun he's ever had.

And then, all of a sudden, Bomar is gone—just gone, like he was never even there. Way across the range, I see Rhetor Croupo kneeling on the ground with his lazel ready to shoot. I wonder if he *did* shoot, if he saw what Bomar was doing and nulled him right there, and for a second all I can think is, *He just* killed *Bomar!* But there would have been a bluish shadow and some of the ground where Bomar was standing would be gone, too, and there isn't any of that.

And then I see Bomar. He's on the ground about five meters away, and looks totally confused—until he sees Fontanus Charles standing over him. Then he just looks scared.

□————————□

TWENTY-THREE

JAX

Charles is another of our city's fontani, one of the oldest anywhere. He looks like he's maybe forty, but he's been fighting since the very beginning of the war, more than five hundred years ago. He's one of the best in the Legion, even though he doesn't look very tough at all. He's short and pale and a little flabby, and he has a round chin that makes his head look kind of like an eggplant, especially since his forehead goes way up with only a little curly hair around the top and sides. The first time I met him, I was thinking this exact thing, and he probably guessed because he said, "Oh, judge me by my size, do you?" He used this weird voice that reminded me of a frog, but he was smiling like it was supposed to be a joke. "When five hundred years old you reach, look as good you will not," he said, in that same froggy voice. I was starting to think he might be crazy. The words all made sense, but they were in a different order from the way people usually talk. But then he said, in a totally normal voice, "Just kidding. You'll probably look a lot better." Since then I've learned that Charles can be really helpful; you just have to ignore him whenever he does something weird, which is often.

Rhetor Croupo has come sprinting from across the range, his face all tight and mad. He stops in front of Charles. "Fontanus Charles!" he says, saluting. "I appreciate the help, sir!"

Charles returns the salute. "Thought it would be a shame to have you null one of your cadets," he says. "The Legion needs everyone it can get, even the exceptionally stupid." Charles turns to Bomar. "How would you like to be a test subject for new artifices, Cadet?"

"Whatever happens will be better than he deserves, sir," says Croupo. He looks down at Bomar, too. "Cadet Bomar! Understand that any of the three people standing before you now—Fontanus Charles, Fontanus Jax-ten, and I—would have been entirely justified in ending your life before you could further endanger your fellow cadets. You will get to your feet and thank Fontanus Charles for saving your hide. You will then report to your section adjutant and wait until I am ready to escort you to the Cura-tor's office."

Bomar has started to cry, but he does what Rhetor Croupo says. When he goes to where Elessa is waiting with the other cadets, they all take a few steps back, like they're afraid they could get in trouble just by standing too close. I actually feel kind of sorry for him.

"Is there anything else I can do for you, sir?" Croupo says to Charles.

"No, thank you," Charles answers. "I'm just here to borrow one of your cadets for the day." He grins at me. "What do you think, Jax? Fancy a field trip?"

"Field trip" is another of the weird things Charles says. It means when we travel somewhere outside Ninth City "for educational purposes," as he puts it.

"Where are we going?" I ask. Charles's field trips are usually fun, and they're always exciting. Sometimes we practice the different techniques fon-tani use in battle. The reason we need to leave the city to practice is that, when we're sparring, it helps to be far away from anything we wouldn't want to break by accident. Other times, Charles just takes me places he wants me to see. Once we went really far south to watch glaciers, which are big cliffs of ice, falling into the ocean. There would be this sound like thunder, and a whole sheet of ice would gush down into the water. It was awesome. You'd never believe how different other parts of the world can be.

Every so often, we'll visit one of the old cities, too, the ones from before the war. That's usually not so fun. Once we went to Tokyo, which Charles said used to be one of the biggest cities in the world. Millions and millions of people lived there, and all of them died the day the Valentines came—all except the three who turned out to be fontani like Charles and me. Two of those fontani have been killed in the war, Charles said, and one is still fight-ing at the Front. Now Tokyo is just a few crumbly old towers. Charles used to live in a city called Vancouver, and there's even less there. He was the only survivor. So yeah, going to the cities isn't much fun. I'm a little nervous about this field trip but definitely excited.

"You've won an all-expenses-paid trip to sunnnnnny Bermuda!" Charles says in another of his weird voices, kind of half singing. As far as I've been able to figure out, "all-expenses-paid" means absolutely nothing.

Bermuda is Charles's name for Area 22-53, an island way out in the middle of the ocean. Technically, it's part of the Ninth Principate, but nobody actually lives there.

"Why?" I ask.

Charles raises his eyebrows. "Why do you think?"

"They've found another fontanus," I say automatically.

"Fontana, actually," Charles answers, smiling. "A girl, right around your age. The censors asked me to give her a little crash course on the history of the Valentine War."

"So she's from the settlements?" I've always been surprised at how little the people who live in the settlements actually know about our war with the Valentines, which is practically nothing. I guess we've got our reasons for "keeping them in the dark," as Charles puts it. For one thing, we can't really explain about the war without explaining about thelemity, and everyone seems to think that if the settlers knew about thelemity, they'd want it for themselves, too, and the problem there is we barely have enough fontani to power the cities, let alone hundreds of settlements. Well, maybe not *everyone* thinks that way. There are a few people, mostly at the Academy, who think we should tell the settlers everything, the way Charles is going to do for this one girl.

"No, actually," Charles says. "The censors did find her in one of the settlements, but she comes from the unincorporated peoples."

Now, *that's* surprising. Before the war, the world was divided into a lot of different territories called "countries," which Charles says were a little like our Principates only they usually had more than one city, and people could be spread out all over the place instead of walled up in a city or settlement. The countries were always squabbling over things, and sometimes even fought *against* each other, but after Romeo destroyed pretty much the whole world, the people who were left joined together to fight back. Eventually, they built the Principates, each with a big piece of the planet to defend, with one city to do the fighting and a bunch of settlements to help out. But there were some people left over, people who went into hiding when the war started or were someplace so isolated they didn't know what was happening and never ended up in a city or settlement. These people are called "the unincorporated peoples." They have little societies all over the world, most of them living the way people did thousands of years ago. Kids at the Academy say the nocos live in caves, or huts made of mud or grass, that they wear animal skins and fight with spears and arrows—not that any of us has ever *met* one. "Really?" I ask Charles.

"Really," he says. "Learning she's fontani has been something of an adjustment, as I'm sure you can understand. I think you'll be able to help her get used to it." He pauses, the way he does when he's getting ready to say something he knows I won't like. "And I'd like your help getting her under control once she goes active."

We'd been walking away from the firing range, but now I stop in my tracks. I should have figured out what Charles had planned, but I didn't even think about it, probably because I didn't want to. When fontani first get their power, they lose pretty much any sense of where they are or what's happening. It's sort of like being in a dream. The problem is, they can also do all these unbelievable things. Imagine a dinosaur sleepwalking, and you've pretty much got the idea. "Like a bull in a china shop" is how Charles puts it. It all means the same thing, which is that new fontani are *really* dangerous. That's why we take them to Bermuda before they go active: because there's about a thousand kilometers of ocean in every direction, so it's less likely they'll destroy anything important. We also make sure to have other fontani nearby, experienced fighters who can keep the new ones from doing too much damage. Bermuda is a total wreck, by the way.

Charles doesn't have much trouble figuring out what I'm thinking. "You can stay behind if you want, Jax," he says, "but this is your best chance to find out what it's like to face fontani who don't necessarily have your best interests in mind—and that's something you need to learn before you find yourself up against a Valentine Zero."

I know Charles is right. Romeo has fontani, too, same as us, and the better I get at fighting them, the more use I'll be to the Legion. But it gives me a bad feeling, like standing alone in the Forum the last time Romeo attacked. Instead of answering Charles, I ask, "Was Rhetor Croupo really going to null Bomar back there?"

"No," Charles says, laughing a little. "I'm sure Croupo had some non-lethal artifice ready. And I was watching the entire time, ready to step in if things became too unruly. I just wonder why you didn't stop Bomar yourself."

That's a good question. It wasn't that I was scared, not exactly. I knew that lazel couldn't hurt me. I could have grabbed it right out of Bomar's hand and not been in any danger at all, but I didn't think to. It just seemed like the sort of thing a teacher should do, or a fighter or a leader, someone like Croupo or Charles or Vinneas. "I don't know," I mumble. "I guess I thought I'd do something wrong."

"Not a problem," Charles says, still smiling. "You'll figure it out with practice. But I want you to understand that I wouldn't have left you alone with Bomar if I didn't think you could handle him, and I wouldn't be taking you with me today if I didn't think you were ready."

"Really?" I'm not so sure. If Charles thinks I'm ready to fight other fontani, he might be crazy after all. I mean, we've done a lot of sparring, but I still can't really imagine what it would be like.

"Really. But listen, let's start out by meeting her. I'll be training both of you from now on, so you might as well start getting to know each other now. And if you think *you're* nervous, imagine how she must feel. A few days ago, she didn't even know there *was* a war. Now people are telling her we can't win without her."

That I get. I'm still not totally used to the idea that the Legion could really need me for anything.

"What do you say?" Charles asks.

"I say let's go." I try to sound confident, even though I'm not.

TWENTY-FOUR

JAX

Charles has a velo waiting, which surprises me until I remember we're going to meet an inactive fontana. Normally, when Charles and I go on a field trip, we just fly, but if we do that today, we'll risk sending this new girl active, which would be very bad for anyone who happened to be nearby.

The trip seems to take forever, though really it's less than an hour. Most of the time it feels like we're not moving at all because there's nothing to see but the ocean and a few clouds. Charles talks the whole way, asking me about the Academy and the cadets in my section. He's seen a lot of generations go by, and he's always interested in "what the kids are doing these days." For some reason, he thinks it's incredibly funny that sixth-classers at the Academy are referred to as "Dodos."

"We'll be seeing one of your old schoolmates today," he says just as Bermuda comes into sight, a tiny patch on the ocean below. "Name of Vinneas. Said you were friends. Very young for the censors, I thought. Well, most legionaries look like children to me, but this one seemed younger than most."

Vinneas—I'd completely forgotten he was with the censors now. Everyone at the Academy was surprised when we found out he was leaving, but it was an even bigger shock to hear he'd been assigned to the censors. Vinneas had one of the highest cumulative scores ever in the Academy's Combat Exercises, and in three years of commanding practice battles, he'd never lost once. On top of that, he'd just been made Procurator, which is pretty much the most important position an OA can have. They wouldn't have done that unless they expected him to end up leading troops or advising on tactics. All the censors do is count up the supplies we get from the settlements. But if it means Vinneas is going to be there, I think I'm glad he ended up with them.

Thick gray clouds have come rolling over the ocean, but they part as they get close to the harvester stationed above the island of Bermuda. By the time we circle in to land, the sky is cloudy everywhere except the puddle of sky where the harvester is, floating like a big, wingless duck in a circle of sunlight.

Vinneas is waiting for us in the landing bay. I thought I was getting used to seeing older people salute me, but it's still a little strange when Vinneas greets me that way. At least it's the only thing he does that reminds me of my rank in the Legion. When he talks, it's like we're just friends from the Academy. "At last, the reinforcements have arrived!" he says with a grin.

He's with another censor, an older man with bushy cheeks who Vinneas introduces as Reggidel. "The girls are waiting in the next room," Reggidel says gruffly. He smiles like he's a little amused and a little annoyed. "Let's hope you two have more luck than we did."

"Been giving you some trouble, have they?" Charles asks, like he already knows exactly what sort of trouble.

"We haven't gotten off to the best start," Vinneas admits. "Nothing you two can't handle, I'm sure."

"What do you mean? Is there more than one?" I ask.

"Naomi, the girl we suspect of being fontani," Reggidel explains, "and her sister, Rae."

"Rae is revenni, as it turns out," Vinneas adds. "We'd like to bring her into the Academy as well. She's proving somewhat reluctant."

Wow, *sisters*. At Ninth City, you almost never see siblings at all, and especially not two people with the same mother *and* the same father. I wonder how much they'll look alike, whether they'll be like the twin boys from Sixth Class Section A, who're about the only other siblings I've ever seen together at the same time.

"We'll be our charming selves," says Charles. "Can't promise any more than that. Ready, Jax?"

I don't think I am, but I nod anyway.

"Well, I suppose that's it, then," Reggidel says with a sigh. He motions toward a door at the end of the bay. "Right through here. Guard your man parts, everyone."

"Recruiting Naomi has been a little traumatic for Censor Reggidel," Vinneas whispers, though Reggidel hears him anyway and kind of grunt-laughs. I want to ask what they think is so funny, but then the door opens, and I'm looking right at them, Naomi and Rae.

They aren't at all what I was expecting. They aren't in furs, and they don't have crazy hair or lots of scars or weird jewelry or anything. They look like people you might see at Ninth City, although their uniforms are white, which is a little strange. White is the color you wear if you're not part of the Legion or the Academy, and at Ninth City that pretty much means very young children and criminals.

They aren't identical, either, like the twins from Section A. Some things about them are the same, like their eyes, which are big and light brown, but you'd never get the two of them confused. One is a lot taller than the other, for one thing.

"Jax, Charles," Vinneas says, "meet Naomi and Rae." It turns out Naomi is the smaller one, which makes sense because Charles said she would be my age, and we're about the same size. Her hair is almost the exact same color as her eyes, kind of like coffee with cream, and she has freckles that same creamy color. Rae must be older. She looks like she spends a lot of time outside, and her hair is much lighter, and she's *extremely* pretty.

"Vinneas tells me you're going to explain everything," Rae says, sounding really mad. She seems to be talking to Charles, but I think the one she's really angry with is Vinneas. She's speaking Aux, which is surprising. I'd heard the nocos all speak languages from the old world, but her Aux is perfect. She has a weird accent that makes her words kind of float. "That will be a fine piece of magic, I expect, reasoning a little girl into your war."

"It isn't just our war," I say, without even thinking. "It's yours, too. It's everyone's. Everyone in the whole world."

Rae had been glaring at Charles and Vinneas, but now she looks at me and suddenly she seems more sad than angry. I can feel my face getting hot. When she speaks again, it's almost like an apology. "I can't understand what sort of people need to send little children warring."

"Why don't we all have a seat," says Charles, "and I'll tell you."

The room we're in has an oval table, and we each pick a chair and sit. It's a little awkward because the table is pretty big, and Censor Reggidel seems to want to sit as far from Rae and Naomi as possible. Rae still looks a little mad, but she smiles at me as she sits down, which makes my face even hotter. I smile back, though, until I notice Naomi watching me, and she *does* look mad. I decide to just keep my eyes on the table while Charles tells the story of the Valentine War.

He starts with the world how it used to be, with countries and billions of people living everywhere. Back then, there was no such thing as thelemity, and people built houses and machines sort of like they have in the settlements today, but all of that changed the day the Valentines came.

The reason we call them the Valentines is that the day they first attacked, February 14 on the old Western Calendar, was called "Valentine's Day." We still don't know what the Valentines call themselves because we've never been able to talk to them. We don't even know what they look like. People had all sorts of different names for them early in the war, but "Valentine" is the one that ended up being the most popular. It used to mean something totally different, but not many people remember that now.

We never saw them coming. All at once, cities just started disappearing. A city would be there, everything totally normal, then it would be gone, nothing but rubble and a cloud of dust. By the time we figured out we were under attack, half the cities in the world had already been destroyed. We tried to fight back, but the Valentines had thelemity, and our strongest weapons were next to useless. They probably would have killed every single person on the planet, except for one thing: It turned out we could use thelemity, too.

As far as anyone knows, there have been fontani and revenni in the world as long as there have been people. The reason no one knew until the Valentines came is that revenni can't do anything without a source of thelemity, and fontani won't produce thelemity until something happens to activate them. The only time fontani become active—as far as we've seen, at least—is when someone nearby uses thelemity for something. Think of it as a candle lighting another candle. And when thelemity is used as a *weapon*, any fontani nearby are almost guaranteed to go active. So when the Valentines attacked, they activated the first fontani on Earth. Pretty soon, we had fontani all over the world.

There aren't many things stronger than fontani. You can't even compare them to people, or animals, or machines—they're more like stars. Just one is more than a match for pretty much any army you can think of. But they're also very rare. We think the Valentines brought somewhere between ten and twenty fontani when they first came to Earth. But this was a world with billions of people, remember. Within days, we had hundreds of our own fontani, enough to chase the Valentines away from Earth, back the way they came.

What we learned was that the Valentines didn't come from someplace far away—at least, not anyplace we could have ever found on our own, by walking or flying or blasting off to the stars, for example. They were from another world entirely, a world *parallel* to ours, and they had used thelemity to open the way from there to here.

They'd made a kind of rip in space, up in the sky between Earth and the Moon. It's still there today, a passage we call Lunar Veil. When the Valentines tried to escape from our new army of fontani, we followed them back through Lunar Veil, and on the other side we found an entire other universe. The Valentines had opened another gate there, which led to another universe, and another gate, and another universe. We kept chasing them, going from one world to the next, until finally we got to a place where there were reinforcements waiting to hold us off. That was when the real war began. We've been fighting them ever since, in all sorts of different worlds, but we've never found the place they call home, the world where they started out.

We've learned a lot about thelemity, too: how to build huge cities right out of the earth, how to design thelemic tools you don't have to be revenni or fontani to use, how to fight an enemy that uses thelemity as a weapon, how to travel between the different parallel worlds—the Realms, as we call them. The front line of the fighting stretches across fifteen different Realms now. The only thing that hasn't changed much since the beginning of the war is that, without fontani, we don't stand a chance.

When Charles finishes talking, the room gets so quiet I can hear my heart beating in my ears. And then Rae says to Charles, "You still haven't told us why you need Naomi." Her voice is low and dangerous, and I'm glad there's a big table between her and us. "You say you were there when the war began. Where are all your hundreds of other fontani?"

"Some are still fighting," Charles answers. "I returned from the Front about three months ago. But I know what you're asking, and I'll tell you the truth: Many of them—most—have been killed in battle."

"We don't send children into combat," Vinneas adds quickly, "not if we have any better choice. Fontani like Jax typically take indirect roles, such as powering a city's defenses while more experienced fontani are away in battle."

"But you will," Rae answers coldly. "You will send them if you decide you must."

"If we could afford to shelter children like Jax from the war, we would," Vinneas says, sounding annoyed. "What you have to understand is that fontani are extremely scarce. Talent with thelemity isn't inherited genetically, and if there's a way to bestow it on someone, we've never discovered it. All we know is that fontani and revenni generally come into their ability sometime around the age of nine or ten. That, and we need as many of them as we can get. They're the only chance we have."

Rae stands, pushing back her chair, and shouts, "Well, you can't have *her*!" so loudly that I jump in my seat. For a while she just stares at Vinneas, then she says, more quietly, "We're going home, both of us."

For the second time, I speak up without even thinking about it. "It's not so bad, not really," I say, "being in a battle. I've never fought the Valentines for real, but I practice a lot with Charles. And I know it'll be dangerous, the real thing, but it's a lot less dangerous for people like me and Charles than for everyone else who has to fight. The legionary's first rule of battle is to keep your fontani safe. So we just do our part because they're all risking their lives to protect us."

Rae only stares at me, so I keep talking, "And it's true what Charles says, that fontani are really hard to kill. Do you know what a volcano is? I've been *inside* of one, and I hardly even noticed."

She breaks into a smile then, sad but still very pretty. "You're a fine boy, Jax," she says. "If this Legion was full of men like you, I would count myself fortunate to be part of it. But Naomi and I have no use for the kind of protection your comrades are offering. We've done well enough by ourselves until now. I think we'll keep it that way."

I know I shouldn't feel happy, because the Legion really does need both of them, but I still get kind of giddy, talking to Rae. Vinneas is obviously frustrated, but Charles doesn't seem upset. Censor Reggidel just looks glad to be left alone.

And then Naomi speaks for the first time. She'd been so quiet until now, I thought she must be very shy, but she's just as forceful as her sister. What she says is "You can count me in."

TWENTY-FIVE

NAOMI

I am alone on an island, a place they call Bermuda, or Area 22-53, depending on who is speaking. To me it is merely a forlorn strip of land foundering in the middle of the sea, stranded among high waves and dark clouds. Rain comes down in puffs and gusts, and though I have been afforded tall boots and some manner of slicker for protection, my face is already damp with water the wind is flinging every which way. At the same time, warm sunlight shines across my back through a gap in the clouds, a pillar of brightness sparkling with errant raindrops and trimmed in the unlikely gamboling of rainbows. The ship, what they call a "harvester," rises into the circle of cloudless sky, shrinking away as it flees my island, until at last it is lost in the glaring sun, and the clouds roll in, washing the light away like dust taken in a breeze.

However fierce the storm here on Bermuda, I imagine it is no more than a whisper compared to the one raging aboard the harvester. By the time I set forth for this island, Rae had worked herself into a temper fit to make anyone nearby fear for his life. She was particularly dire with Charles and Vinneas, railing at them in language it would have shamed our mother to hear. Of everyone, only Vinneas was fool enough to attempt any defense, perhaps because his command of English was good enough to understand her anger but not so perfect that the precise details of her threats and oaths were readily plain. Reggidel, meanwhile, sat well back, grinning as though he could imagine no finer entertainment. By now I expect Vinneas is regretting his resistance, as Rae is not one to be quelled with words. She will keep up her fury until this business on the island is settled, and heaven help Vinneas if anything goes wrong. She has promised to flay him alive and see him dragged twenty miles by a horse saddled with his own tanned hide. For me,

Rae had only kindness and concern, riding down to the island with me and running out into the rain to hug me long and hard, saying, "I'll come back for you, Sunshine. I promise. We won't go far. I won't let them."

Not two sunrises ago, I would have counted her words and embrace finer comfort than all the world's plushest luxuries, but I responded with nothing but a stiff-shouldered shrug. Since the moment Rae appeared, back from the dead and gathering me up in her arms, she has placed herself between me and every possible danger. In truth, it was a tremendous relief to be under her protection; I did not know how desperate and afraid I had been until she was with me again, hackles raised in my defense, and felt a measure of calm and safety I thought I had left behind forever in New Absalom. I have the notion Vinneas himself was mightily surprised when he went from champion in my sister's eyes to lowest of all the Earth's vermin once she heard the Legion's plan for me. But up there on the harvester, as I listened to her snarl and snap at those Legion men, I came to a realization. It was something that boy said, Jax (what a name!), how all the Legion's soldiers had a duty to protect him—and me, were I to join—and how he considers it his responsibility to do the same for them. To Rae I am still a child, not to be trusted with my own affairs, but I have changed since the Valley of Endless Summer. I learned I could be a protector, too. That is what the Legion is asking of me now, and I mean to do it if I can.

As the last glints of sun pass from the sky, I find myself wishing Rae were here, so I could tell her how wrong she is about me. I could summon her now, if I wished, but it would mean abandoning my test and admitting she was right. In my hand is a small device, a handle like the grip of a pistol, cast in black metal with a red button set into the top. I have merely to depress this button, and a flying machine will be dispatched to retrieve me. I am free to use the button at any time, but I resolve not to do so until I know for sure whether or not I am "fontani," as they say, one of these creatures that make magic the way the sun does light and heat.

The black handle with the red button has one other feature of note: an array of glowing numbers counting slowly toward zero, representing the time remaining for the other players of this game to arrange the details of my test. At present, the harvester bearing Rae and Vinneas and Reggidel is busying itself with getting as far from me as possible. Meanwhile, Charles has taken his place elsewhere on this island, at a specific point roughly a mile from where I stand. The exact distance between us is known as a "yiell," meaning the span thelemity will project from any one source—in this case, Charles. The limit of one yiell from Charles's position is marked on the ground before me, a line in yellow paint. Already I have caught the scent of brimstone crackling in the air, as it sometimes does at the edge of anyplace filled with the magic of thelemity.

When my counter falls to zero, Charles will perform a trick called "shading." He will no longer be merely fontani, a simple source of power, but a weapon, "fontani usikuu." This will alter the nature of his thelemity, a shift akin to music's dropping or rising in key, so subtle as to be indiscernible by anyone except other fontani. Once this is done, I will walk across the yellow line, and if I am indeed fontani, as everyone seems to believe, I will "shade" as well and become "fontani usikuu." Or so I have been told.

I still do not quite understand what it means to shade, or to be fontani usikuu. According to Charles, it is a thing easier experienced than described, hardly worth discussing until you have witnessed it firsthand. He did try, but it was difficult to take him seriously. Not only did his admonitions sound like so much fanciful nonsense, but Charles himself freely admitted that nothing he told me now would make any difference once the shading began. Vinneas, Reggidel, and others of the harvester's small crew had any number of poetic descriptions of fontani usikuu, none of which made any obvious sense. Near as I have been able to learn, it means to become a being cloaked in magic, like the calm at the center of a spinning storm. The one thing Charles was sure to make clear was that, whatever happened, there would be no danger to me.

I do not share Charles's confidence. As the little lit numbers click away, I feel the fear pooling in my belly. I was so sure of myself when I stepped onto this island, so determined, but in the wind and wet, my banner of courage has gone to tatters. It is as if I can see what awaits me in the swirling spray beyond that yellow line, rainy images of a long war spanning worlds and worlds, and I yearn to return to my old life, to be safe in New Absalom with Rae and Mama and Baby and all my coda with me, close around warm fires and the snow deep outside and danger far away, and know nothing of thelemity or these creatures, the Valentines.

In my hand, the counter has fallen to zero. I raise my eyes to the yellow line, some ten feet distant. It seems so harmless, a drizzle of paint on uneven concrete gathering water in shallow puddles. I will not allow myself to fear a color, or a shape. I draw one long, slow breath and begin to walk.

The line nears, and I close my eyes, feeling the wind tug at my flapping hood. It will come any moment now, the change, the shade. I steel myself, knowing there can be no retreat from here, and summoning every bit of nerve I have left, I take what I know must be the last few steps toward whatever strangeness awaits.

TWENTY-SIX

NAOMI

Nothing happens. Only when I am sure to be well past the yellow line do I stop walking and open my eyes. The island of Bermuda remains, trees bowed beneath the gathering storm, spray soaking every rock and bush. Before me are the remnants of an ancient road, broken and over-grown, not a splotch of yellow to be seen. Turning, I spot the dreaded line fully twenty paces behind me. For a time, I can only stand there looking at it.

I wonder whether I have failed in some essential piece of my test, whether there was some incantation I was meant to recite, some occult password I neglected to call. I stomp on the ground, as if that might shake my power loose, then cross the line again at a full run. Nothing still. I leap over it and back, walk down its length, arms extended as though to bal-ance on the branch of a tree.

At last I am forced to conclude that everyone was mistaken about me. I am no being of war and magic after all, only a girl splashing in the rain, and I must press my red button or spend the rest of my life on this deserted island.

The button illuminates beneath my thumb, signaling that my only duty now is to wait for rescue. I reason it will be best to seek refuge from the in-clement weather, since I am not to become any great force of nature myself. There is little nearby that would pass as shelter, but not far off I spot a num-ber of crumbling structures, relics of this island's long-departed denizens. I choose the tallest and set off in that direction, and soon I am walking the streets of a forgotten city.

It is as fine a place as any my people have chosen for our winter refuges, excepting perhaps New Absalom and one or two other shroomtowns. The buildings here are sturdy and well formed, many standing above their first story, a feature I have rarely seen in so ancient a place. As I walk wide avenues fringed in brush and rubble, gazing up into dark windows, I catch sight of something that gives me pause. There, at the base of an especially grand edifice of arches and pillars, is an open door spilling light outside. After staring at it a good while, I conclude it must be Charles. He has deduced that I am not one of his fontani after all and chosen this place to keep me in comfort and company until the others arrive.

The doorway and surrounding stonework are ornate and very well maintained considering their age, and I wonder whether this island is quite so abandoned as I have been told. The place I find inside is warm and brightly lit, with quiet music playing from a source I cannot quite discern. It is a long room with high ceilings, orderly and clean, with tall windows all down one side. Along the interior wall is a high, lacquer-topped counter with stools beneath and backed by shelves of multicolored bottles. The space throughout is filled with circular tables, each ringed with chairs and covered in a white cloth that falls nearly to the wooden floor. Every table is empty, save one by the far wall, where a man sits by himself, facing me.

The man looks up as I step into the room. I can make out little about him beyond his vague shape, but it is plainly not Charles. "Ah, Naomi," he says, standing, "I've been waiting for you." His voice is friendly, warm and welcoming, like the place around him. "Please, come and sit with me."

He is a stranger to me, but somehow I have the impression that we have met before. Unsure, I glance back toward the door and the rain outside. "This is no day to be wandering about," the man says. "Let's wait out the weather together. I've ordered us some food."

The mention of food decides me soundly in his favor, as I realize I am famished. My boots leave sopping footprints as I cross to the table. "Here, let me take your coat," says the man, moving swiftly to my back. He pulls out the chair opposite his even as he lifts the slicker from my shoulders. The table has two places set, each with a gleaming white plate and an arcane array of knives and forks. Next to the utensils aligned along the man's side is a pair of horn-rimmed spectacles. They seem very familiar somehow, such that I am sure I've encountered their like before, though where I cannot say. I am still contemplating them when the man takes his place in front of me and sets the spectacles on his nose and I get my first good look at him.

He is tall in stature, and slim, dressed immaculately in a suit of delicate cut and subtly complementary patterns. His cuffs are fastened with
studs rather than buttons, and he wears a glossy necktie done up in a fine
little bow. He has a long face with clever features, a good fit for his build,
and though he is plainly not a young man, his skin has the smooth luster
of a walnut. He wears his thick hair long but slicked back. It is white at
the front but deepens to gray along the ridge of his head. The overall effect
is of something at once complex and effortless. I do not think I have ever
met such a dapper person. The only feature I cannot quite discern is his
eyes because the light has caught his spectacles in such a way as to turn
the lenses a blank and glaring white.

"Horrible out there, isn't it?" the bespectacled man comments. We are
seated near a window, rainwater running vigorously down the glass.
Through the blurry rivulets, I catch sight of gray streets, figures leaning
into the wind as they rush past. "You must be chilled to the bone. We shall
have to warm you up immediately. How do you feel about lobster bisque?"

My feelings regarding lobster bisque are indeterminate because I do
not know what lobster bisque is. I have eaten lobsters before, abominable
creatures resembling gigantic cockroaches my coda will sometimes pull
from the ocean in baskets baited with scraps of garbage. The meat is tasty
enough, but hardly worth the work of prying it from their unpleasant tails
and claws, at least not when there is fish or venison to be had more easily.
I do not care to guess what part of the lobster the bisque might be, but as
it turns out, bisque is a kind of soup, creamy and warm, in which the lobster plays hardly any part. My appraisal is favorable overall; I end up clean-
ing the bowl with my fingers.

"No need to rush," says the bespectacled man. He has been served
bisque of his own but has not so much as lifted his spoon. Instead, he
watches me, smiling, from behind his inscrutable blank lenses. "There's
plenty more coming."

The next course is something called a "burrito." It consists of a full meal
of rice and beans and seasoned meat and innumerable other additions
cleverly rolled into a patty of thin, soft bread, so that the whole thing can
be eaten by hand, and each bite brings forth the full flavorful symphony.
This burrito is served with strips of potato, similar in conception to what
Mama or Rae or I will sometimes fry up over the fire, but so different in

effect as to seem an altogether separate variety of food. Lastly, there is ice cream and chocolate cake, which by my reckoning ought to be renamed ambrosia of the gods.

"Did you enjoy your meal?" the bespectacled man asks when the last bite of cake is gone. "The menu here is not usually so . . . inventive."

The question is quite unnecessary, as I am presently engaged in licking the plate, but I answer nonetheless. "Yes, thank you." I set the plate down, and a man in a white jacket arrives to take it away. I had not noticed him before, but I realize he must have come and gone throughout the meal, bringing out food and afterward clearing what leftovers remained. I study the man in the white jacket as he removes the bespectacled man's uneaten cake and drooping ice cream, but no matter how I angle my head, I cannot get a clear view of his face.

As he departs, I see the room is full of people. Every table is occupied, crowded with well-turned-out men and women, all engaged in quiet but animated conversation. Along the tall counter, more figures sit sipping from oddly shaped glasses while a man in gartered shirtsleeves pours from the multicolored bottles. Though I cannot recall seeing these people before, I have the impression that they have been here all along. And no matter where I look, I cannot make out a single pair of eyes. Those who do not have their backs to me are always arranged so that some object happens to cover their faces: a shoulder, a glass of wine, the buds of flowers leaning from a vase. The music that was playing when I arrived is still audible beneath the low chatter, and I see that it comes from a machine set in one corner of the room, a wooden box with a large horn attached to project the sound, which carries an odd, swaying tune, unusual but not unpleasant, and a scratchy quality I had not heard until now.

"I'm very glad," the bespectacled man says. "I tried to order things you would like."

"Why didn't you eat anything?" I ask, turning back to him.

"I wasn't hungry," he replies kindly. "Now, I was hoping you would do me a small favor."

Inclined as I am to repay this man for his generosity, I have learned never to agree to a favor before I know what will be asked of me. I try without success to look past the gleam of his spectacles. "What do you want me to do?" I ask.

He reaches beneath the table and produces a rectangular wooden case, which he sets before me, flicking the latches open as he does. Inside is a fiddle, a lovely piece of work. Like the man and his spectacles, there is something familiar about this instrument. "Where did you get this?" I say, running a hand along one wooden curve.

The bespectacled man does not answer. Instead, he says, "I would very much like to hear you play, Naomi. Would you do that for me?"

The request is neither onerous nor unreasonable. I think I would have been happy to play even if this man had not just treated me to the finest meal of my life. I lift the fiddle from its case and discover it warm to the touch. Its weight and balance remind me of holding a living thing, at once heavier and lighter than it appears. As I set the fiddle to my arm, a smile spreads across the bespectacled man's face. He makes a sign to someone I cannot see, and the swaying music ceases with a loud scratch. The silence that follows is warm, inviting.

I take up the bow and draw one long note across the strings.

For a moment, I see the rushing ocean, waves flashing in the sunlight.

The bespectacled man is watching me, his mouth drawn into a delighted smile, cheeks crinkling around the edges of his horn frames. "That was wonderful, Naomi," he says. "Please, again."

I can think of no reason why I should not oblige him. Indeed, though I had hesitated, fearful of overstepping myself, I am eager to continue playing. Again, I bring down the bow, drawing out a second note, lower and richer than the first. With it comes a blast of open air, spinning sky: a high, bright sun.

"Splendid, splendid," the bespectacled man says, clapping his hands once. "Don't stop now. Go on, play whatever you like."

But I have lowered the fiddle, unsure of myself. Something here is not right. "What is happening?" I ask him. "Who are you? What is this place?"

An image has risen from the back of my mind, a blurry tableau of faces. They are people I do not quite know, wishing me luck on an errand I do not quite recall. And then the bespectacled man speaks, and the picture fades.

"This is a restaurant, Naomi," he answers soothingly. "You know that. And I am your host. You and I have just shared a lovely meal, and now you are delighting me with your wonderful music. You do like to play, don't you?"

"I do," I admit.

"Then please, play on."

It is all the invitation I require. My song is slow at first, but quickly gathers pace. It seems the fiddle itself is urging me on, all other thoughts gone in the joy of the music. Again I see the sky, now streaked in wispy clouds, and water below, rushing waves reflecting the sun in a glittering tumble. There is something else, too, a shadow behind the glare and sparkle. At first I think it must be somewhere beneath the ocean's surface, a sea monster traveling at fantastic speed, but there is no swell in the water as such a leviathan would raise. I strain for a closer look, and the waves part, as though pressed aside by some immense force. Mirrored in the ocean's surface I see the silhouette of something large and swift moving with liquid sleekness. Its shape changes from one moment to the next, and like drifting clouds, it now and then takes on familiar forms: a bird in flight, a running cat, a woman's body tucked into a dive, a bullet.

There is a second reflection, too, high above. I look up into the blue sky and spot a dark shape crossing the sun, and behind it another, like the shadow of a shadow. All around me, water sprays into the air with the force of my passing, drops glinting in the clear light. The two shadows know I am here. They alter their course, diving toward me.

"Naomi!"

It is a voice I know, and hearing it trips up my song in a jumble of notes. The bespectacled man appears just as upset as I am at the interruption, though no one else nearby has noticed. Casting about for the source of the disturbance, I see a boy standing just inside the restaurant's entrance. He is dressed in a very odd costume: an overlarge shirt and bill-brimmed cap, each emblazoned with some bizarre design. He is not only calling to me but already on his way to my table. Fortunately, a doorman in a black jacket has spotted him and steps in to discourage the boy's advance.

"Naomi!" he calls again, jumping and waving for my attention. "It's me, Jax!"

Again I have the feeling that there is something peculiar about this place. For half a second, this Jax appears to me as two people: the one in a long shirt and cap, and another in a dark uniform. The second Jax seems about to speak to me, but then he vanishes. "I think I have met that boy somewhere," I say to the bespectacled man. "Can we invite him over?"

"Most certainly not!" the bespectacled man says, with a laugh of amused indignation. "You must be mistaking him for someone else. The boy could not possibly be an acquaintance of yours. Look at him—he's a filthy street urchin!"

And truly, the boy Jax does seem immoderately grubby. Now that I have a moment to inspect him more closely, it is plain he is fresh out of some gutter or other declivity. He is in desperate need of a bath, and the outlandish smock he wears in place of a shirt is deplorably soiled, his hat ragged and sweat-stained. I, meanwhile, have on a fine blue dress and white blouse, and my fingernails are clean. I do not know how these details escaped me before, for it is obvious this boy has no business in decent company. Yet he remains vocal in his bid for my attention. Other guests have begun to glance in his direction, frowning with distaste at this rude interruption to their supper.

It is embarrassing to be included in the noisy scene Jax has made, and I am relieved when the doorman finally takes hold of him and, with a firm hand, leads him out of the restaurant. But I am sorry, too, once he is gone. Perhaps it is the imploring look in his brown eyes or how wretched he seemed as the doorman hauled him away. A patter of raindrops against a nearby window reminds me of the biting weather, and I feel guilty knowing Jax has been cast out into it.

The bespectacled man takes note of my distress. "I'll speak to the maître d'," he says with an indulgent sigh. "The boy will be given something to eat and a warm place out of the rain. But I do hope you can agree we could not allow him to stay. Before one may enter civilized society, one must be prepared to behave in a civilized manner. You understand, don't you, Naomi?"

I believe I do. Jax was disturbing the order of this place. "Yes. I think so."

My companion smiles, spectacles aflash with candlelight. "Wonderful. And with that settled, do you imagine we could continue our little concert?"

I had been waiting for just such an invitation. The renewed sound of my fiddle pleases the bespectacled man immensely, and as the notes gather, one of his hands rises into the air, tracing a gentle motion in time to my music. "What are you doing?" I ask, pausing midtune.

His hand goes still, his posture shifting, like someone awakened from a dream. His rapturous expression shifts to a small, embarrassed grin. "I seem to have become a bit carried away," he says. "Your music was so enchanting. Did I disturb you?"

"No." In fact, I cannot remember ever having played so well. Each of his gestures seemed to add precision and flourish to my music, as if we were somehow playing together. "I am only curious."

"An old habit of mine," he says, his smile taking on a more bashful tint. "I was a conductor once, the leader of a symphony. Your playing took me back to another time, I'm afraid. I hope you can excuse a foolish old man his eccentricities."

"No excuse is necessary. It was only something I had not seen before." Though even as I say it, I wonder if this is true. Have I seen someone else "conduct" in that way? Was it something Papa used to do? "May I play again?"

"I would like nothing more," replies the Maestro.

But even as I raise my bow to continue, there is a jarring thud at my window: Jax has appeared on the street outside, his face pressed to the glass. Somehow, he has become even filthier, as if his first act upon leaving this restaurant was to locate a pile of dung and roll in it. When he sees me gaping at him, he begins to pound with his palm, calling out in a voice that seems muffled to me but must be atrociously loud to be heard through the glass. I watch his lips form my name, and anger rises in me. The rain has become a cold slush, but I am not sorry for Jax anymore. He is nothing but a nuisance.

"Ignore him, Naomi," the Maestro says serenely. "Someone will be along to deal with him soon. Play on."

And sure enough, once my song begins again, two men arrive to confront Jax. They are tall, burly, and uniformed in crisp blue suits, badges of authority gleaming over their breast pockets. I feel confident they can take Jax someplace away from this weather, but more importantly, away from me. Jax, for his part, is fast losing enthusiasm for the task of rapping at my window. The sleet has turned to snow and begun gathering in wet piles on his shoulders and cap. When one of the men, tall helmet pulled low over his eyes, calls for Jax's attention, Jax drops his arms and turns away, ready to concede.

But just as the uniformed men are about to lead him away, someone else appears by Jax's side. The newcomer is neither hostile nor imposing, but he cuts an elegant figure in his black hat and long, fur-trimmed coat.

He carries a slim, silver-tipped cane in one hand; the other he lays in a firm but friendly fashion on Jax's shoulder. Instantly, the men in uniform become deferential and eager to please. I cannot quite hear what is said, but it seems this man is explaining that Jax means no harm and is indeed a fine and upstanding young man.

To my astonishment, he is not far from the mark: Though I have not seen it happen, Jax appears to have undergone a good scrubbing, and his tattered outfit has been exchanged for a clean set of tan trousers and a trim blue jacket. He still wears his ridiculous cap, though that, too, has been washed, and no one now objects to it. Indeed, the two uniformed men are fully satisfied with whatever tale they have been fed and presently proceed about their rounds, leaving Jax still outside my window. The man in the fur-trimmed coat tips his hat. Somehow, the falling snow does not seem to touch him.

Jax's eyes have come back to rest on me, though his new friend continues watching the uniformed men as they walk away. When they have disappeared from view, he bends to the street and clears the gathered snow from a patch of cobbled sidewalk. With the utmost ease and nonchalance, he pries up one of the paving stones and hefts it, as though testing its weight, then, with a casual sweep of his arm, hurls it through my window.

The glass shatters, as does a small, flower-filled vase on my table as the stone rolls over the place settings and onto the restaurant floor. The weather gusts in through the broken window, and suddenly I am surrounded by a riot of wind and snow. The Maestro leaps to his feet, a roar of outrage on his lips, but the man in the coat has already stepped into the restaurant by way of the shattered opening, daintily navigating the shards of glass with the aid of his cane.

"Howdy, Naomi," he says, using the cane to tip back his hat, flashing a jaunty grin and laughing eyes. "It's me, your old buddy Charles. This has been an adventure to be sure, but I think we've had enough for today. What do you say to putting down that violin?"

"It is a fiddle," I answer, wind howling around me.

"The fiddle, then. How about you give it to me?"

"Don't listen to him!" shouts the Maestro, his voice barely audible over the storm. Excepting myself, Jax, the Maestro, and this Charles, the restaurant is empty now and seems like it has been abandoned for years. Snow covers the floor and piles in banks against the walls; long daggers of ice hang from the ceiling. But I do not intend to give in, no matter the weather. I raise bow and fiddle to begin a new song, but before I can produce a single note, Charles lunges forward, seizing my fiddle by its slender neck.

I start back, angry and affronted, only to find I am no longer in my restaurant. The Maestro is gone. There is dirt beneath my feet, and Charles is beside me, holding my wrist. In place of the elegant coat and hat I remember, he has on a black military uniform. We are in the midst of some torn-up wilderness, sundered ground and broken trees all around.

Charles releases my arm. "That was quite a performance, Naomi," he says, oddly cheerful given our desolate surroundings. "The three of us are going to learn a lot from each other, I think."

"What happened?" I demand, confused and angry. The ground patters softly as small rocks fall from the sky like sparse rain. "How did I get here?"

"You flew," Charles informs me. "Very majestically, I might add. And what happened, Naomi, is that you experienced being fontani usikuu."

I cannot quite hide the fear I feel at his words. I remember now the things Charles told me about what it meant to shade, how I would find myself in another place filled with strange and alien sights, shifting and fluid as a dream, though to me it would be my real life, if I remembered it at all, that would seem unreal. It came to pass exactly as he'd said, and all that time, while I played my fiddle, I was not master of myself. I traveled all the way here, wherever this is, without even knowing. I am glad Charles has turned to search the horizon and does not see my face. Something thuds into the earth next to him: the stump of a fair-sized tree. "Now, where has Jax gotten to?" he wonders. "Ah, there he is."

Jax has appeared atop a mound of heaved-up earth. He slides down, bouncing on his rear for balance, and comes running toward us. "You got her!" he shouts to Charles. He sounds mightily surprised about it. "Hey, Naomi," he says, scampering to a halt. "That was great!" He appears nearly as pleased with himself as Charles.

"Yes, fine work all around," Charles agrees. "All right, let's go get something to eat. For some reason, I'm really craving a burrito. Jax, why don't you lead the way?"

Jax nods, as though all of this makes perfect sense, and begins walking into the desolate landscape.

"Pay attention, and stay close," Charles says, urging me forward. He points toward Jax. "The force is strong with this one."

"What is he talking about?" I ask Jax, falling into step at his side.

"Just ignore Charles when he says stuff like that," Jax says. "He can be pretty weird sometimes."

TWENTY-SEVEN

TORRO

I've figured out why no one ever comes back. From the Front, I mean. It's actually pretty obvious once you know a few things.

Optio Sorril laid it all out for us our first day at Limit Camp. We all went into this big room, all the new recruits, and we sat there while she told us about the war and how it started, and how if we don't beat the Valentines, everyone in the world is going to die. It was a pretty big shock, I'll say that much. Hexi was sitting right next to me, and her mouth was all hanging open, but Spammers gave me this sideways look and rolled his eyes, like he couldn't believe the Prips actually expected us to swallow such a monumental load of crap. There were a lot of people there just like us, all dragged from some settlement or other, and you could tell a lot of them felt the same way.

Sorril didn't expect us to believe her, though, not right away. She said we were going to have to get used to a very different, like, reality than the one we knew, and that would take some time. We would have a lot of questions. So for now, we'd split up into groups to talk to people she'd brought in from the Legion. We could ask them anything. I ended up in a group with this sort of fat old Legion guy who said he'd been at the Front, that he'd actually fought the Valentines. Spammers was in the same group, and he asked so many questions, it was like the kid couldn't stop talking. He was trying to catch the Legion guy in a lie, but the guy had an answer for everything. Also, he was missing a leg. He said the Legion had real good medical people, like they could practically bring a guy back from the dead, but there were some injuries they couldn't heal, and his leg was one of them. That's the only reason he wasn't at the Front now—because of his leg. After the Legion guy left, I expected Spammers to start going off about how it was all crap right away, but he didn't. He got pretty quiet, like he was thinking real hard.

And the thing was, it did kind of fit. I mean, we always figured there was something weird going on with the Prips. Like, whenever they showed up for the draft, they'd bring that big ship, the harvester, and it would just float there, even though it was obviously real gigantic and heavy. So you knew the Prips could do way more than we could, like with machines and everything. We'd talk about it all the time, my kiddos and me, about what sorts of stuff the Prips had, like flying cars and moving stairs and three-dimensional telecasts and whatnot. But no one ever guessed anything like this thelemity business. That stuff is berserk, it really is. The first time I floated up into the harvester, I was pretty sure I'd just died or something. And then we got on board and the walls would like *talk* to you and doors appeared out of nowhere and every time you wanted to sit, a chair would just grow up out of the ground. I thought I'd gone crazy. So after all that, it's actually not so hard to believe a bunch of aliens appeared out of nowhere and started trying to kill everyone. Spammers is probably way more like analytical about it, though.

Anyway, when old Sorril showed us these moving pictures of the Valentines the next day, I wasn't as blown away as everyone else. I'd seen moving pictures before, naturally, like on telecasts and entertainment programs. What I mean is, seeing all that wasn't what made me believe in the Valentines.

Sorril started off with these pictures from before the war, what she called the "Common Era." There was some footage of people living out in like hellion territory, all alone in the middle of nowhere, but most of what Sorril showed us looked kind of like Granite Shore, only the houses and vehicles were a little strange. What really got me, though, was the way people dressed, everyone different from everyone else. Like you could see a thousand people, and no two would have the exact same clothes.

Next we saw pictures from "Valentine's Day," which was the day the Valentines showed up, obviously. Most of it was this real shaky footage of people running and explosions and all of that. You couldn't really see what was happening. The only clear shots were of the sky with all of these crazy lights shooting all over the place. I'm sure it was scary being there, but it was hard to tell, just watching.

The last thing Sorril showed us *was* pretty scary. She got rid of the machine she'd been using to show us that old footage, then sort of waved her hand, and these new pictures appeared out of nowhere. Sorril told us we were looking through the eyes of a soldier fighting at the Front, in a battle that'd happened about twenty-five years ago, our time, but it wasn't like any battle *I'd* ever seen. The ground was very crumbly and sort of fuzzy green, like moldy bread, and the air was kind of green, too, and hazy. Up ahead was something that looked like a wall of smoke rising out of the moldy-bread ground. Pretty soon, though, you realized it was really a battle, and what you thought was smoke was actually everyone fighting. They'd made themselves into this big floating wall, way up in the air, but they were so far away, you couldn't really see them all individually and whatever. It really did look like smoke, the way it swirled and swept around, but that was just the battle going up and down and in every direction. Something on the other side was trying to break through the wall, and after a minute, a little sliver of the battle broke off and came floating toward us, still looking a lot like smoke until it got close and turned into these things crashing down right on top of us.

Sorril stopped the picture then, so we could get a good look at the things falling out of the sky. They reminded me a bit of spiders because they had eight legs and no real face, though really they were pretty different from spiders. They were much bigger, for one thing, and half their legs pointed up, like arms. Also they didn't move the way spiders do. When Sorril started the picture again, they kind of galloped along. It was more like, if you took two really huge dogs and sewed them together, sort of back-to-back, then covered them in shiny black metal, that'd be pretty much what was coming down on you there.

The things, Sorril said, were called "Valentine Type 3s." That wasn't how the Valentines actually looked, of course. What we were seeing was a kind of armor. The Valentines had all sorts of fighters, and since we didn't know exactly how one was different from another, we categorized them generally by size and what they do in battle. The Type 3 was the infantry type, roughly human-sized. We'd be learning about all the other types, too, but the Type 3 was the one we'd be fighting the most.

Sorril turned off the pictures then, and for a while she just sort of looked at us. She said there was a lot we still didn't know, not just about our enemy but about the world we were being asked to defend. What she wanted us to understand was that it was *our* world, and we were fighting for everything and everyone we'd ever known. Now it was time to learn how. If we thought the Valentines looked scary, just wait until they saw the fighters she'd make out of us.

She was pretty convincing, old Sorril was. People started cheering even before she was done talking. Mersh was so loud he left my ears ringing. Even Spammers didn't smirk the way he usually does when he hears people talking about the Legion. But all I did was stare into the space where the moldy-looking ground and the green sky had been. By the time Hexi started shaking my shoulder and asking if I was coming to dinner, almost everyone had already left. She probably thought I was just stunned from getting my first look at the Valentines, but what got to me about that battle wasn't *what* we would have to fight. It was *where*.

The Realms were a big part of Sorril's speech that first day, about how the war started and everything, but I don't think most people really understood what she was talking about. I mean, aliens trying to kill us, that wasn't too hard to imagine, but I couldn't quite get how there were all these other worlds out there, places that were real but also sort of not real because they didn't exist anywhere we could see. It was pretty confusing. The one-legged Legion guy said it was like if you spent your entire life living in one room, and never left because you didn't know what a door was or how to work one, so when you finally went to another room, you'd think it was a whole different universe, but really, that room had been there all along. And that's how it was for us. Before the Valentines came, we didn't know the Realms existed. We thought our world was the only one. But it turns out there are doors between the Realms, too. You just need to know how to open them. I guess that kind of made sense. But it wasn't until I saw that battle, with the moldy ground and the two armies crashing into each other in the middle of the hazy green sky, that it really got to me how the Realms were someplace *else*.

Some of the Realms are supposed to be sort of like Earth, with air you can breathe and water you can drink and everything, but a lot of them aren't. A lot of them are totally different, like the place with the hazy green sky and the moldy ground. The real crazy thing, though, is it's not just the air and water that are different in the Realms. *Time* is different, too. So one day here isn't the same as one day in the other Realms. Because the world where we live is really just another Realm anyway, one Sorril calls "Hestia." And for some reason, time moves faster here than anywhere else we've seen. What that means is, if you're in the Realms for a year and come back to Hestia, a lot more than a year will have gone by. How much depends on which Realm you go to. So a year in some Realm might be twenty years in Hestia, or it might be fifty years, or a hundred. It's *always* more, though. No one knows why. That's just how it is. So even though to us the war with the Valentines has been going on for like five hundred years, out in the Realms it's only been thirty or forty. That's what old Sorril'd meant about the battle happening twenty-five years ago "our time." Most everyone who'd been fighting was still out there at the Front if they hadn't already been killed, and for them it'd maybe been only a couple of months. There are actually people alive now who were *there* when the Valentines first attacked. Hearing that about knocked me out of my chair. I realized something, too. I knew why no one comes back from the Front. The truth is, some of them *do* come back, like the one-legged guy, but when they do, there's no one left who remembers them.

When I saw that battle, the place with the moldy ground and the green sky, that's when it finally hit me. Even if I survive the Front, Camareen won't be here, or if she is, she won't be the Camareen I remember. I would have done anything to get her back. Now I know I never will.

That night, I find Camareen's music, the sheet Mersh brought for me with her words at the bottom. *Come back.* That's all she had time to write, probably the last thing I'll ever have from her. I think about what it would be like, really coming back. Everyone in the Legion does at least three tours at the Front, six months each, with maybe a month in between to rest up. So say two years for me. Here, in Hestia, that's like fifty to a hundred years, depending on where in the Realms you're fighting. Let's say I make it. I'm maybe nineteen or twenty, and Camareen, if she's around at all, is seventy or eighty. I try to picture her with white hair and wrinkles, but I can't. All I see is her green eyes.

Spammers sees me sitting there with the sheet of music, and he guesses what I'm thinking in about five seconds. He's a real smart guy most of the time. "Hey, boyo," he says, sitting down on my bunk. "You just can't stop getting shat on, can you? We'll have to work on that about you."

"You'll want to stand back a bit," I say. "Don't want any splashing on you, next time the shit starts raining down."

Hexi bounces onto the bunk beside me. "Optio Sorril says that's pretty much what war is, for us legionaries," she says. "Getting shat on, I mean. Only one to blame is Romeo."

"Romeo" is another name for the Valentines. Early on in the war, people started calling them the "Unknown Alien Race," which seems like a good name to me, because at least it says something about them. A lot of people spoke English back then, not just bivvies and hellions, and in English, "Unknown Alien Race" shortens to "UAR." They had this special code to keep different letters from getting confused over the radio, and "UAR" was "Uniform Alfa Romeo." Pretty soon, everyone was just saying "Romeo." It's how most legionaries talk about the Valentines, like they're all one person or something, so it's kind of weird hearing Hexi talk that way. It's also weird hearing her say "shat."

"So think about it like this," Spammers says. "You're just getting some practice ahead of time. When we're really knee-deep in shit, you'll feel right at home."

"You two sound like you wouldn't mind a little shit," I say. I'm not surprised to see Hexi in a good mood. That girl can always find something to be happy about. It's like her special talent. But Spammers, that's strange. His chipperness isn't nearly as sarcastic as usual. Those two aren't the only ones acting noisy, either. There are about fifty of us in the barracks, some from Granite Shore but a bunch from other settlements, too, and everyone seems excited to start training after listening to old Sorril.

"Don't tell me you're completely uninterested in learning how to fight with this thelemity stuff," Spammers says. He says it like he knows I'm only pretending not to care, and that annoys me. And sure, I can see what he's talking about. I was completely impressed when Sorril took down those bivvies, even though she's an old lady and they're like bloodthirsty savages and whatever. But somehow it doesn't seem to matter.

"Come on, Spams," Hexi says. "I think Torro wants to be alone."

"Yeah, I suppose." Spammers gives me a kind of friendly slap on the back. "But just think, kid. Maybe this isn't so bad. Say you get back in a hundred years and the war's over. Just stop by old Granite Shore anyway. You can bet Cammie's great-great-granddaughter's going to be every bit as fine-looking as Cammie."

"Spammers!" Hexi squeals, punching him in the shoulder. "That's *disgusting*!"

"Why?" Spammers asks, laughing. "It's not like they'd be *Torro's* great-great-grandkids. And the best part? There'd probably be a whole bunch of them. Just think, all those little Cammies. Why limit yourself to just one, right?"

"You're sick, you know that?" Hexi says. "Really sick!" She's kind of laughing, too, though.

"*That's* how they should convince people to join the Legion. Offer everyone a great-great-granddaughter orgy."

"*Spammers!*"

But by then, even I'm laughing.

TWENTY-EIGHT

TORRO

I'm a pretty crappy legionary, as it turns out. The first couple of weeks aren't so bad, because it's about the same as militia training back at Settlement 225. We go for long runs and do target practice with the same old rifles and run obstacle courses. I really don't mind, but a lot of the other recruits start getting annoyed after a few days. They thought by now we'd all be flying around and playing with guns that could shoot lightning and fireballs and whatnot. I almost feel sorry for Mersh, he's so disappointed. The only other people who don't seem to care are the bivvies. They just do what old Sorril tells them and hardly ever say anything. And then one morning, Sorril gets us all out of bed way before the usual wake-up and tells us to report to the armory. Today's going be our first lesson in ingenized warfare.

Waiting for each of us in the armory is a bunch of curvy pieces of metal, kind of like the shells off a crab or lobster. Sorril says they're the best infantry protection the Legion has, the D-87 Pan-Climate Enhancement Armor, but it really does look like someone's just got done eating a lot of big metal shellfish. The D-87s are "ingenized" equipment, meaning they're made to work with thelemity. To make us "more effective fighters," as Sorril puts it. I'm not totally sure what she means, but I start to get it pretty quick once I put on my D-87s.

Some other people have already started trying to get into theirs, but they're having a lot of trouble. The D-87s come in all these different pieces, and the pieces don't really fit together very well. I pick up one of the shells, and it feels like it's made of lead. The whole suit must weigh like a hundred kilos. Sorril tells us we have to start with the center, the part that sits on your shoulders. I find the piece she's talking about, and even though it's just as heavy as everything else, once I get it over my head, it suddenly weighs nothing at all. When I fit on the next piece, the edges just sort of melt together. By the time I've put half the suit on, I actually feel *lighter*.

Spammers starts laughing to himself, and I figure he's probably surprised at how light the suit feels, too, because he's got most of his on, but when he sees me looking, he strikes this heroic-looking pose, and I get what's so funny. He looks almost exactly like the people on the murals from the factory caf back at old S-225. Like, this whole time we'd been thinking how stupid it was to believe people in the Legion actually wore armor like that, and now it turns out to be pretty much true.

The real crazy part comes when I put on the helmet, though. Unlike the rest of the suit, which is kind of dull gray, the helmets are clear, so you can see right through them, but once I've got my head inside, everything goes black for a second, like blinking your eyes, and when I can see again, the whole world is different. It doesn't feel like I'm looking out through some helmet. I can't even tell the helmet's there. But all of a sudden the air tastes a little cleaner, and the colors are sort of brighter than usual, and I can hear everything around me real clearly.

"I know why they left those helmets off the murals," Spammers says. His voice sounds different, too, like I can somehow hear *more* of it. "You look *scary*, boyo."

There's no mirror or anything around, and no one else is wearing a helmet, so I pull mine off and look at it, but it's gone clear again. "What'd it look like?" I ask Spammers.

"Didn't you just look right at me?" Hexi says. She was getting dressed right next to me, and that's the only reason I know it's her talking, because her voice sounds totally different, low and a little echoey. And she doesn't look like Hexi at all. She's got all her armor on, including the helmet, which isn't clear anymore but that same gray. Where her face should be there's just a bunch of glowing yellow lines. They look sort of like cracks, the lines do, zigzagging out from a spot at the center like a window that's been hit with a rock.

It takes me a second to catch my breath. "Hey, Hex!" I say. "How'd you get that on so fast?"

Hexi yanks off her helmet and looks at it. The front turns clear again pretty much instantly. "I had it on the whole time," she says, sort of confused.

It turns out the D-87s are made so that when you've got them on you can see through other people's helmets. It makes things easier to communicate or something. You can also talk to each other from real far away, like a radio but way better, and outside the suit, it doesn't make any sound at all, in case you need to sneak around and don't want anyone hearing you. And that's only the beginning.

Once everyone is suited up, Sorril takes us through the same exercises we've been doing for weeks, and they're so easy, it's almost funny. You can do a whole obstacle course or run fifty kilometers and hardly even notice, or shoot your rifle one-handed and hit the target like it's nothing. In the D-87s, every single recruit is fast and strong enough to take on a whole squad of militia. We can see and hear things we couldn't before, and even sort of sense things nearby without looking. It makes me wonder why we spent all that time doing normal training, until the end of the day, when Sorril takes us to one last obstacle course.

It's on the far side of camp, the course is, close to the forest. The new course looks about the same as the ones we've been doing all along, with climbing walls and ramps and swinging rings and so forth. The only thing that's really different is that in some places the trees and ground and the course generally are all piled up with snow.

Right away, people start nudging each other and grinning. Yesterday, this would have been a pretty tough course, but it's nothing now that we've got our D-87s. Even the snowy bits won't be any trouble, since the D-87s are made to keep us warm in like outer space, so who cares about a little snow? But there's something a bit off about this new course. Maybe it's the weird smell in the air. It kind of reminds me of that place where we got off the train from old S-225.

I figure it out when the first recruit hits a snowy patch and just falls over. Where the snow is, there's no thelemity, and our D-87s won't work. Even though I'm ready for it, it's still sort of a surprise when all of a sudden my helmet blinks out, and I'm staring through my clear visor, and at the same time, my whole suit gets unbelievably heavy. The thing really must weigh like a hundred kilos minimum. At least I don't collapse the way some people do. By the time I make it to the end of the course, my D-87s sometimes working and sometimes not, I'm sweating like a lunatic and so tired I can barely stand.

That's why they call this place "Limit Camp": because it's built right where the thelemity coming from the city in the middle of the valley runs out. When you've got thelemity, it basically forms this big bubble around its source. The space inside the bubble is called the "umbris," and the space outside is the "aeter." If you're in the umbris, you've got like an everlasting supply of thelemity, but in the aeter, anything ingenized is just deadweight.

Optio Sorril tells us we have to be able to survive in both. Some battles move so fast that your source could go out of range at any time, leaving you in the dark. That's another way of talking about the aeter. Dark. Our D-87s are made to keep us alive pretty much anywhere, but without thelemity, we're next to useless in a fight, so we have to be ready to find our way back to the umbris, or at least hang on for rescue.

It's a pretty scary thought, being out in some world where there's no air, or it's so cold you'd freeze solid in two seconds flat, or so hot it'd boil you right in your skin, and suddenly the only thing keeping you alive is this heavy metal suit and the little tank of air stored inside for emergencies. I try not to think about it too much, but that isn't so easy when old Sorril is reminding us all the time how we have to be ready for anything, or else the Realms will kill us way before Romeo does. According to Optio Sorril, this is the part where we'll find out what sort of legionary we have inside.

The legionary I have inside is unbelievably lousy, I guess. The branch of the Legion we're all training to join, namely the infantry, is called the "milites." I was a pretty good soldier back in Settlement 225, but I have to be about the worst miles ever. Honestly, the worst. The fact is, fighting Valentines is about way more than just finding something to hide behind while you fire your rifle at anything that moves, which, when you get down to it, is pretty much the whole strategy in the settlement militia.

In the Legion, you still need to be able to hide and shoot, of course, though most of the time they actually give you something to hide behind. The Legion has these things called "assault platforms," which are basically little flat spaces big enough to hold about ten milites, all surrounded by shields and barriers and whatnot to protect you when the shooting starts. The problem with assault platforms is, most of the time while you're on one just shooting away, the stupid thing is going to be flying way up in the air. When old Sorril showed us that battle in the moldy green Realm, the wall we saw floating in the sky, the one that looked like smoke, that was actually made up of hundreds and hundreds of assault platforms, all hovering over one another, and every one was stuffed with milites like me.

So we'll be on these big old platforms, floating around in the sky while half-spider, half-dog things try to kill us. And even worse, once the fighting starts, there's no guarantee we'll even get to stay on our own stupid platform. The assault platforms will be maneuvering around according to what's happening in the battle, and a lot of times we'll have to get to some other platform, like if the fighting happens to be concentrated there or whatever. But the platforms are all floating, remember, so you can't just run from one to another the way you'd run from tree to tree if you were out fighting hellions for old S-225. Instead, you have to kind of *fly*. That's the part that completely flattens me. The flying.

One of the things our D-87s can do, see, is change gravity. I'm serious. It only really affects the suit and whoever's inside, though. What it does is, it lets you change which way gravity pulls you. So say you're standing on the ground like any normal, sane person, but you want to get to something above you. You can flip your personal gravity, and you'll fall *up* into the sky. That's what it's called: "personal gravity." You can also just make yourself totally weightless, which is how they teach us to move from one assault platform to another. You push off the platform where you're standing and float until you get to the next one, then adjust your gravity so you can stand there. The platforms are all double-sided, so there's always someplace to land. If you need to get somewhere really fast, you're supposed to just *fall* in that direction, then flip your PG at the last moment so you don't land too hard and splatter yourself. And *that's* what it's like fighting the Valentines: everyone flying and falling and spinning all over the place. I get queasy just thinking about it.

The obstacle courses old Sorril gives us to practice personal gravity are pretty much impossible. Impossible for me, anyway. Spammers and Mersh and Hexi, they all get it pretty quick. But I'm terrible. Like, I'll be running down a course, and I'll get to some pit, and I'll know I'm supposed to flip my PG so I can walk upside down on the ledge way above the pit, but instead I'll end up falling in, or I'll miss the ledge and go tumbling off into the sky until I get stuck in the safety nets they hang around the courses to catch idiots like me. For some reason, I just can't get the hang of it. Most days, I end up puking in my helmet at least once. If there's anything more disgusting than puking inside your own stupid helmet, I don't know what it is.

"Try not to think of it as flying," Spammers tells me. We're in the armory, and I'm trying to wash the puke off after a particularly embarrassing run.

There are bits of egg in my hair. "Think of each surface as its own planet. The world is round, so everywhere you step, down is a slightly different direction. If you walked to the other side of the planet, you'd be upside down from where you are now, but it wouldn't feel strange because to us the world always feels flat. The platforms are that way, too. The ground is wherever you're standing."

"That's like real profound, Spams," I say, giving my helmet another rinse. The D-87s actually do a pretty good job of keeping puke away from your face, once you've gone and vomited it up and everything. I know Spammers wants to help, but I'm not in the mood for it.

Today was even more terrible than usual. I guess there was some big attack on the city a while back that has everyone on edge. It's why they had that special ancillary draft, the one that got Hexi and Spams and me called up, and now the whole Legion is on high alert. Anyway, they were doing drills in the city, and old Sorril brought us in so we could all get a taste of what it's like to be in the middle of a battle. Right as we got there, they started firing the City Guns. I'd only been to the city a few times since we got into training, and I'd thought these things were buildings, but they're actually gigantic cannons, and when they get going, you'd swear you were about to die. It's sort of like the way a real loud noise will mess up your ears for a few seconds, only the City Guns, they don't just mess with your ears. They mess with your eyes and your tongue and your brain, too. And while all that was going on, old Sorril had us running exercises. No big surprise I didn't make it.

"Or you could try keeping your breakfast down," Mersh suggests. He's only joking, but it annoys me. Mersh is pretty good with PG, and it's sort of a shock to find out he's actually better than me at something. Seeing all those guns really got Mersh going, too, and as a result he's decided to be an even bigger turd than usual. A couple of recruits laugh like Mersh has made the world's most hilarious joke.

"Real helpful, Mersh," Hexi says. "Don't worry, Torro," she tells me. "Optio Sorril says some people take a little longer to acclimate to manipulated gravity. You'll get it soon."

Only I don't get it soon. I actually get worse, if that's possible. The training keeps getting harder, and after our like introduction to the City Guns, we hear them pretty much every day, even way out at Limit Camp. It doesn't stop there, either. Other parts of the Legion start running exercises in the valley, and pretty soon you can hardly go anywhere without getting yourself nearly blown up. They have these things called "equi," which are basically gigantic versions of our D-87s, only the people inside can use thelemity even without ingenized weapons like lazels and so forth. *Those* kiddos get up to some seriously crazy crap. They can set practically a whole forest on fire like it's nothing, or even change gravity—sort of like we do with PG, only they can use it on *other people*, to like just squash them in their tracks. And that's only if they don't step on you first, or like explode your skull or whatever. Mersh can't get enough of it.

In no time, I'm starting to feel queasy even before I get to spinning and falling and everything on the courses. So while the other recruits are all doing this crazy stuff, like jumping way up and swiveling midair so they land standing sideways five meters off the ground, or running along a balance beam that happens to be all tied up like some big thick bootlaces, I'm mostly falling flat on my butt or getting sick in my helmet. You can tell everyone's getting tired of me, even Optio Sorril, who never gets sore at anyone.

One day, halfway through afternoon training, she just pulls me right off the course. "Why are you hanging back, Recruit?" she asks. She's not wrong—about me hanging back, I mean. The course today is like this big twisting vine, with branches swinging around all over the place. I was looking up at it, trying to pick out a path where I wouldn't just fall off. I already felt sort of dizzy, even though I wasn't moving yet.

"I'm a little afraid I'm going to be sick, ma'am," I tell her.

"And is this how you intend to behave when you meet the Valentines?"

"It isn't about intending, ma'am," I say. "It's just what usually happens. So yeah, I guess I will. It stands to reason. Logically, I mean."

It's obvious old Sorril is pretty sore at me, just from the way she's standing, sort of looming over me, even though she's shorter than I am. "I've been watching you, Recruit," she says. "There is absolutely nothing that should prevent you from being an exemplary legionary. The trouble is that you are not making the necessary effort. You would not be the first recruit to resent being brought here, or the first to allow your anger toward those you consider responsible—me, your settlement, the Principate—to interfere with your training. But this cannot continue."

I hadn't been thinking about how I left Granite Shore, actually, how old Cranely got me called up so someone else wouldn't have to go to the Front, but I am now. I start getting pretty mad. And I start thinking, like, maybe

I'd have an easier time if you Prips hadn't been lying to me my entire shitty life. Maybe we could have been practicing this stuff at old S-225, so I'd have a chance to figure out some of this crap before you dragged me off to be eaten by homicidal aliens. It'd feel pretty good to yell all of that at Optio Sorril, probably, but I keep my mouth shut.

"At the beginning of your training, I promised to make a volunteer of each and every recruit," old Sorril says. "For most, learning that we are in a fight for the very survival of our species is enough. But if preserving the lives of every human being in existence does not motivate you, I urge you to find something that does, because I will not send an incompetent legionary into battle. You will volunteer to fight, or you will volunteer for the dungeons. The choice is yours."

TWENTY-NINE

TORRO

The next day, Sorril announces we'll be having our first official combat exercise. We'll be in a real battle scenario, with a mission to accomplish and everything. She looks right at me when she mentions the mission part, like having a mission is supposed to mean something extra for me. She probably wants me to know I've got more to do than just finish the exercise. I've got to find my *motivation*. That speech she gave me sure didn't do it. I went back to the course all right, but I finished about a thousand times slower than all the other recruits. If I can't get good enough to fight with everyone else, I guess old Sorril'll end up throwing me in prison just to keep me out of the way.

Our mission today is actually pretty simple: kill as many Valentines as we can. They won't be *real* Valentines, of course. Instead, there'll be these things called "V-spheres," which are basically targets that move around and shoot back at us. We'll be divided into squads, and whichever squad destroys the most V-spheres gets a special dinner and no chores for a week. A lot of the other recruits look around at me when Sorril mentions the competition part. I know what they're thinking. Everyone wants to win, and they know with me on their squad, they won't stand a chance.

We'll be traveling the way actual milites would for a real battle, using these things called "tetra fortresses." A tetra fortress is basically a whole bunch of assault platforms all stuck together in a big ball, layers and layers of them, with a few people in the very middle to control the whole thing. Us milites all load up onto the platforms and sit there while the fortress flies into battle. When it gets where it needs to be, the assault platforms just launch off. "Like seeds from a dandelion" was how old Sorril put it. She showed us a couple of her moving pictures, and those fortresses really do kind of look like dandelions, with all the little bits peeling off and floating away. Once our platforms are detached, we've got to maneuver into position, making a wall or whatever kind of formation works for that particular battle. We've practiced flying around on the assault platforms a bit, but this time we'll be using an actual tetra fortress, and we'll have an actual source we're supposed to protect.

That's what most battles are really about, when you get down to it—the source. Or the sources, depending on how many there are. The official term is "fontani," which is the name the Prips made up for them, but a lot of the time it's easier to just say "source." Battles basically revolve around the fontani, which makes sense, because they're how we get our thelemity. No source means no thelemity, and no thelemity means you're pretty much dead. If the Valentines get your source, they can just pull back and pick you off like nothing. The Valentines have sources, too, though—the Type os, or just Zeros for short—and if we can get old Romeo's sources, the Zeros, that is, like kill them or trap them or make them run away, then we've more or less won the battle. Most Valentine fighters actually self-destruct the minute they go dark. As milites, it's our job to make up the main lines of battle, protecting our sources and pushing forward into a position where we can go after the Zeros. There's a lot more to it, of course, but that's the basic the idea.

For this exercise, there's going to be a real source out there with us, and we'll have to keep the V-spheres from getting anywhere close. Any squad that lets one past loses automatically. Old Sorril is about halfway through explaining the different formations we'll be using when someone in the back starts to laugh. It's one of the bivvies, the real scary one they call Thom. He had to shave his beard and cut his hair, but he's just as scary as ever.

"Something you would like to add, Recruit Thom?" Sorril asks. She's pretty annoyed about being interrupted, that's obvious, but I'm a little surprised she asks Thom a question instead of just ordering him to leave. He doesn't really speak Aux.

"Pawns," Thom answers in his thick bivvie accent, a big smile on his scarred old face. "We are pawns."

I've never heard that word before, "pawns," but I guess the rest of the bivvies all have. They start laughing, too.

I figure Thom must have said something pretty rude, but Sorril doesn't seem to care. "Thank you for your contribution, Recruit," she says. "Please hold any further comments until the briefing has concluded." The bivvies don't say anything else, but they keep grinning the whole time.

At the end of the briefing, Sorril divides us all up into squads. Each squad is ten people, enough to fill one side of an assault platform. In the Legion, every squad of milites has a leader, the "Decurio," who gives the orders and so forth. Decurios are usually more experienced milites who've been trained to lead, but for this exercise, they'll just be recruits who've done particularly well in training.

I don't get chosen for Decurio, of course, but Mersh and Spammers and Hexi all do. They're real good recruits, it turns out. I actually end up in Mersh's squad. Nobody's really that happy about it. The other recruits think we're like destined to lose with me there, and I'm not exactly pleased to be taking orders from Mersh. Mersh is pretty nice about me messing up his chances to win, though. "Just stay low and try not to do anything," he says, giving me a little punch on the shoulder.

The exercise starts out pretty good, or not that bad, anyway. When the briefing's over, we put on our D-87s and line up to load into the tetra fortress. It's waiting for us in a field behind the barracks, this big dark gray ball with a few numbers in yellow along the side, floating about three meters off the ground.

We've got to use personal gravity to get inside. I try to think of the fortress as kind of its own planet, like Spammers said, which isn't too hard, since it really is just a great big ball. It works. I hardly get queasy at all, even when I'm inside, and I have to jog along the curved floor to find my platform.

There are a lot of recruits in the exercise with us, like from other Limit Camps and whatnot, so it takes a while before everyone's ready, but eventually this little voice in my helmet announces that our fortress is lifting off. Really, though, it doesn't feel like we're going anywhere. The walls and floor don't rumble or anything like that. I probably wouldn't know we're moving at all if that little voice didn't keep chiming in to say how far we are from our launch point. We're all sitting in a line, my squad is, our backs against the side of the assault platform that'll face the battle, and Mersh starts getting into the old strategy a bit, telling everyone to look for the biggest concentration of V-spheres and aim there.

I guess I drift off for a little about then, because the next thing I know,

Mersh is yelling, "Ten seconds to launch!" and the little voice in my helmet is telling me the same thing, and suddenly the platforms around us start falling away, and we're out in the middle of the sky.

It's a sunny day, and clear, and we're way, way up above the ground. I'd almost forgotten it was winter, but everything below is covered in snow. Over the edge of my platform, I can see a forest all like blanketed in white, the trees getting smaller and smaller every second. Other platforms float around us, with recruits loaded up on both sides, and I'm just glad I didn't end up on the side facing the ground. As I'm looking around, I hear Mersh yelling for me to get into position. Everyone is already over by the platform's forward wall, ready to shoot. I scoot in next to him and get my weapon ready just as the first V-spheres appear.

All the recruits are armed with lazels, just the way we would be if this were a real battle. They're much easier to use than the rifles they gave us in the settlement militia. For one thing, you don't have to worry as much about wind and distance and whatnot, since lazels shoot energy instead of bullets. I'm actually not too bad with the old lazel, at least when I'm shooting targets, and that's all the V-spheres are, really.

The V-spheres come down at us like a sheet of rain, and our platform rotates to face them, Mersh shouting at us to open fire. Another good thing about the lazel is you can shoot forever, and it'll never run out of ammunition as long as you're someplace that has thelemity, so we just let loose as those V-spheres come charging in. Everywhere we land a shot, some sphere or other gets wiped away in a blue-white shadow, but we've hardly gotten started when they all swerve back, pulling away into the sky. Our platforms have no problem keeping up, so we just follow, spreading out to give everyone a clear shot. We're moving pretty fast, but our suits keep us from feeling it, the same as they keep us from feeling the cold and wind, even though we're getting real high off the ground—three or four kilometers, probably. Pretty soon we're riding in and out of these big, thick clouds, with huge white slopes towering over us like mountains.

We've done a pretty good job thinning out the V-spheres by then. There are only a few left, whirling around and shooting at us. But just as we swing over this one very tall cloud, a whole new swarm of V-spheres rises, heading straight toward us. Mersh shouts for everyone to aim for the front edge, where the V-spheres are thickest, but even though that area lights up blue like crazy, the spheres keep coming. After only a few seconds, it's obvious they're going to crash into us. Even I can tell.

"Break 'em up!" Mersh yells.

Lazels do more than just shoot those little blue needles of light. They're made for close combat, too. They've got something a bit like the bayonets we had back at old S-225. What you do is you split the lazel into two pieces, so you're basically holding half in each hand, and when you do, each piece turns into a kind of weapon. There's what we call the blade, which is basically a big knife, almost a meter long, and the buckler, which is more like a shield. They're both made of that same blue-white energy the lazel shoots, only a lot stronger. The blade is like a hundred direct hits in one, and the buckler can fend off just about anything, even a blade.

"Break 'em up!" is Mersh's order to draw our blades, so we all step back from the platform wall and pull on our lazels. In a flash, everyone has a blade in one hand and a buckler in the other. Just in time, too, because the V-spheres are coming down on us. A lot of Valentine fighters have blades like ours, but fortunately the V-spheres don't. Instead, they have little glowing spots they try to bump you with. If one touches you, your squad loses points. Also, it really knocks you over.

For a few seconds, our whole platform is crazy with V-spheres and blades hacking away. I get sort of scared one of us'll accidentally hit another recruit, which would be just as bad as getting slashed by a Valentine, but pretty soon there are only a few V-spheres left, then none. We didn't let a single one past. The whole squad is pretty happy, but me especially, because it looks like I made it through the exercise without completely screwing up. Maybe we didn't get the most points, but at least it wasn't my fault.

And then out of nowhere my helmet goes black, and when I can see again, the sounds and colors are different. For half a second I have no idea what's going on, but then the platform starts to tilt, and I get it: We've gone dark. I don't know how it happened, but my blade and buckler are gone, like I'm just holding two halves of a lazel, and I can see my reflection a little in the clear surface of my helmet. I start to wonder why my D-87s don't feel heavy yet. Then I realize it's because I'm falling.

This is bad. I mean, we're totally screwed, me and all the other recruits. It's not like we have parachutes or anything. We might as well be a bunch of rocks standing on bigger, flatter rocks, for all the flying we can do. Up above, other platforms have started tumbling like great big snowflakes, recruits spinning off, flailing in their heavy suits. I look around and see the recruits on my platform lifting off as we gather speed. Mersh is near the back, and he gives me this big surprised look as the platform drops out from under him.

All at once, I get this idea. I don't know where it comes from, really, but for some reason I just feel like we've all got to stick together. I reach for one of the handles on the platform and pull myself down, then start making my way around, grabbing any recruit I can reach and motioning for them to hold on. It isn't easy because the platform has started going end over end, and people are sort of floating away, but we're all falling at about the same speed, so mostly everyone is within reach. But a few are way out there, like Mersh, and they can't seem to get back. We've dropped through the clouds now, and those snowy trees are getting closer and closer. And even though it seems totally pointless, I get a few recruits to make a sort of chain, like one person holding on to the next person's ankles, so I can swing out and grab Mersh and the rest.

The last recruit from our squad has just grabbed onto our platform when suddenly my helmet blinks again, and the platform starts to slow, then swoop upward. Our thelemity is back. We barely have time to feel relieved, though, before a new wave of V-spheres comes flying up out of the snowy trees. I just sort of gape at them, but Mersh yells for everyone to open fire. A few recruits managed to hold on to their lazels, but mine is long gone, so I run for one of the extras stored at the side of the platform, then start shooting away with the rest of my team. There aren't many V-spheres this time, which is good because we're the only platform doing any real shooting. Most of the others are almost empty, with recruits floating all around, trying to get back into position using PG. By the time they do, my squad's already cleaned up pretty good.

It turns out us going dark was all part of the exercise, to like test how we react to being totally helpless. Since there was no way any of us would survive that kind of fall, we were supposed to just hang tight on our platforms and hope our thelemity came back before we ended up splattered all over the place. So what I did was exactly right, not that it was some brilliant strategic maneuver or anything. It just seemed like everyone should stay together. I didn't even notice we were upside down half the time. But it meant my squad was the only one ready when that last wave of spheres came, so at the end, when they count up the points, we've got the most by far. For the first time since I got into this stupid Legion, I'm a big hero. After old Sorril reads off the scores, my whole squad gathers around, slapping me on the back. And then I puke in my helmet.

I don't even mind the puke much, though. I'm already all sweaty under my D-87s, and anyway, I'm sort of used to puke by now. The recruits from my squad actually think it's sort of funny. They give me a hard time, of course, but in like a friendly way. After Sorril dismisses everyone for supper, Spammers and Hexi come over, and Mersh tells the whole story, making me out to be some kind of tough guy. You can tell he's not just saying it, either, because he sounds annoyed it wasn't him saving the day and everything.

Just as Mersh is getting to the part where we all go dark, I see that bivvie girl, Naomi, over with some other recruits. It feels like a dream, sort of, because I can't quite understand what she's doing here. She looks real different from the last time I saw her. Her brown hair is all combed and tied up, and she's dressed in black like a Prip. It makes me pretty sad, thinking about little Naomi being in the Legion. She doesn't seem too upset, though. Actually, she looks quite happy. She's talking to the other bivvies, and they're all real excited about something. The bivvies were about the only other recruits to stay with their platform during the exercise, but I don't think that's what's got them all worked up. Even that guy Thom looks happy. It's hard to tell, because his face is so mean and everything, but I think he's smiling.

Mersh is about finished with his story, and people start giving me a hard time about the puke again, telling me to go wash up or they won't sit with me at supper, so I start heading for the barracks. I'm just about there when I hear someone behind me say, "Torro."

It's Naomi. I'm not quite sure how she got all the way over here. I didn't see her coming or anything. But I say, "Hey, Naomi. Good to see you."

She looks like she's about to say something, but then she gets a good look at me and sort of pauses. "You are covered in vomit," she says.

"Yeah, that was me," I say. "I'm the vomiter. You know, like, gravity and everything."

Naomi nods, like she's not very surprised I'd puke on myself. "I was rude to you the last time we saw each other," she says. "You tried to show me kindness, and I repaid you with scorn. I would like to apologize."

It takes me a minute to remember what she's talking about. It all seems like a long time ago. "Oh sure, whatever, no problem," I say. "What are you doing here anyway, if you don't mind my asking?"

"This exercise was for me as well. My instructor is teaching me to navigate in battle. He wants me to understand that a great deal will depend on me."

I don't quite know what she means, but then I get it. "You're a source, you mean?"

"I am. Please forgive me for leaving you and your fellow soldiers. I was assured no harm would come to you."

"It wasn't so bad. No harm done and so forth."

"I'm glad."

She doesn't say anything else, just sort of looks at me, so I say, "What were you guys talking about over there? You and your people, I mean?"

She smiles then, not at me, but like she's remembering something. "I had good news for them. My sister, who we thought had died, was found alive and well. We sent a message to our mother today."

"Hey, that's great!" Suddenly I feel real happy. Like, I don't even know this sister, but I'm still happy.

I guess Naomi's the sort of person who doesn't talk just to say things. I mean, it's obvious she thinks it's great her sister's back, but I just said that, so she doesn't need to say it again. All she says is "It was good to see you, Torro. I suggest you have a bath."

She's about to go, but then I blurt out, "Hey! Hey, Naomi!"

She turns around and looks at me. "Yes?"

I guess I *am* the sort of person who talks just to say things. I didn't really have anything to tell her. I just wanted to talk to her a little more. Now I don't know what to say. "Hey, what are pawns?" I ask, because it's all I can think of.

"What do you mean?" she says. She looks pretty confused.

"I heard your people say it a while back. They said we're pawns."

Naomi thinks about that a minute, then she says, "It is from a game my people have, a game of strategy, called chess. There are several different pieces, each with its own role and abilities. The pawn is the most abundant piece, but also the weakest. Chess is a game of battle, and pawns make up the front line."

"Yeah, right." I feel a little sick all of a sudden. Those bivvies were right. Pawns. That's exactly what we are.

"Pawns are small, but they are also very important," Naomi says. She's probably figured out what I'm thinking. She's being pretty nice about it, too. "You and I can play a game of chess sometime, and I will show you. For now, I must go. My instructor is waiting."

She tilts her head toward a sort of short, chubby guy standing off toward the barracks. I hadn't seen him before, and I don't know how Naomi did, since he's behind her. I'm about to say something, but then the chubby guy sort of shimmers, like there's a shadow passing over him. Some of the recruits heading off to supper call for me to come along, and I wave to them, to like let them know I'll be along shortly. When I look back, though, Naomi and the chubby guy are both gone. It's just me and the other pawns.

THIRTY

RAE

When I heard I would be attending an Academy of magic, I was prepared for the place to be somewhat mystifying in its habits and culture. Tales make up a kind of currency among my people, and in our stories, witches and wizards are common. They are a favorite especially of children, who will wait excitedly all day for the next installment of whatever saga is being told around our fires, but also in the townships, where any mention of things supernatural is roundly discouraged, and is as such irresistible to everyone, the authorities most of all. One tale I have always loved tells of a school for young magicians, a rambling castle of infinite mystery, filled with monsters and spirits and delightful clutter. It is as if this Ninth City were made to be as unlike that place as possible. Though it is built on magic, it seems composed entirely of straight lines and even curves, of bold and heavy geometry. This city does not ramble. Everywhere I look is clean, towering symmetry. In my travels, I have surveyed some of our continent's more repugnant locales, but this must be the least magical place I have ever visited.

The Academy itself has the outward appearance of a bunker built to repel the aggressions of flaming meteors, or such is my impression of the blocky buildings along its farthest exterior, within shouting distance of the city's limits. What I find beyond is a city within a city, a warren of narrow streets and buildings tall enough to tickle the clouds, interspersed with courtyards varying in size from a few feet in diameter to a scale so vast that my entire coda could circle our wagons three times around and have room to spare, all of it rising in tiers like battlement walls toward Ninth City's center, where stands the crown of buildings known as the Forum. The farther up you go, the more the architecture softens, from the blunt stone slabs of the exterior to something reminiscent of an old church in the center, but always there is the sense of facing a wall, something built to keep outsiders at bay.

Beyond the high parapets and steep, cliff-like towers, there is one more barrier yet to pass: the "entrance evaluations" required for all new arrivals to the Academy's School of Rhetoric. For long-standing cadets, those who have already been through the School of Grammar, the evaluations are a deal more involved, lasting a full month and granting those who distinguish themselves a speedy track to power and prestige. In the case of myself and other recruits culled from outside Ninth City, expectations are not so high. The Academy's Board of Examiners has allotted me one day, and they make it clear even that is likely more than necessary to get the measure of me.

I cannot allow that sort of insult to pass without comment, but my objections are met only with a soliloquy on Academy policy, which prescribes this manner of truncated testing as a way of looking after the safety of its recruits and the sanity of its Examiners. The Academy's training is so rigorous and thorough, I am told, that it is pointless as well as dangerous to hold new recruits to the same standards as those advancing from its lower schools. At the conclusion of my first year, there will be a new round of examinations in which I will have the chance to compete with Academy cadets on an equal footing, but just now I am deemed likely only to waste the Examiners' time and injure myself in the process. I tell them I've had seven solid years' learning on my own, but all they do is smile and say they doubt it's the sort of education you get at the Academy. "Damn right," I say. "I guess you never met a Walker before."

They haven't, either.

The venue for my entrance evaluations is an exercise ground nestled amid a hive of fields and arenas, some so bizarre in composition that I cannot begin to imagine what sort activities are conducted there. I am somewhat relieved to see the place my Examiners lead me is among the least supernatural in character, its only unusual feature being a tendency of the terrain suddenly to change shape or altitude. There is a game in progress when we arrive, something that involves groups of cadets rushing back and forth across turf constantly rearranging itself into mountains and valleys, but the sport is broken up, its players unceremoniously banished, and the ground flattened to make room for my first test, a run of fifty laps around a track raised out of the ground just for me.

Instead of taking their games elsewhere, the displaced cadets retire to a set of nearby stands and erupt into hoots of encouragement as I complete each circuit. My last burn of speed earns a round of appreciative applause and approving mutters from my Examiners as they confer over their timepieces. "Let's start her on course five," I hear one of them say, a tall, older man, with a high forehead and face built perfectly for looking down his nose.

There is an outbreak of booing and raspberries from the cadets in the stands, who I gather had been hoping for a different result. I for my part would just like a few minutes to catch my breath. I watch with some concern as the field's flat track forms itself into an uneven terrain of hurdles and pits and scaling walls, until I notice my Examiners have again turned their attention my way. "Let's move, Recruit," says the old man, his tone all weary forbearance.

His obvious boredom pricks my pride, and I decide to make an example of "course five," not so much navigating the thing as running roughshod over it. Courses eleven, fifteen, and twenty-one all get the same treatment. When I finish course twenty-four, I am made to stop so the collar I have been fitted with to prevent me cheating by magic may be inspected. I wait with satisfaction as the Examiners confirm the honesty of my performance, then summon course thirty to great adulation from the audience of cadets. It is a diabolical assortment of rings and bars and precarious points of balance, much of it passable only by sheer muscle. But climbing trees and rocks and the faces of cliffs is all in a day's work for a scout of the Autumn Walkers, and if called to, I can hang by my arms all day.

"Hardly one cadet in a hundred finishes course thirty," my stern old Examiner confides after I have done just that, thereby earning the courtesy of being spoken to directly, it seems. I've discovered he is a Praeceptor of the Academy, which is to say the head of one of its three schools—Philosophy, in his particular case.

"Your lessons could use a few more mountains," I reply with a grin.

Next comes the test in marksmanship. I have a chance to rest and work the tightness from my forearms as a firing range is erected and the weapon I am to use demonstrated. I am glad to learn no magic will be required, as my only experience with the Legion's weaponry had been as a target, and I am not eager to attempt it for the first time when my reputation is at stake. The gun I am given is, overall, not so different from the rifle I've carried in my saddle holster all these years—only a deal lighter and deader in its aim. Once I've got the hang of it, I pick off my targets as easy as popping the heads off daisies.

"Unarmed combat is scheduled next," the Praeceptor of Philosophy tells me after an extended conference with his fellow Examiners. "Normally at this point we'd have the recruits pair off and demonstrate on each other, but as you're our only recruit today, and rather older than most, I and the other Examners have arranged for a sparring partner more suited to your circumstances."

"All right, bring him out," I say. "No sense fooling around." The crowd in the stands has increased since my examination began, and I wonder if my opponent might be sitting up there, but as I look down the rows of cadets, I see a new wave of excitement, and turn to find the Praeceptor has removed his jacket and donned a magic-dimming collar of his own. He watches me down his long nose, rolling his neck and cracking his knuckles.

He seems somewhat ancient for a fair fight, but I have watched many a thick-necked young ogre fall to men older than he, and I know to approach with care. Sure enough, he squares off with a stance I have never seen before, and though I have youth and strength on my side, and my own method of weaponless fighting learned among the scouts, the simple economy of his movements is such that I have difficulty keeping up. But I have tricks enough to take him by surprise once or twice, nor does he quite anticipate my willingness to take a beating for the chance to deal one out. It is plain also that he does not expect me to be anything but a simple and forthright brawler. By the time the Board calls a halt to the fight, I am down spitting blood, my left arm hanging limp, and a black eye forming, but the Praeceptor of the Academy's School of Philosophy has been put on his back twice and awarded a swollen mouth and a brace of broken ribs in the bargain. With a bloody grin on his lips, he helps me to my feet, our spectators roaring with delight at the unexpected spectacle of our duel.

There is a sort of intermission while I and the Praeceptor are ministered to by a specialized sort of physician called a "chigurrus." His techniques must be similar to those that healed my broken leg, because in minutes my opponent and I are both of us nearly good as new, though the Praeceptor has swallowed one or two teeth, which we're told may take some days to regrow. Meanwhile, the geography of our activity field has altered once again, this time into a set of small and generally uninteresting booths and stations.

When the chigurrus has pronounced me once again fit for testing, my Examiners remove my collar and set me to what they call "a series of simple exercises involving thelemity." Our audience of cadets, which had been clamoring for a battle royal between myself and several other notable school officials, emits a groan of disappointment. The exercises are simple indeed, intended only to get an idea of my natural talent, a thing I am assured can only take me so far.

At my Examiners' request, I conjure a small globe of light, cool a glass of water by touch, incinerate a block of wood, cause a ripe apple to dry and wither. The final task involves putting a ball through a hoop some two hundred yards distant, a difficult problem as the misty claws of my influence do not extend nearly so far. My solution, to fire the thing in cannonball form across the field, garners less-than-universal praise from my Examiners, but I can hear some of them chuckling as the ball lands, smoking and deflated, on the hoop's rim, resting a moment before sliding down and through.

I reckon I am about on pace to begin my Academy career as the greatest cadet ever to walk its hallowed halls—until I am introduced to the written portion of my evaluation. I am escorted to a large hall filled with long tables and there subjected to the most bewildering interrogation I have ever endured, what is called a "standardized test."

Mama and Papa took sound interest in their children's education, and I always considered myself furnished with decent knowledge of the world and its workings. I have a good head for sums, enough to keep track of my family's trades and calculate using the odd weights and measures of the townships. I understand the human form well enough to patch it when it's hurt or slice it into choice fillets. I know which plants are good to eat, which have salubrious qualities, and which you'd want to think twice about putting in your mouth. I can navigate by the stars, render a landscape in pen and ink with passable verisimilitude, and recite long stretches of epic poetry from memory, though I have been told my performances lack dramatic flair. But the entirety of my life's learning is not enough to answer even one of these questions with any confidence. It does not help that the entire test is written in Aux, which I do not read nearly so well as I speak it, but even were it not filled with unfamiliar words and turns of phrase, I doubt I could suitably follow one question in twenty.

A few pages in, I have utterly exhausted my training in numbers, and my mastery of the natural sciences gives out soon after. I begin flipping through the great block of paper that comprises my examination book, just to confirm the rest is more of the same. At the end is a section devoted to an area of learning called "irrational mechanics," which I gather to mean the study of magic, though this is by no means a certainty from the problems I read:

1. Explain three significant distinctions between ingenic and palaketic devices, citing practical examples for each.

2. List the five canonical methods for composing compound infusions, along with their primary and secondary syntactic styles.

3. Describe the simplest process for clearing a path 3m high by 3m wide through a wall of solid iron 10m thick, using only techniques derived from manifestation. Assume efficiencies of 1.00 for all basic energies, with the exception of heat (2.00), muity (0.75), akyrity (0.50), electricity (2.50), and viaty (2.75). Show your work.

I am rereading this last question, trying to puzzle out the meaning of the word "muity," when I hear a loud throat-clearing and discover my examination proctor standing over me. She has been introduced to me as Praefector of the School of Grammar and is the only member of the Board left to supervise me, a job she plainly resents. She is small but ramrod straight, and like my other Examiners, rather advanced in years. The entire left side of her head, from her cheek to the top of her scalp, is marked with a strange crisscrossing pattern of purple-red, like a projection of light or shadow that colors everything it touches, whether skin or hair or, alarmingly, her whole left eye. Grammar is the school for the Academy's youngest cadets, and I can only imagine the terror this woman must inspire there with this blank red eye, now turned disapprovingly on me. It seems I have been laughing at my test, and my proctor is interested to know just what I find so funny.

"I thought you all were trying to save time on this evaluation of yours," I say, and go on to explain how if that was the case, we might have skipped the whole standardized test beyond the first three pages or so. I point her to the section on irrational mechanics by way of demonstration, and she flashes a grin that makes me think she might not be such a despot after all.

"The objective of this examination is to correctly complete as many questions as possible in the time allotted," she says, inspecting my papers. "I have never seen a settlement recruit finish so many as to render it necessary to venture into the final section. They do, however, typically answer more than ten."

My response is that ten was something of an achievement for me, and moreover I am at this school to fight, not fill out questionnaires. This time I get a full, earnest smile, enough to feel sure I have been understood. Regardless, I am not encouraged to continue my examination.

It seems even my poor performance in the area of standardized testing is not enough to keep me out of the Academy: That very evening, I receive word that I am to begin my studies at the School of Rhetoric the very next day as part of Sixth Class Section B.

I am so eager to embark on my instruction in sorcery that I arrive at my classroom fully an hour early. I claim a desk at the front and arrange my study materials neatly on top, then, realizing more than fifty minutes still remain before the start of lessons, commence a full inspection of the room. It is disappointingly plain, the desks spaced evenly in rows facing a longer table with what looks like an ancient slate blackboard hung behind it. The walls are decorated with charts and tables and figures, some bearing a word or two I recognize, though never enough for me to decipher the thing's full meaning. There is also a map of what I know now to be the entire planet, a scope I still find difficult to credit. From my seat, I trace out the boundaries of the world I knew from within the world as it is.

Presently, the sound of boisterous voices begins to fill the hall outside, growing louder and closer but then hushing suddenly at the edge of the classroom. I look away from the map to discover myself the target of several pairs of saucer-sized eyes. A crowd of children has become wedged in the doorway. The clog becomes tighter as more arrive, but none appears willing to enter the classroom. At last a sharp voice from outside sends them running, and from their midst emerges an older girl in black. This, I presume, is our teacher, or rhetor as they are called here. She is perhaps a year or two my senior, but appears younger thanks to a generous serving of pimples and baby fat.

"Section B, to your seats," she commands, and the younger children reluctantly obey, their orderly movement impressive even in their agitated state. Our rhetor, meanwhile, takes up a position before the larger desk.

Her gaze comes to rest briefly on me before flicking back to the class as a whole. "We have a new sectionmate with us today, Cadets," she announces. "Everyone, please say hello to Cadet Rachel."

The ensuing chorus of young voices comes perfectly synchronized but with a clear note of uncertainty—a note that strikes home with me, too. Only now are the precise details of my arrangement beginning to dawn on me. It was made clear from the start that I would be a special case: by age nineteen a student from this Academy should either be off to war or graduated to some advanced training, and I was suited for neither. Without refinement, my magical talents would be wasted in battle, while lessons for rising officers were years beyond my current state of learning. I would have to begin at the beginning, which I now understand means in a classroom full of children. Fair enough. I know the time is coming when these people will send my sister to war, and for the right to fight at her side, I would have gladly walked barefoot over hot coals. Sitting with a gaggle of twelve-year-olds cannot be so bad. Only the desks are a little cramped.

The majority of section B has settled in, but one boy lingers at the edge of my desk, a towheaded little snap bean who takes a step back the moment he sees I've noticed him. "Hey there, little man," I say. "Don't worry. I won't bite."

The boy seems to interpret my assurance as meaning the precise opposite. His response comes in tones so low and shy that I can scarcely hear them. I can make out only the Aux word for "desk."

Our rhetor resolves the confusion. "That is Cadet Chyffe's desk," she informs me. "Yours is located at position twenty-one." She points me toward a desk at the rear of the class, the only one left empty. I stand, gather my books, and offer Chyffe my apologies. He only goggles back as I make my way to my desk.

It is just as small as all the others.

THIRTY-ONE

RAE

My reputation has preceded me to the School of Rhetoric, that is clear enough, but I have still to learn the particulars, as no one seems willing to speak to me except under the most extreme duress. My fellow cadets appear under the apprehension that I am some dangerous beast, near mythical in character and prone to sudden acts of violence, an attitude our rhetor only encourages. Her name is Svetli, and for the entirety of our first lesson, she acts as though she has been forced to teach with something horrible caged in the back of her classroom, studiously ignoring me except for furtive glances to ensure I have not escaped.

I spend the majority of this time struggling to hold in feelings of confusion and impatience. The trouble is not my reception here at school but the present subject of learning. As soon as Rhetor Svetli was satisfied I was unlikely to spring up and tear out the throats of her charges, she commenced a lecture on what she called the "laws of motion." There has been a great deal of talk about "velocity" and "acceleration" and "kinetic energy," all with accompanying graphs and figures, which I have dutifully copied despite not understanding a jot of it. I keep waiting for Svetli to segue into some area of magic, to explain how speed and vectors relate to conjuring fire out of thin air, but she only goes on making diagrams of falling apples and orbiting planets.

After what I judge to be nearly a decade, I have reached the limit of my endurance and cannot restrain myself from asking when we're going to learn a little magic. My question draws nervous titters from the class and a withering look from Rhetor Svetli. "We do not teach *magic* at the School of Rhetoric, Cadet Rachel," she says. "If *magic* is something you wish to learn, I suggest you find a goat and attempt to read its entrails. *Irrational mechanics*," she continues, once renewed giggling has subsided, "is part of your afternoon curriculum, as I am sure you can divine by consulting your schedule."

I am of a mind to inform this Rhetor Svetli that since my sister happens to be the one making the goddamn magic, I'll call it whatever I goddamn please, but restrain myself by a firm exertion of will. Naomi has laid a strict interdict upon me not to embarrass her at our new school, and as I have already been found guilty of several infractions—among them publicly hugging and kissing her and calling her "Sunshine" within the hearing of others—it has been explained to me in no uncertain terms that any further misbehavior will see me tossed into the fire, where there will be great wailing and gnashing of teeth. Therefore, I muster the smile Papa imparted to me for use with people who, for reasons of politics, I am not allowed to whip bloody, and set myself dutifully to the study of so-called classical mechanics.

The morning is a grueling one, and by the time Svetli finally lays down her chalk, my hand is cramped from furiously copying her entire oeuvre. Worse still, my labors have left me no wiser, as I discover when Svetli asks us to apply what she has taught us to a "problem set" of new and diabolical equations. Once I have copied these as well, I subtly reconnoiter the activities of my fellow cadets. While I plainly outclass them all in penmanship, to one degree or another each has succeeded in transforming Svetli's set of jumbled numbers into the precious and sought-after answers. The boy seated ahead of me, a chubby, snub-nosed cutie, has long since concluded the first question with the simple answer of "52 kph."

"Hey," I whisper. When he doesn't seem to hear, I lean forward, close enough to touch him, and say again, "Hey."

He gives a start and looks back, first with terror, then murderous annoyance. "We're not supposed to talk," he says sternly.

"Sure," I agree. I reach over and point to his page. "But how'd you do *that*?"

He rolls his eyes contemptuously, then returns to his work. "Magic."

The composition of the class has altered somewhat by the time of our fabled afternoon lessons in irrational mechanics. Only a few of us from Section B return, those with some talent in magic, while the rest are sent off to more theoretical pursuits on the subject, and the remaining seats are filled by other Sixth-Class cadets of the "revenni" persuasion. I look around for Naomi, only to recall that she will be off with Jax and their special tutor, an exceedingly strange man named Charles. I catch a few of the newcomers sneaking looks at me, and even one or two smirking in a way that leads me to conclude I have become the subject of fun.

We have a new rhetor, Danyee, who is less of a sourpuss than her predecessor but still a good way short of friendly. Nevertheless, my dissatisfaction with her lesson is just as fierce. The first thing she does, after writing "Irrational Mechanics" across her blackboard, is instruct us to open our workbooks to Chapter Three. Fear seizes my heart then, and when Danyee begins to fill the board with strings of numbers and letters and symbols, if anything more obscure than those from our lessons in nonmagical motion, my disappointment is such that I fear I will expire on the spot. By the time Danyee divides us into groups of two for practical exercises, I am well into designing my escape from this heathen hellhole.

My addition to this class has resulted in an odd number of students, and because I am to blame for the confusion, as well as an untutored barbarian, I end up in the one group of three. Among my unlucky partners is none other than Chyffe. To my surprise, he bears me no ill will for stealing his desk and goes so far as to introduce me to our third member, a freckly boy named Kenut. The two of them graciously exclude me from the particulars of our assignment, conferring quietly over readings and equations while I observe from a distance. Eventually, however, they appear to reach an impasse. Their distress is such that I am moved to ask just what in the blazes they're trying to do.

Both regard me a moment, perhaps weighing just how much my limited intellect can handle, then Chyffe bravely sallies forth. "We're supposed to be making light," he says. "We've got to control the wavelength to get six different colors, and they've all got to match up so when we merge them together, we get one white light." He accompanies his explanation with animated gestures toward his notebook. "We've worked out four of them, but we still have to do red and violet. Those are the hardest," he adds gravely.

"Well, let's see what you've got," I say. "Maybe I can help."

The boys appear dubious, but they oblige. At their instigation, four pebble-sized sparks flicker to life in the air above our congregated desks. I can feel the power used to do it, almost like a breath of wind.

Kenut and Chyffe, though obviously pleased with their work, remain apprehensive. "We're way behind," Chyffe says. "Look. Elessa's group already has all six."

The classroom has taken on a mottling of colored hues, tiny lights dipping and swaying over sheets of calculations. Most other groups have produced at least five.

Now, here is something I can do. The smoky cloud of influence I first felt here in Ninth City has been with me all this time, alive and part of me, but idle, resting, as my legs will while I am seated at my desk. Now I summon it to motion, concentrating on the space above Chyffe's notebook, pinching the cloudy essence into two needlepoints. Two sparks burn to life before me. I turn and flex their energy until one is red and the other purple. By observing the lights of other, more successful groups, I am able to adjust my own to the exact right hues.

Chyffe and Kenut watch, mouths gaping, until at last, Kenut hollers, "Whoa! That was awesome!"

These few words unleash a torrent of verbosity in Kenut. He proves to be a naturally gregarious person when not cowed to silence by an intimidating figure such as myself, all of which and more Kenut explains in lurid and excited detail in the last minutes of class, before inviting me to join him for supper at the cafeteria, a gesture Chyffe seems to consider a wild and reckless act of courage, though he agrees to come along. By the meal's end, the three of us are thick as thieves.

Kenut and Chyffe, and the rest of Sixth Class with them, have been intensely curious about me since yesterday, when rumors began to spread of a barbarian girl crashing like a frothing juggernaut through an F-Level obstacle course before going on to murder the Academy's Praeceptor of Philosophy. I gather from Kenut and Chyffe's description that there has been some embellishment surrounding my entrance evaluation, and the same proves true for perceptions of me personally. I am said to be fully two and a half meters tall, with arms like thighs, thighs like tree trunks, and a forked tongue capable of prehensile movement. Other, less reliable accounts report that I am a cannibal and drink blood for my morning repast, that I am a simpleton and have been seen marking my territory with urine, that I have six fingers on each hand and webbed feet. Kenut admits that seeing me in the flesh is something of a letdown, especially once I have presented my disappointingly ordinary tongue for inspection, but he is quick to assure me that the way I really look isn't so bad, either.

Now that my new friends have seen the articulate soul beneath my fearsome exterior, and been assured I would rather dine on cafeteria food than children's brains, they accept me as one of their own. Chyffe eagerly brokers my admittance to the camaraderie of boys in Section B, where I am much admired for my record scores in physical training and the scars on my neck and ear, regarded as tremendously exotic in a place where most wounds heal quickly and without any trace. It is also to my advantage, I suspect, that I am the only female in Section B, Rhetor Svetli included, with any chest to speak of. The girls are not quite as friendly, but I plan to win them over by degrees.

Kenut and Chyffe lay public claim to me as their partner for exercises in irrational mechanics, and for a time we are the cream of Rhetor Danyee's class. Chyffe has a knack for working out the nuts and bolts of just about any problem Danyee can throw at us, while Kenut is an artful translator, able to talk me through the steps required. All I have to do is sculpt the world and its powers according to Kenut's instructions, adjusting according to my own instincts, then enjoy the envious glares of any cadet near enough to witness. While I doubt our reign can continue forever, I expect it to end only when Rhetor Danyee decides to break our group apart. Instead, it suffers a slow decline, beginning with the day Danyee announces we are to begin learning "infusion."

Until now, our study of irrational mechanics has been restricted to a broad category known as "manifestation," which as far as I can tell just means doing things with magic—excuse me, *thelemity*. To quote a local expert, namely Rhetor Danyee, manifestation concerns the creation of "impermanent artifices," which is to say magic that will work only with the active involvement of its creator. I have the feeling that manifestation is where my true talent lies, and I am not eager to venture into new territory. Danyee's first lecture on infusion only confirms my fears.

The discipline of infusion involves the study and manufacture of "permanent artifices" that, once created, will continue to act on their own until whatever task they've been set is complete. There are innumerable methods of infusion, most of which revolve around reciting a lengthy set of instructions and giving these life by means of thelemity. It would be confusing enough, even if the language used were not so arcane as to be nearly unintelligible. Thelemity does not respond to plain speech, it seems, and so we are taught to rely on bizarre dictionaries of terms, phrases that loop and zigzag and turn back on themselves, and interminable patterns of repetition. I lose my grip on the idea about halfway through my first lesson and never get it back, instead trusting Kenut and Chyffe to carry me through.

I succeed in convincing myself that my failures with infusion are of no consequence. The field of battle is no place for lengthy artificing, and it is a rare situation where a soldier will be called upon to create a paper windmill that turns indefinitely of its own volition, as we do at the end of that first class. I have plenty of experience with this kind of excuse, as I have already made it with my other failings at the Academy, which have been numerous and severe. In barely a month, I have already proven myself a fine dunce in a variety of sciences, both theoretical and applied. But in the practical art of manifestation, I remain unmatched in all of Sixth Class, and that, I reason, ought to be enough for whatever sort of warrior they train in this place.

Not everyone's opinion of me is quite so indulgent as mine. Rhetor Svetli, who in my first days at the Academy made noises to the tune that I have no business in her class, now treats me as a void into which knowledge vanishes without any hope of return. Worse still, Rhetor Danyee doggedly insists on attempting to engage me in learning. Her thesis is that the only way to really produce great feats of thelemity is to master the theory behind it. She is right, at least to a degree: Already I have watched Kenut and Chyffe and others around me progress by leaps and bounds, and while I am still well ahead, the gap is narrowing. Perhaps I would have more patience if Danyee's lessons did not sound like a foreign language to me. On top of that there is my pride, already smarting from seeing me landed here in this land of Lilliputians. It has a way of speaking for me if I'm not careful, and when Danyee starts in with that superior tone of hers, the result is usually a good deal of glibness from me and on occasion a smart little magic trick conjured to show just how well I can do without her instruction. But though I'd never say so to Danyee, I have my doubts, and never more so than when I first encounter the subject of irregular energies.

"Irregular energies" is the term used in irrational mechanics for the sort of power never posited or credited to exist before thelemity arrived to upend our general notions of reality. Those forces observed to govern the world throughout most of its history, such as light and heat, gravity and electricity, we refer to as "regular energies." With thelemity's aid, we are able to generate and control these in uncanny ways, but in all other senses they remain Nature's accustomed tools. But thelemity has also given us powers Nature herself never conceived or if she did thought it better not to mention. These are our irregular energies.

For our first lesson in irregular energies, Danyee introduces us to a force called "akyrity." She has chosen it specially because we cadets have a deal of experience with it already from our time on the firing range. Akyrity is the primary ingredient in "null," the artifice that comprises our lazel's most popular ammunition. I had imagined null to be some deeply complicated concoction, but as Danyee explains, it is made almost entirely of akyrity, albeit with several important refinements. We will study how this power is packaged and amplified and stabalized for use in combat during our fifth class year—for now Danyee only wants us to learn its laws and properties and have some hands-on practice.

I know what it means when Danyee begins talking of properties and laws, and settle in to wait while she fills her blackboard with the usual scrawlings, rousing myself only once she begins circulating handfuls of unshelled peanuts, intended as victims for our practical exercises. I watch Kenut and Chyffe work away at their legumes with excruciating slowness, devoting minutes on end to shaving away a single snowflake-sized sliver from the outer shell. When they and the rest of the class have about exhausted themselves, I decide it is time to sail in. I draw in my steam-like cloud of influence, concentrating it around the peanut I have chosen for destruction. But for the first time since I took up manifestation, I find myself unsure what to do next. In the past, I have always been able to bring off whatever effect I chose, even one I had never tried before. So long as I knew the general specifications, it was like molding a sculpture from clay with a rough drawing to go by: not always perfect, but usually close enough. Here it is as if I have been tasked with bringing out some impossible shape, one that looks fine on paper but won't work in the world of solid things. I hover, searching for some inroad or beginning, feeling the scrutiny of Rhetor Danyee and the whole class as well. Finally, I pounce, and though the peanut does disappear, it is not with the whitish shadow of akyrity I saw other cadets produce, but a rollicking explosion that leaves a dark black smear in the center of my desk.

Kenut and Chyffe assure me this poor performance was a fluke. Everyone has bad days, and soon no peanut will be safe from me. But at our next session, as my friends pop off pill-bug-sized bits from their targets, mine continue to evaporate in puffs of yellow fire. It isn't long before most everyone around me can obliterate a peanut's shell with hardly any damage to the fruit inside, while I continue to fill the classroom with fragrant, roasted bits.

It is my first real failure in what I had come to consider my area of expertise, and though Kenut and Chyffe seem to consider my disgrace unimportant, my confidence is shaken. I worry that I have reached the limit of my ability, that I am destined to be surpassed by the children of Sixth Class, a group known in Academy parlance as Dodos. I even consider going to Rhetor Danyee and prostrating myself, swearing to follow her tutelage, though I know she will insist I devote as much time to learning algebra and chemistry as I do to violent magic. I can endure all that and more if it is the only way of becoming the soldier I need to be. And then I discover the magic of animation, and I wonder how I could ever have worried at all.

Animation is one of the many strange disciplines of magic made possible by irregular energy. As Rhetor Danyee describes it, animation is "a process of thelemic manipulation whereby human vitality is extended into an inanimate object," meaning that animation, properly used, lets you take something and move it like part of your own body. Danyee mesmerizes us with a series of impressive demonstrations, riding a chair with animated legs at a crisp trot around the classroom, encouraging a potted plant into a vaguely indecent, belly-waggling dance, causing a human shape to rise from a bowl of ordinary water, even inducing her own hair to stand on end.

For our own experiments, Danyee provides us with a claylike substance known as "bloog." According to our rhetor, bloog is a highly complex invention and not the unappealing slime we might easily mistake it for. Different materials pose different levels of resistance to animation, and bloog is made to be as easy to animate as possible, seemingly at the cost of texture, appearance, and smell. We roll the bloog into long, thin sections, our faces screwed up at the distinctly rancid odor, then hold one end, trying to force through enough of our will to set the other end waggling. Most cadets achieve no more than a listless and erratic jerking, but my first try yields the impatient flick of a cat's tail.

After my disgrace in the matter of peanuts and akyrity, such success comes as a welcome relief. I can safely say animation feels more natural, more innate, than any variety of magic I have experienced to date. Danyee had likened the process to pulling on a pair of gloves, or slipping into a suit, but to me the sensation is more of cooperation, of guidance. Like riding. A person must be in physical contact with an object in order to move it by animation, and so as we progress upward along the evolutionary scale, from bloog worms to bloog pancakes to multilegged blobs of bloog, we begin attaching ourselves by long cords so that our creations might wander freely about. And where most cadets are often reduced to dragging theirs along, mine positively prance.

Sculptures like those we make in class, miniature creatures brought to life by animation, are called "equulei," and as one would expect from a troupe of militant twelve-year-olds, no sooner have we mastered making our equulei walk than we are making them fight. The battles generally take place just beyond Rhetor Danyee's supervision, but only because to have a rhetor watching cheapens the fun. The Academy is in full favor of cadets battling their equulei, as it develops a diversity of skills germane to our war against the Valentines. Nearly all the Legion's more potent weapons employ animation to some degree or other, and skilled "animi," as practitioners are known, are in great demand.

My first battle comes during one of our frequent outdoor sessions. I am promenading my equuleus through the Academy courtyards like a lady out with her lapdog, when suddenly Kenut and Chyffe charge from behind a row of hedges, wild war cries on their lips. I'm no stranger to boys' roughhousing, but the visceral sensation when Chyffe's equuleus collides with mine takes me by surprise. My equuleus responds with a decisive counterattack, and in moments has reduced both assailants to formless piles of mud. Cheers erupt from nearby cadets, even as challengers line up to unseat me from my place of glory. After that, not a single lesson in animation ends without my equuleus surrounded by the splattered remains of its rivals.

My renown spreads, and in relatively short order I am the undisputed equuleus champion of the Sixth Class. Even Rhetor Danyee is impressed, going so far as to suggest that if I hone my skills with some extra studies, I might stand a chance of getting into one of the Academy's elite training programs, once I'm in Fourth Class and eligible to apply. My fellow Dodos think I ought to try now, sure the Academy would make an exception, since I'm already nineteen, practically an old lady. The plans I've begun fashioning for myself are even more ambitious. I've got it in my head to join the Legion now.

The way I see it, the sooner I start, the better I'll be when Naomi comes up to fight. Cadets who try to join up early face a good deal of hoop-jumping, but I figure I might have a shot once I show them what I can do.

I'm wrong, though, and it doesn't take a trip to the Legion's Basilica to find out how wrong. A guided tour of the Academy is plenty.

THIRTY-TWO

RAE

One day, as the revenni of Sixth Class are convening for another afternoon lesson in irrational mechanics, Rhetor Danyee tells us to leave our work at our desks and line up by the door. Today, we will be visiting the Fabrica of Ninth City.

Her announcement is met with considerable excitement, and not only because we'd been expecting a particularly difficult exercise in infusion. The Fabrica is where all the city's marvels of thelemity are designed and created. Normally, Dodos aren't allowed beyond the boundaries of the Academy, but Danyee has secured special permission on the theory that seeing what can be achieved through research and scholarship will motivate us in our studies. Also, she has found a competent and responsible party to act as our guide. Danyee herself will be attending a special training session for rhetors only; from her demeanor, I suspect this "training session" will involve more than the usual amount of heavy drinking for Danyee and her fellow young rhetors.

"Cadets," Rhetor Danyee says, motioning toward the classroom door, "I'd like you to meet Kizabel, an Officer Aspirant from the Academy's School of Philosophy."

Officer Aspirant Kizabel seems far too petite to contain all the achievements Danyee lists to her credit. In addition to having her own workshop at the Fabrica, practically unheard of for anyone so young, Kizabel is an artifex, a maker of artifices, whose creations have been used all over the city. The mildly disheveled state of her black uniform and her unkempt spray of hair convince me she's every bit the prodigy Danyee claims—if I show up to lessons with so much as a hair or button out of place, I can expect hours of extra chores as punishment. And yet no one blinks an eye over our rumpled pocket officer.

We wait, expectant, to hear what wise words this tiny titan will have for us. Slowly, a wicked grin spreads across Kizabel's face. Her blue eyes glint. "So," she says, "who wants to blow something up?"

The Sixth Class is overwhelmingly in favor of explosions. We are almost too excited to keep proper formation as we march down the Academy's halls, toward the School of Philosophy, home to pursuits so scholarly that most cadets cannot even pronounce the things studied there.

The Fabrica is a great block of unadorned stone adjoining the School of Philosophy. Aside from its size, it is so unremarkable, especially with the palatial towers of cadet dormitories visible above, that we begin to think the promise of pyrotechnics was simply a ruse, a suspicion that only deepens as Kizabel ushers us through the bland stone interior, plain gray walkways broken only by the occasional door of cloudy metal. At last, Kizabel stops before one of the doors, presses a hand to its smooth surface, and says, "Hey, Ooj, it's Kiz. I've got those Dodos I told you about. Can we come in?"

We are admitted into a wide room filled with icy, sterile light and figures hunched low over enticing pieces of sparking and smoking equipment. At the far end stands a tall man with long curly hair: Philosopher Oojtelli, or "Ooj," as he prefers to be called.

"Philosopher" is a term used for scholars who have reached the Academy's highest levels of learning, regardless of whether their studies involve the mysteries of existence. Ooj's interests have to do with warding off hostile thelemity. His theories would be exceedingly useful to the Legion if he could only find a way to profitably apply them, but on that account, he is a long way from success.

Ooj directs our attention to a room below, where a lone watermelon stands, adorned with his invention, a circlet reminiscent of a princess's tiara. As cadets crowd against the observation window, Ooj fires a blast of energy at the melon, which explodes spectacularly. "It works about one time out of twenty," he says, and in support of this claim solicits volunteers from the Sixth Class to detonate several more melons. One lucky fruit does survive, only to suffer a grisly fate during the next trial. Ooj shakes his head in speculative lamentation, then loads a new melon to riotous applause.

Before our tour of the Fabrica is finished, we have witnessed everything from a hailstorm conjured inside of a glass ball to a new and highly controversial brand of magic that purports to create living beings out of pure thelemity, though the results we see are even less successful than Philosopher Ooj's warding crown. We have worn every sort of protective gear imaginable: helmets, face shields, gloves, smocks, small metal tabs we are mysteriously told to hold beneath our tongues in the presence of an experimental lie detector. The Philosophers we meet never seem put out to have their studies interrupted by a gaggle of Sixth-Class cadets. On the contrary, they're only too glad to leave off work to explode things with us. Kizabel they treat as a colleague; often I will notice one of them in grave technical discussion with her while another entertains us with some marvelous trick.

The only thing at the Fabrica we do not see, it seems, is Kizabel's own workshop. "That's because I skipped it on purpose," Kizabel says when one brave cadet finally mentions this discrepancy. "It's at the far end of the Fabrica, back near the Academy, and if anyone found out what an abysmal mess it is, I'd be thrown out then and there."

There are a few laughs, but the overall disappointment is plain.

"There's nothing interesting in there," Kizabel says. "And anyway," she adds, noting our lack of conviction, "I haven't been working at the Fabrica much recently." She pauses, apparently coming to some decision, and brings out the mischievous smile that has become a familiar and welcome sign of impending adventure. "Follow me."

Kizabel leads us down a tumble of hallways, mazelike in their blandness, until we reach a small door set inconspicuously into a long wall. "I'm going to show you what I do," Kizabel says, hand on the door. "Keep quiet, and don't touch *anything*. Anyone starts acting up, and I take us all back to the Academy. Got it?" Her voice is serious, but she's still grinning, an indication that we are all misbehaving together.

"Yes, ma'am!" the cadets reply as one. By tacit agreement, Kizabel and I have been pretending that her tour of eleven- and twelve-year-olds does not contain a rather large nineteen-year-old girl. I have kept to the back and said little, and she and her philosopher friends have mostly ignored me, something I take as a kindness. But at the sound of my "yes, ma'am!" her eyes momentarily meet mine, then dart away as she whispers a word of passage to the door, and I know she is embarrassed for me, her oversized Dodo.

Our promise of good behavior lasts only until the first cadet gets through the door. The place beyond is built on a scale for giants, a great open room where we become mice scurrying from a hole. The giants themselves stand in long rows, each in its own stall, dark and still, like statues set into niches along some endless hallway. But I know these are no simple sculptures, that not long ago they were alive, their faces glowing like the light of a brazier. Kizabel shushes the cadets, who are nearly delirious with excitement, though there is still a smile behind the finger she puts to her lips.

"Now," Kizabel says, "I expect you've all guessed where we are. This is the Stabulum, specifically the wing that houses the Legion's equi. You've all heard of the equites, of course. What you probably don't know is there's a lot more to getting an equus into battle than just finding some hotshot jockey to pilot it. Keeping these big guys in fighting shape is how I spend most of my time."

When people think of equi, Kizabel tells us, all they imagine are the equites flying around whipping Valentine ass. But equi are complex and beautiful machines, and to help us appreciate them, she intends to introduce us to some of the people who work their tails off so the equites can go out there and steal all the glory.

As Kizabel takes us down the aisles of silent giants, I lag behind, feeling each one a looming, menacing presence. Equi work by animation, same as equulei, but the little clay toys I send running and skipping through my lessons are as different from these behemoths as a puddle from the raging ocean. Looking up into their dark faces, Vinneas's words come back to me: *Eques. It's a type of warrior. The closest word in your language is probably "knight."*

We come to a halt at the feet of a statue built from what looks to be pale greenish stone. It's forty feet tall at the very least and encased in scaffolding, globes of floating light bobbing up and down its frame. Human shapes, lit by intermittent bursts of glowing color, work along wide platforms, or else by some trick of gravity crouch directly on the thing's body, sticking off in all directions like barnacles from the hull of a ship. The equus itself is clearly damaged, the green stone cracked and torn to reveal metal ligaments beneath, all of it looking strangely like wounds you'd see on a person or other meaty creature, not a hulk of metal and stone.

Kizabel is plainly a favorite here. Workers of the Stabulum spot her a good way off and welcome her with hoots and jests. She hollers back, and one artisan leaves off his labors, swinging down toward us on what appear to be inky-blue tentacles, which retract into an egg-shaped package at the small of his back as he sets his feet on the ground. He introduces himself as Hezaro, and at Kizabel's urging begins describing the highly involved process of returning this equus, named "HeavensHammer," to working condition.

"Poor girl had a run-in with a Valentine Type 6," he says gravely, rubbing his stubbly chin. The "girl" is HeavensHammer, which as far as I can see lacks any demonstrably feminine attributes. "Beastly thing nearly tore her in half, but we'll have her up and about in no time. Would have been sooner, but there were a lot of bad cases after that last incursion. We've been working day and night to get through the backlog."

The cadets are overflowing with questions, though to Kizabel's chagrin, they have more to do with combat than the repair and maintenance of equi. I leave them to it, sinking back from the swell of excited faces and voices bright with inquiries on magical firepower and aerial acrobatics. My attention is elsewhere, fleeing down the seemingly endless gallery of statues. Those nearby are almost identical to HeavensHammer, but farther on I spot several other configurations, different in stature and the lines of their armor. I don't realize I'm looking for one thing in particular until I see it: a familiar shape, last glimpsed silhouetted against the setting sun, head and shoulders above the trees. I glance back toward Kizabel and the cadets, all occupied with Hezaro and HeavensHammer, then slip quietly away into the Stabulum.

THIRTY-THREE

RAE

A small army of giants is waiting for me, stationed side by side, all armored in the same gray stone, each posed identically to the next, heads sleek and alert but blank of any life or consciousness, all exactly alike save for a row of numbers and letters stenciled in yellow across the chest. Printed on the one nearest me is:

IX EQUITES 126-011
THUNDERWALKING

The markings always begin in the same way, with "IX EQUITES 126," but the final number changes on each statue, as do the words written beneath. After "011 THUNDERWALKING" comes "009 WARRIORSVOW." I walk slowly down the row, past "007 FALLINGLEAF" and "005 LANCELIGHTNING." Finally, I see it, the last in the line of gray stone monsters, "IX EQUITES 126-001 FIRECHASER."

Somehow I recognize it immediately, even before I pick out the spots on the armor, lighter in color than the rest and shiny like newly healed skin, where my bullets left their pipe-bowl burns. I am tempted to give the thing a hearty kick, even though I know it's all dead stone and would probably break my toe.

From behind me, someone asks, "What are you doing, Cadet?"

I turn to find myself beneath the glare of a rugged brunette, slim-hipped but strong about the shoulders. She's roughly my age but wearing the black uniform of the Legion. "This is a restricted area," she says. "How did you get in here?"

Why I don't just tell her I'm on a tour of the Stabulum I can't exactly say, but I expect it has to do with her tone and generally impertinent attitude. "Just admiring my handiwork," I tell her. "Can't help being curious, after a fight, to see how the other guy came out."

The girl's mouth twists in confusion. "What?" She seems prepared for further interrogation but pauses as two more bodies come jogging up, one male and one female, likewise clad in black and with similarly sturdy and mostly neckless physiques.

"Who's this, Sensen?" asks the man of the group, taking me in. He's unusually pale and has been attempting a goatee with mixed results.

"No clue," Sensen answers, scowling. "I found her hanging around FireChaser. Said something about inspecting her handiwork."

"Probably just some splatterhead volunteer from the Academy," says the other newcomer, a smaller, curlier-haired replica of Sensen. "Who cares? Come on—it's your turn."

Across the span of the Stabulum, I see more black-uniformed shapes gathered below another equus of the same breed as FireChaser and his neighbors. They've plainly been engaged in some game—cards or dice maybe, the sort soldiers play to pass time between battles, the sort I used to play with the scouts of my coda—but now they're coming my way.

"We can't leave some random cadet hanging around our equi," Sensen says hotly. "And she's not a volunteer. Look." She points to my collar, and the six black dots pinned there. "She's Sixth Class. No way she's trained to fix an equus. I'm reporting her. What's your name, Cadet?"

"Her name is Rachel."

It isn't the deep, echoing voice I remember from my cell, but I know it's him. Bad Cop. The man in black. Imway. He's just as I remember him, neck coiled with muscle, bronzy hair combed back, silver spectacles perched on his sloped nose. "She's one of the unincorporateds we picked up in the valley," he says, stepping up beside Sensen.

Sensen is outraged. "They let a noco into the Academy?"

"Don't be so surprised," I say, jabbing a thumb toward FireChaser. "If I could take you on in one of those, imagine what'd happen in a fair fight." I offer Imway a jolly grin, but he meets me with quiet indifference.

"How about now, then?" Sensen says. "I'll let you ride my Shadow." She nods to the equus next to FireChaser, IX EQUITES 126-003 SHADOWSINGER. "Imway will use FireChaser. We'll keep it to arm wrestling,

I think—there isn't room for anything else in here—but that should be enough for you to show us how a fair fight would go, right? Unless that was just talk."

"Fine." I don't think I'd be able to decline a challenge like that even if I wasn't so proud of my talents in animation. My old self, that girl who'd never turn down a dare, comes swaggering back. I'd thought she was gone for good, but ever since I started at the Academy, she's been following me around, always up for the juvenile high jinks of my fellow Dodos. There's no holding her back now. I don't even wait for Imway to agree but walk up to ShadowSinger and lay a hand against its ankle.

I won't admit to this gob of bullies that I have no idea how an equus works. Instead, I rely on my experience with equulei, reaching out, searching for that place within an object that allows you to take hold of it, like a saddle to seat your soul. It's there, like always, and when I touch it, I feel the equus come to life. And then the stone beneath my hand lurches, knocking me away.

I stumble, barely keeping my feet, as ShadowSinger's face blooms into glowing red. There's a flash of movement, a fist coming down on me, then I'm in darkness, shaking with the force of a terrible impact.

When the ringing in my ears finally starts to fade, I hear laughter, and Sensen's voice, muffled by the dense stone around me. "Oh, sorry. I forgot Shadow's security settings. Can't have every idiot who wanders by riding my equus."

"Very funny, Sen," Imway says. "Now let her out. She's learned her lesson."

But I haven't learned my lesson. I've figured out where I am, trapped like a bug beneath ShadowSinger's cupped hand, and I'm ready to be turned loose. No sooner has the darkness lifted to a view of Sensen's smirking face than I've landed my knuckles on her nose.

My left cross is a little rusty, but still enough to put her squarely on her rear. Blood comes pouring out of her nostrils a moment later, and she holds up a hand to stem the flow, looking wide-eyed from me to her reddened fingers while comrades crowd in to help her. I'm waiting to see if she'll get up when Imway steps between us.

"Walk away, noco," he says coolly. "We'll forget about this. Just walk away."

"Make me." He's too close to get in a good swing, but I hold his eyes, waiting. "I still owe you a broken leg."

He watches me a moment longer, impassive behind his silver frames, then heaves a resigned sigh. "Have it your way."

His friends have gathered behind him, all of them pleasingly dumbfounded. Sensen is on her feet but shows no interest in coming back for another round; she only watches me, eyes narrowed, as Imway approaches the man beside her. He's holding a steaming cup, though he seems to have forgotten about it until Imway casually dips one finger inside. When Imway withdraws his hand, the liquid comes with it, pale tea bouncing like a big heavy drop about to fall. Only it doesn't fall; it rises as though preparing to drip upward, then stalls in midair, a globe of hot tea balanced on a thin liquid pillar. Imway has animated the young fellow's drink.

"I'll make you a bargain," he says, extending his palm like he's offering me the dollop of tea. "If you can knock this out of my hand, I'll let you break any one of my bones you want." With his free hand, he points to the little stream connecting the floating globe to his palm. "All you have to do is touch this part here. That will break the connection. I'll be drenched in hot tea, and you'll get to choose what to break and how to break it. I'll give you three tries. If you fail, you leave quietly. Deal?"

"Deal." He must have some trick planned, some strategy, but I'll just have to figure it out. And how hard can it be, really, to poke a little glob of weak tea?

"Whenever you're ready."

I lead off with a headlong charge. I may be lacking as a scholar in most areas of study, but in matters destructive, I have made a point of honing my skill. For all the new sorts of artifices I have learned, I retain a penchant for the explosive—I have been practicing one fiery technique in particular, and now seems the just the time to show it off. I make it to within five feet of him, too, gathering up my magic to knock him down like a tin figurine, but just as the first slivers of yellow fire begin to appear, the energy inexplicably fizzles. A sudden rush of air sweeps my legs from under me, and I land on my side, feet kicking over my head.

Imway hasn't moved. All he says is "One."

All right, so he's better with magic than I am. No big surprise there. And I don't know how he snuffed me out like that. But I don't have to tackle him or smite him with lightning from on high; I just have to pop that floating globe.

I get up and back away, unsure just how far his reach goes or what his next attack will be, though it seems he's content to let me move first. I cast about for a better approach than the one I've just tried. Around Fire-Chaser's feet are scattered scraps of metal and stone, probably shaved away during repairs, and these give me an idea. Seizing half a dozen smaller chunks with my magic, I sling them into the air, a long arc with Imway's smug head as the ultimate destination. Each is somehow batted down before it reaches its mark, sent clattering harmlessly away by the intercession of an unseen force.

"Shall we call that two?" Imway asks, or starts to, until he sees me coming at him. This time I am able to let loose with my favorite artifice, a golden fist of flame. My blood is up, and as a result the detonation is considerably greater than I had planned. The fire engulfs Imway completely, and I have just enough time to worry that I have taken things too far before the whole inferno dies out at once, as though swallowed up in a deluge. Again, there is no obvious evidence of magic, only Imway, his pose and bored expression unchanged, and another gust of wind to put me on the floor.

I've begun to wonder whether Imway might have some version of Philosopher Ooj's warding gear until I see a faint ruffle in his neatly combed hair, and I understand: He's animating the air, turning it into a kind of equulus to keep me away. I'm impressed. Air is exceptionally hard to animate, let alone powerfully enough to fling a healthy, fully grown girl around like a sack of beans. And there must be something else in there, too, some other magic to undo my artifices.

"You know, this isn't terribly fair of me," Imway says. He strolls toward FireChaser and lifts something hanging on the wall. I consider taking a run at him while his back is turned, but he'll be expecting that. "Here," he says, tossing me what looks like a thick black belt. "Wear this MSR. Maybe that will even things out a bit."

Murmurs and chuckles from the gallery. What Imway called an MSR is the thing I saw that man, Hezaro, use to move around while he worked on HeavensHammer. If nothing else, those tentacles should lengthen my reach—if I can make the thing work, that is.

I fix the belt around my waist, then grope about for something to animate. It's there, a sort of presence I can take hold of, and when I do, inky-blue tentacles spring out, lifting me off the ground. The chuckling stops then, and when I discover certain of the tentacles hold magical tools that seem like they'll serve nicely as weapons—a long, blood-red stinger being of special note—tense silence rises in its place.

The MSR makes me faster than I can believe, but not fast enough, not by a long shot. As I take my first gliding steps toward him, Imway changes his stance, turning to face me sideways, and the air around him assumes a faint red glow. And then he charges. I whip at him with the MSR's tentacles, only to see them lopped off by invisible blades, their liquidy shapes splashing like raindrops, my stinger and other weaponry shattering. The next thing I know, the tentacles holding me up have been sliced away, and I am once again on the floor, now borne on a slick of fragrant goo. I slide to a stop just short of Imway's feet.

"Three," he says. Lukewarm tea splashes beside my face. "Good-bye, Cadet Rachel. I trust you can see yourself out."

Seeing myself out isn't necessary. A whole tour of Sixth-Class cadets has watched my duel with Imway to its inglorious conclusion. Imway doesn't get ten steps from me before Kizabel accosts him, berating the whole gang of equites for misuse of Stabulum equipment and conduct unbecoming of legionaries, and in front of Academy cadets, no less. She makes no allowance for Imway's rank or authority but lays into him the way a rhetor might some misbehaving cadet. Imway endures the scolding silently, with the sour look of a child about to be sent to bed without supper.

The Academy cadets, meanwhile, are in full agreement that today has been the best of their little lives. Despite my unappealing smell, I am welcomed as a hero. Not only did I ride an MSR, I got into a fight with a real eques, and none other than Imway, one of their most revered deities. To their minds, this makes me practically a legionary myself, but I know that isn't true.

Imway did have a nasty trick to beat me: being the plain better fighter. I thought I was closing the distance between myself and the Legion—that I was almost there, in fact. I didn't mind if my skills had about reached their peak, so long I had only a little left to go. Now I know how far away I really am. I may be preeminent among the Dodos, but I am no match for a trained soldier. Perhaps, with Danyee's help, I can improve myself enough to join my fellow cadets in their slow climb through the Academy, even insinuate myself into some quicker track toward enlistment, but either way it will be years and years before I'm ready for the Legion, if I make it there at all.

And by then, my sister will be gone.

□———————□

THIRTY-FOUR

KIZABEL

My imaginary friend thinks I need to get out more.

"I'm not imaginary!" Lady Jane protests. "I may be *insubstantial*. I may be *ethereal*. But I am *not* imaginary. It isn't like you're the only person who can see me. Not that it matters," she adds, pouting with theatrical prettiness in a black evening dress,[1] her preferred attire whenever I am in overalls and drenched in muck. "No one ever visits us anymore. I miss my boys."

"They're not your boys." I am well up inside the Project, rooting around in the core, and my voice echoes impressively, assuming exaggerated registers whenever I activate my fusing wand. The Project's central webbing of gwayd canals stretches above me like a dense canopy of interlocking branches. I run my fingers across each canal, glancing now and then at the schematic displayed in a curtain of mirrors hanging at the edge of the Project's exposed chest cavity. There is a burst of bright blue light each time I sever or fuse a connection, illuminating the delicate veins of the smaller canals, some barely the breadth of a finer-than-average human hair. Production-line legionary equi generally don't require this kind of precision, but compared to the Project, legionary stock equi are about as sophisticated as comedic flatulence.

"Well, they're certainly not *your* boys," Lady retorts. The schematics, full of my latest scribbly and more-than-a-little-ad-hoc designs, are pushed aside to reveal Lady's scowling face. She has acquired one of the cigarettes

---

1 Lady Jane is weirdly obsessed with old Common Era motion pictures, and often chooses her costumes based on depictions of CE culture therein, something she can do freely and at will, not being constrained by the limitations of material existence.

seen so often in CE movies and smokes it officiously from a long black holder.

"You're right about that," I mutter. She's referring to Vinneas and Imway, both of whom used to spend the bulk of their free hours here but have become notably scarce since going on active duty for the Legion. Vinneas at least has the excuse of travel-necessary-to-the-continued-viability-of-the-war-effort, but as far as I can tell, all Imway does is hang around the Stabulum playing whist or tarot with the other equites and occasionally interrupting my repair work to insinuate that my time would be better spent polishing his precious FireChaser. I'm willing to admit (privately anyway) that the shop hasn't been the same the past few weeks, but Lady's sulkily employed tones of high tragedy and melodrama are beginning to grate. I blame the movies.

One benefit to being largely ignored by your two best friends, however, is that it gives you more time for your hobbies, and the Project has seen marked improvement as a result. "Would you mind holding those schematics back up? It's hard to work with your face in the way."

"*Your* face, you mean," Lady points out, rudely but not inaccurately. The two of us are physically identical, in a dermo-musculoskeletal sense. "And who cares what I do anyway? We imaginary friends are known for our flightiness."

"Oh, Lady, no reason to get offended. I only said that because you're not real. Now move."

"Sheesh" is Lady's take on my attitude. "I was only joking. Maybe if you'd leave the shop once in a while, you wouldn't be such a great big phenomenal bore. You've got yucky bags under your eyes, and you've already inverted two gwayd links." Lady rustles the schematics, pointing out the faulty connections with a hand sheathed in long gloves, then watches through a pair of unnecessary opera glasses while I make the suggested adjustments.

I give the core a final once-over, devoting special attention to the film of viatically conductive material along the grips and back of the throne, before pulling myself up by the chest cavity's rim. "You ready to give this a shot?" I ask Lady, rolling up her curtain of mirrors and tucking it beneath my arm.

She speaks in a muffled voice, for effect. "Does my opinion actually matter?"

"Not at all. That was a rhetorical question."

My work suit is thoroughly spattered in glowing blue gwayd,[2] and even though the stain is already fading, I brush at it offhandedly, feeling the distant tingle, like a sleeping limb coming back to life.

"Then allow me to rhetorically tell you this is a waste of time." Lady has reappeared on her wall, watching me through the mosaic of variously sized mirrors as though from behind a fence. She puffs dramatically on her cigarette, exhales. "You've already reconfigured the core a million different ways. If you'd only swallow your pride and—"

"Just go see if the testing floor is clear."

Lady, huffing with offense, flounces from view. When she returns, her evening wear has been replaced by a wholly gratuitous array of protective equipment, apparently meant to signify some ludicrous amount of impending danger. Safety goggles and other precautions that might be considered sensible had Lady an actual corporeal body to injure mix freely with accessories plainly intended as hyperbole: a helmet from some extinct CE sport, oven mitts, pillows belted to her chest and back. "All clear," she says, mumbling around her mouth guard. "Let's get this over with."

The blank wall behind me evaporates, revealing the empty expanse of Testing Floor Sixteen. Until recently, all work pertaining to the Project was restricted to my own facilities. I have everything necessary for partial activations, basic durability and performance trials, fabrication of materials.[3] But ever since we progressed to full activation, Lady has insisted we move someplace where our tests will not result in her needing to replace her mirrors every other day. Because the Project violates just about every

---

2 One of the Project's many marvelous and revolutionary innovations; gwayd in the Legion's ranks of battle-ready equi tends to be red or orange, occasionally yellow.

3 Though, admittedly, very little of the corresponding safety and containment equipment. Brewing the components for an equus from scratch (a necessity as most of the parts needed for the Project were nonexistent until I invented them) involves more than a few rather delicate and volatile processes, none of which an aspiring philosopher like myself is authorized to perform on her own. Requesting a viatic ontologressor or plystecratic sheath would have telegraphed what I was doing to the whole Academy, so I decided to do some by-the-seat-of-my-trousers flying. There were a few dicey moments, but it all worked out just fine, not a single disaster worth mentioning . . . luckily. Thelemic toxicity is highly unpleasant and not exactly easy to explain to one's research advisors.

rule the Academy has, not to mention a number of Fabrica regulations pertaining to the treatment of dangerous materials and Stabulum protocols regarding disposal of same, all experimentation must be conducted covertly. The present time is 0239 hours, and TF 16 should be abandoned until 0600 at least.

Though smaller than most equi active in the Legion, the Project is still large enough that his head would punch through the ceiling of my workshop when standing at his full height. He spends most of his time in a knee-hugging crouch, encased in a nifty contraption of my own design that Lady fondly calls the "egg crate." The crate is a sturdy cube of reinforced interlocking framework, infused with customized weightlessness artifices that allow me to convey the Project's multitonne bulk with ease. Once the Project is settled in the center of Testing Floor Sixteen, the egg crate pulls clear to reveal his full, glimmering splendor.

I will admit that to someone without my overwhelming maternal investment, the Project would cut quite the ghastly figure. When fully arrayed in the armor I'm building to his measurements, a marble-quartz amalgam that finishes to a gallant and heroic white, I have no doubt he will be absolutely magnificent, but naked as he is, the impression is more of a flayed corpse. Stripped-down equi are always mildly unsettling, too thick about the shoulders and limbs to be really human, with the head—undersized, eyeless, mouthless—hinting at alien or potentially demonic lineage. The Legion's current models are all built with single-alloy thurgomuscle, though, which at least gives their exposed bodies the clean, machined look of an anatomical model cast in metal. The Project's muscle, by contrast, is a never-before-seen composite conceived and fabricated entirely by me, which demonstrates unheard-of levels of speed and power in early-stage testing, but also has an unfortunate combination of greasy opalescence and deep gunmetal coloring that, in certain lights, gives it the look of dark meat on poultry.

Once he's up and running, the Project will be absolutely worth the absurd amount of time I've spent assembling him, the risk of expulsion-slash-incarceration, and the fact that I can no longer eat fried chicken. All my experiments, all my calculations, all my instincts, tell me he's already stratospherically more advanced than anything the Legion has. But before he can begin trampling notions about the limits of equus design, not to mention what a cadet who's failed her general exams three times running[4] can accomplish, I have to calibrate his interface, matching the movements of the mighty beast to the intentions of the frail human being inside. For that, I have to activate him all at once, so that I can tweak and tinker with his fine motor functions. In this regard, the Project has proven somewhat uncooperative, no doubt due to the delicacy of his groundbreaking design. Fully activating an equus for the first time is like setting the keystone into a newly built arch: All the supporting forces are coming together at this single point, and once that's stable, you've got a nearly unshakable whole, but unless it's done just right, the whole thing falls apart. In the Project's case, the pieces that need to be held in suspension—the nebulous structures of artifice that make him a magnificent, animated symphony instead of a creepy hunk of inert material—are singularly and exceptionally precarious. With the exception of his frame,[5] every bit of him, down to the tiniest filament of muscle, constitutes a feat of engineering previously thought impossible, all of it woven together with a system of artifices so elegant and complex that likening it to the corresponding blocks in a normal equus would be like comparing a dragonfly to a paper airplane. Needless to say, not an easy puzzle to assemble on the fly. This will be my fifth attempted activation in as many weeks.

Equi can only be fully controlled from inside their core, and since the Project doesn't have working entry protocols, I have to just climb into his open chest cavity. I settle onto the throne and begin strapping myself in,[6] running through the activation checklist in my mind. Throne contact? Check. Starting posture? Check. Sensory receptors? Almost completely lacking, but we'll add those later. Hardheaded determination and unreasonable sense of optimism? Check.

From the direction of my workshop, Lady Jane's voice echoes across

---

4 Only because of the Academy's ridiculously arbitrary and outmoded requirements, I might add.

5 Constructed mostly out of skeletons scheduled for disposal. Further misconduct for which I could be strung up by my thumbs.

6 Fully functional equi keep their animi in place by means of dampening artifices, with actual physical restraints only activating in scenarios involving loss of thelemity or gwayd failure. The Project lacks all such safeguards, of course.

the testing floor. "I'm just going to go ahead one more time and register my opinion that this is a horrible idea."

"Noted," I say, adjusting the armrests and grips. "Here we go!"

I take a deep breath, close my hands around the Project's grips, and settle back into the throne,[7] trying to imagine myself seeping down, flowing out into the great metal body, imbuing it with my soul or essence or whatever part of you makes an equus work. Above me, the branching gwayd canals begin to glow a gentle blue. Animation has always seemed a pretty frivolous study to me, but since beginning the Project, I've been working on perfecting my skills.

I shut my eyes, tell myself I *am* the Project. His arms are my arms. His legs, my legs. I can feel it starting to work, feel the shiver down his spine (*my* spine), spreading out toward the extremities. Sensation flows into the tips of his fingers, and I'm thinking this might really work, when suddenly the Project's fist clamps shut and swings wildly to the side.

"Gah!" I shout, trying to restrain the hand, but it won't respond. I open my eyes just in time to see the egg crate fold with a shrieking groan as the Project's right arm smashes into it. I concentrate everything on seizing back control of the arm, but just then it goes dead, and the Project's left leg kicks out, launching us up and back. No sooner have I shifted attention to the leg than the Project's torso begins to twist and his head to jerk, then the rest of his body, activating and deactivating in random, manic spasms. In moments, the egg crate has been flattened, its hyper-durable structure crumpling like wet paper as the Project thrashes and rolls across the testing floor. I see, alternately, ceiling, floor, ceiling. Distantly, I hear Lady screaming for me to hit the kill button, but centrifugal force has made my own personal arm almost too heavy to move, my vision dimming as the blood rushes from my brain. And then the Project pauses, like he's catching his breath, and it's enough for me to punch the big red button marked "Oops" mounted above my head.

There is a series of popping explosions as the Project's gwayd canals blow. Glowing blue gwayd sprays freely over the testing floor, gushing from predetermined cut points at the Project's wrists, elbows, knees. A particu-

---

7 Actually just one of my reading chairs bolted into the Project's chest cavity—serviceable but somewhat hack in appearance compared to legionary thrones with their ergonomic design and exemplary lumbar support.

larly heady jet from the neck coats the walls blue as the Project continues to convulse, but more slowly now, until, finally, he slumps, crashes to his knees, and collapses sideways to the floor.

Everything is silent except for my breath and the last glugging flow of gwayd. I watch the weakening dribble of blue drip from the edge of the Project's chest cavity, things still spinning, but only in a dizzy psycho-perceptive way.

Again I hear the echoing voice of Lady Jane. "Kizabel? Are you dead?"

Not unsurprisingly, I've survived. Forgetting the Project's posture, I pull at the straps holding me to the throne and fall nearly a meter to the testing floor with an ectoplasmic splash of gwayd. Slowly, heart still thudding, I get to my feet and regard the Project, a gruesome, otherworldly rag doll splayed in glowing blue muck.

"You piece of shit!" I scream, kicking him in his metal knee. I'm furious; I was so sure this time it would actually happen. "You stupid, shitty piece of shit!"

Lady Jane stays quiet until I've tired myself out. "We can try again," she says. "I've checked all your calculations. He's going to work."

"No, you were right." I flop down, leaning on the Project's shin, my feet and legs tingling in the centimeters-deep flood of gwayd drenching Testing Floor Sixteen. "None of the new configurations have made any real difference. The problem isn't with the gwayd canals."

What am I even doing? I've been at this for eighteen hours straight, on top of thousands already spent, ignoring my courses, hardly leaving the shop except to find food or visit the Stabulum. I would have to sit down and seriously review my mental records to recall the last time I saw non-artificial sunlight or had a conversation lasting more than two sentences with a sapient being I didn't build myself. And why? For what? Because I'm convinced the Project is oh-so-important, more than just another of the cute, silly toys everyone thinks I'm such a genius at building?

If Vinneas were here, he'd give me his patented even-the-worst-debacle-has-its-funny-side grin and set to pulling my problem apart, turning it upside down and inside out. And Imway, he'd be lounging somewhere flipping playing cards into a hat, unconcerned with the fact that I'd just laid waste to everything within a thirty-meter radius and asking when I'd be done with this Project of mine already so he could take it for a spin, as if my most devastating setbacks were simply details I was guaranteed to work out sooner or later, as if the most infernal equus I could design wouldn't dare—or even contemplate—not working for him, and in all likelihood being infuriatingly right. But they're gone, both of them, Vinneas off to an endless succession of godforsaken settlements, Imway on permanent vacation in his own bloated ego. Leaving me sulking and far too close to a full-blown wallow.

"You'll figure it out," Lady says.

I sigh, heave myself up, start wringing out my suit. "Yeah, I know." The trouble is, I think I already know what's wrong, and it's not something I can fix myself. "Let's go back to last week's design. That was the best so far. You make the adjustments. I'll try and clean this place up before some-one sees it and throws us in prison."

"Will you at least consider asking—"

"*No*," I say, probably a little too harshly. "Now, are you going to do what I asked, or will I have to make another instara who will?"

"I worry about you, that's all. If you keep this up, you're going to hurt yourself. And what happened to me being your imaginary friend?"

"You're not imaginary."

In my workshop, Lady has conjured an enormous desk behind her mirrors, cluttered with messily leaning stacks of paper and vintage calcu-lating machines. She wears a short-sleeved button-down shirt, front pocket stuffed with pens, and a necktie of nearly unthinkable ugliness. Regarding me seriously from beneath a transparent green visor, she says, "I'm still your friend."

THIRTY-FIVE

KIZABEL

Without the egg crate to help, it takes the better part of two hours just to transfer the mess I've made from Testing Floor Sixteen back to my workshop. Fortunately, TF 16 has endured so many scrapes, dents, and miscellaneous thelemic traumas over its lifetime that the Project's latest tantrum adds little to the general wear and tear, and gwayd vanishes on its own after a few minutes, saving me the two weeks it would have likely required to mop up an equivalent amount of oil, say, or actual organic blood. I've only just got the Project and the remains of the egg crate piled in a mountainous heap, the whole thing covered by an (admittedly pretty lame) concealment artifice, when TF 16 starts to light up. Lady seals the wall of my workshop mere seconds, I can only assume, before whoever reserved the 0600 slot saunters in, coffee and croissant in hand.

Once I've changed into my Academy uniform and consumed, at Lady's insistence, 1.4 muffins and a glass of milk, I'm just in time to be half an hour late to my morning lessons.[1] My tardiness earns me three hours of work detail—nothing I can't handle, since I can apply the time I've logged volunteering at the Stabulum.

I spend the rest of the day a shuffling sleepwalker, distant and glassy-eyed, dreaming only of the Project swept untidily into a corner of my workshop. I'm expected at the Stabulum by 1600, but when my lessons let

---

1 The Academy's policies regarding academic absenteeism are alarmingly strict, and students not in good standing attendance-wise at the end of a given scholastic period are ineligible for advancement exams. I'm dangerously near my limit, which is no good if I ever intend to get my career out of the humiliating state of confusion it's presently in.

out, I take a detour through the School of Philosophy, toward the stubbly outer tower where Dr. Afşar[2] keeps his study.

The Doc[3] is widely considered one of the founding fathers of irrational mechanics and could easily have an office right next door to the Curator but has chosen this remote spot largely to avoid the worshipful attention of academics and officials who grew up studying his work. He spends most of his time in the Realms, advising our commanders at the Front, but makes a point of returning to Hestia every so often to catch up on advancements in the field he helped build.

Since it isn't unusual for fifty years or more to have passed between one visit and the next, the Doc always finds himself somewhat behind the cutting edge. Most of his time is spent reading and muttering in good-natured astonishment over the things we fast-timers have been up to in his absence, but occasionally he will have questions his books can't answer. In such instances, he requests a tutor from the Academy, an OA where possible, as these tend to be relatively untainted by respect for his reputation. Fully accredited philosophers and other senior academics, he's found, often shy away from telling him when one of his theories has been disproven.

When Dr. Afşar needed someone to explain the current state of ingenic and thelemically engineered materials, the Curator sent me in. I was halfway through a description of the Euvoria Process before I realized the surrounding research, developed almost thirty years ago, thoroughly discredited Afşar's Third Hypothesis—proposed, of course, by Dr. Afşar. Ever since, I've had a standing invitation to visit his office any hour of the day or night.

The Doc greets me with his usual "Ah, Miss Kizabel, welcome, welcome." Like most veterans,[4] he speaks with an accent, in his case from

---

2 Yes, that's right: *the* Dr. Afşar, as in Afşar's Theory, the Afşar Effect, the Afşar-Epstein Principle, Afşar's Laws, and so on.

3 Short for "Doctor," a CE academic distinction equivalent to our "Philosopher;" not to be confused with *medical* doctor, roughly synonymous with a legionary medic of class five or higher.

4 Dr. Afşar has never been in combat, as far as I know; the term "veteran" has come, at least informally, to include anyone who has visited the Realms, and connotes not only a person who has been to war but also someone displaced in time and culture.

Turkey, the Doc's CE nation of origin. "What brings you to my corner of our illustrious Academy?"

One of Dr. Afşar's many wonderful attributes is his broad disregard for the rules and conventions of Principate society. His attitude seems to be that since he was here first, his way of doing things takes precedence. For the most part, people just go along with it. I've seen him affect a kind of doddering obliviousness if he happens to offend someone but only to mask his general indifference. I get the feeling that this new world of ours isn't entirely real to him, that he walks among us like a ghost, gliding through our architecture of laws and regulations like mist. It means I don't have to be coy when I tell him about the Project. I lay it all out for him— my ideas, my triumphs, but mostly my woes—while he makes us tea.

Dr. Afşar keeps a pot of tea perpetually brewing in his study and drinks constantly as he works, a practice he claims aids in his thinking by forcing him to take regular bathroom breaks, during which time he can assimilate whatever he's just read. His teapot has a strange double-stacked structure, like one teapot whose lid is for some reason yet another teapot.

"A fascinating enterprise, this Project of yours," he says. He has set out two tulip-shaped glasses and fills each practically to the brim, first pouring dark tawny tea from the top pot, then diluting with hot water from the bottom. The concoction, delivered to me on a tiny saucer, steams with a violent, near-boiling intensity, like an active volcano. "I can see why you would take the risk of assembling it yourself. A machine with the capabilities you describe would be very valuable to our Legion."

This is why the Doc is my favorite. Rather than lecturing me on the many and really quite ludicrous dangers involved in the Project's more-high-octane parts, he has chosen to aid and abet. And it's true: One reason I risked starting the Project at all is that I'm certain my transgressions will be completely glossed over if I can ever get him to work. People around here will overlook a lot of tomfoolery for the right results. I try to take a sip of my tea, just touching the liquid to my lips. The heat is alarming. "I won't know for sure until I activate him," I say.

"That is the way with thelemity, isn't it? We've been studying it for five centuries, and there's so little we really understand." The Doc guzzles freely; his tongue must be the consistency of rhinoceros hide. "Every time I come back to Earth, I expect someone will have it all figured out. Greedy of me, I know, thinking I can simply travel through time and return to all my questions answered. But you and your Project are proof we're making real progress. I still remember the first equi—our soldiers rode on top of them, did you know? Like gigantic horses. The innovation of putting a person inside is quite new—to me, anyway. That's where the word 'equus' comes from. It's an ancient word for 'horse.' But I'm sure you knew that." He smiles, setting down his glass. "This problem with your Project must be worrying you more than I thought. Usually, I can rely on you to stop me with a snide comment whenever I become tedious."

"I'm sorry, sir. Would you like a snide comment now, or should I wait for the next time you descend into tedium?"

"No need to exert yourself." Somehow he's finished his tea and started on a second glass. "Now, as for your Project, my first instinct is that there must be some trouble with the power systems. The type of erratic activation you describe is most often the result of uneven or incomplete animation, or of inconsistent signals from the core structure. I think, however, that you have already figured out the trouble but are as yet unwilling to accept the truth of it."

"Well, yeah, I've got a few ideas," I admit, stammering slightly in surprise, "but you know volumes more than I do. You were the first to devote any real scientific attention to animation, right? You and Dr. Xiao."

"Very true," the Doc allows, "but I am far from current in the field as it is. You, Miss Kizabel, are yourself appreciably better versed in the present state of the art. And so why come to me? It could not be for my expertise. I rather think you are here to talk yourself out of something or into it."

"You really are a genius," I say, forcing a smirk. He's right: For a while now I've known, or at least strongly suspected, that the Project simply won't activate without more power. He's more demanding than a normal equus: Those marvelous new muscles, his unique internal arrangements, it's all too much for me to animate on my own. I thought if I reworked his gwayd canals, made them more efficient, I'd be able to get him working, but I was wrong.

If I want to activate the Project myself, I'll have to take him down to the skeleton and rebuild him, swapping out most of my custom parts for the boring, everyday, unexceptional stuff of legionary stock equi. I get a strangled, sweaty feeling just thinking about it, not because I'll have to start over—I've done that often enough—but because it means compromising the Project and everything he could be, just because I'm not good enough to make him work. It would be the same as giving up. All that time in the lab, missing school and sleep and all but the barest simulacrum of human contact, for nothing.

Even after I've finished my tea and left Dr. Afşar's study for the Stabulum, I still hold out the hope that I'll stumble onto some miraculous solution. I go as far as describing my problem to Hezaro while we're working on HeavensHammer, phrasing things in terms of purely theoretical conjecture, supposed rumors among splatterheads[5] of highly experimental equi losing control during activation. His analysis only confirms what the Doc told me, and what I already knew myself. Maybe when the Project is perfected and refined and free of hiccups, I'll be able to pilot him myself, but if I want him to activate now, I'll need an expert.

When Hezaro calls a break, I excuse myself from the crew's usual fare of instant noodles and obsessive equus-related banter and make my way down the stalls to where the 126th have made camp. It's common for fighters in the Armored Cavalry to hold vigil around their rides, particularly when they're on standby, but the 126th takes this reasonable gesture toward readiness and magnifies it to the point of absurdity. They're the newest equites in the Legion, only just promoted from the Academy, and they like playing soldier so much they'll hardly stop even to sleep.

They're in their usual spot, under the stern gaze of StarHunter, flinging playing cards around and filling the Stabulum with brassy laughter. Sensen, their self-appointed guard dog and all-around dealer-out of shit, intercepts me as I walk up with a "Who goes there?"

"It's me, Kizabel," I say, "as you can obviously see from where you're standing."

"Sorry," says Sensen, whose understanding of remorse is, as far as I can tell, abstract at best. "We've been keeping a tighter watch lately. Can't have superfluous personnel hanging around in case we need to sortie. Anyone without business here will just have to move along. You understand."

The way she's looking at me implies that I am one of the superfluous

---

5 Splatterhead, *n*.: anyone with a deep technical interest in animation, specifically in reference to equi; derives from the distinctive "splattering" of gwayd that often occurs during the repair, maintenance, and construction of same; used both as an endonym among splatterheads and pejoratively by those who lack proper understanding and appreciation for their artistry.

personnel who will just have to move along, which is ridiculous because I'm here almost every day doing bodywork on FireChaser. "Sure, I just need to talk with Imway."

I start toward the table where the rest of the 126th is still sitting, and Sensen steps to the side, like she's planning to block my way, but just then, Imway calls out, "What's up, Kiz?" He's tilted back on his chair, feet up, grinning at me over a fan of cards.

"I need your help with something," I say.

Imway hands his cards to Allomar, who's been observing the game over his shoulder, and leaves the table. Imway always has time for me—I'm looking after his baby, after all.

FireChaser was damaged on the escadrille's first sortie, but as her injuries are 100 percent superficial, utterly lacking in functional consequences, she isn't exactly top priority for the repair crews. It drives Imway bonkers, though, having his equus all scratched up like that, so I'm giving her a full polish, thereby earning me his professional gratitude and broad tolerance from the rest of his escadrille—most of them, anyway.

"So what's up with Sensen?" I ask once we're out of earshot. "She's acting like I ate the last nonfat yogurt."

Imway glances back to the table, where play has slowed somewhat to allow the 126th to mutter among themselves. "Oh, yeah, right," he says. "*That.* Not important." He smiles rakishly. "Certain people don't think you should be hanging around anymore—can't be trusted with our equi after what happened."

The way he says "certain people" leaves little doubt that Sensen is one or all of the "people" in question. "What happened," I can only assume, is a reference to one of my cadets breaking Sensen's nose. There wasn't any lasting damage, though for a while Sensen was rather entertainingly disfigured. Why this should reflect on me is anyone's guess.

"You've got to admit it wasn't your smartest move," Imway says, once I have solicited his opinion on the matter. "Bringing those cadets in here, with all this valuable Legion equipment. Pretty immature, if I had to describe it."

"*Immature?*" I scoff. "Are you serious? This from the guy who destroyed an MSR just to make some kind of macho point?"

Imway sighs the sigh of an exhausted adult beleaguered by stubborn children. "The situation was out of control, Kiz. I had to regain control. I don't expect you to understand."

"What's *that* supposed to mean?"

"It's not supposed to mean anything. You just don't know what it's like to have people under your command. I'm responsible for my 'drille, and—"

"And because I can't pass my stupid leadership quals, you think I don't know what it's like to be responsible for people."

"I didn't say that."

"I'll have you know I was hosting a *really excellent* tour before you started beating up one of my cadets."

The accusation makes him flinch, I'm pleased to see, but it doesn't slow him down. "She's a noco, Kiz, and she was holding a grudge against me from when we captured her tribe out in the valley—her tribe that had been out there for months, *attacking the city*. If you'd given any thought at all to the people you were leading, you might have guessed she'd cause problems. Or did that big brain of yours just happen not to notice how one of your Sixth-Class cadets was—I don't know—pretty obviously not twelve years old?"

"Sure, fine, but how was I supposed to know you would start a fight with her?"

"She started the fight, not me."

"Great excuse, oh exalted leader. Is that the sort of responsibility they teach you in the Legion? *'She started it'?*" I perform this last statement with an exaggeratedly infantile whine. "You're an *eques*, Way. You should be able to handle some random noco without burning down most of the Stabulum in the process."

He shakes his head, sighing another of those the-life-of-an-adult-is-a-thankless-one sighs. "Listen, I already got a citation for conduct. I don't need you mad at me, too. Let's just forget about it."

I'm not quite ready to stop being mad, but Imway chooses this moment to unleash one of his more charming smiles. He possesses conspicuously greater than the usual allotment of handsomeness, an endowment of fine-tuned physical refinement that seems neither reasonable nor fair, cutting a shining and burnished figure that brings to mind a sculpture of some BCE pagan god—Apollo or Ares, maybe—trimmed in silver spectacles. A soothing fog settles over my mind, convincing me that I don't want to fight with Imway, that I am eager to see us on good terms once again. This is how almost all of my arguments with Imway end, and most of the time,

I'm seriously pissed off with myself a few hours later, but somehow even knowing this ahead of time never seems to matter. "Sure, fine, great," I say.

"And I'll let you keep working on FireChaser, of course," he adds magnanimously.

That breaks right through my dreamy little interlude. "*Excuse* me?"

"FireChaser," he says, as if I could possibly forget what his equus is called. "Some of the others—you know, they don't think I should let you work on her anymore."

"*Let* me work on her?"

"Yes, right, after—but like I said, forget about it. I'm squad dek, and I make the calls, so that's the end of it."

I am without words. Thirty seconds or more pass during which all thoughts come in sputtering, inarticulate bubbles of rage, while Imway continues grinning his silly, self-satisfied, stupidly handsome grin, until finally I say, "Listen up, Way." I advance, poking him in the chest. "I don't come in here and polish up that equus of yours because I *enjoy* it. It doesn't plug some cosmic emptiness in my soul or fulfill me in a hundred magical and ineffable ways. I do it as a *favor to you*, because we're *friends*. Everyone here is prodigiously, overwhelmingly busy, and you know what? I just realized it's *irresponsible* of me to waste my time buffing out scratches just so you can have a pretty ride. I'm done. Good luck finding someone else who'll give a shit about your baby's boo-boo."

Imway doesn't appear to have heard me. His grin has not faltered; animal magnetism continues to flow from him unabated. "You don't mean that, Kiz," he says.

"I do mean that, Way. Why don't you learn to do your own work, or better yet, get Sensen to do it? Or that noco—she was pretty good with an MSR. Maybe you could ask *her*."

"Kiz," he says, cajoling. "Kizmeister. Kizerino. Kizopolis. Don't be like that. Come on—what did you want to ask me anyway?"

I'd been almost ready to relent, to give in, because the truth is I *do* like working on FireChaser. She's an awesome machine, and it's strangely calming, tuning up an equus like that, getting her to sing for you. But now Imway has reminded me why I'm here: to ask for his help with the Project. Except now I'm never going to ask.

I was wrong before: Imway and I *aren't* friends. To him I'm just another splatterhead, an interchangeable piece of equipment, my only standout trait being that he can get special treatment from me by flashing that stupid beautiful smile of his like an all-access VIP executive-level badge. I'm 99.999 percent sure it wasn't always this way with him. There was a time in our not-so-ancient history when we really did matter to each other. But not anymore. Somewhere along the line, I became a brain with a wrench.

I have no trouble envisioning what it would be like introducing him to the Project, what an insufferable jerk he'd be about it. If we ever did get the thing working, he'd probably just strut around telling people how he'd invented this fantastic equus with a little help from good ol' Kizabel.

"Forget it, Way," I say. "You're on your own."

And so, it appears, am I.

THIRTY-SIX

KIZABEL

For the rest of the evening, my mind is a scribbly black cloud of resentful wrath. The crew on HeavensHammer gives me a wide berth as I bash bits of armor back into place, while Lady, sensing my dark, choleric state, forgoes her usual cheeky greeting when I return to the workshop, posting her revised gwayd schematics without a peep. I growl ferally for several minutes before collapsing into an insensate coma, awakening hours later feeling more coherent but no less irate.

As soon as I get my hands on the Project, though, the inclement weather inside my skull begins to clear. Working on the Project is like that: I can't keep a bad mood going. Before I know it, I'm securely in my groove, sealing broken gwayd canals and singing along as the Clash[1] echoes through my workshop, while Lady putters around in the guise of a CE 1950s housewife—an uncharacteristic show of solidarity for my cleanup efforts, though only a token one as she remains unsullied by the rigors of manual labor, shuffling nimbly in high heels and pearls, lavender dress spotless beneath a crisp white apron.

I have the Project hoisted up by his armpits—an undignified pose but better than the way I left him—and am perched atop his head when from below comes a strange, ringing sound. I look down to see Lady, leaning on a vacuum cleaner[2] with a telephone[3] wedged against her chin. "Hold on, I'll

---

1 While the past five centuries have seen startling advances in the field of irrational mechanics, not to mention overall military badassery, wartime society has proven a virtual wasteland artistically, especially when it comes to music. With very few exceptions, the only music worth listening to is prewar, as I have been discovering with Lady's help. The two of us have been cultivating a particular taste for CE 1970s British punk rock.

2 CE domestic housekeeping technology.

3 Vintage CE communication device.

ask her," she says, then calls up to me. "Hey, Kizabel, there's someone here
to see you."

"Who is it?"

"Her name is Rachel Ochre," Lady says, without having to inquire by
way of telephone. "She came by a few times while you were out, too."

I can't think of anyone I know by the strange name of Rachel Ochre,
but then it hits me: the Amazon. That giantess I had to lead around all day,
looming behind my tour of Sixth-Class cadets. "Tell her I'm busy."

Lady mutters into her telephone, then calls to me, "She says she'll wait,
if you don't mind. She seems like a very polite girl," Lady offers, since she
can tell I'm annoyed.

"Fine, fine. Tell her I'll be there in a minute," I grumble, and proceed
to dismount and conceal the Project.

I'd forgotten how pretty she was. To the extent I concerned myself
with Cadet Rachel Ochre at all, the image in my mind was of the brawl-
ing, slavering barbarian Imway described—quite at odds with this tall girl
in her immaculate gray cadet's uniform, hair done up neatly like an artifact of antique brass; even the dark birthmark on her neck is more of an
accessory than a blemish. And not a drop of drool anywhere.

"Hello, Miss Kizabel," she says, tentative, words colored in her noco
accent. "May I come in?"

However friendly she looks, I'm not about to let her anywhere near the
Project. I lean against the door, blocking any view of my workshop. "Let's
talk here. You realize it's practically 0400, don't you?"

"I'm sorry to disturb you," she says bashfully. "I'd heard you keep odd
hours, and anyway I couldn't sleep." She pauses, gathering herself for
something, it seems, and says, "I'd like to ask you a favor."

That word, "favor," and this girl's overall manner of a supplicant seeking the wisdom of some eminent individual, are all that keep me from
shutting the door in her face. "Go on," I prompt her.

"I was wondering if you would be willing to tutor me."

"The Academy has plenty of tutors, Rachel Ochre," I say, probably
playing up my exhaustion a little more than necessary. "I can put you in
touch with a few good ones, but it's not something I do myself."

I'm about to step back into my shop, but she actually reaches out to stop
me. "Please. The Academy people aren't about to teach me what I need to
know. They'll insist on me 'establishing a firm knowledge base' and 'achiev-

ing a broad and well-rounded education.'" She uses these familiar Academy phrases fluently and without any trace of an accent, a pitch-perfect impression of a Sixth-Class rhetor. "I don't have time for that. I need to be ready to fight for the Legion, and soon."

"And what makes you think I can help?" I say, more put off than ever. "I'm not in the Legion, and you've never seen me fight."

"You don't have to fight to know *how* to fight." She has become insistent, eager, excited. "You *understand*, and that's what matters. Today in lessons, we were discussing Mr. Philosopher Oojtelli's experiment, and every cadet there knew more than our own rhetor because *you* had explained it to us. Even I got it, and if you'd seen me in class, you'd know that's something."

I'm flattered, sure. My ego is purring comfortably under this girl's well-executed deep-tissue massage, but that doesn't change anything. "Listen, Rachel Ochre—"

"Just Rachel is fine. Rae, if you don't mind."

"Right, Rae. I'm sorry, but I simply don't have time to take on a student."

"I don't expect you to do it out of charity," she says, desperation flickering behind her eyes. "I'll find some way to pay you back—clean up your workshop, or run errands, or bring your supper from the cafeteria. Whatever you need."

"I'm just too busy right now. Between school, and volunteering, and—" I almost mention the Project, but stop myself. "I just have too much to do."

Rae is crestfallen. "Will you think about it?"

"Sure," I say, feeling guilty somehow. "But, Rae, honestly, there isn't much for you to do around here."

At this point we are interrupted by the clatter of Lady Jane shouting angrily from my workshop. "Oh come *on*! You can*not* be serious!" Her tone is that of a person who can simply no longer hold her tongue. "Are you really going to stand there and tell this girl that there is *absolutely nothing she can help you with*?"

Rae's eyebrows furrow at the sound of my distinct vocalizations emerging from this unexpected vector. She glances in the direction of the voice, then back to me, attempting stoically to retain a neutral expression as Lady continues berating me.

"This is the girl from the Stabulum, isn't it?" Lady yells. "*Isn't it?* You told me all about how she piloted that MSR, and on her *first try*. And you're just going to act like you can't think of anything she could possibly do for you? Are you *insane*?"

"We don't even know if we can trust her!" I retort, addressing Lady over my shoulder at full volume.

"Like you're going to find anyone better!" Lady scoffs. "If she wants to learn badly enough to *get you supper*, I bet she can keep her mouth shut about *certain things*."

"I do know how to keep a secret," Rae interjects meekly, obviously bemused at my apparent shouting match with myself.

I look her over, appraising. Lady didn't see Rae piloting that MSR, but if anything, my post hoc description only downplayed how impressive it was, her operating those tentacles like she was raised part cephalopod. Even Imway would have had trouble pulling that off on his first try. So maybe.

"I do have one thing you might be able to do," I say. "Meet me tomorrow at 2300 in Lab III. And bring your R-102s."

Her initial reaction is of almost giddy relief, but then she hesitates. "What are R-102s?"

"R-102s?" I say, momentarily at a loss for a description. "They're, um, for swimming. A swimsuit. You would have been issued a pair when you started at the Academy."

Understanding blossoms on her face, and she smiles. "Where I'm from, we usually just swim in our birthday suit," she explains. Seeing my confusion, she clarifies, in a stage whisper, "That means naked."

I shut the door, feeling genuinely hopeful, to find Lady Jane grinning at me. "Oh, I *like* her."

THIRTY-SEVEN

KIZABEL

Cadet Rachel Ochre, who I am to call Rae, is waiting patiently for me outside Lab III when I arrive at 2317, not at all impatient over my seventeen-minute unpunctuality.

"I've got the R-102s underneath my uniform," she informs me as I open the laboratory door. Demonstrating sound common sense and logical reasoning, she has brought a towel as well. "Are we going swimming?"

"We're going to measure your viatic output," I tell her. Before us, Lab III slowly illuminates to reveal a large, square room, virtually empty save for a shallow pool of water set into the center. The pool is circular in shape and divided into several smaller concentric rings by means of retractable dividers, an arrangement that has the look of a gigantic liquid bull's-eye.

Most theories of irrational mechanics posit that, within an umbris, there is an infinite and inexhaustible quantity of thelemic potential. No one has figured out a way to actually prove this, or to measure thelemity directly, nor have we found a reliable way to quantify the ability of a given revenna or revennus to absorb and harness its energy. The only thing we can do, it seems, is measure thelemity's effects—that is, the results brought about by thelemic manipulation; *exempli gratia* if someone is manifesting electricity by means of thelemity, we would measure that manifestation in watts; if the energy in question is heat, we would measure in joules, *et cetera*. Animation, unknown before the war, was first described by Dr. Xiao Jyun Zi, who called the energy used to bring inanimate matter to life "viaty." The basic unit of viatic power, equal to the energy required to animate one cubic centimeter of distilled water, is named the "xiao" after her.

I am about to explain all of this to Rae, my first lesson as her tutor, when she says, "Oh, for animation, right?" She has already removed her jacket, kicked out of her shoes, and begun working on her trousers.

"That's right." I have with me no fewer than five notebooks of calculations and designs, which I set down on the squat, podium-like structure overlooking the circular pool. "Have you already had your efficiency evaluations?"[1]

"No, but we've studied it some in class," she says.

"Great." I do my best not to sound like I expected her brain to be more or less blank of all relevant education, which was absolutely the case. I think back, trying to recall what I studied when I was in Sixth Class. "So you're learning about irregular energies?"

"Only that one really," she says, and adds with a self-effacing shrug, "I'm a dud with all the rest I've tried."

That doesn't surprise me. Manifesting irregular energies without at least some understanding of the underlying theory borders on impossible. If Rae can animate by instinct alone, she's an even better prospect than I'd hoped. We'll see.

"All right," I say, once I've managed to activate the lab, the circular pool lighting from below with a soft white glow, the clear barrier over the water retracting just enough to expose the center of the bull's-eye. "Go stand in the middle there. When I give you the signal, I want you to animate as much of the water as you can."

The central pool holds 250,000 cubic centimeters of water, covering Rae to the ankles. If she can animate the whole thing, it will be an output of 250,000 Xi (xiaos, that is), or 250 kXi (kilo-xiaos, known informally as "kicks"). I'll need her to produce at least 4,000 kicks if she's going to have any hope of getting the Project to work.

Twenty minutes later, Rae is floating neck deep in a pillar of water nearly three meters tall, holding steady at 5,000 kicks like it's nothing.

---

[1] Revenni can vary drastically in their ability to manifest different energies, and as it's believed a person's capacity to harness thelemity remains relatively constant, we explain the difference in terms of efficiency. The same revenna might be capable of creating a virtual thunderstorm of electric power yet unable to generate enough heat to light a match; we would say such a revenna has high efficiency for electricity and low efficiency for heat. Cadets usually have their basic efficiencies measured sometime during their fourth-class year, but as Rae is old enough to have graduated Rhetoric entirely, it occurs to me she might already have taken this test, in which case I could have just asked for her score and saved us all some time.

"How am I doing?" she asks, treading water, wet hair toffee-brown and slicked over her head.

"Good," I say, furiously scribbling readings into my notebook. "Stupendous. Exemplary. You ready to try the next ring?"

She bobs up, legs kicking through the suspended water. "Let's do it!"

I introduce her to the Project that same night. Rae is exactly what I need, and though the Project is a long way from ready, I decide there's no point in remaining mysterious. Lady takes the unexpected company in stride, altering her homemaker's outfit to play the gracious hostess, apologizing profusely for the state of our workshop and its resemblance to the site of an extinction-level natural disaster, while I dismantle the concealing artifice at the corner of my workshop.

It occurs to me only after the artifice has dissolved from its skewed, cubist-looking representation of empty space—little more than token camouflage, I admit, and not nearly enough to dissuade anyone intent on finding the Project—to the Project himself, hanging from the ceiling like a side of meat, joints mangled from blown gwayd canals, knees dragging, knuckles resting palm up against the floor, that, excepting yours truly, Rae is the first real, actual, physical human being to see him. A wave of nervous apprehension rushes over me, and I wait, breath held, for her reaction.

But Rae is already approaching the Project, extending her hands, reverently taking one of his massive fingers between her palms, and when she looks back at me, it is with the awed, rapturous expression of someone who has just been handed a newborn infant. "What's his name?" she asks, voice slightly lowered, as if to avoid waking the Project from his slumber. Somehow she knows, instinctively, that the Project is a "he."

"His name?" I say disingenuously; I was not prepared for this question.

"Yeah," she says, half mocking now. "They all have names—something to strike terror into the hearts of your enemies, right? So what do you call him? SkullBreaker? PuppyEater? GrannyDisemboweler?"

I might as well tell her. We're in this together now. "Snuggles."

Rae lets loose a single bright peal of laughter. "Snuggles! I love it!"

"I want you to help me make him work," I say. "Someone has to animate him, so I can get his functions calibrated. It won't be easy, but I'm sure you can do it."

"Think about it before you say yes," Lady says, her foreboding tone only a little ironic. "He's a mean one, is our Snuggles."

"Aw, no way," Rae demurs, gazing fondly up at the Project. "He's a pussycat, you can tell. Just look at those eyes."

"He doesn't have any eyes," I feel obliged to point out.

"Guess I'll be careful, then."

In relatively short order, Rae has become a common fixture of the workshop, though as the Project still requires a good amount of stitching up following his last attempted activation, most of her time is spent listening to me and Lady lecture on various topics in irrational mechanics, I in my work suit reassembling the Project's mangled mechanisms, Lady in tweed and owlish spectacles strutting in front of a dusty chalkboard.

I had expected Rae's background in theoretical irrationality to be spotty at best. Instead, it turns out to be more or less nonexistent, the upshot being that everything I've seen her do, from grand feats of animation to a few crude but pretty spectacular manifestations, she has pulled off with little more than intuition and natural talent. No surprise, then, she'd be defeated by irregular energies, which are essentially nonintuitive and unnatural. In the case of regular energies, she has a whole lifetime of experience to use as reference. She can feel her way to the desired result. Feel doesn't work for irregular energies—most of them, anyway—because they fly in the face of the ordered universe we've always known. Akyrity, for example, takes a big steaming dump all over the first law of thermodynamics, and even if that isn't something most people recognize on sight, it still gives us the willies. Asking Rae to manipulate a force like that is like asking someone with no formal training in mathematics to multiply imaginary numbers. So step one for her will be to fill in gaps. I fish out all the textbooks I absconded with from Grammar and assign them as homework. Rae is less than overjoyed but acquiesces when I explain this reading is required and nonnegotiable.

Per Rae's request, we focus on subjects relating directly and unambiguously to combat. Contrary to her own self-assessment, she has a good, intuitive grasp on one of the most important and fundamental concepts in irrational mechanics, to wit, that mastery thereof is as much art as science.[2]

---

2 It would not be wholly inaccurate to say thelemity has a mind of its own. No matter how precisely an artifice is designed, there's always a degree of uncertainty in the execution, and very often whatever quirks come up seem more like the whims of a mischievous personality

"Like giving orders to a willful child" is Rae's analogy, delivered like a girl who's had a good deal of experience in that area.

We've been discussing compounding,[3] a topic essential to creating complex artifices but also necessary to making effectual use of thelemity in combat. When Rae first came to me, the very mention of compound artifices sent her into paroxysms of despair. To her, the subject was as unintelligible as a foreign language, which in a sense it is. The method the Academy teaches for composing artifices relies on heavily stylistic diction and syntax, creating verbal traps and cages with the goal of limiting thelemity's opportunities to go rogue and muck things up. It works well enough, but if you haven't been raised to it, the general impression is of so much gobbledygook. On top of that, most high-level compound artifices, by dint of their length and complexity, are also infusions, a subject in which Rae has already declared herself an ignoramus and an unteachable clod.

Once Rae understood that the Academy's labyrinthine style is only a means to an end, that there are multiple methods of producing the same effect, just as the same artifice can yield varying results on different occasions, it didn't take her long to come around to the one thing every good

---

than the workings of impersonal natural phenomena. The prevailing theory is that thelemity does not actually *want* in any real sense, that what looks like the exercise of free will in a given artifice is in reality the unconscious influence of the revenna producing the power, a kind of human contamination to a force that would otherwise be as sterile and predictable as gravity. But whether thelemity is putatively *alive* or not, it definitely acts that way, and so from a practical standpoint we have to treat it as such if we're to have any hope of getting it to work for us. A great many people never quite come to grips with this—the idea of living inside some deific, semi-sentient amoeba is existentially disturbing, not to mention totally icky—but not Rae.

3 Put simply, compounding (as the term implies) involves layering or combining a series of artifices to create a unified effect. Say, for example, you wanted to use thelemity to whip up a batch of chicken soup. You could compose an artifice to tackle the whole process at once, but that would be a long, difficult process, probably a bigger hassle than just going ahead and cooking the soup yourself. But if you divide the task into a number of smaller components—a kinetic artifice to chop and mix the ingredients, a thermal artifice to heat the broth, *et cetera*—not only would you end up with a much more manageable task, you could also use those pieces, with only minimal rearrangement and alteration, to make beef stew or clam chowder or any number of other recipes. A lengthy chicken-soup artifice, by contrast, would only make chicken soup.

artifex understands: that manipulating thelemity is about persuasion, not command.[4]

What all this means in Rae's case is that memorizing the Academy's usual canon of artifices is going to be disproportionately less effective for her compared to your average cadet. Instead, I give her exercises to help translate them into her own vernacular. After that, her progress is exponential. In hardly any time at all, she's writing basic infusions, generally on topics tending unnervingly toward gratuitous violence.

I'm curious to learn why Rae is so anxious to fling herself into a war she's only recently discovered, a war that was fought to a stalemate long before she was born and shows no indication of resolving itself anytime soon, but asking would be nosy and rude, and so I know Lady will say something if I just wait.

What we discover is that Naomi, the Legion's newest fontana, is actually Rae's baby sister, and Rae's single-minded determination to join the Legion is all about watching the girl's back. Not to protect her—Rae has few illusions about being anything but a squashable bug in a duel between fontani—but just so her sister won't have to go to war alone. Vinneas had described to me the frankly horrific series of events that led to that little girl's ending up in the Legion, and listening to Rae talk about her I feel outright ashamed at my own petty motivations. Whenever the subject of Naomi comes up, I find myself silently focusing on my work while Lady assures Rae we'll have her fit for legionary duty in no time.

And the work does progress quickly: It isn't long before Rae and the Project are both ready for some partials. I'm not at all surprised to learn Rae was a standout anima in her Sixth-Class lessons, but all the raw talent in the world wouldn't be enough to safely attempt activating an uncalibrated equus, let alone an experimental model composed largely of my own cockamamie inventions.

At the Academy, Rae could have expected at least a year or two fooling

---

4 The volumes of hyperprecise, legalistic language filling the Academy's libraries are an attempt to turn thelemity into something standardized and generic, something that can be taught and controlled. But you can never completely filter out the chaos and subjectivity from something inherently chaotic and subjective. Standardized artifices try to say everything, to cover all possible avenues, when what you really want to do is say the *right* thing, the way a single line of poetry can hold more meaning than a thousand pages of instructions. To really make an artifice work, you've got to understand what you're doing and why you're doing it.

around with bloog-sculpted dogs and cats, followed by another year working her way through a program of increasingly complex and demanding
equulei, before they let her anywhere near a working equus,[5] but lacking
any of the necessary training equipment, we'll just have to hook her up and
see what happens.

The first attempt is only a minor disaster, which to me translates as
almost unprecedented success. With great gentleness and many words of
apology, I remove the Project's arm, detaching the shoulder at the socket, and
mount it on the mostly refurbished egg crate in a position allowing ample
support and range of motion. Rae I seat on a makeshift throne at the crate's
center, about where the core would be were we dealing with a full equus and
not a disembodied arm, and connect her by means of a thick, sapphire-
colored cable of twisting gwayd canals. She has no trouble projecting herself
into the arm, and the twisting and flexing exercises she performs at my
request are convincing if a little clumsy, until I ask her to count to five on the
Project's fingers, and at four the hand goes rigid and chops violently downward, shattering a row of bookcases.

"Oh, Kizabel, I'm sorry!" Rae gasps, gwayd-covered and gazing in
self-recriminating horror at the surrounding devastation, the Project's arm
like a fallen tower, limp but for the hand's clawlike rictus.

"Are you kidding?" I say, emerging from behind the overturned desk
where I'd taken cover. "That was fantastic!"

"But I wrecked half of your workshop, and his arm—there's glowing
blue blood everywhere!"

"It's called gwayd," Lady chimes in, her costume construction-themed
for the evening. "It transmits viatic energy through the equus—people
would never be able to animate something that big and complex without
it. It's a lot easier to replace than blood and only stains your clothes for a
little while."

"You destroyed an eighth of the workshop at most," I add.

Despite my protestations and insistence that this was probably the best
activation the Project has ever seen, Rae blames herself entirely for the
damage. "I've never had one of these guys get away from me like that," she
says. She spends the rest of the night collecting the ruined bookshelves'

---

5 Which even then would have been some agreeable old model, well loved and well dented by
a thousand wannabe equites, and not my high-strung and finicky Project.

scattered contents, mostly obsolete infusions composed in my early days at the Academy, which I would be just as happy to throw out.

Further partials go just as well or better, and soon I am confident enough in Rae's burgeoning talents that I cease taking the Project apart, ministering to him piecemeal, and set my sights on a full trial.

Rae's skills improve in roughly inverse proportion to the quantity of undemolished items within the Project's reach, but even after the workshop is fully tidied of all damage and clutter for which Rae can claim any responsibility, Rae tidies on. She has decided that "straightening up a bit" will be among her services to me, and perseveres against my conviction that the workshop is straightened quite enough as it is. Lady, who has been after me for months to remedy the so-called deplorable confusion of my offices, only encourages her, tutting in annoyance as Rae unearths one layer of ancient sediment after another, squealing with exaggerated horror over moldy pizza and melted candy bars. Rae, meanwhile, frequently stops to marvel over some old experiment or other, a practice I'd find far more irritating if it weren't for her obviously earnest appreciation. The bottom layers of clutter are mostly early work that seems silly or pointless to me now, though occasionally Rae does find something I'm pleased to remember, as when one night she exclaims, "Is this an *underwater city*?"

I'd almost forgotten about *Associative Architecture*, and when I see her holding the skinny little green-leather-bound book, I feel a warm and welcome flush of pride. "It is," I say, straightening up from my position over the Project's spine. As yet he's little more than a torso and collection of limbs, but that will change quickly.

"And people can really live there? Normal people? Not—" She waggles her fingers to indicate the kinds of dubious unnatural transformations that might allow a human to survive underwater.

"Definitely," Lady says. If anyone was more obsessed with *Associative Architecture* and its more fanciful applications than I was, it was Lady. Behind her, the reflection of my workshop disappears, replaced by a metropolitan scene with seaweed and blooms of psychedelically colored jellyfish drifting over the streets. "The theory is completely sound. We spent weeks working out the proofs, Kizabel and Vinneas and me."

Rae, who has been gazing in wonder at my drawings, suddenly looks up. "Vinneas helped make this?"

"It's all based on his theories, actually," I admit, hopefully with less tetchiness than I feel. "What you're holding there is his First-Class thesis at Rhetoric, *Associative Architecture in Large System Dynamics*. It's about altering basic aspects of reality on an extensive scale. Caused quite a stir when he presented it at the Academy. If he wasn't already top-ranked for the School of Philosophy, that alone would have got him in."

"What about you and Lady?" Rae asks, brow furrowed with suspicion.

"We got credit for helping with the proofs and calculations. Or I did anyway," I clarify when Lady makes a face. "And we got this lab."

"What a horse's ass!" declares Rae, sneering. "And you let him waltz away like it was all his idea?"

"Well, associative architecture *was* his theory," I'm obliged to point out, though Rae's indignation does give me a small twinge of satisfaction. "We've been able to tweak certain basic features of the world for a long time—it's how we change the weather in Ninth City. But Vinneas was the one who figured out a way to apply almost any artifice to a wide area by altering the way thelemity actually flows within that space."

"*Emotions*, especially strong ones, influence how thelemity behaves," Lady says excitedly. "And if something really big has happened in a particular place, it can leave behind a kind of echo that does the same thing."

Rae has turned speculative. "You mean like someplace haunted."

"Exactly!" Lady squeals.

"Well, sort of," I clarify. "Certain types of events can leave an impression that alters the way thelemity works. Associative architecture is about weaving together those kinds of impressions to create effects on a broad scale. It's a little like changing a person's behavior, or way of thinking, through training and repetition."

"It's totally awesome, is what it is," Lady concludes.

"In theory," I add, before she can get too carried away. "We never actually got to try any of it out."

Rae is crestfallen to learn there is no actual underwater city. "Why not?"

"We would have needed to borrow a whole lot of fontani from the Legion, for one thing. And then there was the small matter of building an entire city at the bottom of the ocean. No way the Consulate was going to devote those kinds of resources to a school project. We did have a lot of fun, though."

There are actually two versions of our underwater megalopolis, dubbed

EASSaC-1 and EASSaC-2,[6] one in which our aquatic citizens are endowed with the ability to process water via their natural pulmonary systems, and another where the whole city is encased in a bubble of air that continually renews and circulates of its own volition. Both lacked any obvious value to the war effort. The same could be said of the city we designed to allow each inhabitant his or her own customized day-and-night cycle, the one where every physical action triggered a corresponding audible effect, creating a symphony out of the residents' daily activities, and just about every other example of the flurry of whimsy filling the final section of *Associative Architecture*, devoted (somewhat facetiously) to "practical applications."

"But you really could build it, right?" Rae contends hotly. "They've got you sneaking around just to work on Snuggles, and you made a goddamn underwater city!"

That has been my opinion in a nutshell for nearly a year, much of which time I spent partly convinced I was insane, delusional, or both. But seeing Rae so searingly furious over the necessary secrecy of my work is another shot of jet fuel to my ambitions.

Full activation of the Project, when it comes, is almost anticlimactic. I'm working around the core, fully assuming I have a long way left to go, when suddenly I realize all the gwayd canals are in place. I step back, glance at my schematics, give the Project a full once-over. Lady and Rae, noticing my change in rhythm, make inquiries. "I think we're ready to go," I tell them, still not completely sure.

"Then let's go," Rae says, enthusiastic, confident.

I'm still having difficulty sorting the trepidation from my sense of accomplishment. "Now?"

"Now. If you're ready, I'm ready."

I am expecting a fusillade of objections from Lady, but all she says is "I'll check the testing floor." She returns furnished for lighthearted outdoor spectating: a peachy sundress and wide-brimmed straw hat, binoculars hanging around her neck. "All clear!"

We're ready. I know it. If I were to delay things now, it would only be out of reluctance to entrust my Project to someone else. And so I cart Snuggles onto the testing floor and help Rae inside.

---

6 Environmentally Adjusted Strategically Subaquafied City 1 and 2, respectively.

"All right, just like we discussed," I call once I've returned to the relative safety of my workshop. "Just see if you can stand him up. Nothing fancy. Got it?"

Rae, settled onto the throne in the Project's open chest cavity, holds out one fist, thumb extended upward.[7] She sets her hands to the grips, closes her eyes. Slowly, the core comes to life, bathing her face in soft blue light, and the Project goes from rigid metal to living, moving thing, his body stretching, straightening, and finally standing in the center of Testing Floor Sixteen.

I wait, breath held, for something in him to come apart, wincing at each unsteady quiver of his limbs, each unexpected jerk of his digits, but his hands do not turn to fists, his spine does not twist, his legs do not kick and flail, and some ten meters above my head, Rae's voice rises in a whoop of excitement, and in my workshop, Lady whoops, too, leaping wildly as confetti and balloons shower inside her mirrors.

After that, things are almost unreasonably easy. We start on calibrations that night—we're too excited to do anything else, even celebrate—adjusting the Project's interface, smoothing out his functions, preparing him to cooperate with a human rider.

Each session brings new leaps in functionality, first in coarse, general-type movements, then in ever-finer gestures. Before long, those huge metal hands can hold an egg without breaking the shell. Processes and protocols fall neatly into place. We close Rae up in the core, equipped with a breathing mask and emergency beacon, but life support and sensory systems activate without a hitch. The masterful white armor, engineered weeks ago in an unwarranted flight of optimism, fits perfectly, the gleaming helmet glowing with an elegant blue pattern like stylized wings.

It's only a matter of time now until I can unveil the Project. Dr. Afşar will help me with the blowback from city and Academy officials, and so will Vinneas, once I bring him in on the secret. I'm a little sad to be so nearly finished, and it's not only nerves over the inevitable uproar once my off-hours shenanigans are revealed. I'm fairly positive Rae has amassed the requisite proficiency with equi to get herself fast-tracked into a training program for animi, meaning I'm about to lose yet another friend to the

---

7 The "thumbs-up"—a general signal of acknowledgment and approval among her people.

Legion. That was the deal all along, true, but it still glooms up my success. We'll be at the Academy together at least a while longer, though, and she's promised to help me demonstrate Snuggles when the time comes to really put his majesty on display.

And then, one evening following an unusually long session at the Stabulum, I arrive at my workshop and the door won't open. "Lady?" I call, confused. "Lady, what's going on in there?"

The voice that responds is not Lady Jane's but the pompous creak of a Fabrica instarus. "Officer Aspirant Kizabel," it says loftily, "you have been misbehaving. This workshop has been host to a shocking collection of violations, among them Fabrica Safety Code section ten paragraph five, section twelve paragraphs one, four, nine, and fifteen, section twenty paragraphs six, eight, twenty-four—"

Suddenly, the voice stutters and descends into mumbles, then tweaks to a higher register before bubbling out. A beat later, Lady's voice emerges from the door. "Kizabel? Is that you?"

"Lady! What happened?"

"It was Imway," she says. Her speaking volume spins erratically from soft to loud. "He came by, said he wanted to apologize to you, and when I said you weren't here, he asked if he could leave you something and I—I let him in. I didn't think he would see your concealing artifice, but he did, and—"

"It's all right, Lady," I say, urgent now, because her voice is becoming more garbled as the Fabrica instarus tries to reassert himself. Even through my panic, I'm impressed she's held him off this long. "Do they know about—about my assistant?" If Rae isn't already in trouble, I don't want to land her there.

"I don't know—I don't think so. I'm so sorry, Kizabel. I thought I could trust him. I just wanted the two of you to make up, and—"

Lady's voice shrinks to nothing, and the Fabrica instarus returns. "Access to this workshop is revoked until further notice," he croaks. "All items within are hereby impounded, your naughty little instara included. You will report to Curator Ellmore for disciplinary action at 0900 tomorrow. That is all."

THIRTY-EIGHT

JAX

It's been a great game so far, a lot of good plays but no one getting slaughtered. It's warm and sunny out, not too much wind, with a few clouds gliding slowly across the blue sky—a perfect day. The field is all thick green grass, not a dry patch anywhere except for the diamond of soft dirt and the bases at each corner, all of them empty. All around, the other team waits for the pitch, hunched and ready to react, their faces shadowed beneath the brims of their caps. On the pitcher's mound, a tall girl with long, skinny arms chews on a wad of gum, watching the batter like she's trying to read his mind. Finally, she winds up and throws, and there's a crack as the ball shoots out over first base. By the time someone chases it down, the batter is rounding second. He stops at third, our whole team cheering, waving his hat while the pitcher scrapes her cleats in the dirt, waiting for the next player at bat. Which is me. I'm up next.

I'm not terribly great at hitting, or even very good, but I'm getting better. I have a lot of time to practice. The girl's first two pitches are way outside, and I let them go by. "Good eye!" shouts the kid on third. The pitcher glares at him, like now that he's got a hit off her, he should at least behave himself, and he gives her a friendly wave. The next pitch is perfect, straight down the middle and only a little fast. I know I should take the easy base hit, but suddenly I want to kill it. I know I can.

But right as I'm about to swing, I see something out of the corner of my eye: a man standing behind the fence way at the other end of the field. He's too far away for me to really make out anything about him, but from the way he's standing, I know he's watching me. And now, even though I still get a pretty good piece of the ball, instead of zooming out across the field, it pops high over second base. The center fielder just waits and grabs it as it's coming down, and I'm out, and the inning is over. But I still love baseball.

Baseball is my favorite game in the world. Not many people know this about me. In fact, not many people have even heard of baseball, since practically no one plays anymore. Charles knows about baseball, and I guess Ninth City has its own league, which is a bunch of people who get together and play sometimes, out in the valley, but almost everyone who plays is a vet, and vets are always doing weird things, so no one really pays much attention. At the Academy, just about everything cadets do is training for war, and that includes the games. Charles gets annoyed sometimes that cadets never actually *play*, which to him means doing something just because it's fun, not to practice combat skills. According to Charles, doing things for fun is what being a kid is all about, which means when you're in a war, no one is really a kid. He seems to think that's a bad thing, though if you ask an actual kid, most of them aren't terribly thrilled to be treated like kids. But maybe Charles has a point because I really do like baseball. I liked it from the beginning, from the first day I played it, even before I knew it was called "baseball."

It was a perfect sunny day, even more perfect than this one. I was walking along a curving, sandy road when I heard kids shouting in high, excited voices. I followed the sound to a stretch of dry, patchy grass beside the ocean. It looked like the kids were just standing around, watching one boy who was holding a sort of wooden club. Some of them were spread out over the grass, with the rest just sitting in a row on a beach behind the kid with the club. For a while nothing happened, then one of the kids on the grass threw something, and the kid with the club took a swing.

There was a loud, sharp crack, and everyone looked up, following something through the air. I looked, too: There was something small flying way overhead. It soared up and up, and I remember thinking it was going to hit me, but then it landed with a thud a few meters away and rolled to my feet. Everyone on the beach was pretty excited, which made sense in a way. The thing at my feet was a small white ball, and hitting it so far with just a little club seemed extremely impressive.

One of the kids who had been standing on the grass came jogging my way. He was a little older than me, maybe fourteen. He had a soft red hat with a long bill that covered his eyes, and a thick leather glove on one hand. He raised the glove to me, sort of like a salute, and said, "Little help?"

I just looked at him, trying to figure out what he meant. Then, after a second, I got it. I picked up the ball and threw it to him. It was a pretty pathetic throw—he had to lunge to get it—but he didn't care. "Thanks," he said, folding the ball into his big leather glove. "Hey, you wanna play? We could use one more."

I did want to play, but I said, "I don't know how."

"It's easy," said the kid. "I'll show you."

"So it's like a game?" I asked.

"A game!" The kid laughed. "Baseball is life, my man! Come on." He ran ahead, back toward the field and the ocean, shouting, "Jax is on our team!"

That was the day I joined the Legion.

It was also my first visit to a mijmere—*my* mijmere, I should say. A mijmere is sort of like a dream, but also sort of real, kind of halfway between. To tell the truth, no one knows *exactly* what mijmeri are, only that they're created whenever fontani shade into fontani usikuu.

When all that power starts flowing out of you, it makes kind of like its own little world. The things there are real, like really real, like if you go swimming in a mijmere and don't dry off before you leave, your hair will stay wet. But mijmeri are also like dreams, because things can change every time you look. Like in a dream, you might be standing in your classroom at school one minute, and the next you're in the middle of a desert, or you might find a bottle lying on the ground, and when you open it, a whole ocean's worth of water comes pouring out—that kind of stuff can happen in a mijmere, too. Most people who study mijmeri think they're real places that are being created out of pure thelemity second by second, forming to the thoughts of the fontani at the center. But like I said, no one knows for sure.

Only a few things never change in a mijmere, and one of those is the Theme. In every mijmere, there's always something happening, some activity the whole world revolves around. We call that thing the Theme. For me, it's baseball. I don't know why; it just is. Every time I visit my mijmere, there's a game of baseball going on. Maybe I'm playing, or maybe I'm watching, but there's always baseball somewhere. If the game stops, my mijmere disappears, too, and then I'm not Jax the invincible fontanus, I'm just Jax the twelve-year-old kid, no superpowers or anything. For a while anyway. I can get my mijmere back, of course, just not right away.

All fontani have a Theme like that. For example, in Charles's mijmere, he's always traveling down a road, just walking or riding, going nowhere in particular. Fortunately, you never get tired in a mijmere, so it's easy to keep your Theme going, especially when your Theme is something fun like baseball.

It's the other team's turn at bat now, so I head for the outfield. The kid who made the three-base hit hurries to catch up with me. He's the same one who invited me to play that first day, and he's been here every time I've come back. All fontani have someone like that, one person who's always waiting for you in your mijmere, who helps you out and gives you advice. It's another one of the things that doesn't change in a mijmere. We call this person your Genius. Mine is this lanky kid with the red hat. I've never found out his name. I just think of him as the Kid.

"Hey," says the Kid as we jog toward the outfield. "Did you see that guy over there?" He nods in the direction of the fence, toward the man who messed up my swing. I can see him more clearly now. He's short and ratty-looking, with a lot of chin stubble and a tattered overcoat covered in rust-colored dust. He looks strange and out of place beside this nice green field with the rows of small, neat houses behind him, trees along the street swaying in the summer breeze and birds chirping in their branches.

"Yeah," I say. "I saw him."

"He's pretty creepy. You think we ought to call the police?"

I take another look at the rusty man, and he looks back, right into my eyes. I recognize him now: It's Charles. "Yeah," I say to the Kid. "Let's call the police."

If I can see Charles in my mijmere, it means I'm in trouble. Charles will be in his own mijmere, walking along his road, but he's here, too, because his mijmere is bashing up against mine. That's how fontani fight one another: by crashing their mijmeri against each other until one of them breaks. Charles says it's like a wrestling match between different realities. Whoever wins gets to control the whole world. My mijmere must be weakening, or else Charles wouldn't be able to just hang around like that.

Charles isn't trying to hurt me, of course—we're only sparring. But if I want to learn, I have to treat this like a real fight, like Charles is actually some hostile fontanus, a Valentine Type Zero. I've got to use my mijmere to stop him. "Calling the police" is one way to do that. "Police" is what the Kid calls the law-enforcement people here, and since this is my world, anyone I don't want around is automatically a criminal.

The main thing to remember when you're in a mijmere is always listen to your Genius. As long as your Theme keeps going, just about anything can happen in a mijmere. You could end up pretty much anywhere, and a lot of time it'll be someplace you've never seen or heard of, someplace where you don't know the rules, like when I saw those kids playing baseball by the beach. Your Genius is sort of like your guide. The Kid always gets what's happening. He helps me figure out what to do.

The police arrive a few minutes later, two of their old combustion-powered cars pulling up on the street behind Charles. Men in blue uniforms get out and walk over toward Charles, but I don't see what happens next, because just then the batter hits a fly ball to left field, which is my position, and I need to chase after it. By the time I've caught it and tossed it in, one of the police cars has pulled away, and a policeman from the other is coming my way. "Excuse me, son," he calls out to me, "can I talk to you a minute?"

I glance over at the Kid, who only shrugs a kind of *sure why not* shrug. I run over to the officer, a big round man with a shiny silver badge on the left side of his chest, his blue hat worn low so it covers his eyes.

"I'm afraid you kids are going to have to move on," he says. "You see that man over there? Well, this is his property, and he doesn't want anyone playing here."

He points back at Charles, who's still by the fence, only he's not so ragged and dirty-looking anymore. He's wearing a nice suit with a vest and pocket watch. The colors around him still seem rusty, but it's more because of the light than actual dirt, like he's standing under a different sun than the one shining down onto my field. Behind him, the neighborhood of clean little houses is gone, and instead there's only a flat open plain with a wide road running through, thick clouds of dust hanging in the air. I can only hear one bird singing now, in a weird, slow melody, not very birdlike.

Charles is overpowering my mijmere, turning it against me. Before, he was just some old stranger, but now he owns the land where I'm playing. That road is from his world. It's flooding into mine, taking it over. None of that is any big surprise—Charles always wins when we spar. But he doesn't usually win so quickly.

"Tell him we'll keep the noise down," I say to the policeman. "He's not using the field, and we don't have anything else to do. It's better than causing trouble, right?"

The policeman nods. Policemen hate when kids "cause trouble." "That sounds fine, son. Just remember, I'll be keeping an eye on you."

"Great, thanks!" I say, starting back toward the field.

"You know, son," the policeman adds, "he did say you could play all you want if you'd let him join in."

This is an old trick. If I let Charles into my game, he'd have no trouble breaking it up. You never let an enemy near your Theme. "Sorry, no room!" I yell, and run back toward the game.

I'm not lying about there being no room. Pretty much as soon as I thought it, more kids started wandering up out of nowhere to join the game. The field is full of them now, all making a lot of noise while they wait to play. When they see me coming back, they start shouting and clapping. "Hey!" someone yells. "Who's the old weirdo?"

"No one important," I say, and now it really does seem true. Charles isn't *literally* no one—he's still there—but he doesn't look rich and powerful anymore. His clothes have started falling apart again, and the hair on his chin is back. He's still covered in red, rusty light from the sun in his world shining into mine, but the neighborhood of little houses has closed in around him, and people have started peeking out of their windows. In one of the yards, a dog starts barking, and another joins in across the street. Charles is almost surrounded.

The Kid strolls up beside me, smacking a baseball into the palm of his glove. "Looks like that guy's worn out his welcome," he says. "He sticks around much longer, people are gonna run him out of town."

I'm winning. It doesn't seem possible, but that's really what it looks like. Charles is in big trouble. My mijmere has built up this little neighborhood and turned him into someone the whole town's against. People are coming out of the houses now, gathering on the street, all staring angrily at Charles. Kids from the baseball field are walking slowly toward him, holding bats over their shoulders. I can't believe it: I might actually beat Charles. This world is almost mine. All I have to do is go for it.

But I don't. I'm about to, but then I think, I can't really be winning. Maybe it looks that way to me, but I must be wrong. This is *Charles Cossou*, one of the best fontani in the Legion. And who am I? Just Jax. I'd never actually do it. No way.

Right as I'm thinking all this, a huge raindrop falls right in front of me, so big you can almost hear the *sploosh*. Where it hits the ground, the grass turns yellow and brittle, like the water is making things dry instead of wet. A second later, another drop falls right beside it, leaving another dry patch behind. Then another falls, and another, each one drying up more of the grass, and suddenly my big green field is turning to gravelly dirt. Rusty dust fills the air like a fog, and suddenly there's a rumble from the sky and a big crack of red lightning, and rain comes gushing down.

The rain now is real, wet rain, and everything is soaked in seconds. It washes the dust from the air, and I can see that my little town is gone. Where it used to be, there's just a flat plain filled with slippery mud and a few dead trees, going on forever. Charles is right there in the middle of it, watching from beneath a big black umbrella.

All that's left of my baseball field is a small patch of muddy grass. Most of the kids are gone, and the few that are left are dashing to get out of the rain.

"Wait!" I call, sprinting after them. "Come back! Rain delay! It's just a rain delay!" If I can stall them long enough, maybe I'll be able to bring the sun back, but as I'm splashing toward home plate, the kid who'd been waiting around for the next pitch lets his bat drop, and it lands in the mud, and with that my mijmere is gone and I'm way up in a big blue sky, thousands of meters above the ground.

THIRTY-NINE

JAX

For a few seconds, I sort of float there, then the wind presses my hair back, and I start to fall. I can see the ocean far below, the shadows of clouds moving slowly across the waves and the sparkle of sunlight on the water. Charles and I always spar in places like this, places far away from anything we might damage.

The whole fight might have felt like a dream to me, but while I was in my mijmere playing baseball, I was also here, over the ocean, swirling through the sky. When you're fontani usikuu, you're really in two places at once: your mijmere and the actual real world where everyone else lives. And you're doing two things at once: whatever you do in your Theme and tearing around as a big hurricane of thelemity. With practice, you can learn how to control the hurricane, to aim it and get it to do what you want. When you're in a mijmere, the real world shows up in a million little ways, like if you're dreaming about a train whistling, then you wake up and find it's really your teakettle going. But until you start to see how the two worlds fit together, it's a lot more like sleepwalking.

That's one reason why new fontani are so dangerous, why we take them to Area 22-53 to activate—because while they're dreaming in their mijmere, they might also be ripping through mountains and knocking over entire forests. I'm not joking: Fontani usikuu can really do that. So if we're going to practice fighting, it's best to do it where there's nothing around that we don't want to wreck by accident. The first thing your mijmere wants to do is protect you, and it doesn't care how it makes that happen or who else gets hurt. It's one reason why new fontani are so strong: They're just trying to defend themselves, and there's nothing to distract them from doing it. Charles says if you can put your whole mind to a single purpose, your mijmere will take care of the rest, but I haven't quite figured that part out yet, which I guess should be pretty obvious from the way I just got my butt kicked.

Close by, there's a cracking sound like a falling tree, and when I look I see something in the sky. Really, it must be falling as fast as I am, but it looks like it's hanging by a string, swinging slowly toward me. It's a person, and I know who it is way before she's close enough to see clearly: Naomi.

We were supposed to be taking Charles on, two against one. According to Charles, two fontani should almost always be able to defeat one fighting alone, as long as the two are working as a team. So that's what Naomi and I are trying to learn. We're supposed to be getting our mijmeri to meld together, which would make us way stronger than we would be on our own. But we haven't quite gotten the hang of it, and so here we are, both our mijmeri broken, falling through the sky.

Naomi glides past, the wind kicking her braids around, and even though we're falling straight toward the ocean, she's still able to give me a long, scolding look. She's mad at me, probably because she thinks it's my fault Charles beat us again.

I put my hands up in a shrug, which is supposed to mean, *I don't know what went wrong.* She doesn't look convinced, but it's hard to tell because we're falling so fast. Neither of us is scared of hitting the ocean—this isn't the first time we've lost to Charles, and we know he's just letting us feel what it's like to end up without your mijmere to protect you.

Sure enough, I'm only in the air another second or two before I'm swallowed up in a cloud of rusty dust, then I'm standing beside a long black road as some gigantic, combustion-powered truck roars past. When it's gone, I see Naomi on the other side, wearing a blue-checkered dress and black shoes and holding her fiddle case in one hand. I reach up to feel my head, knowing there'll be a baseball cap there. This is how we usually look when we show up in Charles's mijmere.

I check the road to make sure there are no cars coming, then run across to Naomi. In my own mijmere, I'd be completely safe, but here I could get flattened for real, so I need to be careful. Naomi has already started walking, and I run to catch up. "I guess the plan didn't work," I say.

Naomi doesn't say anything, only looks at me with her serious brown eyes, obviously still annoyed. That's something I've learned about Naomi: She won't talk just to make conversation, and if you say something obvious, like I just did, she won't say anything back. She'll just glare at you in a way that makes you wonder why you opened your mouth in the first place.

Most of the time I feel like an idiot around her, but once in a while it's kind of awesome. Like one day in Section E. After Bomar got put in "alternative corrective education" for the lazel incident, they gave Naomi his desk. Probably the Academy decided it would be convenient, since we're the only two fontani in Sixth Class, and the whole School of Rhetoric for that matter. Anyway, Naomi's sister, Rae, ended up in Section B, but since she's revenna, she has afternoon classes with some of the cadets from E, and one day Naomi overheard Elessa telling some of the other kids how sad and pathetic it was to have this big dumb noco girl hanging around in Sixth Class, and how the Academy should just send her off to the Front so she could at least do something useful.

If Naomi was like Bomar, someone who liked to show off and bully people, it might have been really bad. I could tell she was mad by the way she narrowed her eyes, focusing in on Elessa. But instead of doing something crazy, Naomi just walked up to her and stood there, very close, looking her in the eye. For a long time, she didn't say anything, and everyone froze to watch. And then, in a voice so low you had to lean in to hear, Naomi said, "You do not know what you are talking about. I suggest you shut your mouth unless you want to demonstrate yourself an even greater fool than you already have." It was like Elessa just shriveled up. Nobody has said anything bad about Rae since, and the best part is Naomi didn't use any of her powers. But I bet being on the wrong side of that stare was no fun at all.

"Did you go after Charles like we planned?" she asks finally.

I wish I could do Naomi's *that's obvious why are you asking me?* look, because I'm a little insulted. "Of course I did!" I say.

"Then where were you while I was fighting him?"

"I was fighting him, too! Or didn't you see me falling out the sky with you after? I wasn't doing that for fun, you know."

She gives me another long look and says, "How can he beat us that easily?" She sounds angry but not with me.

We're walking by a lonely little building pushed up close to the road, and I decide to study that instead of looking at Naomi. It has tall windows with cans stacked inside and big signs everywhere written in what I think is English. Through the window it's dark and empty. The only sign I can read says, "Gas 10¢/gal."

"I don't know," I say. "Experience, I guess. We need more practice."

That's pretty obvious, but Naomi doesn't do her staring thing. She's actually been getting better pretty fast. She can already navigate her mijmere well enough to travel around without wrecking everything in sight and has even gone on a few legionary maneuvers. I'd been training with Charles almost a year before I had enough control to be around anyone else. "Our enemies will not wait for us to learn," she says, her voice quiet and hard.

She's right, of course. Romeo isn't going to leave us alone just because we're not ready. I feel like I should say something encouraging, even if it gets me another Naomi glare, but she's looking ahead, toward something coming down the road.

It's an old man, shambling angrily toward us. He has a fat gray beard and long, matted gray hair covering most of his face; all you can really see of him is a lot of crooked teeth. "Hey! You kids!" he shouts, waving a walking stick at us. "Get off my road! Go on now, no one wants you here!"

I'm a little startled at how loud he is, but I'm not scared, and neither is Naomi. The old man is Charles's Genius. Like the Kid, he doesn't have a name as far as anyone knows. Charles just calls him the Tramp. Genii are probably the weirdest part of a mijmere because they act so much like real people, unlike the rest of a mijmere, where everything's always changing. Pretty much everyone agrees mijmeri are more than just whatever's inside fontani coming out—how else could I end up playing baseball when I'd never even heard of it? So maybe Genii are like that, too, things from somewhere else that somehow find their way into our dreams. But sometimes I think it might be the other way around—like maybe when I go to my mijmere, I'm actually in the Kid's dream. Or maybe the mijmere is just where we happen to meet up. Genii are always looking out for their fontani, but they're usually not very nice to other people visiting their mijmere. Charles says the Tramp has a good heart and a great sense of humor, but he totally creeps me out.

A little way down the road, I see Charles walking slowly toward us. He's wearing an old suit, a bit like the one he had on in my mijmere, and an old, roundish hat. "It's all right, they're with me," he says to the Tramp.

The Tramp glares back at Charles, then looks at Naomi and me suspiciously from beneath his long hair. "Arright, arright," he mutters to Charles, and goes shuffling past, grumbling to himself something that sounds like "Damn kids . . . damn cheeky kids . . ." I almost laugh because his grumpiness reminds me a little of Naomi.

"So," Charles says, tilting back his hat so he can smile at us. "That could have gone worse. Room for improvement, true, but at least you're moving well."

"How were you able to fight us both at once?" Naomi asks.

Charles sets off walking in the opposite direction from the Tramp, and we follow. "The same way I fight one of you alone," he says. "I turn you into something I can deal with, something my mijmere gives me power over. You, Naomi, were a bird sitting on a roadside fence. Jax, you were a stray dog. It's about focus—you have to be able to pour yourself toward your goal completely. And confidence." He looks over at me. "Jax, you had an opening that would have let you hold me off at least a little while longer. Why didn't you take it?"

"I don't know." My face flushes, and I can feel Naomi glaring at me again. "My mijmere just kind of broke down. It wouldn't do what I wanted."

"It did exactly what you wanted," Charles says. "You weren't sure you could take me on, and so your mijmere tried to pull away. Made it easy for me to wash right in."

"I still wanted to *win*!" I say. Charles is always saying how understanding yourself is one of the most important parts of using your mijmere, but he's had like thirty more years' practice. "You're just way stronger! What was I supposed to do?"

"That's why I'm teaching you to cooperate," Charles says. I think he's pleased I asked, though I don't know why. "Even if your enemy is far more experienced and powerful, working together can turn the battle to your advantage."

"You seemed to have little trouble with the two of us," Naomi says.

"That's because you weren't working together."

"Yes we were!" she says fiercely.

"Yeah!" I say, glad we're on the same side. "We had a plan!"

"You coordinated your movements," Charles says. "That's different from working together. From my perspective, each of you was alone. Think about it like this: Did either of you see the other in your mijmere?"

I don't have anything to say to that. If Naomi was close by, she should have shown up in my mijmere, even if she was just something small and insignificant, like how to Charles she was a bird, and I was a dog. But I wasn't even thinking about her—I was too busy with Charles. I'm guessing things were also like that for Naomi because she doesn't answer, either.

"I thought so," Charles says. "Attacking at the same time may give you an edge, but it won't make any real difference unless you combine your strength."

"And how do we do that?" Naomi asks.

"You have to share your world, learn to exist side by side. Make a place for each other within the worlds you've created for yourselves."

"That is a very vague answer," she says.

"Well, it's a very vague concept, and an even vaguer skill," Charles answers. Somewhere in the distance, car horns begin blaring. Charles tilts his head, listening. "And unfortunately we'll have to leave today's lesson there. Something has come up."

Wind gusts over the road, enveloping us all in a cloud of red dust. When it clears, we're back at the Academy, in one of the big courtyards at the School of Rhetoric. The place is totally empty, and I immediately know why: The incursion alarm is screaming all around.

"I've got to go," Charles says. "Jax, you'll be expected at the Forum. Take Naomi with you. I'd rather the two of you stick together."

"All right," I say. By now I'll be able to shade again if I have to.

Charles raises a hand, like he's going to tip his round hat to us, even though it's not there anymore, then he's gone, and Naomi and I are alone.

"I have heard that sound before," she says, so softly I almost don't hear her over the alarm. Her eyes are wide, staring around at the buildings above. She actually looks a little scared. "What is it?"

"It's the incursion alarm," I tell her. "It means we're under attack."

PART THREE

SOMETHING
SO WONDERFUL

FORTY

VINNEAS

L ife on a harvester gets interesting near the end of a mission. "Surreal" is probably a better word. The hold is stuffed to bursting with everything from granite to grapes, crude oil to raw sugar, chickpeas to live chickens, even assorted hazardous (explosive, corrosive, radioactive) materials sprinkled through to liven things up, but walking the storage aisles, where aged beef carcasses hang next to stacks of honeycomb still crawling with live bees, seems ordinary compared to visiting the habitation decks above.

By the time we've passed through four or five settlements, there is room aboard only for a skeleton crew of pilots and materials handlers; our liaisons from the Academy and the Legion have flown back to their respective institutions, leaving their new recruits behind on the theory that these will be adequately cared for in our capable hands. It isn't a bad theory, in principle—transit from our last stop back to Ninth City usually takes less than a day; how much can go wrong?—albeit one that can be thoroughly disproven by even a single visit to the recruits' quarters.

The kind of mayhem that ensues during the last leg of a mission is, I think, entirely predictable given the factors involved. Take a large group of people, remove them from their homes—against their will, for the most part—and place them in cramped (though not uncomfortable) quarters, all in an environment so strange and alien that only the most mentally unbalanced of them could reasonably have expected to wind up anyplace like it. The only mitigating factor, as far as I can see, is that the shock of encountering thelemity for the first time tends to send a fissure through the more or less universal sentiments of resentment and fear settlers hold when it comes to the Principate. Some cling to their old notions, their hatred too useful and loyal a standby to relinquish, but far more often the reactions I see bear indications of awe, excitement, and hope—the idea that this great ship, with all its marvelous inventions, is reason enough to believe our destination will be better than the place we left behind.

I don't mention how commonplace thelemity seems when viewed simply as a tool, or how even something so wonderful sours when used for war. The goggle-eyed gapers, babbling effusively over a toilet or a reading light, help distract from those who interpret thelemity only as further confirmation that we of the Principate are thieves and kidnappers, ascribing all kinds of sinister notions to this awesome power we've been keeping secret all these years. The rumor that thelemity is somehow generated by harvesting human souls usually begins to circulate within twelve hours, a matter complicated by the close resemblance such an outrageously paranoid theory bears to the truth.

Our passengers' rampant hostility aside, meeting them has been an education. Not always a pleasant one, to be sure—I've learned to have an artifice on hand to dry spit from my face, and my vocabulary of colorfully derogatory regionalisms increases hourly—but it's allowed me a unique perspective rarely available to someone from the cities. In a way, I and all my comrades back home are in a position very similar to these draftees, filtered and categorized and sorted so that we might be optimally utilized in service of a single overriding goal: victory. We may occupy different positions in the larger structure, but all of us—cadets, officers, soldiers, settlers—are alike in that our lives are circumscribed by the all-consuming imperative of war.

The difference is that those of us raised in the cities have had our entire lives to prepare for the moment when we'll be called to Earth's defense. The exigencies of our society, and the responsibilities that society demands, are impressed upon us from our earliest days, and if the reality of it is less than cheerful, at least we know what that reality is. Such courtesy is not extended to the settlers. Instead, we raise them like livestock, one more quota to be delivered on time. An old adage goes that the first casualty of war is truth, and that seems to be the general opinion around the Principates. But the more I see of the settlements, the more I question how necessary this deception of ours really is. Certainly, a larger dose of truth would go a way toward reducing the bedlam that always ensues on harvesters like mine, deemed inevitable by a leadership that has never been punched in the jaw by a fifteen-year-old lumberjack who blames you for the disappearance of every friend she's had since she was nine. At the base of things, the settlers are no different from us. This is their war, too, and I think they would fight alongside us if only we gave them the chance.

And then, too, there are the unincorporated peoples, left to their brutal, bloodstained world. I sometimes find myself picturing Rae, and those scars along her neck and ear. I can't even imagine the sort of life she lived before she wound up in that holding cell of ours.

Reggidel has, over years of experience, become adept at staving off the chaos constantly threatening to overrun our new recruits, going so far as to develop a series of lectures and demonstrations that amount to a kind of "introduction to thelemity." He allowed me to sit in on one such seminar, and afterward pronounced me fully trained in recruit orientation, informing me that I would be looking after such matters from now on so that he could devote his time to reading the latest entertainment texts from the settlements.

When I get to the ship's mess, I find him nose down in a text entitled *The Ravishing of Block 99*, so engrossed that my arrival goes unnoticed despite the strong smell of smoke that follows me in. Entertainment texts are, like crusty milk, a taste Reggidel acquired in the settlements and shows no desire to relinquish despite the wide availability of more wholesome options. Known variously as fuzzies, wipers, pulps, and canners, en-texts are designed mostly to give the horrendously understimulated minds of our settlers something better to do than stew bitterly over being worked to death sixteen hours a day. The texts carefully avoid any and all sensitive issues while reinforcing the prevailing social order wherever possible. Corruption is unerringly punished, hard work and faith in authority rewarded. For the most part it's a lot of love triangles—or, more accurately, love polygons of several more than three sides—notable for their strained drama and implausible sex scenes. There are a number of long-running series, with new installments generated at a startling pace. Reggidel's favorite is Block 99, about the erotic goings-on at a housing project in the fictional Settlement X, an average place but for the unusual percentage of attractive residents and the improbable frequency of exciting events (fires, earthquakes, "hellion" raids, and so on).

As entertainment texts are one of the few commodities abundant in the settlements but scarce in the cities, Reggidel makes a point of stocking up during every mission. His appetite shows all the signs of real addiction, something Reggidel himself acknowledges, proclaiming that I'd understand if only I would stop being such a snooty Prip and give Block 99 a chance. My response, that I'll happily read the whole series if he takes care of the recruits, is met only with a low chuckle and the rustling of pages.

"It looks like we've got a few passengers in the early stages of IED," I say now, brushing ash from my ruined jacket. Thelemity affects all living matter in one way or another, the smell of ozone or sulfur at the edge of a thelemic field being the most oft-cited example. Most people experience only a passing tingle or a brief sensation of falling the first time they enter an umbris, though occasionally the results are more spectacular. In the recruits' quarters today, I was presented with a boy suffering from some alarming changes in skin color, a woman with pale green mushrooms growing along her arms and forehead, and an elderly man who had begun sneezing a flaming goo not unlike napalm. Symptoms of Irrational Environment Disorder, or IED, tend to present as minor versions of the activation surges experienced by revenni, though really the condition is more similar to motion sickness.

"We're going to need more pugmento tablets," I inform Reggidel. "Actually, we should be distributing them as soon as the recruits get on board." I remove my still-smoldering jacket. "Before they start setting people on fire."

Reggidel has fixed himself a plate of crusty milk and crunches thoughtfully. "Applesauce works just as well," he says over a mouthful of gooey bread, still not looking up from his book.

"*Almost* as well." As I inspected the recruits suffering from IED, the whole room was silent, as though bearing witness to great wisdom and power. Since we were out of pugmento tablets, I administered doses of applesauce, also known to mitigate the symptoms of IED, and curing such an exotic condition by such ordinary means only confirmed my powers in the eyes of our recruits—not before I'd taken a blast of flaming snot to the chest, however, though the fire burned out quickly enough that the only lasting damage was to my uniform. "And the recruits would know that if we bothered to educate them about thelemity before they ended up with fungi sprouting from their eyebrows."

"We gave them those pamphlets, didn't we?" Reggidel, who knows mention of the pamphlets will only rile me more, pointedly licks a thumb and turns another page of his book.

"Yes, the pamphlets, which are about as informative as that book you're reading."

"Don't bring Block 99 into this." Reggidel's strategy is generally to sit calmly by whenever I feel the need to vent my frustration over the Principate's recruiting techniques. He doesn't see the point in arguing, especially when there is shocking betrayal and meticulously described nudity afoot at Block 99. Now, with his bland, faintly wearied tone, he seems to be inviting me to argue with myself, since he can't be bothered, and I'm about to take him up on it when the soft light overhead dims, then rises into a jarring red.

The calm, friendly voice of the harvester's lead pilot descends out of the air. "Good afternoon, everyone. Unfortunately, it seems our return to Ninth City will be temporarily delayed. We'll be setting down in the next ten minutes or so and switching over to conventional power. Please note that all processes requiring thelemity will be unavailable. Thank you."

"Aw, crud," Reggidel grunts. He slaps his book closed and lays a hand on the table in front of him, calling up to the navigation deck. "Hey, boys," he says. "What's going on? We go dark, and it's going to be a riot in here."

"I'm sorry, sir," the pilot says. "Ninth City just sent word of an atmospheric incursion. Glazdell is leaving to support the defense forces."

Glazdell is the fontana assigned to provide our harvester with a steady source of thelemity. Typically, anyone traveling beyond a city's umbris has to rely on vehicles that operate within the everyday laws of physics, but the harvester is far too large and cumbersome to remain aloft by means of mere aerodynamics. It's a testament to the importance of our mission that the Principate is willing to commit a source to us full-time—except when Romeo rears his faceless head, that is. This will be the third time we've had to go without thelemity since I joined the censors, and beyond the general tension inherent in every incursion, it's always a minor disaster for the cargo, much of which the harvester isn't equipped to deal with under conventional power and will thus have to be dumped. But that isn't what worries me now, not what has me dashing to Reggidel's side.

"Where is it?" I ask, leaning over to speak with the pilot. "Where was the incursion detected?"

"Sixth," the pilot says, "but the enemy is moving. Command expects we'll engage over Third or Fifth."

Reggidel has produced a small flashlight and sits back, aiming it at his book. "You should probably go see to the recruits, make sure no one's panicking." He's got more to say, but I'm not listening. Someone *is* panicking, and that person's name is Censor Vinneas.

FORTY-ONE

VINNEAS

I run for my quarters, pull out the maps and almanacs beneath my desk, and flip madly through, comparing charts and figures, already knowing what I'll find but hoping I'm wrong. I'm not. Though it's daytime in the Third Principate, the Moon will be right overhead.

"Bresley," I call, summoning the harvester's instarus. "I need to put a communication through to Curator Ellmore at Ninth City."

Bresley's voice emerges, patient but also imperious, from the nearest wall. "Sir, Ninth City will be under incursion protocols by now. Moreover, we will be going dark in—"

"Yes, thank you, Bresley. That's why I need to speak with the Curator now. Tell her it's an emergency."

Bresley sighs resignedly. "Very well, sir."

Within an area powered by thelemity, the available methods of tele-communication are so numerous that deciding which to use can take longer than the communication itself. If you want to contact someone *outside* an umbris, however, the options dwindle drastically, since that requires generating a signal capable of traveling through a medium devoid of thelemity. Instari hate doing this, and Bresley conveys his annoyance by humming peevishly as he raises Curator Ellmore. But it works. After a few very long seconds, I hear her say, "Vinneas? Are you there?"

"Here, ma'am."

"You'll have to make this fast. I'm expected at Command."

"Yes, ma'am, I'm sorry, but it's important."

"Your instarus mentioned as much. Please, proceed."

"We need to close Lunar Veil immediately."

"Vinneas," Curator Ellmore says, in a way that conveys both familiarity with the topic and reluctance to revisit it.

"This attack, Curator—it isn't just a raid," I press on. "It's a full-scale assault. The Valentines are here now—or they will be if we don't close the Veil right away."

"I hope you've got some evidence for me."

"Look at this." I hold up one of my maps and then, realizing the Curator will be able to see neither me nor it, tell Bresley to open a visual feed, a task he accomplishes promptly if grudgingly. Curator Ellmore's office appears in my wall mirror; through the window behind her, I can see our defense forces taking to the air over Ninth City.

"Here," I say, pointing to my map. "The incursion began over the Sixth Principate, but the Valentine forces are moving toward Fifth and Third. There are plenty of better targets they might have chosen. The only way their movements make sense is if they're heading for Lunar Veil. This is it, Curator, the attack I've been talking about. This incursion—it's meant to support a larger force about to come through the Veil."

Lunar Veil is the most heavily trafficked gateway into the Realms, and the only one of any real importance because it opens the route to the Front. It isn't so much a doorway as a hazy place where our Realm, Hestia, meets the one next to us, a mostly abandoned place we call Dis. For the space of several kilometers in the upper atmosphere, always along the line between Earth and the Moon, these two Realms mix like fresh- and salt water at the mouth of a river opening into the sea, a cloud of brackish reality swirling like a storm. Lunar Veil was how the Valentines first came to Earth, and if they plan to return in force, the Veil is how they'll do it.

"You know perfectly well what will happen if I show up at Command arguing that we have to close Lunar Veil because the Valentines are acting strangely. Imperator Feeroy will assure everyone I'm overreacting, that the Valentines have been acting strangely for months."

She's right. There have been three incursions since I left Ninth City, and while each time another Principate was able to successfully fend the enemy off without Ninth Legion's participation, all have followed the same pattern: Whereas past attacks always consisted of swift raids on targets necessary to supply our Legions at the Front, in these recent incursions the Valentines have held back, giving our forces time to engage. In every instance, such "lingering" (as Imperator Feeroy put it) has allowed us to escape with our centers of population and production untouched, albeit at the cost of greater damage to our defense forces. Recent numbers put battle readiness in some Principates as low as 50 percent, mostly due to disabled or grounded equipment. It's a trade we were happy to make, since weapons and soldiers are relatively easy to replace, whereas losing a city or a settlement would disrupt supply to the Front for years. Generally, that isn't a bad overall result, logistically speaking—unless there's a major attack on the way. Unless Romeo was just softening us up for the real assault.

"That's true, they *have* been acting strangely for months," I say, "and this is why. They were trying to weaken our short-term defenses."

"Which would be a complete change from the tactics they've relied upon for the last three centuries."

"Yes, ma'am, that's right. And I believe it's because something has changed at the Front. You've seen the data." We still don't know *how* the Valentines are sneaking into Hestia, appearing out of nowhere in our atmosphere, but Kizabel and I proved pretty conclusively that when they do, it has something to do with our losses in the war. "If there was a way to communicate directly with our forces at the Front, I think we'd learn they've suffered some sort of setback, one that has allowed the Valentines to mount a major offensive against Earth."

"Were you aware, Vinneas, that Imperator Feeroy has been telling a story that is almost the precise opposite of what I'm hearing from you?"

"No, ma'am, I wasn't."

"According to Feeroy, the recent increase in the severity of incursions is a sign of desperation. He argues that the Valentines are overextending their resources in one final attempt to regain momentum in this war, a war we've been winning for years and which, if we can maintain pressure at the Front, is about to turn decisively in our favor. Can you guess which of these theories has been the most popular?"

"But Feeroy's theory is completely unsupported by the facts."

"Imperator Feeroy has woven a plausible explanation for events as they present themselves. You, Vinneas, would have us close Lunar Veil, thereby disrupting our supply line to the Front, just to hold off an attack that would likely eradicate us anyway. Feeroy is promising us victory, and all we have to do is continue on as we have. Unless we can prove your theory definitively, I'm afraid we'll find very little support."

She's right, of course. Feeroy's narrative is immeasurably more attractive than mine. Heck, *I'd* like him to be right. But he isn't. Feeroy and the rest of Command are reacting to the situation as they want it to be, not as it is. I shouldn't be surprised—filtering the facts to present the rosiest possible picture is part of human nature—but I am. We're trusting these people with the lives of everyone on the planet. They're supposed to be able to face harsh realities, make tough decisions. And if I can't make them listen now, this war is going to be a whole lot shorter than everyone expects.

"Put a flash on the Veil," I say.

"What?"

"Flash the Veil. Disrupt the connection between the worlds—that will let us see what's on the other side." Most of the time, Lunar Veil is almost invisible, just an expanse of seemingly empty air. If you were to fly into it, you might observe a shift in the stars above, or an odd doubling of your vision as one Realm transitioned into another, but more likely you wouldn't notice anything amiss until you found yourself on the other side. Under the right conditions, someone could pass through without even realizing the change. The entire Valentine Host could be waiting on the other side, and we wouldn't know it. We have a small base just beyond Lunar Veil, a waypoint for troops and supplies, but unless I'm wrong, they've already been overrun, and since most types of energy—radio waves, for example— can't cross the boundary between Realms, there's no easy way to check in. But a large discharge of thelemity along that boundary will cause the two sides to momentarily separate, like oil and water, allowing a brief glimpse from one world to the next. "When we do, the Valentines will be there, massing for an attack."

"Vinneas," the Curator says, "the enemy is headed for the Veil right now and will likely arrive before our forces can intercept. Executing a flash will require breaking through a good-sized contingent of Valentine fighters."

"That's exactly their plan!" I shout, unable to restrain my frustration any longer. "They'll hold the Veil until their forces are ready to come through. If I'm right, and we don't do anything, Earth is done. The Valentines have probably already captured Dis, and are mustering to invade Hestia. Closing the Veil now is our only chance to mount an effective defense. Isn't it worth the risk to know for sure?"

Each of the passageways out of Hestia appears and disappears on a schedule coinciding with the movement of some astronomical object relative to Earth. Lunar Veil, which is associated with the Moon, becomes accessible roughly once every month. Gateways like Lunar Veil are typically only permeable for a short time unless they're held open by a process known as anchoring. If we were to undo Lunar Veil's Anchors now, it would close almost immediately, but we would have to wait a month before we could open it again.

"A month here translates to days or less along most of the Front," I say. "Best case: We look, Dis is empty. There's a short hiccup in the lines of supply. Command can blame me."

A shadow of Curator Ellmore's wry smile briefly crosses her face. "You're too low on the food chain to absorb that much blame," she says. "And as far as Command is concerned, any delay is too long. Our operating directive is to concentrate all available assets at the Front. Even a small interruption will be seen as an unacceptable setback."

"As opposed to the sort of setback we'd see if the Valentines capture Earth?"

This time Ellmore really does smile, albeit weakly. "I'll find a more diplomatic way to put it when I make my recommendation to Command," she says. "I don't believe I mentioned Imperator Feeroy has been given full authority over Ninth City's defense forces."

I sit back in my chair, the red light around me taking on a slow, underwater quality. If Feeroy is in charge, we're in bigger trouble than I thought.

"I've made this case to Command before," the Curator is saying, "but you've given me something new to work with. Maybe I can convince Princept Azemon or Dux Reydaan to listen. But I'm afraid any orders to the defense forces will go through Feeroy first, and I doubt he'll care much for attempting a flash, not when it means risking his exemplary kill ratio on a frontal assault."

"Try one of the other Principates," I say, not bothering to hide my desperation. "Third maybe, or Sixth. They might listen."

"I don't think they'll take my call, not in the middle of an incursion, but I'll try. Wish me luck."

When her image vanishes, I stare at my reflection, unable to quite believe what's just happened. I'd come to accept politics as a necessary part of life at Command, to see the muddy maneuvering of bargaining and influence, the interplay of rivalry and ambition, as an unavoidable aspect of governance. But I always believed that when the time came to make a crucial choice, our leaders would act with only the interests of our world in mind. I was wrong, and because of that, we're about to be wiped out. It just doesn't seem real, that after five hundred years, the war is going to end like this. It could all be over in an hour.

I can't let it happen. "Bresley?" I say. I can feel an idea forming, hazy and soft, but focusing fast. "Are you still in contact with Ninth City?"

"Yes, sir, but—"

"Find Officer Aspirant Kizabel for me. She might still be at the Fabrica."

"Sir—"

"We don't have a lot of time, Bresley. Please."

"Yes, sir." Some of Bresley snootiness has gone, and he searches without humming this time. Possibly he's been listening to my conversation with Curator Ellmore and knows what's at stake. "Sir? I've found her. She's at the School of Rhetoric."

Rhetoric? I would have expected her to be at her workshop, or else at the Forum with Jax. I don't know if she's been keeping up our appointments since Imway and I joined the Legion, but I hope so.

"Vinneas?" Kizabel's image swirls into view, blurrier than Curator Ellmore's had been, and darker. She looks thinner than I remember, and exhausted, like she hasn't slept in weeks. "What are you—"

"Kizabel, listen. I need you to go to your workshop, or your quarters, someplace with a cog radio, and turn to the channel for long-distance recreational communication."

"What?" she says. A baffled shake of the head. "Why?"

I'm about to tell her, but it's too late: The lights around me go out, then, after a few beats of total darkness, in which the air becomes noticeably still and silent, conventional power kicks in, and the room fills with cold, fluorescent light and the whirring of fans circulating air. I run down the hall to the communications room, trying not to think about the anarchy no doubt unfolding in the habitation decks below. I just hope Kiz has taken my request seriously.

The communications room is empty, the harvester's entire crew probably up above decks, getting some air while they wait for the power to return. We're out in the middle of nowhere, a hundred kilometers at least from anything Romeo might conceivably choose as a target, though that won't do us much good if the whole Valentine Host comes crashing through Lunar Veil.

I switch on the radio and turn to long-distance recreational, a channel reserved for cadets with an interest in conventional communications, meaning it would probably be free even if we weren't in the middle of an incursion. "Kizabel?" I say, depressing the transmit switch. "Kiz, are you there? Come in." Nothing. I try again and am similarly disappointed. And then I hear a distant, electronic whine, and Kizabel's voice comes crackling through the speaker.

"Vinneas? Is that you?"

"Kiz, yes," I say, relieved. "I'm here."

"What's so important you've got me using a stupid cog radio?"

"Your equus—does it fly?"

Silence, then, "I don't know what you're talking about."

"The equus you've been building secretly in your workshop for the past several months," I say slowly. "Does it work?"

Another long pause. "Yes," she says finally.

We have a chance, then—a very, very small chance. I take a deep breath, going over the possibilities in my mind, calculating and considering my plan. How sure am I the Valentines are really coming? How sure am I we can stop them? Sure enough to ask my friend to do something that will almost certainly get her killed?

"Kiz." For a few frantic seconds, I rack my brain for another alternative—anything else—and come up with nothing. It's got to be Kizabel, this girl I've known since we were six years old, or the world. I have to ask her, and if she refuses, I have to convince her.

"Vinn? You still there?"

"Kiz," I say again, exhaling, doing my best to hold my voice steady. "I need you to do something unbelievably dangerous."

FORTY-TWO

IMWAY

Flying an equus takes discipline. Training and dedication and talent, but discipline above of all. It's something you never truly understand until you've felt one of these giants come alive at your touch. The uninitiated see only the colossus of metal and stone, the suit of armor that allows a creature of mere meat and bone to contend with a horde of alien machines. And with good reason—we equites are trained to make it look easy. Only after we've proven ourselves a hundred times over are we finally given an equus of our own. We're taught to fly, yes, and to fight, but beyond that we're taught respect. The equus, more than any other weapon we possess, is attuned to thelemity's primal currents, its wild and chaotic nature. The power an equus wields is a force, like the wind or the tides, a force that can turn on you at any moment and rewards carelessness with swift and decisive brutality. Respect your equus, respect its power, or it will kill you. That's something every eques learns early on.

Cruising speed is a perfect example. Legionary equi are capable of attaining tremendous velocities. The average equus in Ninth City's defense force could travel from Earth's surface to the Moon in under an hour, assuming an unobstructed route and a constant and reliable source of thelemity. The trouble is that thelemity is rarely available in constant and reliable quantities—at least not when you're moving at three hundred thousand kilometers per hour. At that speed, you would shoot through a first-factor umbris—slightly over three kilometers in diameter—in about four-tenths of a second. Once you're out the other side, your equus turns back into a pumpkin, as the saying goes. No few headstrong recruits have ended their careers plummeting to Earth in a fancy-looking hunk of rock and metal that used to be a fully functioning equus. It happens often enough that we have a name for it: blasting out. The faster you go, the smaller those little bubbles of power that fontani project seem. On your way into battle, flying in formation with a source at the center, you might well be positioned right up against the edge of the umbris, so close that a single mistake will send you careening into the aeter. Traveling at cruising speed is a little like riding a cresting wave. Thrilling, but constantly poised on the edge of disaster. To make it as part of the Legion's Armored Cavalry, you need the nerve to toe that edge, but—more importantly—the discipline to never venture over.

Right now we're traveling at roughly 2,000 kph, just under twice the speed of sound—generally considered a safe speed for a full-sized sortie, one that includes infantry and artillery in addition to the faster and more maneuverable Armored Cavalry, otherwise known as the equites. Speeds for an emergency intercept run three and four times the rate we're moving now, and that's only when we're planning to remain within Earth's atmosphere. Once you leave Earth, you leave the world of quadruple-digit velocities behind also. But today our orders have us heading for the Second Principate—a hop, skip, and a jump, relatively speaking—and only in a reinforcing capacity, as reports tell us the Sixth and Third Legions have already engaged the enemy.

That isn't to say we're attending as casual spectators. No one's bringing any party favors today. Our sortie consists of seven full cohorts, more than two-thirds of Ninth City's active defense force, strung out in an arcing line five hundred kilometers long. We have a complement of five fontani—further evidence that Command isn't screwing around—each projecting a sphere of thelemity and traveling at supersonic speeds, surrounded by a swarm of legionaries hanging on for dear life. First, Second, and Fifth Cohorts, those weighted most heavily toward armored fighters, are clustered together in the lead, moving in close formation. If we're ordered into battle, they'll be the ones to breach the enemy lines. The rest of us are dotted behind, one cohort per source, trailing all the way back to Ninth City, where Seventh Cohort has just launched. My 'drille—126th Equites, Sixth Cohort Armored, Ninth Legion—is with the next bubble out.

We're at the rear of the formation, just the place for a 'drille of jockeys who have yet to dance with Romeo toe to toe. We've been on active duty only a few months, though it feels like years since I was dismissed from my afternoon lessons with orders to report to the Curator's office. My hopes for the meeting were low. Joint exercises with the Academies of Fifth and Eighth Cities had concluded only days before, and the celebration afterward had gotten notably out of hand, especially among the Ninth Equites Aspirant, who had dominated the field. As Decurio, responsibility for the squad's behavior rested solely with me, and I was prepared for a full dressing-down. Instead, I found Dux Reydaan, Ninth Legion's highest-ranking officer, seated in front of the Curator's desk. While Curator Ellmore looked on coldly, the Dux explained that he would be inviting me to graduate to active duty with the Legion's equites. Of late their ranks had dwindled to a dangerous low. While there was no shortage of volunteers, so few successfully completed training that it was becoming infeasible to supply armored fighters to the Front while maintaining a stable defense force at home. He wanted to see whether there was a future in accelerating the training program for certain exceptional candidates, and having watched my Ninth EAs in the recent exercises, he decided it was worth a shot. The Curator didn't try to hide her disapproval but stressed that if I wanted to volunteer, there was nothing she could do to stop me. I could have two days to decide whether to accept the Dux's offer and recommend eleven other animi from the program, enough for an escadrille. "If you don't mind, sir," I said, "I can tell you now." Joining up wasn't a question. I'd spent the past five years training for this moment. As for my recommendations, I could think of at least twenty animi who could have held their own with the Armored Cavalry, but as it happened, my first string numbered exactly twelve fighters, myself included. I doubt it was a coincidence.

Now we're on our third official sortie—fourth counting that first mission rounding up nocos in the valley—flying in close formation at the tail of Sixth Cohort. Though we've already settled into cruising speed, I'm keeping us in the tighter spiral formation—typically used only during the chaotic moments directly following launch—as a reminder to stay sharp. One false move, one misjudgment in course or heading, is still enough to put you outside your umbris. Maybe Seventh Cohort would dive to catch you, and you'd get to spend the rest of the mission as the rookie who couldn't control his equus, but more likely you'd drop like a stone—because you'd be inside of one. Assuming your safety gear deployed properly, you'd still have two or three days to cool your heels, all alone in noco territory, before anyone bothered to track you down, so the Legion could give your equus to someone who actually had the chops to fly it.

Once we clear the cloud deck, however, I give the order to relax formation. From here, it's a straight shot to our destination over the Second Principate. Ahead, I can see the shimmer of another umbris, Fourth Cohort buzzing inside like a swarm of gnats, and further still the marble-sized umbris carrying Third. Blue horizon stretches on every side, fading to black overhead, while a daytime moon looms, pale and huge.

My order to relax formation is also the signal that conversation beyond orders, acknowledgments, and status updates is now allowed, and Ottumtee, who can't stand long silences, speaks up almost immediately.

So what are the chances we'll see combat this sortie? he asks from his equus, 126-005, call sign LanceLightning. It isn't exactly his voice I hear—more an impression of it. During missions, equi most often communicate by Directed Speech, a method that solves many of the problems inherent in traditional verbal communication. By conveying words directly from the speech-generating area of one brain to the speech-interpreting area of another, DS cuts down on opportunities for misunderstanding—particularly useful during the confusion of battle—without requiring you to decipher another person's actual thoughts, a process so cumbersome it makes interpreting garbled radio signals seem simple by comparison. An interesting side effect of DS is that it often doesn't sound much like the person's actual voice— what you hear is how that person sounds to him- or herself. Ottumtee, a tall, sturdy guy with a voice so deep he usually sounds like he's speaking from the bottom of a well, comes across as smaller and younger over DS, and his wry, almost sarcastic tone, easy to miss in normal speech, stands out more clearly.

Slim to none, Iftito answers. He graduated from the SoR near the top of First Class, and could easily have gone on to intensive studies at Philosophy if he hadn't been picked for the Equites Aspirant. He can always be depended upon for accurate information delivered swiftly and free of ornament. In person, people often find him abrasive, but the voice coming from his equus, 126-011, call sign ThunderWalking, is unexpectedly silky in tone.

Well, Pelashwa says, *that all depends on how you define "see." I'm sure we'll have a perfectly good view of the battle.* Pesh and Ottumtee are close friends, and she'll take any opportunity for banter. Her equus, 126-007, call sign FallingLeaf, sidles up to Thunder but stops short of giving him a playful bump, something she'd do if we weren't on a mission.

That's if the battle is still going on, Midmurro interjects. *Sixth and Third Legions should have things pretty well mopped up by the time we get there. The only reason we'd have to engage is if we were all pretty thoroughly buggered already.* Midmurro is an excellent flier and extremely resourceful, but I nearly left him out of this 'drille because of his obnoxious habit of playing the utmost authority on any and all subjects, especially those he knows nothing about. There are hundreds of scenarios that could end up with us in combat, and in only about half of them would we be pretty thoroughly buggered. Fortunately, no one else in the 'drille takes him very seriously.

Shut up, Middy, Sensen snaps. As the oldest in the 'drille—she was in her last few weeks as an Officer Aspirant when we were promoted—Sensen has assumed the role of unofficial disciplinarian, making it her duty to curtail all behavior beneath the dignity of the Legion. It's a job I'm glad to leave to her.

A few moments of silence pass, then Pelashwa says, *So when you say what are the chances, are you looking for like an over/under or what?*

Are you offering odds on whether we get into it today, Pesh? asks Uo. He's one of the few exceptions to the rule that equites, as a type, are highly competitive and rigidly self-motivated. Despite being ranked fourth in overall scores back in the program, he comes off as easygoing to the point of laziness.

I just want to get back to our game of tarot before someone messes with my hand, Pelashwa answers. *I've noticed every time we leave in the middle of a game, the cards mysteriously shift in certain people's favor.*

Are you accusing me of cheating? Uo asks, his voice ringing with insincerity over DS.

You're on record as admitting you cheat on almost every hand, Ottumtee points out.

It's all part of the game, Uo insists.

Isn't cheating by definition not part of the game? Pelashwa asks.

Let's call it extraregulatory strategy, then, Uo clarifies.

And what exactly are your "extraregulatory strategies"?

For tarot? Mostly just stacking the deck so I get better cards.

That's cheating!

I actually would settle for just a look at a battle, Ottumtee says, apparently trying to get the conversation back on track.

I would like to officially extend my invitation to shut up to Uo and Pel-

ashwa, Sensen says. *Ottumtee, too, actually. Why don't all three of you just— did anyone just see that?*

Something has just flashed by to our right, an object moving so fast it was little more than a pale-colored blur. Immediately, I order my 'drille into combat posture. Though it takes less than a second, by the time we've readied our weapons, the object is well past—already barely a speck shrinking into the distance as it races alongside Sixth Cohort.

I reach out to the DS conduit reserved for officers and raise Centurio Kitu, the commander of Sixth Cohort. *Sir,* I say, *FireChaser here, Decurio of the 126th. We've spotted an unidentified object moving in your direction at high velocity.*

We see it, Chaser, Kitu replies. He's a veteran of the Realms, with three tours and hundreds of enemy kills to his credit. Rumor has it in all that time he's never raised his voice once, even with a pair of Valentine Zeros bearing down on him. *We're trying to make contact now. Maintain your position and wait for orders.*

Understood, sir, I reply, then open communication to my 'drille. *Did anyone get a good look at that thing?*

It looked like an equus, says Iftito, *but it definitely came from outside this umbris, which suggests an artillery shell, most likely from a City Gun. Based on its trajectory, I'd say it came from Ninth.*

Each city of the Principates is equipped with an array of heavy artillery, massive guns that can stretch two hundred meters or more into the sky. Aside from fontani, which are in extremely scarce supply, the City Guns are the most powerful weapons we have. The equipment required to operate and maintain them is too elaborate and cumbersome to transport into battle, meaning their primary function is long-distance bombardment. They fire shells loaded with ingenic ordnance, using thelemity to launch them out into the aeter, where they might travel thousands of kilometers under conventional ballistics before reaching their target— always within another umbris, where the shells again use thelemity to do their deadly business. During a battle, it isn't unusual to see shells from the City Guns whistling down onto the enemy—a few well-placed shots can be enough to take down even a Valentine Zero—but no one from Sixth Cohort has called in an artillery strike today. We're still a long way from the enemy, and it wouldn't make sense for Ninth City to be attempting a shot like that when Sixth, Third, and Second Cities are so much closer to the battle.

Could it be a misfire? I ask.

Possibly, Iftito says, *but that thing isn't moving like a shell. If I had to guess, I'd say it's under human control.*

Impossible, Sensen snaps. *Where could an equus have come from? It didn't just drop out of the sky.*

A few seconds later, Sensen gets her answer. The object, whatever it is, has continued across our umbris, if anything moving faster as it shot past the rest of Sixth Cohort. Iftito is right about its movement: Artillery shells generally follow the dictates of gravity up until they reach the vicinity of their target, but the streak of white that blasted past us moments ago seems to be consciously avoiding collision, dodging around gunships and tetra fortresses, accelerating past the waves of equites that swerve to intercept, moving ever closer to the front edge of our umbris, a dangerous place to be at such a reckless velocity. The object gives no indication of seeing the approaching aeter until, a mere split second away, it suddenly spins, dips, and shoots almost straight up, rocketing away into the sky.

Problem solved, I guess, says Uo. Whether the object was an artillery shell, an equus, or something else, it won't be much of a threat to anyone now, unless it happens to land on some unlucky noco out in the wilderness somewhere. Given our position, it's more likely to drop harmlessly into the ocean.

No, look! shouts Haiyalaiya. Her equus, 126-012, call sign EndIsWaiting, is positioned at the top of our formation, giving her the best view of the unidentified object's ascent, and after tracing the arc of its flight, I see what she means.

My eyesight has always been my least impressive physical attribute. Since I was ten, I've needed spectacles to see anything farther away than my toes. FireChaser, by contrast, has senses far keener than any flesh-and-blood creature humanity has ever encountered, and while we're flying, her eyes are my eyes—although Chaser doesn't have eyes in the traditional sense. She's a model C-47 Courser, equipped with a lattice of sensory receptors providing 360 degrees of vision, extending well beyond the spectrum normally visible to humans and with resolution fine enough to count the hairs on a flea.

I have no trouble following the tiny white speck as it moves through the sky. Though it must have turned back to inert matter moments after it left the umbris, it still had enough momentum to carry it a significant distance. As I watch, it arcs through the air, tips, and sails gracefully downward, dropping neatly into the umbris where Fourth Cohort is flying, some fifteen kilometers ahead of us.

No way, Midmurro says. *Absolutely no way.*

Did that really just happen? Pelashwa asks.

Whoever's inside that thing is absolutely batshit, Uo agrees admiringly.

None of us has ever seen someone jump from one umbris to another like that. It's possible, obviously, but judging the proper angle and velocity to make the shot is extremely difficult, akin to sinking a pebble into a cup floating in the center of a competition-sized swimming pool. Even as I think about it, I realize the unidentified object must have performed this same feat at least once already. That was how it appeared behind us, seemingly out of nowhere: It must have jumped from Seventh Cohort's umbris the way it just jumped from ours. But why? Assuming you can make a shot like that, there are few situations in which it would make sense, let alone be worth the risk of missing and grabbing nothing but aeter.

Before I can contemplate the possibilities any further, Centurio Kitu's voice comes through over DS. *All units be advised: Our defensive perimeter has been breached by an unidentified object that appears to be an equus of unknown design. Object has ignored attempts at communication and is to be considered hostile. Assume battle positions and prepare to match speed and heading.*

We're going after it? Midmurro asks, incredulous.

Kitu isn't going to commit an entire cohort to chasing that thing down, I say, *but he has to assume we're in a combat situation. We're going to consolidate with Fourth Cohort and increase speed to the intercept site. Time to form up, everyone. It's about to get tight in here.*

There isn't a stray comment, not an unnecessary syllable exchanged as my 'drille glides into position. Later, there'll be quibbling over cards and whether this counts as seeing combat, but for now everyone is prepared for the real thing. In moments, Sixth Cohort has doubled its speed, every unit locked in steely, rail-rigid flight.

Ahead, Fourth Cohort has reacted to the mysterious intruder just as we did, shifting into battle formation and hastening toward our destination. The unidentified object, meanwhile, has performed the same trick again, jumping ahead to the umbris where Third Cohort is flying, and then once more to the larger formation of First, Second, and Fifth, Ninth Legion's vanguard.

What is it doing? Midmurro wonders aloud. Once again, no one speaks up to chasten him; we're all asking ourselves the same thing. The unidentified object may not be an artillery shell, but that doesn't mean it couldn't be carrying some kind of ordnance. At the same time, it's hard to imagine any objective that would make sense. For some reason, I think of Centurio Kitu's description, *an equus of unknown design*. It makes me uneasy, though I couldn't say why.

Unlike the cohorts farther to the rear, Ninth Legion's vanguard is already in battle formation by the time the unidentified object drops into its umbris. First, Second, and Fifth Cohorts aren't taking any chances; instead of waiting for the object to reveal its intentions, they immediately move to engage. The formation's rear swirls back, blazing with flashes of color as deadly weapons come to life, promising the object's swift and merciless end. But the glowing trail of combat continues across the umbris, flaring here and there through the vanguard's formation amid sudden ripples of motion, until the object erupts from the other side, trails of angry energy—spikes of white-blue null, gouts of fire—close on its heels dissolving as they splash into the aeter, dying out as they pass beyond the range of the thelemity that makes them possible.

It seems there's cause for concern after all. This is the second time our unidentified object has survived something that should have destroyed it—and that's if you consider the four leaps from Seventh Cohort to the vanguard as a single near-death experience. It isn't too surprising that something moving that fast could get by a few cohorts unprepared for its unlikely arrival, but the vanguard, already in position to fight, should have made short work of it. If that really is an equus, it's way ahead of anything we have in the Legion.

We're approaching the intercept point now, close enough to see the battle already in progress. The sky below Lunar Veil glows with cross fire, the pinprick bursts of lazels, the sweeping curves of dogfighting equi, the sustained flashes of the gunships. Above, Lunar Veil is just discernible in the place where the blue light scattered through the atmosphere dims to black, a subtle shift in the pattern and color and texture of sky, swirling slowly like an image reflected in the surface of a pond.

Sixth and Third Legions have already engaged the enemy and appear to have the situation well in hand. Both have deployed their tetra fortresses, creating two parallel walls to hem Romeo in while the equites stab inward from the edges and gunships lance supporting fire from above and below. The Valentine incursion force, squeezed from two sides, looks to be on the verge of retreat, moving upward toward the Veil as though preparing to escape into Dis. It would be a poor strategy—they're a long way from the Front, and we've got an outpost on the other side of Lunar Veil that would be able to join the battle—but it's one of the few options they have left. If they keep fighting, it won't be long before their sources are trapped. After that, it's all over.

The unidentified object lands at the very edge of the skirmish. It isn't as spectacularly difficult a leap as the ones that came before, since the umbris surrounding the battle is larger. Umbrae grow in size the more sources are inside, and depending on how many Zeros Romeo brought with him, this one should be at least ten to twelve kilometers across—bigger once Ninth Legion joins the fight.

Despite the distance between the unidentified object and the battle in progress, Sixth Legion's rear guard breaks off to pursue. They'll have had word of the object's unusual behavior and won't want to risk its getting close enough to disrupt the ongoing rout—say by detonating some nasty artifice along a wall of assault platforms or amid a cluster of gunships.

The unidentified object, however, ignores the battle and pursuing fighters. Instead, it angles upward, toward Lunar Veil. This alone probably keeps it from being annihilated by Sixth Legion's rear guard, which gives chase nonetheless, firing a few distant bursts as the object accelerates into the sky. There's no chance of catching it now: It shoots straight up until at last it exits the umbris, disappearing into Lunar Veil like a stone dropped into a pond.

FORTY-THREE

IMWAY

This move, dashing into Lunar Veil, doesn't make any sense. The spaces between worlds—areas like Lunar Veil, where one Realm meets another—are the only places, other than the direct vicinity of a source, where thelemity is known to exist. That equus—if it was an equus—will be able to make it to the other side, but once it gets there, it'll be stuck. The Legion keeps an outpost in Dis, the next Realm over, though generally at a safe distance from the Veil. All the unidentified object will be able to do is float aimlessly until one of our patrols picks it up and captures whoever's inside.

Well, that was a lot of fuss over nothing, Uo says.

Stay sharp, I say. *That battle isn't over. Centurio Kitu will probably order us in any—*

I break off; something has happened. To the naked eye, it wouldn't look like much, but through FireChaser's enhanced vision, the shock wave of energy is obvious. My first thought is that our fontani must have moved in to engage the Valentine Zeros, but then I see that the disturbance is coming from Lunar Veil. At first slowly, then all at once, the Veil changes, its reflective surface turning transparent to reveal a view of Dis, the Realm beyond.

Most of the Realms humanity has visited contain a solar system moderately similar to our own. The planets there may be different from Earth—many are uninhabitable to human beings—but the basic setup is usually the same: a star with a few orbiting satellites. Dis is a notable exception, a wasteland of space populated by little more than drifting clouds of gas and dust.

Only the Dis we see now isn't empty.

It's easy to miss how large Lunar Veil really is when its façade blends so neatly into the sky, but as it flashes into transparency, a startling scene is revealed. In the foreground, a battle is in progress—hardly more than a skirmish, but it comes as a surprise, since our outpost in Dis hasn't reported combat of any kind. Compared to what we see in the space beyond, however, a few scattered fighters is almost beneath notice.

A Valentine army is arrayed across the dark sky, waiting rank upon rank, while in the barrenness of Dis, further swarms trail steadily closer through the distance of space. As we watch, a shudder moves slowly across the Valentine lines: Lunar Veil is transparent to them as well, and they've seen us.

All of this happens in a flash—hardly a few seconds, but enough time to survey the scene and count five heartbeats thudding in my ears—and then the Veil returns to its glassy, watery blankness. In those few moments, however, the lines of battle are completely redrawn. Instead of a dangerous but manageable incursion of Valentine fighters, we're dealing with a full-on invasion. The Valentine army we saw through the Veil was plainly gathering for a massive assault. Their strategy would be to take us by surprise, pouring through Lunar Veil all at once before we had time to react. By showing us what's on the other side, that unidentified object has ruined Romeo's plan. At this very moment, word will be spreading around the world for an emergency lockdown of Lunar Veil. And the Valentines won't wait for us to shut them out—they'll try to rush through before the Veil closes. Though we can't see it yet, the attack has already begun.

My cohort is close enough to get a good view as the first Valentine fighter descends out of the Veil, like the opening drop of a coming storm. A fraction of a second later, two more emerge, then a continuous flow of fighters too numerous to count, raining down onto the gathered ranks of Sixth and Third Legions. The Valentines show no hint of tactics or organization; this is an all-out charge, plain and simple.

The downpour quickly envelops the smaller Valentine force waiting beneath the Veil—guarding it, I now understand, from anyone who might consider peeking through. Sixth and Third Legions, though they didn't know it, ended up providing a screen that allowed our unidentified object, the equus of unknown design, an open path to the Veil. Now the two Legions, so much in command of the battle only seconds ago, see their lines broken apart beneath a deluge of enemy fighters, and the blue-black sky lights up in rainbow hues as both sides descend into combat.

Centurio Kitu's voice, measured in his signature calm, rings out over DS. *All units, prepare to engage. Your objective is to slow the enemy's ingress into Hestia until we can close Lunar Veil.* There's no need to relay Kitu's orders to my 'drille. Every fighter in Sixth Cohort has heard him.

Lunar Veil isn't normally a stable passage into the Realms. In the early years of the war, we were able to open it only once per month, and only for a few hours. Resupplying the Front was a complex and inefficient affair; if we didn't get everything through during that one narrow window, we'd have to wait an entire month before sending anything else. It was decades before we learned we could keep the Veil open indefinitely using a series of ingenic dynamos, called "Anchors," positioned strategically around the world. Right now, legionary detachments will be destroying or disabling Lunar Veil's Anchors, and once that happens, the Veil will close in a matter of minutes. The question now is how much of that Valentine army will make it through beforehand.

Sixth Cohort moves in, vibrations from the initial clash of combat reverberating around us. Already, the first wave of Valentines has begun to flow outward from the battle. They won't want to engage us here, won't want to hang around with nearly three full Legions to challenge them; instead, their goal will be to spread across the world, striking our weakest points. With their Legions occupied here, Sixth and Third Cities will be almost completely undefended. Ninth City, too, has committed the better part of its defense force to this operation. If one of those Zeros manages to get a clear shot, we may have nothing to come home to.

Everyone in Sixth Cohort is well aware of the stakes, and we hold nothing back. By the time the Valentine fighters come flooding our way, we've spread into a wide net, equites charging while tetra fortresses launch a wall of assault platforms in concave formation. My 'drille is in position near the top, S-Cannons and WhiteLances ready. *Stay close,* I tell them. *I want overlapping attacks—no one goes anywhere alone. And keep an eye out for Zeros. Romeo is trying to rush by, but he can't go anywhere without his sources. We hold the Zeros back, everyone else stays too.*

That's all I have time to say before the first volley from the gunships lights up the oncoming Valentine rush. There's a series of flashes, the air distorting with the discharge of force as the enemy's front line twists and collapses, the sleek multilimbed bodies of the Valentine fighters burning and contorting and fizzling out of existence. And then, all at once, they're everywhere. For one terrifying moment, I'm sure my 'drille is gone, that the wave of battle has swept them away, until I recognize Sensen's ride, Shadow-Singer, to one side, and Allomar's, StarHunter, on the other, and see that my 'drille has followed my orders exactly. We're all together, each covering the others, cutting through everything in our way.

From the number of Valentines still coming through, it's clear the planned attack would have been devastating, but even our brief glimpse beyond Lunar Veil was enough to tell us Romeo wasn't quite ready. Once his plan was revealed, he had no choice but to try to get as many troops across as possible before the Veil closed. As a result, the Valentine charge is a disorganized motley of different units, allowing us to take advantage of each one's weaknesses. Our gunships, safely ensconced behind a protective wall of assault platforms, pick off lone Valentine Type 5s and 6s—the general equivalent of our equi—and blast away indiscriminately at smaller units. Our equites, meanwhile, are free to range through the battle, dismantling heavier fighters while trampling the pesky Type 3s that might trouble the milites manning our fortresses. This the 126th does with ease, most of our time being spent wading through floods of Type 3s—enough to bother a lone equus, but no problem at all for a full 'drille moving as one.

Still, the Valentines keep coming, pouring through the Veil. We're slowing them down, but there are too many for us to completely hold back. Clouds of energy light up the sky as Valentines breach our walls of assault platforms, clawing through the cracks they've hammered in our defenses and tearing apart the milites who try to hold them back. Equites rush in to close the spreading gaps, only to be mobbed and overwhelmed by Romeo's fighters, the daytime sky staining sunset red with gwayd.

By the time Centurio Kitu announces that the Veil is closing, I know we're in the middle of the biggest battle Earth has ever seen, and it's far from over. Once Lunar Veil is sealed, we'll have to deal with all the Valentines that made it through. Already, there will be Zeros streaking toward our cities, raiding parties headed for helpless, isolated settlements, the potential targets far too numerous for us to defend them all. There's no telling how much damage they'll do before we can hunt them all down. After that, there will still be the matter of an entire Valentine army waiting in Dis for Lunar Veil to open again.

I lead my 'drille through a thick clump of 3s, while overhead a sustained strike from a team of gunships dismantles a pair of huge Type 6s leg by leg, bright purple gwayd rushing from each blasted limb and spattering down onto us. Over DS, I hear Ottumtee call out, *Chaser, I've got a bead on a Zero.*

I respond quickly. *Where?*

Just beneath the Veil.

Lunar Veil is still swirling, but slowly now, its liquid quality fading away, as if the sky itself were hardening in place. In a way, that's exactly what's happening: The fluid connection between worlds is being blocked off, the Veil becoming impermeable. Already, the influx of Valentine fighters has dwindled nearly to nothing, and what few make it through rush immediately for the outer edges of the action. Only a thin cloud of Valentines remains near the Veil, and at their center, the dark energy of a source.

All sources—Valentine Zeros as well as our own fontani—share a distinctive, easily recognizable profile: a roil of darkness outlined with gleaming bursts of light. The best description I've heard came from one of my rhetors at the Academy, a two-tour vet with a face pocked and scarred by deflected shards of null. What sources look like, he said, are rapids on a river, only instead of water, what's churning around is the darkness of space, and instead of foam at the edges, you have stars. Not the words I'd choose, but they get the idea across.

The source Ottumtee pointed out is the expected ball of sparkling blackness, but its behavior is unusual. Rather than joining the battle, it hovers in place, moving in tight, erratic circles. There are only two reasons that might explain this type of movement. One is that the source's supporting troops are near the edge of its umbris, and it needs to retain tight control over the thelemity it's projecting. The other is that it's fighting another source. There's no need for a source to worry about its umbris in a battle of this size, which means what we're seeing up there isn't one source, but two.

Looks like a duel, I say. We won't be much good in a fight like that. To a source, an equus—even a whole 'drille—is about as dangerous as a horsefly. We might get in a bite or two, but that's all. The only real chance of defeating a source—aside from throwing another source at it—is to trap it in the path of a whole lot of firepower. It wouldn't accomplish anything to call in Sixth Cohort now. The battle is still too hot to organize the sort of coordinated strike we'd need, and even if we could, the fact that two sources are fighting here means one of them is ours, and right now we can't tell which is which. To make any meaningful difference, we'd have to wait for a lull in the duel. I'm about to report Ottumtee's sighting to Kitu and order my 'drille back into battle elsewhere when something in the swarm of Valentines catches my eye.

At first it's only a glint of white among the tangle of enemy fighters, but then the tumble shifts, and I see it's the unidentified object, the equus of unknown design—only now that it isn't streaking across the sky, I can pick out more of the details, and I realize the design isn't completely unknown.

I've seen it before—in Kizabel's workshop.

We're going in, I tell my 'drille. *Spiral formation.*

There isn't a lot we can do in there, Chaser, Iftito cautions. *Maybe if we hang back, wait for the gunships—*

We're not going after the sources, I say. *We're going to bring back that equus. You can bet there will be people waiting to speak with whoever's inside. Surround and extract, understood? And be careful—we don't know what it can do, and no guarantee it's friendly.*

No guarantee it's friendly? Pelashwa says incredulously. *It basically just saved Earth from total destruction.*

The white equus—I can't think of it as an unidentified object anymore—appears to be mostly unarmed. It darts and weaves through the sparse cloud of Valentines, dealing out punches and kicks—attacks more appropriate to a schoolyard brawler than a refined weapon—whenever an enemy ventures too close. The Valentines, in turn, seem more concerned with intervening in the duel going on above. Presumably, they know which source is theirs and are trying to turn the fight in its favor. The white equus appears to be trying to fend off these same attacks, and taking a good amount of punishment for its efforts. Its armor is cracked and split in several places, and it sheds shimmering blue gwayd with each twist and turn.

Just be careful, I repeat to my 'drille. *Everyone fall in.*

I report the situation back to Kitu, let him know my plan. *Very good, Chaser,* he says. *Swift wings and sharp blades to you.*

Sharp and swift, sir.

We're swift, and we're sharp. The Valentines aren't expecting us, and we're able to cut well into them before they have a chance to respond. The first curl of Type 3s is rearing back to challenge us when from above there's a sound halfway between thunder and an infant's shrieking, like the sky is splitting open and not enjoying the experience one bit. FireChaser's senses quake and blur, and when she can see again, the air has filled with a faint pinkish haze scattered with what look like glowing embers. The boiling energy of sources in combat is now completely still, surrounded by a dense ring of burning air. The duel is over.

All fighting in the vicinity of the surviving source ceases. The Valentines know as well as we do that the victor here could easily wipe every one of us from the sky. In a few seconds, that's exactly what will happen to one side or the other, depending on whose source won, but no one wants to be first, and general wisdom tells us that the first to run will also be the first to die.

As steadily as I can, I scan through my roster of fontani for Sixth, Third, and Ninth Legions. To the naked eye, all sources may look like rivers of darkness, but each has its own unique flow of energy, and if this is one of ours, I should be able to identify it. But my search comes up empty. Either FireChaser's sensory arrays are still too garbled to pick this source out, or it wasn't on our side when the battle started.

We're dead, Midmurro says. *It's a Zero. We're all dead.*

Shut up, Sensen snarls.

Everyone cool it, I say. My voice is steady, but I know if we're facing down a Zero, our chances of getting out of this alive aren't good. Our best shot would be to make killing us more trouble than it's worth. *On my mark, I want you all to shut down and drop. It might not go after you if you don't look like a threat.*

What are you planning, Chaser? Pelashwa asks.

My plan, if it deserves to be called a plan, involves what I'm sure will be a very brief rush into the airspace of this possible Zero. Hopefully, the split second of distraction I provide will be enough for the rest of my 'drille to get out of sight.

But before I can make my move, the white equus, which had been hovering nearby, falters and begins to sink, too damaged to remain aloft any longer, and, reflexively, I move to intercept.

It takes less than a second, but when I look back, the Valentine fighters have been reduced to a few misty clouds of gwayd.

Uo and his ride, SunOnWaves, dip down to help me hold the white equus, which struggles weakly in our grip, while the rest of my 'drille surrounds us, everyone still watching the lone source floating above.

Guess it wasn't a Zero, Ottumtee comments.

Maybe it forgot which side it's on, posits Uo.

But it wasn't one of ours, either, right? Pelashwa says. *So who is it?*

The source answers for itself. A woman's voice comes ringing through our equi, vibrating with the dangerous energy audible in communications with fontani. *This is Fontana Malandeera of the Twenty-Second Legion,* the source says. *I must speak with your commanders immediately. There is urgent news from the Front.*

FORTY-FOUR

NAOMI

To attach overly much significance to any single experience or event strikes me as silly, but I cannot help thinking of the first time I saw the Valley of Endless Summer, what I now know as Ninth City, as the moment everything began to change. Until then, my life was an endless succession of dirt roads, of mountains and forests and nights spent in fields amid a circle of wagons, always in some new spot but never anywhere truly different. I knew of nothing more alien than the townships, with their paved streets, their smoking chimneys, their fearful citizens rushing among close-set houses. But as I stood atop the Great Ridge, looking down onto that terrain of summer amid a land enshrouded by winter, I felt the world expand around me. It was as if I had spent my life locked in a high tower, never knowing anything of the land below until one day I climbed down and set my feet on solid earth. Now it seems each step brings me to some strange new frontier. Every time I look, the world's boundaries have shifted again.

Even to say "the world," as if this one place contains the sum of all existence, is a mistake. The ground we tread is only a single point in an infinite web of worlds—the Realms, they are collectively called, though I have been learning their individual names as well. Our Realm, everything from the center of the Earth to the farthest reaches of the night sky, is called Hestia, named after the goddess of hearth and home in some ancient religion. The Realms found beyond Lunar Veil are not titled so sensibly. Instead, they have names such as Oz and Perelandra, Neverland and MapleWhite. Nonsense words, which Charles tells me come from imaginary countries described in old stories. I suppose I can understand why the explorers who first saw these places, at sea in a universe expanding beyond all reason or understanding, would seek out some familiar and comforting reference. I only wish the names they chose were not quite so ridiculous.

From Hestia, these Realms lead away in a line of ten, each connecting to the next like beads on a string. To reach any one, you must first travel through one of its neighbors. A person cannot go from Hestia to Barsoom, the fourth Realm distant, without first traversing Dis, Oz, and Arda in that order. And before that, you must cross the murky passage of Lunar Veil. There are other gateways out of Hestia, each attending on some celestial body: Mercurial Veil, Jovian Veil, and Saturnine Veil to name a few. It is presumed that the egresses from our Realm, like the Realms themselves, are beyond counting, perhaps one for every star in the firmament, even those too small or distant to see from Earth. Lunar Veil and the Realms beyond are significant for one very important reason: They constitute the path that brought our enemy here.

This string of ten Realms is known as the Corridor, largely because travel therein follows a single, fixed path. It seems odd that we would think of a succession of Realms, each as large and complex as our own, as something narrow, but I suppose this is so when compared to what follows. As with Hestia, the Realms of the Corridor branch out in multitudinous directions, but only by walking these ten in order can we find our way to the Front. The tenth Realm of the Corridor is called Wonderland, and from there the Realms bloom into a web of interconnected realities as intricate and convoluted as a rabbits' warren. We call this tangle of worlds the Lattice, and it is from somewhere inside this maze, we believe, that the Valentines originate.

In contrast to the Realms of the Corridor, with their fanciful titles, those of the Lattice are designated by strings of letters and numbers, a system I find nearly as incoherent. We do not know how many worlds the Lattice contains, only that, unlike the Corridor—which we believe began as a tunnel of exploration, newly discovered and never settled—the Lattice was claimed and cultivated long before our armies arrived. We have seen few Realms therein where the Valentines did not maintain some presence, though never have we encountered anything like a permanent colony. All we have ever found are military outposts, which have taken strong and universal exception to our presence in their domain.

Drawn out as a map, the Realms as we know them look something like a tree. Hestia is at the root, and from there the trunk of the Corridor grows, eventually spreading its branches to become the Lattice. The ragged edge of the uppermost boughs represents the Front, the line of Realms where our Legions are locked in combat with the Valentines. According to Charles, the beginning of the war was a time of chaos, when muddled clashes would roll from Realm to Realm, and the lines of battle shifted dramatically and often. Since then, the fighting has settled along a frontier of fifteen Realms, and while it is not unknown for one side or the other to advance or retreat, for the past three hundred years, the Front has been little but a slow and grinding stalemate.

All of this has been part of my education at the Academy of Ninth City. Khorography, as the mapping of the Realms is called, is part of the quite overwhelming field of Khorology, or study of the Realms, and one of several topics in which I have received remedial instruction, albeit the only one with Jax as my teacher. It is no simple subject, but Jax is a capable tutor, affable and never haughty about his superior knowledge. He can be quite funny at times, though if I am honest, I must admit I do not fully understand his sense of humor. Often my first clue that a joke has been made is Jax's sheepish grin, his way of apologizing for digressing, something I am sometimes impatient with him about. But I am grateful for his help, and never more so than today, as it helps me understand the debate now under way in Ninth City's Hall of the Principate, where the fate of Earth and its inhabitants is being decided.

Two days have passed since battle began in the skies beneath Lunar Veil, and only now is the general state of emergency being lifted. I grew concerned when Charles had been gone an hour, though Jax assured me it was common for surface evacuations to last through the day whether or not there was any danger. "The Legion doesn't want nonessential personnel running around until all the fighters are back in," he said, but I could tell his show of confidence was largely for my benefit.

It was getting on toward dusk by the time Charles returned, and it was only to bring news that the battle had spread. Our enemy was at large, and it was possible he would target Ninth City. We must be prepared to fight.

"There will be another fontana here in the city with you," Charles said, "but she may not be in a condition to fend off a Zero by herself. If there's a strike on Ninth City, she'll need your help."

Charles himself was to rejoin the battle. He had returned only to see us and to escort reinforcements back into combat. The air over Ninth City had filled with the buzzing specks of soldiers and fighters rising and descending among the tall buildings. When they had collected overhead, hovering like a cloud of midges, Charles looked at us, and said, "You can do this. You just have to believe in yourselves and each other." And then he was gone in a gust of wind and light.

"At least there are three of us," Jax said, watching the fighters disappear into the darkening sky. In the low light, the great peaks of Ninth City seemed lonely as mountaintops. "No one's heard of more than one Zero trying to strike a city at a time. Three against one should be OK."

I could tell he was nervous; so was I. We have both progressed in our training, but we are plainly a long way from being able to contend with a source of Charles's prowess. Only that day he had defeated our best efforts with hardly a breath of exertion. Charles has promised that with practice, I will be better able to control my mijmere, but I wonder sometimes whether his assurances are merely nice words meant to prop up my spirits. In our skirmish, I had built a concert hall to hide in, with balconies full of gracious and appreciative onlookers and an orchestra flooding the place with music, which I have come to understand is my Theme. But even before Charles began his attack, I heard a discord rising. My Genius, the man I know as the Maestro, was able to quell the disorder, but by then Charles had smashed through the doors, and my symphony was in ruins.

Jax and I both knew a Valentine source would likely be too much for us to contend with, and there was no telling whether this fontana Charles had mentioned was a seasoned warrior or untried amateur. I wondered why she had not come to wait with us at the Forum. Was she afraid?

As darkness fell, a heavy quiet descended with it, the kind of silence that precedes a storm, or a stalking predator, when even the birds and insects cease their chatter. It seemed to me something terrible was trailing us, misting our necks with its hot, cloudy breath. The night was cool, and I thought I smelled fire on the air. I wondered where Mama was just then, and Baby Adam, in the midst of such peril. And I thought of Rae. I knew she would be down in the city's shelters, but I had the strange feeling she had found her way into danger, and this frightened me even more.

Just then I would have given my eyeteeth to be anywhere else, anywhere but this plain of stone, with the night and our foes coming for us. It was my first real taste of the work I had been recruited to perform, and

I did not know how anyone could bear something so lonesome and desolate. I had joined the Legion to be a protector, and now it seemed clear I lacked the stomach for it.

The City Guns began to rumble then, stark pillars of light illuminating the sky. Suddenly, I felt something close around my palm. Jax had slipped his hand into mine. I did not feel it happen, nor could I say what his intentions were. Normally, I would have pulled away with some sharp remark at his presumption, but I did not. To my surprise, his touch reassured me. It told me that if I had to fight, I would not fight alone. He said not a word about it, and neither did I.

We waited all night, alone in the Forum, while the City Guns roared out their thundering tattoo and the sky rumbled and shimmered and glowed with the fury of distant battle. All across the horizon, armies wielding weapons of thelemity tore rips and scratches bright with blossoming color, displays I once considered wonders and called by such whimsical names as angel's stitches and moon babies but now knew to be only the tracks of this endless war.

Charles did not reappear until the following day, just before noon. He looked tired, weariness I knew must be more mental than physical. Visiting a mijmere has a way of restoring a person's constitution. Jax and I had each shaded once or twice over the course of the night, whenever we became fatigued, though never for very long, as we did not fully trust ourselves to control that sleepwalking power in the midst of a city.

"The fighting's over," Charles told us, "the worst of it, anyway." His voice and expression indicated the worst was bad indeed. "Romeo doesn't have enough strength left to try for another city. We're safe for now. Go get some sleep. There will be a meeting of the Consulate in the morning, and I want the two of you there. Whatever they decide, it will concern you both."

Charles was not inclined to say more, but it was plain from his demeanor that our situation was grave. I retired to my room, not expecting to sleep much, but was unexpectedly overcome by a deep and heavy exhaustion. It was a feeling I knew well, the kind of tiredness that comes after a day of strenuous work, or a long journey through the cold, but it seemed unaccountable when I had done nothing more than stand around the Forum, occasionally visiting my mijmere. For all it lacked sense, it was real enough: I was asleep in no time.

FORTY-FIVE

NAOMI

In the morning, I returned to the Forum with Charles and Jax. There was a good-sized crowd, a strange sight after so many hours there with only Jax for company. Most present were Academy cadets, though I picked out legionary uniforms as well. A number of dark figures were making their way toward the Hall of the Principate, a gloomy stone structure occupying one full side of the Forum, and Charles directed us to join them. They led us to a large, vaulted room equipped with heavy, tiered seats, like a lecture hall at the Academy only far more imposing. At the bottom was a flat, round space, with twelve figures seated along a steep stone platform above.

"Those are the Princepts of the twelve cities," Charles explained, "also known as the Consulate. They make all the major decisions regarding the war."

I knew as much already; the layout and functions of government among the so-called Incorporated Peoples of Earth were also part of the Academy's curriculum. I even recognized Consul Seppora, the leader of the Consulate, elected from among its members to wield executive power and cast tie-breaking votes. From my vantage, she seemed very old and frail, her face thin and her hair so white as to be nearly translucent. She looked almost about to nod off until I realized she was actually watching the room through keen, hooded eyes. Azemon, Princept of Ninth City, sat beside her, and seeing him raised a question in my mind. In addition to being Consul, Seppora was Princept of Fourth City. Why weren't we meeting there?

When I posed him this question, Charles did not answer immediately. Instead, he directed me toward one of the auditorium's middle tiers, where three empty seats waited conveniently for us. Only when he was seated, with Jax and me on either side, did he say, "The reason the Consulate is not meeting at Fourth City is that Fourth City was destroyed yesterday morning."

The even tone in which Charles made this report surprised me. I had not been part of this place very long, but I knew there were only twelve cities like ours in the entire world. They differed from Ninth City in some of their particulars, but each was a vast center of population, home to millions of people. "Did anyone survive?" I asked.

This time, Charles did not respond at all, and I understood his silence to mean the worst had happened. I felt a pang of shock and pain at the thought of so many people gone in an instant, and I thought, dizzily, of how the same might have happened here, with only Jax and me to stand in the way of disaster. I suspect Jax was having similar thoughts; he had become very pale.

The room around us, noisy when we arrived, began to quiet. A man had appeared below the ledge where the Consulate sat, calling for order, though the real source of the room's newly subdued temperament was Consul Seppora herself, whose hooded gaze swept over the room, spreading silence as a knife does jam.

When she spoke, her words, magnified to fill the room, cut through any lingering whispers. "This assembly of the Consulate of Earth will now commence," she said. Her voice had a hard, metallic edge to it, whether natural to her speech or an artifact of the magical means used to enlarge it I could not say.

Consul Seppora did not busy herself with preamble. She launched right into the matter at hand. "Recent events have convinced the members of this Consulate that the threat facing Earth is greater than we once imagined. Our purpose today will be to evaluate that threat and determine what actions are necessary by way of response. We will begin with reports from the twelve Principates and from the Front, after which we will hear recommendations before making our final decision. The first report will be from Imperator Feeroy of the Ninth Legion."

Imperator Feeroy was another figure I recognized. He was the head of Ninth City's defense force, outranked only by the Dux of Ninth Legion and Princept Azemon himself. Feeroy was a narrow man with a squinting, aggressive posture that reminded me of a hen surveying the ground for some tasty morsel to strike at. His present demeanor lacked that hunched eagerness, however; instead, he seemed strained, a slick sheen of sweat shining on his forehead and neck. I did not know why this should be. From the sound of things, Ninth Legion had acquitted itself admirably. Indeed, it was one of our own fighters that revealed the true nature of the Valentine attack: that it was no simple raid but the spearhead of a greater invasion. And yet Feeroy shied modestly from any credit, insisting that what mattered now was not the battle behind us but the danger ahead.

The reports that followed were not nearly so gracious, nor so encouraging. One by one, representatives of each Principate described how they had weathered the recent attack. First the Dux, as the head of each Legion is called, would set forth any military activity and losses, then the Praetor would describe the state of the city and settlements within the Principate's domain. I began to wonder why Feeroy had been the only one to speak from our Principate, when the Dux of Ninth City rose and began detailing our Legion's participation in the battle over the past two days. Feeroy, I realized, had been brought in only to narrate the turning point, the moment when the greater Valentine force first appeared.

Certain of these representatives were introduced with the word "provisional" appended to their title, and this, I learned, meant the title's former holder had been killed. It was the Dux Provisional of the Fourth Principate who brought news of the near annihilation of Fourth Legion, and the Praetor Provisional who told us of the destruction of Fourth City. Twelfth City had also fallen, and Sixth as well, and every Principate reported sweeping devastation among its settlements.

I could not help picturing Settlement 225—Granite Shore, as I knew it—and the people there, Mama and Baby and nearly all that remained of my coda. I listened with my heart in my mouth as Bennereg, Praetor of Ninth City, read the list of settlements lost from the Ninth Principate. When he passed over 225, I thought I would weep from relief, but, thankfully, I kept my eyes dry. By the time the last of the Principates had reported, the mood in the hall was heavy with defeat and despair. But the bad news had only just begun.

A woman seated among the lower seats stood and walked to face the Consulate. She was compact, sturdy, with short, spiky hair and clean, angular features. I could tell she was fontana, like me, by the gold pin at her neck, but that did not explain the reaction she drew from the assembly, the murmurs of concern I heard all around. I understood when she announced her name, "Fontana Malandeera of the Twenty-Second Legion."

The Twenty-Second was an expeditionary Legion; she had come from the Front.

For nearly an hour, Fontana Malandeera told us the story of her last days at the Front. It began with victory, or the appearance of victory. After years of fruitless struggle, our forces succeeded in breaking the enemy lines, winning a series of decisive engagements all along the Front. The Legion pursued its advantage, chasing Romeo's scattered forces, beating our enemy back whenever he turned to fight. In a matter of days, we had advanced farther through the Lattice than in the past two decades combined. By the time we finally encountered a new line of entrenched resistance, we had seized no fewer than thirty Realms. Confident in our methods of war, and hopeful that Valentine power was finally eroding, we prepared to fortify our positions and consolidate our gains.

We expected a renewed offensive once the Valentine Host had a chance to regroup, and readied our forces to deflect a strong frontal assault. But what came was no simple counterattack. The Valentines struck from our rear as well, descending on Legions still vulnerable from our swift advance. Nor was this any mere incursion, simply a pack of token marauders snuck through our lines to cause disorder among our ranks. It was a full host, pouring after us through Realms we had only just taken from the Valentines, Realms we had scoured for any sign of our enemy and thought utterly secure. Somehow, Romeo had insinuated a vast army directly behind our lines. Everyone agreed this should have been impossible, yet clearly it was not, for here the Valentines were, breaking our Legions apart.

Surrounded, wedged into indefensible positions, cut off from any retreat, the Legion resorted to its most desperate option, the final fail-safe in case of utter defeat. They closed the Front. They shattered the Anchors used to hold open the portals between Realms, allowing the passages to collapse and effectively halt the enemy's advance. Those passages could be opened again, but not for some time, and until then the great Valentine Host would be chopped into disparate pieces, its strength divided. Only a small portion of Romeo's forces, those at the very rear of his attack, remained with a clear path to Earth, and what was left of the Legion vowed to delay them long enough to send warning of the Front's collapse.

Fontana Malandeera was the one chosen to bring this message, and she raced toward Hestia with all the speed her magic allowed, knowing Romeo was following just as swiftly behind. But when she reached Dis, she found the enemy waiting to meet her. It was as she attempted to fight her way through—hopelessly, it seemed—with more Valentines swarming about her every moment, that the space below opened to a view of Earth, where she witnessed another battle in progress: our own Legions fighting beneath Lunar Veil.

All of this Fontana Malandeera recounted to us in the most matter-of-fact style, with no indication that it might well be the worst disaster ever to befall the human race. "What remains to say others have told better than I can," she concluded.

The air in the auditorium had taken on a stale, suffocating feel. I had only been part of this Legion a short while, but news of its defeat struck me like a punch to the gut. I could only imagine how those around me, bred to fight this long war, must feel. I glanced at Jax; he sat perfectly still, jaw set, staring at some point in the distance.

"Fontana Malandeera brought with her messages from her commanders, which verify her testimony," Consul Seppora said once Malandeera had taken her seat. Already, some in the assembly had begun to protest, shouting that Malandeera's tale could not possibly be true, but the Consul's clipped declaration silenced them. "We have every reason to believe the Front has dissolved and that our Legions there no longer represent a viable defense. We must proceed under the assumption that the Valentine Host will be able to move unchecked toward Hestia.

"By closing off the Front," Seppora went on, "our Legions have delayed the Valentine advance, but only for a time. Based on the information brought to us by Fontana Malandeera regarding the composition of the Front, we estimate that the Valentine Host will reach Earth in force within seven years, our time. A smaller but still substantial portion could arrive in as few as thirty-one months. The remainder, that fraction not caught when the Front was closed, is already here, held back only by Lunar Veil, which will open again in twenty-eight days." She paused, allowing us to absorb the meaning of her words. "We therefore have twenty-eight days to act. The Consulate will now open the floor to recommendation and discussion."

That was hours ago. Since then, the debate has gone on and on. The consensus seems to be that we would stand only a slim chance of defeating the enemy presently waiting beyond Lunar Veil. The Valentines will have time to muster a well-ordered attack, while our main advantage, the City Guns arrayed across our planet, has been crippled by the loss of three of our cities. Even if we are able to prevail in the coming battle, we would not survive the ones to follow. Earth is by all accounts a strong place to stand and fight, but only if there is someone to do the fighting, and it will take time to rebuild the Legion to a strength capable of resisting the Valentine Host. The most optimistic estimate I have heard for this task is twenty years. Others proclaim twenty-five, or thirty, or fifty. But all agree it will require many more than the seven years now left to us.

Somewhere amid the discussion, the endless review of figures and time-tables, catalogues of our remaining defenses and the coming waves of Valentine fighters, the notion comes to me that a decision has been made, something everyone knows but no one is willing to voice. It hangs in the air like a ghost, floating silently down the aisles of arguing men and women.

Imperator Feeroy is the one to finally set it loose. He stands before the assembly and announces that we must leave Earth. We can escape through another of Hestia's gates before Lunar Veil reopens. If we close Saturnine Veil behind us, it will be some thirty years before it becomes passable again, and by then we can be gone without a trace, so lost among the Realms that the Valentines will never find us. When the time is right, we can settle again. We can find a new home, a new Earth. It is the only way to ensure humanity's survival, he says.

The protestations that follow are only for show. No one wants to advocate the surrender of Earth, but all are willing to be defeated in their determination to stay. I am reminded of the night my coda settled on Granite Shore, listening to them debate whether to go north and die of cold or head south and die at the hands of hostile tribesmen. To me, our discussion now feels just as hopeless. Though I find myself admiring Feeroy's courage in saying what no one else would, I feel certain that if we abandon Earth now, we will never be safe. But what can I say? No one will listen to me. What good is a feeling compared to the vicissitudes of war, to doom-filled forecasts, years of repairs and recruitment to reassemble our Legion, and the threat of an invincible enemy relentlessly pursuing us?

I am afraid to look at Jax, or Charles, afraid I will see in them this same conviction, this foggy but powerful perception that leaving Earth would be a fatal mistake. And then I hear the voice of Princept Azemon speaking over the surrounding din. "Consul Seppora," he says, "there is another proposal I think the Consulate should hear. If you would please acknowledge Curator Ellmore of the Academy of Ninth City, I believe she can explain further."

I follow the room's collective gaze down to the steely figure of Curator Ellmore, and beside her, Vinneas.

FORTY-SIX

KIZABEL

While Curator Ellmore delivers an eloquent and politically dexterous account of the poor decision-making that led us to this dire state, carefully avoiding any assignment of blame while simultaneously issuing an unequivocal I-told-you-so to everyone who saw fit to ignore Romeo's perplexing behavior over the past months, praising Vinneas's foresight and tactical wherewithal without dwelling too long upon the details of his actions, insubordinate and not-quite-treasonous-but-with-a-strong-scent-of-mutiny as they were, I flip nervously through my notes. The heavy stack of diagrams, maps, schematics, tables, and figures I've spent the last twenty-six hours preparing looks unnervingly similar to the delirious scrawlings of an insane person—which, incidentally, is about how I feel. Insane. Vinneas, meanwhile, is utterly self-possessed, casually jotting notes on a small pad of paper, his only accessory.

The Consulate towers over us, its members listening intently, their expressions ranging from intrigued to concerned to potentially cannibalistic. I decide Consul Seppora is without question the most intimidating person I have ever seen. For all her aged frailty, she has the scaly, contemplative demeanor of a slow-moving reptile capable of snapping out with blinding speed, and I get the sense she could literally bite my head off with her crocodilian jaw. For the fourth or fifth time since sitting down, I tip my coffee cup to my lips and find it empty. In the lower right-hand corner of his notepad, Vinneas has doodled a castle surrounded by mounted knights. Stifling a yawn, I attempt to discreetly rub my eyes and roll the kinks from my neck.

I spent the first night of what is now being called the Battle of Lunar Veil in an uncomfortable cell in Shelter Block East, the guest of Ninth

City's Gendarmerie.[1] I will be the first to admit that I was apprehended under decidedly incriminating circumstances, having first gained access to the Fabrica by underhanded means, then outright broken into my former workshop, strong-arming a duly authorized city instarus in the process. But I still don't think the pair of gendarmes who discovered me in the wreckage of my workshop, cackling to myself beneath a Snuggles-shaped hole[2] in the ceiling, needed to tackle me quite so enthusiastically.

When I objected to this unfriendly treatment, I was informed that during incursions, the entire Principate was considered to be in combat, and anyone taking advantage of the general distraction for the perpetration of mischief was in fact aiding the enemy and should be treated accordingly. At that point, it's possible I might have claimed my so-called mischief was actually part of a plan to save the world, and on that count I was doing a whole lot more than a couple of potbellied gendarmes like the ones carrying me down to Shelter Block East. Needless to say, things did not improve. Names were called, accusations leveled, and, in the end, I was deposited in a locked cell[3] to wait out the remainder of the incursion.

It was an awful night, not so much because of the cell itself—which was small but generally not so bad—as my increasing certainty that the world was about to end. Vinneas was right about the impending Valentine invasion, I was sure of it, and if Rae was going to reveal the truth, I knew she had to do it soon. The more time passed, the surer I became she was dead, and we were all going to die, too.

But then, sometime around 0630, I heard shouting from the direction

---

1 A branch of the Legion tasked with policing activity within the city, composed mostly of legionaries who washed out of more elite fighting units and who thus suffer from feelings of inadequacy and a sense of underutilized potential, which, combined with a frustrated desire to get out and shoot something, often means an unpleasant experience for anyone who happens to fall into their clutches. This is especially true during incursions, when the city's defense force is engaged in actual combat with the actual enemy, and the gendarmes are subsequently both at the height of their power and most aware of their diminished status vis-à-vis the rest of the Legion.

2 Just a normal explosion-type hole to the untrained observer, but I was fairly sure I could trace a few lines of the Project's familiar frame in the blasted-out raggedness Rae and Snuggles left behind as they exited my workshop.

3 With actual metal bars, no less—a precaution to keep me from escaping if the city lost thelemity.

of the room where my captors had retired to their all-important duty of drinking and telling dirty jokes, and Rae appeared, frog-marching the gendarmes to my cell, her accent, usually easy enough to understand, rendered incomprehensible by her rage. I learned afterward that she had come with orders for my release from Princept Azemon himself, but at the time, she appeared to have freed me with pure righteous fury.

No sooner had the door to my cell opened than Rae threw herself at me, encircling me in her long arms and practically lifting me off the ground. "It worked," she said, releasing me and clasping my hands.

Finding myself on the verge of tears, I took a moment to clear my throat to avoid any sort of emotional lacrimation. "They closed Lunar Veil?"

She nodded hesitantly. "Some of the Valentines got through. The fighting is still going on, but the Curator and Princept Azemon say the worst of it is over. We're all right for now."

"What about Snuggles?"

Rae's expression took on an aggrieved twist. "Oh, Kizabel," she said. "I don't know. He was in bad shape by the time we got back. I had them take him to your workshop." She smiled weakly. "The Curator says you can have your workshop back, by the way. They'll even fix the ceiling. Do you want to go see him?"

What I really needed was sleep. I'd dozed off once or twice during my captivity but had been too worried and terrified overall to get any useful REM. But at the present moment, I was more interested in how Rae and Snuggles had fared in the battle. The two gendarmes, who had been listening in frowning befuddlement to our conversation, moved aside at a contemptuous glance from Rae, and we joined the columns of cadets and citizens just then being allowed to leave the shelters.

As we walked, Rae narrated the battle. Snuggles had performed even better than I'd hoped, allowing Rae to puddle-jump to the head of our formations and wing past a skirmish already in progress, all with only minor damage as far as I could tell. Rae was somewhat less informative on the subject of Snuggles's injuries,[4] but by the time we reached my workshop, I was beginning to think they weren't as bad as she imagined.

---

4 Probably because this was her first time in combat. Animi experience damage to their equi much as they would an injury to their own bodies, but what feels like a mortal wound may in fact be pretty inconsequential from the perspective of engineering and repair.

Lady Jane was waiting for us, a blur in the brushed metal of my workshop door. "You did it!" she squealed. In the background, I heard loopy CE jazz music, one of the songs she played in celebratory moments. "We're not all dead!"

"We might all still die," I felt compelled to point out.

"With that attitude, you can just stay outside, thank you very much," Lady answered.

I didn't feel like arguing, and to be honest, I was pretty proud of myself, and of Rae, and of Lady, who had played her own part in our continued existence, overpowering the instarus that had been posted to keep me out of my workshop. In the spirit of the occasion, I offered her the sincerest "Yippee" I could muster.

"Good enough, I suppose." Lady sighed, pulling back the door for us. The scenery behind her mirrors showed the aftermath of a wild party, a landscape of collapsed chairs, smashed glasses, balloons drifting among overturned bottles of champagne.[5] My workshop was in a similar state of disarray, as was to be expected following the hastily arranged launch of an experimental and still-somewhat-unpolished equus.

The wall to Testing Floor Sixteen was open, and there Snuggles knelt, looking just like the statue of an ancient armored knight carved in white marble, luminous in the new daylight shining through the hole in my workshop ceiling. The cracks and erosions scarring his armor only added to his antiqued appearance, though if you looked closely, you could see a few spots of exposed thurgo-muscle glinting like shards of metal in white sand.

"I think I broke him," Rae said miserably. "By the time we got back, I couldn't get him to fly anymore. He could hardly walk. Imway and his people had to carry us most of the way," she added.

"What?" Imway still occupied the number one spot on my shit list, and hearing his name in the context of our present victory[6] made no sense at all. I whirled on her, not sure I'd heard right, but the disgusted look on her face told me I had.

---

5 A grape-based alcoholic beverage, notable for its effervescent carbonation and popularity during CE festive occasions. Not so different from Fizz, presumably, though I've never tasted it myself.

6 A precarious and maybe only temporary victory, admittedly.

"He and his people were the ones who pulled me out of the fight," she said, then smiled. "He thought he was rescuing you, because of Snuggles."

Recently, my feelings toward Imway had rested largely along the resentful/homicidal end of the emotional spectrum, but hearing this caused an unexpected blip. If Rae was telling the truth, Imway had dived into an ongoing battle to rescue me—or a person he thought was me. Maybe our childhood friendship still counted for something after all.

Once Snuggles was escorted back to Ninth City and his rider's identity revealed, no one could quite decide what to do, except for Rae, who was so exhausted she could barely stand and promptly collapsed in a heap. It was solidly six hours before she was either conscious or coherent enough to explain what had happened. I decided I couldn't begrudge her the nice night's sleep she'd had while I was cooped up in a four-and-a-half-square-meter cell worrying myself to death, given that she'd made it a priority to track me down as soon as she had regained the ability to form complete sentences—but mostly because of the disconsolate way she was now looking at Snuggles, like he was some adorable but pitifully injured woodland creature.

"He'll be fine," I told her. And he would. Snuggles might have been almost inoperable at the moment, but he'd be an easy fix. The symptoms Rae described—the lag in responsiveness, her own debilitating exhaustion—were textbook gwayd loss. It was obvious he'd sustained a number of small injuries, and without any active sealing or cauterizing artifices—among the many finishing touches I'd left out during his hurried launch—he'd leaked gwayd at an absurd rate. I was impressed Rae had been able to keep him moving as long as she had; the strain must have been enormous.

"Really?" Rae asked, as if she didn't dare hope.

"Oh, sure. Flesh wounds only. I've done worse just testing him out here. We'll have him back on his feet in no time—maybe even a few hours, if you're up to try an activation later."

"I thought we were celebrating!" Lady shouted indignantly.

I was already feeling better, bubbling with the energy I get whenever there's real, interesting work to be done. "This is how I celebrate," I said, already searching for my tools amid the debris of the workshop.

I had erected the still-slightly-mangled egg crate and was stripping Snuggles from his armor, Rae playing tinker's assistant, running for riggings and materials and answering questions regarding the Project's function during his first long flight—already I'd begun to imagine a few tweaks and improvements—when from the direction of my workshop door I heard Lady say, "Well, look who's decided to show his face!"

My first guess, based on Lady's saucy tone, was that it had to be Imway—I gathered from Rae's incipient scowl that she thought the same— but the rejoining voice belonged to Vinneas. "Lady! It's been ages. So lovely to see you again. Having a party?"

"All by *myself*," she answered, slurring[7] somewhat, "because everyone else is being *tedious.*"

"Unconscionable," Vinneas answered, then paused. I had climbed down from the scaffolding around Snuggles, and when Vinneas saw me, he crossed the room in five long strides and clasped me to him. "Great work, Kiz," he said, voice barely above a whisper. "I don't know what I'd have done if anything had happened to you out there."

"Yeah, no problem," I said. It was my second very-tall-person hug of the day, and I was quite overcome. So nice to know your friends care. "I was actually pretty safe, down in the shelter holding cells. Rae did most of the dangerous stuff."

Rae had been standing quietly a few steps back. Vinneas actually looked confused to find her there—a rare moment when he seemed unsure of himself. "Hello, Vinneas," Rae said.

After the enthusiastic squeezing I'd received from both of them, I expected Vinneas and Rae would have some similar greeting for each other, but all that passed between them was a tentative smile, followed by several seconds of silence and hesitant shifts in posture—awkwardness, I realized with an insightful jolt, that resulted from as-yet-unexpressed romantic sentiments. An excited sound almost like a chirp escaped me before I could stop it, and I had to pretend a sudden tussive fit to avoid suspicion. This was big news. Imway, as one would expect from a gorgeous macho jerk, was quite the ladies' man, but I'd never known Vinneas to show any interest in females as such. Lady had obviously reached a similar conclusion: She was

---

7 It was entirely possible Lady had managed to get drunk. Instari live by the rules they create for themselves; if Lady decides to conjure alcohol, it could very well impair her cognitive functioning.

giving me the bawdy eyebrow waggle she used to denote steamy drama afoot.

"Rae," Vinneas said, overcoming his uncertainty by an obvious outlay of effort. "You took on half the Legion and an entire Valentine army for us. Thank you. I hear you fly like a shooting star."

Rae rewarded him with a sparkling grin. "Don't forget Lady."

"Yeah!" agreed Lady. "You know what those assholes wanted to do to me, Vinn? They were going to *archive* me, bottle me up in some snow globe and file me away as an example of an interesting but volatile and ultimately failed artifice."

"Ingrates and cretins, all of them," Vinneas affirmed, "and, unfortunately, it looks like they'll need your help again."

When Curator Ellmore learned a mysterious equus had appeared beneath Lunar Veil to miraculously unmask a shocking Valentine offensive, she immediately recognized Vinneas's work and arranged to have him brought by velo from the harvester where he'd been stranded when the battle began. While I was stewing in prison, and Rae was in an insensible vegetative state, Vinneas had been privy to the worldwide chaos of the battle and the feverish scrambling as our leaders attempted to figure out what to do next.

The situation was bad. Earth's Legions had been reduced to a fraction of their former strength, yes, but that was nothing compared to the news from the Front. Rae and Snuggles weren't the only exotic objects Ninth City's defense force recovered during the battle. They'd also brought back Fontana Malandeera of the Twenty-Second Legion, sent to us on orders from our commanders at the Front. Our former commanders at the former Front, that is. From the sound of things, we were all pretty well and truly screwed. Vinneas had spent the night listening to officials in cities across the world frantically deliberating over a list of dwindling and increasingly unattractive options.

"They want to abandon Earth," he told us now. "All the Princepts agree. The Consulate is meeting here tomorrow, and they'll make it official then."

Rae and I were gaping at him, speechless; the only sound was Lady's light snoring. "We can't leave!" Rae shouted. "There has to be something we can do!"

"I've listened to the analysis," Vinneas said. "It seems like the only way to save humanity."

"But you have a plan," I said, finishing his thought for him. He had that look he gets when he's holding on to an idea, something elaborate and enormous and crazily grand, and even before he said it, I knew I'd do everything I could to help.

"There's a chance." He met my eyes, grinning. "Do you still have your copy of *Associative Architecture*?"

FORTY-SEVEN

KIZABEL

And so here I am, nearly two full sleepless day-and-night cycles later, with plans for a prodigious and fearsome world-saving weapon crammed into half a dozen folders, plus all the data sets and proofs and engineering summaries and architectural details I thought I'd need to make my case, piled into a mountainous mess of papers I have to keep straightening and adjusting to prevent the whole thing from spilling humiliatingly onto the floor in front of the Consulate and a good portion of the remaining leadership of the Twelve Principates. Curator Ellmore has finished her speech, and as she returns to her seat, Vinneas rises and walks, with that unerringly confident manner of his, to lay out our plan before the Consulate.

The argument he makes is simple. For what little we know about our enemy, there are a few certainties. We know their military strength outstrips ours. Until recently, we had reason to consider our forces evenly matched—the Front had been at a stalemate for centuries—but no longer. Compared to the Valentine Host presently on its way to Earth, our remaining defenses are so minuscule as to be insignificant. We know, too, that the Valentines possess an understanding of thelemity, and of the Realms, far greater than our own. For all our efforts to discover the secret behind their regular incursions into Hestia, how they are able to bypass our lines at the Front—and perhaps the Realms themselves—to appear without warning over Earth, their method remains a mystery. This is only a single example, but it is telling evidence that the Valentines may possess capabilities we haven't yet imagined. In fact, Vinneas says, there is only one advantage we can claim with any confidence over our enemy: time.

Of all the Realms we have seen in centuries of exploration, Hestia, our home, stands out in one crucial regard: Time here moves faster than any-where else. There is no way to know for certain how unique Hestia is in this respect. If the Realms are truly infinite, as we suspect, then there must be some other Realm careening across time at an even greater velocity. But we have never encountered such a place. Indeed, we have yet to find a Realm where time moves more than a tenth as quickly as it does in Hestia. Moreover, there appears to be a trend in the speeds at which different Realms travel through time: The farther you proceed into the Lattice, the slower—on average—time flows. All available evidence indicates that no Realm the Valentines presently occupy can keep pace with time in Hestia. And this asset, time, outweighs everything the Valentines have in their favor. In matters of war, time trumps all.

Given enough time, we can close the distance between ourselves and our enemy—build a stronger Legion, advance our mastery of thelemity—and perhaps one day surpass them. With time on our side, Vinneas argues, we do not merely have a chance of defeating the Valentines. Victory is all but inevitable. And if we surrender time to our enemy, defeat is just as certain.

"Very eloquent, Censor Vinneas," Consul Seppora says, once Vinneas has finished. "You make an excellent case, and I doubt anyone in this room would disagree with your central premise. But, unfortunately, time in this instance is not on our side. We are facing the imminent arrival of an enemy we cannot hope to defeat."

"Cannot hope to defeat *yet*," Vinneas replies.

I suffer an involuntary cringe at his presumption in correcting the leader of the Consulate, almost expecting her to lean down and crunch his skull for an afternoon snack. Instead, Seppora's thin, saurian mouth stretches into something like a smile. "Explain, please."

"As Fontana Malandeera described in her report," Vinneas says, "when our forces realized they were about to be overrun, they closed off the pas-sageways leading between the Realms along the Front, leaving a signifi-cant portion of the Valentine Host without any clear path to Earth. The Valentines will have to wait for those passages to reopen—perhaps only a matter of days from their perspective, but for us, it will mean a reprieve of months or even years. If we could close off other Realms along their route to Earth, we would delay the Valentine Host even more—possibly long enough to mount a convincing defense."

Muted discussion has begun pattering through the crowd behind me, but Consul Seppora remains unmoved. "I do hope you have more for this Consulate than *possibly*, Censor."

"Small Valentine raiding parties may be capable of reaching Hestia by some unknown alternate course," Vinneas continued, "but the main body of the Valentine Host will have to advance through the Realms the same way we do. If that were not the case, they would be here already. Once the Valentine Host enters the Ten World Corridor, it will have only one path to Hestia. I propose that we send as much of our remaining Legion as we can spare into the Realms to close off the Corridor before the Valentine Host arrives."

The ambient chatter has become too noisy to ignore, rising as more and more people begin to understand what Vinneas intends. Consul Seppora raises a hand for silence. "And you believe such a mission would serve a useful purpose?"

"Yes. If we are able to seal the first four Realms leading away from Hestia, we will delay the Valentine Host an additional fourteen years, as viewed from our perspective on Earth. If we can close five, that total will rise to twenty-four years, allowing us more than twenty-six years in all to prepare for the earliest estimated arrival of the Valentine Host. Given the enemy positions outlined in Fontana Malandeera's report, an excursion of the sort I'm proposing should be able to secure at least five Realms—and with them, twenty-six years—before encountering any serious opposition."

Consul Seppora examines Vinneas closely, while on either side members of the Consulate whisper to one another. "And when they *do* encounter opposition, Censor Vinneas?" Her implication is clear: Will this be a suicide mission? From the discussion I hear rising once again around the room, most people consider the question a nonissue; sacrificing a few legionaries to salvage the entire war sounds like a steal of a deal.

"The expedition would have no immediate way back," Vinneas admits, "but it could easily escape the oncoming Valentine Host by simply exiting the Corridor. As you know, every Realm, including those along the Corridor, branches outward into a potentially infinite number of other Realms. The expedition has merely to choose one such passageway to remove itself from the Valentine Host's path. The Host itself will be unable to follow without further delaying its advance on Hestia. If, as we all hope is the case, our renewed Legion is able to repel the Valentine attack and retake the

Corridor, we will be able to retrieve the expedition then. From the expedition's perspective, it may be only a few years' wait."

The despair, so palpable here only a short while ago, has begun to recede, to reshape into something like hope. But not everyone is convinced. Nearby, someone signals for Consul Seppora's attention. When he stands, I recognize the gaunt face and beady eyes of Imperator Feeroy.

"Consul Seppora," he says, "if I may address the Consulate. I am familiar with Vinneas and know him to be a very intelligent young man, but he has little experience in the practice of war, and I believe he has ignored one very crucial detail."

"What detail would that be, Imperator?" the Consul asks.

"The Valentine Host is not some distant threat to be countered by long-term strategy, a problem we have years to solve," Feeroy says. "The first wave is here, right now, waiting to invade. There will be no delaying the attack. In twenty-eight days, the Moon will be aligned to reopen Lunar Veil, and Romeo will have a clear path to Earth. Tell me," he says, turning to Vinneas, "how does that fit into your proposal?"

"In order for the expedition to succeed in its mission, we will first have to defeat the Valentine vanguard," Vinneas says, like a man checking items off a to-do list. "With proper planning and preparation, I believe we can win a decisive victory over the enemy forces stationed in Dis."

"A decisive victory?" Feeroy repeats with an incredulous chuckle. "How exactly do you imagine such a thing is possible, Censor? The Legion is scattered and crippled, our defenses and infrastructure in complete disarray. Three of our cities have been destroyed, and it will be years before those remaining return to their full strength. There is still fighting in progress all over the planet. From what I have been told, there is a rogue source—probably activated accidentally during the battle—that has yet to be brought under control and may very well cause further destruction. Enough of our tetra fortresses and gunships have been damaged or destroyed that we would be hard-pressed to mount an effective defense at Lunar Veil, let alone launch an expedition into the Corridor afterward. And even if we could muster the necessary strength, how would you manage to move a force sufficient to fend off the remnants of the Valentine van? Most of our long-distance transports were at the Front. I doubt those left on Earth would carry half the legionaries required, let alone enough food and supplies for all the years you plan on waiting for rescue."

Vinneas had expected precisely this argument and told me to be ready once it came up because I'd be getting my turn with the Consulate very soon. "Our cities can provide all the resources we need," Vinneas says.

"Our cities?" Feeroy scoffs. "What good will our cities be to us at Lunar Veil, or out in the Realms? It isn't as if we can take them with us."

Finally, Vinneas allows himself a smile. He turns toward Consul Seppora, "If you please, Consul, I'd like to introduce my colleague, Officer Aspirant Kizabel, to explain the logistics of our proposal."

That's my cue. Feeling thoroughly light-headed, I descend to face the Consulate. Once again, I have visions of being devoured alive, only now the imagery is far more real and splattery, with lots of animals-savaging-one-another-in-the-wild gore.

Imperator Feeroy is so offended by my presence that he momentarily forgets his manners. "Officer *Aspirant*? You brought a schoolgirl to lecture the Consulate on strategy?"

"Kizabel is eminently qualified to speak on the matter at hand," Vinneas answers coolly. "She is an accomplished faber and artifex, who contributes regularly to studies at Ninth City's School of Philosophy and to repairs at Ninth City's Fabrica. I can provide further references for her work, but I am certain her competence will be readily apparent once she is given a chance to speak."

"She is a *student*, Censor," insists Feeroy.

"As was I, until about two months ago, and you, Imperator, sometime before. In fact, I would venture to guess every member of the Consulate has had some experience with our Academies at one point or another."

"I should think Censor Vinneas has earned the benefit of the doubt," Princept Azemon says from Seppora's side. The implicit reference to Vinneas's warnings about the coming Valentine attack delivers a visible sting to Feeroy.

"At this point, we must be prepared to judge ideas on their own merit, whatever the source," Seppora agrees. She turns her small, glinting eyes on me. "Please, proceed."

"Right, great," I say, fumbling through my folders for the plans I need. "Well"—I stammer a few fractured syllables, cough into my hand—"as Censor Vinneas said, with the exception of fontani, our cities are the planet's best weapons. They're a lot like the fortified positions we build at the

Front: self-sustaining, with everything required to conduct ongoing operations. They can maintain battle spires—which launch troops and assault
platforms more effectively than tetra fortresses—and heavy artillery far
more powerful than our gunships. I'm talking 160, 208-soul guns. All of
which requires a great deal of supporting structure, not to mention an
operational framework too large and complex to easily or efficiently carry
into battle. That's why our cities are arranged as they are, laid out to jointly
defend the planet. But what if it were possible to create a city that moves?"

Carefully, I lay my plans across the floor and stand back. From my
pocket, I produce a cantivel[1] containing a projection artifice. At a flick of
my thumb, my scribbled and amended and appended designs rise lumi-
nously into the air over my head, giving the Consulate and everyone else
in the room a good, clear view. "This is IMEC-1," I say, very conscious of
the vast volume of attention now focusing on me. "As you can see, it possesses all the attributes of a fully functioning city, including living and
working areas, sustainable supplies of food and water, and facilities from
which to launch military sorties. It differs from other thelemically powered cities in only one significant way: mobility. By rendering the offensive
and defensive capabilities of a fortified city portable, IMEC-1 would make
the ideal base of operations for an expeditionary force. Even considering
the Legion's losses thus far, it could be fully staffed while leaving ample
support behind for the continued defense of Earth."

As I transition into a description of the IMEC's basic design and function, making sure to linger on the theory that makes the whole gorgeous
contraption possible,[2] my blueprints multiply and metamorphose, depict-
ing the city from numerous angles and levels of detail, diagramming
everything from the layout of the streets to the internal plumbing to the
prevailing weather patterns. What we have, now parading before the
assembled bigwigs of the Incorporated Peoples of Earth, is nothing less

---

1 Any device made to store artifices for later use; especially useful for pacifers, since they're
  unable to create artifices on their own, though revenni like me also find them expedient.
  Basic cantivels usually take the form of a small metal disk, which can be activated by moving a finger or thumb across its surface.

2 With copious supporting notes and citations, naturally. Never has an urban layout been
  more thoroughly researched and referenced than that of IMEC-1.

than a fully fledged flying city. Or, as Rae so enthusiastically put it, "A real live Laputa,[3] you goddamned loony beauty!"

The overall effect is at once disarmingly simple and deliciously complex, a complete—and, I hope, believable—picture of a city capable of surviving anything either the Valentines or the Realms can deal out. We started with EASSaC-2, that brilliantly impractical, fanciful spree from *Associative Architecture*, pillaging the work we'd already done on establishing habitable environments under conditions not traditionally ideal for an air-breathing, terrestrial, human community and applying it by strenuous mental acrobatics to the various horrific scenarios to be found beyond Lunar Veil, including but not limited to: the vacuum of outer space, toxic and corrosive atmospheres, deadly high-energy radiation, extreme gravitational forces, temperatures exceeding 1.9×10^7 K and approaching absolute zero, and swarms of alien insects carrying flesh-eating alien microorganisms. Getting the whole thing into the air was simple when compared to building what is effectively a mini-ecosystem not only capable of supporting the population of a major city but able to survive travel at interplanetary speeds. The same innovations that go into Personal Gravity can be used, with a little elbow grease and the help of associative architecture–type applications of large-system dynamics, to put a city in the sky.

But it's obvious what's got this auditorium of eyeballs so fixated isn't the equations for shockingly authentic artificial sunlight or the thelemic schematics for circadian stabilizers. It's the dramatic (if conceptual) views from the IMEC's towers, the pristine fields and sparkling waterways suspended in the midst of space. I've given these people the next best thing to walking around inside the place, and in a few moments, they're going to have that experience, too. Here I'll admit to an unprofessionally egotistical thrill, since those spectacular high-rez designs are all me. Vinneas's skills lay mainly in theory, not producing pinup-quality renderings of drop-dead-sexy engineering. You could frame this presentation and hang

---

3 A reference to a story popular among Rae's people, concerning the adventures of a CE-period explorer who visits a number of fantastical locales, among them a flying city. I try not to take it as an ill omen that our plan has been anticipated by a satirical fairy tale, or that this explorer, one Gulliver, also encountered a land inhabited by sapient, talking horses, an idea that the story apparently places on an equal level of plausibility with our current strategy for saving the world.

it in a gallery, and if you did, the smugly stylistic signature at the bottom would say, *Yours truly, Kizabel.* Also, *Up yours, Academy review board.*

But not everyone is as impressed with myself as I am. The esteemed Imperator Feeroy can hardly wait for me to finish my presentation so he can get up and say something condescending. "Clearly you have put a great deal of energy into this invention of yours, and I assure you it is very impressive," he says, sounding less impressed than annoyed. "But perhaps you have forgotten that we have only twenty-eight days until Romeo is free to continue his invasion. How much time do you estimate will be required to launch this—what did you call it?"

It's written right there, at the bottom of the main diagram, but I don't point that out. "IMEC-1," I say. "Ingenically Mobilized Expeditionary City. One."

Everyone is watching me now, anxious to see how this squabble will play out. The fate of Earth could depend on whether or not I know what I'm talking about. Only Vinneas is smiling, looking like he's thoroughly enjoying the show. This must be how he keeps so calm all the time—he plans everything out in advance. Even people like Imperator Feeroy aren't so scary when you already know what they're going to say.

"Yes, of course." Feeroy chuckles nastily. "How long do you think it would be before your IMEC is prepared for battle?"

"Twenty-three days," I answer without hesitating.

Feeroy's sneer drops away, and for a second I see it isn't me he dislikes. He doesn't care about me at all—except that, as far as he's concerned, I'm wasting time that could be put to better use securing the survival of humanity. "You must be mistaken," he says, startled. He gestures to an aerial view of IMEC-1. "It would take years to erect that artillery array alone. How do you expect to build an entire city in twenty-three days?"

"I don't. Twenty-three days is how long it would take to assemble the underlying thelemic architecture and initialize the systems necessary to get the IMEC airborne, habitable, and combat-ready once the basic physical structure is complete."

He lets loose an exasperated laugh. "And what good is it to know we can make a city fly if we don't have time to build a city?"

"We don't need to build a city," I answer. "That part of IMEC-1 is already finished. You're standing in it."

FORTY-EIGHT

TORRO

It isn't like I thought building a floating city would be *easy*. Not even building it, really, since we're using good old Ninth City, but even with the thing already there, no one expected getting it into the air was going to be like a simple process. At Limit Camp, they teach you about thelemity a little, how in some ways it works the same as a sort of machine, only you can't see all the gears and levers and engines and whatnot because they're made out of this invisible force. So I knew there'd be more to it than just waving your hands around a little and the whole thing taking off. First we had to put together all the little working parts—what the Prips call "artifices"—that make up this invisible machine that's supposed to keep a whole island in the air. I don't really know how I thought we'd do it. Maybe I was picturing some glowing crystals or something. But I definitely didn't think it would be like this.

For the past week or so, we've been building houses in the middle of nowhere. No kidding. I mean, I suppose it isn't really *nowhere*. We're out in the valley around Ninth City, not too far from our old Limit Camp, in fact, but it feels a lot like hellion territory, with all the empty fields and forests and no roads or fences or factories anywhere. Just the sort of place where there might be hellions waiting to skin you alive and eat your eyeballs and whatnot. It makes me kind of nervous, even though all I have to do is find a hill or climb a tree, and I'll be able to see Ninth City. At least I'm not the only one here. We've got three whole squads, and, of course, the place doesn't look totally devoid of like human habitation because we're building these houses, but somehow that only makes everything seem creepier because no one's ever going to live in them.

The reason I know the houses aren't for anyone in particular, or really anyone at all, is because as soon as we're done building them, we burn them down. Like, we'll spend days putting up these cozy little cottages, arranging them all in rows, and we'll make the beds and set the tables for like a nice meal, with actual food and everything, then once the Immunes have come through to make sure everything is done right, we just set it all on fire. And that isn't even the strangest thing we've done. Not even close.

We've been at it for a little over two weeks now, building good old IMEC-1, that is. It all started with the attack, naturally. We spent the whole thing down in the shelters at Limit Camp, and even though no one told us what was happening outside, we knew something was wrong. It wasn't our first trip to the shelters or anything, but they'd never kept us down there more than a few hours, and this was going on a full day. But then the alert ended, and it was like everything went back to normal, the same drills and PT and lectures on how to stop yourself bleeding to death from a severed arm and so forth, until a couple days later, when Optio Sorril called the whole camp together, just like she did that first day, when she told us all about the war and the Realms and the Valentines and so forth. I'd thought that was all bad enough. This was even worse.

What old Sorril had to tell us was that we'd basically just lost the war. She didn't say it that way, of course, but it was pretty obvious what was going on. While all of us recruits had been down in the shelters, there'd been this huge battle going on all over the world. It wasn't just some little atmospheric incursion the Legion could clean up in a couple of hours, either. This time old Romeo'd sent a whole army, the biggest Earth had ever seen, and the reason he could drop this like big horde right on top of us was that he'd already killed off everyone at the Front.

What made it even worse, for me anyway, was that the whole thing, the Front getting overrun and everything, had all happened months ago, before any of us had even been recruited. It had just taken the Valentines that long to get here because of how much slower time moves in the Realms. So everything that had happened, getting drafted and dragged out here and puking in my helmet and whatnot, none of that mattered. I could have been back at Granite Shore with Camareen this whole time for all the difference it would have made.

Everyone was real upset, you could tell. Poor old Mersh was actually crying, and if you looked around, you could see other people were, too. I mostly just wanted to hit something, but I didn't. No one moved or made a sound—unless they were already blubbering and couldn't help it— because Sorril was still talking. The people in charge had come up with a plan to get us out of this mess, and we were supposed to help. We were going to build a fortress, an actual like flying island, that we could send into the Realms to hold the Valentines off. If it worked, everyone back on Earth would have something like thirty years to get ready before Romeo's big army, what Sorril called "the Valentine Host," finally got here. Long enough that we'd stand a good chance of fighting Romeo off. If the plan was going to work, though, we had to have the whole flying fortress ready to go in twenty-five days.

We were supposed to have another two months or so at Limit Camp before we officially joined the Legion, but there wasn't time for that anymore. As of that moment, old Sorril said, we were all part of the Ninth Legion, Third Cohort, Twelfth Century. If we'd made it the whole way through training, we'd have all been assigned to different parts of the Legion, but the way things were, they'd decided to just make us our own new century.

Sorril had to pick a few of us to be squad leaders, too, and good old Mersh was right at the top of her list, thanks to how well his squad had done in combat exercises. Kiddo went from recruit to Decurio in two seconds flat. I think he was kind of disappointed it happened so quickly. He'd been excited about the ceremony they do when you finally graduate into the Legion. But he got to choose his own squad, and he made sure to get me and Hexi and Spammers, so we could all stick together.

We started work right away. Optio Sorril brought in these two guys from a part of the Legion called the Immunes, basically legionaries like us but specially trained to build big complicated things like flying islands. The Immunes were here to supervise our work on the fortress, which they were calling IMEC-1. They called up the Decurio from each squad and told everyone else to get into our D-87s and report back and bring our trenchers along.

Trenchers, also known as U-55 entrenchment tools, are sort of like lazels, only you use them to build things instead of blow things up. If you've got the right materials and know what you're doing, you can make your own shelter pretty much anywhere, including outer space. You can even make things float, mostly rocks and logs and so forth, if you don't have anywhere good to build. I figured we'd be doing something like that, maybe making floating blocks to build this floating fortress, but I was way off.

Once we all suited up, Mersh told us we'd be going to the South Piazza. We'd all been there a couple of times since we finished our first four weeks of training and they started letting us out on recreation. South Piazza is one of the few places in Ninth City where people go just to relax. When we got there, though, it was totally empty, except for people in D-87s like us. Our job, Mersh said, was to draw lines. We were supposed to set our trenchers to make contrasting marks, then draw all over South Piazza. Not just anywhere, of course. Each squad had a square twenty meters across to work on, and we had to make the lines according to this very specific diagram. It wasn't easy, because you couldn't really tell if you were doing it right, and if the Immunes decided your line wasn't exactly perfect, you had to start over. Spammers got the hang of it pretty quick, but the rest of us made a lot of mistakes. As soon as we finished one twenty-meter square, the Immunes would come in and start drawing even more things, mostly weird-looking symbols and little pictures, like of animals and people and whatnot. Meanwhile, we'd get another twenty-meter square of Piazza and have to draw all over *that*.

It all had to do with thelemity, obviously, but none of us could figure out how. We heard about other squads going down to the main city shelters and just gutting the place, pulling out all the beds and supplies and everything until it was all just a big empty space, then, when that was all done, the Immunes told them to cut their thumbs and leave one fingerprint in blood on the wall. Seriously. The Immunes never told us why we had to do all this stuff, or if they did, they'd say something pretty unhelpful, like "this is going to be an ocularoclastic node" or "we need to redirect the cephaloparisic flow through this area." It became a sort of joke in some of the squads. Whenever we had to go take a piss, we'd say something like "I need to flobnob the groobinwhistler."

It took two days to finish the whole Piazza, and as soon as we were done, they sent us to this big flowery field just outside the city and told us to start burying little statues of animals. Like, we got boxes and boxes filled with these figurines of cows and pigs and whatnot, and a map of the field with marks all over it telling us where to dig and how deep to bury each one. It was a little like assembling something at a factory, how precise everything had to be, only instead of a 1.25cm screw or whatever, you had a statue of a chicken. After that, we went to a lake, and they gave us all cups filled with some liquid, oil if you were a girl and water if you were a guy, and had us walk around the place in a big circle exactly seventy-nine times. That was it. Next they had us lighting candles and putting them on tree branches. Every day it was like we had some new crazy thing to do.

This one time they brought us all to some great big field and taught us a game called football. It's a little like dash, a game we used to play at old S-225, only there was no punching or eye-gouging allowed. We played all day, and it was actually pretty fun, up until the end, anyway. When we were all tired enough to drop, the Immunes had us play one last round, only this time they told us exactly how it was supposed to go, like who was going to win and by how much and so forth. Spammers nearly messed the whole thing up by scoring when he wasn't supposed to. It turned out he was pretty good at football, and I guess he didn't like throwing the game, even if it was for the preservation of humanity. Or maybe it was because Mersh was on the side that was supposed to win and he was being kind of a turd about it. Anyway, the Immunes made us start over, and I guess that time we got it right because now here we are burning down houses.

The trenchers actually make the whole job pretty easy, relatively speaking. They look sort of like giant-sized spoons, the trenchers do, and in addition to drawing really nice-looking lines, they can move and reshape just about anything you want. For example, if you've got a block of stone, and you want it to be shaped like something else, a cone or a ball or a little truck or whatever, your trencher can do it in about a minute, less if you really know what you're doing. So building a house isn't anything like as hard as it would be back at Granite Shore, where you'd have to dig the foundation and nail together the walls and shingle the roof and so forth. Here you just sort of wave your trencher, kind of like you're spreading something out, and the walls practically build themselves. The Immunes give us all the materials. We just have to reshape them and put them together according to the plans. We use wood, mostly, so the houses will burn. Our trenchers can set the fires, too. They really are handy little things. You can even use them to fight, if you happen to lose your lazel. It's only the little fussy parts you have to do by hand.

"Why do you think they have us make the beds?" I ask Spammers as we're doing just that. Each cottage is a little different, but there are always a few bedrooms and a few beds to make.

"No idea," Spammers says. "Good thing we're trained for this kind of sophisticated and demanding work, though."

We all got a lot of practice making beds at Limit Camp. On your first day, they teach you this very specific way of doing it, and after that, they're always real like persnickety about it. I doubt we were actually preparing for something like this, but it certainly didn't hurt. "But I mean, what's the *point*," I say to Spammers. "If they're going to burn the whole thing down anyway, why make the beds?"

Spammers rolls his eyes. "The thing you've gotta understand about this thelemity crap, kiddo, is there's *no* understanding it. It's strictly for crazies."

I kind of agree. If thelemity is about building invisible machines, then this one has to be the screwiest machine of all time. Most machines, you can look at them and at least sort of tell what they're doing. Like you have a machine that takes cans and fish, and it makes canned fish. But if there's some way burned-down houses and buried pig statues come out to be a flying island, I don't know what it is. "At least we're doing something to help, right?" I say.

"You sure about that, boyo?" Spammers says, doing the old skeptical eyebrow raise. His enthusiasm for the Legion hasn't really stood up to working on the IMEC, especially since he came down with that case of IED. We've had to go in and out of the city's umbris a lot, and that hasn't been good for some people. A few days back, just before lights out, Spammers was lying on his bed and suddenly he started sprouting big, shiny green flies. They just came out of his skin like bubbles out of boiling water, and in no time there was a huge cloud of them buzzing all over the place. All he had to do was go take some pill and he was fine, but it was pretty uncomfortable for a while, and ever since, he's been real grumpy. I don't think that's a very unusual way to feel, though, when flies start coming out of your skin.

He's not the only one getting kind of irritable, either. We all are. They feed us all right, but we're lucky to get four hours of sleep at night. If you get too tired, they give you this drink called raspalji. It's about the most awful thing you've ever tasted, but it makes you feel like you could pull up a mountain and grind it to bits with your teeth. You're not allowed more than one dose every two days, though, and we're all still tired most of the time.

"Think about it," Spammers is saying. "Say we really *are* done. Old Romeo's coming, and there's no way to stop him. You think those Prips are gonna *tell* us? No way. Everyone'd panic. But if they give us a whole bunch of pointless things to do, keep us tired and distracted, well, maybe they'll be able to evacuate everyone important before Romeo gets here. Because you *know* they don't have enough of those great big flying machines to take everyone along, especially turds like us."

"If that's what they're doing, why tell us Romeo's coming at all?" I ask. "Why not just pretend everything's fine and sneak off when no one's looking?"

"Too late for that," Spammers says. He doesn't sound that concerned, though. "Everyone already saw Romeo coming in here and kicking the crap out of us. If the Prips tried to get away now, people would know something was up."

It isn't completely implausible, that's for sure. But I really do think this IMEC business is for real, however crazy it seems. The Prips may be a fat bunch of liars, but if they were planning to screw us, I know Naomi would tell me, like she told me about Granite Shore.

It was still pretty soon after the attack, and I was in real bad shape. The work hadn't gotten too tiring yet. I was just so worried. I'd been thinking about how we'd all just skipped up into the Legion, and how that was probably to make room for a lot of new recruits, which meant there were probably going to be a lot more extra drafts or whatever Ghalo called them out in the settlements. And that got me thinking about Camareen, and whether she was safe, and I thought about how a bunch of cities had been destroyed, like completely blown out of existence, and how that probably meant some settlements were gone, too. There wasn't really anyone around to ask, but I got one of the Immunes talking, and he said some settlements really *had* been destroyed. He couldn't tell me which ones, though, only that there were a lot, and he definitely didn't remember whether Settlement 225 was one of them. By the end of the day, when they sent us off to our new barracks, I was going pretty berserk. And then I heard someone say my name, real quiet, right behind me. I turned around, and there was little Naomi.

"Your home is safe." She just came right out and said it, like she could guess what I was thinking. "Settlement 225 survived the battle."

I said, "How did you know I—?" I was going to say, "How did you know I was worried?" but I couldn't even finish, I was so surprised.

"You cannot rest easy while people you care for are in danger," she said. "I have seen enough of you to know that."

"Thanks, then," I said.

"You would do the same if I needed something it was in your power to give. Please, convey what I have told you to your kiddos, with my regards." It was funny hearing her say "kiddos," since that wasn't how she usually talked. It made me think of that night back on Granite Shore, when we all threw in to bring her people that food. I guess this was sort of the same thing. I was going to thank her again, but she'd already disappeared, just like that.

"Well, if they were going to make up some big distraction," I say to Spammers, "don't you think the fake jobs they gave us'd make a little more *sense*? And hey, tuck in those sheets, boyo. You're getting sloppy on the corners!"

We're just finishing up when we hear Hexi yelling from the hall. "What are you two *doing* in here?" A second later she's at the door, looking annoyed. "Hurry up, will you? We're falling way behind Second Squad. Mersh is getting ready to blow an artery or something."

"You mean *Decurio Mezzivish*?" Spammers says. Out of all of us, Spammers is having the most trouble accepting Mersh as dek. Listening to Mersh order him around bothers Spams even more than being all lousy with green flies. I can relate. Mersh is a pretty good dek, except you can tell he enjoys it a little too much.

"That's exactly who I mean," Hexi says, all curt and whatnot. "Now get those corners straightened, and let's burn this place."

Mersh is waiting downstairs with the rest of the squad. When Hexi tells him we're done, all he says is "We're going to have to do better on the next cottage. I want four more completed by the end of the day. No more horsing around, got it? Miles Spammachen! What are you doing?"

The minute Mersh gave the order not to horse around, Spammers immediately started horsing around. There's this big bowl of fruit on the cottage's kitchen table, and Spammers'd been reaching for an apple sitting right on the top. He obviously wasn't going to take it, like he was making this jokey-looking face and everything, but Mersh decided to yell at him anyway.

"That apple looked a little out of place, sir," Spammers says, real casual. "I was just going to rearrange it a bit."

"Leave that to the Immunes," Mersh snaps. "You have your orders. Now get moving."

Spammers makes a very crisp salute. "Yes, *sir*!" I'm pretty sure he's making fun of Mersh a little, but Mersh doesn't notice.

FORTY-NINE

TORRO

We actually do get five more cottages up before another squad finally comes to relieve us. Mersh yells at everyone the whole time, the way our squad leaders did back in settlement militia, and you can just tell he's enjoying himself like anything. They let us have a few hours' sleep, then we're back at it before sunup, but we've only done two more cottages when the Immunes come through and tell us to report back to the staging area, the place where they keep all the different building materials like wood and shingles and bedsheets and bowls of fruit.

Old Sorril's waiting for us, looking about how I feel, which is to say totally exhausted. She's smiling, too, though. When the whole century is gathered up, she tells us we've done it. IMEC-1 is ready for launch. There'll be plenty more to do once it's up and flying, but we're finished with the really hard part. They're giving us the rest of the day off, but we'll probably want to stick around to watch the launch, since it'll be the first time anything like this has happened in the history of humanity and whatnot.

Everybody's pretty excited, not just because it's some big historic event but because we've hardly had any time to ourselves since the IMEC got started. Sorril's got us all some beer and aquavee, and I'm a little inclined to just get completely drunk, but instead I end up hanging around with Hexi and Spammers. There's a lot of food left over from the cottages, mostly apples and pears and so forth, and even though I'm not all that hungry, I feel obliged to have some, since until now we've hardly been allowed to touch this stuff except to stack it neatly in bowls.

So I sit there like compulsively eating fruit while Hexi gives Spammers a hard time for not believing in the IMEC. Legionaries are supposed to give each other a hard time every so often, and Hexi's been practicing. She's not so great at it just yet.

"Still think the IMEC's all a hoax?" she says, trying to elbow Spammers in the ribs but getting his shoulder. Lately, he's been pretty vocal about that theory of his, the IMEC being a sham, I mean. We've all heard it.

Spammers has this orange he's been cutting up with his trencher, and he squirts it at her. "Maybe. Maybe it won't take off at all. Maybe the Prips just want us all in one place so they can sneak away somewhere else. We'd all feel pretty dumb, then, wouldn't we, waiting for a floating island that doesn't even exist?"

"Not as dumb as you will when it actually happens."

"I'll believe it when I see it."

We sit around all morning, and nothing happens, but then about noon-time Sorril shows up and tells us the launch'll be starting soon. We can watch from the fields where we were building those cottages, only we're advised to stay at least fifty meters back from the burned-down wreckage unless we want to end up with the world's worst case of IED. Our whole century sets off in a big rambunctious pack, though Spammers is pretty quiet, probably thinking about those green flies.

There's plenty of space to watch, since we had to clear out all the trees to make room for the cottages, and the cottages were all built in this big, long trail, like you can look left or right, and the piles of blackened and collapsed cottages seem to go on forever. Hexi and Spammers and I get a spot near where we'd been working the other day, and the rest of our squad comes along, including Mersh, even though he doesn't seem to enjoy the idea of like fraternizing with legionaries under his command. There are a couple other squads around, but mostly the place is pretty empty.

No one says much of anything. I think we're all a little nervous. And then Spammers blurts out, "So what exactly is supposed to happen?"

"Be quiet!" Hexi says. She's already getting upset. Spammers has a lot easier time upsetting her than the other way around.

"What? It's not like I'm going to break the IMEC by being too loud."

"You don't know that!"

"They built something under the city," Mersh says. He's drinking a beer, the same kind with the red can you'd see back at S-225, and smiling this real smug smile. "You remember how they cleared out all the main shelters? There's a whole complex down there now. Artifices and stuff every-where. They call it the Myria Engine."

"At least it's got a better name than IMEC-1," Spammers says. "Was that really all they could come up with? IMEC-1 sounds pretty dumb, if you ask me."

Mersh doesn't even look at him. He just takes a sip of beer and keeps talking. "The Myria Engine runs the whole thing. They'll get that working first, then start up the rest of the IMEC."

"How'd you find that out?" I say. I'd been peeling a banana I brought with me, getting ready to eat it, but now I'm interested.

"Need-to-know basis, boyo," Mersh says. "Couldn't always be stop-ping work to explain things, could we?"

That gets me pretty irritated. Like, how can anyone tell what I need to know? It would have been quite helpful if someone'd thought to tell me Granite Shore hadn't been blasted to a million pieces, for instance. And like, maybe if the Prips'd told us all from the beginning what was really going on with this war, things would be different now. Maybe Spammers wouldn't be so mad about working here, or so suspicious about this plan with the IMEC. I think that goes for just about everyone from the settlements. It's hard not to be suspicious of the Prips, even though it turned out there's all this like firm and convincing evidence the war is really real after all.

I don't see how only telling Mersh about this Myria Engine thing accomplished very much, either, aside from making Mersh real pleased with himself. Spams and Hexi look annoyed, too, and I wonder if they're thinking what I am, about not trusting the Prips and so forth. Anyway, Mersh doesn't notice because right then, something starts to happen.

All of a sudden, I get this weird, topsy-turvy feeling. It isn't quite like walking into an umbris, where you can't tell if you're happy or mad, and everything smells like rotten eggs and so forth. It's more like the air starts to tighten, like the whole world is a rag someone's wringing out. It's over almost immediately, but you couldn't miss it.

"Nobody laugh if I puke," Hexi says.

Spammers sits on the ground. "I think I'll be too busy puking."

Even Mersh forgets how important he is for a second or two, just drops his beer and kind of ducks like he's expecting something to fall on him. I guess no one thought he needed to know what launching the IMEC would be like. I don't really pay too much attention to Mersh or his foaming can, though. I'm too busy watching the sky.

Up until a minute ago, it was a normal sunny afternoon, but now, everything's gone dark purple, like it's already dusk, and if the sun's out anywhere, I can't see it. A little above the trees, though, there are a few glowing spots of light, like maybe it's still sunny in other parts of the valley.

Suddenly, Hexi grabs my arm. "Look!" she says, pointing ahead, toward the burned-down cottages. A kind of mist has rolled in over the ground, low and pretty wispy, the sort you see over the water sometimes on cold mornings. But Hexi isn't pointing at the mist, not really. She's pointing at things *inside* the mist. At first they look like trails of light, the way sunlight reflects off the edge of sharp metal, but the more you look, the more you can tell the lines and edges are shaped like *people*, walking all over the place and just going about their business. Most of them are moving around the burned-out cottages, and I realize they're acting the way real people would in cottages that *hadn't* burned down. A few are even floating in the air, where the upper floors would have been.

"What are they?" Hexi says, not to anyone really, but we all look over at Mersh, since he's the one with all the answers. Mersh doesn't even seem to notice us. He's just staring at all the glowing shapes bustling around the ruined houses.

The next thing that happens is the ground starts to move. Not where we're standing, fortunately, though it takes me a minute to figure that out. It looks like this huge wall of earth just comes rising up in front of us, with the burned cottages and the glowing people on top, and you can see the rocks and roots and like layers of dirt in the wall, but you can't really tell if the people and cottages are going up or we're going down because the wall is so long you can't see the end of it. And then it lifts away, and there's open air underneath, with a few little clods of dirt and whatnot dropping off into the huge pit the whole thing left behind. There has to be ten whole meters of empty space beneath that wall of dirt before it finally hits me that the thing is actually *flying*.

For a while we all just stand there, staring up at the land lifting away, but then I notice something strange. I mean, something else strange, aside from the whole flying-island thing. Even though the ground is still moving, the burned-out cottages and the glowing people don't seem to be going any higher. The reason is that the whole stretch of land around them is *tilting*, like turning into a pretty steep slope, actually. It all looks real precarious, once I realize what's happening, like the ruins of the cottages should be sliding right off, but they just stay where they are, and soon it starts to feel like we're looking down at them from above, even though they're still pretty much in front of us.

Nearby, I notice that a whole lot of Immunes have showed up, and they've got out those plans they're always carrying around, the big sheets of drawings that tell you where to build your cottages and bury your pig statues and so forth. They're crowded around, arguing over something, and every so often one points up at the tilting land and back at the plan.

Mersh has seen them, too. "You all stay here," he says. "I'll see what's going on."

It doesn't work out so well for him, going over there. He's only about halfway to where the Immunes are when one of them looks up and starts yelling at him, this very small, very intense girl with short black hair and sharp blue eyes. "You!" she says, pointing at Mersh. "You there. Were you in charge of the squad working this area?"

Mersh stops in his tracks, but it's too late to get away, and the girl makes him come over and show her which cottages his squad was building.

"Shit, kiddos," Spammers says, kind of dazed-sounding. "I think we're in trouble." He's staring up at the IMEC like it's about to come crashing right down on top of him. I look, too, but can't think how I'd know if something was wrong, since pretty much *everything* looks wrong.

Spammers points, jabbing his finger. "There, right there. See that kid? That little kid?"

It takes me a while to find what he's pointing at, but eventually I see him, a little glowing boy. He isn't moving around the way all the other glowing people are. Instead, it looks like he's pointing back at Spams.

"Is he *pointing* at us?" Hexi says.

That isn't the only thing that's a bit off, though. All around the little glowing boy, the ground looks sort of funny, like a wrinkled blanket, with the wrinkles getting bigger every second. And even though everything nearby looks completely fine, that patch and everything on it, the grass and weeds and whatnot, is waving around like it's in the middle of a windstorm.

Spammers says, "You remember yesterday, when I pretended to take that apple?"

"Spammers!" Hexi shouts. "You *didn't*!"

"I wasn't going to take it!" Spammers is already getting defensive. He tends to get pretty defensive when he knows he's done something wrong. "If Mersh hadn't been such a turd about it, I wouldn't have done anything!"

"Did we break it?" I ask. I've noticed a few other places where the ground seems not to be floating away quite as well as the rest of the IMEC. Some pieces have even started peeling off, spilling dirt and rocks and grass down the sloping edge, like the ground is starting to dissolve.

"I don't know." Spammers looks about ready to drop dead. "And I *ate* the apple, too. What does *that* mean?"

It must be why the Immunes are here, because we messed something up, and now the IMEC is falling apart. Mersh is still over with them and obviously wishing he wasn't, and the intense-looking girl is like interrogating him and some of the other Decurios while another of the Immunes holds a little swinging thing on a chain over some of the plans. I'm trying to figure out what's happening when the girl looks up and sees me. "Hey! You there!" she shouts. I try to pretend I didn't hear her, but she's already coming my way. "Yes, you, the one with the banana! I'm talking to you!"

I'd forgotten all about the banana, but I'm still holding it, all peeled and ready to eat. I guess there's no chance she means someone else. I'm the only one holding a banana. "Yes, ma'am," I say.

She holds out her hand. "Give me that. Your trencher, too."

I do what she says, and before I know what's happening she's used the trencher to hurl the banana right at the IMEC. It shoots straight for the burned cottages and glowing people all roaming around in the mist. About halfway there, the banana catches on fire, just lights right up. It pretty much disappears before it gets to the IMEC, but the little boy who'd been pointing at Spammers seems satisfied. He stops pointing, anyway, and as he walks away, the ground where he'd been standing stops moving.

She hands me back my trencher. "Thanks, Miles," she says, using my rank, miles, meaning just a normal, ordinary guy from the milites.

I'm pretty impressed. I knew you could use a trencher to launch things like that, but setting something on fire midair can't be easy. "Sure," I say, "no problem."

She's already on her way back to the Immunes, though, shouting, "There! Was that so bloody difficult?" One of the other Immunes starts to argue with her, but she says, "We can do a full repair later. For now, we need to keep all this shoddy workmanship from getting any worse." Someone else speaks up, and she yells, "I don't *care* whose fault it is! Now patch the rest and let's get out of here!"

"So did we break it or not?" Spammers whispers.

Hexi shoves him. "We'll know when it falls on us."

It doesn't fall on us, though. Actually, we're able to fix things up pretty quickly, once someone brings back a few bowls of fruit. I guess Spammers wasn't the only one sneaking a bite here and there because there are plenty of other spots around the cottages where the ground doesn't quite hold together. Throwing fruit stops them from sliding away, but it doesn't exactly melt the dirt and everything back into place. Instead, the piled-up ground just stays the way it is. Mersh is stuck hurling apples with the rest of us, on orders from that intense-looking girl. It turns out her name is Immunis Kizabel, and she's the person who *designed* the whole crazy IMEC. I'd heard of her, of course, but I'd been imagining some old lady. Immunis Kizabel is probably only a little older than my kiddos and me.

"Seriously," Spammers says as Kizabel and the other Immunes rush off to some other part of the island. "I'm never going to understand this place. Not ever."

About two hours later, we're looking up at a genuine flying island. It didn't come together exactly the way I expected, just lifting out of the ground like a cookie from a sheet of dough or whatever. Instead, it kind of folded together like a box. The finished thing is really two flying islands stuck together, kind of. Like, the place where we'd been working on those cottages actually ended up on the *bottom*, and so did a few parts of the city, and a bunch of other trees and meadows and so forth. There's even a lake, right in the center, and when you look up at it, you can see the land below reflected in the water. It makes Spammers and me kind of dizzy, doing that, but Hexi can't get enough of it, seeing Limit Camp and our bunks and the mess hall and everything, all far away and upside down in this great big lake in the sky.

"I wonder if the harvesters and everything have to turn upside down to land up there," Hexi says later while we're waiting for transportation to IMEC-1, formerly Ninth City. We're outside the umbris now, and the light has gone back to normal. It's late afternoon and cold enough to see your breath.

Spammers groans. Hexi has gotten better at giving him a hard time, I guess. "I don't think I'll ever get used to living on that thing," he says. "But hey, maybe we won't have to, if we're lucky."

Hexi looks over at him. "What do you mean?"

"Think about it, girlie. They've got to send that thing off into the Realms, right? Well, they can't take *all* of us with them, can they? Who'd hang around and watch out for Earth for the next thirty years? I know Torro's thought about this, haven't you, boyo?"

I hadn't, actually, but I'm thinking about it now, even though I'm trying not to. I'm a little scared that if I let myself think about it, something'll go wrong.

Spammers is grinning at me now. "So say they decide to leave good old Twelfth Century behind! They close up the Realms, and we don't have to go to the Front. Maybe we have to stay on a few extra years with the Legion, but who cares? We'll be the first legionaries to get home without having to leave for fifty years first!"

Hexi is getting excited now, too. "Hey, maybe we can all go start our own settlement!"

Spammers laughs. "Just like old Mersh said! Unbelievable!"

But there's one other thing, something they don't mention. No way they'd've forgotten. I guess they just don't want to talk about it.

There's a great big army of Valentines out there, waiting for old Lunar Veil to open so they can storm on through and kill us. Before this flying island can go off on its jolly way and leave me and my kiddos behind to start our own settlement or head back to Granite Shore or anything like that, we've got to deal with Romeo. Maybe we all *will* get to stay on Earth, but first we've got to make it through this battle alive.

FIFTY

VINNEAS

Of all the considerations necessary to uprooting a vast metropolis and outfitting it for combat across a series of hostile alien worlds, the most troublesome by far is deciding who gets to run the thing. Kizabel would accuse me of trivializing the staggering amount of work and aggravation that went into getting IMEC-1 both literally and figuratively off the ground, of belittling what herculean feats the straining backs of humanity's defenders have wrought, and, of course, she'd be right, but however banal the negotiations surrounding the IMEC's administrative status—its place within the Legion and *vice versa*—may seem when compared to the apotheotic spectacle of plucking an island from the earth and setting it in the sky, I have a feeling the consequences will be every bit as convoluted and thorny.

The IMEC had its share of detractors—for the most part venerable military chiefs who objected to gambling the future of the human race on some half-baked scheme cooked up by a couple of untried novices. However, once the Consulate had voted—unanimously—in favor of commissioning what was decried variously as "a schoolboy's farcical toy" and "a suicidal monstrosity," it seemed just about everyone in the upper echelons of the Legion and Principates of Hestia considered him- or herself the natural choice to command the aforementioned toy/monstrosity.

The trouble—most of it, anyway—arose from the fact that IMEC-1 fell rather mistily into a gray area between several preexisting authorities and institutions. It was a city, obviously, but it was also a weapon of enormous power—or would be, if we could get it to work—as well as a military base, one which would house practically everything that remained of the Legion. Who, then, should be in charge? Should Princept Azemon, who had governed Ninth City for the past fifteen years, continue to do so after its transformation into a flying fortress? Most certainly, in the opinion of Princept Azemon. Or should the IMEC be entrusted to someone prepared to lead in an exclusively military capacity? According to various individuals prepared to lead in an exclusively military capacity, the answer was a resounding yes. To further complicate things, all twelve of Earth's Legions would be represented in the IMEC's garrisons. At the Front, where every Realm had its own supreme military commander, this wouldn't have been a problem, but on Earth, the Dux of each Legion is traditionally answerable only to his or her Princept and the general directives of the Consulate. The idea that any Legion—even the Fifth, whose numbers had been reduced to the extent that it could no longer form even a single full cohort—should cede command to another Legion's Dux was, apparently, so insulting as to be unthinkable.

Had there been time to bicker and scheme and maneuver, it's likely anyone with a remotely reasonable claim to the IMEC would still be bickering and scheming and maneuvering, but fortunately—for the purposes of expediency, anyway—the world was about to end, and so the debate only lasted about three hours. The decision Consul Seppora handed down was that, while each of the twelve Legions would remain under the leadership of its respective Dux, ultimate command of IMEC-1 and its legionary detachment would fall to Ninth City's own Dux Reydaan, who would be responsible for all tactical and strategic decisions. To the whole assembly's credit as soldiers, the ruling was accepted immediately and without argument, though I suspect the general stoicism resulted in part from Seppora's promise to revisit the issue after the coming battle, assuming the destruction of humanity hadn't rendered it moot.

Following the meeting, Curator Ellmore was heard to comment that the truly tragic thing about what was now being called the First Battle of Lunar Veil—rather optimistically, I think, since a Second Battle of Lunar Veil would be conditioned on our ability to build a flying island—was that most of our military leadership survived. I don't completely agree, especially as I'm now part of the military leadership, but I see her point. None of our officers wanted to be left out of the upcoming glorious mission to save humanity, and as a result, they continued to squeeze themselves into the chain of command well after all the top spots—and indeed, any conceivably useful position—had been filled. Even after its thorough renovation and expansion, the Dux's Basilica feels overcrowded.

At first glance, the interior of the Basilica looks much as it did in its former life as the center of Ninth City's military operations: an enormous space, comparable in size and composition to the largest cathedrals and mosques of the Common Era. At the center, beneath the huge, vaulted dome, is a dynamic model of Ninth City, popularly referred to as the Board. Our assets and defenses, our fighters—and, when relevant, the enemy's—are all represented in pieces of carved stone, easy to differentiate by size and color as milites, equites, artillery, *et cetera*. The pieces move independently, shifting across the model city or floating above as corresponds to the motion of their counterparts in the world outside. On unexceptional days, the Board has the languid, almost hypnotizing peacefulness of a koi pond. Today, it more resembles a wasps' nest, though the image of a pond lingers with me, especially given recent alterations to the Basilica's floor.

Whereas Ninth City, like any reasonable human dwelling, was set firmly and dependably on the ground, IMEC-1 is afloat and exposed to attack from all angles, and to account for this new range of peril, the Basilica's soaring interior has been mirrored downward to accommodate a new Board, with our double-sided city floating in the center. It would be easy to mistake the Board's lower half for a reflection in the polished stone floor, but a closer look reveals that the two sides are very different, each with its own geography, its surrounding pieces moving on their own unique errands.

To avoid distinctions such as "up" and "down" or "top" and "bottom"—meaningless, even harmful when operating in a world where orientation is often relative—the IMEC's two surfaces have been given direction-neutral names. The "red" or "city" side bears the closest resemblance to the old Ninth City, supporting its most recognizable landmarks, including the Forum, of which the Basilica makes up a prominent portion. The "green" or "country" side is more residential in character, its skyline less ambitious, hosting the majority of the IMEC's open space and its only large body of water. Both sides are equally well protected, however, bristling with our towering City Guns and battle spires, amply supplied with garrisons ready to sortie at a moment's notice.

At present, the model of IMEC-1 is a grid of carefully arranged pieces. The Board, so frantic since this morning, is quiet but for a few buzzing circles of last-minute positioning and preparation. Here inside the Basilica, the scene is more frenetic. Officers jog back and forth carrying messages and orders along a layer cake of platforms extending nearly floor to ceiling—or perhaps ceiling to ceiling is the better description. Gravity reverses at the level dividing the Basilica's mirrored halves, so that from each side's perspective the other appears upside down. Climbing from one to the other is a simple if bowel-jabbing procedure, though it's difficult to shake the subliminally disorienting sense of passing into some reflected, parallel world.

Every piece on the Board, from the heavy, rounded cubes representing full cohorts to the starlike, luminous specks that mark our fontani, carries an abundance of information. The exact content of that information depends on the subject in question and its position relative to the IMEC. In the case of distant enemy units, we may get only a grainy visual, but if a squad of milites happens to be marching past the Basilica, we can watch them from any angle we choose, read the condition of their bodies and equipment, gauge their morale, see through their eyes, smell through their noses. Instruments for reading such intelligence—some large and baroque, others small and fragile—are mounted along the platforms that encircle the Board, the densest clusters indicating posts where commanders roost to observe and direct the Legion's movements. Low-ranking officers like me are issued only small durbunler, devices similar to binoculars in design and appearance and—with a little imagination—function.

Fontanus Charles Cossou joins me while I'm standing along one of the platforms, scanning the IMEC's City Side. As the lenses of my durbun pass over each piece, the legionaries signified sweep into view. I've spotted a cohort of milites loading into one of the battle spires, and by adjusting my durbun's dials, I can observe them filing onto the assault platforms circling up the spire like kernels on a cob, taking their places in quiet rows, nervously fiddling with their lazels and adjusting their armor.

"They're ready," Charles says. He's watching the pieces on the Board, but the way he says it makes me think he can see those milites better than I can.

I lower my durbun to salute. "There are a lot of inexperienced legionaries out there, sir. I hope we did enough to prepare them."

Charles doesn't acknowledge my salute. Like many of the oldest veterans, he doesn't put much stock in legionary protocol. "You've given us a chance, Vinneas," he says. "That's what we needed more than anything. Assuming this contraption of yours holds together."

"I've made sure there's a supply of bubble gum and duct tape on hand, sir," I say, my standard response to concerns regarding the structural or conceptual soundness of IMEC-1. I've heard a lot of these over the past month, and few have been delivered with a grin, like this one from Charles. Having accepted my proposal, the Consulate felt obliged to transfer me over to Command, officially to advise on the preparations for defending Earth. As far as I've been able to discover, my duties consist solely of absorbing frustrated rants from my fellow officers whenever we encounter any kind of problem or setback. For this, I have been awarded the foolishly lofty rank of centurio. I might have been made an optio or tesserario, except that I was already a censor, and despite being a dead end in terms of rising to the highest levels of the Legion, the censors do head up their own division of operations, making them equal to centuriones in the overall chain of command. The Consulate couldn't very well *demote* me for my part in our new plan, so here I am.

"Excellent," Charles says, still grinning. "We'll do the rest. Or they will," he concedes, indicating the milites and several other pieces gliding across the Board. "If all goes according to plan, I won't come into it at all."

"You're part of the reserve?"

"Heading it up, in fact. I was just conferring with Feeroy."

He nods toward a platform a few levels above ours, and when I look past the expanse of drifting pieces, I see Imperator Feeroy glaring down at us. Despite how virulently unpopular his plan to evacuate Hestia has become, Feeroy remains adamant that it is our best and safest option, and other commanders have seized upon his conviction to distract from the fact that they had been just as vocal in favor of evacuation back when the only other option seemed a gallant but doomed last stand. With Dux Reydaan assuming command of the Legion overall, Feeroy might reasonably have expected the Ninth would be his. Instead, under the logic that a commander so eager to avoid a fight should have that portion of the Legion least likely to see combat, he has been assigned the Legion's reserve forces, who will wait behind on Earth and join the battle only if summoned. I can't help respecting Feeroy's commitment to his beliefs, but that doesn't keep him from blaming me for everything that's happened. I doubt it helps any that his decision to ship me off with the censors is the reason I'm now the Legion's youngest centurio. In terms of angry tirades, he's been my best customer so far.

"Has he told you anything about his plan for us out there?" Charles asks.

"No."

"You should ask him."

I watch as Feeroy studies the movement of pieces across the Board, far more intent than I would expect of a commander who will be leaving the majority of his troops behind. Something in his expression makes me uneasy. "Here's to hoping you miss the whole battle, then," I say to Charles, though one thing I've learned about plans is how quickly they can fall apart.

"Adventure, heh. Excitement, heh. A Jedi craves not these things." Charles grins at me in a way that makes me feel I must be missing something. "But promise you'll let me take this baby for a spin once we're off in the Realms," he adds, turning to look down at the hefty, goldenrod-colored piece used to represent the IMEC.

"It's a deal."

He steps back and surprises me with a sharp salute. "I'll see you at the victory party, Centurio."

When he's gone, I continue scanning the IMEC, looking over the disposition of our forces. No doubt there are several officers around who'd like to expend some nervous energy by shouting at me, but as I see it, my real job is worrying about strategy. For all my glib comments about gum and duct tape, I know the IMEC is far from perfect, that there are still bugs and glitches, problems with its layout and function a month simply wasn't enough time to fix, even with the entire Legion working nonstop. I tune the dials on my durbun, surveying first the overall placement of artillery, then the blocks of troops positioned around the city. I'm panning past a crowd in the Academy courtyards, where some of the cadets recently inducted into the Legion are mustering, and over toward the Stabulum, when a huge face abruptly pops into my field of vision.

"Hey there, Vinneas! Looking for me?"

I take a surprised step back, but when I lower my durbun, I'm alone on the platform.

The voice of Lady Jane emanates from the railing in front of me. "Ha! Scared you!"

I raise my durbun again and adjust the view to bring Lady Jane into focus. Once work on IMEC-1 began, Kizabel and I were able to convince the Consulate that Lady Jane would be a resource vital to finishing the project on time. She's been indispensable in helping us respond to the contingencies of putting the theory and design of the IMEC into practice. The rest of her time she spends making a gleeful nuisance of herself.

"I hope you don't plan on sneaking up on people like that while we're in combat," I say to her. "Someone is going to mistake you for a secret Valentine weapon."

"The Valentines don't have anything this pretty" is her reply to this sensible concern. Despite her jaunty attitude, she's plainly anxious about the prospect of battle. To bolster her confidence, she has donned the flamboyant uniform of a CE eighteenth-century field marshal.

"Of course. How could I have been so careless?"

"So," she says, ignoring my question and assuming a singsong tone. "Who were you looking for?"

"Just making sure we're all in position. Reviewing the troops."

"Really?" She smiles slyly. "It seemed a lot like you were looking for *someone.*"

"Listen, Lady, maybe you can help me with something." It isn't just a blatant, artless change of subject. I'm still thinking about the look on Feeroy's face as he scrutinized the Board, like he was following some pattern I couldn't quite see. Feeroy's ego may on occasion override his more reasoned faculties, but he remains an experienced commander with an extensive combat résumé. And if something about the battle now taking shape has caught his attention, I want to know what it is. Looking at the Board more closely, I've already got an idea.

"Lady, where would you say Romeo has the best chance of breaching the IMEC's defensive perimeter?"

"That isn't funny, Vinn." Lady's face registers offense that I would even suggest such a thing. "We've got battle spires and guns covering the whole thing. We're one big enemy kill zone."

"Say you had to chose a spot. Which would it be?"

She's quiet a moment, and when I look through my durbun, I find Lady with her field goggles turned toward the real-life image of IMEC-1. "Well, I don't know, Vinn," she says. "I mean, it isn't like we're invincible or anything. The IMEC does have its flaws, though if you tell Kizabel I said that, you're a dead man."

Lady Jane is beginning to see what I see, what Imperator Feeroy saw. IMEC-1 is arguably the most devastating war machine mankind has ever produced, but it was still jury-rigged in under a month.

"And anyway," Lady is saying, "that perimeter is huge. There isn't any one place . . ." She trails off.

There it is. I feel something cold tingle at the back of my neck, the fear I've been working to get under control all day. IMEC-1 doesn't have any single, disastrous weakness—not that I've been able to find anyway, and I've been looking—but it has cracks, faults, fissures; places where coverage from our artillery isn't quite perfect, places where the vagaries of artifice or geography create blind spots in communication or command, places where the city's layout makes it difficult for milites and equites to mount a strong defense. If I can see those weaknesses now, how long will it take the enemy to find them and press?

Our only chance of winning this battle was to introduce something new, something to offset Romeo's advantage in numbers. IMEC-1 will do that, so long as the City Guns keep firing. But if we lose the IMEC, we lose our one solid advantage, and if that happens, we lose everything.

"Vinneas?" Lady asks. She must be thinking along the same lines I am; there's a tremor in her voice. "What are we going to do?"

I'm not sure there's anything *to* do. We've prepared all we can. Now it's up to our legionaries to pull off the victory.

I shut my eyes, intending to block out everything—the Board, the Basilica, the fretful officers bustling along ladders and platforms—and focus on the problem at hand. Instead, I'm visited by the last view I had through my durbun before Lady Jane made her theatrical entrance. A scene from a Stabulum: the crowd of soldiers waiting for the order to launch, the tools of their trade lining the walls like ancient suits of armor, and Rae, in the black uniform of a legionary eques. She would have caught my attention even if she weren't already on my mind, I think, the one still figure in the last moments of lurid anticipation before a fight.

She stood apart, her head bowed, those lovely features serene except for the slightest furrow, hinting at some deep focus. At the time, most of my attention was occupied by the sharp internal tug that goes off whenever I see her face, but looking again now, I can't help wondering what was on her mind. The idea comes to me, suddenly, that she might have been praying. Most religions popular in CE society are alive and well among the unincorporated peoples, after all. In any other person on any other day, I wouldn't give it much thought one way or the other. Spiritual inquiry isn't forbidden in the Principates, only discouraged in favor of more practical applications of the supernatural. Instead, I find myself hoping, more powerfully than I thought I could hope for anything, that there was indeed a prayer somewhere in her silence, and not only that, but that something out there will hear her and keep her safe.

Several levels above, Dux Reydann stands at his command post, calling for our attention. The Basilica goes quiet, frozen but for the Board and its orbiting pieces. The blue sphere representing Earth falls slowly away from the model of IMEC-1, even as a glittering spark that must be Charles Cossou drifts down to rest on the planet's surface. Reydann raises his voice to address everyone below, his words magnified in the enormous space: "Sound the General Call to Arms."

There is a clattering of feet as everyone runs to their stations, the sound soon lost in the rising roar of the city's battle call.

PART FOUR

THE KEEP

◻──────◻

FIFTY-ONE

RAE

I am among the giants now, a soldier commissioned to ride as the heart and mind of a metallic titan. Eques is how we're titled in the Legion, but I've decided the translation Vinneas proposed, "knight," is a poor description. It's true we wear armor of a sort, and on occasion will wield a sword or shield after a similar fashion, but our lives are utterly lacking in the noble and courtly ways that always featured in Papa's tales of knight-errantry. In place of solemn oaths and trials of temperance and virtue, my mantle of knighthood was bestowed after a stern lecture and five days of determined bullying.

The lecture came courtesy of Centurio Kitu, chief of the Sixth Cohort's Armored Cavalry. In language altogether eschewing the flowery grace notes of chivalry, I was informed that the experimental equus I had debuted during the Battle of Lunar Veil, confiscated promptly thereafter, had since proven so damnably temperamental toward new riders that it was decided inducting me into the Legion would be easier than convincing that fitful beast to accept someone with any actual training or experience.

There was a place for me in the Sixth Armored, provided I could satisfy my superiors all that fancy flying of mine was no fluke, and swore to obey orders from now on. Any sign I was contemplating some rogue stunt, or exhibited the mutinous predilections one might expect from a girl who'd already stolen Principate property and used it in complete disregard of legionary mandate, and I would be locked someplace safely out of the way, that uncooperative equus of mine dismantled to hinder any further mischief. It was more than I could have hoped for, or so I thought, until I discovered Kitu meant to place me with the 126th Equites, under the command of none other than Bad Cop Imway.

I learned later that Imway was as unhappy with this arrangement as I was. He lodged a formal protest with Kitu, arguing that the effectiveness of his unit depended upon intuitive trust and synchrony borne of long association, harmony my presence was sure to disrupt. Kitu's answer was that the 126th was by far the greenest squad in the whole of Sixth Armored, with the least rapport to disrupt, and unless I proved incompetent or insubordinate, I would remain under his command. That said, Imway would have the chance to expose me as anathema to disciplined combat. Had there been time, I expect he would have taken months to test and torture me, but as it was, my gauntlet lasted less than a week.

The 126th made the most of their opportunity, sabotaging me at every turn, provoking me with relentless assaults upon my honor and person, daring me to prove myself unworthy of the name eques, a distinction that by their reckoning I had not earned and sullied by mere association. None of it was any real surprise. I had engaged in personal combat with their commander on two separate occasions and struck down another of their number with a sucker punch to the face. On top of that, I was the greenhorn of the group. Even in my coda, it was common for our scouts to greet new riders with a small taste of the hardships our world could offer.

I persevered, knowing that if I balked or rebelled, I would be out of the Legion faster than I could say Peter Cottontail. What I did not expect was the abruptness with which the trouble ceased. From the close of my fifth day with the 126th on, not a single harsh word or look was cast my way. Whatever they thought of me, orders were orders, and there was more at stake now than pride. I was impressed in spite of myself.

Since then, relations among the 126th have been marked by professional coolness. I've had the notion certain grudges and resentments have merely been set aside pending hostilities with a more dangerous enemy, but it's plain as well not all my new comrades took pleasure in tormenting me. A twinkling, moon-faced girl bearing the complicated name of Haiyalaiya, who during long-distance maneuvers clipped my ankle and nearly sent me crashing into some frigid arctic ocean, came to me with tears brimming in her large eyes and a lengthy apology for each and every act of cruelty she had been obliged to commit, several of which I failed to remember. Sensen, meanwhile, was sure to let me know she would never willingly occupy any sky with me in it, and only her orders and duty to the Legion now keep her from kicking me like the cur I am. For a time she made a point of referring to me as "Thirteen," a contemptuous allusion to my designation in our unit, but the name failed to gain purchase. To the 126th I am Rachel, Eques Rachel should an extra level of formality be required. That is how I know what distance remains between myself and the others. No one calls me Rae, and though it's common for equites to reference one another by the names of their mounts, no one mentions mine, probably out of fear of accidentally cracking a smile.

Kizabel and I both agree that to rechristen the equus she built and I rode into battle would be as unlucky as renaming a ship and as offensive as defacing a work of art. We have remained steadfast in this conviction against all inveigling, invective, and complaints about the dignity of the Legion and the solemnity of war. As far as the Sixth Cohort is concerned, I ride the X-2020, the model number assigned to Kizabel's singular design, but legionary protocol requires every equus bear a name inscribed on its breastplate, and no exceptions have been made for this one:

IX EQUITES 126-013
SNUGGLES

He's something of a runt compared to the other equi of the 126th, the StarHunters and RuinMakers and FireChasers, all Coursers, as their model is called, taller and broader than my Snuggles, but no match for his speed and power and grace. His white armor has been patched and polished, and fairly glows beside the deep, stony gray the others wear. Beneath that smooth plate, he has been prepared to do violence, armed with an assortment of deadly tools befitting an equus of the Legion.

Today, the Stabulum is deafeningly loud, thunderous with the pounding of hands and feet as the Sixth Armored awaits the call to battle. Lunar Veil cannot be opened except during the span of a few hours each month, meaning that the day and time of this fight was set the moment we decided to make our stand. Rather than leaving us each to hold a quiet and lonely vigil as the hour drew near, the planets and stars grinding down like the gears of a watch, Centurio Kitu summoned us all to the Stabulum, and, with artful speechifying and heroic words, worked the Sixth Armored into a lather hot and fine enough to shave a man's face. We are to fly with the vanguard, the first charge to break the enemy onslaught and win the Legion a foothold in battle. It will be a perilous enterprise, but Kitu has us eager for it. I feel the excitement as much as anyone, but I leave the fervor behind, so that I can say good-bye.

I have a ritual, one Reaper Thom taught me to perform whenever the time comes to risk my life. I close my eyes, and in one breath I set aside the world and everything in it, all the loves and hopes I have ever felt. Once there is nothing for me to lose, I can fight without hesitation or fear. This came foremost of all Thom's lessons to me, before shooting and riding, before learning how to grip a knife. He would never have taken me on as his pupil were he not certain I could cast my life away at a moment's notice, step out of it like a second skin. But I had watched Papa die, seen my brother and sister taken. I knew how it felt to lose everything, and I could find that feeling again.

It is what I did each time I rode out with the scouts. While Mama kissed the part in my hair and implored me to come back to her, and heard me promise I would, what I was really saying was *Good-bye*. I say it now, silently, amid the pulsing shouts and stomps echoing down these corridors of giants.

Good-bye, Mama.
Good-bye, Baby.
Good-bye, Naomi.

It is as if I have shrugged off a warm blanket before a chilly wind. I am lighter, colder, alert, awake, free. I am ready for war.

The call isn't long in coming: a booming howl, loud enough to drown out our racket and every thought but the summons to battle. The walls and roof of the Stabulum glow with red light as equites sprint to their posts, and in the rows of stalls, towering shapes begin to stir.

Snuggles responds to my touch like a living thing, growling and keen for a fight. He kneels, laying one great hand on the ground to lift me aboard. His fingers have grooves where I can stand, handles I can grip to steady myself as I rise toward his core. His interior abounds in comforts and niceties missing when he was only Kizabel's Project, but he is the same Snuggles, the same fierce spirit I came to recognize in our first weeks together. The core folds around me like some huge and gentle palm, and I awaken to the formidable strength and senses of his giant's body.

I am reminded momentarily of Envy, my companion on so many journeys, killed in the desperate flight to Granite Shore. I am glad I did not have to watch her fall, her beautiful black-and-white coat marred in blood, her strong legs slack in death. She would have done anything for me, I know, and proved it on more than one occasion. And while I have been told time and again that unless joined to a human spirit, equi are nothing but dead rock, I feel a similar connection with Snuggles now, the will to face any obstacle and never stop running so long as the heart this beast and I share keeps beating.

Like the others of my escadrille, as a war party the size of the 126th is called, I keep my mount in a kneeling position as Imway calls each of us to count off. Above, the ceiling of the Stabulum pulls slowly back. It is an hour or so after dawn in this part of the world, a dry southern continent where we have awaited the reopening of Lunar Veil, and the light stretching over the Stabulum's rows is the rich, juicy orange-pink of a ripe peach. As number thirteen, I am the last to sound my readiness for launch. Once that is done, Imway waits half a moment, then orders us together up into the glowing morning.

We rise into a sky swarming with equi of the Legion. Ours is not the only Stabulum mounted onto this flying fortress, and as we spin over dizzying views of towers and spires and sinister barrels of artillery, I mark glinting armored figures streaming from points all across the island, gathering and parting like shifting ocean waves. Sun shines across the tides of hard-plated bodies, and for a single breath I am taken by the beauty of this scene, the fighters sparkling and prismatic as spray washing over the city's stone peaks.

I sense Imway issuing orders by Directed Speech, the peculiar form of communication equi use, and obediently I circle Snuggles into cruising formation. The 126th has altered its habitual flight patterns to account for my presence, generally by wedging me someplace out of the way. While most of them have acknowledged my skill in flight, I am not trusted in battle, and whatever position I occupy is presumed to be our weakest point.

The vanguard has begun to gather into a sweeping arc some distance ahead of the IMEC, and Imway guides us toward our position, slightly to the right of the formation's apex. We have with us fighters from all twelve of Earth's Legions, including the overwhelming majority of our Armored Cavalry, a force built for swift and powerful assaults. Two fontani fly close behind, each a seasoned warrior, I've been told, though to me they seem nothing but small blossoms of sparkling night, an unlikely thing in this warm and lustrous dawn. I cannot keep my mind from wandering to

Naomi—another fontana, as she is, posted behind us on Earth—but my thoughts are distant, abstract, as though they belong not to me but some figure from ancient history, sentiments found in the journal of a person long deceased.

Ahead, Lunar Veil has begun to shift, the twist of its edges rendered distinctly in the morning's brilliant pastels. I have one last glimpse of us as shimmering droplets, now descending toward a vast surface of stirring water, and then the battle begins.

The first wave of enemies arrives like a flock of sparrows descending from a cloud, a scattering of dark specks swooping suddenly across an expanse of bright pink. Hardly have the Valentines made their appearance than they are met with a clattering of explosions, artillery rumbling across our mobile fortress. The sky before me explodes with incongruous colors, concussions shaking through the clouds and down into my armor to rattle my very bones. Distantly, I note my quickening heart, everything beyond this place and time receding into shadows, faces I loved taking on the pallor of ghosts.

Even before this first volley is finished, a second hits, fired from one of our cities below, so far from here that it is hidden behind the curvature of the world, yet still close enough to level its guns at Lunar Veil. When the sparks and thunder clear, all but a few of the invaders are gone. Of special note among the survivors is a single point of darkness, hanging in the sky like some backward reproduction of a morning star: a Valentine Zero.

Our enemies will have expected a vigorous defense. Very likely they had an idea of the placement and armament of our cities and knew their opening gambit would incur a heavy cost. What they did not expect was that we would bring one of those cities with us into battle. Where the Valentines might have counted upon a lull in our bombardment as each spray of shells crossed the long miles from our stationary guns, time that would have allowed them to recover and maneuver, our flying fortress is ready with a new barrage almost before the last one has ended. The shots pass neatly through the formations of our vanguard, causing no more disturbance than a warm wind, and collide with the faltering enemy. There is another jangle of reverberating flashes, and when it passes, the sky it leaves behind is empty. Even the Zero's dark star has fallen.

I hear Imway ordering our party to hold steady, but there is no waver in our ranks nor anywhere along the vanguard's line. We keep our course while the call and answer of gunfire goes on, the flak and debris of spent energy and shattered enemies whirling with our passing.

The Valentines are slow to relinquish their offensive, but they are no fools, either. Once two more swarms of shadowy shapes have sallied from Lunar Veil, only to be flattened beneath the determined hammering of our guns, the Valentines perceive the danger, and fighters cease to emerge from the sky.

Centurio Kitu orders the Sixth Armored to close ranks. The time has come to move, to press the advantage we have won before the enemy can gather up some new strategy. The vanguard bursts forward in a roar of speed, and together we charge into Lunar Veil.

The last time I came this way, I did not realize I had entered another world until I was nearly back out of it. It was only after poor Snuggles began to succumb to his injuries, rent to shreds by horrible talons and jaws, that I took in the night around me and the distant view of Earth like a patch of blue glimpsed from a well's bottom. I recall some disappointment that I would not get to die under my own sky, but I have never been overly concerned with the choices denied me, and this seemed no great tragedy. What mattered was that my task was accomplished, and there was nothing left to do. The crossing now is much the same: a shroud of mist hiding the world from sight, then a wide sky of alien stars. I do not wonder if I will see Earth again. The place is one more pale memory, and I have a new errand before me.

Gradually, I perceive the 126th on my wings, and the lines of the vanguard spreading wide on either side. Imway calls out, warning us to brace for combat. Already my senses have begun to prickle across the many articles of mayhem at my disposal, bolts and pulses of destroying energy I can wield like arrows and scythes and long-reaching fists, and the slender, chalk-white lance we carry for close combat, now forming in my hand like a crackling icicle as I sight ahead, waiting for the enemy to appear.

It seems at first that there is nothing before us but a haze of dust sprinkled across the firmament, but with alarming speed those far-off specks become glinting motes, and the motes a multitude of terrible monsters, all claws and teeth forged in sleek, matted metal. I have one brief instant to contemplate this flying wall of blades before it comes crashing onto me.

It is chaos, simple and complete. The enemy is all around, a multitude of metallic creatures built for war. They come in all sizes, configured according to their preferred mode of attack, arms to slice and grapple, mouths to bellow out fiery blasts, bodies built like bullets or the jagged edge of a saw. Their ranks extend in every direction, twisting and curling like thorny vines. Snuggles and I circle and dip, striking out at the seemingly endless tangle of foes. The voices of the 126th fill my mind, calling out warnings and advice, and without quite realizing it, I have joined in, registering dangers and opportunities, offering and summoning assistance. Imway can be heard above them all, coordinating our maneuvers, rallying and guiding our attacks.

We set upon a collection of good-sized fighters, flattened shells bristling with clawed arms like nightmarish crabs, and cut them to pieces with our lances. The Valentines use animated armor much like our equi, and each cut draws a splash of gushing, bright green gwayd. Their fighters are different from ours in at least one respect, however: They destroy themselves the moment they are defeated, crumpling like burning paper until only twisting threads of ash remain. It shakes my rhythm, the first time an adversary folds and vanishes under my blade, but only the once. My enemy is the spirit inside the armor, and once that is gone, it makes little difference what sort of husk is left over.

The crab-warriors dispatched, we turn to join another unit from the Sixth contending with a long, tangled thing that brings to mind an endless, razor-legged millipede. We have turned over a rock, and now we must tangle with every awful creature hiding beneath.

The vanguard has hit with speed and power, but our momentum can't last. I count at least five Valentine fighters for every one of ours, and once we've exhausted the first feverish exchanges of our assault, it's plain the shock we delivered is quickly passing. Soon, we will have to deal with our enemy's full and enraged strength.

I find myself with three equites of the 126th, isolated among a forest of Valentine claws and teeth. Without any of us announcing an intention to do so, we draw our lances and edge together. We fight head to toe, so that each has plenty of room to strike, cutting back the horde around us. But the whirling attacks edge closer, advancing and retreating but slowly constricting around us, until the vise is so tight we can hardly move without angry thorns digging into our armor.

The deepening danger and desperation of our position sharpens my focus, and as I work Snuggles farther into the fray, he responds with a surge of eager power. We were both fashioned for this work, each in our own way, and it feels natural to our shared body, neither one of us drawing back, even from oncoming death.

As a pair of pincers narrowly misses my shoulder, I spot a hole in the attack, like a worn patch of cloth, and aim my lance there. My comrades do the same, and together we shred our way out, a luminous pea soup of gwayd splashing away in heavy globules. Only when we are clear, floating above a new onrush of enemies, do I understand what allowed our escape. Our city has found its way through Lunar Veil, guns blazing to scatter the Valentine lines.

A voice I recognize as Haiyalaiya's springs into my mind. Her equus, 126-012, EndIsWaiting, hovers at my shoulder. *Hot boiling shit! Glad you're on* our *side!*

The rest of the 126th has joined us now. We close ranks and dive back into the fight.

FIFTY-TWO

NAOMI

A solemn mood has fallen over the Basilica of Tenth City, quite a difference from when I arrived this morning. The lively scene then reminded me of my coda readying to break camp for some long journey. I suppose that is not so strange. Our Legion was about to set forth into another world, after all, though no one here would be going anywhere. From where I stood, there seemed nothing so solid and stationary as this Basilica, with its stone walls and ceilings high enough to dwarf the tallest pine canopies of the northern forests. The great map at its center, what they call the Board, appeared as delicate as the rest of the Basilica was sturdy. By the look of it, a loud cough might have brought the whole thing tumbling down. I found myself thinking of Baby, and the way he would play soldiers with chess pieces, arranging knights and castles in elaborate formations without any regard whatever for the rules of the game.

Likening the Basilica's Board to a chess square seemed apt enough once the call to battle came. The silent concentration of those gathered around was as tense and focused as that attending the pitched grudge matches between Reaper Thom and Randy Tinker Bose. You could almost forget that somewhere, real soldiers were fighting, until the order came to fire Tenth City's guns.

The report of our first fusillade sent a shudder through the Basilica's floor and proved the Board was more robust than it appeared, for not a piece was knocked out of place. Instead, a scattering of small green orbs appeared above our position and sailed toward the site of combat. When they found their mark and word came back of a direct hit, you would have thought we'd won the war, the way people cheered. But I suppose we had to take our victories where we could.

I knew Rae was somewhere among those specks and blocks, and my sentiments then were much the same as those I felt whenever she went scouting. I was afraid she might not return, true, but such a possibility never seemed real to me. I could not imagine the enemy that would be too much for my sister. Far more genuine was my dread that when the time came for me to stand in her place, I would not live up to the example she had laid out. And here she was riding forth again, and me at the rear, my nerves quivering at the mere echo of battle.

After two more volleys, each as successful as the first, the great double-ended pyramid used to signify our flying island met the wide disk marking the border of Lunar Veil and dissolved into a scattering of golden fairy dust. Thus ended our part in the fighting, or so we are given to hope.

Most of our commanders now appear at a loss for what to do next. We all know the fate of the world is being decided at this very moment, but to us it is as if we have loosed an arrow and now can only wait and hope it finds its mark. We cannot even watch because Lunar Veil is by its nature impassable to nearly all signals that could bring us news of the battle. Legionaries who only minutes ago were feverishly coordinating our attack on the Valentines now stand motionless along the tiers of raised platforms, staring at the Board as though, by dint of sheer concentration, they might see past the curtain of sky. Only the man standing beside me seems to suffer no uncertainty regarding what the situation requires of him. "Back at it, gentlemen and ladies," he bellows into the Basilica's quiet. "This still is an active engagement. You've all got your orders, and none of those include using your mouths as flytraps. If you're monitoring an observation post, keep at it. Everyone else, get moving."

His name is Legatus Cressock. He is the commander in charge of the Legion's reserve here in Hestia, an older man but very hale in the way all aged Principate people seem to be, with broad shoulders and a shock of thick gray hair. We met a day ago in the briefing where the order of this battle was first laid out for me, and he was friendly enough then, like a gruff but gentle old hound. In combat he directed his troops with stern good humor, but as with everyone here, he underwent a change as IMEC-1 disappeared into Lunar Veil. There is no joy in his smile as he watches his soldiers busying themselves with the defense of Earth, and his hands grip our platform's railing as though he intends to squeeze the life from it.

Charles said almost nothing throughout the whole opening skirmish, trusting in Cressock's expertise and speaking only when he wanted to make some point of instruction to Jax or myself, but now he says, "No need to tire them out, Legatus. It's going to be some time before we have any real news from Dis. If Reydaan decides to call in the cavalry, you'll want everyone fresh."

Charles has already explained our part in the present engagement, and even had he not, the briefing we attended with Legatus Cressock, and numerous others before and after, were education enough. We are part of the Legion's reserve, the portion held back from combat so that we may seize any opportunities that arise in battle, though it is obvious to everyone that the opacity of Lunar Veil will make seizing opportunities difficult. For that reason, Charles says, we may also think of ourselves as an extreme rear guard, left behind to thwart any enemies who find their way past our main force. In the case of a rout, it will be up to us to make Earth's last defense, but that piece of our mission is unspoken, and no one speaks it now. I wonder, though, if it is this possibility of a final, hopeless fight that now hangs so heavily over the Basilica.

"Something of a lost cause, staying fresh," Cressock says with what sounds to me like bitterness. "This situation is going to wear on them whether or not anyone is shooting at us. At least if we keep them busy, they won't have time to dwell on a situation they can't do anything about." He looks over to where I am standing with Jax. "This is your first action, isn't it, ma'am? I know Fontanus Jaxten has stood for the city during an incursion before."

Legion people are always highly formal and polite. I like that about them. "This is my first assignment, sir, but I have joined Jax on one previous occasion. Nor am I a stranger to organized violence. I have seen a deal of it elsewhere."

"Organized violence," he repeats, his eyes crinkling at the edges in a way that makes me think he approves of my comment.

"I will own that is something of a contradiction in terms."

Cressock lets out a short, barking laugh. "Then you already know more about war than I did the first time I saw combat, and I must have been nearly twice your age. The Legion will be in capable hands with you. And you, sir," he says, nodding to Jax.

"Legatus," Charles interjects, somewhat sharply it seems to me, "I think it's about time we got ready to move. It's earlier than scheduled, but a little practice now should make the transitions smoother later on, wouldn't you agree? And it'll keep the troops busy."

Charles is referring to the way Lunar Veil drifts constantly over Earth, following the path of the Moon. With time, it will pass beyond the sight of Tenth City and the range of its guns. The reserve will have to move if we intend to keep watch for anything coming through, but I had thought that necessity was still some time away.

"Yes, sir, I think you're right." The grim set has returned to Cressock's face. "Let's see how speedy these old dogs can be about prepping for the trip."

"Jax, Naomi," Charles says, looking down at us, "why don't you go and see if you can find Malandeera at the Forum. I'll coordinate with the Legatus and his people and meet you outside."

Jax was quiet all throughout my conversation with the Legatus, and he remains so until we are nearly out the Basilica door. "I'm not crazy, am I?" are his first words to me. "You heard that, right?"

I ask him to be more specific. "Something weird was going on back there," he says, "with Charles and Legatus Cressock."

Now that Jax has mentioned it, I think he is right. It was as though only part of what passed between the two men could be heard in what they said. "Cressock was angry about something, I think," I reply. "It must be some recent development, as I met with him only yesterday, and he seemed genial enough."

"And did you see the way Charles got sort of mad at him?" Jax asks. "When he started talking about going off to war the first time? What was up with that?"

"Cressock was not the only one," I say. Jax has me pondering now, thinking about the heavy atmosphere that seemed to hang everywhere in the Basilica. Tension over the ongoing battle, yes, but something else as well. Could it have been fear? "Is that how your commanders usually act—during an incursion, perhaps?"

Jax shakes his head, brows furrowed. "No. That was just . . . weird."

As a description, "disquieting" would serve as well as "weird." But I have no good explanation for the behavior of Charles and Cressock, and I doubt Jax has, either, as I conclude from his silence as we emerge from the Basilica onto the Forum of Tenth City.

It is a far less pleasant city to look at than Ninth, I have decided. Close living is a common feature of all Principate cities, which endeavor to contain as many people as possible within thelemity's limited purview. But whereas Ninth City's geography of towers and battlements appears to follow some natural organizing principle, like a grove of tall trees that arrange themselves to leave ample sunlight and air to breathe, Tenth City has the look of a mouth crammed with too many teeth. The smooth, gleaming blocks appear to jostle for space, uncomfortable in one another's presence.

Like Ninth, Tenth City is built around a central Forum with a fountain of extravagant and symbolic design adorning its center, and that is where we find Fontana Malandeera, her eyes turned skyward. It is possible to discover a great deal about the world from one's mijmere—even things hidden from human sight—by cultivating a kind of double vision. As a baby crying in its crib may become a mewing cat in the dream of its sleeping mother, so the details of reality find their way into a mijmere, and often something invisible to the casual observer will become glaringly obvious through the eyes of fontani usikuu. Charles has said that with practice it is possible for fontani to look across great distances even without the aid of a mijmere, but I am still some way from learning this trick.

As we approach, Jax calls out, "Can you see anything?" Meaning has there been any news from Dis. Because of the obstacles Lunar Veil poses to communication, messages between the Legion's main body and its reserve are to be sent in the form of signaling rockets. But time in Dis moves slowly by our reckoning here in Hestia, and I doubt the fighting there will be past its first few minutes—much too early for there to be anything of significance to report. If Jax is already looking for news, he is more anxious than I thought.

"Clear skies," Malandeera says, turning a rueful smile our way. "No doubt our boys and girls are already making a mess of things."

Fontana Malandeera has made no secret of her dissatisfaction at being assigned to the reserve. As the only legionary to return alive from the Front, she considers it her duty and privilege to heap a measure of ruin upon the hordes that killed her comrades and pursued her the long way to Earth. Fontani will be at a premium in this battle, however, and while the Consulate has decided there must be at least four of us in the reserve, no commander was willing to give up a trusted and familiar fighter so that Malandeera of the Twenty-Second Legion could have her revenge. Though Malandeera plainly disagrees with these orders, she is a loyal legionary, and her stance is closer to impatience than anger.

I have an idea to question her about the scene we witnessed in the Basilica, but Jax is quicker with his queries. "Do you think they'll call us in?" he asks. It is an attempt at swagger and not at all convincing. "When will we know?"

"Can't say for sure," Malandeera answers. "It's been a long time since I've seen signal rockets in a battle. But I think there's reason to hope you two have a long wait coming before you end up in the thick of things." That rueful smile appears again. "Not too long, though."

Here is another odd comment. The Consulate has already debated which portion of the Legion should embark into the Realms if we are victorious today, and while nothing has been decided, most are of the opinion that our youngest soldiers—namely Jax and myself—ought to remain behind for what many are calling the "MapleWhite Campaign." If the mission succeeds, and the Valentine Host is delayed sufficiently for the Legion to rebuild, it will be twenty years or more before Earth sees any fighting more serious than a routine incursion. Perhaps this is what Malandeera meant about hoping Jax and I will have a while to wait before we see real battle. But how long would be "too long"?

I am about to request a word of clarification when I spy movement over the skyline of Tenth City. Our fighters have begun to rise over the stony spearpoints of buildings in preparation for the coming journey. I pick out the armored figures of equi among them, and the heavy globes known as tetra fortresses.

Malandeera has observed them also. "So soon?" she asks.

"That's what we came to tell you," Jax says. "Charles thought it would be a good idea to go a little early. For practice," he adds uncertainly.

If this news surprises Malandeera, she does not show it. "I suppose it isn't too long until we pass out of range," she says, turning again to look at Lunar Veil. "What have you two done with Charles, then?"

Charles, however, has just emerged from the Basilica, and so can speak for himself. There is no doubt in my mind that our commanders would have preferred to bring him into this fight. The only reason they relegated him to the reserve was that doing so meant Jax and I could be sent along with him, thereby depriving our main force of only one experienced source where it might have lost three.

"All right, everyone," Charles says. "Ready to play leapfrog?"

By "leapfrog" Charles means our plan of jumping from city to city to keep pace with the movement of Lunar Veil. Each city along our path has a full complement of legionaries crewing its guns. All they need to be ready for combat is a source of thelemity. As Lunar Veil passes beyond one city's range, Jax and I are to fly ahead and make sure the next is fully powered. Once we arrive, Charles and Malandeera will follow with the remainder of the reserve. That way we will always have guns ready to fire, even if the Valentines attack while most of the reserve is in transit.

But I am not quite ready to forget the strangeness I sensed in the Basilica. I search Charles's face for any clue of what might have caused it, and finding none, I ask, "Charles, has something gone wrong with the battle?"

Charles appears surprised. "Why would you say that, Naomi?"

I do not quite know how to respond. There is nothing in particular I can cite as cause for my unease, and if I try, I will likely sound silly. And yet I have a notion Charles knows what I mean to ask, and also the answer, only he has decided not to tell me.

"This is a tense situation, Naomi" is what he says instead. "We each have our own part to play. I'm sure I can count on you and Jax to do what's right."

Whatever is going on, I have had about my fill of it. I open my mouth to say as much, but just then Jax says, "Yes, sir," at the same time resting a hand on my shoulder, and in a puff Tenth City is gone. In place of the jagged stone towers and moody sky, I find myself beneath a canopy of thick green leaves luminous with summer sun. It is a whole new world, built faster than the blink of an eye when Jax shaded beside me, and my own mijmere sprang up in response, yet it feels like a place I have known forever. Before me stretches a rolling, grassy hill dotted with gaily attired figures, all in various attitudes of leisure. The air carries the scent of herbs and wildflowers, and gentle music played on strings.

"He isn't going to tell us, Naomi," Jax says. He stands in the same relation to me as before, only now he wears a long, smock-like shirt and a "baseball cap," his usual attire when he appears in my mijmere. Outside this place we are already moving toward our destination at considerable speed, crossing lakes and forests and deserts like twin bolts of lightning, but here only an easy stroll is required. I have on a light, long-sleeved dress and wide hat with an excessive amount of frill. I know Jax does not see this world quite the same way I do. To him, we will likely be at one of his baseball games. The essence of things will be the same, however: We are situated together in some friendly manner.

Only I do not feel friendly just now. "Charles is hiding something from us," I say. Pulling down my hat to keep the sun from my eyes, I set off in the direction of the music, which I see is coming from a quartet arranged on a small hillock nearby.

I set a good pace, and Jax must hurry to keep up. "Maybe he is, but he must have a reason, right? Charles knows what he's doing."

I glare at him from beneath my hat. "What makes you so sure? It could be that something has happened, and he doesn't want to tell us."

"Well, it can't be about the battle," Jax says. "We haven't heard anything yet."

He is right about that, at least. "My sister is fighting out there right now." I cannot quite keep the quaver from my voice.

"I know," Jax says. "And she needs us to do our part. Everyone does. Maybe that's why Charles hasn't said anything. Maybe he doesn't want us getting distracted."

Likely that is the explanation, knowing Charles. "How long is too long a wait to fight the Valentines?"

Jax crinkles his nose at me. "What do you mean?"

"It was something Malandeera said. That she hoped we'd have a while to wait, but not too long. What do you think she meant?"

"I don't know." He ponders, then says again, "I don't know."

"She meant something, I'll tell you that."

"Yeah," Jax says with a sigh, "maybe, but you know what we can be sure about? Everyone wants to win today. Charles, Cressock, Malandeera, the whole reserve. They're doing everything they can to make that happen. So that's what we've got to do, too."

"You're right." It's true. I dislike being lied to, but there is not much I can do about it now, and winning this battle is far more important. If I have to bite my tongue, that is what I will do.

A gust of wind has begun blowing toward us, visible in the flapping of ladies' dresses and of blankets laid over the ground. "We're nearly there," I say to Jax. "Are you ready?"

"Yeah, let's go."

Together, we turn our faces into the rushing air. All at once, the sun-drenched hillside burns away, and we are in a stone plaza much like the Forum of Tenth City. There are differences enough in the shape and arrangement of this place, however, to be certain we are somewhere else. Also, the time of day has changed. The sun, just risen when we departed, now waits somewhere below the horizon. Only a few minutes have passed, if that. It is simply that we are now considerably farther to the west than we were before, and the sun here occupies a different place in the sky.

The air is chilly, but within seconds a warm breeze begins to blow as the power Jax and I have brought with us brings this new city to life. On every side, strange sounds screech and clatter, each a sign for some different magic taking shape. The city's great guns groan and pivot into alignment. Far away on the horizon, Lunar Veil shimmers like an expanse of deep water.

Jax's eyes are on Lunar Veil as well. "Do you think they'll be all right?"

I do not know what to tell him. I dearly hope they will, but we are in a war, and in war, anything can happen.

FIFTY-THREE

KIZABEL

Under zealous cross-examination, I would probably be forced to admit I'm the teensiest bit disappointed no one at Gun Red Fifteen seems to know who I am. After all, we're currently battling a terrifying alien threat on a flying island *I designed*, not to mention the leading role I played in putting the whole extravagantly-baroque-jigsaw-puzzle-of-a-thing together. Anyone who wanted to add a little poesy to the overall affair might have titled me the grand impresario of IMEC-1, though, of course, no one did. I realize the present situation offers a profusion of other more pertinent subjects for contemplation, including but not limited to moral and philosophical examinations of my relatively short life to this point and any number of ontological speculations. My comrades out there in the melee are probably far more concerned with simple, cerebello-medullary subthoughts, procedural memory and fight-or-flight stuff, but working heavy artillery lends itself more to introspection in a cerebral, prefrontal sense, and right now, I'm thinking I'd like it noted somewhere that I really did help build this thing.

As far as anyone on Red Fifteen knows, I'm just another gun monkey who, due to my singular lack of combat skills, is useful in battle only as power for the heavy artillery. The lack-of-combat-skills part is perfectly true, but I *was* invited up to Command to advise in case my expert knowledge of our Ingenically Mobilized Expeditionary City was required. The trouble with the invitation was that it came from Vinneas, who understands IMEC-1 just as well as I do and who also happens to be a strategic and tactical wunderkind, something I most certainly am not,[1] all of which

---

1 Humanity has yet to invent a game of strategy at which I show appreciably more aptitude than a trained pigeon. I am, however, fabulous at badminton. My scores were on record at

made the invitation feel more patronizing than anything else. At least on GR-15, I'm doing something useful, *videlicet* blasting Romeo into a million microscopic smithereens. The Legion's heavy artillery is all palaketic,[2] meaning it has to be crewed by revenni like myself. Every time our gun fires, a little bit of that power comes from me.

Gun Red Fifteen is a seventy-two-souler,[3] and like all the big guns aboard IMEC-1, it's nicknamed after some outstandingly violent geographical feature back on Earth—"Old Faithful" in this case, a title that as far as I can tell is at least half-ironic. "Faithful" is indeed one of the oldest pieces of artillery still in operation, and while it's every bit as accurate as the new 144s and the massive 208s,[4] it has developed something of a personality over the years. It is occasionally slow to fire, as though registering disapproval of the choice of target, and is suspected of holding grudges against crew members who insult or mistreat it. Faithful's loyalty is irreproachable, however. A strict yet respectful gun commander is usually enough to curb any misbehavior, and fortunately that's what we have in Tesserario Leuvenven.

The tall and barrel-chested Tessie Leu makes for a formidable presence as she marches along our gun's upper levels, gathering information from spotters and calling out adjustments to the trajectory of fire, all while maintaining a steady slew of orders to us gun monkeys below. I have a theory that the main requirement for gun commanders is not any kind of technical skill but the ability to issue repetitive commands for long periods

---

the statistical cadet register of the Academy of Ninth City, and I hope still are, despite the fact that Ninth City technically no longer exists.

2 Palakesis is a technical process used to alter or enhance a thelemic artifice. Whereas ingenic tools and weaponry, such as the trencher or lazel, employ a steady amount of ambient thelemity to power a predetermined or already existing artifice, palaketic devices magnify and direct new artifices as they are created. The process could be crudely compared to the way a megaphone magnifies and directs sound. Palakesis allows for a higher level of potency and control than ingesis, but can only be initiated by people capable of thelemic manipulation.

3 That is, fueled by the collective energy of seventy-two revenni, an arrangement known as a "seventy-deuce" among people familiar enough with such high-powered weaponry to adopt a slangy tone.

4 For some unknown reason, heavy artillery tends to work best when its gunners come in multiples of eight.

of time without becoming droning or dull. Tessie Leu has the at once martial and matronly air of someone used to dealing with large numbers of small children, an attitude I think would be appropriate even if this gun weren't crewed mostly by kids fresh from some Academy or other—which, as I deduce from the bug-eyed youthfulness around me, it is.

I've only seen Tessie Leu once before today, during a thirty-minute orientation session after I was assigned to Old Faithful, and I expect the same goes for my fellow gun monkeys. This is no elite, highly coordinated unit; gunner training takes all of five hours, and that's about four-and-three-quarter hours longer than necessary.

Crewing a piece of heavy artillery is possibly the simplest job in the Legion. The only conscious participation required is the most token sort of focus, summoning up just enough will to get to that nebulous state before intention forms into an actual artifice—after that, the gun takes over, grabbing hold like a hand clasping a hand, drawing the power out through you, and deploying it to deadly and destructive effect. I'm sure if the Legion could think of a way for the gun to do everything, they'd have us strapped to a stack of bunk beds, more milking cows than monkeys, but current state of the art still calls for this modicum of active involvement.

Every gun is equipped with a series of levers arranged around its base like spokes on a wheel, and each lever has a row of gun monkeys[5] to work it. The levers operate by a mechanism resembling a hybrid between oars on an ancient galley ship and the hammer of a CE Old West pistol, the kind that had to be cocked before firing. At Tessie Leu's command of "power!" each row heaves back on its lever, and as we do, Old Faithful drinks up energy through us. The next step is to duck back, reflexively covering our ears and preparing for the burst of sound and shock and psychic queasiness that accompanies the discharge of so much universe-altering force. We get a few breaths to recover, then Tessie Leu is back, calling for another round of power.

Needless to say, there isn't a lot of opportunity for gun monkeys to get acquainted, to develop close personal relationships and overall *esprit de corps*. Most of us weren't even assigned to a specific gun until two days ago, when Command finalized its deployment for the rest of the Legion and

---

5 Usually eight in number, to be specific. Old Faithful is sometimes referred to as a "9-8'er," meaning it has nine rows of eight gun monkeys each.

started filling in the artillery with whoever was left. But despite knowing that we are, if not outright dispensable, for the most part fungible and interchangeable, morale among the gun monkeys of Old Faithful is at a raging, thunderous high.

Part of the credit goes to Tessie Leu, who somehow manages to imbue our limited interaction with a measure of affection and encouragement, peppering her one-word commands with grains of reassurance and motivation that would doubtlessly come off as cheesy in other contexts but seem heart-swellingly inspirational in the midst of a battle, when the capacity for irony is largely nonfunctional. Nor does it hurt that we've seemingly got Romeo bent over our collective knee and are presently spanking his ass to a fine ruddy pink.

Before the General Call to Arms went up, we were all scared more or less completely shitless—in some cases literally, I'd wager, based on the suspiciously foul atmosphere around the benches circling Old Faithful's trunk. Tessie Leu had a speech prepared, of which I remember exactly nothing thanks to the thudding rush in my ears and the suddenly overwhelming importance of little details of the kids around me. The boy sitting to my right, for example, has an array of freckles along one hand in the exact configuration of the Big Dipper,[6] and the girl to my left is a dead ringer for the female lead in one of the old CE films Lady Jane is always trying to get me to watch, a particularly disturbing example in which the apparent heroine is murdered only a few scenes in. I was alternately watching Big Dipper trying to steady his shaking hands by gripping the lever in front of us and recalling flashes of the scene in which my other neighbor's doppelgänger was stabbed to death in the shower by a cross-dressing psychopath, when all at once the sirens went off and Tessie Leu was shouting at us to move. The ensuing sphincter-loosening terror passed almost immediately once we set to work, and soon my whole bench was moving together, Big Dipper and *Psycho* Girl and the rest all rocking back and forth as one.

It was some time before my mind came around to the fact that there was a battle going on, and I began to take heed of the spotters mounted alongside Tessie Leu. I'm not very well versed in the brevity code used to reference targets and threats and vectors for large-soulage firepower, but I

---

6 A northern-hemisphere stellar constellation also known as Ursa Major.

quickly learned how to pick out the reports of a confirmed hit. Tessie Leu
has begun keeping us up to date as well, now that we gun monkeys have
found our rhythm and the necessity of shouting us back into synchrony
has become less pronounced.

From where I sit, it seems Old Faithful has proved a terror to Romeo's
creepy-crawly hordes. Our spotters have already awarded us credit for taking out several of the colossal Type 7s that typically wreak havoc with our
infantry, along with no few raiding parties of 5s and 6s and whole swarms
of 3s. They've even lauded us for making the final strike on two separate
Type 0s, though as Zeros almost never go down except under sustained
fire, it wouldn't surprise me if ten or more other guns were making the
exact same claim.

As much as I enjoy hearing what a murderous, steam-rolling juggernaut
we've become, the whole thing feels weirdly abstract. No one down here
can see what's going on, and despite the sounds filtering in from outside—
a lot of booming and banging combined with the kind of nightmarish
squealing you'd expect during a fire at a menagerie of imaginary mutant
monsters—it's hard to imagine how anything we're doing relates to the
actual fighting. Imway's always talking about the rush of combat, but this
feels more like doing laundry. Once the back-and-forth of crewing takes
over, it's surprisingly easy to get the Valentines and their Hieronymus
Bosch–inspired swarms out of your mind.

In fact, it's entirely possible accounts of our rampant butt-kicking are
being inflated all around, but we gun monkeys are letting ourselves believe.
Big Dipper, who spent the first two pulls of our volley dry-heaving onto his
knees, is now the most enthusiastic gunner on our bench, while *Psycho* Girl
has left off her earlier fear-drenched porcine squealing for something more
like a wolf's growl. Every time news comes down of another hit, the benches
of Old Faithful shout back in unison, a wordless roar that somehow artic-
ulates both a jeer to the enemy and a cheer for our gun as a whole.

And because it seems our interactions with Romeo are strictly of the
our-steel-toed-boot-to-his-face variety in terms of one-sided wreckage,
no one on the benches is prepared when we end up getting stomped
instead.

I don't know if someone up in Command saw the tides of battle taking an unfavorable turn, if our fighters on the front lines knew they were
being beaten back or outflanked; maybe our spotters were restricting their

reports to the sunny and fair. Whatever the reason, we gun monkeys see only clear skies ahead right up until the first figurative clap of thunder.

Between one shot and the next, Tessie Leu's usual call of "power!" changes to "hold!" About half of us let out the triumphal shout that's become as much a part of our rhythm as anything, and three full benches go through with their pull, only to come to an abrupt halt when they see everyone else stalled in attitudes of confusion and dawning fear.

Tessie Leu walks calmly to the console at the edge of her platform, and as she leans in, conferring with Command, silence descends over Gun Red Fifteen. For the first time since the Call to Arms, I get a serious earful of the battle, the tremors of other guns and the steady oceanic sound that must be the generalized combat beyond. An image of the huge umbris of thelemity surrounding us pops into my mind, our fighters swirling with Romeo's like weather patterns over a planet. I doubt Tessie Leu takes more than a few seconds to confirm what she's heard from Command, but the moment seems to go on forever. You can almost see the foreboding sweating from Old Faithful's gun monkeys. When Tessie Leu speaks again, her orders are sharp and forceful.

"Masks up! Straps on!" she calls, circling Old Faithful to address each row of gunners in turn. "Raise masks and strap in! Now!"

A visible shudder of shock rattles down the benches. We all understand the plain, face-value meaning of her words, how these translate into specific actions we're being asked to perform; what doesn't quite register is the reasoning behind them. Minutes ago we were winning this battle, but if we're hearing Tessie Leu right, Gun Red Fifteen is in serious peril. Whatever our status is in the overall fricassee of cross fire, whether the fontani of IMEC-1 have been killed or routed or just got distracted chasing a ball of string, one thing is clear enough: Thelemity is about to become very scarce around here, and probably our lives with it. We're about to go dark.

Our Ingenically Mobilized Expeditionary City works so smoothly most of the time that it's easy to forget the whole self-sustaining flying island concept actually depends upon a frankly ingenious diversity of artifices, without which this place would be little more than a gigantic boulder sprouting a few building-shaped crags. Among the IMEC's many lovely amenities are a breathable atmosphere and consistent gravity, both perfectly mimicking the environment of Earth, homey comforts that really show their value in a Realm like Dis, which has neither.[7] Artillery gunners are all issued a set of D-55 Tactical Survival Attire,[8] featuring masks that, when closed, effectively seal the wearer off from nearly any environment not hospitable to human life, as well as straps we can attach to our benches or other handily placed buckles to keep ourselves in place in the event that gravity becomes unreliable.[9] Until now, the only feature of our D-55s we've had cause to use has been the remarkably effective cooling and sweat-wicking system, but from the sound of it, there's a good chance this place will become weightless and airless very soon.

For all the imperative significance of her orders, Tessie Leu has to issue them twice before any of Old Faithful's crew reacts, and even then compliance is spotty at best. The network of clips and straps that seemed so simple during training now strike me as bafflingly counterintuitive and complex. Only the knowledge that a solid jolt in zero gravity could launch me at neck-breaking speed into the nearest wall focuses my attention enough to hook myself in. I pull up my mask and feel it close around my face, a vacuum-tight seal that will keep me breathing at a pressure of one Earth atmosphere for five hours at least, more if I can stop hyperventilating. I've got everything in place and double-checked when I remember our emergency safety protocol says to raise masks first, and I'm actually about to pull straps and mask and start over when I realize how pointless and potentially-life-endingly-stupid that would be.

Hardly have I taken my first breath of D-55-conditioned air when a furry disorientation passes through me, and my mask fills with the smell of rotten eggs, one of the many unpleasant odors that sometimes arise when thelemity meets the mundane world. My involuntary jerk of surprise as I feel myself lifting gently from my seat sends me shooting forward, but my straps tighten, holding me in place. My head swims with the woozy

---

7 The IMEC's customized gravity is also pretty handy should you happen to find yourself in any significant gravitational field, even one similar to Earth's, but not favorably aligned with same.

8 Essentially a version of the D-87 Pan-Climate Enhancement Armor lacking both the armor and the enhancement.

9 Note, however, that the straps are only helpful in the case of *decreased* gravity. Under increased gravity, D-55s are about as useful as a paper bag—a paper bag filled with squished human remains if the gravity gets too high.

feeling of dangling over a cliff's edge, accompanied by panic-level heart palpitations that won't go away no matter how much I remind myself I'm all locked in and safe as can be under the circumstances.

As incompetent as I was in deploying my safety gear, most of my comrades have fared still worse. Two gun monkeys from the bench ahead of me bounce into the air, propelled by some careless pressure against floor or seat that wouldn't have mattered were there gravity around to provide a counteracting force; one manages to grab a nearby handle, but the other snatches only open space as he floats gently and helplessly upward.

Beside me, Big Dipper has made the same mistake I did regarding mask-and-strap order, but hasn't progressed past his straps. Fortunately, Old Faithful, and every other heavy gun aboard IMEC-1, has an air lock that slams shut when the thelemity cuts out, thus sparing Dipper from imminent asphyxiation. He does start to rise from his seat, however, causing him to flail even more frantically. I reach over and pull him back down, and after bonking him on the head as a reminder to close up his mask, I get to work on his straps.

My strap-work is quicker the second time around, but not quick enough. I've only got Dipper about half-secured when the world suddenly turns white.

My next sensation is of bouncing around like some crazy, high-energy particle, the straps holding D-55s to the seat tensing to absorb the force of my movement. I'm left with a gyroscopically spinning brain and the understanding that there's been some kind of impact or explosion. Without thelemity, all the nifty countermeasures that protect IMEC-1 from attack will be disabled, allowing Romeo to sit back and shoot proverbial fish in a barrel.

Ironically, the one weapon he can't use directly against us now is thelemity. Thelemic artifices can't last outside an umbris, meaning any weapons that rely on thelemity for their destructive output won't work. That doesn't mean Romeo can't use thelemity to fire some good old-fashioned explosives, however, or pelt us with projectiles thelemically accelerated to superhigh velocities. And if our heavy artillery has been as pivotal in this battle as we down here were given to understand, Romeo will want to get rid of us as promptly as possible. Probably Old Faithful was targeted in the very first volley.

Whatever that blast was, it didn't hit us directly—if it had, the atoms of my brain would no longer be sufficiently interconnected to ponder the matter—but it came close enough to hurt. To my left, through eyesight that keeps sliding askew and spasmodically righting itself, I spot an elephant-sized hole in Old Faithful's side, and beyond stars and dark sky intermittently visible between flashes of colorful strobing light.

A hazy, mostly incomplete thought floats across my consciousness, something on the order of *Hey! We're in a war! Fancy that!* With calm near to paralysis, I note bits of debris pinging off of my mask before exiting into the general vacuum, and a floaty feeling in my limbs quite separate from the literal weightlessness of zero G. *Is this really what all the fuss is about?* is what I ask myself. It seems so silly. We're just a bunch of junk drifting through space, fighting over other junk floating through space.

The two rows of benches nearest the hole in GR-15 are mangled and splintered, their levers twisted to uselessness, their former occupants all gone, most likely pulverized in the blast or sucked through the breach as Old Faithful explosively decompressed. Dazedly, I realize my own bench is almost empty—everyone from *Psycho* Girl on has simply vanished, leaving only me and possibly Big Dipper of the eight who had been here I'm-not-quite-sure-how-long before. I swivel to search for Dipper just as his limp left arm connects with my mask.

He's still there, in body if nothing else, floating half a meter above his seat. His incompletely affixed safety straps kept him tethered in the overall area of our bench, but he must have been whipped around quite a bit. Also, he never got his mask up. I yank him down, and have his mask closed and sealed before I notice the blood trailing from his nose and the bloated, bluish tinge of his face. My sense of time is too addled to know whether he's been exposed to the vacuum in here for fifteen seconds or fifteen minutes, but I'm afraid all the friendly atmosphere in the world won't do him any good.

My distress at the possibility that Big Dipper might have been killed is as unexpected and overwhelming as the impact that likely killed him. I am seized by the sudden conviction that if this boy is dead—this near-complete stranger whose name I don't know and whose voice I wouldn't have recognized if replayed for me in crisp high-fidelity sound—the entire world and life itself are totally and absolutely without meaning.

After a few panicked and confused moments, during which I become determined to at least finish strapping Dipper in, I happen upon the diagnostic patch on the thigh of his D-55s. The pressure and temperature inside his suit are both good, and to my astonishment there's the blip of a weak but consistent pulse. By some improbable happenstance, he's alive.

High above, the top of GR-15 lights up with a halo of chattering light—our antibombardment batteries getting to work. They'll slow Romeo down, but without thelemity, I can't imagine us lasting long. Already, another barrage has started falling, each impact shaking Old Faithful like a bottle of bugs in the hands of a mean-spirited child, flinging poor Dipper around like a rag doll. I hold on to him, trying to keep him safe until the shaking stops, and I can finally close up his straps.

FIFTY-FOUR

TORRO

Out here, you could see the whole thing happen. Well, not the *whole* thing. This battle's so big, there's no way to really keep track of it all at once, especially considering how there's fighting all over the place, including both sides of the city, and we've got to pay attention to shooting old Romeo at least part of the time. But you really can see quite a bit from an assault platform. Like, you can see old IMEC-1, or most of it anyway, and the great big net of assault platforms around it, and the cohorts of equites and whatnot we've got chasing Romeo all over the place, though they're mostly way out and just look like a bunch of whizzing, popping lights. So when those Zeros got onto old IMEC-1 and the whole battle started going pretty much to crap, I had about as good a view of it as anyone.

We'd launched out from one of the battle spires on IMEC-1 with about a million other assault platforms and formed up into a wall just like we learned in training. Only this wall was pretty different from the ones we'd practiced because instead of making a big solid stack of platforms, we left several pretty large gaps. The whole thing looked more like a fishing net than a wall, actually, and in fact that's sort of what it was. A net, I mean. The way all our platforms were laid out, the Valentines would be kind of funneled toward the gaps, but that put them right in the path of the big guns down on IMEC-1.

We were all nervous as anything, of course, me and the rest of my platoon. Everyone else in the Twelfth of the Third, too, I bet. We knew how to fly an assault platform, but this was our first real battle where someone was really intentionally trying to kill us. And if that weren't bad enough, this was supposed to be like the most important battle ever. Like, if we lost, that was pretty much it for Earth and everyone. Old Romeo was just going to march in and kill whoever was left. Optio Sorril was pretty clear about that. As we were waiting to load up into our battle spire, she gathered our whole century around, the Twelfth Century, that is, and told us with that easygoing smile of hers that if there was anything we cared about, anything at all, we were fighting for it now.

That got to me a bit. I mean, I've never been like ecstatic about the Legion and everything, and I'm not too fond of the Prips, but I do care about a few things. I really do. I kept thinking about that as we put on our helmets and climbed to our platforms, and I was still thinking about it when we launched. I watched old IMEC-1 get smaller and smaller behind us, and all the other platforms flying around all over the place. I felt pretty strange, but I had a hard time deciding why, and before I could, Mersh started calling me a lazy turd and yelling for me to get to my firing post.

I was pretty sure we were all about to get blued right there, though I was planning on having a like pulmonary embolism first. Then I got my lazel up and saw no one was really coming at us. What was going on was this other part of the Legion, the vanguard, had already flown ahead to clear the way for everyone else, and now that old IMEC-1 had arrived in the thick of things, we were off to help them out.

Those kiddos from the vanguard were really going at it. You could see them flying around like crazy, just slashing and blasting away. They were giving it to Romeo pretty good, but I think they were glad when we showed up. When the big guns down on IMEC-1 got going, whole chunks of Valentine fighters started to just disappear, like they'd been drawn there on a blackboard or something and someone came with an eraser and wiped them away. It didn't take old Romeo long to figure out what was happening, though, and he kind of pulled back a bit so his fighters weren't completely out in the open and everything.

Anyway, at first there wasn't all that much to do. We'd built our wall or net or whatever of assault platforms, and Romeo knew the minute he got close we'd just give him another round from the big guns, so he was trying to stay out of the way as much as possible. That wasn't terribly easy for him, though. The guns were going pretty much nonstop, really rumbling away so much it felt like an avalanche inside your head. You could see all these huge swarms of Valentine fighters, just thousands and thousands of them way out ahead, and big flashes of light going off right in the middle of them, like when lightning strikes inside of a cloud. Meanwhile, whole cohorts of our guys were out there chasing Romeo's fighters around, trying to bring them closer or trap them someplace where our guns could really chew them up.

From our perspective, there wasn't all that much to do, except every so often when one of those Valentine swarms made a run for our part of the net. They would sort of swirl around a ways out, and once in a while one little stream of fighters would break off and come at us. We'd fire our lazels and the pair of 13mm auto-ingens mounted on our platform, and eventually the Valentines would turn around and fly away. Usually, before they even got very near us, a few of the guns down on IMEC-1 would see them and let loose with a close-range attack. Anyone who's watched a chain saw going to work on a tree can about picture what that looked like.

Those big guns didn't let up for a minute, but after a while I started to worry about the wall or net or whatever. Our platforms were all in pretty close, relative to everyone out there chasing Romeo around, but it still must've taken a crazy number of us to cover old IMEC-1 from like every conceivable angle. In between runs, I'd get a look around, and I started to notice the net sort of looked like it was thinning out in some places, and in others it'd been kind of bent out of shape. I pointed that out to Spammers and Hexi, and I think they were a bit concerned, but Spammers just said formations never last very long anyway, and Hexi agreed. Mersh told me to shut up and worry about my own area of operation. I still felt sort of nervous, though, like I was supposed to be doing something but didn't know what.

And then this one time, old Romeo really came in crashing at a bunch of platforms just above us, and while I was craning up to shoot them, I saw something big had changed. I didn't even know what at first, until I looked more closely at the other end of our net, and there was nothing but a lot of empty space. Assault platforms can be hard to spot if they're not grouped especially close together or lighting up the way they do when they're shooting, and I'd thought there just wasn't very much happening, but in fact someone'd torn a huge hole right through the net protecting old IMEC-1. I looked down at the city, and even though it was difficult to tell with the guns going nonstop, I thought I saw some fighting down there.

I called up Mersh through my helmet. "Hey, Mersh," I said. "I think there's something going on down on the IMEC."

"Eyes forward, boyo," he said. "Our orders are to make sure no one gets past. How're you gonna do that if you're looking the wrong way?"

"Yeah, but, Mersh, you should probably just take a look. Maybe these guys'll come our way if they need to make a run for it."

Mersh did take a look, too. He even seemed a little surprised, but all he said was "Command'll know all about that. If they want us to do something, they'll tell us."

And sure enough, about two seconds later, Mersh sort of cocked his head, like he was listening to something, and I knew he was getting orders from Optio Sorril or maybe someone even higher up. Mersh took another look below, and this time he really was worried, no question about it.

He was looking at some fontani flying over the city—or sources, I should say. Fontani are ours and Zeros are Romeo's. These starry things had to be both, I thought, because of the way they were moving, really tearing around the city but not going anywhere in particular.

Pretty much our whole platform had turned around to see what Mersh and I were looking at, and when Mersh noticed, he started yelling again about getting back to our posts. But before anyone could move, there was this terrible ripping sound. I thought old IMEC-1 was about to split in half or something, that's how loud it was. Half a second later, it came again, though this time it sounded more like breaking than ripping, to be precise. Nothing really happened to IMEC-1, though. Instead, all those sources just stopped their crashing around and hung in the air awhile, kind of twirling a little bit. While that was going on, Mersh got another call from Sorril or whoever, but no one paid much attention to him.

Then, suddenly, three things happened pretty much all at once. Mersh yelled, "Fall stations!" and at about the same moment those sources disappeared, and my D-87s went dead. I couldn't really say which I noticed first.

Only one thing could have happened. Some of Romeo's Zeros must've gotten past our net and onto old IMEC-1, and wiped our fontani out almost before we knew what was going on. After that, the Zeros would have just taken off, because if we had no sources left, those great big guns that'd been giving Romeo such a monumental pain in the ass wouldn't work anymore.

Zeros move so fast they could've flown right by our platform, and we wouldn't have known, but it was pretty obvious once they were out of range. My helmet just went black, then clear, the way it does when we're all out of thelemity, and that was pretty much that.

FIFTY-FIVE

TORRO

Fortunately, all us milites know how to act if we go dark. We've practiced so many times, it's practically instinctual. "Fall stations" is the command to grab onto some secure part of the platform, and I think we'd have done that even if Mersh hadn't given us any orders at all. Dis has hardly any gravity, so it isn't like our platform is going to immediately drop out of the sky, either. We stay pretty much where we are, and so do all the platforms around us, hanging there out in space. That's probably the best thing about our present situation, though. Even though I watched everything happen down on IMEC-1, I still can't completely believe it's all true. Like, unless I'm really, really wrong, the whole battle just turned over on us.

Something crackles beside my ear, and I hear Spammers say, "Well, shit," through my helmet radio.

"Shut up, Miles," Mersh says.

"What do we do now?" Hexi asks.

"You shut up and wait for orders," Mersh answers.

"Mersh is right," Spammers says. "We'll want to be in position in case some of our fontani make it back."

"Did you just say 'Mersh is right'?" I ask. But it's true. In fact, Mersh and Spammers are both right. Pretty soon someone's going to notice the guns on old IMEC-1 have stopped, and they'll come back to help us out.

The trouble is, no one comes back. I think some of our cohorts out there try to swing around toward us, but there are all these big clouds of Valentines waiting to tangle them up, and I guess they don't make it very far. I bet the Zeros that just finished with old IMEC-1 are in a pretty good position to get in the way of anyone trying to get back, too.

"Yup, any minute now," Spammers says. He's doing his thing where he pretends something really awful is just like a minor inconvenience or whatever, but you can tell he's as terrified as anyone else.

"They must have us blocked off," Hexi says. "That's what they'd want to do, right?"

Mersh looks like he's about to tell us all to shut up and wait for orders again when he catches sight of something down below. He rushes to the edge of the platform, and the rest of us follow. At first it's hard to tell exactly what's happening down there. The air all over IMEC-1—or I guess it's just empty space because the air's all gone—anyway, suddenly there are all these chunks of rock and whatnot flying around over the city, and several of the buildings have sort of shifted, like the tops of them are facing a little in the wrong direction. This one very large gun has gone kind of crumbly in the middle, one half of it floating slowly away from the other. And then the bottom edge of another gun bursts up in a cloud of dust, and the whole thing tilts to the side like it's going to fall, only it just sort of hangs there. It *would* fall, I bet, if there was any gravity to pull it down.

Hexi says, "They're shooting at us."

They definitely are. From the other side of our platform, we can see one of those big clouds of Valentines floating off ahead, all lit up and letting loose with everything they've got. Their sources must be just far enough back that their umbris won't reach us, so they'll be using weapons that can blast us without needing thelemity—bombs and bullets and whatnot. Some of the other assault platforms near ours have already been hit, either broken apart or sent spinning off into space, but old Romeo isn't really aiming for us. He wants those big guns.

The antibombardment arrays on old IMEC-1 have mostly started up by now, and that's enough to intercept at least some of Romeo's shots. The space over the city is filling with flashes and explosions and clouds of debris and so forth. But it's pretty obvious they can't sit through all that forever.

All we can do is sit there and watch it happen. I start thinking about when Hexi's number got called in the draft, and it was like she was choking or dying or something, and even though I wanted to help, I couldn't think how, like there was this big gap between us, so big I could never get to her. It's a real cruddy feeling. It makes you want to jump off a cliff, like even that would be better than doing nothing.

"So how about those orders, dek?" Spammers says to Mersh. "We're not going to just let Romeo wreck the city, are we?"

I've about decided there isn't much we *can* do, aside from sit here and hope some of our fontani make it back, but then Mersh says, "Command wants us to stay put until the Valentines have deployed their ratters."

I'd forgotten about the ratters. They're the fighters Romeo sends in when we've all gone dark and can't defend ourselves. They've got these big, long, nasty tails they can use to drink up thelemity, sort of like an electrical cord. They can't use ingenic weapons, but they've still got ingenic armor, so as long as part of the tail is connected to an umbris somewhere, the ratters are pretty much invincible. No way our antibombardment guys will be able to stop them.

Once I know they're coming, I have an easy time picking out the ratters' nests from the rest of the Valentines, the ones doing all the bombarding, I mean. The ratters are really kind of dull-looking compared to all those flashing lights and whatnot. They whip out from the nests, and for a while they don't really seem to be going much of anywhere. It's pretty uninteresting, in fact, until they start speeding up. Then they come straight at us.

Mersh yells, "Fall stations!" again, and we all duck just as the first ratters come through, hitting our wall of assault platforms like they're diving into a lake or something. Wherever they hit, platforms go spinning away into space or down toward IMEC-1 or just smashing into other platforms nearby. Even when the ratters have already gone past, their tails keep whipping around, and any platform that gets too close ends up about broken in half. If we could just cut those tails, the ratters would all shrivel up the way Valentines always do when they go dark, but right now we don't stand a chance of getting through that armor.

Two more waves of ratters come diving down, and all we can do is hold on to our platform and hope we don't get hit. Finally, I hear Mersh on my radio. "Everyone all right?"

It doesn't seem possible, but we are. The cloud of Valentines out there seems to go on forever, and each nest must be sending out like twenty ratters at a time. When I raise my head to look around, though, it's obvious most of our platforms haven't gone anywhere. Compared to our whole wall, the ratters—even like a couple hundred or thousand of them—are really pretty small, and just like all the Valentines bombarding old IMEC-1, they're after the guns, not us. If the Valentines wanted to take our platforms out, they'd have better ways to do it than throwing ratters at us.

When everyone's reported that we're still alive and so forth, Mersh gets on his radio to check in with Optio Sorril. Over the side of the plat-form, I can see the ratters ripping up the city, tearing through bridges and buildings and leaving explosions everywhere, their tails slicing everything they touch from the ground on up. One tail just misses our platform, and takes two others with it as it swings by, but Mersh doesn't even look up. Finally, he kind of nods, and I can see his mouth forming the words "Yes, ma'am." He looks around at us, and it's almost like he's forgotten where he is and who we all are.

"Hey, Mersh, boyo," I say, "what's going on?"

Mersh gives his head a little shake, like he's clearing something out of there, then he stands up and tells Hexi to open up our platform's auxiliary armament locker. It's full of all sorts of special equipment for when you need more than just a lazel.

"Here's the plan," Mersh says. He says it slowly, almost like he's mak-ing it up as he goes along. "In 360 seconds, we're going to launch from this platform toward the Valentine formation. Once we're inside their umbris, we will either cut the tails on those ratters or destroy the nests with ingenic mines. In both cases, we should be able to breach their armor using the blades on our LL-40s."

I think we waste about a hundred of our 360 seconds just staring at him. Finally, I say, "Mersh, that's completely nuts. I mean, I'd take forever to fly all the way over there, and we'll be getting shot at the whole time. You know we will. And then what? We're supposed to just walk up to those nests and start hacking away?"

Everyone's quiet a minute, then Mersh says, "Those are our orders. Unless we do something now, the ratters will destroy every gun on IMEC-1, and that will be the end of this battle. Anyone who doesn't want to come can stay behind. I'm sure you'll be useful if any of our fontani make it back."

We all know he's telling the truth. Someone's got to stop those ratters. And as we look around our platform, it's obvious no one's going to sit this out, not when the rest are about to go out and risk getting killed.

"All right," Mersh says. "Everyone grab two mines and line up forward side." He looks over at Spammers. "Spams, you set up the slide gun and cover us."

The slide gun is one of those auxiliary weapons we keep around for special occasions. It isn't as powerful as the 13mm autos, for example, but it'll work pretty much anywhere and can fire either conventional or ingenic rounds. I'm expecting Spammers to make a joke or something, but all he does is salute, say, "Yes, sir," and get right to it.

The rest of us follow Mersh around to the front of our platform and line up with our feet on the flat metal and our heads facing the enemy. The cloud of Valentines is still shooting at us as much as ever, only now instead of being in front of us, it's like they're above, and we're looking up into some stormy sky full of lightning and crazy, swirling suns. The tails from the ratters are like fishing lines, or maybe ropes you could use to climb into the sky.

"Ten seconds," Mersh says. "Launch on my command."

We crouch, ready to jump off and fly and just hope we make it to that umbris before something shoots us down. I don't even think about what we'll do if we actually get there. What I do think about is the first time I met Naomi, when she caught me by surprise with that great big pistol of hers. I couldn't tell you why. I just see those old woods with everything wrecked all around, and her big eyes watching me over the barrel of that gun.

"We'll make it, Torro," Hexi says. She's right beside me, and, somehow, she's still smiling.

I just smile right back as best I can.

"Three!" Mersh yells into our ears. "Two! One! Launch!"

FIFTY-SIX

TORRO

We push off together, directly toward the cloud of Valentines. Our assault platform falls away beneath us, and it's like we're in this endless, weightless jump. From all along our net of platforms, other squads rise with us, and suddenly there are people in D-87s all around, thousands of us, first in a flat line, then more like a flock of birds as we separate out a bit, some moving a little faster or slower. I get the feeling we must go on forever, like there's no way old Romeo could kill us all. He sure gives it a try, though.

Here and there through our big flock or whatever, people start spinning out of control, just getting knocked down like they've been hit by an invisible brick or something. Romeo's started aiming for us, and out here in space we've got no cover at all. Our only chance is to make it to that umbris, and from here, it looks like it'll take years to get there.

Every second, more of us are getting hit. Nearby, I see two guys from my platform get stabbed out of the air and go falling away out of sight. I'm about sure I'm next when not so far ahead the empty space lights up with little glowing red speckles—ingenic shells from our slide guns going live. Spammers and everyone back on the platforms must have got them working. I can just make out a kind of deeper red farther on, where the shells must be hitting the Valentine lines. The umbris is coming up fast now, and in no time I'm sliding right past those red speckles. It's like I've dived into some tingling bath. My D-87s come back to life, and, instantly, I feel a whole lot better.

I can finally get a good look at the enemy, too, now that my helmet's working again. The ratters' nests are by far the biggest things in sight, probably a hundred meters across at least. The tails coming off have a kind of wavy, rounded look, sort of like tentacles, but they're also a bit furry, like they really might be the tails of gigantic rats or something. Flying nearby are a lot of smaller fighters, though they're still bigger than your average miles. Type 4s, probably. They're flattish, like saw blades, and they spin very rapidly, spraying huge shells or whatever that move so fast you can't even see them—or anyway I couldn't until my D-87s started up again.

Spammers and our kiddos with the slide guns are already doing a pretty good job keeping the blade-things busy, and I'm just thinking I should be getting after those nests when Mersh hollers, "Get moving!" right in my ear. I unsling my lazel and set my personal gravity to full fall in the direction of the nearest nest. That should get me there in the shortest time possible with the least chance of getting killed. Most of the other milites around me seem to have the same idea, and it turns out we're all wrong.

Several of them are pretty well ahead, since they didn't stop to look around and like take stock of the battlefield and so forth, and it doesn't take those saw blades long to swing around and start laying into them. They can fire null in addition to their heavy shells, the saw blades can. A few of our guys break up their lazels and use the bucklers to block the incoming fire, and that works real well as long as there's only one saw blade shooting at you. As soon as two come at you from different angles, though, you're pretty much done. I watch at least ten people ahead of me get cut apart, slashes of white-blue just slicing through them. Scraps of D-87s fly past my head, probably with bits of people inside, and I think now's a good time to start like contemplating a change in strategy.

I give up on falling straight to the nest and angle my PG so my body swings to the side and goes tumbling toward one of those huge ratter tails. It's a drop of maybe fifty meters, and I hit hard and almost roll off, grabbing on with both arms until I can stand up. I'm pretty dizzy, but at least no one's shooting at me. I call out to Mersh and the rest of my squad, "Find a tail and land on it! They won't be able to shoot at you without risking cutting off their ratters by accident!"

No one answers, though. I look up the way I came, but I can't see a single person from my squad anywhere. The whole place is a mess, just lousy with saw blades and ratter tails and flashes of null going back and forth and milites everywhere getting completely blued. I'm starting to think my whole squad must be gone when Hexi swings up from underneath the tail where I'm standing. She shifts her PG, does a little dip, and lands beside me. I don't know what else to say except "Hexi!"

"You always were easy to pick out in a crowd," she says. Mersh has found us, too, and a bunch of other milites, some from our squad, some not. I'm glad as anything to see them.

There's pretty much only one way to go from here, and that's right down along this tail we're standing on. It's basically a big hairy bridge leading right to one of those nests. The surface is covered in crawly-looking Type 3s, the kind with arms and legs all over the place ready to rip you apart, what we generally call Swarm Tactic Skirmishers, or just skirms. They started bunching up around this tail as soon as we landed, and now they're galloping right toward us.

Hexi and me, we start right in with our lazels, but Mersh and the milites closer to the nest break out their blades and bucklers instead. That really does the trick. The bucklers fend off most of the fire coming from those skirms, and meanwhile everyone else has a clear shot with their lazels. We push our way down the tail, using our PG to stick to it on all sides. There are a lot more skirms down on the nest, rushing to climb up after us, but someone's already shooting them to crap from somewhere up above.

That's when I remember our slide guns. It must be Spammers and everyone back on the platforms helping us out. I turn, expecting to see him there, now that I can use my D-87s to look way out into space, but I can't pick him out in all this big mess of fighting.

"Torro!" Hexi calls. "What are you doing? Let's go!"

Mersh and the rest are already charging toward another herd of skirms. They've all got blades and bucklers out, just hacking away. I pull my blade, too, and follow Hexi, but only after I've checked behind us one more time. The trouble is, the reason I couldn't find Spammers is because where he should have been, there was only a bunch of torn-up platforms and hunks of scrap, bits of armor and empty space.

The skirms certainly aren't pushovers, that's for sure. They've got blades of their own, long, hooked ones that can come scratching out of any one of their eight arms or legs or whatever. Mersh is really getting into it with them, but he isn't so distracted he can't give orders. "Torro! Hexi! See if you can plant a mine in this thing!"

Some of the milites who came with us down the tail are already like attacking the problem, but they aren't making a whole lot of progress. That weird metal fur we saw on the ratters' tails is all over the nest, too, and it keeps getting in the way. I'd thought it was a trap or something, but it's actually a kind of armor. Every time you take a swing at the nest, some strand of fur or whatever stabs out and knocks your blade away.

Trying to get past the fur gets real annoying real quick, and pretty soon, Hexi and me are both starting to panic. We've figured out we can cut through the fur if one of us gets it to extend and the other slices it from the side, but that only works one strand at a time, and clearing enough space to plant a mine would take about 850 years. And all the time, more skirms are coming, swarming out from the side of the nest. Mersh keeps screaming at us to hurry up. He's starting to sound pretty tired, and I doubt it's from yelling. Finally, Hexi goes a bit berserk. She takes her lazel and starts shooting the side of the nest like crazy, making a bunch of those hairs stand up all at once.

"Do that again!" I shout. She shoots again, and this time I cut through each piece of fur that springs up when she hits it with her lazel. The whole patch comes away with a pretty satisfying scratch.

After that, it's no trouble to cut a hole into the side of the nest. I drop one of my mines through and tell Mersh we've done it. I think we're just in time. There aren't too many of our milites left. Mersh is breathing real hard when he orders us all to get clear so he can null this stupid nest. In this case, getting clear means just launching off into the battle. Not a very safe plan, but better than staying here, I guess.

Hexi and I flip our PG and fall up away from the nest, and about half a second later the place where we'd been standing like collapses in on itself. A pack of skirms comes leaping up after us, but before we can get out our blades, someone shoots them apart from below. Mersh and some other milites are still down there, fighting to get away from the nest. I watch three and then four more jump off into space while Mersh hacks through a couple more skirms, and he's about to launch, too, when one of the skirms buries a blade in his leg. I'm thinking somebody's got to get back there and help him, but at almost the same time, there's a gush of white-blue from inside the nest and part of the thing just kind of crumbles and falls off. A lot of the skirms that'd been chasing us crumble away, too. I don't see many other milites getting away, either. And no Mersh. I try to get him through my helmet, but he won't answer.

"Torro," Hexi says, sort of hesitantly.

I think she's worried about Mersh, too, so I say, "We'll find him, Hex." I'm starting to feel pretty queasy, though, like I couldn't really have seen what I just saw. A skirm blade is going to take off a lot more than your leg. "He's out here somewhere."

"No, Torro, look. The nest."

The nest wasn't hit quite as bad as I'd thought. There's an ugly, kind of caved-in place where I dropped that mine, but nothing much has happened to the rest. There are still plenty of ratter tails squirming around all over the place. I bet the mine only got one or two of them, if it got any at all.

"It didn't work," Hexi says. "Torro, we can't leave the nest like that. We have to go back."

She's right. I mean, like, I know she's right. If we don't do something about this stupid nest, all the ratters at the other ends of those tails are going to be loose on old IMEC-1, messing with our guns and killing everybody.

So we reverse our PG and go back, aiming for the collapsed spot in the side. At least there we won't have to cut through the nest to get another mine in, or that's what we think until we see that silvery fur or whatever is actually growing back. There are still plenty of skirms, too, and when they see us coming, they rush in to meet us, shooting away with those terrible old legs of theirs.

We use our bucklers like umbrellas against the needles of null flying up at us, and land right in the middle of a huge crowd of skirms. They pounce on us immediately, and I start really like regretting the decision to come back. We probably won't make it ten steps, let alone over to the hole we blew in this nest. That's what I'm thinking, anyway, when another squad of milites drops down, sending the skirms spinning.

Actually "squad" probably isn't the best description. There's only four of them. They really lay into those skirms, though. One of them calls to me, "Let us finish your work, pawn," and I recognize the voice, and the weird accent. When he turns around, I see it's that real scarred, scary-looking old bivvie, Thom. The milites with him must be the other bivvies from his tribe, little Naomi's friends.

Together, the six of us, Hexi and me and the four bivvies, fight our way toward the hole in the nest. It isn't easy, with the skirms hounding after us and the hole getting smaller every second as more of that silvery fur grows back. By the time we get there, all that's left of the damage we did before is a pretty small gap.

Hexi runs over and jams her buckler into the hole to keep it from closing up completely. "Get a mine, Torro!"

I pull the second mine I brought from our platform and slam it down on Hexi's buckler.

"Blast!" old Thom yells. "Set it to blast, boy!"

Hexi says, "He's right! Null will only take out a little piece—we've got to blow it apart!"

The mines we brought can use different types of energy, same as our lazels. Null is usually the best when you want to destroy something, but that didn't work out so good last time. I set the mine to blast instead of null and just hope old Thom knows what he's talking about. Then I kick Hexi's buckler down into the hole.

"Make your move, pawn!" Thom shouts. He's the only one of the bivvies I can still see. Everywhere else is all skirms and blades. I grab Hexi and set my buckler underneath me and blow the mine.

Suddenly, we're way up above the nest, like we've been instantly transported there or something. I think the nest must have ballooned out or maybe in and just thrown us here, because it kind of shudders a few more times, then breaks apart in this terrific explosion. The shock of it knocks me tumbling back, and I lose track of Hexi, like she must go off in some other direction. I can't see her anywhere. I try to steady myself with PG so I can find her, but my D-87s aren't working right. They're slow and heavy, and there's some like yellow cracks in front of my face that make it hard to see straight. When I try and wipe them away, the fingers on my D-87s won't move. They're stuck to some other pieces of armor, what looks like an arm, just hanging there off my suit. Which doesn't make any sense at all. That was the hand that was holding on to Hexi.

I remember one of those skirms jumping at me just before the mine went off, and I guess it must have damaged my suit or something. The more I try to move, the more I feel like I'm swimming through something very thick and heavy. Eventually, it's like all I can do is float. So that's what I do. I float. And I wonder what the chances are that if I just keep floating, I'll eventually end up back home.

FIFTY-SEVEN

JAX

I don't see it when the signal rocket comes through Lunar Veil. I've been watching the sky for almost an entire day, waiting for some sign of the battle, and so of course as soon as I doze off for five seconds, *that's* when the rocket appears. I'm not mad I missed it. It's not like I'm superexcited for news from the Legion. I'm more nervous than anything, or to be totally honest, probably halfway between nervous and scared stiff. When you're afraid of what the news will be, sometimes you'd rather have no news. What I especially don't like is how the rocket only came once I was almost asleep. Good news doesn't sneak up on you that way.

It isn't easy to communicate between one Realm and another. Radio signals and stuff like that mostly get blocked out by passages like Lunar Veil, meaning most ways of talking over long distances won't work. Messages between Earth and the Front were almost always delivered in person. For this battle, though, the Legion needed to be able to communicate quickly with the reserves, so they decided to send basic messages using signal rockets. Each color of rocket means something different. Green says the battle's over, and we've won. Yellow means the Legion wants the reserve to come help. Red is for enemies incoming.

Naomi's afraid, too. I can hear it in her voice when she says my name, and when I open my eyes, I see it in her face, even though it's dark out. Up in the sky, the rocket looks almost like just another star, except for the way it's sliding through the air. Then it explodes into an incredibly bright yellow, enough to light up the entire sky. For a few seconds, the whole Forum looks like it's late afternoon, with long shadows stretching everywhere.

"They're calling in the reserves," I say, though what I'm really thinking is *At least it's not red*. In a way, though, yellow is worse. Red could just mean a few Valentines had slipped past our lines, like in an incursion. But with yellow, we know the Legion's going to need us to join the battle. It could be that we've got Romeo on the run, and they just want us to help finish him off, but somehow I doubt it.

I don't expect Naomi to say anything. For one thing, that gigantic yellow rocket makes it pretty obvious we're getting called in. For another, Naomi has said practically nothing since the battle started. She thinks everyone is keeping some big secret from us, and that has her sort of mad. I don't see how it matters that much. We're busy fighting a war. There isn't always time to explain every little thing.

So I'm pretty surprised when Naomi says, "What happens now? What do we do?"

"We wait for Charles, I guess." Now I'm starting to feel scared for real. I don't know why, but thinking about forming up with all the reserve fighters and flying out over Earth and into Lunar Veil is worse than thinking about the actual battle.

There isn't really any waiting to do because Charles and Malandeera are already coming our way across the Forum. Naomi jumps down from the fountain where we've been sitting and goes to meet them, walking with long, angry steps.

"Charles," she says sharply, "tell us what is happening."

Charles looks surprised, but he still sounds confident. "The Legion has called in the reserve," he says. He grins at me. "Wide-awake, Jax?"

"And that is all you know about the battle?" Naomi demands. "If we're to join this fight, it will do no good to keep the particulars from us."

"All I know about what's happening in Dis is what that rocket has told us," Charles says, looking up at the little yellow light still hanging in the sky. "We won't learn much more until we get to Dis and see the situation for ourselves. However." He looks Naomi right in the eye, then turns to me. "However, only Fontana Malandeera and I will be going to Dis. The Legion has other plans for the two of you."

"What plans?" Naomi asks. It's obvious she's concerned, and I feel my stomach do a few flips, too.

"You have a different mission, every bit as important as ours," says Malandeera. "While Charles and I lead the reserve into Dis, you and Jax will take the Legion's remaining long-distance transports and evacuate Hestia."

Naomi shouts, "No!" at about the same second I yell, "What?" We both thought everyone had given up on the idea of evacuating.

"The reserve's commander, Imperator Feeroy, wanted a fail-safe, a last resort in case the Legion was defeated," Charles explains. "He convinced the Consulate it would make sense to have an evacuation party ready. They have selected a group of knowledgeable and capable people whose job it will be to establish a new home for humanity, and eventually rebuild the Legion. Jax, Naomi, you have been assigned to accompany them as their fontani."

"Do not ask this of us, Charles," Naomi says. "Please. You know running will serve nothing in the end."

"Charles isn't asking," Malandeera says. "Those are your orders, passed down directly from the Consulate." Even though she's being pretty stern, it's the kind of extra sternness you hear officers use when they're issuing orders they don't agree with, like they're being stern with themselves, too. I remember Malandeera saying she hoped it would be a while before Naomi and I had to fight, but not too long. This must be what she meant. If we evacuate now, we'll probably never see the Valentines again. We'll just be running away forever.

Naomi looks from Malandeera to Charles. "This is what you would not tell us. The others all knew, but you said nothing."

"No, not everyone," Charles says. "Legatus Cressock will be responsible for leading the evacuation, so of course he knew, and most of his officers were informed. But the rest will be just as surprised as you are. The Consulate thought it would be counterproductive to issue evacuation orders before they became necessary."

I think about how unhappy Legatus Cressock seemed back at the Basilica. Now I understand why. I can tell Naomi's totally furious, but I'm not sure how to feel. My whole life everyone's told me the one thing I have to do is fight the Valentines. Now Charles is saying the exact opposite. I'm definitely not one of those people who couldn't wait to get into a real battle. To be totally honest, I really hoped the war would end before that happened. I'd daydream about someone's coming, maybe in the middle of class or a firing drill, and telling us we'd won, that it was all over. Everyone would get up and cheer, and it would be like we didn't need to train for the Legion anymore. We could just do whatever we wanted. But I never thought it would happen like this.

"Legatus Cressock will be along soon with an escort from the evacuation group," Charles is saying. "From there you'll head for Jovian Veil. Very probably that's as far as you'll go—if we can win this battle, all you'll end up doing is flying out and back.

"I trust you," Charles says firmly. "Both of you. I've seen how strong you can be. You know what's at stake. You know who is depending on you. I'm sure you'll do what's right."

I've been looking at my feet while most of this was going on, but now I notice Charles watching me, and I realize he's waiting for an answer. I have no idea what to say. I'm relieved I won't have to fight, but in a lot of ways, this is even worse. How am I supposed to start a new Earth? I don't even know what to do on this one! And leaving everyone behind, not just the Legion but pretty much all the people on the planet, it feels pretty awful. But those are our orders, right? Hasn't someone else already made the decision?

"OK," I say to Charles. "You can count on me."

We all look over to Naomi, but she doesn't say anything. Her face is all crunched up, like a piece of paper, her mouth pressed tight. It's like she's holding something back, and I think maybe she's about to start crying when she jerks her chin in a nod. Even though it's only the tiniest little movement, it says *Yes, I understand* and *Go away, I don't want to look at you* at the same time.

Charles actually seems happy with Naomi's answer. He smiles like he's got just what he wanted from us, and it's a real smile, not the fake kind. And then he says to Malandeera, "After you, please."

The air shakes, like it does sometimes when nearby fontani summon up their mijmeri. Charles and Malandeera disappear, then reappear in the air above the Forum, looking like two clouds of darkness and stars. I can still tell them apart pretty easily, of course. To most people, mijmeri all look alike, but they're only the same the way all trees are the same, or all birds. It's easy to pick out the differences if you know what to look for. Malandeera's mijmere is smoother than most, like something that might have come out of a factory, even though it's constantly changing shape. Charles's mijmere, on the other hand, is kind of shaggy, like a wild animal, or someone who really needs a haircut.

Charles and Malandeera float there, a few hundred meters overhead, while across the city fighters from the reserves rise into the air, ready for action. Soon they're speeding away toward Lunar Veil, getting smaller each second.

Naomi doesn't say anything, and I don't, either. We just watch as Charles and Malandeera and the reserves disappear into the ceiling of stars. The Forum is totally quiet, and with just Naomi and me standing there by the fountain in its center, the whole place feels huge and really lonely, like a great big desert somewhere. It reminds me of that first time I had to stand for Ninth City during an incursion, before I met Kizabel and Vinneas and Imway. But they're all gone now, and so is Ninth City, and I might never see any of them again.

"This is wrong." It's Naomi, but I'm not sure if she's talking to herself or me. Then she looks right at me, her brown eyes wide. "Jax, this is wrong. We cannot abandon Earth."

"Those are our orders," I say. "You heard Charles."

"Charles does not believe in this plan any more than I do. That is the reason he kept it from us."

"No, he didn't tell us because he was *ordered* not to tell us until we needed to know. Besides," I say, thinking suddenly that it's really important I get her to understand, "it's the right plan. You and me and a few fighters wouldn't make any difference out in Dis—"

"We are fontani, Jax," Naomi snaps.

"Yeah, sure, but Charles can beat both of us without even trying, right? Maybe we'd help a little, but what are we really going to do? With the evacuation party, we're making sure we don't get wiped out completely."

"And what does that matter in the end?" Naomi doesn't look scared anymore—she's turned very serious. "Who will we be saving? Me and you and a handful of others? I would rather throw my weight behind those fighting for us even if it is only the weight of a feather."

"It doesn't matter if you don't like our orders," I say, but at the same time, a little part of me kind of agrees with her. There's no way we can evacuate anything but a small fraction of the people on Earth. If we go now, and the Legion loses, we'll be leaving everyone else completely unprotected. They won't even have a source to power their defenses. "We've got a job to do."

"I'm glad that is how you feel," Naomi says. She takes one step back, moving away from me, then another. "It lessens the cost of what I am about to do." Her hands must be sweating because she wipes them on her jacket. "It will be only the weight of a feather."

"What do you mean?"

"Jax, I am going to join this fight."

I think I must literally have heard her wrong. "You *what*?"

She just looks at me, as serious as ever. Her words work around my brain, almost like she's saying them again. "But we've been *ordered* to evacuate!" I'm probably starting to sound whiny, but I don't care.

"I intend to disobey those orders," she says. "I am beholden first to my conscience, and I cannot leave others to fight for me. Not when there is something I can do to help."

"Going with the evacuation *is* helping! They need us to keep the Legion going! We have to keep humanity alive!"

"My aim is not to protect the Legion, or even our species. What matters to me are the people all across Earth, and those fighting for us beyond this world. They need us, not in a hundred years, or five hundred, or a thousand, when we have built a new Legion and founded a new Earth. I will make my stand for them now. They are the center, the keep of our castle."

I try to think of anything I can say to change her mind, but when Naomi's set on something, there isn't much that can stop her.

"Good luck, Jax," she says. "I hope we meet again soon."

And then she disappears, and I'm alone in the dark Forum.

FIFTY-EIGHT

JAX

For a while, I don't know what to think; I just float around in my own head, my brain numb, like, *What just happened?* Naomi seemed like the most careful, most serious person I'd ever met, adults included. How could she just fly away like that?

That last thing she said, about the keep of a castle, runs circles through my brain. I didn't think much about it at first, but now it seems important. A keep is something from a time called the medieval period, before things like electricity and automobiles were invented, when people would fight with swords and arrows and horses and metal armor and stuff like that. We learned about it at the Academy, in History of the Common Era. Back then, they had castles, huge stone fortresses for defense, and the keep was the strongest part of all, usually behind the innermost wall. It was where everyone would go when the rest of the castle had been taken over by enemies. The place to make your last stand. What Naomi was saying, I guess, is that she can't retreat anymore. For her the keep isn't a place, but the people she cares about. If this is going to be her last fight, that's where she wants to be. I'm not sure I totally get it, but I'm starting to see she had her reasons.

I must be totally distracted trying to figure all of that out, because someone walks up behind me, and I don't even notice until he says, "Fontanus Jaxten, sir. It's time to go."

It's Legatus Cressock. Behind him are two rows of men and women, younger than he is but still pretty old, also in black. It makes me think of the Academy, the way they're standing there, like a rhetor with a bunch of cadets.

Legatus Cressock salutes. "I'm here to escort you to your evacuation transport," he says. He glances around, eyebrows lowering. "Where is Fontana Naomi?"

"She, um," I say, clearing my throat, "she's not here."

"Not here? Where is she?"

I feel weirdly embarrassed, like I haven't done my homework. I point toward Lunar Veil. "There, I guess. In Dis."

Maybe Legatus Cressock is surprised, but he only hesitates half a second. "I'm not sure I understand you, sir."

"She went to fight. To join the battle."

I notice the people standing behind Cressock looking sideways at each other, but I don't feel embarrassed anymore. I'm not even thinking of them, or my orders, or even the Legion. I'm thinking about Lunar Veil, and everyone out there—Naomi and her sister, Rae, and everyone from Ninth City. My hands have clenched into fists.

"And I'm going, too." The words just come out; I hear them from far away, like I'm not even the one talking.

Now Cressock really does look surprised. "Sir," he says, "our orders are to evacuate to Jovian Veil. The transports are waiting."

"I know." Usually it would make me totally nervous, telling an officer I wasn't going to follow orders, but right now it feels good, like it's what I should have been doing all along. "But I'm not going with them."

No one says anything to that. They all just look at me. I try to explain. "Look, it's like, if we go now, and leave everyone on Earth behind, and everyone in Dis, too, it's like we've already lost."

They only keep staring, like I'm speaking total gibberish, or that's what I think until I notice a few are nodding, almost as if they're waiting for me to say more. The problem is, that was about the only answer I could think of.

"It's like the keep," I say hurriedly, remembering how Naomi put it. Only when I try to explain it, the whole thing comes out all jumbled. "Like a castle. And the keep is where you stand and fight when there's nothing else left."

What's so crazy, though, is that they actually seem to get it. Most of them are nodding to themselves now, like I've just said the profoundest thing in the history of profound things. No one tries to argue with me, or tell me I'm in trouble for disobeying orders.

I take a deep breath. "All right, I guess I'm going," I say. "I'm sorry you won't get to evacuate. But don't worry—you won't be missing much. We're going to win. I promise."

I've already turned to go, and I'm about to shade into my mijmere, when Legatus Cressock says, "Sir?"

I look back; no one has moved. "Yes?"

"We'd like permission to come with you."

I feel my determination tangling up, like I've started running, then tripped. "You do?"

"The Legion left behind a good-sized complement of fighters to escort the evacuation, sir. Since there will be no evacuation, I hope you will allow us to accompany you into battle."

"You want to go with me?" I stare at Cressock and the lines of legionaries. "All of you?"

"I think I speak for everyone assigned to the evacuation when I say those orders never sat right with any of us," Cressock says. "The Legion's mission is to protect the people of Earth, and the people of Earth are here. We'd much rather be out there with you, sir." From behind him come murmurs of "Yes, sir" and "Absolutely, sir," even a few outright cheers.

I know I should try to look tough and brave, but I can't stop myself from grinning. They're all total strangers, but knowing they're with me makes me absurdly happy. "Then let's go!"

For the first time since we met, Cressock smiles for real. In a deep, sharp voice, he shouts, "Move, legionaries! I want every fighter we have in the air in five minutes!"

Five minutes later, we're speeding toward Lunar Veil, Earth down below, totally dark at first, then warming up with pinks and oranges as we rise through the atmosphere, and the sun peeks over the horizon. Legatus Cressock and his fighters surround me like a cloud. They're a mini-Legion, everything from gunships to tetra fortresses to equi. I have to fly slower than I'd like to so I don't leave them all behind, but that shouldn't matter much, since time here moves so much faster than in Dis. I'll be coming in almost right behind Naomi, and even Charles and Malandeera will have been there only a few minutes at most.

I've never been to any of the Realms besides Hestia. I don't even think about it until Lunar Veil is already so close it takes up almost the entire sky, and then I'm like, *Oh crap!* But going through doesn't feel weird at all. You could totally not even notice you'd gone to a whole other world, except Dis is so much emptier and colder than Hestia. It's the way I always imagined outer space: no moon or planets, only random hunks of rock floating around and one small, lonely star for a sun. Also, in Hestia there wasn't a huge battle going on everywhere you look.

Everything is tangled and confusing. It's like there are a hundred different fights happening all at once, most of them way far apart from one another. Each one is like its own separate galaxy of color and motion, swirling and flashing with blasts of light. The only place I don't see some little pocket of fighting is behind me, in the direction of Lunar Veil.

This definitely isn't how I thought the battle would look. Before the Legion launched into Dis, I went to a briefing with Charles, and the commanders there told us to expect a concentrated fight centralized mostly around IMEC-1, since that's where we'd have our heavy artillery. The City Guns were going to be key to this battle. But what's happening now looks like the opposite. The *exact* opposite, even: I don't see IMEC-1 anywhere.

What I do see are Charles and Malandeera, and Naomi, too. They're way ahead of me, flying like they've got someplace urgent to go, with fighters from the reserve close behind them. I feel a little nervous, like they'll be angry when they find out I didn't evacuate, but I'm not going back, so I'd better just let them know I'm here.

Ever since I launched off from Earth, I've been surrounded by my mijmere, but I've focused almost all of my attention on the real world. I needed to see where I was going, and I didn't want to accidentally swerve off somewhere and leave Legatus Cressock and his fighters in the dark. Usually, I have a lot of trouble paying attention to two worlds at once, but right now it feels totally natural. I let myself submerge into the world of my mijmere, hoping I'll be able to talk to Charles and Malandeera and Naomi there.

I'm in the stands of a huge baseball stadium, sitting in a hard plastic chair. It's nighttime, and the only light is coming from a mostly full Moon. All the lights in the stadium are out, including the great big tall ones above the field. Still, I can tell practically every seat around me is filled. People are murmuring and talking in the dark, and every so often I hear someone scream or cry out. "Charles?" I say. "Naomi? Are you there?"

Someone next to me nudges my elbow, and I hear the voice of the Kid. "Tough break. Everyone all set for the big game, then this happens."

"Why is it so dark?" I ask.

"No power," says the Kid. "Must be a busted fuse. If someone doesn't get the lights back on, it's Game Over."

"Did you see any of my friends?"

"Yeah, I think so. That prissy girl and the hobo-looking guy. Some lady with them, too. I think they went to see if they could get the lights working."

"Show me the way they went."

Out in Dis, I can already see what they're trying to do. Charles and Malandeera and Naomi are headed for IMEC-1. It's still far away, but I've spotted it now. The reason I didn't notice it before is that it almost looks like just another rock floating through space. But my friends are aiming straight for this particular rock, and when I look closely, I can see the buildings and City Guns and the ring of defenders floating around it. The one thing I don't see is a single spark of thelemity. That's when I know for sure: IMEC-1 has gone dark.

Now it makes sense why everyone seems to be fighting in little pockets all spread out away from each other. The reason the battle looks like it's broken into a million tiny pieces is because that's exactly what's happened. Our fontani must be trying to get to IMEC-1, to bring back thelemity and get the City Guns going, and the Valentines are doing everything they can to keep them away. And that means IMEC-1 is where I need to be.

Legatus Cressock and everyone from the evacuation force has already figured all of this out. As soon as I start toward IMEC-1, they accelerate right along with me. Charles and Malandeera have a good head start, and for a while it looks like they won't have any trouble getting there, but then, out of nowhere, two Zeros come streaking through the sky like meteors. Even though I've never seen a Zero before, I know that's what these are. Friendly fontani wouldn't attack Charles and Malandeera, of course, but I think I'd be able to tell these were Valentines anyway. They just *feel* like strangers.

Instantly, Charles and Malandeera are swept up in a big, roaring fight. They're some of the toughest fontani the Legion has, but even if they weren't, they'd have the advantage. The Zeros came alone, and Charles and Malandeera have their reserve fighters. A few equi or gunships wouldn't stand much chance against a Zero all by themselves, but in a battle between sources, they can be enough to tip the balance.

I know Charles and Malandeera will be fine, but I'm still nervous for them. The Zeros out there are probably trained fighters, picked specially to come to Earth and finish us off. Romeo wouldn't have sent just anyone. Like some kid who wasn't even supposed to be part of the battle to begin with. Who was supposed to run away. Those Zeros would probably laugh if they knew I was out here trying to stop them. If Valentines *can* laugh.

In my mijmere, I'm climbing over people in the dark, trying to get to the end of my aisle. Everyone's grumbling at me to get moving, and when I try moving faster, I stumble and step on an empty seat where someone's spilled a drink, and my foot slips on the wet plastic. I'm about to go headfirst onto the concrete underneath when the Kid grabs hold of my arm.

"OK?" he says, pulling me the last few steps to the aisle. He hands me something small and heavy: a flashlight. He's got one, too, and he shines a bright yellow beam toward a tunnel leading beneath the rows of seats. "Over here."

We've barely got inside when we hear the sound of fighting somewhere nearby. It's hard to say exactly what's happening, but there are crashing noises and scary, popping sounds and voices.

"That's Charles and Malandeera!" I tell the Kid.

"We should go around," he says.

"Don't they need our help?"

"We have to get the lights working first. Once they're back on, there'll be plenty of people to help."

He's right. I don't like the idea of leaving Charles and Malandeera behind, but I make up my mind quickly enough when I hear other footsteps running toward us.

Somewhere in the darkness ahead, I hear Naomi call out, "Come on, Jax! They're on their way!"

Out in Dis, another Zero has appeared, heading right at us. Naomi is already closing in on IMEC-1. Her mijmere is easy to spot, with its spiraling, twirling edges. It looks the way I bet music would if you could see it.

I push to follow her, but I'm also afraid of leaving Legatus Cressock and the rest of his fighters behind. If Naomi gets to IMEC-1 first, I'll be able to slow down a bit, but I don't think that's going to happen. This new Zero is already almost on top of us.

Deep beneath the stadium of my mijmere, Naomi calls out, "Keep going—I'll hold this one off!" I can just see the glow of a flashlight up ahead, casting her shadow against the wall of the tunnel. I skid to a halt as another shadow appears beside Naomi's. It's shaped almost like a person, but gigantic, and some parts, like the head and hands, aren't quite the right shape. "Go, Jax!" Naomi yells. "Go!"

The Kid shoves me toward another tunnel. "Down here," he whispers.

I don't want to leave Naomi behind. She's never fought another source on her own, let alone a Valentine Zero. But as I fly past, Legatus Cressock and his fighters peel away to go and help her. It's the right plan. They wouldn't be able to keep up at my full speed, and this way Naomi stands a better chance against that Zero.

It's really up to me now. Naomi and Cressock and Charles and Malandeera and the whole reserve are all fighting to give me a shot at getting to the IMEC. It doesn't matter that they'd all be better at this than me. I'm the one who's here, so I'm the one who has to do it. I aim myself straight ahead and go.

"Hurry!" the Kid yells into my ear. "We're almost there!"

IMEC-1 is close now. Just a little farther. I don't even have to make it all the way there, I know, just get close enough for my umbris to reach some of the City Guns. If I can get power back to those guns, they'll be able to help Naomi and Charles and everyone else. But a second later, I kind of wish Cressock had stayed with me. More Zeros are coming. The Valentines know what I'm trying to do, and they're sending everything they've got stop me.

In my mijmere, I'm running flat out. The beam of my flashlight bounces crazily, sending shadows everywhere. The Kid is a few steps ahead, urging me forward. "It's right up here!" he says. "Only a little farther!"

Heavy footsteps are coming our way through the darkness: another Zero heading straight for us. Somewhere ahead is the switch to bring back the power, and I've got to get there before this Zero does. I'm getting ready for one last burst of speed when suddenly the Kid yells, "Stop!" and half a second later I run straight into his back.

"What are you doing?" I scream. "We're almost there!"

Just then there's another scream. It's low and twisted, and it can only be the Zero. The tunnel lights up with bolts of hot blue, and the air fills with a thick, sizzling smell.

Out in Dis, there's a huge explosion over IMEC-1, the kind of explosion you'd expect if a whole bunch of heavy artillery opened up all at once. The weird thing is, none of the artillery is working. There was only that one Zero flying down to block my path. I was sure it had me—it had reached just about the perfect spot to strike—and then, out of nowhere, it exploded.

"What happened?" I ask the Kid.

In my mijmere, he turns his flashlight toward the wall of the tunnel. There, in big orange letters, are the words CAUTION: ELECTRICAL HAZARD. Not so far ahead, the floor is covered with thick black cables. Some of them are torn or frayed. As we watch, they let loose a few bright sparks, each with a loud snap. Lying across the cables is what looks like the shadow of a tall, heavy man, but when I turn my flashlight to get a better look, it fades away.

The way to IMEC-1 is clear. And I've figured out what happened to that Zero, sort of. Floating just over the city is a huge cloud of artillery shells, the kind the City Guns use for long-range attacks. They won't do much of anything without thelemity, but once they're inside an umbris, they're deadly. These ones are just close enough to IMEC-1 that they'd be easy not to notice—floating there inside our ring of assault platforms—and just far enough away that they wouldn't damage the city or any of our fighters if they went off. I don't know how they got there, but I do know that when that Zero hit them, it set off a whole bunch at once, and left plenty of space for me to fit through.

I make my way carefully past the shells—or the electrical cables. Whichever world I'm looking at, they could fry me if I make the wrong move.

Down in my mijmere, the Kid points his flashlight at a wall of switches. One row is connected with a big lever, and I pull it back, snapping all the switches at once. Suddenly, everything is washed out in blinding white light and a roar that whumps into me like a gust of wind. When my eyes adjust, I'm in a tunnel leading out onto my baseball field. The lights shining down are so intense that I can barely see past the first patch of green grass, but I can hear the crowd, everyone cheering their heads off.

The Kid runs toward the sound, and I follow. As we're running, he lets out a whoop and kicks over a trash barrel standing by the side of the tunnel; it falls, spilling a few small metal cans onto the ground. The Kid stomps on one, crushing it with a crunch. Then he crushes another. A can rolls against my foot, and I step on it, feeling weirdly satisfied as the metal crinkles beneath my shoe, before I walk out onto the field.

I'm standing on IMEC-1, what's called the "green" side, or the "country" side, probably because of all the trees and green fields. It even has a lake. But it also has plenty of heavy artillery, and I've landed near a row of guns, coming down so hard that I send bits of rock and dirt flying into the air. All around me are what look like big metal snakes. They seem to be hanging from the sky, trailing way off toward some of the Valentine formations above. I realize these must be the fighters Romeo uses on us when we're out of thelemity. Aeter-Capable Troops, or ACTs, though a lot of people just call them "ratters" because of their tails—those things I thought looked like snakes. Only I don't see anything attached to the tails now except maybe a little crumpled metal. As I watch, the crumpled parts begin to fizzle away, and the tails start doing the same thing.

I'm wondering what could have happened to those ACTs when two more of the ratty fighters drop down in front of me. In my mijmere, two metal cans have fallen at my feet. When I see the cans sitting there, I get it. I know just what to do: I smash them. At the same time, the ACTs shudder and implode.

Legionaries armed with lazels have come out from the guns nearby, but when they see I've taken care of the ACTs, they salute and run back inside. Already, some of the other guns have started to fire. All through IMEC-1, things are starting to work again. The air is returning, the gravity, too. The huge lake on Green Side, which had floated partway out of its basin, comes splashing back down, waves running over its banks and flooding the slopes nearby. Between the rumbling of guns, I can hear smaller battles: legionaries fighting back against ACTs.

This isn't the time to stand around. Right now I'm the only source in this whole city, meaning I'm as dangerous to those ACTs as the ACTs were to everyone on IMEC-1 before I got here. My job now is to keep Romeo from doing any more damage.

But when I try to fly again, I just stumble forward and trip. I fall hard on the ground—only it isn't the ground of Green Side on IMEC-1. It isn't any ground I recognize, either. And I'm not in any world I know. I'm someplace else.

□————————□

FIFTY-NINE

JAX

When I get to my feet, I'm in a tall room with dark wooden walls. I'm standing on a thick, heavy rug, which must be what tripped me. From above, I think I hear the sound of a crowd—very, very faint, and muffled like it's coming through a staticky radio. In front of me is a huge wooden staircase, and underneath that a door with a tall man standing in it dressed in a black suit and black tie. The doorway is dark, and the shadows keep me from seeing any of his face above his lower lip.

"Good evening, sir," says the man in the black suit, "and welcome. The master is expecting you. This way, please."

He waves a hand toward the staircase. He's wearing white gloves, which seems strange, but I don't question it. I just go up. The stairs are so wide that the man in the black suit could walk beside me, but he doesn't. He follows close behind, almost breathing on my neck. I can still hear the muffled sound of a crowd, getting louder as we climb.

The place at the top of the stairs is a lot like the place at the bottom: high ceilings and wooden walls. There's a big old Common Era clock, the kind with only twelve hours on the face, but there are no hands to tell the time.

"Through here, sir," the man in the black suit says, gesturing to a pair of double doors. He makes it sound like an invitation, but I get the feeling that if I don't do as he says, something bad will happen to me.

Past the doors is a room with books everywhere, stacked in shelves so tall, they have a ladder attached to reach the ones on top. One wall has an alcove with a hearth and a crackling fire burning inside, and in front of the fire are some very comfortable-looking leather couches and chairs, and a low table. There's also a small box that casts flickering light into the room, cold light that looks strange beside the warm glow of the fire. The box seems to be where the sound of the cheering crowd is coming from.

At the far end of the room, a man sits at a wide, heavy desk cluttered with papers and a complicated-looking machine. The word "typewriter" floats suddenly into my head. The man has swooping brown hair and a neatly trimmed beard. He doesn't seem to notice us; it looks like he's got his attention half on his papers and half on the flickering box.

"Master," the man in the black suit says. "Your guest has arrived."

The voice surprises me, it's so close. The man in the black suit is towering over me, and even though between the flickering box and the fire there's plenty of light in here, I still can't see his whole face.

Right then is when I figure out I'm in a whole lot of trouble. I don't know this man or his "master." I don't know where this house is or how I ended up facedown on a rug back in that hallway. And no matter how the shadows in here move, no matter which way I look, the eyes of the man in the black suit stay hidden. I'm in a mijmere—*someone else's* mijmere.

I think back to the battle in Dis. It seems like it all happened a long time ago, in another life almost, or a dream. I'd just returned thelemity to IMEC-1. There was still a lot of fighting going on, but now we had a chance. And then I ended up here.

Another Zero must have attacked me after I landed. It probably came through the same way I did, only a few seconds later. We're fighting each other right now. As soon as I think it, I know it's true. And if I don't recognize this place, and there's no baseball happening anywhere, it means the Zero is winning. It must be insanely strong to have completely swallowed me up like this, before I had a chance to fight back or even notice what was happening. Maybe even stronger than Charles. It's probably not too far from totally overpowering me. After that, it'll be able to fit me into its mijmere however it wants. It could even turn me into an empty can and crush me, the way I crushed those ACTs.

The man at the desk looks up from his work, fixing me with pale blue eyes. He must be the Zero. This isn't how he really looks, of course. My mijmere is still strong enough that he looks like a person to me. To him, this place will seem like a library on his world—if the Valentines even have libraries—and I'll look like a Valentine.

The Zero smiles at me with teeth streaked yellow. In a voice as smooth and polished as his wooden desk, he says, "Ah, wonderful. Please come in and have a seat. I'll be with you in a moment." His smile gets bigger—a little *too* big. "Can I offer you some refreshment? A drink, perhaps? Or a sandwich?"

"No," I say, then, because he only smiles at me some more, like he thinks I'm just lying and I really do want a sandwich, I say it again. "No."

"Let's get you some water anyway. In case you change your mind." He looks past me, toward the man in the black suit. "And some cookies, too."

"Yes, sir," the man says. He bows and steps away, closing the doors as he disappears.

The Zero goes back to his papers, making marks on each sheet before adding them to the pile on his desk. When he sees I haven't moved, he says, "Do sit down, please. It makes me anxious, having someone standing around like that while I work." He marks one last page with his pen and gets up from the desk. "Right there will be fine," he says, pointing to one of the couches by the fire. When I still don't move, he smiles an extra-wide, extra-yellow smile. "I can have my man restrain you if necessary. I don't think either of us wants that."

He's right. He has most of the power here. I'm all alone, and almost everything in this world is on his side. As I settle onto the couch, I get a better look at the box making the crowd noises. On the side facing the Zero's desk, there's a rounded glass panel, and inside of that is the image of a baseball field. In the back of my mind, I hear the word "television." But this isn't just any baseball field—it's *my* baseball field. I recognize it right away. So maybe I'm not totally powerless here after all. My game is still going on. It may be shut up in a little box, but at least it's here somewhere.

The Zero pours himself a glass of brown liquid from a heavy, clear bottle. "So," he says, "let's begin with your name."

I don't say anything, but the Zero catches me looking at the television. He walks over and turns a small knob beside the picture panel, and the sound of the crowd fades to nothing. "I'm enjoying the game, too, but please, let's try not to become distracted," he says, settling onto the couch across from me. He folds one leg over the other and smiles at me again. "Your name, please."

"Jax." I don't believe for a second that I'm here for some friendly conversation. He's trying to weaken me, to absorb me into his mijmere. He could probably kill me right now—hit me with that bottle of brown liquid, or throw me into the fire—but I'd be able to fight back, and my guess is he doesn't want to risk getting hurt. He'd rather wait until I'm too weak to do anything. I'm getting there, too. The television's picture has begun to jump and roll, static gathering like snow over the field. Pretty soon, it'll cut out completely. I'm not sure why he hasn't turned it off himself, actually. But if telling him my name slows him down, I'm glad to do it.

"I do love athletic competitions, don't you, Jax?" the Zero says, nodding toward the television. "A far better use for our energies than war, wouldn't you say?" The picture rolls again, and the Zero leans over. I'm sure he's about to flip the television's power switch, but he only plays around with a little antenna on top, like he's trying to tune the game back into focus. "My apologies. The reception here is atrocious."

I realize with a bolt that the Zero doesn't know baseball is my Theme. To him, it's only entertainment.

"If it's distracting you, just turn it off," I tell him. My mouth is totally dry, but I think I sound confident enough.

"Oh, no. It's no bother. The sound keeps me company. This place can be so gloomy." He looks back at me, then notices something over my head. "Ah, here we are."

The man with the black suit is standing at the door again. "The water you requested, sir," he says. "And cookies. I took the liberty of providing some milk as well." He sets the tray in front of me. "Will there be anything else, sir?"

"No, thank you," the Zero says, looking at me the whole time. He keeps his eyes on me as the man in the black suit leaves, like he's waiting to see what I'll do. I stare at the tray, the crackling fire reflecting in its silvery surface. There doesn't seem to be anything wrong with the water or milk or cookies, but I still don't want to touch any of it.

"Well, Jax," the Zero says with a sigh, like he's getting down to business, "this *is* a sorry state in which we find ourselves, isn't it? I will admit I never thought much of your people, but I never expected they would send *children* into battle. Look at you—you're nothing but a cub!"

"No one sent me," I say, trying to sound calm. "I came on my own."

The Zero takes a drink of his brown liquid, watching me over the rim of his glass. "Is that so?"

"I was supposed to evacuate."

"And instead you charged heroically into a losing fight," he says, like he's finishing my sentence. "Well, *bravo*. Good for you, Jax. Truly."

"I didn't have a choice," I say, feeling suddenly angry.

"Oh, now you're just being silly. There is always a choice. As you said, you were supposed to evacuate. You could have left this war behind, but instead you chose to make your stand. Not the most prudent idea, I'm afraid."

"That's not a real choice," I snap. "Just like I didn't have a choice about being in this war to begin with. None of us does. If we don't fight, you'll just kill us."

"That's likely true," the Zero admits, "but it's still your choice."

"Not a very good one."

"And then," he continues, like he hasn't heard me, "who's to say your people *didn't* choose this war?"

"Me. I'm saying that."

"And how do *you* know? Were you there when it began?"

"I know people who were."

"And you simply take them at their word?" He laughs. "What else *would* they tell you? They want you to fight, don't they? They want you to believe you have *no choice*. But if you allow yourself to think about it, Jax, really *think* about it, you'll realize you know almost nothing about this war you've been convinced you have to fight. I'm right, aren't I? I can tell by the way you're frowning to yourself."

He sips his drink, watching me, but I don't have anything to say. "You don't even know what it is you're fighting," he says, sounding like he's teaching a lesson in class. "And if you don't know *what*, how can you really say you know *why*?"

"That's easy," I tell him. "We're fighting because you're trying to kill us."

"Well, yes, I suppose you've got me there," he says with a chuckle. "I *am* going to kill you. If it's any consolation, I can assure you I won't enjoy it. I will kill you because it is my duty. You understand duty, don't you, Jax? I'm sure your people teach you all about duty. It's such a convenient way to relieve oneself of the burden of choice."

He's watching me again, and I try my best to look him right in the eye. It isn't easy. He seems like a normal, polite, kind of oldish man, but there's something not right about him. His yellowy teeth seem sharp and almost rusty, and there's red around the blue of his eyes. He uses a calm, friendly voice, but he's talking about killing me. Right now, though, I want all his attention on me because I've heard something. When the man in the black suit left, he didn't completely close the door, and now there's music coming through, soft and muffled like the sound of my game on the television, but getting louder. Fiddle music.

"We should probably just get this over with," I say. "I'm sure you're extremely busy, right?"

"Oh, not at all! And you haven't even touched your cookies."

I haven't. I've been concentrating on that music. I'm imagining a forest outside the windows, filled with flocks of singing birds and wind whistling through the branches, that old clock in the hallway ringing, ice clinking in the Zero's glass—anything to bring music into this room.

A loud *crack!* comes from the direction of the bookshelves, and a second later there's the soft, fuzzy sound of a fiddle playing. What looks like an old, dusty-looking radio has suddenly started working. Needles in lit dials on its face bounce back and forth with each staticky note.

The Zero looks over his shoulder toward the radio. "Finicky old thing," he says. "Naturally, it waits until I have company to start working. One moment, Jax."

He starts to get up, but I say, almost shouting at him, "You looked pretty busy when I came in. What were you doing?"

That stops him. His yellow smile stretches out again, and he lowers back onto the couch, blue eyes burning. "You know, Jax, I suppose you're right. Why prolong the inevitable, eh? I've enjoyed our conversation, really, but the time has come to bring it to an end."

Maybe he's waiting for me to say something back, but instead I take the whole tray of water and cookies and milk and throw it at him. Then I kick over the table. If this were a normal house, one I could leave and actually hope to get away, that's exactly what I'd do. But this is a mijmere, and I can't escape by running. So I don't. I make a dash for his desk.

I get about halfway around the couch before he grabs me and slams me to the ground. He's insanely strong—stronger than anyone should be.

"Such awful manners," the Zero snarls. He doesn't sound polite anymore. Behind him, the fire roars and blazes, turning him into a reddish shadow. "I'd hoped to conclude our acquaintance in a civilized manner, Jax, but it seems quick and dirty will have to do." Leaning beside the hearth is a heavy metal rod with a handle on one end and a spike on the other. The Zero grabs the handle and swings the rod back, ready to bash me with it.

But before he can bring the rod down, there's a loud screeching sound,

a mess of musical notes. When the Zero turns to look, something thuds
into his stomach. He lurches forward, and whatever it is hits him again,
colliding with his knee. When he stumbles, I see Naomi standing over him,
holding her fiddle case.

I think she must have hurt the Zero pretty badly, but he's more surprised than anything. He whirls on her, letting out a growl that doesn't
sound human at all, and swings his metal rod at her head. She blocks it with
her fiddle case, but the force of it knocks her to the floor. The Zero swings
again, and this time he catches her on the arm, making her cry out in pain.

"So very sad," the Zero says, though he sounds extremely pleased with
himself.

Naomi raises her case to block his next attack, but the rod smashes
straight through. The case shatters, and she disappears with a little musical
twang. Her Theme has been stopped, and her mijmere has collapsed. To
this Zero, she's completely powerless. She could be anywhere in his mijmere
now, or anything: a ceramic doll on the mantel, an image on a piece of paper.
I have maybe a few seconds before he kills her.

"Not so gallant anymore, are we, Jax?" the Zero says, turning toward
me. He must mean because I let Naomi take him on all by herself. But he
didn't know what I was doing all that time. When he sees me, his smile
clenches tight.

Naomi gave me a chance, and as soon as the Zero had his back turned,
I went for it. I knew if I was wrong, we'd both be dead like *that*, but it was
our best hope of getting out of this alive, and anyway I'm not wrong. I
grabbed all the papers from the Zero's desk, and now I'm standing in front
of the fireplace, with every one of them piled in my arms.

He forces a laugh. "What do you think you're doing, Jax?"

"Just going to burn a few papers. Too much clutter in here, right?"

"Dear me, Jax, don't be foolish. That won't—"

Maybe he's about to say burning his papers won't do anything, but I
never find out, because right then I heave them all into the fire. The whole
stack lands right on the burning logs, and a few flaming pages flutter out
like fiery bats. The Zero lunges for them, but before he can touch even one,
the whole room vanishes, burning away like just another piece of paper,
and the next thing I know I'm back in my stadium, the one where I went
when this battle began.

"Whew. That was close," says the Kid. He's munching peanuts from a bag. Down on the field, the game is well under way. The lights are up, and in the distance, I can see colorful explosions—though not like something from a battle. These are more like happy explosions.

"They're called fireworks," the Kid says, sounding a lot like the voice in my head that told me about typewriters and televisions.

"Naomi!" I shout. "Where is she?" For a second I'd forgotten about the whole fight with the Zero.

"Right there." The Kid points down toward the field. Naomi is off to one side, sitting on a stretcher. A man in white is wrapping her arm in bandages, and another is holding a cup of water for her to drink. Her head is bandaged, too, but she doesn't look badly hurt. She sees me and nods, smiling. "She'll be fine," the Kid says, and I know he's right. Once her mijmere comes back, she'll be able to heal herself pretty well, but until then this is about as good as I can do for her.

"What about the Zero—the man from the library?"

The Kid only grins and nods toward the concrete beneath our seats, where he has a cockroach trapped beneath a clear plastic cup. "Pests," he says. "Huge problem around here. We'd better take care of this one."

Without his Theme, the Zero's mijmere has collapsed. He's only a bug to me now. But for some reason, I don't want to just squash him—or have the Kid do it, which would be almost the same thing.

That Zero was terrible. He would have killed me and Naomi both. If I let him escape, he'll try again. But he was right about one thing: We don't really know anything about the Valentines. I wonder if anyone's ever tried really *talking* to a Zero. What if, instead of killing him, I found a way to capture him? We could learn from him. Wouldn't that be better?

But while I'm thinking about all of this, a heavy black boot stomps down on the plastic cup, crushing the bug-Zero underneath. I look from the boot up to the person who's just jumped over the seat beside me. It's Fontana Malandeera. She's in heavy, dark clothes, and there's soot all over her face. She twists her foot, grinding the cup into the concrete. "Let's go, Jax," she says. "This fight isn't over yet."

SIXTY

IMWAY

We're all alone out here. Our last contact with IMEC-1 came in a rush of radio traffic, a single message repeated on every available frequency: *All units, return to home.* After that, everything went to shit.

The 126th was tasked, along with the rest of Sixth and two other cohorts from Ninth Legion, with isolating and neutralizing a full wave of Valentine fighters. The enemy outnumbered us five to one, with four Zeros to our single fontana, but with IMEC-1 behind us, the odds were solidly in our favor. Beyond that, our source was Fontana Nellope, one of Ninth Legion's best. We already had two Zeros down, and quite a nice panic under way in the Valentine ranks, when our artillery support abruptly dried up. Without the constant hammering of ordnance to keep her opponents in line, Nellope was quickly surrounded, forced into a fight on the enemy's terms with no prospect of retreat, and all of us with her.

Our one and only goal now is to get Fontana Nellope free of this battle, and that means helping her defeat the two Zeros hemming her in. Nellope is an experienced and formidable fighter—in her three tours at the Front, she's defeated no fewer than ten Zeros in single combat—but that doesn't mean taking on two sources at once will be a simple matter, not when they know how to use the numerical imbalance to their advantage. The whole of Sixth Cohort will seem like little more than a cloud of buzzing mosquitoes to any of them. But mosquitoes can be distracting, and for Fontana Nellope, some strategic distraction could mean the difference between triumphing over these Zeros and being snuffed out. If we can divert either of her adversaries for even a fraction of a second, it could give her the opportunity she needs. That means we have to try.

I've led the 126th on three runs so far. Three steep dives over battling sources circling one another in a dance like something halfway between stalking predators and orbiting moons. Each attack lasted only minutes, but in that time we've taken more losses than in the entire preceding battle. Hitting a Zero means flying low and fast over a sea of roiling energy, where one thoughtless wave can crush an equus like a cracker. On our first run, Koleg and Midmurro took hard lashes that left them clinging to the emergency safety gear inside equi suddenly reduced to dead husks. On the next, a swell of stars rose and completely swept away three more of us. Uo, Pelashwa, and Rachel—all of them gone before anyone could react. We looked for them on the next pass, but found only a few drifting shards of armor.

The 126th is holding together. My equites are as frosty and precise as when we sortied from Earth—more so, if anything, since we reached the tipping point toward mayhem—but they're balanced on a knife's edge, fueled by a cocktail of training and determination fortified with adrenaline. We've never lost one of our own before, and here we are down three. As we circle through the storm of fighters—both legionary and Valentine— seeking our next avenue of attack, I can't help wondering how long we can keep this up.

The time to move will be just as Nellope's orbit reaches its farthest separation from the Valentine Zeros. It isn't an easy point to spot, but I have to trust myself. There are people who claim they can tell one source from another simply by the look of an individual mijmere, but I've never quite mastered the technique. Fortunately, sources project a wide variety of radiation aside from visible light—everything from heat to noise to high-energy gamma rays—and each has a kind of signature, a combination of patterns and energies unique to that source. It isn't quite as reliable or consistent as a fingerprint, but it's a dependable enough way of spotting our own. Fontana Nellope profiles powerfully in hard X-rays and magnetic pulses, and through FireChaser's sharpened senses, I pick her out easily as she draws away from the two Zeros, one of which shows up mostly in infrared, the other in microwaves with ripples of electricity. When I judge the moment is right, I order the 126th to draw weapons and fall in.

We've covered roughly half the distance to the target before resistance begins in earnest. A swarm of Type 5s—the style sometimes called waspies for their resemblance to gigantic versions of stinging insects, but more formally designated as Mid-Range, Mid-Power Interceptors, or MMIs—

banks out of the melee and takes up a parallel course. I bring the 126th in fast. MMIs can be dangerous if they get you in their sights, but they aren't made for close combat. Once we lay into them with our WhiteLances, there isn't much more to say. The fight slows us down, but we come out well enough: all eight remaining equi still combat-capable. Iftito loses Thunder-Walking's right leg from the shin down, and Xempa takes some damage to LoyalShield's off hand, but it isn't enough to hamper our mission. You don't need legs to fly, and one-and-a-half hands is plenty to swing a 'Lance.

An encounter with a second drove of MMIs—a variation more like dragonflies in shape than wasps this time—brings an unexpected boon. As we're closing to engage, another escadrille of seven equi swings in ahead of us, catching the MMIs in an impromptu pincer maneuver. They're from Third Cohort, flying big A-12 Destriers, and when I contact their dek over DS, he suggests we team up for the coming run.

They fall in behind, guarding our formation's rear as we make our approach on the first of the two Zeros. I remind my 'drille to set their WhiteLances to maximum extension—no sense in getting closer to a Zero than we have to. The Destriers from Third do the same, and together we cut downward into the Zero's surface, raking it with our blades and adding a liberal peppering from our S-Cannons.

Our combined efforts, easily enough to level a small neighborhood, can't be more than a sharp pinch to this Zero, but we're unpleasant enough to draw some notice. The boiling black surface bulges, and we pull away just as it whips toward us—a careless swat that could have wiped us out completely.

Keeping formation with the Destriers from Third, I lead the 126th into the next part of our run. We're all set for a repeat performance of our last successful attack when I catch sight of a string of Valentine fighters sweeping in behind us. Bulky, five-armed Type 6s, a profile usually designated as Heavy Breach Troops, or HBTs. They can cause havoc among unsupported infantry, using their speed and mass to smash whole lines of assault platforms, but they're hardly a threat to a solid complement of equi—or so I think, until an HBT latches onto one of our Destriers and pulls it down into the Zero we'd been about to hit. A geyser of energy stabs out from the Zero's surface, and in a blink, both HBT and Destrier are gone.

I've never seen anything like this from Romeo before, but it doesn't come as a complete surprise. Valentine fighters will self-destruct just to avoid capture; a suicide attack is only a few steps away. Romeo has us well enough outnumbered that he could trade fighters one-for-one and still come out of this battle with a full-sized regiment left over. Those HBTs wouldn't stand a chance against us in normal combat, but they only need to stay alive long enough to drag us into the nearest mijmere. Even after we aim our S-Cannons back and begin shooting them down, the HBTs keep coming.

The Destriers from Third fall with sickening speed. A few turn to fight, but the HBTs carry so much momentum that even badly damaged, they're enough to drag an equus the relatively short distance to either of the two Zeros. Only one Destrier makes it out alive, when a stray explosion leaves it disabled and too far away for the HBTs to hit without giving up any chance at the 126th—a far juicier target.

I have to act now. If the 126th doesn't change tactics, we're going to end up like our comrades from Third. Scenarios flash through my mind as I run down our options. There aren't many. If we stand our ground, the HBTs will overwhelm us. If we keep running, they'll catch us—our Coursers are fast, but once those HBTs get moving, they're faster. We've got to outrun them or fight, and we can't outrun them.

I instruct the 126th to prepare for running combat. The longer we keep moving, the better chance we have of getting clear of those Zeros. *Don't let the HBTs latch onto you,* I tell them—obvious advice, but I've found in situations like this, the obvious is usually the first thing you forget.

The HBTs swing onto an intercept course, spreading out to better avoid our fire and put themselves in position to surround and envelop us. They've just begun to overtake us when my radio spits out a spray of static, and I hear a woman's voice say, "I believe now is the time to make your stand, man."

At the same moment, three HBTs burst apart in a spray of purple gwayd, and several more shudder beneath the impacts of cannon fire. A group of equi has hit the HBTs from behind, raking through them in a high-speed dive. I give the order to attack, and the 126th charges the suddenly disrupted formation of HBTs with renewed determination.

It isn't just that we've seen the chance to come out of this alive. There's more to this rescue than that. I have to jettison some past assumptions, but I realize now the interference from three battling sources could easily have disrupted attempts to locate our lost 'drille-mates. And there's no mistaking the three equi that have just joined the fight: I'd know Pelashwa's FallingLeaf and Uo's SunOnWaves anywhere, and there isn't an equus in the Legion I'd confuse with the X-2020.

I have to give it to Kizabel: That toy of hers can really move. It's fluid, balletic, and blindingly quick, so that from one attack to the next, the HBTs hardly have time to react before they're coming apart at the seams. Rachel's fighting style is more brutal, more reckless than the tersely efficient technique they teach at the Academy, but it's effective enough—graceful even, when fitted to the liquid speed of the X-2020. But it isn't until we've nearly finished with the HBTs that I see what that speed can really do.

Between our resurrected equi catching those HBTs off guard and the boost they gave to our numbers, the situation has turned firmly in favor of the 126th. It isn't our most elegant fight, but there's no room for finesse here. We've lingered too long in the vicinity of hostile sources, and it won't be long before we draw their serious consideration—or, more likely, end up heedlessly obliterated when their battle with Fontana Nellope resumes. What matters now is dispatching these HBTs and vacating the area as soon as possible. No time to worry about losing points for style. We've culled almost enough of the grapplers to be confident of a clean getaway when a savage string of curses erupts over DS. It's Sensen; an HBT has latched onto her equus, directly over ShadowSinger's core, and begun dragging her down.

I've been cutting my way through a pesky cluster of HBTs, and, by the time I disengage, two more have landed on Shadow, swallowing up both of her legs and one of her arms. Already I'm afraid they've taken her too far for me to do any good. The full kinetic force of an HBT is enough to overpower even the most determined equus; three HBTs together can push a Courser faster than I can fly. I tuck into a dive anyway. I won't leave Sen to burn out if there's even a small chance I can make a difference. I've only begun gathering speed, however, when a blur of white streaks past. Ahead, I see the X-2020 plummeting after ShadowSinger.

Sensen doesn't let the fact that she has absolutely no chance of breaking loose keep her from fighting back. She strikes out furiously with Shadow's free arm, an effort that does little aside from adding topspin to her descent. With a final twist, Sensen and the three HBTs plunge the last of the distance toward the nearest of the two Zeros.

The grappler holding Singer's legs hits the mijmere first, dousing the surrounding space in purple gwayd, followed by a splash of red-orange as the Zero swallows up Shadow's lower half. I wait for the next burst of gwayd, the one that will signal Shadow's core being crushed and Sensen with it. Instead, there's a flash of white as the X-2020 crashes into the knot of HBTs.

Rachel is not gentle with her rescue. She cuts hard into the HBT wrapped around ShadowSinger's core, slicing off two of its five arms and a good chunk of Shadow's armor as well. But it gets the job done: The HBT goes cartwheeling away, gushing gwayd. Before the remaining HBT—the one holding Shadow's arm—can react, Rachel swings her WhiteLance up, severing the entire arm at the shoulder. The grappler, whose strength had been fully committed to winning that arm, springs free, the force of its pull propelling it directly into the mijmere below.

One arm holding ShadowSinger's dismembered frame, the X-2020 climbs away from the Zero's roiling surface. Close behind, the HBT that lost two arms to Rachel's first attack comes spinning back, ready with the other three. Rather than trying to knock the HBT back with her cannon, Rachel lets go of ShadowSinger and tackles it. The two tumble back toward the Zero, already receding as it moves for another bout with Fontana Nellope. It looks as if both the HBT and X-2020 are going into the mijmere, but then they spin, skidding across its surface, both obscured in a spray of purple gwayd until the X-2020 rises, the HBT nowhere in sight, dissolved by the Zero's surface.

Rachel has the X-2020 back on course well in time to retrieve the badly damaged ShadowSinger—or seize, I should say, as Sensen seems determined to rejoin the 126th under her own power. Not much chance there: ShadowSinger's emergency systems have kicked in to bring gwayd loss down to a trickle, but that's about all she can do at this point. Even Sensen's attempts to shrug off the X-2020 look halfhearted. When she contacts me over a private DS conduit, her voice sounds distant, like something shouted from a high tower.

I think that noco just saved my life, Chase, she says, resigned.

It certainly looked that way, I admit. It looked like more than that. I've never seen an equus get that close to a Zero—not willingly—and come away unscathed.

This doesn't mean I have to be nice to her from now on, Sensen declares firmly.

I think we'd all be disappointed if you were, I assure her. *Rachel would probably take it as an insult.*

The bitch did *cut my arm off.*

I'm sure she'll find a way to make it up to you. I call up my full 'drille then, ordering them to get themselves out of the fighting while we await the opportunity for another run. *And special thanks to the rescue squad,* I add. *It's good to have the three of you with us again.*

It's good to be back, dek, Pelashwa answers. *You might want to relay all of that to Rae personally, though. She's radio-only.*

For the first time since it reappeared, I take a solid look at the X-2020. Now that it's released ShadowSinger into the care of two other equi, I can see the long gashes where some Valentine blade or claw gouged into the white armor, glowing dim blue from the gwayd pulsing beneath. The head's front plate is mostly missing, torn at a ragged angle, like something big got in a good hard bite.

She earned that topside damage crashing head-to-head with a Type 7, Pelashwa explains. *Got the three of us out of a very tight spot. Not the move any sane person would have used, though. The girl is certifiable, but she sure can fly.*

I key my radio to raise Rachel in the X-2020. "Nice work out there, Eques," I tell her.

"Piece of pie," she calls back through a scatter of static. It's the same voice I heard just before our clash with the HBTs. *Time to make your stand, man.* I didn't recognize it at the time, but now it seems obvious.

"You good for another round?" I ask her. "This battle isn't over."

"Fit as a fiddle, but I broke that mind-reading radio, and I'm having a little trouble telling our people apart. Who'd I go after back there, anyway? Is he all right?"

"You couldn't see the identifiers?"

"Well, no, not exactly. Snuggles is short a few pieces just now."

Again, I consider the X-2020's ruined top unit. The sensory array must be almost useless. "Are you telling me you're flying *blind*?"

"*No,*" Rachel says defensively. "I can still see heat and a few other things."

Unbelievable. "What were you thinking? Can you even tell friendlies from hostiles in that thing?"

"Well enough to pull *your* big red rear out of the fire," she says.

It's a fair point. I tell Rachel as much, then open up to the rest of the 126th over DS while keeping my radio transmitting to the X-2020. We may have our lost fighters back, but we're still up to our asses out here and sinking.

The catalogue of energies radiating from Fontana Nellope's mijmere has become erratic, her signature patterns changing to match those of her enemies. Meaning she's starting to weaken. We don't have much time left to help her through this fight. As Nellope orbits back toward the pair of Zeros, I search for another opportunity, anything that will give us a chance at one more strike. Even if I have to risk myself and what remains of the 126th on odds so long they might as well be nonexistent, our chances will still be better than if Nellope goes down.

And then, just as Nellope draws in for her next dive, the swing of her descent suddenly ceases. It's disorienting to watch, a splintering burst of sky and stars. A fraction of a second later, I see the reason behind her abrupt change in course as the space around the enemy sources lights up with detonations bright enough to overpower every discharging weapon nearby. When the disrupting energy clears enough for me to see, both Zeros are reeling. Only one thing could have produced an effect that powerful: a full artillery strike from IMEC-1.

I can't explain it—last I heard, the IMEC was dark with no prospect of rescue—but I'm not going to argue. My 'drille has already come to the same conclusion, and their shouts of jubilation are such that I need to tune them out to raise Centurio Kitu over DS, even as a new barrage explodes across the enemy's mijmeri.

Kitu has only just confirmed what the 126th has already guessed—that IMEC-1 is somehow back in the fight—when both Zeros break from their pursuit of Fontana Nellope. It's as if they've disappeared altogether, until I think to look outside our umbris and see them retreating away into space. They've cut and run.

I ask Kitu whether we're planning to pursue, knowing as I do that the probability of catching them now must be close to zero.

Not today, Chaser, he answers. *Command wants us to consolidate around IMEC-1. The Valentines are attempting an ordered retreat, and we think it's time to add a little disorder. See how many we can get before they escape. The more we polish off now, the fewer we'll have to deal with later. Get your wounded someplace safe and form up.*

I relay Kitu's orders to my 'drille. *I'm afraid Shadow's going to have to stay behind,* I add. *Activate your beacon and settle in, Sen. We'll be back for you as soon as we can.*

Hope you brought a good book, Ottumtee quips.

Kiss my ass, Otto, is Sensen's reply.

Everyone stay cool now, I warn them. *Having the enemy on the run is no reason to get sloppy. It's looking like this party is almost done, so anyone who gets themselves killed now is going to be in trouble, understood?*

Affirmatives all around.

It's an unnecessary warning—not because the 126th is too disciplined to become careless, though I'd like to think that's true also. As we fly to join the rest of Sixth Cohort, already the Valentine fighters we pass have begun to sizzle at the edges, taking on the brittle look of dried mud or ash as they crumble away.

SIXTY-ONE

RAE

When I think on Death, I imagine her as a child, a girl in a white dress with untidy hair, running barefoot through the battlefield, collecting lives like wildflowers. She goes about her work without malice but spares no more mercy for her quarry than would any lighthearted thing for a daisy or dandelion that has captured her fancy. I have never seen much benefit in appealing to her sentimental side or bidding for her favor with promises or gifts, but it seems to me there is a certain etiquette to be observed in Death's presence. It is simply this: Do not try to keep your life from her, do not clutch it to your breast or hide it beneath your hat. If she has a place for you in her basket, she will find you out one way or another. Instead, go to her at the outset. Take your life and put it in her pocket. Say to her, *You just hold on to that for me.* At least then your hands will be free to fight.

We have become well acquainted, Death and I. I have learned the sound of her footsteps and the tunes she hums at play. There were times when she held my life in her hands, lifted it to her lips, and twirled it between her fingers, contemplating its color and scent, the leaves shivering in her chilly breath. But on each occasion she has deemed it wrong for her arrangement and set it loose to fall, fluttering, behind her.

I have been spared once again. When the last shots had been fired in the Realm of Dis, my life was there on the field of stars, waiting for me to gather it up. For a little while, I even harbored the notion it had come back in colors brighter and more brilliant than I remembered. I know now that was a false hope.

The battle did not end when our enemy broke and ran but lasted for many wearying hours after, during which my escadrille was tasked first with chasing down a portion of the Valentine fighters flying about on various troublemaking ends, a job my comrades called "mopping up," then with helping contain the damage to our city. IMEC-1 had been badly shot up, its skyline cracked like a brawler's teeth, and we were needed to clear the streets of rubble and quell areas of supernatural upheaval.

By the time Snuggles and I returned to the Stabulum, we were in a thick haze of exhaustion. I am proud to say I was able to dismount under my own power, a claim not every eques out that day can make, though I will admit to somewhat losing track of my cardinal directions after my feet touched the ground. Snuggles had his wounds attended to first, was doused in a greenish cauterizing fire, then a sort of sealing orange foam before I was permitted to step free, at which point I was met by a curtly unfriendly medic who examined and questioned me and finally informed me I had a ruptured eardrum and moderate subconjunctival hemorrhaging but no life-threatening injuries. After scrawling a green number "3" on my uniform, he departed in search of more serious cases, delivering a stiff nod and a "Nice work, Eques" like a final dose of medication.

I spent an unknown period of time sitting where I was, dazedly observing the mayhem of the Armored Cavalry's return, before another passing medic took pity on me and pointed me toward the Stabulum exit with assurances that beyond lay a station where I would have my choice of coffee, tea, or juice, and as many cookies and crackers as I desired. I was on my way to this promised land when from the direction of my retreat came a familiar and welcome voice: Kizabel.

"Rae!" She was out of breath, something I might have taken note of under other circumstances. Kizabel does not run anywhere if she can help it. "You made it! You guys were fantastic! I—*gah*!" she cried, having taken me in. "Look at you! Vinneas said you were all OK! What happened?"

I gathered she must mean my subconjunctival hemorrhage and damaged ear, and briefly narrated the events that had brought me here—all at an unnecessarily high volume, I was later informed.

"Well, you look awful," she said candidly. She too had a green number "3" traced across her chest. I was about to ask how she had earned it when she added, "I bet we can get you cleaned up before Vinneas finishes whatever tremendously important thing he's doing over at the Basilica."

She was speaking too quickly, even for Kizabel, and I had trouble keeping up. "When did you talk to Vinneas?"

"Just now. A few minutes ago. He saw you were about to land and asked me to come find you, since I'm nonessential personnel at the moment, and he's being tremendously important, as I believe I've already mentioned."

A hazy warmth pulsed through me then, something excited and expectant, at the news that, from whatever high vantage Vinneas occupied, he had marked my return, picked me out amid all the whirling confusion, noted me specially. The feeling was brief because on its heels came the question of why he had sent Kizabel running down here for me. "Kiz, what's wrong?" I asked, fear bubbling in my gut. "What happened?"

I think Kizabel saw the distress come into my face, and in an effort to head off my panic, she made what turned out to be a poorly calculated assurance. What she said was "Don't worry. Naomi's fine."

A few moments passed while I sank into pure, cold dread. "Where is she?"

Kizabel seemed to realize her error and hurried to salvage the situation. "There's no reason to worry. Really. Just stay calm. Everything's OK."

"Kizabel!" I screamed, feeling the wildness begin to take over. "Tell me where she is!"

Amid all the noise and commotion of the Stabulum, the urgent calls of medics, the oaths of injured equites, and the screeches of their equi, I was still loud enough that people turned and looked.

Cornered, Kizabel opted for a different tactic. "At the Academy's infirmary. It's only protocol, I promise," she assured me. "Rae, listen to me. She's perfectly fine. We can go see her right now."

I did not wait around for further invitation but set off at a run in what I judged to be the direction of the Academy. Kizabel rushed after, keeping me on the correct general course and offering apologies for me whenever I bowled over some unsuspecting person. Fortunately, the city was full of legionaries dashing about on urgent errands, and my heedless and uncivil behavior fit nicely into the general traffic.

By the time I reached the Academy's infirmary, I was just about out of my mind with terror. Had I simply stopped, taken a few breaths, and listened, as Kizabel kept hollering after me to do, that journey might have been a deal less desperate, but it would not have helped much. Nothing would satisfy me until I had seen Naomi.

And there she was, as Kizabel said she would be, with no outward appearance of harm, propped up in a small white bed and wearing a wide grin seldom seen on her somber face. I went to her, at first not even daring to touch her, then taking her little face in my hands, holding her chin and cupping her skull and running my fingers over her, searching for any sign of hurt.

Naomi responded to my concerns by struggling and swatting me away. "Rae!" she shouted. "Will you stop it! Let go of me and quit fretting, you old nag!" This protest, and others in a similar vein, finally set me at ease. I had detected some tenderness in Naomi's arm that worried me, but if she was calling me names, there could not be much wrong.

Above her protestations, I heard laughter around us, and looking about discovered that Naomi occupied the middlemost in a long row of beds, all filled with convalescing legionaries overflowing with mirth at the scene I had made. Naomi, humiliated at being mothered over in front of her fellow soldiers, laid into me further, which only increased the general merriment. But I could tell, even if Naomi couldn't, that this was laughter of fellowship, and when it subsided, I was given to learn just what sort of reputation I had soiled with my mollycoddling.

My sister was a hero. Naomi told part of the story herself, and soon Kizabel, who I had left behind in my final sprint through the ward, arrived to fill in the details she had intended to give me before I went running through the city like a lunatic. Kiz had some official intelligence courtesy of Vinneas but could narrate the important parts firsthand—as could every legionary in the ward, I discovered, when several piped up with their own versions of the story. It seemed they all remembered exactly where they were and what was happening when Naomi's valor tipped the scales of battle. So did I, once I'd heard enough of the story to understand what had happened.

When IMEC-1 went dark, and the heavy guns fell silent, and our enemies threatened to overwhelm us, it was Naomi who fought her way in to give us another chance at victory. She had been one of several, true. It was thanks to the combined efforts of the Legion's reserve that we were saved. But Naomi, and the little gentleman Jax, were the ones who made the final push to revive our fortress and its cannons.

Naomi suffered a broken arm in the fight, but thanks to the healing powers of fontani, the bones had already mended. She held up the disputed arm for me to see, wincing as she worked her fingers but determined to demonstrate her soldier's grit. "Charles says I'll be good as new in a day or so," she said proudly. "If I work at it, I'll be able to heal up faster pretty soon. I could maybe even fix your eye. Does it hurt very badly?"

My eyes had shut to allow me better focus on the multifarious work of gathering up my scattered wits. Seeing Naomi healthy and in the flesh helped immensely, but I still had to reassemble my understanding of the world and its present order. I had departed Earth believing my sister as safe from the Valentine hordes as any human alive. She was to be left behind the rest of the Legion, and I had it on good authority that even if the reserve was called to battle, she would be traveling in the opposite direction. Now I was faced with the business of reconciling my memories to the truth that, in the very worst moments, she had been in the thick of things.

"Naw, it doesn't hurt," I said. "Just looks bad is all."

"Rae, I am all right," Naomi replied sternly. "Truly. Don't cry like that."

A few tears had indeed gotten away from me and were plainly the source of much embarrassment to Naomi. I mopped the culprits up best as I could. "You're right. I'm sorry."

"We won, Rae," Naomi said, slowly, as if this was a complicated matter demanding careful explanation. "I was afraid at first, but there was always someone to help. I wasn't alone more than a minute before Charles swooped in and sent me to fight with Jax. And we did it. Jax and I beat a Zero together. The next one I'll whip all on my own. You watch."

At that, the room of laid-up soldiers loosed a hearty hurrah. I mustered what I thought a convincing smile. "I'm sure you will, S—" I began to say "Sunshine" but stopped myself just in time. "Sure you will. Everyone back home will be so proud of you." I was proud of her, too, but somehow I couldn't bring myself to say so.

"They were here!" Naomi said excitedly. "Reaper and Apricot and the Simons, too! Simon Rumble had a little shriveled-up ear and said the magic they'd use to grow it back was going to turn it blue, and when the medics told him it wouldn't, he asked if they could make a blue one for him anyway."

She went on a few minutes longer before one of the attending doctors came to shoo me out. Naomi, still boasting, consented to have her hair smoothed back and her forehead kissed, after which I exited the ward to the shouts of soldiers who believed their recovery would also benefit from some kissing.

Kizabel was waiting for me outside. She had backed off to allow me some privacy with Naomi but now was eager that I not be angry with her.

"Rae, I am *so* sorry! I had a whole plan for how I was going to tell you. I drew a flow chart and everything. And then I got there and I saw you and I completely blew it."

"It's all right, Kiz. Everything's fine." I had begun to cry again, and felt exceedingly foolish about it. Everything was indeed fine, or as fine as I had any right to expect. Naomi was safe as she could be, circumstances considered; so was the Earth and everyone on it. My friends had come back with all their stitching more or less together. Naomi said it herself: We won. So why was I carrying on like this? "Just ignore me. I'm being silly." I drew her in for a hug, and again noticed the "3" on her uniform. "What happened to you?"

"Oh, nothing catastrophic." She waved a hand dismissively. "Just a little IED mostly. Nothing I can't sleep off. Hey," she said, new excitement in her voice, "let's go see Vinn. I bet things are cooling down at the Basilica by now."

Kizabel seemed to consider a visit to the Basilica one of her more brilliant ideas and was crestfallen when I begged off, claiming exhaustion as my excuse. Really, I was feeling very much out of sorts and unsure how I would stand up to further company. Sitting with Naomi had left me a deal more injured than the whole fight that came before, though I didn't feel it properly until a while later, when something happened to prod that same hurt spot again.

The something was named Vinneas. He was a handsome man I thought I remembered from a long time ago, though when I finally saw him again, I had the notion we'd last met in another life, or at least another world. By then, the IMEC had returned to Earth so that repairs could benefit from the rapid pacing of time there, and I, along with the rest of the 126th Equites and every able-bodied soldier of the Legion, was laboring day and night to set our fortress back to rights. Vinneas, too, had been swallowed up by this monumental task, and while I had never entirely lost track of him, would often note the print of his mind in some plan we'd been assigned or recognize a familiar turn of phrase in orders coming down from Command, it nevertheless wobbled my sense of time and place when, at the end of a long shift, I spied his tall frame at the edge of the Stabulum.

He was engaged in animated conversation with Imway, but the two broke off as I walked up. In place of the cool enumeration of my disciplinary failings Imway usually offered by way of debriefing, he said only,

"0600 tomorrow, Eques," and departed. For Vinneas he had what appeared to be a consoling pat on the shoulder, albeit delivered with a sly, sideways smirk.

Vinneas, meanwhile, was grinning heartily. "Rae," he said, in a voice from long ago, "walk with me?"

Silently, I counted up the days since we'd last spoken face-to-face: nearly a month. Naomi and Jax were not the only ones to emerge from the battle with a gleam of newly burnished heroism. Vinneas had won his share of renown as well, albeit for strategy rather than daring. While our ranks of commanders were planning how they would mow the enemy down, Vinneas had spied how the fight might go wrong and devised a scheme to win back our advantage. He laid a trap of magical ordnance, fired alongside the signal rockets that would summon the reserve, and when rescue came—in the form of young Jax—there was a sky of sleeping thunder waiting to clear his path to our fortress. It was all done so deftly— the enemy's movements predicted so perfectly, its advantage so thoroughly undone—that you'd almost think nearly losing the battle was part of the plan all along. The success of his gambit made Vinneas quite a favorite at Command, but it seemed glory did not particularly agree with him. From a distance, he had seemed taller than I remembered, but I saw now he had grown inward instead of upward. I realized I had never properly thanked him for his attempts to ease my mind over Naomi, though I sensed mentioning this now would disappoint him, so I said, "Of course I will. Lead the way."

The route he had in mind took us away from the Stabulum toward the outermost avenues of the School of Philosophy. Most of Ninth City's Academy had been requisitioned as housing for the IMEC's overpopulation of soldiers, but Philosophy was fully returned to its former function and consequently one of the city's few quiet places in our present state of upheaval. Later, I decided Vinneas must have brought me there specifically because he expected I would lose my temper at him and hoped to limit the number of witnesses.

We talked idly over our activities of the past weeks. He asked after my health, and I was pleased to report a complete recovery, particularly of my subconjunctival hemorrhage, which, I had discovered, referred to a burst blood vessel in the eye, painless but grisly to look at. It was plain, however, we were simply passing time, and so it came as no surprise when Vinneas said, "I have something to tell you. Something important. It won't be general knowledge for another day or two, but I wanted you to hear before they made the announcement."

Whatever news he had, it seemed to cause him physical pain. "The Consulate has finished making its assignments for the MapleWhite Campaign," he said. "They've decided to include the entire Ninth Legion."

I was quiet for a minute, thinking this over. The MapleWhite Campaign was the official name for the Legion's upcoming expedition against the Valentines. MapleWhite was the fifth Realm along the Corridor, the last we would have to seize in order to delay the invasion the necessary twenty years, and thusly both the objective of our mission and a natural title for the overall affair, though in informal moments I had also heard our voyage referred to as Operation Hairball and the Doorstop Maneuver, generally by toiling legionaries debating whether or not to join up. The Legion had put out a call for volunteers shortly after our return to Earth, but if what Vinneas said was true, it had not been entirely satisfied with the results.

"I suppose we'll be going on a journey together, then," I said. It was a notion I'd pondered in some detail, having signed up along with the rest of the 126th the same day recruitment for the expedition opened. I had no doubt Vinneas would as well, and could remember thinking there were worse fates than sharing an island with him.

"Yes, all of us," Vinneas replied carefully. "All of Ninth Legion, including Naomi."

Here was what had been weighing on him. I was glad I could at least answer calmly. "I know."

"How?" he asked, his face startled and relieved in about equal measure. "It's still classified information. Even the unit commanders won't know until tomorrow."

"Maybe some young officer went and blabbed to one of his friends. It's been known to happen." I let him work that over a bit before I said, "No one told me. I only knew Naomi had volunteered. She expects I'll try and stop her, so she's been avoiding me, getting ready for a fight." I'd been halfway to a smile, but it soured the second I felt it coming.

"It's still possible she'll have to stay behind," Vinneas said. "There's a motion under consideration before the Consulate to make an exception for Naomi and Jax. A lot of people think twelve is too young for Maple-White."

"It won't work. If Naomi's set on going, she'll be riding this island as sure as you or me."

"There's a chance she won't," he persisted. "A significant chance, in fact. Curator Ellmore made a hard push to set an age limit on MapleWhite, and even though the Consulate voted her down, it was obvious she got to them. No one wants to send children on a mission like this, Rae," he added plaintively. "This really could go our way."

His voice touched something off in me, and before I knew what was happening I'd bitten down on him, hard as a steel trap. "It won't," I said, all sharp and cold. "It won't ever go our way. I don't care if you have everything laid out fair and fine from here until Judgment Day. There'll always be something waiting out there to cut you down. So don't tell me about *significant chances*, and don't come to me with your stories."

It was not what I said as much as how I said it, though once I had time to think it over, it seemed to me the words carried a deeper meaning of their own. But just then neither of us could miss the violence in my voice. For one blood-blind moment, I was sure I hated him, and if anyone had asked me why, I would have hated them, too.

"Rae." The injured look that crossed his face in the second before he gathered himself up was enough to bring me back to my senses, or partly anyway. Vinneas only meant to help, to deliver a little good news with the bad. It was brave of him, especially considering how he must have thought I'd take the bad part. He couldn't have guessed the good news would cause all the trouble.

I badly wanted to take it all back, but the very thought of touching him or saying a single kind thing set glowing the same pain that made me strike out to begin with. So I put on the calmest voice I could and a smile that wouldn't have fooled anyone, and said, "It was good to see you, Vinneas. And don't worry, I won't say a word about anyone's giving away secret military intelligence," and left him there in the lonely alleys of Philosophy.

SIXTY-TWO

RAE

I was upset with myself for a long while afterward, doubly so because I couldn't puzzle out where all that anger and hurt had been sitting, or why, days later, it wouldn't seem to go away. All I had done was read Vinneas out, a feat I had accomplished often enough before without any serious regrets, but the ache now was nearly as bad as what I'd felt by Naomi's bedside. It was this last notion that helped me locate the trouble. When I finally sat down, gritted my teeth, and set to probing those two wounds, I discovered both had landed in nearly the same place.

It started with the battle for Dis, as the skies cleared of magical fire and the swarms of enemies thinned to wisps. The thrum of combat began to fade, and all at once it hit that we had done it. We had won. For a few glorious minutes, out there among the stars, it seemed absolutely anything was possible. I allowed my imagination to run away with me, and it turned out to be a dangerous mistake.

For nearly half my life, and surely since I became a scout, I have known my future in all but a few particulars. I was Reaper Thom's best student, and if I managed to outlive him, I planned to be his successor, his likeness in female form, a bullwhip maid with knives for hands and bullets for eyes. Protecting my coda was to be my sole purpose. I would have no family aside from Mama and what I watched Naomi and Adam build for themselves. The only true uncertainty was how long I could go before something put an end to me. Given my record to date, I allowed myself even odds of making it to twenty-five.

I did have one grand ambition, a dream so fragile and tenuous I never spoke it aloud, not even to Thom, for fear it would break at its first taste of open air. It was this: that Naomi and Adam would never know Death on the same close, personal terms I did, would never require expertise in bloodshed, never make violence their profession. I nurtured this fantasy secretly, planning and plotting but never letting myself believe it might truly come to pass. When Naomi accepted a place in the Legion, I resigned myself to giving it up completely, at least where she was concerned.

And then we had won. The battle was over, our enemy put to flight. The danger had not passed, it was true, but whatever happened now, for a while this war would leave Earth behind. And it would leave Naomi, too. Lunar Veil would close her in, and she might not see war again for years and years and years. Maybe ever. She could have a real life.

That was the headiest of the fantasies I'd entertained, but it wasn't the only one. For all the grim prospects I'd foreseen as a scout, my scouting days were over. It seemed now as never before there might be more I could give than my last breath. I had an idea or two about where I'd go making offers, too.

I think of Vinneas more than I would care to say. In idle moments, he often appears unbidden, strolling from a crowd of unconnected thoughts. I have convinced myself, too, that it would not be overly vain or confident to imagine he regards me differently than your average soldier of the Legion. When I stop and consider the matter, I feel sure there has always been something between us beyond what the circumstances called for, something unique to us. I thought I might like to find out what that was. But not anymore. I see now that to attempt any such thing would be unwise at best. At worst it would be horribly cruel to everyone involved.

For this reckless wishing of mine, I received a pair of solid knocks, blows I might have withstood were I better prepared. When I saw Naomi in that infirmary, it seemed the entire world had broken in two. I knew well the thrill running through her, the sense of invincibility after a brush with Death. It was how I felt after my first battle. My sister was a soldier now, and all the things I'd wanted for her were so many ashes. And then later Vinneas came and tried to revive that old hope, with all the hope I had for him bound up in it. It was more than I could stand.

It wasn't Vinneas I hated; it was the world. I hated it for being a place where hope was something dangerous and cruel, where anything sweet and bright and good lasts only for a beguiling flash, just long enough to make you want more.

These are not happy thoughts, but now I've had them, at least I can patch myself up and avoid wandering into further danger. I can't stop loving Naomi, or dodge the pain of seeing her grow up too fast, but I can cast off my fantasies of coming home one long-distant day to find her the head of some great household, a grandmother several times over. I can stop wanting things I'll never have and chasing things I'll never get to keep. I can try to forget I ever met anyone like Vinneas.

It all turns out to be easier than I would have thought, for a while anyway. IMEC-1 remains in dire condition, and there is little time to spare for self-pity. Alongside my fellow equites, I work twenty and thirty hours at a stretch. Our island's faculty for altering the laws of nature has been employed to provide a constant supply of daylight, and in that insomniac blur, I can scarcely tell one hour from the next, let alone recall any notions I'd once held out for the future—until one day after a long shift I return to my bunk and find a letter waiting, addressed to me.

I share a room with three other equites of the 126th, but all are so fixed on sleep that the thick envelope sitting atop my pillow goes largely unnoticed. I take it outside to read, prying the seal open with my fingers. It is from Mama. Communication over legionary channels is still restricted to official wartime functions, but somehow she has found a way to get this message to me, sending her love and news from all our friends, written out cleanly in her careful hand.

Much has transpired since I last had word of my coda. Jenny Sullivan has had her baby, a boy she named for his grandfather. The decision raised some eyebrows, as Marcus Sullivan was a lifelong reprobate and in the opinion of many should not be leaving namesakes. Meanwhile, Chloe Hollis, cousin to Naomi and me, has finally decided to marry and brought a hefty slice of her new husband's family with him into our coda, which has required adjustment in certain quarters. I am assured any brawls that have broken out were civil, restricted to fisticuffs only, with guns and knives never coming into play. Most significant of all, we have left the township of Granite Shore and are presently engaged in establishing a permanent settlement of our own. The site is none other than the Valley of Endless Summer. As yet we have hardly more than a few foundations, but Mama reports swift progress, as well as sightings of wild horses in the countryside that could provide us a new riding stock. The letter concludes with an invitation to come and visit, once I and the other Walkers of the Legion are allowed enough leave from our duties to make the journey.

I read the letter twice through, then stand there, holding it and think-ing of all these people I used to know, off in their new home. I try to picture myself among those young families and fresh houses, or out chas-ing mustangs through the valley. What comes instead is a view of the Great Ridge and the spine of snow-covered mountains, and one thought: A coda that has ceased wandering has no need for scouts. I shut my eyes and try again, bearing down hard on my imagination, and suddenly I hear a burst of air and look to see the letter has caught fire in my hands.

In half a second all that remains is a shower of ashes and a single scrap of paper pinched between my fingers, which likewise vanishes in a puff of flame as soon as I let it loose. The bits of ash float away, borne off by a small current of air, and I watch them, thinking, *Good. That's the end of that.* I wipe my smudged hands on my uniform and go to get ready for bed.

The incineration of Mama's letter seems to me a definitive conclusion of the matter, and I put it out of my mind. It does not occur to me that this might be premature until some days later, and by then, Reaper Thom Mancebo is at my door.

He comes knocking in what, for me at least, amounts to the middle of the night. I am awakened by a startled shriek to find Haiyalaiya, who usually occupies the bunk above mine, standing at our open door with the sinister apparition of Thom before her. Though the room is dark, and it seems impossible Thom could see anything inside from his place in the hallway, I have the impression he has already picked me out.

Haiyalaiya has gotten over the shock of Thom's arrival and begun demanding his name and rank and intentions banging on the doors of tired legionaries attempting to get some much-needed shut-eye.

"It's all right, Endie," I say, joining Haiyalaiya at the door and using her equus-derived nickname as a gesture of informality. "He's a friend."

Haiyalaiya appears dubious but doesn't argue, preferring to get back to the business of sleeping. I join Thom in the hall, which is busy with groggy-eyed legionaries on the way to and from long, laborious shifts. "What is it, Thom?" I ask tiredly.

As an answer, Thom fixes me with his steady marksman's stare. Thom and I do not need to speak to make ourselves understood, and I know right then he's found out about the letter; what I can't puzzle out is how. I get my answer, or part of it, a moment later, when Thom produces the letter itself, the ashes reassembled and held together by some manner of artifice. It looks like a reverse of itself, the paper ash-black and the written words white, but it's Mama's letter all right.

"Where'd you get that?" I ask. Thom only goes on watching me, not accusing, but full of reproof. "Look," I say irritably, "it was an accident. I didn't mean to torch the damn thing. It just happened."

Thom does nothing to indicate he believes or disbelieves, or has even heard what I've said. His gaze doesn't waver, and its steadiness keeps pulling words out of me. "No, I wasn't going to tell you about it," I grumble. Now that I've been caught, I'm turning cranky and sullen. "I'm sorry I burned it, all right? But it's done, and Mama would have sent another eventually." And then I add, "Anyway, I'm not going."

At this Thom folds the magically reconstituted letter and places it in his jacket, then returns to staring, still manifestly unsatisfied with my accounting of things.

"You do what you want," I snap. "I won't be flying all the way to that valley just to see a few half-built houses."

Again no answer from Thom. It seems I am speaking to a statue set in a pose of eternal questioning. I've had about enough of it. "Because, Thom," I say hotly, "it'd be a great big waste of time. Mama and Baby and everyone will want to see this place, too, right? So let them all come here if they want to say good-bye. I don't need to get settled in with everyone, then just turn around and leave again. There's no goddamn point."

My voice breaks then, and I have to shut myself up. The last time Reaper Thom saw me cry, he was pulling a bullet from my gut with a pair of pliers, and I don't want to soil my record.

Thom, for his part, seems finally to have heard me. He frowns and slowly nods, like he's been listening to a story he already knows by heart and only needed to remind himself of the last few details. "Follow me," he says, and sets off down the hall without further explanation.

I would much rather go back to bed, but I feel now I need to prove something, to myself if not Thom, who is generally immune to rhetorical displays. So I follow. It turns out we don't have far to go.

The place Thom has in mind is the School of Rhetoric, a short walk from my quarters, since like most cadets newly enlisted in the Legion, I have been billeted in the Academy itself. I make an unusual sight travers-ing the halls in my standard-issue sleeping gear, however, and soon the odd looks begin to wear on me. I am on the verge of mutiny, of demanding to know why we're here and what could be so important that it was worth depriving me of sleep, when Thom stops in his tracks, a hand raised for silence. At first all I hear is the babble of voices and shuffle of footsteps, but then something else comes lacing toward me. Music.

Music is perhaps a generous description; more accurately it is a feral screeching fit to wake the dead. But it is also a sound I will forever associate with melody: the sound of a fiddle. Thom waits until he is sure I've heard, then continues onward. I go with him, curious to learn the player's identity, but also drawn by something deeper and older.

The perpetrator of this particular racket is Fontanus Jaxten, as I discover when the noise ceases with a screech, and from a classroom up ahead, his voice emerges. "I suck at this," Jax declares. "I totally, completely suck."

The next voice kicks my heart into a clumsy lurch. Naomi. "You've barely even tried," she says.

"Well, it's obvious how much I suck," Jax insists. "You heard it, too, right?"

"You were the one who wanted to learn." Naomi's tones are heavy with exasperation. "And first you've got to hold it right. Give it here. I'll show you."

The tune that begins then is one I've heard a thousand times, and I can truthfully say I have never known anything so beautiful. Thom has halted a little past the classroom door, the light from inside falling just short of his face. He motions for me to join him, the way he would out in the woods if he'd spotted some spectacular bird and wanted me to see without startling it off.

I peer inside. There is Jax, sitting atop a desk and frowning in concentration, and beside him Naomi, Papa's fiddle on her arm.

"She's good," Thom says, low enough that even I can hardly hear him. "You were, too."

"No I wasn't," I say.

He laughs softly. "No, not so good. But you liked it. You shouldn't have stopped."

That last part is true enough. I never had talent the way Naomi does, but I have loved the sound of the fiddle ever since I was young, and when I played, I put my heart into it. But after I began scouting, there was never any time—I was either riding or too tired from it to play. Nearly two years went by before I decided I was in desperate need of practice, but when I finally got hold of a fiddle, somehow playing didn't seem worthwhile anymore.

I suppose that was about the time I had my first good long look at the road ahead of me. What I saw was no place for fiddling. I thought it would be the same for Naomi, that going to war would cut her off from the girl she was before. But seeing her now, hearing her play, I know that isn't so. She's still Naomi, still my solemn, thorny, wonderful little sister. And she's stronger than I am, strong enough to become a warrior without losing herself to it.

"You may get rusty," Thom says, "but you never forget."

Our eyes meet just long enough for me to understand why it was Thom brought me here: to show me that, despite everything I feared for her, Naomi would be all right. Naomi, and maybe me as well.

Suddenly, the music breaks off, strings squeaking. "Who's there?" Naomi calls. "Rae?"

"Hey there!" I say, sidling to the doorway, guilt written all over me.

My sister takes me in, eyes narrowing. "What are you doing here?"

"Oh, just out for a walk."

"You are wearing your pajamas." Naomi's tone indicates she considers such behavior improper but not out of character for me.

"I was with Thom," I begin, only to discover the subject of my half-formed excuse has become a distant figure fast disappearing into the Academy's crowded labyrinths.

"Is something wrong?" Naomi asks, eyeing me more carefully now. "Did something happen?" An odd look has come over her, familiar and disorienting at once. It takes me a second to recognize it as the same fear I feel whenever Naomi herself is in danger. She has added up my abrupt arrival, my disheveled appearance, my overall state of confusion, and assumed terrible things have befallen people she loves.

"No, no," I say. "No, Sunshine, nothing like that. It's all good news. We've had a letter from Mama."

SIXTY-THREE

VINNEAS

'm only an hour or so late to the party—well in time for the official send-off of our expeditionary force—even if from my perspective it's been more than three days since the whole celebration began. IMEC-1 was fully restored and furbished for its mission well before the Consulate and the Legion's upper echelons had attended to all the crucial executive decision-making necessary for that mission to begin, and so they decided to just go forward with the launch and catch up with everyone later. Boredom is a great enemy of armies, deadly as any salivating alien horde, and there seemed no point in making the whole expeditionary force—nearly half our remaining military, along with certain academics and other special-ized passengers—wait around while a few stuffy bureaucrats went about their stuffy business. Far better to let our heroes fly ahead to Dis, where hours and hours of tedious administrative chores on Earth would pass in the time it took to pop a few champagne corks. It was the right idea, undoubtedly. I only wish one of the stuffy bureaucrats wading through those hours and hours of tedious administrative chores wasn't me.

One benefit of staring extinction in the face is that it has finally shaken us from a few of the more entrenched and dogmatic policies we've assumed over the past few centuries—among them, our long-standing campaign of duplicity and misinformation among the settlements. Preparing Earth to repel the next wave of invasion will require the complete and combined efforts of everyone on the planet, and it was decided the best way to secure the necessary level of cooperation would be to finally bring the settlements in on the full truth about our war. Part of me will be sorry to miss what may be the greatest overhaul to society since the establishment of the Principates, but the rest is just glad to be spared the hassle of sorting through the bedlam that will doubtless become a worldwide reality for much of the near future. What the end result will look like, I can't say, but if we of the MapleWhite Campaign ever do make it back to Earth, I expect we'll find it a very different place from the one we left behind.

It's been just under six weeks, or roughly forty hours—depending on whether you're counting time in Hestia or Dis—since the first wave of the great Valentine Host was finally dispersed. In that time, we've set into motion the machinery that will, if all goes according to plan, yield a fully restored Legion in under twenty years' time, and successfully rebuilt our flying city—a process that involved a deal more actual building than getting it airborne in the first place—with a few notable improvements. Even Kizabel, who violently denies the merest suggestion that her baby could ever have been flawed in any way, will admit the restored version may possibly be *more* perfect than before.

Sorting through the aftermath of the battle wasn't easy, not by any means. There were too many losses we simply couldn't repair or replace. I can say with confidence that reviewing the casualty reports for the encounter at Dis was the worst experience of my life. I knew, intellectually, that we lost even more people during the opening attack, when the Valentines had a clear shot at our cities and settlements, and I understood the toll would have been incalculably greater had we evacuated as Feeroy proposed. But even so. This was the one scenario in which people died as a direct result of my actions. Staying to defend Earth was my idea; if it weren't for me, it's likely this battle would never have happened. Meaning that, in a very real sense, each of those lost lives is on me.

I can't help thinking how many might have been saved if only I'd been a little smarter, acted a little faster, planned a little better, worked a little harder. I tell myself the Valentines were always the aggressors, that I did only what was necessary for our survival, that every life lost should only motivate me further to end this war any way I can. But there are still days when it seems nothing can justify something so destructive, days when it feels like I've left a gaping wound in the universe, a crater in reality, that will never heal no matter what I do.

And then there are days like this one.

The festivities awaiting me, which began three days ago in Hestia and have been continuing in Dis for a matter of hours, are part victory celebration, part memorial service, part *bon voyage* party, all wrapped up in a careful schedule of elaborate meals, inspirational speeches, moments of silence, congratulatory toasts, and assorted binge drinking, culminating in a rousing valediction to Earth as our expeditionary force begins its heroic mission to close our home off from the rest of the Realms.

But as the velo I'm riding passes through Lunar Veil into Dis, at the rear of a formation carrying the last of the officers who so selflessly delayed their participation in this momentous event, it's apparent those already at the celebration couldn't wait for the show to begin. Even from this distance, splashes of light and color—all impromptu artifices, by the look of them— can be seen spattering like raindrops across the bubble of atmosphere surrounding IMEC-1.

Or perhaps I should say "the Keep," as people have popularly come to refer to our expeditionary city. I haven't yet discovered the origin of this *nom de guerre*, but there's little question it has become so ubiquitous over the past month as to replace the official designation of IMEC-1 in all but the most formal and technical contexts—much to the chagrin of Kizabel, who considers her presence one such formal and technical context.

To see it now, with its gaily illuminated buildings and streets brimming with revelers, its lush forests and pristine lakes, you'd never guess that only two days ago, local time, the Keep was a virtual ruin, a confusion of rubble and wreckage. In fact, if it weren't for the arrays of towering City Guns and toothy battle spires scattered across its surface, one could easily mistake the Keep for a perfectly ordinary, peaceful, everyday flying city.

Mine is the last velo to land, lowering onto a wide grassy lawn in the Academy's outer courtyards. I join a line of officers filing inside, where Dux Feeroy waits to greet me with one of his signature noncommittal nods. I'm almost certain he still despises me, but it wouldn't be politic to let his dislike show, seeing as he and I are widely viewed as the heroic duo that rescued the Legion from the brink of devastating defeat.

As commander of the reserve, Feeroy was the natural audience for my budding thoughts on worst-case scenarios, but more importantly, he was the only one who would even pretend to listen. I'd already approached— or tried to approach—every superior officer from Reydaan on down, and no few subordinates as well. None wanted anything to do with me or my worries over problems it was too late to fix. I was informed—with such consistency that I began to wonder whether there had been some kind of internal memo on the subject of never even contemplating retreat—that what mattered now was winning this battle, not what would happen if we lost, and anyway, weren't contingency plans a matter for the reserves?

The plan I had in mind wasn't perfect—in fact it was flawed in more ways than I cared to count—but it was better than nothing, which was what we had until then, and it was simple enough to implement. Most importantly—as far as anyone in the Legion is concerned, anyway—it worked, and far better than I could have hoped. The Valentines took some pretty extreme risks trying to capitalize on their advantage after IMEC-1 went dark, and when our guns came back online, large portions of their forces were caught out in the open. Faced with already heavy losses, they chose to retreat rather than risk annihilation. As a result of this stunning reversal, and also because almost no one in Command took any interest in my last-minute preparations, Feeroy and I were both left looking pretty good once all the smoke had cleared. Feeroy, along with the rest of Command, was perfectly happy to ignore the fact that the only reason any of us are still alive is that the evacuation force disregarded orders and joined the battle, but that doesn't keep him from blaming me personally for their insubordination.

While I'd like to believe Feeroy's loathing of me is a loathing tempered with respect, the best I've seen thus far has been cool indifference with a hint of contempt—all of which can be awkward, since I'm now part of his advisory staff. Another bit of administrative business that needed to be taken care of before we left was my latest promotion. I am now Legatus Vinneas, head of Ninth Legion's Fourteenth Cohort. Not bad for a legionary whose only discernible duty during the last engagement was self-appointed worrier.

When I request permission to be excused from the officers' banquet slated to follow this evening's closing of Lunar Veil, Feeroy consents with lordly indifference. What I do with myself is beneath his interest, is his stance, though he doesn't pass up the opportunity to get rid of me as soon as possible. "You may want to watch the closing someplace other than the Dominium," he says, referring to the building formerly known as the Hall of the Principate, now home to the offices of Dominus Reydaan, the Keep's supreme commander. "The crowds will make it difficult to slip away afterward."

"My thoughts exactly," I say, saluting. "Thank you, sir."

When I was at the Academy, we would occasionally form classes up at the Forum for review, and it always felt like the place was so big, you could keep adding cadets forever and never run out of space. But today, the great stone plaza is overflowing from every side, and the crowd becomes denser the farther you go. The Legion domiciled on the Keep is now comprised of four full Legions—the Second, the Sixth, the Tenth, and, of course, the Ninth, each supplemented with reinforcements from the others remaining behind—and it feels like each and every one of those legionaries must be wedged in here with me.

I try to make my way without accidentally bumping anyone or treading on the multitude of toes crisscrossing beneath me like roots in an especially overgrown forest, though it quickly becomes apparent most people neither notice nor care when I blunder into them. The noise is fantastic, shouts and laughter punctuating the general human babble and the pervasive swell of music—that truly dreadful stuff always commissioned for official events.

The Font of the Principate—Old Fife, that is—looms tall over the sea of dimly lit faces, itself covered in the shadowy figures of legionaries stacked into a teetering tower silhouetted against the subtly starry sky, pouring down cheers of triumph at having climbed so high. Here and there at random, artifices pop upward with sparkling loops and darts, then bloom into pearls and blossoms of luminescence that shimmer a moment and disperse into the expanse of stars, sometimes leaving behind a sharp bang or prolonged howl and a scattering of excited applause.

It takes me nearly half an hour, but eventually I work my way around the stage erected outside the Dominium and duck into the long passageway leading beneath—the same trip I used to make during every atmospheric incursion, back when I was still with the Academy and this place was still the Hall of the Principate. Sounds from the Forum echo with a weird, eerie ebb and flow, then fade almost completely as I emerge onto the balcony on the opposite side.

It's certainly crowded, but not nearly so much as Curator Ellmore—or I—expected. I realize the odd sensation I experienced in the passageway must have been an artifice erected to discourage unwanted guests from finding their way out here; though whether it was put in place by the people on this balcony or the officers who will be enjoying their banquet on another patio above us—and no doubt would prefer to be spared the drunken shouting of common legionaries—I don't know.

No sooner have I stepped out from the tunnel than one of the figures gathered along the balustrade shouts, "Vinn, is that you? I thought I smelled you over there!"

The voice belongs to Imway, who greets me with an enthusiastic and slightly inebriated embrace. "Nicely done, Vinn!" he says, sniffing me for comic effect. "Been celebrating without us? You smell like you've finished two bottles of aquavee and taken a bath in a third. Better hope no one from Command sees you like that!" The joke being, of course, that I'm someone from Command.

"A drink or two may have spilled on me while I was en route," I concede.

"The trick is to get the drink into your mouth first," Imway tells me sagely. "Here, I'll arrange a demonstration so you can get an idea of the fundamentals."

He slaps a hand onto my shoulder, guiding me toward the waiting group of legionaries. Most of them are holding small silver cups, though I notice a few have dropped theirs to stand at attention, a hint of unease in their postures.

Fortunately, Imway and his escadrille have all known me long enough that their first instinct is to punch me in the shoulder rather than salute, and soon everyone else is following their example of informality, my new rank—still only a few hours old, as far as anyone present is concerned—mostly forgotten. The 126th is all here, and they know that's something worth celebrating: Very few fighting units made it out of the battle so completely intact. As I share hugs and toasts and slaps on the back, however, I notice one eques is conspicuously absent.

"Rae's down in the city somewhere," Kizabel says, apparently having noticed me searching the little crowd on the balcony and made an unnervingly accurate intuitive leap. She, too, has brought a group with her—most of them new faces I assume are gun-mates from her stint as an artillery-woman. "She went to check on her sister. Said she'd stop by a little later."

"Sure, excellent," I say, trying not to sound disappointed. By the knowing smirk on Kizabel's face, it's plain she isn't fooled one bit. "It's just that I've hardly seen her since we went back to Earth," I explain lamely.

Kizabel and I worked together closely while the Keep was under repairs, but in all that time, I barely had more than a glimpse of Rae, mostly at the Stabulum, where Snuggles was undergoing painstaking restoration. Re-restoration, rather. Kizabel was less than satisfied with the repair team's initial efforts and insisted on rebuilding everything herself. All company other than Rae could expect to be chased off in a hail of execration and dented machine parts. I'll admit to being more than slightly jealous that an equus had more visits from Rae than I did but also somewhat relieved. I did something to offend her sometime in the recent past, but because I haven't figured out what or when, my attempts to fix things have relied on reasoning that amounts to little better than random guessing. I'm a bit afraid to find out whether I still rate as scum. I put my chances of success at around one in twenty.

"Oh yes, absolutely," Kizabel answers, now grinning openly. "Well, you're trapped on a floating island together, so odds are you'll run into each other eventually."

It's an awfully big flying island, big enough that two people might not see one another very often if they don't make a point of it, and I'm about to say as much to Kizabel when I spot Fontanus Jaxten lingering at the edge of the balcony. Recalling the effect distinctions in rank had on this crowd, I opt for a comradely nod of acknowledgment rather than any greeting involving the word "sir."

"Jax!" I call, motioning him over. "Glad you could make it!" I say this even though, in truth, I'm not very glad at all. A significant faction within the leadership—Curator Ellmore among them—believed younger legion-aries ought to be categorically banned from MapleWhite, and while I don't completely agree, I have a hard time justifying the decisions that allowed Jax to take part. Granted, he and Naomi—another of the Legion's youn-gest fontani—were instrumental in our latest victory, defeating a Valen-tine Zero not far from where we're standing now. Jax does look more mature—taller, leaner, with fewer marshmallowy qualities than he had the first time we met, a seeming eternity ago but in reality only a few months—but he's still obviously a child. It may be a simple matter of perspective—no doubt I look as young to Curator Ellmore as Jax does to me—but still. He isn't even thirteen.

Jax's recent experiences have lent him a new self-assurance, and he converses confidently with the older legionaries around him. He is remark-ably well informed on military politics and seems particularly interested in my opinions regarding how the Keep will perform in the likely event of a second engagement with the enemy during our upcoming mission. When Kizabel launches into her by-now-familiar tirade on the churlish popular habit of referring to IMEC-1 as "the Keep," he comforts her in a way that implies a shared understanding of humanity's natural ingratitude. We haven't been talking long, however, before he asks me for the time.

"I should go," he says, after I've fished out my watch and showed it to him. "I told Naomi I'd watch the closing with her."

The closing of Lunar Veil will mark the official end of our victory party and the beginning of our mission into the Realms—though I have no doubt the general celebration will continue in an unofficial capacity for some time afterward. Already, the Anchors holding Lunar Veil open have been disabled, and soon the Veil will collapse, sealing us off from Hestia. A moment before that happens, however, there will be a flash on the Veil, giving everyone gathered across the Keep one final glimpse of Earth.

"Did they cancel Reydaan's speech?" I ask. The flash is supposed to coincide with the climax of a laudatory homily from Dominus Reydaan, but my watch tells me we're only minutes away from our big farewell, and I have yet to hear a peep from the Dominus.

"It's been going on for a while," Jax says. He indicates the corridor leading out to the Forum, and I recognize the faint whisper of Reydaan's voice echoing through. Whatever artifice has sealed us off from the Forum must also be blocking most of the speech; fine by me, since I've proofread the thing enough times to know we're not missing much.

Kizabel, who has drunk a little more than is good for her, begins teasing Jax about preferring the company of a female over that of his old and loyal friends. Having been on the wrong side of Kizabel's teasing myself, I decide to intervene. "See you later, Jax. Say hello to Naomi for us."

Jax gives me a grateful look. Kizabel, by way of adieu, shouts at him, "And tell Rae she needs to stop prancing around the city and get over here!" I can't be sure, but Kizabel seems to have intended this comment more for me than either Jax or Rae. There are a few snickers, but Jax simply nods, as though in confirmation of an order, and vanishes, leaving only a puff of air and a hiss of static.

"Fontani," Kizabel muses wonderingly, while along the balcony people holler with drunken approval of the display. "What I wouldn't give to be able to do that."

"It would make life more convenient," I agree. As if in illustration, the air crackles again, rushing this time like a miniature tornado. The sound of howling wind is quickly replaced with an excited whoop, followed by delighted laughter, as of someone who has received a startling but not unwelcome surprise.

Rae has appeared out of thin air, not much more than an arm's length away. It turns out Jax delivered Kizabel's message as instructed, then took the extra step of bringing Rae directly to our balcony. I'm not sure if he did this out of courtesy or as part of some treacherous conspiracy with Kizabel, and I don't particularly care. Either way, it means Rae is here.

Kizabel's reaction leads me to suspect collusion on some level: She's the first to respond to Rae's arrival and gives the strong impression of not being taken entirely unawares. Her greeting consists of a broadside tackle, which Rae absorbs easily, squeezing her arms around Kizabel's shoulders and lifting her several centimeters off the ground, the two of them cackling maniacally over what can only be some inside joke between them.

The full roster of the 126th Equites is next to crowd around, jostling in with boastful salutations, hearty embraces, and sloshing cups of aquavee. I am at once stunned and unsurprised to see Kizabel directly in the middle of it, trading backslaps and good-natured verbal abuse, a head shorter than anyone else but solidly holding her own. There was some tension between Kiz and the 126th a while back, a falling-out in which Rae, if I recall correctly, played a supporting role, but it looks now as if all unpleasantness has been relegated to the world of bygones, brushed away as petty differences tend to be when the world is on the brink of obliteration.

That's my impression, in any case, until Imway wades into the scrum, wearing the magnanimous grin of a host arriving late to his own party. For the most part he is received exactly as his demeanor anticipates, with toasts and clasped hands and loud laughter, but a few steps from the center of the group his gallant warrior's smile abruptly drops, replaced by an expression of confusion and dawning outrage. In the next instant he is all hail-fellow once again, fist raised to accept a cup of aquavee passed his way by shouting comrades, but there remains a slightly petulant set to his jaw, easily missed by anyone who hadn't witnessed this brief interruption to his bonhomie. Of the sight that upset his usually unconquerable confidence,

I've caught only the tail end, but it's telling enough: Kizabel wedging her way from Imway's pack to rejoin her new gunner friends.

So far as I can tell, the only other person who took note of this exchange is Rae. She catches my eye across the crowd and, with a single look, manages to convey not only that, yes, I did in fact just see what I thought I saw, but also that there's a good deal more to the story. Whatever that is will have to wait, however, because several equites of the 126th have taken it upon themselves to include me in the festivities, by force if necessary.

"You do always travel in style," I say to Rae, once her welcoming party has absorbed me fully enough that I can speak to her directly.

The comment is well received among the equites, for whom traveling in style is an occupational ideal. It strikes them as the highest form of praise, inciting a raucous round of toasting "to traveling in style." A bottle of aquavee begins making the rounds, but when it settles in Rae's hands she passes it on without drinking, receding a few quiet steps from the crisscross of laughter and clinking glasses.

"Don't feel like celebrating?" I ask.

"Just the opposite," she says, wiping one laughter-induced tear from the corner of her eye. "Today, I'm doing nothing but."

"I was afraid we wouldn't see you."

She looks over at me, smiling. "Oh, I wore out my welcome pretty quick everywhere else." She glances over toward the other equites, half of whom have, for reasons not entirely apparent, descended into fits of laughter. "I'd have shown up earlier if I'd known what kind of welcome I'd get. Had a notion Sen would want a go at me once she got into the hooch. Thought you'd be gone, too, off in some smoky room somewhere with all the other bigwigs."

"Wore out my welcome," I say with a shrug. And then, carefully, "And you weren't the only one concerned about venturing into dangerous territory."

"Oh?" Eyebrows raised; brown eyes playful. "Dissension in the ranks?"

"No. You."

"Me?" She looks surprised, but that sense of play hasn't totally gone.

"I had this idea you were angry with me."

The expression that crosses her face is one I've never seen on Rae. I'm not entirely sure, but I think it could be embarrassment. "I did, too," she says. "But I wasn't. I was angry, and you were there. It looks the same from a lot of angles." Rae shakes her head as though clearing away a thought. "It wasn't your fault. I was just so goddamn tired of good-byes."

This more to herself than me. I think I know what she means, but I can't imagine any way to tell her so without sounding like an idiot. Claiming I understand even a tiny part of what Rae has been through could very well be the biggest lie I've ever told. I rack my brain for the right thing to say, trying to spot the potential pitfalls, to chart a way through. But my only certainty is that Rae is a spoiler of strategy.

I'm saved from just blurting some clumsy, half-formed reassurance when the light all across the Keep—from the twilight sheen of the sky to the ambient illumination glowing around our balcony's edges—begins to pulse, first welling up so that every shadow and crevice is momentarily filled, then dimming almost to blackness. The same thing is happening everywhere on IMEC-1, I know; it's the call for our attention. On the third ebb, the lights stay down, putting the dark sky of Dis and its great catalogue of stars on full display. The music coming from the Forum has stopped, I realize. Reydaan must have finished his speech. Laughter and applause flicker back and forth over the city in the gathering quiet. The grand finale is about to begin.

Suddenly, the Earth is there, a blue-white balloon of oceans and swirling clouds. It's about the size the Moon appears back home, the slightest crescent slice peeled off from one end. It reflects a pale aquamarine down onto the city, the light shining on the upturned faces looking back. The nascent pockets of cheering around us fade out, and for a second or two, everything is totally silent.

If Rae is not in the mood for good-byes, she won't enjoy this next part.

I'm going to say something, ask if she wants to sneak into a smoke-filled room of bigwigs with me, or just grab her and drag her back to the Forum, anything so she won't have to watch her home disappear, but before the impulse can gather into action, I feel something press against my hand. It's only a brief touch—her palm against mine, the pressure light but firm—but the message it carries is clearer and more powerful than anything I could have thought to say or do. The simple communication of a single, pure idea: possibility.

My first indication that the show is over, the ceremonies officially at an end, is the sound of wild cheering all around. I get the feeling it's been rising steadily for some time. I'm still looking toward the sky, but when I search the spot where our little blue planet had been, I see only a scattering of foreign stars. Earth has come and gone, and we're on our way.

"Don't worry," Rae says, leaning close to be heard over the sounds of celebration. "It'll be there when we get back."

□————————□

SIXTY-FOUR

TORRO

I'm still here. Sometimes I don't totally believe it, even though it's obviously true. Like maybe there was some mistake or something. For one thing, only about half of us from Twelfth made it out of the Battle of Dis alive. That attack on the ratters was what did it, though if you'd asked me right before we launched off after those nests, I'd have said we were *all* about to get blued, not just like 50 percent of us. Maybe that's why everybody from the Legion was so impressed with us afterward—because we'd charged in knowing we had basically no chance at all. Really, though, I wasn't thinking about whether we were going to die. I was mostly just thinking about jumping off that stupid platform. A lot of people from Twelfth say the same thing. And it wasn't like we could have run away or anything. There wasn't much of anywhere to run to.

But, anyway, we all got this big unit citation for valor and gallantry and so forth, the whole Third Cohort, Twelfth Century, I mean. I got the feeling that if you'd been in the Legion a long time, you'd be pretty thrilled to get an award like that, but most of us in Twelfth had never even heard of it. Generally, we were just glad to be alive, the ones who made it back. In fact, the only person I know who'd have been all that thrilled to get an award for gallantry is dead, which as it turns out means he got even *more* awards than anybody. That doesn't make him any less dead, though.

Optio Sorril told us we could take Mersh home if we wanted, me and Hexi and Spammers. I was pretty surprised she even knew the four of us were all chummies. Like, it was obvious we'd all been called up together and everything, since we came in on the same train from old S-225, but there were about a hundred other people on there with us, and somehow Sorril figured out we were the ones to ask if she ought to send him back.

That was what she meant by "home." Old Granite Shore. We talked about it, though, and we decided it wasn't such a good idea. Out of all of us, Mersh was the only one who actually wanted to leave in the first place.

What we couldn't agree on was what to do instead. Spammers didn't want to do anything at all. He said Mersh was gone, and it didn't matter what happened to whatever part was left over. As far as he cared, the Legion could just do whatever it did with everyone else it'd gotten killed. That made Hexi pretty furious. She said Mersh was our friend, not some pile of trash, and it was up to us to do what he would have wanted, and Spammers would have known that if he wasn't such an insensitive turd. I kind of agreed with both of them. Like, Mersh was dead, so he probably didn't care what happened to him anymore, but I didn't want to just leave him with the Legion, either. Also, Spammers really *was* being a turd. The weird thing was, it turned out he and Hex could both have it their way.

We all agreed that if Mersh was going to plan his own funeral, he'd want something big and heroic, and when I asked Optio Sorril about it, I found out that was basically what the Legion was doing for *everyone*. It didn't matter if you'd died fighting off ten million Valentines or two seconds into the battle of a heart attack or like severely impacted bowels or whatever, you were still a hero getting a hero's funeral. Spammers tried to talk us out of it at first. I don't know who he was madder at: the Legion for acting like making a big deal over a bunch of dead people would make up for them being dead, or Mersh, because he really would have just loved the whole sappy thing. Even Spams had to admit it was a pretty impressive affair, though.

It was the first thing we did after the Keep took off from Earth. They had everyone go over to Green Side, because that had the most open space for people to spread out. Green really does feel a little like being out in the wilderness somewhere, with all the trees and lakes and everything, especially since most of the taller buildings are on Red Side, so they're completely out of sight. When we were all there, out in the middle of the woods, all these Legion people started making speeches one after the other about how brave we all were and everything, but especially those who like sacrificed themselves so humanity could live on. All strictly crap, of course. I mean, I'd been in the battle. I knew I wasn't all that brave, and I *definitely* wasn't sacrificing myself for humanity. The only reason I didn't die was that I was *lucky*. The rescue people said if the cuts they found in my D-87s had been any deeper, I would have been blued right along with Mersh, and I doubt that would have made me any braver. What those legionary guys said wasn't all that bad, though. I know Mersh would have liked it.

Once the speeches were done, they let everyone who'd died just float away into space. That morning, me and Hexi'd gone to pick up what was left of Mersh, which turned out to be just ashes in a little stone container, kind of a tube with a raindrop-shaped bead at each end. I should have expected that, since they cremated dead people back in Settlement 225, too, but for some reason I'd thought we'd see Mersh just how they found him. I was pretty glad we didn't. After those skirmer Type 3s got hold of him, there wasn't much left. Spammers says old Mersh came back in three different pieces, and not very big ones, either. This little stone thing was a lot better, real clean and nice-looking and so forth.

We'd given the tube with Mersh in it to Hexi before all the speeches started, and when the last speech was over, the raindrop-shaped beads started to glow, and the thing just lifted out of her hand. It was happening to other tubes all over Green Side, too, and pretty soon there were all these lights rising up above the trees. I couldn't believe how many there were. It was very pretty to look at, but also really awful, if you thought about it for even a second. Every one of those lights had been a person, maybe someone who'd been dragged out of some settlement somewhere and sent off to fight and just wasn't lucky enough to make it out alive.

The tubes kept floating up and up, swirling like some big, glowing river, until finally they just faded away. What really happened was they'd passed out of the umbris surrounding the Keep, so there was no thelemity to make them glow. They were all still out there, floating on their own now. They'd keep going around and around Earth, maybe for hundreds or thousands of years, maybe forever, or maybe they'd eventually fall down into the atmosphere and burn up.

It left me with this crazy feeling, when the lights were gone and there were just the stars and Earth hanging there with just one little sliver missing. I didn't start crying, the way a lot of people did. I was sad, sure. But everything bad that would ever happen to the people in those tubes had already happened. I was feeling sorry for myself, probably. It was dumb, I know. I mean, I was still alive, right? But that was how I felt.

When the lights were gone, people started heading over to Red Side, because there was going to be a huge party at the Forum to celebrate winning the Battle of Dis. Hexi wanted to stay behind for a while, to just sit around and tell stories about Mersh, but Spammers said he'd had enough of this remembering crap, and now he wanted to get drunk. And the truth was, me and Hexi were in the mood to get drunk, too, or at least Hexi was. So we all went to Red Side, and Hexi got one sip of aquavee and started telling stories anyway, and Spams joined in eventually. They looked like they were having fun, but I just started feeling weird and a little sick.

I think I was the only person who even noticed when we finally left Hestia. We'd only been at the Forum a little while, maybe an hour. They had practically everything you could think of to eat and drink, and people were going a little berserk. I think they were all just happy to be alive, especially after that memorial thing with the lights. Hexi had given up on the stories and was just showing off her arm to anyone who would look. It'd been cut off just below the elbow after we blew up that nest, but once they got her to the infirmary, it only took a few days to grow back. She said it still sort of tingled sometimes, but the pink, shiny look it had at first was almost gone, and you could barely see the whitish line where her D-87s had sealed the skin over to stop her from bleeding to death. She kept saying, "It still looks better than beet juice!" and punching me with her new hand. It was funny, I guess. At some point, though, I noticed the stars overhead starting to swim around, and when they stopped, they weren't the stars you'd see from Earth anymore. They were the stars in Dis.

I used to think stars were stars, just tiny glowing dots and whatnot, and I couldn't believe how *different* these were. I tried to point it out to Hexi, but she only kept punching me. It was like no one cared except me. And then I started to feel real sick, like if I didn't get out of there right away, I'd puke. I felt like I was back at Limit Camp, running some topsy-turvy obstacle course, and I couldn't tell which way was up.

I'm almost to the edge of the Forum when someone grabs me by the arm. I'm sort of upset, because I'm still feeling pretty lousy, and I thought I'd gotten away without anyone noticing, and I kind of shove back before I realize the person grabbing me is Optio Sorril. I don't know where she came from, but she isn't happy about getting shoved. I give her the old salute, and say, "Sorry, ma'am. I didn't know it was you."

"Not a problem, Miles," she says. "We've all been on edge the past few weeks. That's what tonight is for, though I'm afraid some of us are already celebrating rather too much." She means everyone around here getting blind drunk, I can tell. I'm probably not the first one today to shove her by accident. "And I have the sense some aren't celebrating quite enough."

"I don't really feel like it, I guess, ma'am."

Old Sorril nods slowly. "It's not too late to change your mind, Torro. I can have a velo ready in ten minutes to take you back to Earth."

Mersh wasn't the only guy from Settlement 225 who had the chance to go home. The day after I got out of the infirmary, Optio Sorril called me to her office. I'd been in there almost a week, way longer than I needed to be. I wasn't even all that hurt. A few patches of skin had gotten messed up from being exposed to outer space, which was easy to fix, but I'd been low on oxygen for a while, so they made me wait around to be sure I didn't have any like permanent brain damage. Anyway, old Sorril and me chatted for a while, then she asked me if I'd like to go back to Granite Shore. I thought she meant with Mersh, to take him home and everything, and I told her me and Hex and Spammers had already decided we weren't going to do that. But that wasn't what she meant. Old Sorril was offering to send me back for good.

The Legion was trying to change the way it managed relations with its settlements, was how old Sorril put it. If we wanted to build a Legion strong enough to fight off the Valentines, we'd need everyone cooperating as much as possible, and the Legion had decided the best way to do that, to like get everyone on the same side, was to be totally honest about the war. They were going to tell the settlements everything—about the Valentines, thelemity, the whole deal. And they figured all of that would sound a lot less like abominably insane if people heard it from someone they knew, so they were looking for legionaries they could send back to their old settlements to explain things. If I wanted, I could be the guy for S-225, what Sorril called a "liaison." She said I'd be good at it because I was so empathetic and personable and whatnot.

It actually sounded like a pretty good deal. All I had to do was tell everyone on Granite Shore how this crazy, made-up-sounding stuff the Prips were feeding them wasn't a complete and total lie, and maybe demonstrate thelemity by showing off with lazels and trenchers and so forth. And since I'd be an officer in the Legion, I'd outrank all the local authorities. I wouldn't have to worry about Qu or Ghalo. I could order around that fathead Gemt whenever I wanted. I could even get Cranely for what he did to me. And I could be with Camareen. Sorril didn't come out and say all that, but she let me know I could kind of pick up where I'd left off. And after ten years, I could choose to stay in the Legion or go and do whatever I wanted. Deals don't get much better than that.

I turned her down, though. I knew even before she finished talking that I wasn't going to do it. I wanted to go home more than I'd ever wanted anything. It was just that I couldn't, not when everyone else was going off to fight. It's crazy, I know. If I'd asked Hexi or Spammers, or anyone from Twelfth, they would have told me to go. I could have said, "Listen up, kiddos, I'm going home to Granite Shore, good luck with the war and everything," and they would have thought that was just great. They'd have been *happy* for me. But I still couldn't do it, and I can't leave now, either.

I tell Sorril thanks, but I'm part of the Keep, and that's all there is to it. I think she understands, the same way Hexi and Spammers would've if I'd gone. She'd have been glad to see one of us get out, but she knows why I can't. As I'm leaving, she says, "Well, Miles. It seems you turned out to be a volunteer after all."

SIXTY-FIVE

TORRO

After that, I just kind of wander around. It's about the first time I've been in the city when I wasn't doing some kind of work. I got put on repair duty approximately five seconds after I'd finished up my meeting with old Sorril, and from there it was pretty much nonstop until now. It feels nice, walking up and down the empty streets.

The streets aren't *totally* empty, I suppose. Now and then, I see someone walking up ahead, or down some alley or something. They're probably people like me, people who didn't want to be at the Forum. I never say anything. I just let them go by. The city is real quiet and peaceful, and I don't want to mess that up. It doesn't even seem like someplace people built—more like people haven't even discovered it yet. Like a deep, dried-out riverbed with high stone walls. You can still hear everyone at the Forum cheering like crazy, but it seems far away.

At some point, though, I hear music coming from somewhere. It isn't that awful Prip music Camareen hated so much, with all the drums and cymbals and whatnot. It's one small little sound, playing a pretty happy little tune that makes me think of something running and dancing. I follow it until I get to a sort of square, where a whole bunch of people are sitting and standing around listening to the music. And right there in the middle is little Naomi, playing.

This isn't the first time I've heard bivvie music. Sometimes when their caravans came through Settlement 225, a few of them would play for us. The best music, though, was what you'd hear at night, coming from their camp. Every so often, Camareen would take me to listen. We'd have to sneak out and like hide in a field so the bivvies wouldn't see us, but it was always worth it. And that's the kind of music Naomi's playing now, the kind the bivvies played for themselves.

I'm imagining Camareen being here, how happy it would have made her to hear this music, when suddenly I get this idea that I'm thinking about Camareen the same way I was thinking about Mersh. What she *would* have liked. Like Camareen is dead, too. And even though she's just fine back on Granite Shore, it's still like she's gone forever because I know I'll never see her again, not unless she lives to be about a hundred and I get back to Earth alive. And what are the chances of both of those things happening? Not very good, I'd say.

As I'm thinking about all of that, the music stops, and when I look around to figure out why, I notice everyone's staring at me. Maybe I made a noise or something, I don't know, but I feel pretty embarrassed, especially since I probably look like I was creeping around in the shadows and whatnot. But then Naomi says, "Torro, come and join us."

I'd forgotten how Naomi's one of those fontani, and how they're supposed to have really fantastic eyesight and hearing and everything. She probably knew I was there the whole time. Now that I'm paying closer attention, I can see that most of the people sitting around aren't even bivvies. There are a few, like that guy Thom and the couple others from Twelfth, and some more I don't recognize that are probably from other centuries. But most everyone else seems like someone you'd meet in the Legion, settlement people and Prips, too, people who could have just wandered out of the city the way I did.

"Yeah, sure," I say. I feel a lot better here than I did at the Forum, and I'm about to go find someplace to sit down, when I realize I've got something in my hand—a piece of paper. It's the page of music Mersh brought me the day I got sent up to the Legion, the one with Camareen's message, *Come back*. I'd had it in my jacket, but somehow I ended up taking it out.

I've stopped short to look at it, and people are starting to stare again. I think about just putting it back in my jacket, but then I say, "Hey, Naomi, can you play something for me? I have a request." I give her the page. "Do you think you could play it?"

She looks it over, all very serious. "This music is not written for a fiddle," she says. "But I will do what I can."

Everyone is watching us now. "It's music," I tell them. "Like, old music, from before the war." That gets people interested. It makes me a little nervous, like maybe they'll all want to look at the page and accidentally tear it up or something, but Naomi asks old Thom to hold it for her so she can read it while she plays, and that settles anyone else's getting anywhere near it.

The song is slow and a little sad, but there's something else to it, too, like something hopeful. It's a real nice song. It really is. But after only a minute or so, it stops. You can tell there's supposed to be more, like from the way the notes are going, sort of picking up, but it just stops right there.

"That's all there is," Naomi says. I think she's a little disappointed, too. "The rest is missing."

I feel like a pretty big idiot. I've seen other songs written down, like when Camareen would play or sing for me, and they're almost always more than one page long. But for some dumb reason I thought this had to be a whole song. I'd been carrying it around all this time, not even knowing it wasn't finished.

"Play it again," someone says. I don't even see who, but everyone else starts saying the same thing. Even though most of the song is missing, there's still something there that gets them. They all want to hear more, even if they'll never get to the end.

Naomi brings up her fiddle again and starts to play.

SIXTY-SIX

NAOMI

The song is titled "Over the Rainbow," with music by Harold Arlen and words by E. Y. Harburg, or so I am told by the bold script at the top of the page, below the proud proclamation "Sung in the M-G-M Picture 'THE WIZARD OF OZ.'" These references mean nothing to me, and I do not expect Torro knows any more than I, for they are written in English, as are the words arrayed beneath Mr. Arlen's bars of notes. The lyrics seem maudlin and daydreaming to me, but perhaps there is more substance to be found in the lines that follow. What those are I cannot say, for the music I have is only a fragment of the whole. I am certain there is more, and would be so even if the lyrics did not end partway through a sentence, for this melody is plainly the opening phrase of some longer composition.

Torro has brought us just the song by which to take our leave of Earth. I wish only that I had more to play. Until now, I have built my performance entirely of tunes learned at Papa's knee, heard a thousand times on wagon trails, scratched out on cold nights, sent dancing or weeping at weddings and funerals, familiar as old friends. They are fine songs, rich with flavors of home, with memories both happy and sad, and when I picked up my fiddle tonight and began to play, they called my people to me as surely as a bugle cry summoning scouts to supper.

Reaper Thom is still here with me, as are Apricot Bose and the Simons Grumble and Rumble, and Rae stayed for a time before running off to chase that boy Vinneas. She even asked for a turn on the fiddle, which was a surprise to everyone. Her performance suffered from a lack of practice, but when you have a face like Rae's, people do not stickle over the quality of your music, and reviews were positive for the most part. It was a large audience indeed: There are more Walkers on this island, I have learned, from other codas, and the sound of these old ballads, well-known to every codesman on the continent, brought them out to listen. Others gathered also, people from cities and townships wandering from the dark streets in ones and twos and threes, strangers at first but friends after sharing this music with us.

And yet until Torro came, it was always the ballads of the Walkers here. I do not think anyone wished to hear the abominable clatter that passes for music in the Legion. Torro's song is something new, something different, a song that belongs to none of us and all of us, and as such is a good melody to embark on a shared journey. We have each traveled our separate ways to this place, but from here on, we go together.

The Consulate made some effort to relegate Jax and myself to duty on Earth, but we remain part of the Ninth Legion, and if the Ninth was to join in this mission, we would not allow anyone, even Consul Seppora herself, to keep us back. The Consulate proved unequal to our determination, especially once Charles took our part. He spoke at length in praise of our courage and fortitude and service to the Legion, and promised to impress upon us by his continued tutelage the importance of following orders. I believe this last comment was meant as an apology for withholding the evacuation plan from us, but I have not yet decided whether Charles deserves to be forgiven, even though his speech was what finally convinced the Consulate to restore our privileges as fontani of Ninth Legion. I think I may eventually offer some terms of peace simply to learn the meaning behind his final argument before the Consulate, the one that seemed to chip away the last of their resistance: "I'm going to need their help with your latest assignment."

After that, only one person made any effort to prevent us from joining the expedition—or, I should say, to stop me in particular. Vinneas visited me privately and with an arsenal of clever and well-reasoned arguments attempted to convince me to stay behind. When that failed, he came as near to begging as a man can while still keeping his dignity, and, if I am honest, went a step or two over the line. I will own that I was a little moved, for I imagined Rae had put him up to it, and if so, the consequences of failure would be harsh for him indeed. Unfortunately for Vinneas, pity was not enough to undo my resolve.

I knew Rae would consider my decision nothing but childish hard-headedness, and anticipated a fiery confrontation. I determined at least to mention the effort Vinneas had made on the chance doing so might spare him some of her wrath. But when I saw her again, Rae did not seem angry, only sad, and when I told her of my conversation with Vinneas, she professed ignorance on the matter.

"I know you can take care of yourself, Sunshine," she said. "You have the bravest soul I have ever known. It is a privilege to fight at your side." It was the first time she had ever treated me like a comrade, and in the pride of that moment, I could even forgive her use of my old nickname.

At the time I did not remark on the sadness I thought I saw in her, and it has not surfaced again. I did, however, recognize the same look in Mama when Rae and I went to see her that last time. My coda was offered a place in the new Ninth City, already being raised on the site of the old one, but they chose instead to build a small settlement of their own, albeit still within the bounds of the Valley of Endless Summer. There they will be free to pursue their own ends, safe within the valley's sheer walls from the harrying of tribal raiders and the harassing authority of such people as Ghalo and Qu. The town they are building, I am pleased to say, bears close resemblance to New Absalom.

Mama did not scold us for throwing in with the Legion or try by any means to keep us with her. She and the rest of our coda, even if they did not fully comprehend the extent of this war, understood that we had embarked on a new kind of scouting, an errand to head off danger before it could strike those less able to fight.

Baby Adam took the news of my departure as a kind of consolation for losing Rae, over whom he wept copious and bitter tears. He wiped his nose on my uniform, then surprised me with a mighty embrace and a "G'bye, Miss Priss," and I felt in him a new and unaccustomed strength, the first spark of the man he might become.

Mama only laid a kiss on each of our foreheads, and uttered her constant "Come back to me, sweet girl." I will admit I shed some tears of my own then, for I knew this would be our last farewell. Rae and I may one day see our brother as an old man, but Mama is already past forty, and I have little doubt the years of our campaign will be more than she has left. That was the only time I truly considered abandoning this expedition, but I had pledged myself to the people of the Keep, and I would not turn my back on them now.

My decision was the right one. I know that for sure, standing here among this motley collection of legionaries, their ears tuned to the sound of my fiddle. This music has enchanted us all, holding us in thrall by its incompleteness. Again and again my audience calls out "encore!" as if they imagine I am holding the rest back. I try making more from what I have, varying pacing and key, looping the last notes back to the beginning, but the result remains jarring, a poor substitute for the real thing. I soon become somewhat incensed with Mr. Arlen's publisher for not being more economical with his printing.

It is during one of my many loops that Lunar Veil finally closes. The flash and the final vision of Earth have already come and gone. What I feel is more like a change in the air, as when a door nearby slams shut. I doubt any of those around me perceive it, except for Jax. I have only to look at him to know he, too, has had this sense of a world shutting away behind us. We are well and truly on our way now. We cannot know what awaits us, only that we will face it together.

This time, as I reach the final notes of Torro's page, I find another line waiting in my mind, and after that another, and another. It is as if this song has been sleeping somewhere in my memory, and only now awakened. I do not know if what I play is truly "Over the Rainbow" as Mr. Arlen wrote it, or if it is some invention of my own; nor does it matter. I allow the melody to unroll before me, feeling my heart lift as I chase along after it, eager for whatever comes next.